Oathbreaker

To request permissions, contact the publisher
srgeorgewriting@gmail.com
Paperback ISBN: 9798218513467
Ebook ISBN:
Edited By: Amanda Mulvaney
Cover Art By: S.R.George
Cover Art Copyright © S.R.George

Other books by S.R. George

<u>The Breaker Series</u>
Bondbreaker

Trigger Warnings
Oathbreaker contains content that may be triggering to
some.
Trigger Warnings include but are not limited to:

Misogyny, Graphic Violence, Graphic Sexual Scenes, Human trafficking, Sexual Violence, Sexual Assault (both mentioned and depicted*), Torture, Kidnapping, Imprisonment, Gun Violence, Drug/Alcohol Use, Child Loss, Emotional Games, Abuse, Racism, Patricide, Discussions of Death, Grief, Domestic Terrorism, and Field Medicine.

If you or someone you know is in trouble, please reach out.
Help is available.

Human Trafficking Hotline: 888-373-7888
Sexual Assault Hotline:1-800-656-4673
Suicide Hotline: 988

*Oathbreaker does contain a depicted rape scene.
It occurs in Chapter Forty-Seven after they leave the ball.
You can skip it if it is too triggering.

It is never my intent to cause harm but it was an aspect of
the story that, for me, couldn't be skipped.

Dedicated to:
All the feral women, who are such joys in my life, even
through all battles you've fought.
This is for you.

Playlist
Rivers and Shores - Full Album - Black Hill & heklAa
Hell Is A Teenage Girl - Nessa Barrett
When Tomorrow Starts Without Me - Trey Pendley
Cravin - Stileto & Kendyle Paige
Rain - Sleep Token
Intrusive Thoughts - Natalie Jane
Ugly Side - Blue October
All Eyes On You - Smash Into Pieces
Comfortable - Victor Ray
Labour - Paris Paloma
Tennessee Whisky - Austin Grigori
Love Me Harder - Steven Rodriguez
Simple Man - Shinedown
Home - Blue October
Speechless - Dan + Shay
Face Down - Red Jumpsuit Apparatus
Girls Like You - Anna Clendening
The Love That You Want - Sleep Token
Sharks - Imagine Dragons
Voila - Barbara Pravi
Empire Now - Hozier

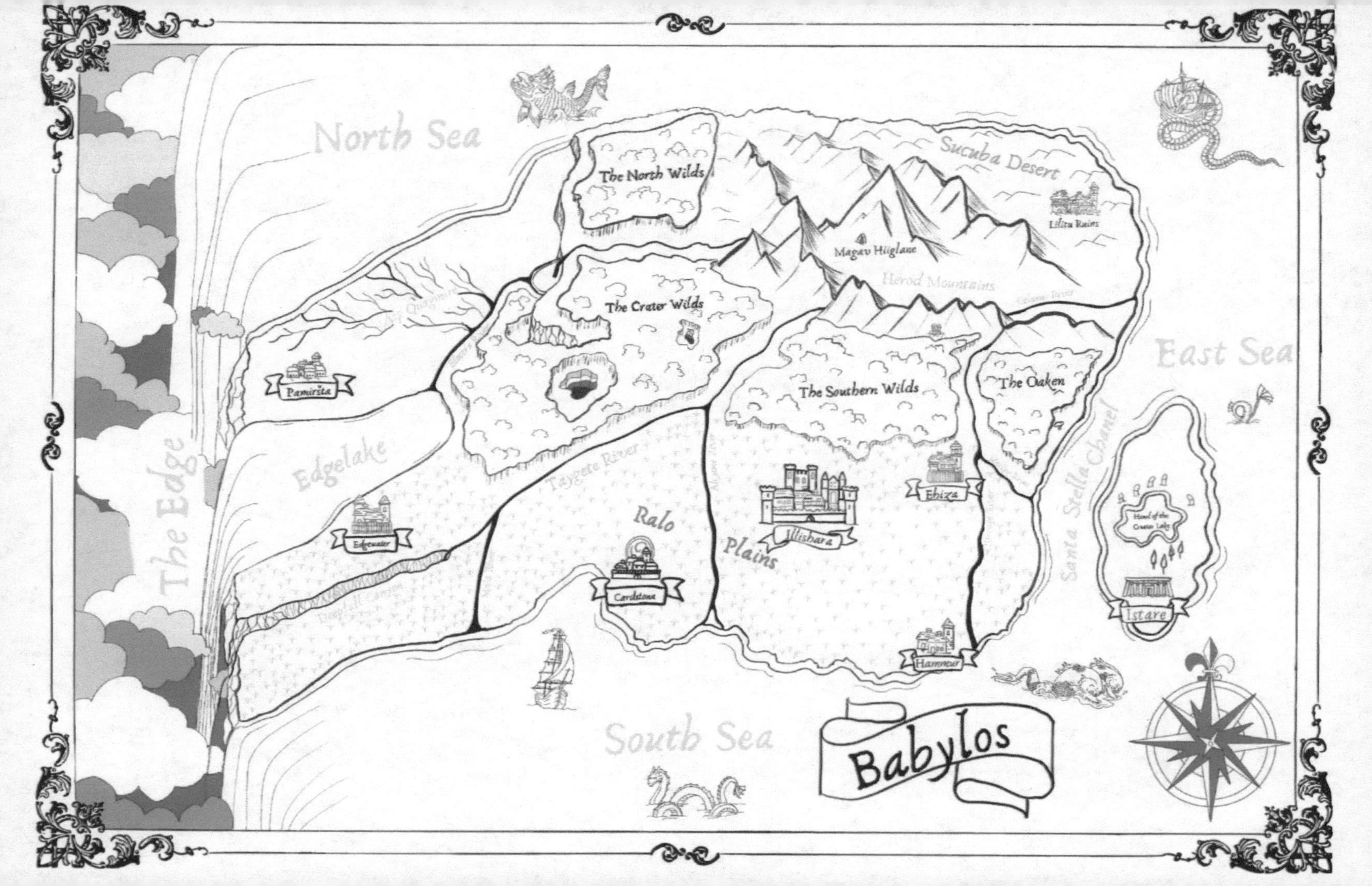

Babylos
North Sea
East Sea
South Sea
The Edge
Sucuba Desert
The North Wilds
The Crater Wilds
The Southern Wilds
The Oaken
Magav Hiiglane
Herod Mountains
Lilitu Ruins
Ralo Plains
Illisbara
Ehiza
Hammer
Istare
Hand of the Creator Lake
Santa Stella Chanel
Edgelake
Edgewater
Pamirita
Cardstone
Taygete River

Oathbreaker

S. R. George

A Breaker Series Novel

Prologue

Our kingdom has always been fraught with its own kinds of war. Not bloody battles nor a slitting of throats, but of a tyranny of a different kind. Wars of gender and class that have separated us from how we used to be. Babylos, the Kingdom of Elves was once a great nation, founded in magic and art. We understood the medicine of the earth. Knew how it breathed and tamed its wild beasts, but like all great nations we were built on the backs of others.

Humans wanted a taste of all that we had to offer and so the first and only Great War of the Modern Era waged. The blood of men, elves, fae, and monsters stained the earth, and the earth wept as its children slayed one another.

The story of us, long since forgotten, said the great creator and the earth agreed. The bloodshed could not continue, living beings should not kill one another for nothing. Thus, they brought upon them all a great cataclysm. All kingdoms fell under the wrath of the earth and the creator who rained fire from the skies, flooded the land, and shook the ancient forests until they yielded. It was then the creator came to the new elf king, King Cardoc, First of His Name, and gave him charge over the elves and only the elves. The young king was brash but yielded to the creator and let the humans free to build their own kingdom and thus the Era of Man began.

A History of Cardoc Raloqen the First by Cypress Crane, First Scholar of the Crown

I shut the dusty tome as the laughter of the young princesses graced my ears. Katrel Gwendolyn Raloqen and her younger sister Tummilia Raloqen were playing tag through the stacks in this great library. I wondered how they would grow up. Will Katrel be noble and brave? Will Tummilia be graceful and wise? Will anyone ever know the truth about them, the children of the king? That Katrel has a fighter's heart behind those copper eyes in her young face or that Tummilia has straw-colored hair laced with copper. I wondered if the king knew what that meant, if he's even noticed her at all after they announced her as a girl. I feared for her to be the second child of the king, my littlest princess.

Katrel jumped behind the stack next to me and placed a finger to her lips. Her long chestnut hair plaited in a braid down her back was the only feature she shared with the king. It swayed over the maroon and gold dress she was wearing as she crouched down.

"*Sortir. sortir. où que tu sois.*"[1] Tummilia's bell-like voice called.

"*Tu ne m'attraperas jamais.*"[2]

I leaned down to whisper to the girl. "Practicing your French today?"

"*Oui, vieux* Cyran."[3] She said, beaming at me.

I flicked her nose. "*Je ne suis pas un vieil homme, petite princesse. Je suis ton enseignant.*"[4]

She glowered at me, but huffed. "*Mes excuses, professeur.*"[5]

I smiled. Yes she would be as brave and noble as those copper eyes said she would. "*Joues-tu bien avec ta soeur, petite princesse?*"[6]

"*Oui Professeur* Cyran. *Je l'ai laissée m'attraper deux fois.*"[7]

I smiled at the little lion's heart. "Go play, keep practicing."

---

[1] Come out. Come out. Wherever you are.
[2] You'll never catch me.
[3] Yes, old man Cyran.
[4] I'm not an old man, little princess. I am your teacher.
[5] My apologies, teacher.
[6] Are you playing nice with your sister, little princess?
[7] Yes, Teacher Cyran. I've let her catch me twice.

"*Merci, Professeur.*"[8]

She peered around the corner, just as little Tummilia came into view. Katrel jumped out at her sister.

"Boo!"

Tummilia screeched, then stomped her foot angrily. "*Pas juste,* Katrel. *tu n'es pas censé me faire peur.*"[9]

Katrel laughed before breaking into a sprint deeper into the library, teasing her sister the whole way. My littlest princess huffed and sat on a stack of books, her bright blue gown fluffing out around her.

"*Ce n'est pas juste Professeur* Cyran. *Ce n'est pas juste.* Katrel *est plus vieux et plus rapide et ce n'est pas juste.*"[10]

"Be that as it may, little princess, if your opponent is bigger or faster than you, you just have to be smarter than them."

"But teacher, how can I be smarter than her? She's older than me."

I smiled at the beautiful little girl with tempest blue eyes, glad that she took after her mother that way. "Well little one, where does your sister like to hide in the library?"

She pondered looking hard at the floor. "Well don't tell momma, but Katrel likes to hide under Scholar Crane's desk."

"Is that the last place she goes?"

The young girl nods vigorously. "Yes. Every time."

"Well, then little one, beat her to it."

"*Merci Professeur* Cyran. *Merci.*"[11] She sprinted off in the direction of the Crown Scholar's desk.

I was not going to rat the child out, but I listened while I shelved the books I'd been thumbing through. They

[8] Thank you, teacher."
[9] Not fair, Katrel. You're not supposed to scare me.
[10] It's not fair Teacher Cyran. It's not fair. Katrel is older and faster and it's not fair.
[11] Thank you, Teacher Cyran. Thank you.

called out to each other trying to find one another. After a half hour of Marco Polo Katrel's keening scream rattled the dust from the stacks of books. I had to chuckle at them, both sweet, wild girls.

"Cyran?" The sweet voice of my longest friend pulled me from the stacks.

"Ciserie. I mean Your Highness." I bowed awkwardly. She was draped in a fine white gown with silver accents, it brought out the luminous quality of her starlight hair.

Her soft chuckle rang like a bell. "Cyran, my friend you can call me by my name. No one is around."

"Very well, Ciserie." I smiled at her. "What do I owe the pleasure of your beautiful face gracing my library."

She returned my smile. "I was looking for my daughters. I hear they make quite the ruckus here when they play."

"Remind you of anyone?"

"Yes, and I do recall your father had a taste for the hickory switch when he was tired of us, Cyran Crane."

"Now, now, Ciserie no need to summon the ass from the bowels of the library. I will still get thwacked with the switch, especially for speaking so plainly with the Queen."

She rolled her eyes, exasperated by my nonsense. "Well, if you happen upon my children, Cyran, will you send them up to me? Katrel has a music lesson and Tummilia has dance."

I nodded my head, bowing at the waist. "Yes, Milady of course. I will round them up and send them to their lessons."

She came to stand behind me. "I will see you soon Cyran."

"Oh, I'm sure we will, my dear. I'll send your daughters."

"Thank you." With that, she left my stack and all I heard was the light click of her heels and the swish of her dress.

*Time means little to those like us who live long
lives, those of us who watch the sunrise and set over the
growth and death of that around us. Growth alone shows
us that time moves and death shows us that it is finite. That
even when we die, time still marches on.*

*The Epitome of All by Cairn Crane, Fourth Scholar
of the Crown*

The playing of the key bones rang throughout the
throne room as "The Sonata of Kings" fell from Katrel's
fingers. Tummilia danced the dance of the same name
before king and court. Her gossamer dress fluttered like one
hundred butterflies every time she twisted and leapt.

I stood back hiding in the crowd, just as enraptured
as everyone else was with the girls. I was just a scholar
after all, not even a Crown Scholar yet, that was my
father's title. Not permitted to write my words to honor
those girls who were already so much more than the king.

Upon his throne King Cardoc, Third of His Name,
watched, his face stuck in a permanent scowl as he looked
upon the presentation floor. Do they not impress you with
all that they have accomplished? Both girls speak and
understand thirty or more languages, both play at least four
instruments. Tummilia is next in line to become the
primess, head dancer of honor, in the royal dance company.
Katrel has a line of suitors asking her for dances at all your
courtly functions. Yet still you watch them with such
contempt.

Queen Ciserie, my longest friend, in contrast to her
husband, smiled at her daughters as they performed their
arts. They are your light, aren't they Ciserie? The only

5

good thing to come from your arranged marriage is your children's lives. I wonder if you begged him for Tummilia's life. Is that why I didn't see you for weeks after she was born or why you only wear long sleeve dresses anymore? Did he hurt you, Milady?

Young Revan Cistern stood close to the key bones pedestal. He, the son of a wealthy merchant, was already climbing the ranks; his goal, as I have heard it, was to be the next Commander of the royal guard. He was brash, outspoken, and one of the king's favored boys. There was a hungry glint in his fine young face that told me that he would go for Katrel's dance tonight, but there is something in those eyes that unsettled me when he looked at Tummilia. The dance finished and the courtiers cheered and clapped. The girls bowed to the king, the only being who wasn't clapping. Undeserving of the crown he wore.

"Well done, young ladies." He drolled from his throne, his voice holding nothing but boredom. "Well done. Now music, dance. Enjoy the feast."

Noblemen swarmed the throne as their sons and daughters took to the floor to dance. Tummilia turned down three suitors as she made her way to the dais and kissed her mother on the cheek, and I crept closer to the royal family.

Ciserie leaned towards her husband. "My King, may I socialize with my court."

He sighed a long-suffering sound. "If you must. Don't stray too far, my prize."

She bowed her head. "Of course, my King."

She descended into the crowd with grace beyond her station, Tummilia at her side, her starlight waves flowing behind her. The way I used to trail behind her when we ran wild through the stacks of the great library as children. Had your father not been station hungry you would have been mine. My Ciserie, but what could two kids do against the king? Oftentimes I found myself wondering what life would have been like had we had the option to deny the king and were able to be together. I make after the gilded women.

"Cyran." The king rarely asked for my presence. Even though I hate him I turn and come to stand before the dais.

"Your Majesty." I said, in a deep bow.

"Cyran Crane, do you plan on following your father's footsteps?"

"It would be an honor, Your Majesty."

"I think you will have a good eye to write the tales of our peoples. You observe and see everything."

"It was how I was taught, Your Majesty."

"Come observe this conversation with the lords and we shall see how that teaching has stuck."

"Of course, Your Majesty."

I came to stand beside my father, listening to lords talk about how each of their sons would be a worthy match for his daughters. On the floor, Katrel stood with her mother and sister at the banquet table where Revan stood chatting with them. The king marked my gaze.

"Lord Cistern."

"Yes, my Lord?" The lord with gold in every aspect of his being spoke.

"Your son Revan is to be a knight soon I hear."

"Why yes, my King. He aspires to be the next commander of your guard."

Commander Tellen scoffed but said nothing as the king narrowed his eyes.

"Interesting. What is his prowess as of late?"

"His swordsmanship, my King. He practices every day without fail."

"What are your thoughts, Cyran?" The king asked.

"I think that he is untested, my King. Revan is a year older than your eldest and he has not yet been accepted as a soldier in the commander's army. Even if his aspirations are to be the next commander, the evidence of his effort is lacking."

The king smiled, nodding at Lord Cistern. "I would

like to speak with the boy."

"Oh course, my king."

"Later. What is it you gentlemen want to share with me?"

The men prattled on forever about the cost of shipping and marriage arrangements that were always open for their sons to take one or the other princess. The discussion was mind numbing at best, watching as Katrel bid her mother goodnight and left the ballroom without a glance at the king. Tummilia was still chatting with Revan, who handed the girl a glass of wine. My heart thudded uncomfortably in my chest. The king cleared his throat and I returned my attention to the men.

"Cyran. What do you think about the cost of antler imports?"

"Your Majesty, I think that the importing of antlers is excessive."

"Oh, how is that?"

"It would take time of course, but we could import deer into the wilds and let them breed for a few years. Not only would we have ample antlers for the artisans we would also be able to use the deer for food, lessening the need to import meat as well."

"Interesting. I'll ponder Cyran, why don't you go and socialize."

"Thank you, my King." I bowed before I made my way through the crowd to Ciserie. She was still by the banquet table chatting with some ladies. I bowed to her. "My Queen, may I trouble you for a dance?"

Her eyes widened with fear glittering in them, but she grasped my outstretched hand. "Cyran, it would be my pleasure."

I guided her onto the floor and began to Waltz. Her lithe body swayed gracefully with the music. "You are very beautiful tonight, my friend."

"He knows, Cyran." She whispered almost imperceptibly.

The fear in her eyes solidified in my heart and the music swelled as if to mock me. "What?"

"He knows."

"Do you know what he's planning? Is he coming after—"

"I don't know, Cyran." She said as the dance came to an end. "But it won't be pretty. Please take care of yourself, Cyran Crane."

With that, she returned to the throne and sat beside the king. He placed a hand possessively on her lap and purred poisons into her ear. I left the ballroom, my heart hammering in my chest. He knew. How long had he known? What was he going to do to us? Creator, please give us protection.

"Stop it." A bell-like voice demanded from a corridor as I passed.

"Come on pretty princess. This will be the best option for you." A male voice crooned.

"Let me go, Revan."

Tummilia.

"Don't be like that." The lord's son purred at her. I turned down the corridor searching for her. "We're having fun."

"No Revan, I most certainly am not having fun."

"Well just relax and I'll show you how fun it can be." He had her pushed into an alcove one hand wrapped in her hair, his mouth pressed to her throat and his other hand was sneaking its way up her dress. Fire burned in my belly as I charged at them.

"Stop."

"Come on Tummi. I'll make you feel good."

"Stop Revan."

"Come on."

I grabbed the young man by the back of his neck and yanked him from her. "Sir, the lady said she was not interested, that means to stop."

He pulled free of my hold and Tummilia curled

around behind, me pressing into my back. "What's it to you, scholar?"

He stank of wine. "Leave her alone."

"Or what, scholar?"

I lunged, disarming the young man and pointing his own sword at his throat. "A scholar I may be, but I am also a gentleman and skilled with a blade. Don't test me, boy."

He paled and took a step back. "My—my father will hear of this."

"What a disgrace to be unarmed by a scholar. I don't think daddy dearest will enjoy trying to rectify his son being weak."

He glowered at me. "Give me back the sword."

I flipped the blade and offered him the hilt. "You should be more careful with who you challenge."

He took the blade cautiously. "Duly noted Scholar Cyran."

"Now apologize to the princess." I stepped sideways exposing Tummilia, she stood tall and held her hands in front of her just like she was taught.

"I apologize, Princess Tummilia, for my forwardness with you." He swayed precariously with the words.

"See that it doesn't happen again." She said with every ounce of royal grace. "Goodnight, Master Revan."

"Goodnight Princess." He bowed and turned, weaving back down the corridor.

"Let me escort you to your room, Princess."

"I would like that." She gave me a sweet smile. "Thank you, teacher."

"You 're welcome, little princess."

She laughed as we walked back to her quarters, where I bid her goodnight. I told her if she ever needed some protection from a gentleman I would always be there. Walking to my own quarters I pondered what the king knew, if tonight had been a test of my loyalty to him or Ciserie, and if that would put what we cared about in danger.

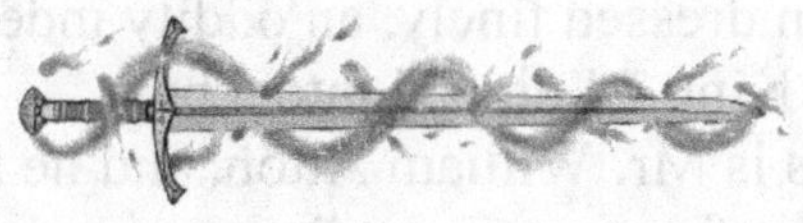

It is a shame that Fire and Light are not allowed to share space. Both are twisting powerful forces that can change landscapes. They could change landscapes if they were allowed the power. The King does not know how to let both flourish and bloom like the wildflowers that they are. Fire and Light are those two princesses. They were forged of stronger things than what he thinks. Chauvinistic fool underestimates the power of women, of those who bring life into the world.

I was there when Ciserie gave birth to both those girls. I watched her scream and cry and bleed as the midwife tried to help her. Where were you? Waiting in court for the announcement of your child's birth, not there holding her hand, helping her breathe. Katrel fought her way from the womb, tearing the queen on her way into the world. You were disappointed that she was a girl, that you did not have a son to carry on your legacy. Tummilia was easier, gentler on her mother. That was a commentary in and of itself.

The Age of Fire and Light, Volume One, by Cyran Aeralie Crane Fifth Scholar of the Crown

A private summons lay upon my desk when I arrived at the library that terrible morning. I should have known that it would be a terrible thing that I was to witness and record. I should have known when the sun had risen into the grey dawn that something malicious was to take place. I should have known as I walked from the library to the throne room an eerie feeling crawled under my skin, twisting around my heart and mind.

"Cyran." The king greets me jovially from his throne. The queen sits beside him not looking at me, but at her hands curled tightly in her lap. How long has it been since your eyes were full of starlight? On his other side sits a human man dressed finely, an oddity indeed.

"My King." I dipped into a bow.

"This is Mr. William Atton, and he has come to pluck a flower from our court."

I furrowed my brows. "A flower?"

"Come, bear witness Cyran, nothing more nothing less."

I took up the free space beside the queen. The men laughed happily plied by wine. "You will see my friend. She is beautiful and fair. Though she serves me very little, she would be a great addition to your collection."

"I hope she is as beautiful as you led me to believe Cardoc. I would hate for our friendship to come to an end."

"You will see." The queen's hands tightened roughly in the folds of her dress. The king waved idly to the guards. "Bring them in."

The princesses entered the throne room. Katrel dressed elegantly in the red and copper gown. Tummilia is in a silver gown that draped gracefully over her body. What was going on?

"My dears, a performance for our guest."

"Yes, my King." The girls said in time.

"Which piece would you like us to perform?" Katrel asked, looking up at her father through her lashes. Still so fierce, endlessly brave and enraged. The king would never be able to quench that fire that burned in her.

The king eyed them. "The Taking of Night."

I looked at the king sideways. Why that piece? It told the story of a star that had fallen to the earth and was forced to become consort to the flame emperor. My heart pattered painfully in my chest.

"As you wish, my King." She said and they both turned from the dais. Katrel going to her key bones and Tummilia to the center of the throne room floor.

The music was beautiful as it flew from Katrel's

fingers and Tummilia's feet graced the floor with the carefully practiced dance. Atton watched, a lascivious glint in his eyes that turned my stomach. The man who was here to pluck a flower watched the youngest princess with a hunger that only men who prey on those less than them have.

"She bends beautifully." Atton said softly to the king. "Untouched?"

"That I am aware of." The king responded just as quietly. "What do you think of my ask?"

"It's a large sum of money, especially in the new world."

"I would drop the price a bit to just be rid of it."

My hands tightened around my ledger; he was selling Tummilia to a human. The summer sweet princess who had done nothing but be born second and a girl. She was loyal to the king. A kindness in the cold of the royal halls. She was her mother's daughter. How could you treat her less than that, Cardoc? How can you look at her and treat her like an object to work out your political means?

"No, no, Cardoc. Your hospitality has shown me how eager you are for us to continue our exchange. You have been an outstanding host. What is one whorelette between friends?"

The king smiled and shook the man's hand. "Then she is yours."

No. No. No. But the scream never left my lips.

Chapter One

Katrel

Babylos was the last place I wanted to go. My homeland had long ago stopped feeling like home. Hours without Tummilia had destroyed me and wounded my heart beyond repair. Though I missed my mother fiercely she never stood up to him. Took his beatings and berating the entirety of my life, and did nothing. Maybe that was why I hadn't thought at all when I ran after my sister. I had only been stopped by Scholar Cyran, our teacher, who had given me a port key to leave the kingdom and placed a sword in my hand for the first time. He had told me to be smart and not come back, I should have listened to that. We had returned to the gilded halls of home, only to be chased out by our father. Niratap was wounded defending us from the horrible man who we shared blood with. How can this be? How can one man hold so much power over me? How do I get us out of this? How—

Shasha landed a left hook on my cheek that sent me flying backward onto the mat.

"Katrel, what are you doing?" Mitta barked from where she was spotting Niratap. "That was sloppy."

"I know." I barked back, eyeing the desert-skinned woman.

Shasha reached her hand out to me. "You, okay? You seem a little distracted."

I wiped my face on the back of my hand before I took hers and pulled myself up. "I'm fine."

"Again then?" She asked, giving me a tentative smile.

This woman who I only paid respect to initially because my longest friend had presented her to us, claimed her as his own. She quickly had become a formidable sparring partner in a short amount of time. In the eight and a half months she had been with us, she had put us in many precarious positions, but she had a fire in her soul that I could admire, one that mirrored my own. She was fearless when it came to our stories or the beasts that stalked the forests around our home. She trained harder than any of us, with the only goal of being strong enough to protect her mate, to protect us.

"Fine." I growled, getting back into my starting stance.

Shasha huffed but matched me. In the time she had been here she had wormed her way into all our hearts, even mine. She had a grace that I didn't think was possible for a being so young to have. From being hunted by a basilisk to defending the male that became her mate with a branch, to standing up for herself against black market denizens who only wished her harm, to pushing without care for herself to rescue him, to charging ahead alone in a raid and standing solo against his captor, to just yesterday when she stood against that kelpie bitch. I held so much respect now for the firecracker that loved so fiercely and freely. She swung her leg into a high kick that I caught flipping her onto the mat, the air left her lungs in a woosh. She pressed her forehead onto the floor gasping.

"What's the matter?" I taunted, feeling the glare, the lord shot me across the room. "Did I take your breath away?"

"You know Katrel." She panted as she came to her knees. "You really are a cocky bitch sometimes."

She swept my legs out from underneath me, and I landed hard on my ass next to her. She was getting faster and stronger every day. I glared at her, meeting her earthen-colored eyes that were always so full of love for every one of us. I laughed and she followed suit, rolling up to kneel beside me. She really was the embodiment of sunlight and joy and that was what made her the perfect match for my friend.

"Fair enough. I will take the loss today." I lay splayed across the mat, sweat clinging to my clothes and skin.

She chortled. "The epitome of grace, Your Highness."

I glared at her, rage surging up in my heart. "Don't call me that."

Her eyes widened at the hardness in my tone. "Katrel I—"

I rolled to my feet. "No. It's fine. You didn't know."

"I meant no offense. I was just playing around." There is a pain in her voice. Regret.

"Don't be hard on yourself." I said unwrapping my hands. "I renounced that title when I left the kingdom, regardless of what my father thinks. I don't want it."

She came up behind me and wrapped her arms around my waist and squeezed me in a tight hug. "I'm sorry."

I placed my hands over hers. She was still so young, untested by the world. My three hundred and thirty years had hardened my heart so quickly, between the men who I had no choice to have in my life to the cruelty the world had shown me so soon. Shasha was still so young, and yet she came up against everything with warmth and kindness in her heart.

"You don't have to be sorry, Milady. I am struggling with what is to come."

She released me and came around to face me. Her hands cupped my face and the ferocity at which she met my gaze stunned me. "You are not going back alone. We will keep you free."

"But—"

"Katrel." Niratap came and stood behind his mate. His towering form was slowly putting back on the muscle that he had lost being incarcerated by that madman. He told us all the time that he was fine, but we all saw when he flexed his hands to chase away the pins and needles that took residence there. He had been tortured, had almost died twice while he was imprisoned, but was still against all logical reason, going to stick his neck out for us. For me and Tummilia.

"My Lord."

"We will keep you free, on my life."

Tears threatened my eyes. "Your life is not worth my freedom."

He arched a brow at me, his face severe. "Isn't it?"

"I don't believe so." I looked down at the floor as fear crawled under my skin. "I should just go and submit to his demands; it will be easier."

"Easier, yes. However, that is not what you want." He said softly.

He knew and still accepted us. "No."

"Then it's settled, my dear. We will go with you and keep you safe. Your father may be a king, but he is not your keeper."

Niratap pressed a kiss on Shasha's cheek and walked to the water station. All of us watched him with concern in our hearts as his long body moved. He flexed his hands before he poured himself a glass of water; Shasha moving to his side on instinct alone. I knew he was pushing, he always did not matter how much we nagged him. Mitta came beside me, her beautiful face placid as she watched them.

"He's pushing too hard again." I said plainly to her.

She sighed. "Yes, he is a full-time fucking job."

"I can hear you." He grumbled. "I am fine. The tingling gets better every day."

Mitta shot him a knowing glare. "Not for one minute do I believe you, you know?"

He shrugged as he consoled his mate, she fretted over him whenever she could. I smiled at them. I wanted a love like that. I wanted to be doted on and worried about, but if my father had his way, that obnoxious lord would be my husband, and I would be nothing more than belonging to him. I swallowed. I had always found men boorish, and their advances annoyed me growing up. I knew then that I was just a pawn for them to use to raise their station, That now outside of Babylos, I found that the vast majority of males anywhere just wanted to hit it and quit it.

Shasha's mother poked her head around the door. She was the spitting image of her daughter. Not as curvy, but their faces were both delicately shaped. "I don't want to bother, but Rogmesh said most of you were here."

"Morning Momma." Shasha said, smiling warmly at her mother. "We're taking a water break, but you're welcome to watch if you like."

"I will admit I'm curious." She said coming up to them.

"Well, I'll leave you to it." Niratap said, giving a tilt of his head to Jazz. " I have work that needs doing—"

"And rest." Mitta growled at him.

"And rest by order of the busybody rakshasi."

Her face went severe and cold. "You need to tell him too."

The lord glared at her and then looked down at his hands. "I know."

"Today, my Lord."

His tail flicked in irritation. "I will try."

"No, you have to." She barked. "Taegan was his best friend. You need to tell him."

He drew a deep breath. None of us had spoken a word to Bastion about Taegan's death, that was a blow that only the lord could deliver. He would be angry that we hadn't told him, we all knew it, but it was Niratap's responsibility to break that pain to him as our leader. Today was Taegan's birthday.

"I will tell him within the hour. Mitta, I wouldn't expect him for his physical therapy today."

"Noted."

He pressed a kiss to Shasha's forehead before he made his leave, and a heaviness settled over my shoulders. Mitta stepped forward offering the woman a chair. She smiled warmly at her asking Shasha what she wanted to practice that she thought her mother would be most impressed with. I listened to them as I walked to the water table, Shasha was sure anything that they did would be impressive for her mother to watch. Jazzera agreed.

Mitta. Since she joined us, I had been fascinated by her beauty, grace, and care. She had been used as a war mount for many years and after some tragedy that she never spoke of, she had left. Left behind her master. Left behind her people. Left it all behind her and stumbled upon us, broken and bloody. My heart skittered with her praise and feared for her when she was away.

Is this what love is, this longing that kills me slowly? Surely, she doesn't feel the same for me. In the two hundred years that I had known her, she had never laid with anyone, never put her heart out for those around her. What kind of sorrow did she hold in her heart that caused her to isolate herself?

Who am I to wonder what kinds of things made Mitta the way she is? I can't even come to terms with the things that happened to me and Tummi. I have never been able to overcome that feeling of weakness and helplessness, that being dunked in acid had burned into my body and memories. The foolishness that was running away from home after my sister with a sword and no training, that had ultimately led to finding a family I would do anything to protect. The betrayal of Tummi being sold without my knowledge, while I was in the fucking room playing the key bones. That room. A shiver snuck down my spine as I shook my head to clear that still hot memory, to banish the flames of rage that continued to spur me on. No. My father would not hold power over me anymore, I would not allow it.

Chapter Two

Mitta

Katrel and Shasha wailed on one another and watching it is something that brings a strange sense of pride to my heart. I taught both everything they know when it came to moving their bodies to defend themselves. Shasha a quicker study than Katrel, but when I had first come to this house Katrel had been so full of rage and fire that she had a hard time finding herself, finding that seat where she was balanced. Now that the day we were leaving to go to her forsaken homeland was growing nearer she was even less grounded than I had ever seen her.

"I hope you have a plan." I said to Niratap who racked the weights below me. His silver eyes met mine and sent shivers down my spine. Even as a predator myself, something about his gaze still stopped my heart. Still caused the wild part of me to freeze in fear.

"I'm going to ask."

"That's it?" I growled at him.

A cocky smile slid over his face. "That is all I've come up with."

"I thought you were cleverer than that. Do you want me to slide on more weight?"

"I think I'm mighty clever in a pinch. No, I think I'm good for now. After a few more sets I'll need to rest."

"Are you pacing yourself?" I was genuinely concerned with his wellbeing despite his flippancy and inherent need to always be in the thick of it. I often considered the benefit of tying him down to get him to heal properly, but I knew his invisible scars were just as important to remember.

He sighed, reaching for the bar to start his next set.

"Yes, Mitta. I am."

"You know I only do it for your benefit. The nagging."

He smiled through his push. "I know."

I glanced at the girls just as Shasha landed a wicked left hook into Katrel's cheek with no resistance. Katrel landed hard on her ass. I barked. "Katrel, what are you doing? That was sloppy."

"I know!" She snapped back, glaring at me across the gym. Before Shasha offered her hand and they went again, blow for blow.

"Have you had that hard discussion with Bastion yet?"

He paused mid-rep, his eyes avoiding mine. "No, I have not."

"You need to do that. Bastion will be concerned when Taegan doesn't reach out."

"Mitta." He growled, racking the weights again. "You don't have to tell me that it will destroy him. I already know."

"Bastion may surprise you."

He sighed sitting up as the girls knocked each other down and laughed. "I know."

The laughter stopped and he rose, stalking towards the girls purposefully as Shasha wrapped her arms around Katrel's waist. I followed behind as he came to stand behind Shasha.

"Katrel." Niratap spoke calmly, his voice was full of care and authority.

"My Lord."

"We will keep you free, on my life." He promised her and I knew it was a promise he would not take lightly.

"Your life is not worth my freedom." My heart broke at her words. Did she not see her own worth? Did she still feel so small compared to her father?

"Isn't it?" He asked, his face severe but kind.

"I don't believe so. I should just go and submit to

his demands; it will be easier." Katrel said, looking down and focusing on unwrapping her hand.

"Easier, yes." he said softly. "However, that is not what you want."

Katrel's voice was small when she answered him. "no."

"Then it's settled, my dear. We will go with you and keep you safe. Your father may be a king, but he is not your keeper."

He kissed his mate's cheek before he loped to the water. My eyes trained on the mobility of his body, his shoulders still caved in slightly, his gait tight on his right side, and then he flexed his hands before pouring himself water. Kozran claimed his prognosis was good, but only if Niratap took it slow, something he failed to do regularly. I was hopeful but his progression was slow, his recovery was not going well.

"He's pushing too hard again." Katrel said beside me.

I sighed. "Yes, he is a full-time fucking job."

"I can hear you." He grumbled as his mate fretted over him. "I am fine. The tingling gets better every day."

I shot him a glare. "Not for one minute do I believe you, you know?"

He shrugged as he attempted to console his worried mate, assuring her he was taking it slow. We all knew he wasn't.

"I don't want to bother, but Rogmesh said most of you were here." Jazzera said, poking her head into the gym.

"Morning Momma. We're taking a water break, but you're welcome to watch if you like." Shasha said warmly around her mate.

"I will admit I'm curious." She said coming to stand beside them.

Niratap shifted his tail from underfoot before he bowed his head gently. "Well, I'll leave you to it. I have work that needs doing—"

"And rest." I snarled.

"And rest by order of the busybody rakshasi." He smiled playfully.

"You need to tell him to."

The lord glared at me, then looked down at his hands. As if his tingling palms held all the answers. "I know."

"Today, my Lord."

His tail flicked. "I will try."

"No, you have to." I barked. "Taegan was his best friend. You need to tell him."

He drew a deep breath; it was a heavy weight that he shouldered. "I will tell him within the hour. Mitta I wouldn't expect him for his physical therapy today."

"Noted."

He pressed a kiss to Shasha's forehead before he made his leave. Katrel's shoulders slumped as if the heaviness the lord was facing had landed on her shoulders. I rolled my own and I moved forward to offer Jazzera a chair.

"What do you want to practice, Shasha? I figure you want to impress your mother with some of the skills you learned."

"I'm sure anything we do will impress my mother when it comes to this." She gestured vaguely at the gym.

"You're probably right." Jazzera said with a warm smile.

"What haven't we practiced since we've returned?"

Shasha frowned at me. "My swordsmanship. I don't feel very confident with a long blade in my hand."

Katrel set her cup down on the table. Her voice was firm as she spoke. "The only way to get confident with a blade is to practice with it. Firearms aren't permitted in the elf kingdom, so you have to be comfortable with a blade."

"Why are firearms not permitted?" Shasha asked genuinely as Katrel went to the rack of blades.

"Because the elf kingdom is resistant to modern

weaponry. It's hard to smuggle a bow or sword into the throne room to kill the king." I said matter-of-factly, nodding my head to the ring by the weapons rack. "Katrel is right, the only way you will learn is to practice."

"Which sword are you the most comfortable with?" Katrel asked, eyeing the rack.

Shasha made her way to the ring with me and her mother in tow. "Um, the short sword I like the most, it's the closest in weight to my dagger."

Katrel grabbed two of the practice long swords. "Long sword it is."

"Why?" Shasha asked. I eyed her trying to decide if it was an actual question or if she was whining. It sounded like whining.

Katrel's brows rose as if she was wondering the same as she handed her the practice blade. "One the long sword is my favorite and two it is the most common sword in the elf kingdom."

"Okay. Not to sound like a broken record, but why?"

"Elves have long been craftsmen and artisans, however throughout the last era elves went to war. Most of them pointless and the only end was to prove that they were a superior race." Katrel said, spinning the blade in her hand. "I don't share that thought, the enslavement of others slows the growth of living beings and society as a whole. Longswords are lethal and when it comes to martial weapons, easy to craft in mass and easy to decorate and embellish. Elves are strong, but as a race, we are not bulky or thick-muscled as the other warrior races like orcs or dwarves."

Katrel took up her fencing stance looking down the blade. Shasha matched her, tapping the tip against Katrel's. "So, elves like being pretty when they fight?"

Katrel glowered at her and swung, the blades coming together with a sharp clang. "Something like that. Be aware of your feet."

"I know. I know." She spat. "Keep moving. Keep space."

Katrel sidestepped a downward slash from Shasha and pushed the blunt tip of the blade to her throat. "Dead."

"You need to mind your timing, Shasha." I said.

"Right." They returned to their starting position.

Katrel pushed again and Shasha retreated. They met blow for blow.

"Shasha. You need to counter, not just parry."

"I know."

"Don't tell me you know. Show me."

Shasha pulled back shifting to the left, Katrel marked it, channeled Shasha's blade, then disarmed her. "Disarmed."

"Shasha, how did that happen?"

"I left a window when I shifted, Katrel acted on the window."

"Correct. Go again."

The clang of blades rang over us and Jazzera came to my side. "Is this how this goes all the time?"

"No. Normally I'm in the ring with her when we practice with blades."

"Then why is Katrel in there with her?"

"Katrel needs an outlet." I said, watching as Shasha took control. "She's spending too much time in her head worrying about what may happen when we enter her homeland."

"X mentioned that last night. That the elf king isn't someone that you would call friendly."

"Luckily, he doesn't venture from his home. I haven't had the pleasure of existing in his presence, but I have heard that he has the propensity for being underhanded. He has traditional elven views."

"Which are?"

"Patriarchal. Women are second class. Objects to be seen not heard. Stuck in time, because the king refuses to move into this century in great leaps. They have a very limited connection to the rest of the world; outside basic internet and light cellular service on the edge of the territory, both of which are limited to trade. Sorry to say you probably won't get your weekly call while we're there."

She nodded, watching as Shasha was disarmed again. Katrel explained how to get out of a disarming maneuver, shifting into being a teacher easily. Jazzera asked. "Are you worried?"

"You want my opinion?"

She smiled. "Shasha told me you were in charge of most of the weapon training and as the head of security I figured you would have insights on how things will go."

"I'm not particularly worried about Shasha. She's resourceful and will be underestimated by everyone around her in Babylos regardless of if they heard about the raid or not. I wish she had more ranged weapon experience beyond her side arm because if combat happens the lord and I would like to keep her out of it. She is great at hand-to-hand and with her dagger. Katrel and Tummilia will also be underestimated because in the elf tradition, it's shameful for women to bear arms. Though commoners, both male and female, usually know their way about a bow."

"I see, what about you? You're a woman."

Shasha gained ground on Katrel pushing in on a block, with a roar. Katrel twisted away from her, getting behind her and slashing across her back. "Dead."

"You lasted longer that time, Shasha. Go again." I said and smiled at Jazzera as they reset, the clang of blades resonating once more. "They will expect me to be highly skilled based on my race. Rakshasi are a warrior race, and no one was exempt from knowing how to fight. Times have changed, but the need for skilled warriors hasn't, most of my kind now work as mercenaries or bodyguards."

"I see. Who else is going?"

"Other than the three of us, Tummi, Bastion and the lord."

"Bastion is still recovering from being shot, isn't he?"

"He is, but it's just musculature and strengthening his right side. Lord Niratap is the only one I'm worried about, not for lack of skill."

"Really?" She asked, as Shasha gained the upper hand.

"He has impressed me with the ease at which he can pick up a weapon and he, through exposure, knows how to work a room. His condition is recovering slowly, slower than I would like, and that concerns me. I don't want him overtaxing himself like he did back in November. I don't know the kind of access I will have to medical supplies there, and they will treat him poorly because he is a monstrosity. They won't see him as an equal, but as some prize to overpower."

"How did he overtax himself?"

"The way magic works a practitioner can draw from either an internal store of mana or external store from nature. The lord has a large store of internal mana; however, his body naturally uses said mana to heal itself." Shasha disarmed Katrel who laughed heartily.

"Disarmed."

"Good, go again. At the auction in November, he protected us with a shield that over drew that store of mana; and it took from his body, crashing his blood sugars. There's a balance and even though his physical bloody wounds have healed, he's only at about half strength and even if we trained every day there is no way to build that body conditioning back in a week."

"Why would they treat him poorly? He is a lord after all, regardless of his race."

"A title that he took from a man he killed for freedom. Not one he had from bloodline. You must remember humans weren't the first to enslave other beings."

She swallowed but watched the girls start again.

"Will he be safe?"

It was my turn to swallow at that. "I can only hope that we are enough. I won't lie to you, where we are going, what we are doing, the risks outweigh any amount of caution that we do. We could walk in there and all be killed, or we could walk out of there with nothing accomplished. I tried to reason with them, but he puts an incredible weight on his word, and he promised those girls their freedom. He will do anything to keep them safe."

"And my daughter will do anything to keep him safe."

I nodded. "Your display yesterday was impressive. You honored her, with your bravery."

She smiled at her daughter. "That kelpie is a bitch."

A belly laugh rolled out of me. "Yes, she is."

Chapter Three

Bastion

I hefted the flour from the pantry storage floor and carried it to the kitchen, feeling back to normal after a slow recovery. Mitta and Dr. Kozran said I was lucky. Lucky the bullet had missed major vessels and muscle attachments. Lucky it hadn't broken any bones which would have slowed my recovery farther, but it wasn't the physical recovery that had me up earlier than most walking the grounds. It wasn't the ache in my other shoulder when rain clouds darkened the mountains that pulled me into the recesses of the house. It was relentless. This need to remember who I was, to remember that I wasn't Mrak, but Bastion.

Remembering who I am was the hardest thing. Ghosts of the terrible things, Mrak had done, I had done, made me feel disconnected from my family and often made me feel like I was pretending to be me. Like Bastion was just a part to be played. Their faces, the faces of the women and boys that I had to hurt haunted me. I didn't want to be that person. I didn't want to hurt others. I didn't want to kill innocents. I hadn't, but I did kill and somehow that made me feel worse. I shook my head walking through the doorway.

My mother tsked wildly at me as she walked in the door, wiping her hands on her apron. "Bastion, you shouldn't be pushing yourself."

"Ma, I'm fine." I protested as I set the flour down on the floor.

"In the last six months you have been shot in both shoulders. I think not."

"Really Ma, I am fine. Mitta cleared me to go back

29

to regular activity a week ago."

"But you should rest and let your muscles heal."

"Ma!" I half snarled.

"Bas. Don't snarl at your mother." Dad said, coming into the kitchen with a sack of potatoes on his shoulder.

"But Da, she's smothering me."

"An' I don't care, you will respect your ma." He sat the sack of potatoes next to my bag of flour.

"This is bullshit." I threw my hands up, as Allipo came into the kitchen as well.

"Bastion!" She snarled. "Respect."

"What, I was cleared to do whatever, why do you insist that I rest. I'm good."

"You indignant child." She spat, grabbing the rolling pin. It had been a long time since she had brandished the weapon at me.

Allipo cleared his throat drawing our attention, a satyrs smile on his face. "Sorry to interrupt this *lovely* family interaction, but Bastion, the lord would like to speak with you."

"Right now?"

"Yes."

Thank fuck. "Where is he?"

"He's in the study." Allipo's face fell a little bit. "Unfortunately, I wish I could spare you from it."

I cocked a brow at him. "What do you mean?"

He shook his head. "That is for the lord to share."

A sinking feeling rooted itself into my core as I walked past the satyr. He wouldn't meet my eyes and dipped his head. What could be so terrible that Allipo wouldn't meet my eyes? I ran through as many scenarios as possible. Had someone died? Was he kicking me from the mission? What was going on?

In the study the lord stood by his window, looking out in the distance where I knew the cemetery grove lay. Someone had left us then, someone important.

"You wanted to speak with me, my Lord?"

He didn't shift from where he stood. Didn't look at me. He just stared out the window and sighed. "Yeah, Bas."

Dread tightened my stomach. "Who?"

He adjusted the cuffs on his shirt, a discomforted tick I had noticed a long time ago. "I don't know how to tell you this."

I closed my eyes bracing myself for the worst. Fuck this was going to hurt. "Just tell me."

I heard him take careful deliberate steps until he stood before me. I braved looking up into his silver eyes, they were red-rimmed and puffy. Damn it. "Bastion."

"Just tell me. Please." I hated the way my voice broke. "Just tell me which one of my friends I'm never seeing again."

Shock and sorrow danced over his face. He swallowed. "Taegan."

I felt my breath leave my lungs. No. "What?"

"He was compromised."

My heart dropped into my belly. No. "How?"

"I haven't gotten a full report. Kallin is lying low."

No. "How did he die?"

"Bastion, knowing will not ease your sorrow." His words were wise, but I needed to know.

"Tell me." Tears threatened my bravery, exposing my broken heart. "Please tell me how my best friend died."

He swallowed again. "Bastion."

I felt the treacherous droplets roll over my cheeks. "He suffered, didn't he?"

"Yes." He didn't have to tell me. I knew. Taegan had been compromised. He had been tortured for information. He had suffered. Alone.

"Did he say anything?"

"He only gave my name." The lord said softly as he flexed his hands.

"When?"

"Back in November."

I must have heard him wrong. "What?"

"I found out in November; he was killed just before Thanksgiving."

"What? You've known for months and didn't tell me?"

"I didn't know how to tell you without putting you at risk and then—"

Then he was captured and tortured. My heart was shattered into little pieces. "Does his mother know? Fuck. What about his body?"

"She does. Kallin took care of it." He said softly, gently. "At the end of the week we'll have a service and bury his ashes."

"She should be here."

"Staspar is going to get her. Kallin will meet him at the airport with Taegan's remains and Staspar will bring them both to the manor."

"Okay."

"Bas, if I would have known I would have pulled him. Hell, I would have gone and collected him myself."

He would have, but he was injured then. Even if he had wanted to, he couldn't have saved Taegan. He had been right about not telling me, my soul was cracking at the loss, a chasm forming where Taegan had been. The wound breaking through all the progress I had been making to me. We were the same age. We laughed and chased each other as kids. Two peas in a pod. My confidant. My fishing partner. My drinking buddy. My best friend. And he was gone. Taegan was gone. He was dead. A wail left my body as the weight of it crashed upon me. Niratap wrapped his arms around me, pulling me tight as I cried. My hands curled into fists, and I screamed. Footsteps thundered into the study.

"What—"

I wept as voices protested at whoever pushed them from the room. I screamed into his chest. Screamed as I shattered. Taegan. You weren't supposed to get yourself killed. You weren't supposed to get caught. Your assignment was safer than mine, in a low-threat area. How? How? This was unfair. It wasn't supposed to be you falling on the sword. It's not right.

I pushed away from Niratap. He was like another father figure to both of us and that sorrowful look in his eyes was a second knife to my heart. He was shouldering blame like he always did when someone fell. His hands were clean of their blood, but his soul stained with the loss. It was too much to grieve with him. Too much to know that even when I was an active participant in his torture that he had been suffering this loss, holding it close to his heart as he was beaten and drowned and restrained. If only to save me from this breaking. I left.

"Bastion."

The cracking in his voice chased after me, but I couldn't. I couldn't do this.

"Bas." Shasha reached for me.

No. Nothing you could say could help this ache. All of your sad faces. All of you have mourned him already, your wounds have scabbed over, but mine—mine are fresh and deep. Taegan. No. no. no. Another scream launched from my soul, as I stormed through the manor. I couldn't sit here and cry. I couldn't breathe the same air as my family when a chunk of my heart was gone. I snatched my guitar from the sitting room, and I left.

Someone called after me, but I couldn't stand the thought of warm comforting hugs and words. No, I just wanted to escape. I just wanted to go back to our young wild days, when we spent days at a time at the fishpond, drinking and dreaming. Dreaming of what life would be like if we didn't have to fight the monsters of the world. What a life full of the things that our time together was, laughter and love. Never again would I hear the bright timbre of your laughter or how your nose crinkled when we danced like fools. Never again would I out fish you drunker than reason allowed or get dunked into the water going after a fish. Never again would we belt those sad country songs out at the stars hoping that they would grant our wishes or pondering the life we would lead. Never again because you are dead.

The fishpond had been our oasis, a hideaway from adult responsibilities that we both planned on taking up. It's been almost four years since I have been here. Four years since I saw you last. Four years. When we were here last, at our pond, you told me that you had found your mother and were working on getting her safe. She was your focus for the next ten months and you had brought her home. She had become another mother to me.

Then I'd gone under, and six months later so had you. I plopped down on the stump that had always acted as a seat around our fire pit, overgrown with neglect from our time away. I busied myself pulling the weeds away.

"What do you think about this, huh? You'd probably tease me about crying over you like I had when you cried over a cookie."

Birdsong was all that responded as I cleared our space, I remembered the first time we'd been here. How you laughed so hard you cried when I dived into the pond after your first fish because it had flopped out of your hand. I wondered if our gear was still where we'd left it.

In the little lean-to we had built to store our fishing gear, the door sat askew, but all our gear was where we'd left it, dried out bait and our cooler we always forgot to take back to the manor. In the back behind our folding chairs, rotted from being left alone out here for so long, sat six bottles of Taegan's homemade mead and two milk crates of beer. I felt tears threaten again as I saw the faded note taped to a bottle.

Bas,

If you make it home before I do. Don't drink all my fucking mead. I have to record it so the girls will believe me when I say you're loose when you're drunk. Fucker.

Tae

"Fuck, you thought of everything before you left didn't you bud? At least I'm alone out here so no one thinks I'm crazy talking to you. Oh well, more mead for me."

I take a bottle of mead and a case of beer to the dock. Those first two beers hit my stomach like stones and had I not planted my ass on the dock prior, I probably would have fallen like a stone into the pond. I felt him all around me, could hear his mad laughter, and could taste all our memories in the mead I chugged from the bottle trying desperately to use it as a band-aid for my aching heart. The sun was starting to sink in the sky, painting the clouds orange and pink.

"You should be here." I said forlornly. The words of a song I never thought would be for my friend slid out as I pulled them from memory. I sighed. "Tae, what even happened?"

Well, do you want the truth or the legend?

I looked to my right on the dock and the spritely faun male with his tawny hair, grey horns, and slate eyes stared back. He was slightly transparent. He smiled at me. I looked down at the pond where I was reflected, and he was not. "I couldn't be that drunk yet that I'm hallucinating."

You're not hallucinating Bas. I'm visiting.

I groaned. "Fuck."

And here I was thinking you missed me.

I rolled my eyes, before laying back and taking three large gulps of the mead. "I did. I do, but you know I don't like this. That I don't enjoy conversing with the dead. It's not fair that you're gone."

He shrugged, looking back over the pond. *We both knew the risks.*

"Yeah." The clouds drifted overhead lazily. "So, what actually happened?"

I got caught in a lie. Trying to dip out to call Staspar, to ask if he knew anything about back-end scales from a satyr named Shists. I misspoke and got pressed, I couldn't charm my way out of it. He shrugged again. *Got jammed, interrogated, and bled out.*

"How did you die?"

Well somewhere in the beating and breaking of my body, boss man decided that he should be able to, you know, thousand cuts kind of bullshit since he couldn't get information from me if he cut out my tongue. He cut me too deep, and I bled out slowly, while he peppered me with questions. It got to a point where I realized I wasn't going to get to go home, I wasn't going to see this place again and I made a choice. I would rather our family know I was gone than die without anyone knowing. He asked who I worked for, and I gave him the lord's moniker. He cut off my ears and I succumbed to my injuries before he cut out my eyes to send back to the lord.

"Jesus." I glugged down the rest of the bottle of mead.

Yup.

"Hopefully I'm not too drunk to remember that and ask about Shists."

K knew I was digging; it may be in his report.

"But it might not. I'll poke if I remember after I'm sober."

He laughed that crazy crow-like laugh. *Fuck I wish I could drink that with you, that's raspberry mead I was super excited to try out when I made it.*

"Well, it's tasty if that eases your spirit."

He smiled. *Not really. How did your assignment go?*

"Well, I got shot twice. Once in each shoulder, which was fantastic by the way. I sexually assaulted the lord's mate while undercover, before she fell into his hands, now were good friends. I had to be an active participant in the lord's torture. Handled people entering the sex trade all while trying to figure out how big the player I was working for was in the monster trade." I shrugged.

How is he?

"He's healing slowly, his nerves are regenerating even slower. We're going to Babylos at the end of next week and I'm worried about him."

He'll be fine, he's resourceful. What do the girls think?

"Katrel is angry. I don't know how Tummi feels, she's been spending a lot of time in her room."

Are you going too?

"Of course, I'm going. Why would I stay behind?"

To heal. To rest. Recover from being deep undercover for three years.

"I can't let them go into danger without me. Not after being unable to protect him."

Taegan glowers at me. *Don't beat yourself up Bastion. You stayed under to keep him and everyone else safe. Had you taken the great risk to try to rescue him yourself or defend him, you both would have probably ended up dead. Black market kingpins are like that. Especially if they feel like they've been betrayed.*

"I know, but my heart is sick with what I had to do to him. To Shasha. Fuck even the fucking around I did with Allipo made my skin crawl. Playing a half-crazy orc really got hard here and there."

But you played it well. He looked back out over the water. *What's she like, the lord's mate?*

"Shasha?" I sat up and grabbed a beer from the crate. "She's pretty amazing. She's fiery and fierce and brave. She's smart and has a drive I don't think I have ever seen in someone. You'd like her."

I bet. He smiled at me. *Don't cry for me, Bas.*

"You make it sound so easy like you weren't an anchor in my life."

Oi, Bas that sounds really gay.

"Says the faun who got us both drunker than creation, flirted with a tree, and then asked if you could suck me off."

He cawed again. *Okay fair, but you're a pretty orc.*

I shook my head. "Gods we were really too drunk that day."

At least we remember it.

I rolled my eyes again. "You are terrible, the worst influence."

I think that we were great for each other, but I think it's time, Bas. Love me. Remember me and our shenanigans, but don't stay here sad and morose like you get.

"I'm not morose." He gives me a look as I open my fourth beer.

You are when you're buzzed and once you get sloshed you most certainly are. There's a sweet spot in between where you are loose, but not sad and stupid.

I glared while chugging the beer in one go. "Get bent."

You first.

I cracked another one open. "I'm going to get sloshed and stupid then."

Fine then. Sit out here and sing sad country songs, before you get so stupid you can't find the lean-to to get more beer and drunk Bas wanders home, howling the saddest songs he knows.

"Could you not haunt my aching heart?" I groaned.

Love me. Mourn me. Remember me. Then honor me, Bas, by not getting stuck and being sad over the fact that you didn't get to say goodbye. That you weren't there to save me. That the lord wasn't available to save me. Don't harbor that in your heart, Bastion. Honor me that way, please.

"Again, it's not that easy."

Well, figure it out. He stands like he is going to

walk away.

"Taegan, you can't tell me to just figure it out."

Well, I am. I can't be here for the things we wanted to do, so now you just have to do them alone or with someone else.

"Taegan." I turned to where he had stood, but he was gone. "Thanks for nothing."

Chapter Four

Tummilia

Dancing had always been a happy place for me. When our mother had pushed me into dance lessons I fell in love. In love with knowing my body. In love with the grace that it gave me. In love with the language of motion. In love with me. After my father sold me away, dance became tainted, twisted into a monster with fangs. Men used me as such, an adornment of lust for them to take advantage of. No one had ever questioned when I pulled back from the merrymaking, only Nira truly understands. I think that strangely the male witnessed enough of my mistreatment to understand why I pulled away.

Men have only stared at me with hungry lust, save my father who always looked at me with a burning rage I never could understand. Teacher Cyran who always had warmth in his eyes, and the men of the house, though Allipo always has mischief in his gaze when talking to any female. Back home the male courtiers all vied for Katrel's hand to dance and when she turned them away, they came to me. As if a dance with me would soothe their wounded pride. Several pushed for more than the dance, more than a glass of wine, but I declined them all. The only time it got farther was a time when the young knight prospect, Revan had slipped something into my wine and taken me from the banquet hall to force himself upon me.

Cyran had saved me then, but when my father sold me away there was nothing he could do. No words he could have said that would have kept me from Atton's hands. William Atton took everything from me. He took my innocence, forced it out of me the night he claimed me as his possession. He took my home from me, everything I had ever claimed as mine, and then gave me a cell to sleep in and gossamer to attempt to cover myself with. He took my joy, forcing me to dance and perform for him, his guests, and his guards.

I had spent the last three centuries trying to find that joy again. Find that little girl who only wanted to dance. Find the woman she had become through hardships and triumphs. Find who I am now. I was strong, brave, and kind, I thought as the cool metal of the pole kissed my palm I repeated that to myself. Alone with only my pole and my mirrors with only my own eyes watching me as I pulled myself up. I danced claiming my body as my own. It's strange, this battle I have with myself. I can give all my goodness to others, but that same kindness I couldn't pour into myself. The song ended and I panted staring at my reflection in the mirror. Who was I? Who was the woman who glared back at me in the mirror?

A heart-wrenching wail echoed through the house, pulling me from the darkness of my own mind. Another scream had me in motion dashing down the hall. I rounded the corner and saw Bastion storming away from a gathering of family, Mitta holding everyone back as he passed. Jazz reached out for him, she didn't even know him, and she wanted to comfort him.

"Leave him be." Nira said coming into the hall, his face sad and forlorn. "He needs to be alone to process."

I swallowed poor sweet Bastion. "Did you tell him?"

Nira looked at me, his eyes held a weight that took my breath. "Yes."

I nodded, what was there to say. Those boys had been inseparable as youths, both taking vows very young to serve Nira's dream of dismantling the force that harmed all of us in one way or another. Shasha wrapped her arms around his waist, looking up at him with love and care in her face. She was a blessing we needed, before we knew we did. In the last decade my friend had pulled away, spending more time away from the manor. Hunting for souls he could rescue searching for more of his kind. She was an anchor that brought him back to us. I didn't pry to what kind of darkness he was fighting both out there and in himself, but Shasha was the light that brought him from his own shadows. I liked her instantly as soon as I watched them interact together. Nira losing his temper was something that we had grown accustomed to, but it was different that first night when he stormed off to lick his wounds. He felt different.

Bastion stormed out the front doors, his guitar slung across his back. Shasha asked, "Where will he go?"

Nira cupped her face. "The fishing pond I presume. Him and Taegan were always there, being young men. Just give him space to process his loss."

"Okay. Do you think he'll be okay?"

"He will. It will just take time."

Mitta smiled. "I think Taegan left a ton of booze out there too."

Nira smiled, but the suffering didn't leave his eyes. "Then I'll keep my ears open for his keening when he comes home."

His parents laughed heartily. Durgash chortled. "Unless he passes out floating in the pond."

Shasha pulled away from Nira, stepping to the Days. "Has he done that?"

They laughed heartily telling stories of his escapades, everyone was enraptured by the tales. Nira tried to relax and put a small smile on his lips. However, he absentmindedly rubbed his sternum, as if it would rub the ache from his heart. I placed a hand gingerly on his elbow and an eerie stillness settled over his body.

"May I speak with you, my Lord."

"Of course." He gestured to his office.

"Nira." Shasha, called bright and bubbly. "Join us for a walk through the garden?"

Softness returned to his face. "Another time, Love, I

have work that needs doing."

Her smile falls ever so slightly. "Okay I'll see you at dinner then?"

"If not sooner, *mo grá.*"

Her smile returned. "Okay, I'll be expecting you."

He chuckled softly before ushering me towards his office. I waited for him to take his seat before I sank into the plush yellow chair. He folded his hands together and rested his chin on top of them, his solemn eyes pinned me. I took a deep breath.

"Do you have a plan?"

He smiled softly. "Why is everyone so concerned?"

I smiled but averted my gaze. "Our father is not a man to take lightly."

"It's not my intention to take him lightly. However, many things have changed in the last three hundred years. We do not have someone to monitor the elf kingdom, nor do we have an in."

"You're not planning on planting Katrel as your in, are you?" The horrible thought came out of my mouth before I could think it through. He glowered at me.

"No. I promised your sister I wouldn't let her be a servant to his will. I gave her my word. Besides, I'm not that desperate to know the inner workings of Babylos, from what I have gathered they trade goods and only rarely have interacted with the black market. Most of that is for medicinal plants and poisons."

"And the sale of women and children."

He leaned back and fiddled with a pen. "Yes, and that."

"I know. I know. Your focus is the monster trade, but prostitution is—"

"I know." He said, his voice grave. "I know, it's close. Too close."

"Do you have a plan?"

"No."

"So, we're what, going to travel to the Babylos,

waltz up to the throne, and tell our father 'no'?"

"I'll ask him to reconsider."

"You think that will work?" I couldn't hide the skepticism in my voice.

"No Tummi. I am hopeful, but no, I don't think it will be that easy."

"What's plan b?"

"I don't have a plan b that won't get us killed."

I swallowed; this really was a suicide mission. "So, we are going in with a hope and prayer."

He sighed, staring up at the ceiling. "You know him better than I do. What do I expect? What should I watch out for?" He looked back at me and the exhaustion in his face made me take a breath. "How do I keep us safe and alive, Tummilia?"

"I don't know him well enough to tell you. Katrel and I were never privy to anything going on. We were just kids back then. Barely of marriageable age when he sold me away."

He stares at me calculating. "A hope and a prayer is all we have then."

"He could just as easily kill all of us except Katrel to further his agenda. Are you prepared for that kind of loss?"

"Tummi. Death and I have been very close friends as of late, so it did cross my mind that this could be a suicide mission. That I could die. That you and Mitta and Bastion could die. That—" he took a shuddering breath. "That Shasha could die."

I swallowed, his fear and pain evident in the lines of his face. "My Lord."

"No. It's alright. Shasha and I have discussed this at length." He stood, opening the cabinet in the wall. "We both understand the risks, and though neither of us want the other in danger, we also won't let the other walk in without each other. We have come to terms with our mortality. My hope is that we will all make it home in one piece."

"And if we don't? Who will you sacrifice to get us out."

He sighed, pouring himself a glass of scotch. "I don't need to answer that."

He was right. He didn't need to answer. I knew, just like we all knew. "You can't keep falling on the sword Niratap. It will get you killed."

"To be completely honest with you, Tummilia." He downed the scotch in one hard swallow. "I am surprised it hasn't yet."

The throne room's marble floors shine offensively in the light from the elk horn chandeliers, crimson velvet drapery hangs about the room. They always made me feel like the throne room was bleeding. Father sits upon his throne, watching me and Katrel as we come into the room. Mother always looks scared anymore, scared for us or herself I don't know. Cyran has stepped into his father's shoes taking up the mark of Crown Scholar, but the man seated next to father on the dais eyes me in a strange way, one that only Revan has ever looked at me with.

Father speaks but his words I don't hear, I respond robotically to his request. Katrel is the one who asked what he wants us to perform.

"The Taking of Night."

Katrel goes to the keybones, and I take my starting spot on the empty floor. My heart flutters uncomfortably in my chest as the man stares at me with that hungry look. It's almost as if his hands are roving my body as the dance begins. Father is smiling at the man and laughing and something sinister twists in my gut.

My chest heaves as the dance finishes and we are both dismissed. Something is not right. Something is inherently wrong with all of this. I turned to Katrel before she entered her room.

"Do you find that odd?"

"What Tummi?" She said exasperatedly, every day she is angrier, and I can't figure out why. "That father wanted to show off his daughters to a merchant friend?"

"No. I've become accustomed to that, but the way he looked at me."

"And how did he look at you, Tummilia? The way a man looks at a woman? Like prey?"

"Well, yes."

Katrel sighs. "When will you learn that we are of marriageable age and as the princesses of the kingdom it is our only purpose to be married off to strengthen the crown whether it be politically or as vessels to create the next kings."

"You make it sound so terrible."

"It is terrible, Tummilia. We as people have no value beyond what we can give to the kingdom. Be it our name or our wombs."

"Katrel!"

"Tell me I'm wrong, I dare you."

"Uh." I can't. She's right and I know it.

"That's what I thought." She opens the door to her room. "You need to realize that we are just pawns in the games of men. Why else waste our morning dolling us up if not for show?"

Her door snicks shut, ending the conversation bitterly. Katrel has only grown farther from me and colder as we've aged. She is the Crown Princess and whoever she marries will be the next king. Father hasn't seemed like he cares about me, or what I do. Though the only men who have ever shown interest in me are the ones my sister rejects. Does that mean they are in it for me or because they just wanted a way into the royal family?

I pushed into my own room contemplating what was to come. Why not have a ball to honor the merchant, who father had sat beside him and called friend? Strange enough that he was human, but the way his eyes roved over my body. A chill crawled up my spine as I closed my own bedroom door. My room is dark and cold, the fire gone out. Strange, before I had gone to dance the fire had been roaring in the hearth. Stepping close, water soaks into my slippers.

"What the—"

A man's hand covers my mouth. "Now, little princess, you're going to come with me."

I froze. I should have screamed. I should have run. I should have fought, but I just stand there. Another man comes in front of me. I can't see his face in the darkness as he collects my hands and ties them together. I wanted to scream, but my voice is hiding from me.

"Such a good little princess." The man chuckles softly. "She's soft, Jacob."

"Elias. Just grab the bag so we can go."

"Do you think William will share when he's had his fun?" He asked the man behind me, as he slid the bag over my head. Tears finally slid down my face. This couldn't be happening.

"Probably. Stay quiet Princess and we won't have to hurt you."

They walked me through the halls of the castle leading me into a room.

"Where do you want her?" The man named Jacob asked.

"Lay her on the bed."

I found my voice though it shook. "I don't know what you want, but my father is the king."

The new man laughed as they sat me on the edge of the bed. "Child. I know that you weren't told about this, but who do you think sold you to me."

"Wh—what?"

"Tie her down Jacob."

"No." I screamed pulling against the men as they

pulled me back over the bed. "Stop."

The man laughed again. "Scream all you want girl. No one is coming to save you."

"No!"

"No!"

I sat up in bed, my heart fluttering rapidly. I wasn't there anymore. I wasn't in that room. I wasn't with those men anymore. They were dead. I remembered watching as Niratap tore through them that night. As terrible as it was, I cried tears of joy when they died, too many of them had laid their hands on my skin. I felt them on my body as I freed myself from my covers. A walk might free me from the nightmares. The gardens were always peaceful even at night, the moonflowers and night roses were in full bloom.

Beyond the hedge a low keening sound drifted on the breeze. "In the arms of the angels, far away from here."

"Hello?" I called back.

There was a strum of a guitar and a splash. "Fekkin ell."

"Bastion?" I said coming around a bend. The young orc was floating in the fountain, his guitar laying across his chest. His cheeks were rosy and eyes puffy. Poor kid.

"Tummi." He cooed, lifting his arms above him.

"How drunk are you?"

"I'm not drunk."

"Denial drunk. Got it." I walked closer to the fountain. "Do you want a hand?"

"Suuuuuuuuure." He flopped his arms down into the fountain and giggled like a toddler.

"Give me your hand, love."

He gave me a haphazard grin but reached for me. "Okay Tuuuuuuuuummi."

"Come on silly boy." I said, reaching my hand out to him.

"I won't pull you in."

"You better not." I hefted him from the fountain and sat him on the edge. "You doing, okay?"

His grey eyes met mine, the sorrow in them made my heart ache. He leaned the guitar beside him and placed his head in his hands. "Honestly, no, but you don't need to worry yourself Tummi. I'm not going to run headfirst to join my friend anytime soon."

"The lord wanted to tell you sooner."

He sighed. "I know, but he couldn't."

I sat next to him and stared up at the stars. "He's watching over you."

"I know he is." Bastion smiled. "He wasn't supposed to be the one to die."

"But it happened."

He sighed. "A slip of the tongue is all it takes."

"Sometimes less."

"Yeah."

"Do you need help getting back to the house? You sound like you're sobering up, but I don't want you getting lost."

"My brain knows where my mouth is, not my legs."

I laughed as I stood, offering my hand. "Let me guide you back to the house then."

"Thank you, Tummi."

He grasped the neck of his guitar before he rose stumbling into me. "You really are drunk aren't you."

"Probably." He tried to step and teetered away from me.

"Not that way. Come with me."

I guided him back through the garden and into the manor. We stumbled up the stairs and down the hall to his room. I flopped him down on his bed before pulling his shoes off and setting them on the floor of his closet.

I took in the space that I hadn't been in for some

years, not since he was a child. Band posters had been tacked to the walls, that alone would drive Allipo nuts, a computer desk sat against one wall and before the fireplace were all sorts of instruments from drums, to keyboards, to a fiddle. Polaroids were tacked to the wall beside the fireplace. Captured moments of the young orcs' life on display. Him with his parents baking bread, to him and Taegan soaked and laughing at the fishing pond. Beyond the collection of instruments is the bathroom that smelled of clove soap. I wet a cloth and returned to the young orc laying in his bed. I sat beside him.

"I'm sorry." He mumbled as I dabbed his forehead.

"It's okay Bas. I much prefer a sense of purpose."

"Why were you out in the gardens?" His voice has taken on a roughness that warms me in ways it shouldn't.

Sweet kid had always been like that, from picking dandelions to give to us to matching us shot for shot in the range, but now he was no longer a child. Could I open myself to him that way? Could I open up to him about the terrible things that had happened to me?

"Tummi?" He pressed, looking up at me.

"I had a nightmare and didn't want to stay in my room."

"Do you have them often?"

"Sometimes." I guess I was opening up. Letting him catch a glimpse of the broken parts of myself.

He yawned. "What was your nightmare about?"

"It's not something that can hurt me anymore."

"Tell me?" His eyes pleaded with me and something in that storm cloud gaze made me want to share that with him.

"It was about the day I was sold. It wasn't a pleasant day for me."

"I still don't understand how a father could sell his children into the trade, especially a king."

"My father never really cared for me. In elf traditions royalty passes from father to son or father to grandson. Royal families have always been lucky since the dawn of our era in history and had sons. Katrel was a disappointment being born a girl and then I was double the disappointment. It was incredibly scandalous for the royal family to have more than one child, let alone another girl. To be honest, since we've been away from home, I realized how lucky I had been being sold off. My father could have easily killed me."

He propped himself up on his elbows. "We won't let him hurt you."

I blinked back tears. "You both have told me that."

"I mean it." He said, gasping my hand. "I will not let him hurt you or your sister."

I wiped my cheeks with the back of my hand. "I should let you rest."

He gripped my hand. "Don't go."

"Bas." His eyes shone with tears.

"Contrary to popular opinion, I really don't want to be alone." He gave a half-hearted tusky grin.

Tears rolled down my face, but against all reason I lowered myself into the bed next to him. He threw the comforter over us and laid on his side. I pressed my back against his chest, wrapping his arms around me. He pressed his face into my hair and breathed deeply. It was strange. Those other men had done similar things. Smelled my hair and told me how delicious it smelled. Told me how they wondered if my body tasted the way it smelled. But when Bastion did it, it made me feel safe. His body was muscled and firm behind me and strong, so much stronger than the little boy I used to sing to sleep when he screamed from colic. I felt him behind me, massive, at attention, and pressing against my ass.

"This isn't fair for me to ask." He whispered against my neck.

"What is it, Bastion?"

"I have for the longest time wanted you, ever since I was old enough to understand the feeling. Tell me no, because I'm drunk and stupid, but I want you Tummi."

Heat pooled in my core. "We shouldn't."

He kissed the back of my neck. "We don't have to."

My heart fluttered. I swallowed, as the words of horrible men haunted me. "You understand what happened to me, right? That I am tainted."

Bastion stilled behind me, his hold loosening. "Tummilia, whatever anyone else has told you, you are not dirty or damaged because of what happened to you."

He pulled away and I rolled to face him. "Bastion?"

He glowered at the ceiling; his face still rosy. "I mean it. You are not broken because cruel men forced themselves upon you. Just forget that I asked. You don't have to stay. I don't want to be one of those men. I don't want to be that way ever again."

My heart cracked at that. I had heard in passing that Bastion had been processing girls while undercover, forcing them into the very bondage we wanted to free them from. "Bastion."

"It's okay." He closed his eyes and even in the faint light I watched the tear roll down the side of his face. "Like I said, I'm drunk and stupid."

I cupped his face and ran my thumb over his cheek. When had he become so handsome? He had a rugged shadow along his square jaw and the scar above his brow that was new. "Bastion. You are drunk, there's no denying that, but you aren't stupid. A little loose with your tongue and body, but never stupid."

"Tummilia." The husky way he said my name sent white hot fire burning through me. I looked down into his devastating eyes. How had I missed that look? The depth at which he felt for me. His hand cupped my face, his calloused thumb marking my soul with the gentle strokes. "You are so beautiful."

"Bastion. We shouldn't." My brain was screaming logic at my racing heart. I had changed his diapers. I had been a teacher and an aunt to him as he grew.

"We don't have to. Regardless of what I want, it is your choice."

It was predatory to want him this way. But I wanted his touch, welcomed it. I wanted to taste his lips and feel him against me. I wanted. Maybe it was the fact that I had never wanted a man's touch since we had been freed; didn't seek nighttime companions like Katrel had, though every morning after she was testy and volatile. Maybe it was the long-suffering loneliness that I had had since my youth, but I leaned into him and pressed my lips to his. His large hand threaded through my hair angling my head to deepen his access to my mouth.

His tongue slid softly against my lips, which I eagerly parted for him. Honey, berries, and spice invaded my mouth as we explored each other. How had I missed this? I was lost, not knowing where I ended, and he began, his fingers flexed in my hair against my scalp coaxing a soft groan from me. His other hand found my hip, this thumb stroking me through the fabric. Was this feeling what left Katrel so angry or was it the lack of spark that angered her, because there was no way this floating happy feeling could be so terrible. He pulled back and I wanted to demand more, but his hooded gaze made my heart skip.

"We should sleep. You may enjoy kissing me, but we are both pretty raw right now. Sex shouldn't be something we share unless we're both sure."

He was solid for a drunk. Wise beyond his years to hold space for our wounded souls. "You're okay with that?"

He smiled, his tusks glinting in the pre-dawn light. "Tummilia. Let's sleep and if tomorrow or the next day your heart still desires me, we can explore each other. I want you, but not as a crutch for my heart. Not to chase the memories of bad men away. I want us for us."

I smiled. "I like that."

I curled against him, and he wrapped an arm around me, wrapping me in his honey and clove spice scent. He was right. We shouldn't dive into each other to comfort ourselves. Shouldn't use each other if we wanted to explore something else. Tonight, we were comforting each other. He didn't want to be alone. I didn't want to be trapped under men from memories and to be completely honest with myself, I probably didn't want to be alone either.

Chapter Five

Shasha

Tomorrow was the funeral for the young man the house had lost. Someone I hadn't had the pleasure to meet, but who had meant so much to my mate. He had been in his office most of the night, creeping in just as the first rays of dawn had begun to peek through the curtains. His face was tight with deep shadows resting below his eyes. We were supposed to train in a few hours, and he was pushing himself. Stretching his energy far beyond what he should, with the unknown before us and the other looming threats especially. Worry filled my heart at how hard he went at it, worry and pride that my mate was such a dedicated leader.

"You know," he murmured, cracking an eye to stare back at me, "it is much easier to sleep without being watched."

"It's much easier to sleep, *mo grá*, when you come to bed at a reasonable time."

He chuffed rolling onto his back. "And how do you know I haven't been in bed beside you all night?"

"Because I woke up when you went to take a shower."

"So, you were pretending to sleep when I crawled into bed and kissed you."

"I may or may not have been waiting for you."

He grinned, but it didn't quite meet his tired eyes. "I was checking in on Staspar and Saara. Making sure they were going to be here on schedule and that they didn't meet any resistance with Taegan's remains."

I frowned at him. "Understandable, but you also need to rest. We are leaving in a week's time and going into the elf kingdom completely blind as to what to expect.

You need all your strength and energy for that."

"You are correct, my love." He ran a hand down my arm grasping my fingers in his.

"Still no plan, beyond saying please."

He snorted. "No. I don't know enough about Elven customs and traditions to build a good enough plan to get us in and out safely. I don't know enough about Cardoc to know whether he will take us kindly or not. From what I do know I can surmise that he won't, and we have to prepare for anything."

"So, we're at a disadvantage."

"A high one at that." He yawned.

"Sleep my love."

"Why? We have training in a couple hours and Staspar and Saara will be here around noon."

"I will send Mitta a text. She will want you rested beyond anything and missing a couple days of training won't do much harm."

"What about—"

"Rest *mo grá*. I will wake you in time to greet the boy's mother."

He eyed me but gave a gentle nod and squeezed my fingers. "Very well, mate. I will rest."

I scooted close to him and kissed him softly. "You have nothing to fear, my love. As long as we are together, we will come out on top."

He kissed me back. "If you believe it, I will try to strive for that."

"Sleep."

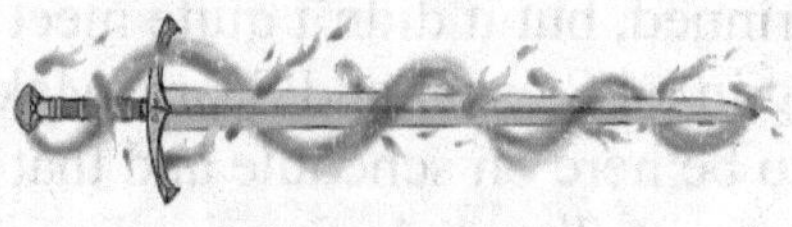

The quiet rap on our door pulled me from my book. A tale of a fair maiden being kidnapped by a dark prince from a fallen kingdom. She had just stabbed the man in the heart and was running from her captors when I placed my bookmark and slid from the bed. Careful not to disturb my mate slumbering soundly as I tossed the sheets over him to cover his ass. The knuckles rapped against our door again as I rounded the bed and padded to it.

"I'm coming. I'm coming." I muttered as I opened one of the doors. My mother stood there with a soft smile on her face that fell as she glanced past me to where Nira slept. "Mom."

"Hey baby girl. I was just checking on you guys, I didn't see you at breakfast."

"Sorry. I should have let you know we were staying in this morning. Niratap had a late night and needed to rest."

"I understand." She looked beyond me to where Nira was half covered in bed, his tail had fallen from the sheets and twitched as he dreamed. "Knowing a story is very different from seeing the evidence of it."

I knew she was talking about the patchwork of scars that laced across his back and arms in varying stages of age. Knew that she spoke from a place of care, but part of me bristled to defend him. "He has lived a hard life."

She huffed. "No need for the tone, child. I meant no harm. He has surprised me more than I could have imagined. So have you."

I stepped into the hall and closed the door behind me. "I'm sorry that things didn't go smoother. That we had to fight each other. To be honest I understand why you kept me so sheltered, especially after I fell headfirst into his world. I understand what it looked like falling for the man who bought me."

"I misjudged him. I only saw the man-eating predator. Not the man and I was resistant to it. Still am if I am honest, but he protected me from the sharp tongue of my daughter and the sharp teeth of that kelpie."

"I appreciate that you didn't cower when he shifted. It is really jarring the first time."

"Don't mistake it, I was scared out of my damned mind." She laughed nervously. "A monstrous creature shapeshifted in my defense against a fae beast. He is definitely a marvel to say the least."

I chuckled. "He wants to be on good terms with you and my father. I don't think when he purchased me that what we have become was his goal, but I am happy being with him."

"You're not scared?"

"Of Niratap? No. I know that he would never hurt me intentionally. We both have tempers and have the tendency to weaponize our words first, but ultimately, we love each other and no spat between us could destroy that. I couldn't explain the feeling of rightness I have, being with him, it's beyond words. We just belong."

"I think I can sympathize."

I looked at her, shocked by her words. "How?"

"I feel the same with Xaevean." Warmth filled my chest as she reminisced. "Ever since I met him. Meant to be."

"I would like to hear it sometime. The story of how you met."

"I would love to tell it to you. When do the other guests arrive?"

"They're supposed to be here around noon. We have about an hour before I have to wake him. Is that enough time?"

Mom beamed. "It is the perfect amount of time."

"We can sit by the fire in our room as long as we're quiet. It's cozy there."

"Alright. Lead the way."

We sat in the soft brown chairs before the fire. I tucked my legs up as my mother glanced at the sleeping man on the bed. I wondered what she thought of it all, with me sharing a bed with a monster. I never thought of him that way, he was just a man to me. Just Nira. Who filled my heart full of love and life and everything I had ever wanted he gave.

"Does it bother you?" I found myself asking, painfully curious.

"What love?" She asked, turning to face me.

"Me and him? Honestly?"

Her face soured and she looked into the fire that was dying in the hearth. "Honestly, I'm still trying to come to terms with it. I don't like it, but the more and more I ponder the reasons why I don't, I find myself with more questions than answers. Is it because of how I was raised? Is it the religion that I love that says he's less than me? Does it feel so convoluted to me because your father is also different? I asked him the other day what he thought, and you know what he told me? He told me that he didn't approve because he was so much older than you. That because he purchased you, he didn't value you as you valued him. He didn't approve because you being with Niratap put you in danger. But if he hadn't have purchased you, you would still be in some sex den or dead. That the way he dotes on you like you were royalty, the way adoration floats in his eyes when you walk into a room, proved that he cared deeply about you and that he couldn't see you in a safer place than next to him."

I wiped my face as tears rolled down my cheeks. "He has some redeeming features, my father, that is."

She laughed lightly. "That he does. Now, I was telling you how we met."

I leaned closer and nodded. "I know the basics, but I want to hear your story."

"Well, I was working at the post office back then. I wasn't much older than you when he walked in. I knew that some young black man had moved to Afton, but seeing him in the flesh was something else. Our hometown is just a bit whitewashed if you get my drift." I did because I had been the only black girl in school. "He was so handsome then, not that he's changed much, apparently elementals are long-lived, but he had one hell of a smile, and he was dressed so sharp. I was beside myself with feelings I had never felt before. It was love at first sight and he came up to the counter with Decan in tow. Decan, that sly devil introduced us did his business and snuck out the door without either of us noticing. He stood there talking to me the entirety of my shift and when I was off, he walked me home. I swooned over him to my mother, and you know how your grandmother was. She told me he was only interested in my virtue and not in me. I told her I didn't believe that. The next day after my shift was over, he was waiting for me and wanted to know if he could buy me a drink. Much to my wild youthful spirit I said yes."

"And then it was history."

She chuckled. "He definitely made me wild. He pulled me out of my shell, like he pulled me onto the dance floor and wooed me. Decan swore to your grandmother up and down that Xaevean was the best man for me, he was good and kind, but your grandmother, ever the witch, drilled him constantly about everything repeatedly. I thought it was her age showing, her memory starting to go. She'd ask him where he was from, who his parents were, what they did, why he moved to Afton, what his intentions were for our relationship that was so fast and hard. I fell so hard, baby girl."

"Sounds like grandma." I remember my grandmother well enough to know she had been a crotchety old biddy who found her senile enjoyment out of harassing my mother at any moment she could. Mom had been the only one of her children who stayed in Afton and the only one with a broken family. My aunt and three uncles ran as fast as they could and as far as they could, only visiting the required Thanksgiving or Christmas. My aunt was the closest, living in D.C., and sometimes made it up for Easter, but now that Grandma was gone none of them visited Afton.

"Then there was this night in February where it was unseasonably warm. Your father took me out to dinner at that Chinese place we like so much."

I laughed. "The weird one owned by that Ukrainian family?"

"Yes, that's the one. Then he took me dancing and after a few drinks we ended up wandering up to the hills and we told each other about our dreams."

"What were they? Your dreams?"

"I wanted nights like that one for the rest of my days. Nights filled with laughter and fun and him. He wanted to be great, but not in the way his father was, in his own way with kindness. We wanted a life together and it was under those very stars he asked me if I'd marry him. It was brash and foolish, we were so young, but I loved him so purely in that moment. I told him I would. The next year we were married before God. His family didn't come, and your grandmother had to comment on that the entire night. I remember what she said to him during the reception."

"What did she say?"

"She said, 'If your well-off politician family can't show up, are you going to show up for my daughter?'"

"No." I said in mock horror, it was definitely something my grandmother would say.

"Yes, and he just apologized. Told her his father was a very busy man and didn't have time to spare. She hissed at him something along the lines of 'not even if his boy was getting married' and your father simply nodded. A year after that you were born, and your father was over the moon. They don't have a very good relationship, your father and his father. I know he said that his father said terrible things to him before you were born, but even now they haven't reconciled."

"Do you think they will?"

"I asked him that the other day and he told me, and I quote, 'fuck that jackass of a man. I don't care if he's my father, he wasn't hurt with me cutting ties and I don't care if he's well off. I'm doing pretty good myself without his old money and old ideas.' And that was all he had to say."

"Ouch."

She shrugged glancing back to where Niratap shifted in the bed. I don't know what she saw looking at him. Did she see the faint hint of his ribs, still visible since his capture? Could she tell which scars were the newest, the deepest lashings from Dravin dipping below the sheet down to the cleft of his ass? Did she see their pink tinge, know that deep x of scarring was only a taste of what he had experienced?

"How is he?"

"Stubborn. Reckless. Tired." All that was true. "He's recovering, slowly for his species, much too slowly for his liking."

"He seems like a workaholic."

"He is, but he manages at least a hundred undercover operatives in various places around the world. He is dedicated to the beings in this house and the creatures he shelters. He oversees and cares for several communities of beings in New York. He's a CI for the FBMI. He's an investor and a player in the underbelly of the world. All while trying to find more of his severely endangered species."

"And then he chose a spit fire as a companion."

"That he did." I beamed at her. "He's been teaching me how to navigate everything in the underground bit by bit."

"Aren't you scared?"

"Of course. It would be foolish not to be, but with him I know we'll be fine."

"Are you worried about going to the Babylos? Worried about him?"

"Yes." It was the only answer I had. "He's not a hundred percent yet and from what Kozran said last week he may never be a hundred percent again. I worry that he's rushing into it with nothing but faith. I love him deeply, but I worry that we are ill-prepared to deal with that chauvinist elf king. I worry he will push himself past his limits, because he feels better and ultimately reinjures himself."

"That is understandable. Mitta shares that concern." I gave her a quizzical look. "We were talking about that the other day, when I sat in to watch you train."

A deep resonating growl pulled our attention back to my mate who shifted rolling onto his back.

"Shit." I mumbled, jumping up and going to his side. "Mom, will you go into the bathroom and wet a rag for me?"

"Yeah. What's wrong with him?"

"He's just having a nightmare." She scuttled off to the bathroom while I gently stroked his arm. "*Mo grá*, I need you to wake up. It's just a nightmare."

His eyes rapidly fluttered under his lids as his breathing quickened. Mom returned to my side and handed me the cool rag.

"Thank you. Step back, just in case, he can lash out when he has them." I patted the cloth against his cheeks and brow as his face contorted. "Niratap my love, I need you to wake up."

"Is he violent when he lashes out?" My mother's voice came from the fireplace.

"Not necessarily violent. I think it just takes him time to come back to reality. Nira, my love."

"Does he have them often?" She asked as he pulled away from me, his hand coming to rest against his throat.

"In recent months, yes." I said shifting to ease his hand away. "Mate, I need you to wake."

He ground his teeth as he arched off the bed, fighting off some phantom aggressor. I wondered if the malice had found him again.

"Do you want me to hold him down?" My mother had crept closer behind me.

"No. I don't want you to get hurt." I stroked his face trying to pull him from the dream. "It will make him panic. Being restrained is difficult for him. Niratap, please wake up."

He gasped and sat up panting. His eyes wide in terror as he took in his surroundings. His gaze stopped on my mother, his head tilting quizzically before his eyes settled on me. He took a deep breath resting his head in his hands.

"Why is your mother in our room?" His voice was rough like he had been screaming.

"We were having a discussion before—" I didn't have to finish the thought, he knew.

He sighed as the tips of his ears pinked, and a tremor rolled down his spine. "I apologize if I startled you Jazzera."

"Don't fret about it." My mother said, turning to the door. "I'll go and get you guys some food."

"Thanks mom." After she slid out the door and it closed with a click, I pressed. "What was it about?"

He took a couple shuddering breaths before he spoke. "Do you really want to know?"

He didn't always share, but it seemed he was open to it. "If you wish to share. Was it the malice?"

"I'm not sure. It might have had a part of it, but it was Atton." He placed his hand against his throat and swallowed a couple times. "He had his hands wrapped around my throat; he was telling me he couldn't wait to break you. Then his flesh started to decay, and his ghoulish corpse was twisting the life from me."

I shuddered at that. "That sounds terrifying, but you're safe now. It was just a nightmare."

He gave me a forlorn look. "I hate that I'm having so many. It either wakes you or disrupts the house and then everyone is fretting over me."

I rubbed soothing circles on his back. "It doesn't bother me. You just went through a traumatic experience. It would be weird if it didn't affect you. You're also being hunted by a creature that can infiltrate your dreams and twist them."

He smirked. "You are a gift."

"As are you. Go get dressed and I'll fix your hair."

"I am fully capable of taking care of my hair."

"Yes, but it helps settle both of us."

He leaned over and pressed a tender kiss to my forehead. "Very well mate of mine."

I had the detangler and brush pulled out when Nira came back into the bedroom. He had on a charcoal suit that warmed his skin and brightened his eyes. He was fidgeting with the sleeves as he padded over to where I sat.

"Come sit."

He smiled softly. "On the floor?"

"We've talked about this, you're too tall otherwise."

He huffed a soft laugh but sat before me with a groan. "The floor is a long way down."

I sprayed his hair lightly before I started brushing out his ends. "I'll help you up, if need be."

He was quiet for a moment. "What were you and your mother talking about?"

His hair detangled easily through the bristles of the brush. "Well, she came to check on us and it evolved into her telling me the story of how she and my father met. Their love story."

"I hope it was enlightening."

I swept his hair back around his antlers. "It was. Would you like me to braid your hair?"

"If it's not too much trouble my love."

"It's not trouble at all." I said, collecting the hair that descended from above his antlers. Starting it off as a partial French braid, I pulled the rest of his hair back into my fingers and finished it out. Snug like he liked it. I climbed over the arm of the chair and walked to the bathroom. "Let me grab the comb and the pomade and I'll smooth out the top. Don't move."

"I won't."

As I came back there was a knock on the door. I called. "Come in."

My mother entered, Rogmesh behind her with a tray balanced on her hip. Rogmesh beamed. "You look mighty sharp, my Lord."

His eyes narrowed in her direction as I tilted his chin up and locked down his hair. A subtle dusting of pink colored his cheeks as his eyes returned to mine. Their intensity never lost its ability to render me breathless. My heart clenched as I shifted my gaze to check my work before stepping back to set the supplies on the side table and offer him my hand. He took it, but barely tugged as he righted himself.

"Thank you, mate."

"Always."

Rogmesh cleared her throat as she passed us. "I made you some cold sandwiches, prepared some fruit and brought some water. Our guests will be arriving in about a half hour's time. Is there anything thing either of you need?"

"No, Rogmesh." I said, my gaze not leaving Nira's. "We'll be down in a few to greet Saara and Staspar."

She smiled. "Leave the dishes, I'll collect them while you get the guests settled."

Nira sat in one of the chairs and uncovered the dish. Two plates with simple chicken salad sandwiches and a pile of early spring berries sat on the plate. The water glasses had the same berries and mint floating betwixt the ice. He looked at her as she moved to leave. "Rogmesh, did Allipo prepare the room I ask him to?"

She paused at the door next to my mother. "Yes, my Lord. The Amethyst suit was prepared to your instruction and the girls cleaned it this morning."

"Alright. Thank you, Rogmesh."

She bowed and exited the room. My mother

fidgeted at the door. I looked at her as I sat. "Did you need something mom?"

"I—" She took a deep breath. "Are you sure you want to go through with all of this Niratap?"

He popped a berry into his mouth watching her as he chewed far more than the berry warranted. His tone was tight when he spoke. "What is this *this* you are referring to."

"Going to the Babylos. Are the risks not greater than your aim? Why go if you don't have a plan?"

Nira watched her, thinking carefully of what he would say as he flexed his hand. I saw it in the sharpness of his eyes. He took a sip of water and when his eyes met my mother's again there was a softness there beyond his anger. "I will never let those girls fall back into bondage solely because I don't have a plan of action. Katrel does not deserve to be a brood mare for her father's line and Tummilia does not deserve to be a plaything that their father can use as a bargaining chip to win favor with others. I cannot and will not allow that. Yes, the risks against us are astronomical, but they are the same if we go or if we stay. Katrel must appear before the king and that is our only option."

"But why is that the only option?"

He relaxed into his seat, his jaw working in irritation. "Going to Babylos is dangerous because yes, I don't have a plan, nor do I have intel that is current enough to make a plan. Ignoring King Cardoc's summons is dangerous because if Katrel, the Crown Princess, doesn't appear before her father he will use the full force of his armies to rain fire on our home. So, no Jazzera, there is not any other option because the two we have could, in all likelihood, get us all killed."

My mother's hand went to her mouth, her skin ashing over. I looked away. Niratap was right. We could die either way and that was a harsh reality I hadn't been preparing to share with my mother. That harshness in his voice hadn't entered his eyes as he told her the truth, only kindness sat in his quicksilver eyes.

"You would put my daughter, your mate, at risk like that?"

Niratap glanced at me, and I gave him a sympathetic look. He shifted in the seat uncomfortably. We had discussed this thoroughly and repeatedly. He had sworn to the girls that they would be safe, that he would be there to keep Cardoc at bay. I didn't want him going. He didn't want me going. He wasn't going without me and thus we were at an impasse.

"Shasha and I have discussed this at length. I don't want her to go, Cardoc is a patriarchal ruler and thus I fear for her safety. She fears for mine since I have not healed fully."

"And he has the tendency to be careless." I interjected.

He gave a tight smile and nodded. "I will do everything in my power to protect your daughter."

"I'm stronger now too, mother. I can protect myself." I felt his eyes at my back as I looked at my mother. "We will be okay."

"I—"

"Jazzera." The force of the command in his voice startled me. I never expected him to use such a tone with my mother and magic crackled in the air. "You won't change our mind; we're going to protect our girls. This conversation is over."

My mother gave a curt nod before she turned to leave. I took a few bites of my sandwich before I looked at my mate. He was watching me, his eyes hard. "Yes, Shasha."

I swallowed, finding my voice. "I would appreciate you not using magic on my mortal mother."

He arched a brow. "How did you know I used magic?"

"I felt it in the air. What did you do to her?"

"It was a small compulsion I told her we were done and to leave." He sighed, frowning. "I did not enjoy doing it."

"She is worried." I growled.

"And I am not?" He questioned, but his voice lacking emotion.

"No, I know you're worried about how this will all go. I know you're scared." I looked away from his gaze. "I know."

He cupped my face and pulled me to look at him. "I am sorry. I will refrain from using magic on your mother in the future and I do understand where she is coming from. You are her child and losing you would be a wound beyond her understanding. I did not mean to cause you harm or anger you."

"I understand why you did it." I said and I did. She would have pushed, and it would have evolved into a fight which was not conducive for what we were about to face. "I stand by your decision. Let's finish eating our guests will be here soon."

I didn't know what to expect as we stood at the base of the steps watching as a black sedan rolled up the drive. The vehicle stopped just before the steps and a familiar red mop of curls exited the driver's side, as Staspar came around, opened the passenger door, and he helped the faun woman. She was stunningly beautiful; her full wavy black hair framed her pale face. Her ash horns were short, and her storm cloud eyes shone brightly as she laid eyes on my mate. Staspar handed her a cane and I finally saw the odd angle of her left hock. Staspar bowed deeply as they came to stand before us, I noticed her hands were mangled as well.

Niratap bowed deeply to the woman as she approached. "Saara, it is good to see you again. I hope your travels went well."

She gave a dip of her chin. "Yes, my Lord. Staspar has been a kind companion for this sour meeting. I hate that this has been such a long wait to lay my son to rest."

Nira's face became somber. "I wish we were meeting under different circumstances."

"As do I." Her gaze landed on me. "And who is the maiden of shadows and flowers?"

"Saara, this is my mate, Shasha." Niratap spoke softly.

"It's a pleasure to meet you." I said, smiling softly. "I didn't get to meet your son, but I have only heard good things about him while I've been here."

"You did not know Taegan?"

"No."

"Shasha has only been in my company since August. She did not have a chance."

She nodded and met my mate's gaze. "Where is my other son?"

Niratap smiled, offering her his arm. "Bastion is hopefully in the kitchen helping his mother cook a grand feast for your arrival."

"You are too kind to me, my Lord." She said using his arm as support.

"No. I have many years of unkindness to make up for, my dear." He said, leading her up the steps.

"It is in the past."

Staspar stood beside me, smiling warmly at me. "Da lord ask' me to s'ay an 'elp her move abou'."

"That is awful kind of you Staspar."

"I 'ould 'ave regar'less. She isa lovely 'oman." His eyes crinkled happily as he offered me his arm. "Milady?"

I took his arm. "So, when we first met. The lord said you looked at me with a different kind of hunger. What did my mate mean by that?"

The satyr flushed brightly, his skin matching that of his hair. "I 'ave no idea of whish you speak of, Milady."

"I'm sorry Staspar. I am only teasing."

He eyed me cautiously. "You 'ave become quite da trickster, Milady."

"I'm glad you noticed." Niratap was chatting softly with Saara. "Did you know Taegan well?"

"Aye. He was a good ki'. Curious an' brave, wild but he was bes'friens wif Bas. Dey were inseparable."

"That makes sense, Bastion took the news pretty hard."

"I am not surprised. Dey were soulmates."

"I thought soul mates were romantic partners?"

"Dey can be, but more offen den not dey are friens. People who are bonded, who jus belong wif one anodder."

Chapter Six

Niratap

Funerals have always been the worst thing in my line of work, for they happened far too often, especially to those who were too young. I wanted to save them all, but that was an impossible ask for one being. Taegan's loss was a wave throughout the organization, many had sent loving notes in their briefs and more had sent money to help support his mother. Everyone loved him. I had loved him and the only people who loved him more was his mother he had only recently found again and his best friend.

Bastion had helped Saara out over the grassy yard to a hidden grove where we buried our beloved dead, every time she stumbled, he caught her. Her second child she called him, with love and grace. Rogmesh and Durgash never minded the woman claiming Bastion as hers; they had done the same with Taegan. The faun boy who we had found after breaking up a trafficking ring. When I met those teary, thunderstorm eyes, I knew the boy would only come with me. The Days quickly thrust the two boys together and as they grew, Bastion pulled Taegan from the shadows that the dens of debauchery had planted in his life. This funeral was different than most.

We gathered around the small grave for his ashes, a simple stone that Saara swore would be all he would have wanted. Bastion had agreed. A somber feeling curled itself around my heart and made it hard to breathe. Shasha had comforted and soothed the rough edges his death had left on my being, but the wound was still open, still oozing. I cleared my throat and stepped forward to the graveside.

"As the sun settles on the earth tonight, we honor

one of our fallen friends. Taegan was a laugh in everyone's heart. He was warm and kind and good. Noble and brave for one so young. Know that you are loved and missed here on this plane and may your soul frolic in the Summerland." I stepped back next to Shasha and she gripped my fingers in her hand, giving them a comforting squeeze.

Rogmesh stepped forward with a bittersweet smile on her face. "Taegan was a wild, unruly child who ran through our kitchen screaming at the tops of his lungs, only plied with chocolate chip cookies or Oreos." There was a chuckle that rolled through the group. "As a young man he was kind above all else. Yes, he was still wild and unruly, but when he comforted a young child or helped an injured creature, the care he put into his being rivaled all others. You will always have a home at our table and in my heart my sweet boy."

Allipo stepped forward as Rogmesh rested her head on her husband's shoulder, tears already rimmed his eyes. "Taegan knew nothing of being a cloven beast. He knew nothing of the dance, the music, the soul of fauns and satyrs alike. He knew nothing of the madness of Dionysus and Silenus. Knew nothing of Greece and had no love for sweet grape wine. But he was the sweetness of said wine. He was a dance of his own. A music that I will never unhear. And a wild mischievousness that will be missed in my heart. May the gods grace you with the madness of Dionysus and may you dance around those pyres and partaketh of that sweetest ambrosia."

Saara cast a look to Bastion who was looking at the small whole in the earth where his friend's body would lay. A sweet smile came to her face as she hobbled forward and, with the help of Allipo and Staspar, placed her son into the earth. "My sweet Taegan. My sweet, sweet babe. You were taken from me so young and taken from this earth to soon. I did not have the chance to know you as I should have, I was robbed of that right to know you. I had all but given up hope of ever seeing you again, but then you waltzed back into my life as a young man full of love and courage. It took my breath away, Taegan. You took my breath away and showered my weakness in kindness. I have loved you since the day you were born, and I held your tiny body in my arms. I will love you until we can dance in the Summerlands together at last."

Tears rolled down her face as she stepped back leaning against Staspar as she cried. Bastion didn't move from where he stood between Saara and Tummi. His eyes not lifting from their hold on Taegan's grave when he spoke. "Taegan. You jackass. You weren't supposed to go off and get yourself killed. We were supposed to get dumb drunk on your honey meads and sing to the moon when our tours were up. We should not be standing here mourning over your dust and memory, but here we are without you. I—" Bastion took a quivering breath. "I was not prepared to lose you, but you bet your ass when I get there Ima beat the ever-loving-shit out of you for leaving me behind."

Bastion was angry and I understood that it came from the part of him that was still young and still innocent. Bastion cleared his throat before he started to sing. It took me several moments to recognize the song. "When Tomorrow Starts Without Me". I didn't know the musician, but the song was something that they would have sung together. There were moments throughout where Bastion's voice shook as he pushed the words from his heart and tears rolled over his cheeks. Two halves of the same coin, those boys had loved each other with a depth that I had never felt for a friend, only for the woman beside me. When the song was through Bastion took a shuddering breath and wiped his eyes on his sleeve. Saara pressed a soft kiss to his cheek.

Shasha left my side and crouched before the small stone that held only Taegan's name. She pushed dirt into the grave and packed it down lovingly with her hands. "I never got the chance to meet you Taegan, but I know you were loved by the people that I have come to love, and that is enough for me, to love you posthumously."

I smiled softly at her as she stood, my sweet mate with her large heart; her returned smile matched my own before she went to stand by her parents, who hugged her. I crossed the circle to where Saara stood and kneeled before her, her hands covered her mouth in shock.

"I am sorry for the loss of your son. I know you disagree that I shoulder the responsibility of his death, but it was my lack of involvement that got him killed. I cannot bring him back, but I can give you something of his to keep." I reached into my back pocket and presented her with the fine bone knife that I had given to Taegan when he had taken his oath. "This bone knife is carved from my antler. My hope is that it will protect you where I failed to protect your son."

"My Lord." Saara whispered, taking the blade in her broken hands. "You honor me, know that I don't blame you for the death of my son because long before, you gave him life when he had none."

I bowed my head to her; if she had wanted to, I would have let her bring the blade against me. I knew she wouldn't, but part of me hoped she would. Take that pound of flesh that by no means would bring her son back. Instead, she placed a soft kiss on my forehead, it was forgiveness I did not deserve.

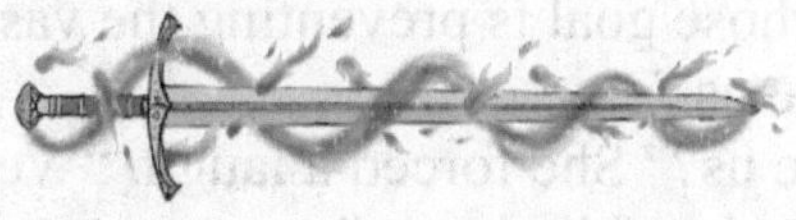

Back in the manor there was music, dancing, and a feast that the Days had prepared complete with all the things Taegan had loved, even chocolate chip cookies. I let Shasha drag me through several dances before I bowed out and the satyrs led her through another. Celebration was a salve to the deep loss we felt, but I needed some air and time with my thoughts. On the terrace leaning against the hedge wall, I sipped my scotch watching my family, the liquor smooth on the back of my tongue.

They were my family. Taegan had been a child to the whole house, and this was the only way we could ever mourn him. The satyr way. Durgash pulled his wife to the floor and spun her in the center of the circle they had created. Saara clapped to the beat in her seat, laughing as the Days danced. Shasha sat with Echo as Dheg pulled Tummi into a dance. Even Dorilody swayed in the corner of the room with a sweet placid expression on her face. The tightness in my chest had eased since the funeral and a sense of belonging took root. Home. I was home. A place that only a few months ago felt lost to me.

Nessa came through the doors and smiled at me. "Brooding in the darkness, brother?"

"No. Just needed some air." A moment of peace to reflect.

She crossed her arms over her chest leaning next to me. "Air or brooding, both seem to be right."

I huffed, swirling my scotch. "We haven't really had a chance to talk, have we Nessa?"

"No, recovering from being prisoners and then you dove headfirst into whatever it is that you do to maintain all of this," she gestured at the revelry, "has kept us both busy."

I sighed. "I run a multileveled black-market operation, whose goal is preventing the vast trade of creatures like us."

"Like us?" She forced a laugh. "Well, it looks like your organization failed you."

I finished my scotch in one heavy swallow, setting the glass on the terrace table. "I didn't know."

"Didn't know what?"

"That you were still alive." I looked at her. She had put on weight and was looking less like a wraith; warmth had returned to her skin and fire burned brighter in her eyes. The long length of her hair was braided down her back and the raven-colored dress clung to her long, lithe body. I never thought I would see her again.

She looked up at the spring sky as if it held all the answers. "I thought the same. After we had been attacked, I thought the worst. So, I went deeper into the mountains and survived out there on wild game. It was a lonely existence. I thought that you had been killed. "

"No, I was just chased off. It was rough at first, being on my own. And then I met someone who showed me kindness, who I loved."

"What happened to them?"

"She was killed, and I was enslaved. I broke free three centuries ago and have built this organization in the hope of destabilizing the very network that captured me."

"And you never thought to come look for me."

"I thought you were dead, Nessa." The air hung heavy between us. I swallowed the lump that was fighting to rise in my throat. "I thought you were dead."

We stood there for a long moment watching the others dance. Bastion downed another beer in a few quick swallows. His father had joined him and whatever they were talking about had Bastion morose; he had seemed distracted too. I wondered if he would be ready mentally to go with us.

"The girl? Is she all you ever dreamed?" Nessa asked, pulling me from my thoughts.

"What?"

"Shasha. Is she all you ever dreamed for?"

I found my mate dancing happily with Staspar. "Yes. She is everything my soul has ached for and more."

"Are you not concerned by our dying race?"

"Not particularly. I was for some time, worried that our species would die out, but now there are so few of us the genetic pool is terribly small. You and I are part of the last generation of bitarogs."

"How sad. Well, I hope you and your little *mutt* have a good life." Nessa dropped her arms and left my side.

"Excuse me." I hissed after her.

"What?" She said, turning to face me, a cruel smile on her lips.

"I must have heard you wrong because I could swear you called my mate a mutt."

"Well, she is, *dearthάir beag*." [12]

"Nessa."

"Niratap."

"Take it back." I snarled low.

"Why?" Her grin growing, she had found something to criticize. She always found something to criticize. "She is a mutt. Half human and half elemental, is she not? Granted, the elemental part of her is the only physically redeeming feature."

"*Soith searbh tóg tú é sin ar ais anois!*" [13] I snarled, the revelry coming to a halt beyond her. Everyone panted and watched us through the door.

"You should watch that anger or yours, *dearthάir beag. Is é an laige is mó atá agat.*" [14] She turned away from me walking back into the dining room.

"Nessa!"

"Goodnight, baby brother." She called behind, not looking behind her as she drifted through the group and out the opposite door.

I rolled my shoulders and gave a tight smile to everyone as I sank into one of the iron chairs. "Please excuse us."

I looked at the stars. Nessa and I had never gotten along. She was sharp tongued and sharp fanged, never once did she back down from a challenge even when that challenge had been me. When we were but pups, she would show me that fiery spirit even more. Part of me was glad that captivity and isolation hadn't killed that in her. Another part wanted to drown it myself. I sighed, pinching

---

[12] Little brother

[13] You bitter bitch, you take that back now!

[14] little brother. It is your greatest weakness.

the bridge of my nose. The woman would be the death of me, or at least my fragile patience.

"Are you alright, *mo grá*?" Shasha asked. She poured scotch into my glass, her warm floral scent mixed with the spice of the scotch. It set my stomach on fire.

"Yes." I said as she set the decanter on the table. She had changed from her black dress into some soft brown pants and a yellow sweater. Her face was pinched with concern.

"Are you though?"

I huffed a laugh. "Yes mate. My sister is just a vapid bitch who seems to frown on all that I have done to survive, while she hid out in the wilds."

"Somehow I doubt that is only what that display was about."

I pulled her between my legs and nuzzled the crook of her neck. "It wasn't, but her bark and bite are things I can handle."

"Nira." She said my name softly with such devotion, such love. I knew I would risk everything for her, everything and more. I just held her close while she pet my hair. Mate. Mine. I could drown in all that she was. Someone cleared their throat in the doorway.

Katrel stood with her hands clasped before her. "I don't mean to intrude, my Lord, my Lady, but I was hoping to speak to you about what your plans are going forward into my homeland."

"Everyone has been asking this past week, it seems. I am merely going to ask for him to relinquish his order and let you go."

Katrel scoffed. "You can't be serious, my Lord."

"I am. It is all I have, to ask."

"He'd slay you for less." Her voice settled into a harsh whisper.

"If that is the cost."

Shasha tensed beside me. I knew she did not like that answer. "I will not allow that."

I gently rubbed Shasha's back. "Be that as it may, my hope, at the very least, is that he grants us penance and we can find another solution while we're there."

"So, we are going to our deaths. Well, your deaths and my enslavement."

"Katrel, really?" Shasha snapped, her patience growing thin with Katrel's disrespect. "He's doing the best he can with what he has available."

"Well, his best is not enough. Pardon the disrespect but this is foolish and reckless. I will just go. The worst that could happen is I get pregnant with a beady-eyed Revan Jr."

"Katrel." I tried for a gentle but authoritative tone. Tried, but I just sounded annoyed. "I will not see you enslaved and used as a broodmare. It's not going to happen. I gave you, my word."

"I don't think your word is enough."

I straightened in the chair. "My word is my life Katrel. I made a promise, and I intend to keep it, no matter the cost."

"Then you are a fool." She stormed away, but the scent of salt bothered me.

"Katrel!" She did not stop, bumping into Bastion as she marched through the dining room. "Katrel!"

I sank back into the chair with a sigh when she disappeared. Shasha pressed into the space between my legs, her fingers trailing lightly over my thighs. "She is scared."

"I know."

"You are doing your best."

"I know."

"My love, you are very tense."

I huffed. "It has been a grueling few days, *mo grá*."

Her fingers trailed over my tail. "That knife you gave Saara, you said it was made from your antler, but your antlers seem intact to me."

A soft chuckle rolled through me as I fiddled with

one of her braids. "I shed my antlers every century or so, part of my natural aging process. That first shed after I freed myself, the girls suggested using them to carve weapons. The knife that I gave Saara was crafted from my last shed for Taegan."

"When will you shed next?"

"Soon. I suspect within the next year or two. Why ask such questions, mate?"

"Curiosity." She looked at me through her lashes, rose dusting her cheeks. How interesting.

"Would my fair mate wish for a blade honed from my antler?"

She smiled. "I would, but I have other desires as well. Ones that could be handled much sooner."

"I see." I shifted, enveloping her. I ran my tongue over her throat, and a heated sigh left her lips. "What desires are those?"

Her fingers curled tightly around my tail. "You. It is always you."

Heat pooled in me, but I was wound too tightly, too volatile, and I did not want to hurt her. "I have a proposition my mate."

"Anything." Her breathless reply made my hair stand on end.

I pulled back, meeting her heated gaze. "I want to play a game."

She blinked. "A game?"

"Yes."

"What kind of game, my Lord?"

"I wish to play a game of cat and mouse."

"And how does one play this game?"

"You run and I will chase. I will give you a head start."

"What happens when you catch me?"

"Unspeakable things will happen to you when I catch you."

She gave me a coy smile stepping back. "Very well,

my Lord. Are there any rules to this game, anywhere I am not to run to?"

"I will be on your heels, my little flower."

She turned. "How much of a head start do I have."

"I'll give you thirty seconds, *mo grá*."

"Very well. I'll see you soon, mate."

She ran and as she rounded the corner of the house my heart sang with desire. I stood, loosening my tie, rolling my shoulders, letting my hunger build.

"My Lord." Allipo said from the doorway.

"Do not wait for us, Allipo."

"Very well, my Lord. Practice caution please."

"We will be safe. Goodnight, Allipo."

The shadows swallowed me as I shifted into my wild form, I went the extra step to use the magic to fold my clothes and place them gently in Allipo's arms.

The satyr smiled. "Thank you, my Lord, you honor me. Enjoy your romp with the lady."

I chuckled before charging after her. In the time she had spent training she had grown faster and stronger, but she was not faster than me. I watched her dive into the hedge maze. My love, where do you plan to go?

I stalked her, catching glimpses of her turning corners. My ears picked her wild laughter. I came to the center of the maze where my mate stood opposite the fountain, breathing hard. She was glorious.

"You found me, my love."

You are so beautiful, and I love you. I stalked her around the fountain. She kept it between us, matching me step for step.

"What are you going to do to me, my Lord?"

Oh, what won't I do to you when I get my paws on you.

"Will you pin me down, my Lord?"

Yes.

"Will you shred my clothes? I'm quite partial to this top just so you know."

I'll let you keep the top then. I like that color on you.

"Will you devour me?"

My mouth watered. *You are a most delectable treat, my love.*

"Will you fuck me?"

Yes.

"Will you fill me?"

A low growl resonated from my chest. *Gods woman. Let me catch you. Let me taste you.*

"Are you hungry, Niratap?"

Starved, love.

"Well, I'm not ready to be caught yet." She turned and ran out of the exit. *Clever girl.*

I followed at a lope. Her scent mingled with the blooms of the garden, but what she failed to hide was the fresh wet earth and spice that was me wrapped tightly around her soul. She darted out of the garden and into the grove of fruit trees, weaving between the flowering trees. Apricot, peach, and cherry flooded my nose, but still the misty forest scent guided me.

I came to the edge of the property and my heart skipped erratically. *My little flower, be careful.*

I picked up the pace listening intently to every snap of a twig or rustle in the leaves. The scent of wildfae was thick and dread filled my stomach as I searched for my mate. Within three steps I shifted into my mortal form.

"Shasha!" A chittering giggle answered me.

"Shasha!"

"Did you misplace your mate, shadow of the forest?" The woods teased around me.

"You better leave her be, wildlings."

"Oh shadow, we would not wish for your fury."

"Then where is she?"

A hand wrapped around the end of my tail. I rounded on them, my talons sinking into the wood of an ash behind them, wrapped around their throat. The being yelped and the familiar tart scent of fear caused me pause. I frowned as the fae giggled around us.

"My love. Did you think it wise to sneak up on me while I hunted for you?"

"You called for me. I answered."

I sighed as the fae chittered again. I pulled my claws free. "Run."

"What?"

"Run, Shasha. For the next time I catch you I will be inside you."

The scent of her desire hit my nose as she turned and fled. I wasn't going to let her get far, just to a different grove where the wildlings wouldn't tease us. Where I could bed her in privacy. I followed behind her, shifting into my middle shape. Claws and fangs, but I could taunt her.

"*Mo grá*. I am quite cross with you for pulling on my tail."

"I was just letting you know I was safe." She called over her shoulder.

"By immediately putting yourself in danger."

She stopped and faced me at the mouth of a soft meadow. Perfect. She put her hands on her hips. "You wouldn't have hurt me."

She was right. Even as I barreled to her, and she turned to run. Even as I tackled and caged her to me so she wouldn't feel the impact of the ground. I wouldn't hurt her, but I was going to destroy her.

She wriggled beneath me rubbing her glorious ass against my arousal. "The more you struggle, mate, the more aroused I get."

She froze. "I thought you said when you caught me you would be inside me. I am terribly empty, my Lord."

I growled. "Not for long."

I held her head to the ground, the earth soft below her, as I used my other hand to pull her earthen toned pants away. She smelled divine, a beautiful feast laid bare for me.

"Do not move." I growled, easing up on her head.

She peered at me. "And if I do?"

My mouth watered at the thought. "There will be consequences for every transgression."

"Oh really." She shifted onto her elbows, defiance glowing. I held her gaze and palmed her supple ass in my hand. I would give her the chance to tell me no, give her the option to end this, but her eyes only heated with desire. I swatted that beautiful cheek.

"Oh god."

"Listen to me and I'll reward you."

"Yes, mate." Her husky voice caused heat to pool in my groin.

"Good." I purred. I wrapped my arm around her hips and pulled her up. I kissed over her cheeks, nipping the sensitive spot I had made. She moaned as I kissed the backs of her thighs. "Are you wet for me, little flower?"

"Nira, please." She crooned trying to take purchase on the ground with her hands.

"No, I caught my dinner. I'm going to enjoy it."

I ran my tongue over her glistening slit. She smelled of summer rain and wildflowers. She tasted like honey-sweet wine. This was heaven and her keening cry of pleasure made me groan. I dove into her warm body with my tongue, lapping up that sweet ambrosia of her body, fangs pricking her soft flesh. She shattered on my tongue, her body tightening around it. I eased her back onto the ground, where she panted. Rose dusting her cheeks and lust burning in her eyes.

"I'm not done with you, sweet flower." I removed her pants completely, tossing them aside. "I want you. In every way you will allow me."

"Take me, love." Her reply was breathless. "Fill me however you wish. Shadows and all."

I positioned her on her knees, baring her sweet body to me. I would never not hunger for her. Never lose this sense of euphoria when she granted a monster like me access to her.

I slid my beastly length against her quivering core. I groaned at the moist heat that greeted me. "You are so ready for me, aren't you, my love?"

"Please."

I rubbed against her again, a pained huff coming out of me. "In due time, mate. I am going to enjoy you. Slowly." At least as long as my resolve held.

I ran my hands up her stomach cupping her fine breasts, letting my claws scrape against her skin. She rocked against me panting like a starved animal. I loved this, her wonton passion and abandoned inhibitions.

I eased my body into hers slowly, enjoying the feel of her wrapped around me. She had taken me in all my forms, welcomed each and every aspect of me. I no longer eased myself for fear of hurting her, but because it tormented both of us to go slowly. I seated myself to the hilt, as deep as I could possibly go.

I groaned. "You feel divine, my little flower."

"Please, Nira."

I pulled my hips back, enjoying the friction and the way her body squeezed. She wanted it rough and wild, but I was enjoying her. I paused with just the tip inside her. "I don't think so."

She gasped as I slammed deep inside her. Slow and hard was how I took her rocking her into the loamy earth. She shattered around me, dragging me with her. I came hard, filling her with all that I was.

"Oh gods." She panted there on the ground as I rubbed soothing circles on her back, letting our bodies settle against one another and settling back into my human skin.

"You are a gift I will never deserve."

She wiggled herself free of me and rolls underneath me. Her hands trail along my collarbone and over the scar from the basilisk. A shiver trailed down my spine. She pressed her hand over my heart.

"Why do you say such things?"

I cocked my head to the side. "I say them because I speak my truth."

She ran her hand up my chest and behind my neck before she pulled me down cradling me between her soft thighs. "I think your supposed truth is a lie that you tell yourself as justification for allowing terrible things to happen to you. I think you tell yourself such terrible things because it's easier than being afraid. That somehow, in spite of being your mate, I will change my mind. That in spite of my love for you, you hate yourself enough to think you don't deserve happiness. You are wrong, my heart."

"You wound me, my love."

She frowned. "You wound yourself. I am not going anywhere. You are mine and I am yours. Wholly and completely. I wish life hadn't been so cruel to someone so good."

I pressed my forehead to hers. "It is the nature of humanity to want control. You and your pure heart won't change that, love."

Salty tears rolled from her eyes. "I know."

I kissed her cheek. "You are too good for this world."

"No, I am not." She kissed me back, those heated brown eyes warming my soul. "I am selfish."

"Yes, but only with me and I don't mind that you are." I ground my hips against her, a flush coming over her skin.

"My love." She crooned.

"My only." I nuzzled the sensitive spot where her neck met her shoulder. Where her scent was the heaviest. "May I?"

"What love?"

The warmth of her voice ignited fire that warmed my belly as lust burned away reason. I growled. "May I take your essence inside me."

A guttural cry escaped her lips. "Please."

I shifted, poised myself at her entrance and kissed

her thundering pulse. "You honor me mate."

I thrust into her as my fangs broke the skin of her luscious throat. I took two deep pulls of her wild winds and flowers laced with torrential forest rain. The taste of her and I danced over my tongue. Her nails dug into my skin, taking blood of her own, and she licked the droplets from my wrists. This was a claiming we needed, reassurance that we were in fact still whole for each other.

I fucked her, lazily rolling my hips against her, kissing the soft line of her jaw, enamored with her breathy gasps and sighs. She licked her fingers taking every ounce of me she could. Fire and wind and water and earth, that was what we were. The entirety of the universe, compartmentalized in this moment. It scared me that we may not have many more of these moments, but only time would tell.

Chapter Seven

Bastion

Fuck this. I hated this. I didn't want to do this. It shouldn't have been Taegan. It should have been me going to the earth, not him. How had I gotten so lucky?

Because you weren't supposed to die.

I sighed. "Are you going to torment me all day?"

As long as you'll listen.

I frowned.

Taegan's spirit sighed. *I hope you're not like this all day. You can't be mad at someone at their funeral.*

"I'm not mad at you, I—"

Mom.

Saara ran her arm through mine, linking elbows with me. "Are you ready for this, my boy?"

I swallowed. "No."

She smiled sadly. "Me neither."

I'm sorry, Mom.

I swallowed. "It shouldn't have been him."

Bas.

"But it was. Now we just have to trust his soul to the gods. He was a good kid, Bastion, just like you." She gave me a gentle tug and we began walking to the cemetery. "I'm done asking the why question."

"Pardon?"

"The whys. You know, why my kid? Why did they kill him? Why didn't he fight? Why didn't he flee?" She shrugged then stumbled a bit. "Damn this gnarled body of mine. He should be putting me in the earth, not the other way around. "

"It shouldn't have been him," I said again sadly.

She chuckled. "He would be quite cross if he heard

us, wouldn't he?"

Taegan walked beside us, his face sad. *Ma.*

"Yeah. He'd probably give us shit about it."

She laughed, stumbling again. "You know. You're probably right. He'd say, 'Ma, it wasn't your fault.'"

It wasn't your fault Ma. I made a mistake and misspoke in the wrong company.

I cast him a glance, his eyes full of sorrow. "That's exactly what he would say. He made a mistake and got caught, it was a risk we all know. If I could take his place I would."

"Don't talk like that, Bastion." She chided. "There is no reason for you to want to take my son's place. You have four parents who love you dearly, many friends who care for you, and that pretty elf girl seems to fancy you."

"Four?" I asked, my cheeks pinking. "What elf girl?"

She laughed warmly. "Your parents by birth, Rogmesh and Durgash, and your adoptive parents, me and Lord Niratap. You know exactly which elf girl I'm talking about; she is very pretty and immensely sweet. Pursue that, I think she fancies you, too."

"It's not a matter of fancying each other, Ma." I said as I clocked Taegan smiling a wild faun smile. "She's above me in many aspects."

"And when should that stop anyone?"

If Tummi is game, Bas, you should just take that leap. I wish I had gotten that chance.

"But what about what everyone thinks? Orcs are viewed poorly by elves. That, and she is a princess."

"Who cares?" Saara sniped. "If you love her, the opinions of the rest of the world matter very little. If you love her and it's true, nothing else matters Bastion, nothing. You have my blessing to pursue her, if that makes you feel better."

It didn't, but as we came into the grove, I pulled thoughts of Tummi to myself, keeping my heart to myself.

It was hard as she came to stand beside me and gave me a sweet-natured smile. I couldn't find the strength in my heart to return it to her. This wound was still so fresh in me, and it was made all the more real by the small hole carved into the earth. Taegan's resting place.

I think I'm going to like the afterlife. Especially if I get to watch over you guys like this.

The lord started the eulogies, his voice clear and somber, the message between the lines was clear on his face. He blamed himself. Every death that happened, he shouldered them, carried their names as scars on his heart.

I wish he didn't feel that way. I knew the risks just like everyone else.

I couldn't respond as Mom went next telling funny stories about our youth and Taegan's love of chocolate chip cookies. Everyone chuckled softly at the stories, even as tears streamed down her face.

Those cookies are the shit. I think I'll miss eating them the most.

Allipo stepped forward, his voice full of warmth as he gave a satyr's goodbye. Blessing Taegan's spirit with the madness of Dionysus. I never understood the Greek god of wine's importance to the fauns and satyrs, but he was most revered by them. His blessing of madness was the highest honor in their history.

As long as Dionysus has a taste for honey mead, I'll be fine. Madness or not.

Saara hobbled forward and with the help of Allipo and Staspar, she placed her son, my best friend, into that little hole in the earth. "My sweet Taegan. My sweet, sweet babe. You were taken from me so young and taken from this earth too soon. I did not have the chance to know you as I should have, I was robbed of that right to know you. I had all but given up hope of ever seeing you again, but then you waltzed back into my life a young man full of love and courage. It took my breath away, Taegan. You took my breath away and showered my weakness in kindness. I have loved you since the day you were born, and I held your tiny body in my arms. I will love you until we can dance in the Summerlands together at last."

I love you too, ma. I'm right beside you always.

I didn't move from where I stood between Saara, who cried quietly against Staspar, and Tummi, who sweetly smiled at me. I saw it even as my eyes didn't lift their hold on Taegan's grave when I spoke.

"Taegan."

Yeah, Bas? Taegan stood opposite the grave from me, his loving smile plastered to his face.

"You jackass."

Oh, this is the conversation we're going to have, eh? His brows furrowed and he put his hands on his hips. *Your eulogy to me is a fight? Why?*

"You weren't supposed to go off and get yourself killed."

Sorry man. I didn't really have a choice in the getting-killed thing. Not to reiterate myself, but I fucked up. Not you.

"We were supposed to get dumb drunk on your honey meads and sing to the moon when our tours were up. We should not be standing here mourning over your dust and memory, but here we are without you."

Taegan smiled sadly at me. *I know man. I know. I really did fuck our plans, didn't I. My mead recipe is in my room if you want to brew more when you run out and I'll stick around a bit to harass you.*

"I—" My breath shook, my heart bleeding out as I forced the words out. "I was not prepared to lose you, but you bet your ass when I get there Ima beat the ever-loving shit out of you for leaving me behind."

Fucking bet. But do me a favor first. Live Bastion. Live for me. Drink honey mead and bellow those shitty country songs at the moon. Fall madly in love with that girl you fancy. Bed her wildly and lovingly. Most importantly I need you to live for me and stay alive for them. They need you.

I cleared my throat, not knowing what song I would sing.

Sing "When Tomorrow Starts Without Me", Bas.

And so I did, the words cracking open my wounded heart, and I let it. Let my voice shake as I sang to my best friend, who stood there without actually being there. Who smiled sadly at me as I sang what he wanted us all to know. That even though he was gone, we would be okay. We just needed to remember that, to breathe and remember him. I wiped my teary face on my sleeve and Saara kissed my cheek lovingly. It was bullshit. This whole thing was bullshit. Saying goodbye like this was not fair.

It's not goodbye, Bas. Taegan said, placing his ethereal hand on my chest. *I'll be here, right here in your heart. Always.*

It was when the third beer hit that I had grown tired of Taegan hovering around me. Though he wasn't the only spirit gracing our house. The male that often stalked after Mitta watched her, leaning against the bar. A fair faun clapped happily watching Dheg with love on her face. Another male stood beside Dorilody watching the merry dances. Taegan wouldn't let me be, he just watched the merry-making and occasionally pushed for me to stop drinking and ask Tummilia to dance. She spun in happy circles with her sister.

Go dance with her, Bas.

I glowered at him as Dad sat on my other side. "Glaring at ghosts. son?"

I cocked a brow at him. "What?"

He smiled softly. "His loss is hitting you pretty hard, huh?"

Harder than you know, pops.

"Yeah." I confirmed chugging the dregs at the bottom of my bottle. "Dad, I just feel lost. I was so sure that once Taegan was home I'd feel anchored again."

I can't be your everything, Bas.

"Why do you feel lost?" Dad asked.

I huffed. "I was undercover for three years. I don't know who I really am. I remember the things I liked to do. I have memories of everyone, but I feel disconnected, like an outsider."

That's a weird way to look at family.

"And you think Taegan was your anchor?"

"He was my best friend, Dad. He knew me better than I did."

Bastion. You're still you. You're still good.

"The undercover hangover. I understand kid. It was really hard on your mom too. She was kinda haunted when she came back and had to rearrange who she was. It will just take time, Bastion. Be patient with yourself."

See, what did I tell you.

I sighed, cracking open another beer. "Dad, can I ask you something?"

He grunted agreeably. "Anything."

"Can an elf love an orc?"

He blinked a couple of times then smiled. "Bastion, an orc can love whoever they wish. It's not the dark ages anymore. Love who you want, just be true."

"Regardless of station or age?"

"As long as you're not trying to diddle little ones, I see no problems with it."

"Gross."

He shrugged. "That's the only thing off limits in my book. As long as your love is true that's all that matters. Your mother and I got married in a dangerous time and a dangerous place, but when love is true it works out. I wouldn't stress over it too much."

A snarl caused all of us to pause as the lord and his

sister faced off on the terrace. She was walking away head held high, waving idly behind her. She said something my alcohol-dazed brain couldn't comprehend, half the words in Irish, as she left through the dining room door. The lord glared after her but did not follow. He apologized to us, and I wondered what they had been fighting about.

Nessa's not fond of Shasha, she was poking at him. I flicked my eyes to Taegan. He shrugged. *You looked curious.*

I sighed. "So, you think that I have a chance with her?"

"With Tummilia? Boy, since you were a teen, you've been in love with her. I say shoot your shot."

"How did you—"

"I'm your da, it'd be pretty short-sighted if I didn't notice when you fancied a girl."

"But—I—"

"Don't sweat it, Bastion. Just talk to her."

Told you.

Mom came up to the end of the table. "You boys need anything?"

Dad wrapped his burly arms around her and pulled her in. "Just you, my love."

He groped her until she swatted him on the shoulder. "Durgash, we're in public."

"Never stopped me." He buried his face between her breasts. I cringed away from them.

"Durgash!" Mom squealed, wiggling in his hold.

That's kinda gross.

I shared a glance with him. I loved that my parents loved each other, I just wished they would love each other a little less publicly sometimes. Mom broke free of Dad's hold. Straightening her skirts she growled. "Now, do you need anything from the kitchen? I'm going to grab another loaf of bread."

I shook my head and Dad said. "Do you need a hand, my love?"

"No, you boys continue your chat, Tummilia offered to help me." She said, waving a dismissive hand as she walked away. She smiled warmly at Tummi, who I hadn't noticed had spun out of her dance and trailed behind her into the kitchen.

I wanted to trail after them, to soak up the sunshine and starlight in that smile. Even with my father's push to shoot my shot, how could an elf like her, a princess no less, ever love an orc like me? I wanted something full of joy and laughter, like my parents had. I wanted a love that was freely given and received. Could she love me like that? I sighed.

"You know son," Dad said, also watching the women head into the kitchen, "your mother and I make love look easy, but it's not."

"What do you mean?"

"Love is a lot of hard work and care. It's not a fifty-fifty split of responsibilities or care. More often than not it's eighty-twenty or one person is giving a hundred when the other has nothing." He nodded toward the lord and lady out on the terrace. "Do you think they have it easy? Do you think that through everything that they have been through and the sacrifices they have made for each other and the rest of us, that they have an easy love?"

"Well, to be honest with you Da, I've never thought that love could be anything but easy. Devotion and care should come easy."

"They do, but there is more to loving someone than how devoted you are or how much you care. Loving someone is work. When you love someone like you say, it never lasts."

"Why?"

He nodded to the lord and lady who were talking to Katrel. "They make sacrifices for each other every single day. Whether we see them or not. They lose sleep over their worries and nightmares. They miss out on things they want to do because the other person needs them more.

96

Shasha didn't have to grab the scotch bottle and take it out there, she could have stayed inside and danced with the satyrs. She chose him over herself. That is love. Sacrifice. So if you want to love Tummilia, you will have to do more than just care for her. "

Go talk to her, Bas.

I sighed. "But what do I have to give, to sacrifice?"

"Sometimes the sacrifices don't make sense. Sometimes the sacrifice is time and sometimes it is blood." Dad shrugged. "That's for you to find out."

I groaned, laying my head down across my arms.

"Go talk with the girl, son. The worst thing that could happen is she'll tell you is no."

Is that what you're afraid of?

I glared at Taegan before I pushed myself up and walked around the table. "Fine, I'll go talk with her."

"Good on ya!" Dad cheered, snatching my beer and finishing it as I turned to the kitchen. Katrel bumped into me. Our eyes met for just a moment, and I saw fire, hot rage burning in her copper eyes, tears threatening to spill. I didn't reach for her as she stormed past, the rage in those eyes scared me.

I took a breath to steady myself and then another before I opened the door and walked into the kitchen, almost running headfirst into the one who I was here to speak with. She was flushed, the deep rose of her cheeks pulling the copper tones in her summer field hair. Her dark swirling blue eyes captured me and held me in their tumultuous churning waves. She was fathomless and endless and breathtakingly beautiful.

97

Chapter Eight

Taegan's funeral was short and bittersweet. All of us had made peace with it. His death was a wound throughout the whole family, those of us in the house and out on missions. Taegan who gave love and care and happiness freely. Taegan who was sweet to a fault. Taegan the fast learner and strong fighter. Taegan, the pure heart. Taegan, the whole family's adopted child. He would be missed. The short procession from the gravesite to the dining hall helped me process this all too familiar goodbye. Parents should never have to bury their children and the ache that thought brought to my heart was almost too much. Libations were the best way to numb that old wound anymore. After a few shots of vodka that pain was just a memory and when the dancing began, the sorrow of the night eased away.

Nessa, the lord's long-lost sister, and Shasha were the only outsiders to the grief. I knew Shasha felt deeply for Niratap, she knew that the loss had deeply affected us, but the way she watched him warmed me more than the liquor did. She pulled him out onto the dance floor, into quite a frolic that he had never really had the opportunity to experience. I wondered sometimes how Bran would have fit into this company. Would he laugh and drink wildly with Durgash? Would he dance with Allipo and Dheg, his heart on his sleeve, like he had with me? Would he respect the man I had come to follow? I had to think he would. Asira would be around Tummilia's age; would she brighten the world with a laugh she never got to use as Tummi did? Would she be a fierce fighter like Katrel? Like myself? I shook my head; sad days are only made sadder with thoughts of things that will never be.

The lord stepped out onto the terrace and his sister followed soon after. I was glad that he had found blood that he thought had been lost to the terrors that were the world we lived in. I hoped that they could reconnect, find the love that they thought had been gone for so very long. They hadn't had any real chance to do that either with everything that had been going on, so much time apart and the lord jumping back into work after his three months out of commission.

"Excuse me." The lord's voice rasped through the doorway.

"What?" Nessa's bell-like voice sounded in mockery.

The lord said something, and she responded, their voices swallowed by the music and laughter of orcs. I strained my ears to capture the low exchange between the two siblings, coming to stand by the terrace door.

"Nessa."

"Niratap."

"Take it back." He snarled.

"Why? She is a mutt. Half human and half elemental is she not? Granted the elemental part of her is the only physically redeeming feature." My heart lurched in my chest. What?

"*Soith searbh tóg tú é sin ar ais anois!*"[15] He snarled and the dancing halted through the music still rang obnoxiously though the room.

"You should watch that anger or yours, *deartháir beag. Is é an laige is mó atá agat.*"[16] Nessa smiled as she turned away from the lord.

"Nessa!"

"Goodnight, baby brother." She called behind not bothering to even turn her head to acknowledge her brother as she left. Haughty bitch.

[15] You bitter bitch you take that back now.
[16] baby brother. It is your greatest weakness.

The lord apologized for their spat and sighed. The dancing and chatter started up again as Shasha flitted out the door with the decanter of scotch for the lord. She would easily mend that wound. I slipped from the party unnoticed and caught up with Nessa on the stairs.

"That was uncalled for." I said to her.

She eyed me with her sharp gaze and huffed. "If you say so. I was just testing my brother's resolve."

"Testing his resolve by disrespecting his mate, the lady of this house."

"I do not care who or what my little brother chooses to fuck. However, I have a right to fear the death of our species. The choice of taking her as a breeding partner is a detriment to us all."

"That is a very old way of looking at things."

"Is it? I wouldn't know." Her eyes narrowed.

"You should apologize to your brother."

"No, I'll let him marinate in it. She's inadequate as a breeding partner and he will see that. She is too young and too inexperienced to handle him. He'll see eventually."

"I very much doubt that."

"We'll see." She turned and ascended the steps. "He is bound to find a bitarog that would be better suited to the task of bearing his young."

"Besides you?"

"Obviously besides me, you wretched woman." She turned and sighed. "*Gobdaw soith.*"[17]

"Do you think that he hasn't searched high and low for more of you? That he hasn't scoured foreign markets and hunted through auction dens for your kind?"

"Then he hasn't searched hard enough!"

I was angry, but she needed to know. "You are the only female bitarog we have seen in at least three centuries."

She glared at me, but her voice wavered slightly. "That makes no sense. It's not possible."

[17] Stupid bitch

"I'm telling you the truth. Apologize to your brother."

She turned and stormed up the stairs and out of sight without another word. I sighed to myself. The woman was vicious, but she had hidden so well in the wilds. She didn't know of his sacrifices, his risks, and all the lives he had saved. Hers included.

At the base of the stairs the warm glow of chandelier light twinkled overhead and the laughter from the dining room filtered into the foyer. It felt strange standing outside the doors watching them, very much like the outsider I felt I was. Shasha was standing between the lord's legs whispering sweetly to him. Tummilia was speaking with Rogmesh as they walked into the kitchen. Bastion and Durgash sat at one end of the table drinking and talking. Dorilody had been dragged into a dance between Allipo, Dheg, and Katrel, while Echo and Eloimaya sat with Saara clapping happily. Katrel spun out of the fray, breathing hard and laughing. She was gloriously beautiful with her bright copper eyes and chestnut brown hair. I wondered if the love and joy that sparkled in her eyes now would ever be mine.

I cursed myself, feeling quite the fool for thinking she would ever want someone like me. Not only was I below her station, but I could also never give her what she needed. Those parts of me had been sealed away, for a long time. I turned away from the revelry. There were plenty of things that I could work on instead of wallowing in self-pity.

The lord had been looping me in with sparse information on the creature that was plaguing the lands around us and the lord's dreams. The malice. From what little we had been able to glean from the scraps of text that the colleges had been able to provide, we knew it was some kind of conjured creature summoned by a necromancer, but there had to be more. The articles on necromancy were vague at best. The two historical texts were written in a confusing turn of phrase that also made me think one thing opposed to another. At my desk again I read the scholar's notes. He surmised that one of the old races might have more information on necromancy and the malice. Many of the occult texts had been lost to history either by church cleansing, ethnic cleansing, or nazi indoctrination.

I rubbed my eyes, it felt hopeless not having enough information about this creature. Though as the days grew longer, the lord suffered from fewer nightmares. It was like the creature was stronger in the darker parts of the year, but I hadn't found anything to validate that. The lack of information rattled me as much as hearing the lord snarl in his chambers from my own when the nightmares roused the house. The haunted look I saw in his eyes the next day when those dreams followed him into the daylight.

Then there was the lack of information on the elf kingdom to worry about. We had no information that was current, everything that we did know was anecdotal from the girls when they were growing up. Katrel didn't remember many of the things we needed, like how the guards were armed or their rotations. Tummilia only had recollections of their rooms and the library to share, happy childhood memories that held little bearing on what we were going to do. Katrel wouldn't share her memories, and I wondered if they had wounded her in some way.

I wondered what kind of man would treat her so terribly that the mere mention of his name caused hot ire to burn in those glimmering copper eyes or the fear that made her delicate hands tremble. Delicate hands that I knew were calloused and hardened by training. Hands that I would love to feel on my body.

I groaned, getting up from my desk and storming into my bathroom. I splashed my face with cold water. What was wrong with me? She would never want for me like I shouldn't want for her. I glared at myself in my mirror, glared at the familiar desert-colored face and dark eyes. That was the problem, wasn't it? I wanted her. I wanted her touch. I wanted her lips on mine. I wanted her hands to explore my body while my mouth explored hers. I wanted to love her. I wanted her to love me, and I shouldn't want that. Shouldn't desire anyone, let alone her.

I stripped from my clothes and curled into my sheets, pushing the knives that I needed to sharpen and oil off the edge of the mattress. I squeezed my eyes shut and tried to picture anyone other than her as I slid my hand down the front of myself over the thin white scar that was just below my left breast and the other that matched it at my waist. So close to being all I had ever wanted. So close and the moment that I had it, it had been taken from me. Hot tears threatened but I needed the other release more.

Heat coiled between my thighs as her eyes glittered behind my lids and even though I shouldn't, it was her hand playing with my swollen clit. Her hand teased my breasts just the way I like. Her fingers curled through my moist curls and inside my needy cunt. Her name was a moan trapped behind my lips. I should have picked Bran or even the boy I'd fooled around with in my youth, but the men didn't cause my blood to sing. Katrel, she made my blood sing and damn me to the forever dark, but I came hard with her name on my lips.

A small gasp pulled me from my thoughts. I hadn't heard the door open, hadn't smelled the salt and flame scent of her. I opened my eyes and felt the flush of my heated body rise anew. I was covered, but it was evident in the air what I had been doing beneath the sheets. I wanted to curl up and wither away right there while she stood there looking at me, a pale rosy, pink crawling over her cheeks.

Chapter Nine

Katrel

This was the only part of the day that affected me, but not because of grief. Taegan had been a sweet boy who loved everyone. It was watching a mother who loved the child she barely knew intern his ashes into the earth. Watching her weep over a loss that she felt so deeply carved a path through my heart. To be loved like that would have been a gift growing up. However, our mother didn't care for what happened to her children, she had never once stood to protect us, she had sat idly by while he honed us as political weapons to serve his purpose. Sat idly by as he paraded us before men in our youth like prized cows. Sat idly by while he sold my sister into slavery.

The wake started with drinks, a toast to a soul moved on from this place. Socializing with each other and offering love to Saara. It was hard to open my heart to someone outside of our little family. I was still resistant to Shasha, but the way she pulled Niratap from behind the shell he put up to protect us, that he used to separate his family from his worries. Shasha soothed the sharp edges of guilt and grief that had hung on him for as long as I could remember. She pulled him onto the floor to dance. There was joy in his eyes as she made him sway awkwardly between Allipo and Dheg. I wondered what a love like that felt like and even as I joined the dance with them there was something aching in my heart. I forgot who I was when I danced and found release from the wild thoughts that haunted me like ghostly hands hanging onto me.

Dance. Mother had said my soul had been too wild to dance, that was why she had put me behind the key bones. Had me learn the complicated ballads of our people.

Pour my fire into something that wouldn't bite me back. I hated playing the keys and the skill had gone unused since I had come for Tummi. I pleaded with her, begging her not to go back to our father. To not go to a home that had never been a home. We had almost gotten Niratap killed, had our mother not told us to leave when we did. The only time in my life that she had ever risked anything to care for us. Niratap excused himself from the dance and Shasha was swept up by the rest of us, spinning and gliding through the riotous dance.

Eventually I stole my sister from Dheg "I will be taking my sister."

"Very well." He bowed out, stepping over to his next victim.

I pulled Tummi into a gentle waltz and asked. "Are you scared, Tummi?"

"Of what, Kat?"

"Of going home."

"Yes and no." She huffed at me.

"That's not really an answer."

She shrugged. "I'm scared of what could happen, of father. I'm excited to see mother."

"I don't know why." I snarled. "She didn't protect you when father sold you as a sex slave."

"She had about as much choice as I did in that matter."

"She should have fought for you, for us."

"I can't hold resentment for her in my heart, Kat." She smiled sadly at me, and it made me feel like she was pitying me. I hated how the hot rage roared in my blood.

I sighed. "Fine."

"You worry too much."

"What are the lord's plans? I know you asked him."

"All I know is that he will keep us safe." She said gently.

I glared at her as she spun me, and then laughter bubbled past my lips. Dance had always made me feel so free.

The lord snarled angrily out on the terrace, the sound caused all of us to stop, the music still playing as we stared. It was a slew of Irish, but the feral growl undertone made my heart flutter uncomfortably in my chest.

His fire-hearted sister turned from him and causally threw over her shoulder. "You should watch that anger of yours, *deartháir beag. Is é an laige is mó atá agat.*"[18]

"Nessa!"

"Goodnight, baby brother." She said, not bothering to turn as she walked through our throng of stunned dancers.

He huffed and rolled his shoulders. "Please excuse us."

Shasha brushed past me as she went into the kitchen, her face set with concern. She passed by me again with a bottle of the Irish scotch the lord favored. She was taking it out there to ease his tension, to soothe him. Dheg pulled me back into the dance, spinning me wildly making me laugh. We spun round and round while the other girls clapped happily. The dizzying pace made my heart sing, but my thoughts were on the future that was so uncertain. I disentangled myself from the dance, breathing hard. I needed to speak to him. I leaned against the doorway and listened to them speak. He was candid, but didn't elaborate on what his sister had said to rile him so.

When quiet descended out on the terrace, I stepped out of the warm glow of the dining room into the pale moonlight. I wrung my hands before me nervously before I cleared my throat.

"I don't mean to intrude my Lord, my Lady, but I was hoping to speak to you about what your plans are going forward into my homeland."

"Everyone has been asking this past week it seems. I am merely going to ask for him to relinquish his order and let you go."

18 little brother. It is your greatest weakness.

I blinked. He couldn't think that would work. I chuffed. "You can't be serious, my Lord."

"I am. It is all I have, to ask."

Fear rose like fire over my limbs making me want to scream, but my voice only came out as a harsh whisper. "He'd slay you for less."

"If that is the cost." He shrugged lightly. As if he didn't care that the tyrant of the Babylos wouldn't care about his pitiable request.

Shasha growled adamantly. "I will not allow that."

"Be that as it may." He soothed his mate. "My hope, at the very least, is that he grants us penance and we can find another solution while we're there."

Hot fear gripped my heart, and I couldn't help it as panic caused my voice to take on a saccharine quality of disbelief. "So, we are going to our deaths. Well, your deaths and my enslavement."

"Kartel, really?" Shasha snapped. "He's doing the best he can with what he has available."

"Well, his best is not enough, pardon the disrespect but this is foolish and reckless. I will just go. The worst that could happen is I get pregnant with a beady-eyed Revan Jr." I would sooner kill myself, but dying to save my family was a risk I could take.

"Katrel." The lord half growled, and half groaned. He was over this conversation. "I will not see you enslaved and used as a broodmare. It's not going to happen. I gave you my word."

"I don't think your word is enough." At least not to keep us safe. Not against the king.

He straightened. "My word is my life, Katrel. I made a promise, and I intend to keep it, no matter the cost."

He would sacrifice and sacrifice over and over again if we let him until he was nothing more than a memory in the wind. I couldn't lose them. I couldn't face being the reason he was killed. I couldn't let him sacrifice his life for me against a man who would view his as worthless regardless of his accolades or given title. A fake courier in his court. The fear bubbled over, and I felt my eyes start to tear up. I turned away from him. I would not show him that weakness. "Then you are a fool."

"Katrel!" He shouted after me as I all but ran from the wake. My shoulder slammed into Bastion as I did. "Katrel!"

I fled. Tears seeped down my face as I ran to my room and slammed the door. My room was dark and cold. No fire burned in the hearth. I avoided fire when I could. It reminded me too much of the night Tummi was taken. The night my blood exploded from me. The night I lost control. It often reminded me of the night I found her too. When I had been too weak to save anyone or myself. When the skin on my back was destroyed in that acid.

I paced the length of my room. I wasn't there. I wasn't being held in a vat of acid, by a dozen men who easily had overpowered me. I wasn't that helpless girl anymore. I wasn't. I wasn't trapped in the castle anymore. At least not right now. I cradled my head in my hands. He was going to sacrifice himself for us. No, he was going to sacrifice himself for me. Me, who was cruel to him when he offered kindness to me. Cruelty was my nature, in my blood. Even so, he was going to ask my father, King Cardoc, Third of His Name, for my freedom. All of this felt so surreal. His convoluted sense of honor was going to get him killed and it would be my fault.

I couldn't pin down the spinning emotions, couldn't stop the torrent of chaos inside me. The rage, the fear, the guilt, and the sorrow that swam in my blood. I felt that crackling power begging to be released and heat pooled in my core. No. No. No. No. A small flame flickered before me on the hard wood floor. I smothered the flame with my palm, savoring the pain through my hand that never could have reached the wailing in my soul. I sat leaning against the thick wooden door, taking in deep draws of air. Trying to calm the beast within me. I stared at my palm watching it start to blister and ache.

With a sigh I stood, leaving my room with its scorched floor behind. I needed to get this treated. I needed to talk with Mitta about the lord's crazy half-brained scheme that was sure to get us in trouble with that terrible, terrible man. Maybe she would have a solution that wouldn't get us killed. I didn't check the dining hall to see if she was there. I simply walked back to her quarters, and knocked quietly on the door, and when there was no response, I knocked again.

"Mitta? Are you in there?" A deep throated groan answered me. Was she okay? Was she injured? "Mitta, I'm coming in."

I opened the door and stepped into her room just as my name left her lips full of heat and desire. She was curled in her sheets, her face angled away from me. The sheets hugged her tightly showing me everything. The beautiful swell of her breasts, one clutched firmly in her hand. The smooth panes of her abdomen only broken by the arm that rested over the top of them, guiding my eyes down to where her hand was working the sensitive space between her legs. A different kind of heat took residence in my core. There was no way that she felt like that about me, it wasn't possible. She was far too beautiful and brave to be interested in someone as cowardly as me. She turned her head, her eyes widening at my presence, a deep flush setting in over her features.

"Katrel." She pulled the sheet tight to her chest. "I—I didn't hear you knock."

I couldn't clam the blooming warmth in my chest. "I burned my hand."

"How bad?" She held the sheet tightly to her chest, coming to my aid without a second thought. Her skin still flushed, a worried crease between her defined brows, her full lips pulled into a thin line.

"I—It's not that bad." I said as she took my injured hand gently in hers, "but it hurts and its blistering."

"Go into the infirmary and run your hand under cool water. I'll throw on some clothes and tend to it, okay?"

I nodded as she turned from me heading to the bathroom, her backside on full display. She had strong legs that led up to a full ass that was curvy and luscious. Her back was well muscled and defined, peppered with fading scars that danced around the white tiger that was tattooed there. Her beast within. I turned out of her room and walked into the infirmary dazed, obeying her instructions. The cool water made me hiss as it danced over my skin, pulling the heat from my flesh.

"What shenanigans are responsible for this?" She asked, as she came beside me. Her footsteps were so light that I hadn't even heard them with my acute hearing.

I deflected, as she took my hand in hers. She couldn't know that I was so weak-willed that I couldn't even control the fire in my veins. "Do you know of the lord's plan?"

Her mahogany eyes flitted up and met mine, before returning to examine my hand. "You mean his plan to 'ask the king to nicely let you go and leave us alone' plan? Yes I asked him last week. I told him he was foolish. He agreed, but we really don't have any information on the Babylos to make another plan. It really is our best option, as much of a hail Mary that is."

She turned to one of the cabinets. I asked. "Do you think that we will be okay?"

"That is completely left to how convincing Niratap can be with your father."

"That's what I'm afraid of." I said as she returned. She opened a jar of pale-yellow salve. "What is that?"

"It's a burn salve. It has lavender, aloe, St. John's wort, and calendula in it. It will help the burn heal, keep your nerves safe, and prevent scarring."

"Okay."

She smeared the salve over my burned palm gently,

then wrapped it with a clean bandage. She held my hand gently in hers, her thumb gently caressing my wrist. Did she realize what that did to me? "That should be good for a couple days. Try to take it easy with that hand, okay?"

"Doctor's orders." I smiled, wanting nothing more than to kiss this beautiful woman.

"Yes, doctor's orders." She moved to the sink, washing her hands. "Will you tell me how it happened?"

My smile fell. "My own carelessness."

She nodded solemnly as she meticulously dried her hands. "Okay, keep the carelessness at bay then. While your hand heals, if the pain bothers you, please take some ibuprofen."

"I will. Thank you, Mitta."

"That is my job. Have a good night, Katrel." She turned from the sink, stepping away from me.

I grasped her hand with my uninjured one and the woman spun to face me. "I meant it Mitta. Thank you."

"Anytime, Princess." She said, I hated that it was like she said it to create distance between us, but I didn't want there to be distance.

"Don't call me that, I'm not a princess here. I'm just Katrel."

She smirked. "Very well. I would help you anytime, Katrel."

I wanted to kiss her at least once. I swallowed. "Why was my name on your lips when you were pleasuring yourself?"

A peachy pink rose over her neck and face. "I— You must be mistaken."

"No, I heard you call out my name. I heard it."

Her brows furrowed. "And what of it?"

Fuck it. "Do you fancy me, Mitta?"

She pushed me against the counter, leaning her face inches from mine. "And if I do?"

"Then kiss me."

She blinked once. Twice. Then her lips collided

hungrily against mine. Everything she gave I gave back. She pressed into me and my hand came to rest against her supple hip. She groaned softly against me, before pulling away. Both of us stood there breathing hard, sizing each other like an opponent. She took a step back.

"Mitta—"

"This was a mistake. I'm sorry." She said sharply and left.

The absence of her warmth made me feel hollow and unwanted. A feeling that I was already accustomed to, but it hurt more now that it was her who had left me.

Chapter Ten

Tummilia

Ever since the day he found out about Taegan, and we laid in each other's arms, I had been battling myself. Between things I wanted and things that the world believed were right. At the funeral, Bastion had sung so beautifully to his friend's grave, and I gave him every warm glance that I could. I didn't know what he was experiencing and couldn't comprehend how this loss affected him. To lose someone so integral to who you were, I wondered if it was similar to what Katrel had felt when I had been sold. It wasn't the same, but loss triggered so much.

Bastion didn't join the dance, preferring the far end of the dining table to the fray of dancers. Satyrs could find reason to dance on any occasion. Allipo and Staspar pulling any willing soul along with them and getting swept into the merry making with everyone made my heart sing. It made me wonder if I would be celebrated. Would my mother mourn me? Would my father? I almost laughed at my own foolishness, that cruel heartless man wouldn't mourn any death but his own.

Shasha bumped into me laughing as Nira pulled her back to him. "Sorry, Tummi."

I laughed, beaming at the two of them. "You're fine, Milady. You keep him dancing and happy is all I ask."

"Now, now Tummi. I cannot be that morose."

"You are." Shasha and I said in unison, both of us busting up with deep belly laughter.

"Well then." He said with a smile kissing Shasha on the cheek. "I will excuse myself to lick my wounds."

"No, don't go." Shasha whined twisting in his arms.

"I just need a moment, my heart." He pressed a kiss

to her lips. "Some fresh air and rest."

"Are you okay?" She asked.

I admired how quickly she moved from the playful battiness to caring for him. He had always needed someone like her. Someone to care for him. Someone who treated him as if his shadows were the sun. I spun back into the dance and Dheg snatched my hand as Echo bowed out to sit.

"Seems you are without a partner, lovey."

"Why sir," I smiled at him as he lifted me up. "I think I was snatched up because your partner needed a break."

He laughed, dipping and hopping about with me in tow. "So maybe you were, but you make an excellent second partner, lovey."

"Excuse me." I huffed as he spun me out, laughing breathlessly as he reeled me back. "But I will have you know I was almost a Primess in the Royal Dance Company."

We separated and Dheg bowed low. "My apologies, lovey. I did not know I was in the presence of greatness."

"Stop that." I swatted at him playfully and he took my hand. "We are the same. My father doesn't want me and I'm not fond of him anymore. I am not a Primess nor a princess anymore."

Dheg smiled, but his eyes didn't crinkle as he pulled me in close, to sway me this way and that. "Apologies all the same, my friend."

"It's fine." I said, pressing a light kiss on his cheek.

Katrel pushed between us then and said. "I will be taking my sister."

"Very well." Dheg bowed and turned in a circle to find a partner, his eyes locking on Dorilody. He sang. "Lody, Lody, Loooody."

"Dheg, don't you even." She threatened, pointing a finger at him. Katrel spun with me in a quick round and I heard Dorilody squeal as he picked her up and spun her.

"Are you scared, Tummi?" Katrel asked, leading us through a gentle waltz.

"Of what, Kat?"

"Of going home."

"Yes and no." I huffed.

"That's not really an answer."

I shrugged. "I'm scared of what could happen, of father. I'm excited to see mother."

"I don't know why. She didn't protect you when father sold you as a sex slave."

"She had about as much choice as I did in that matter."

"She should have fought for you, for us."

I smiled sadly at my sister. "I can't hold resentment for her in my heart, Kat."

She sighed and spun me. "Fine."

"You worry too much."

"What are the lord's plans? I know you asked him."

I knew she would be angry regardless of what the lord decided to do. I shook my head and told her what I believed to be true. "All I know is that he will keep us safe."

She glowered at me before I spun her, laughter bubbling from her. I saw it all the time growing up. How much Kat always wanted to dance and never got the chance to. Mother said she was too wild, the fire of her soul too big to dance. A snarl from the terrace had the revelry coming to a halt beyond her. Everyone panted and looked through the door as Nessa came inside.

"You should watch that anger or yours, *dearthár beag. Is é an laige is mó atá agat.*"[19]

"Nessa!"

"Goodnight baby brother." She called out not looking behind her as she drifted through the group and out the opposite door.

The lord apologized softly before turning back out

---

[19] little brother. It is your greatest weakness.

onto the terrace. Shasha dipped into the kitchen before she rushed out with the bottle of scotch the lord favored. She didn't hesitate, had never once balked at the darker sides of him. That warmed my heart more than anything. It was a shame that we had had to wait for someone like her, so full of light.

I broke away from the dance floor and Kat did the same, going to stand by the terrace door. I took a deep breath and sighed as I walked to where Rogmesh was stacking empty trays. Kat was going to ask the lord his plans and he would tell her. He was honest with us to a fault. I tapped the orcess on the shoulder, needing my curiosity to be satisfied. "Rog, can I speak with you?"

"Of course, sweetheart." She smiled broadly as she set the trays against her hip.

"Can we talk in the kitchen?"

"Ah." She smiled knowingly, as she handed me the trays. "Let me ask my boys if they need anything. Would you grab those other two trays for me?"

"Yeah, I can do that." I said going to the other side of the table.

I watched her with her husband, who groped lovingly at her. I wondered what it was like to be loved so freely. The way Nira and Shasha were with each other, the way the Days were. She laughed happily even as he buried his head playfully between her breasts. I looked away, to be loved like that. I sighed as Rog waved me over and I followed behind her into the kitchen.

"Now what did you need to ask me, love?" She asked, taking the trays from me.

"Is it wrong to," I took a breath, "is it wrong to want a deeper relationship with someone you helped raise?"

She smiled that knowing smile. "Now, who are you fancying, my dear."

I felt my face flush. "I just want to know if it's wrong?"

"Child." She said, even though I was older than she

was. "If you love him, love him."

"But I changed his diapers, Rog!" I sighed leaning against the counter. "And we are so different."

"You are both a different race, yes. But when he smiles at you, does it make your heart flutter?"

I remembered the night I pulled him from the fountain. His goofy grins and gentleness, the memory warmed me. "Yes."

"Then who cares if he's an orc and you're an elf?" She said smiling. "He's fancied you since he was old enough to feel desire. Maybe longer."

The flush crawled down my neck and over my ears. "He what?"

"You heard me. Here hold this for me." She handed me a fresh tray of cookies. "I'm fairly certain that son of mine has thought of you in both carnal and loving ways his whole life."

"Rog?"

"Yes?"

"Does that mean I have your blessing to pursue an intimate relationship with your son?"

"Tummilia, I love you, but please take him. Love him like your heart wants you to. You never know what will happen, you could be a heart match. Take the leap. Talk to the boy."

"But—"

She placed her hand on my cheek. "But nothing. Take the leap."

I turned to the door. "But what if he doesn't want me."

"Child, he does. Durgash and I both know he does. Just go talk with him."

"But how do you know?" I said over my shoulder before the door.

"A mother knows." She said while setting a tray of sliced bread and cheese on her shoulder. "Let's take these out."

I turned to the door reaching for the handle as it opened, and that beautiful fair skinned male stood there. His steel-grey eyes were wide as we stood face to face.

Rogmesh took the tray from my hands. "I'll take these out. You kids have a talk. 'Scuse me, baby."

"Yeah of course, Ma." He said. His eyes never left mine as he stepped out of the way and let his mother by. She closed the door with a kick and then it was just us in the kitchen.

We stared at each other for what seemed like an eternity. The color in his eyes swirled like molten pewter, I could slip into them and ride those churning waves, warmed by the heat I saw in them. His strong jaw met rounded cheeks, boyishness that would never fade from his face. There was a scar that cut through one brow, his short tusks well managed, his lips I knew were soft. I licked my lips in anticipation of their feel on my own. His eyes tracked the motion hungrily. His eyes met mine and something akin to regret crossed through them. What could he have to regret? He took two steps back and the absence of his body heat made me see that we had only a hair's breadth of space between us.

He cleared his throat, rubbing the back of his head. "I'm sorry for crowding you."

I cleared my own throat and looked at the ground, anywhere but those soft, sorrowful eyes. "Don't apologize. I should have moved back."

"I–" He started but never finished.

I looked up at him, my eyes tracing over his strong frame and broad chest to his face which had grown rosy. "You?"

"I–" His brows rose as he met my gaze. "Fuck. Tummilia, I fancy you."

My flush deepened. "You fancy me?"

He began to pace the length of the kitchen, nervously. "Yes. I fancy you and I know you are a princess and an elf but–"

"I'm going to stop you there, Bastion."

His eyes widened. "What?"

"I am a princess, yes, by birth not by choice and my father sold me off because he was ashamed of being a king with two daughters and no sons. And yes, I am an elf and you are an orc, but Bastion, I fancy you."

"What?" He froze and turned to me.

"I fancy you." I took a step toward him. "I fancy you and I think I have for a while."

"Tummi. Fuck I must be dreaming." He rubbed his face viscously with his hands. "This is not happening."

I smiled, coming to stand before him. "It most certainly is. I—I want to love you, Bastion. Will you allow me that?"

He gazed down at me, his hands dropping to his sides. When had he gotten so tall? "Tummilia, I want to love you, too."

My hand shook as I pressed it to his chest above his heart. It thundered under my palm. "I would like that."

A heartbeat.

A breath.

And he had me in his arms. His lips met mine with a ferocity that stole all my reservations about us and ignited them, burning away any doubt. My legs pressed against the counter and my arms wrapped around his neck. I felt him. Every hard line. Every soft curve. For the first time I wanted it, I wanted him. I wanted all the things that I had avoided because other men; men like my father, had only placed worth on the softness of my skin. But when Bastion looked at me with those storm cloud eyes, I felt the caress against my soul. He saw me and all my flaws, all my nightmares and still wanted to love me. He wanted to love me. My hands twisted into his hair as he laid me over the countertop, kissing down my jaw.

"Bas." His name left my mouth in a heated whisper. "Bas."

He looked up, face flush and bright. "Is it too

much?"

"No."

He withdrew, pulling me to sit. "What's wrong?"

I pulled his face to me resting his brow against mine. "Nothing. Nothing, love." Saying that to him made my heart squeeze tightly. "I don't think your mother would appreciate us on her counter."

He coughed and a deep belly laugh rolled out of him. "It's my parents' kitchen, Tummi. I would not be surprised if they had fornicated on every surface in here."

Laughter bubbled up from within me. "You know come to think of it, I'm sure I've walked in on them in the pantry."

We laughed, the sound bouncing around the room and that made me feel whole. How had I missed this? How had I missed him? I let him take my hand and lead me out of the back door of the kitchen. We walked hand in hand around the manor, through the gardens and under a blanket of stars. In the solarium I pressed him against a pillar, my hands trailing up his torso.

I wanted him, though I didn't understand where the desire came from. Didn't fully understand the heat in my belly. I kissed him. His lips met mine with a gentle hunger, letting me lead. Letting me explore the panes of his chest and taste of his tongue. He was honeyed mead, berries and spice that fanned that fire in me, made me light up.

He sighed leaning back against the pillar. His voice was coarse with desire. "I can't believe this is really happening."

"What?"

"You and me. This. I feel like I'm going to wake from a dream."

"I am very much real, Bastion." I said, wrapping my arms around his neck.

"I want you." He groaned, his large hand cupping the back of my neck. "I've wanted you for so long."

"Really?"

His ears pinked. "Yeah. Taegan always teased me about it too. He'd always say, 'just ask her already' and I would tell him 'no', she's not interested in me. I feel kind of silly now."

"Don't be, I wasn't sure the other night. I definitely wasn't sure three years ago. Let's go." I took his hand and led him from the solarium down the hall to my room. I paused before the door, the rush of excitement and fear roiling through me. I turned and asked hesitantly. "No judgment?"

"You saw my space; did you judge me on it?" He said gently, bracing his hands on the door frame, caging me against the door. His soft smile was only broken by his tusks.

I didn't think it was possible to blush more, to have my heart flutter more erratically in my chest. "No."

"Then no, Tummi. No judgment. We both have darkness, and I am prepared. Even if I'm not, your darkness doesn't scare me."

"Bas."

"Are you afraid of my darkness?"

I don't balk. I want him too much to balk. I knew what his darkness was; it was just like mine, the roles only reversed. The sweet kind man before me was not a predator, even if he thought he was. "No."

Something shifts in his eyes, something wild. "Show me your darkness."

I had no other arguments as I opened the door. Taking in my familiar space from the armoire that held my dance gear to the oversized fluffy bed unmade from this morning to the wall of mirrors that reflected us and the pole before it. I switched off the overhead light and it was cast in a warm rosy pink from the mirror lights. His eyes met mine in the reflection then, smokey and full of mischief, but he didn't say anything, just moved through the space and sat on the edge of my bed.

"It's clean." He said testing the softness of my

mattress. "Well, cleaner than mine."

"You don't want an explanation?" I asked, twisting my hands behind me.

"Oh, I do." He smiled that soft smile again. "But I figure you'll explain if you want to."

I swallowed. Nervous energy running through my body. "I dance."

"I know that you dance, Tummi."

I swallowed again. "For myself. I dance for myself."

He cocked his head, but didn't press me. "What are we doing, Tummilia?"

"What?"

He smiled and shook his head, standing. "You and me. In your room. What are we doing? To be honest, I want you in all the ways a man can want a woman, but I'm not going to force you to have me. You said you wanted me." He rubs his face, before opening his arms wide. "I just want to know how you want me. If you want me."

It's a statement. He's not questioning me. It sounds like he's questioning his own resolve. I want him, yes, but—but. "I'm scared."

His smile faltered. "Of me?"

"No." I blurted, crossing to where he stood, pressing my hands to his chest. "No, I'm not scared of you, Bastion. I'm scared that I will disappoint you. That I won't be—"

"That you won't be what, Tummilia?" His voice shook and he fisted his hands at his sides. "That you won't be what I'm used to, because I've spent the last three years taking advantage of women?"

"Bas—"

He side-stepped me. "No, it's okay Tummi. I made a mistake. I'll—"

I looped my arms around his waist. "No. Please don't go."

He sighs. His large hands cupped mine at his waist,

his thumb gently stroking the back of one. "Tell me what you need, Tummilia. Do you need to wail on a male to ease your sorrows? Because I can take it. Do you need someone to listen? Because I'll listen. If you need it, it's yours, just don't break my heart. I can't survive another loss."

I swallowed again, fear stealing my voice. I shifted my hand down his front, feeling him through his dress slacks. He's thick, thicker than any man I'd ever felt, and he was heavy with desire. He made a choked sound in his throat, somewhere between a grunt and moan. I stroked him through his pants, listening to the soft groans, and grunts, and light puffs of air. I wanted him. I wanted to claim who I was. I wanted to not be afraid of sex. Afraid of being used. Bastion didn't want to use me. He was afraid of using me. Afraid that he had become the tormentor he had played for three years. I wondered what he had done in those three years. I pressed my forehead between his shoulder blades, swallowing again as he stilled my hand.

"Do you want me?"

"Yes."

He pulled my hands away, stepping out of reach. "I want you, but I think—" He shook his head defeatedly. "Never mind."

"No, tell me."

He rubbed his face, something he only did when he was stressed and today, he was all mixed up. "I think that we need to reverse our roles."

"What?"

His breath left in a huff as he pulled his tie free and held it out to me. "Reverse the roles, Tummi. Take from me."

"I'm not going to abuse you, Bastion."

"We both need this, I need to—" He growled in frustration. "I need to be vulnerable for once and you need to take control. Just take from me, Tummi, please."

"Are you—"

"Yes, I'm sure. This hot and cold we're doing is

chipping at my resolve. I don't know how much more I can take." Tears rolled over his pale cheeks and his voice broke. "Don't let me become a monster."

"Bas—"

"Take it." He held out his tie again.

I took it, still at a loss. "Bastion, I don't know what you want me to do."

He closed his eyes and though he was trying to hide it by fisting his hands, he was shaking. "Take your pound of flesh, Tummi."

A tear rolled over my cheek. "Bastion, you are not the cause of my pain."

"And you are not the cause of mine. My frustration, maybe." He cracked a weak smile. "Please, Tummi."

"Punishing yourself will not undo the things you had to do undercover." I knew that weight and it was hard to separate yourself from it. The crushing knowledge that you had to play a predator to get a bigger one.

He looked at the floor. "Please."

"What do you want me to do?"

"Tell me what to do Tummi. You have control. Take your pound of flesh for the things I can't right; the wrongs that were cast against you. I consent to whatever you need to release, I can take it. Let me take it."

"Bas."

"Tummi." He smiled softly. "It's okay. Take."

I shook the cobwebs from my head. Bastion wanted this. Wanted me to take a pound for all the things that had been done to me. For all the things that he had done to others, while undercover. My hands shook as I twisted the tie between them. I didn't want to hurt him or use him just to find a baseline. I was no longer weak. I was no longer a victim. Looking at his face I saw the haunted look in his eyes, maybe he did need this. I took a breath to steady my nerves.

"Strip." My voice wavered as I spoke. He reached up to the first done button on his shirt, his gaze locked with mine as he undid it.

I added. "Slowly."

"As you wish."

He smiled and at a painfully slow pace, he undid the rest of the buttons of his shirt. The pale green skin of his chest was grey in the rose-colored light disturbed only by a patch of dark hair in the center that trailed down his stomach and disappeared below his belt. He was beautiful, stunning, and as the shirt fell away my eyes ate up every inch of his skin.

He undid his belt, watching my gaze as he slid it free. He held that out to me as well. I took it. I had no idea what he wanted me to do with it, but I took it and clutched it in my hands as he undid the button and zipper of his pants. He just let them fall to the floor exposing his long legs. He hooked his fingers in the waistband of his boxers and slid them very slowly down those long legs.

Completely bare before me I took in his body. He was lean, with defined muscles and thick limbs like any orc, but his face was soft. His body was not burly like his parents, but closer to that of an elf. His finned ears stood out through his soft shaggy hair; he'd let it grow out now that he was home. The fine trail of hair down his body pooled at his groin and framed his penis in black. It stood proudly on his body, thick with an upward curve. He was tense. He cleared his throat, and I looked up at his face.

"Do I please you?"

I nodded, choking on the lump in my throat.

"Where do you want me?"

Fuck. "On the floor by the pole."

He dipped his chin and sat on the floor. He braced his elbows on his knees as he looked up at me. "What now?"

"Lay down."

He uncoiled his body on the floor, interlocking his hands on his stomach. I stood beside him looking at the lines of his body. He was so beautiful.

"Clasp your hands around the pole."

He did as I instructed, interlocking his fingers. I walked by him watching the rise and fall of his chest. I crouched beside him using the tie to bind his hands. I checked my knots three times.

"Are they too tight?"

"No."

I looped the belt around his forearms on the other side of the pole, cinching it tight. "And that?"

He tested it. "No."

I crossed my legs as I sat beside him looking deep into his eyes. "We need rules. Before we dive into this headfirst. I need you to tell me to stop if it becomes too much."

He sighed. "A safe word."

I nodded.

He pondered. "Axolotl."

I laughed. "Really?"

"No isn't a safe word, love."

I swallowed.

"Neither is stop." My heart began jumping again.

"Bas."

"Even if I beg, Tummi. Unless axolotl leaves my lips, you don't stop."

"Is there anything off limits?"

"I would like to keep all my parts." He said with a smile. "And you probably shouldn't injure me since we're leaving in a week. I'm okay with getting hit and if you want to use knives. For the sake of cleanup and because it's gross, no piss or scat."

"That's gross."

"A hard line then. No extra bodily fluids. Is there anything you want me to call you? Madam? Mistress? Princess?"

I frowned at him. "Don't call me Princess. Mistress will work."

"Very well, Mistress. Are you ready to start?"

God this was hard. my heart thundered wildly in my chest. I took a couple breaths before I shifted over him, straddling his abdomen. "Yes, my pet."

His eyes widened a bit at the name, but he did not object. I ran my hands over his broad chest, pinching his dark nipples, he grunted and arched off the ground with a sharp intake of breath. What was I going to do? I didn't want to abuse him. I didn't want to hurt him.

"Tummi." My name was breathy on his tongue. I looked up at his face pressed against his arm. "Don't worry about me. Just take. Take pain. Take pleasure. Take what you need."

"I don't want to hurt you."

"And I don't want to hurt you. Please take it from me, Mistress."

I sighed and kissed him. His lips were soft and eager against mine. His tongue swept softly against my lip, and I parted for him, our tongues dancing against one another hungrily. I pulled away, kissing down his throat and over his chest. I ran my tongue over his nipple, he hissed and panted in response. I sucked it into my mouth, rolling it between my teeth watching him as he watched me. His eyes hooded, breathing in pants. I traveled across the expanse of his chest and gave the other the same attention. He groaned, arching off the ground. His thick penis rubbed at the apex of my thighs through my underwear. The sensation caused my stomach to tighten and my body to heat.

I ground my hips against him. The choked desperate cry that came out of him spurred me to ask. "Do you like that?"

"Yes, Mistress." He said breathlessly.

I liked that. I kissed just above his heart. He was beautiful. "Do you want more?"

"Yes, Mistress."

I kissed down his stomach, dragging my body against his hard length, paying extra attention to scars that were unfamiliar to me. His breathing became more and more ragged as I moved down his body. I paused just above the lush patch of dark hair and looked up at him. His muscles spasmed in anticipation all the way up his body.

"My pet." I kissed the ridge of his hip.

"Yes, Mistress." He panted.

"Look at me." He obeyed lifting his head to stare down at where I hovered over his body. "I want you to watch me."

He nodded. "Yes, Mistress."

I shifted down between his legs. I dragged my nails over his thighs. His breath hitched, his lids fluttering.

"Eyes on me, pet."

"Yes." I ran my nails over the underside of his thickness, he groaned, his eyes closing shut. "Fuck."

"I said, eyes on me." I gripped his thickness, my fingers unable to close around him, there would be no way he would fit in my mouth. He bucked up into my hand and a delicate bead of fluid appeared at the tip.

"I'm sorry, Mistress." He whined looking back down at me. "It feels good."

I stroked him, the power and control he gave me was a rush of euphoria. "I'm glad that it feels good, my pet, but eyes on me."

"Yes, Mistress." His hooded eyes watched me as I stroked his velvet shaft a few more times, the bead growing heavier at the tip. I wonder what he tasted like. Would he be sweet like honey or salty?

"May I taste you, pet?"

"Please." He moaned.

I enclosed the tip of him in my lips, my tongue sweeping that salty bead of him up. He made a guttural male noise but kept his hips planted to the floor.

"You're such a good pet."

He groaned as my breath danced over his moistened skin. "Anything for you, Mistress."

I ran my tongue along the underside of him. His

breath came out in a rush, and I saw him fight the urge to roll his head back. He was so beautiful. He groaned as I flicked the tip with my tongue. I suckled down the side of his shaft, languishing in the velvet soft texture. He lost the fight watching me, his head falling back against the floor, his body bowing as I explored his length. I noticed crescent shaped scars on the opposite side.

"How did this happen?" I gingerly ran my fingers along the side. He jolted at my question but groaned as I kissed each scar up his shaft.

"Not now." He groaned as I cupped him.

"I asked you a question, pet." I said before lapping up another bead of salty liquid from him.

He inhaled sharply. "Christiana used me as a toy when I first went undercover. Used me and abused me. I resisted and she dug her claws into me."

I looked up at him. "Bas."

"No. Don't pity me. Don't let one bad thing keep you from claiming me. Make me yours, Tummi." His eyes were pleading, begging me not to let this stop. I sucked on the tip, taking his salty sweetness. He groaned. "Fuck. She liked seeing me bleed. Most of the injuries she gave; they would tend. Except for those, it was a way for her to lay claim to me."

Hot anger flared in me. "No one gets to claim you, pet. You are mine." That anger poured from my lips as I kissed down him, the scars fading in their wake. I blinked and he did too.

"What just?"

I sat back looking down at his body. At the thick muscular limbs, velvet soft skin, dark kinky hair, and my heart throbbed with understanding. "You are mine, Bastion. No one else's. Mine."

He watched me in awe as I slipped from between his legs, my hands shaking as I stripped. I felt his eyes eat up my skin as it was exposed to him. My skin took on the rosy glow of the lights, pinkening my body and pulling the

bronze out in my hair. I tucked my arm across my chest.
Our eyes locked.

"You are so beautiful."

I chuffed. "Yeah, right."

He cocked his head to the side. "I think you are."

I stepped forward, letting my hands fall to my side.
"Am I pleasing to you, pet?"

"Yes, Mistress."

"May I, have you?"

"Please, Mistress."

I straddled his hips, his hard length pressing into my
dampened slit. I rubbed against him, needing us both to be
slick for this. Both of us groaned at the sensation. I was hot.
I braced my hands on his stomach as my body quivered
over him. He felt so massive beneath me, I didn't know
how I would manage him, but I ached to have him inside
me. Ached for him to fill me. I rose up and he moaned at
the loss of me.

"Patience, pet."

"Fuck." He growled as I angled him at my entrance.
His voice softened with care. "Take me slow, love."

"I'm not suicidal."

He chuckled, the movement eliciting a moan from
me. I eased the tip of him between my folds, descending
around him. My body shook with need, even with just the
head inside me I was full of him. I took him, letting him
stretch me inch by glorious inch. My body spasmed
halfway down him and both of us cried out with pleasure. If
my brain had not flooded with desire, I would have
admired his self-control. He let me set the pace, even
though he could have forced himself into me and run me
down and I was fairly certain the belt and tie wouldn't hold
him. He let them, let me have him.

When I had him seated, stretching and filling inside
me. I panted with effort; I looked up at his face. He
watched me, his face flushed but beautifully painted with
ecstasy. He swallowed.

"You took me so well, Mistress. I didn't know if you could."

"You are mine. Made for me." I rolled my hips, and he groaned.

"Fuck. Tummi."

I rolled them again, rising and lowering my body around his. The grunts and groans he made fueled me. I came hard, my body clamping down on him like a vice. I rested my head against his chest. When my brain clicked back on, I reached for the belt and tie, untying both of them. His hand descended and rested on my back. He was still thick and heavy inside me.

"May I make love to you, Mistress?"

"Yes."

He rolled us up with ease, his strong hands cupping my ass as he stood and carried me. He eased onto the bed, laying me in the center and staring down at us. His body never left mine. He kissed me. His tongue diving into my mouth, silencing my moan as he pulled his body back. His mouth slid over my cheek and down my throat, his tongue darting out to lick my pulse. He paused, his breath cool on the path of heated kisses as he spoke.

"I will be gentle."

He continued kissing down to my chest. He cupped one of my breasts, pinching the nipple between his fingers and rolling it gently. I gasped as he took the other in his mouth, sucking and flicking my nipple with his tongue. I arched off the bed, burying him inside me. He grunted against me as we settled into my sheets. I wrapped my legs around him, taking him as deeply as I could. He rocked gently into my body and my heart galloped in my chest.

"Do you like that, love?"

"Yes." I replied breathlessly as I rolled my hips to meet his thrust. "You feel so good, Bastion."

"Fuck." He groaned into my shoulder as he found a steady rhythm. Thrusting lovingly into my body, it was such a different experience. To be loved.

I wrapped my arms around his shoulders, kissing his cheek. I whispered. "I love you."

He slowed and turned to face me. "What?"

I felt my eyes tear up. "I love you."

He smiled softly. "I love you too."

"Really?"

"Yes." He was breathing hard. "Yes. For longer than I would like to admit."

I bucked up into him and smiled as he groaned. "I love you, and I'm not scared of this with you."

"Then let me satisfy you." He growled, before kissing me. He pushed away from our embrace, his hands on either side of my head. He continued our slow, methodical tempo, pulling out to the tip and plunging back into me. The thick ridge of his head hit just the right spot, causing me to see stars.

He increased the tempo slowly building to a near frantic speed. I traced my hands along his chest. Never had I found a male beautiful, but Bastion was glorious. My body cascaded over the edge, clenching around him. Milking him over with me.

"Oh, fuck." He pulled out of me, but it was too late. Half of his hot orgasm spilled inside me the other half splashed across my belly and sheets. "Fuck. I'm sorry. I wasn't going to—fuck. Don't move, I'll be right back."

He launched off the bed and into the bathroom. I chuckled, running my fingers through the quickly cooling fluid. It had a velvety texture on my fingers, smooth and sticky. I stuck my fingers in my mouth, it was sweet and salty like toffee. Bastion came out with a rag in hand. He froze beside the bed and watched as I licked my fingers.

"You taste good." I mused.

He smiled a goofy smile. "Do I?"

"Yes."

He climbed between my legs and gently rubbed between my legs. "I didn't mean too—I mean I was going to pull out."

"It's okay."

He looked up at me sheepishly. "Do you have spare sheets?"

"Yes, they're in the closet. Off the bathroom."

I shifted and winced, a sharp ache cutting through my core. He caught me, scooping me up into his arms. He sat me in my reading chair; flipping on my lamp before he went about stripping my bed and putting fresh sheets on. I watched him, idly stroking my clit. This was new for me, wanting a male the way I wanted Bastion. When fresh sheets were on the bed and tucked, he turned to me. I didn't know what possessed me, but I spread my legs wider for him to view me. He huffed, his eyes eating up my skin, lingering at where my fingers idled over my dewy folds. He licked his lips.

" Do you like what you see?" I asked.

"Yes." His voice was rough with desire.

"Do you want to taste me?"

He made a deeply male noise in his throat. "Please."

"Come taste me then, Bastion."

He came to stand before me, his beautiful male form highlighted in pinks and the warm glow of the lamplight. He sank to his knees before me, resting my legs on his shoulders, something in how he watched me, worshiped me with his eyes, made me molten. He held my gaze, searing me with his devotion, as he lowered his mouth to my core. The first gentle passage of his tongue was a lightning strike to my senses. The second ignited a fire in me. And when he pressed himself into me, his tusks framing my slit as his tongue explored me with deep hungry passes, I arched off the chair and he wrapped his thick arms around my thighs, holding me in place for his ministrations. I writhed in his hold as he sucked and licked my heated flesh. He pulled me tight against him, my hands twisting into the dark mop of hair on his head.

"Fuck." I gasped as a violent shudder cascaded through my body. "Bastion, I'm coming."

He groaned into me as his tongue plunged as deep
as his mouth would allow. Lapping up all that my body
gave him. When the tremors ceased, he eased away from
me, kissing down my thigh as he let me slide back into my
chair. His lips were moist with my fluids.

"Kiss me."

He crawled up my body, until his face level with
mine. "Tummi—"

I swiped my tongue over his lips, tasting him and
me mixed there. I devoured his mouth; kissing him
hungrily and loving every press of lips and sweeps of our
tongues. His strong arms wrapped around me, lifting me
from the chair. I wrapped my legs around his waist. He was
heavy and hard against me. I wriggled and he growled into
my mouth.

"Woman, will you ever tire?"

"Of you? Never. I have had a centuries long dry
spell and before that I did not have a choice. I choose you,
Bastion."

"I'm sorry that had to happen to you." He said
softly, tucking my hair behind my ear.

"It happened a long time ago, Bastion." I said as he
laid me softly in the bed. I caught the back of his head with
my hand as he made to pull away. "You are not a bad male
for wanting me."

His cheeks pinked. "I want you, but I don't want to
traumatize you in the process."

"You are not Atton or my father, Bastion. You are a
better man than both of them, a thousand-fold."

"But I've done terrible things like them. I've—"

I pressed my lips to his hushing him. "It was your
job. Nothing more. Nothing less. You are not that male."

He closed his eyes, tears fighting in the corners of
his. He shuddered, fighting the sob. "But I hurt them."

"Yes, but you didn't hurt me." The storm cloud
eyes met mine. "And you weren't there to protect me
either. Your parents weren't even born yet, for fucks sake. I

know how you feel. The lord knows how you feel. We've all played roles where it challenges our being. It's one of the cons of the job. I know telling you to forget their names and faces won't happen. They'll always be with you, but eventually they get easier to carry. Now come to bed."

He smiled softly as I let go of him, scooting over so he could slip under the sheets. I curled against his chest and let him hold me. He rested his chin on my head and stroked my back. Regardless of what happened in Babylos, I was happy to have him here. A slice of pure happiness and freedom before the storm of pain that was sure to come.

Chapter Eleven

Shasha

My parents stayed two extra days, insisting on being there for comfort. I had never known Taegan, but it was nice to know they cared, that my father, despite his misgivings about our relationship, cared about my mate.

"You will call me if you can?" My mother asked for the tenth time.

"Yes, mama."

"Niratap, you take good care of my daughter."

He smiled softly and dipped his head. "Yes, ma'am."

"Remember what I said."

Something shifted in his eyes, but he dipped his chin in a nod. "Yes ma'am. I will try."

"Please do."

"Come on, Jazzy. She is safe with him. "

Nessa walked past us, and I didn't like the way she looked at my parents, like they were disgusting. Niratap tensed beside me as they locked eyes. He leaned down as she started up the stairs, pressing a kiss to my cheek before he addressed my parents. "I hope you two have a safe drive home. I must speak with my sister."

He stepped away to follow her up the stairs. My father watched them carefully and the hair on the back of my neck rose as they made for the gym.

"I don't think this will go well." My father said, stepping around me to go up the stairs.

A snarl resonated from the halls above and my father and I took the steps two at a time. Rounding the hall to the mouth of the gym where the siblings faced off.

Niratap shouted. "What the fuck does that mean,

Ness!"

"Exactly what you think it means, little brother."
She hissed back, turning away from him to cross the gym
floor.

"Hey, both of you knock it off." Mitta growled from
the free weights where she was spotting Dheg.

"Keep your opinions to yourself, bitch." Nessa
barked and I could feel the rage radiating off my mate.

Niratap grabbed her wrists and pulled her to face
him. "You will not disrespect my family in their home."

"Am I not your family?" She growled. "Or has time
made that too large a rift?"

"That is not what I meant, do not twist my words!"

"Ha, that's all you are anymore brother. *Focail.
Gan úsáid mar a bhí riamh. Ar a laghad ar ais ansin bhí sé
toisc go raibh tú i do laonna. Anois, cad é do leithscéal?
An é do stíl mhaireachtála bog nó an leathphór a luíonn tú
leis?*"[20]

"*Féach ort féin, Nessa.*"[21]

"*Nár láimh liom tú a bhrón, ní ligfidh mé duit
caitheamh mar seo liom.*"[22] She wrestled her arm from his
grip.

"*Agus cén bealach é sin, Nessa? Cosúil le soith?
Toisc ón áit a bhfuil mé i mo sheasamh is é sin go díreach
cad atá tú.*"[23]

Her face reddened with ire, and she swung, her
hand clapping sharply against his face. "*Conas dare leat
labhairt liom mar sin. Conas leomh tú.*"[24]

"*Bhuail tú* fucking *dom.*"[25]

---

[20] Words. Useless as ever. At least back then it was because you were a
pup. Now what's your excuse? Is it your soft-spoken lifestyle or the
half-breed that suits you?

[21] Watch yourself, Nessa.

[22] Unhand me you brute, I will not let you treat me this way.

[23] And what way is that, Nessa? Like a bitch? Because from where I
stand that is exactly what you are.

[24] How dare you talk to me like that. How dare you.

[25] You fucking hit me.

"Tá. Bhuail mé fucking *leat. Is leanbh den sórt sin thú,* Niratap."[26]

"Is leanbh mé, Nessa?" Niratap got in her face as he snarled. *"Thosaigh tú é seo le do easpa measa ar theaghlach mo chara."*[27]

"Ní mo locht féin pórú bocht do bhréagáin."[28]

Niratap tackled her to the floor. "Take it back."

She struggled underneath him. "No."

"Take it back!"

"No!" She slammed her palm into his throat. Niratap sputtered and coughed as she kicked him off her. "You made the bad decisions, not me."

Nira lay on his side catching his breath. I wanted to go to him, but my father grabbed my arm. He shook his head, and I knew in my gut that this was going to get worse before it got better.

"If my decisions are so bad. If you cannot stand my presence or my mate then go the fuck home, Nessa." Niratap growled.

She went rigid. "You don't mean that."

He shifted looking up at her. "Go back home."

"You would choose that mutt over me." Nessa flung her arm in my direction.

"I would choose her over everyone." He said with lethal calm. "She is my mate. I chose her. She chose me."

"You can't choose her over me. *Is mise do dheirfiúr.*"[29]

Niratap groaned. "Ness grow up. The spoiled princess routine was old when we were pups."

"Fuck you, Niratap!" She screeched.

"Fuck you, you hateful woman."

"Enough." Mitta shouted at them, neither listened.

---

[26] Yes. I fucking hit you. You are such a child, Niratap.
[27] I'm a child, Nessa? You started this with your blatant disrespect of my mate's family.
[28] Your whore's poor breeding is not my fault.
[29] I'm your sister.

"You both need to calm down."

"If you would focus more on the longevity of our species—"

Niratap scoffed. "Our species was doomed before we were born. Our father fled the first hunt. Our mother died the second. I was enslaved after that. If you are so worried about the species, Nessa, go find a male to mate you, though I don't think any of them would want to have a cunt like you."

She roared, throwing her head back before she leapt on him, slashing her claws viciously as she shifted. Niratap met her halfway, shifting just a quickly. Claws and fangs and fur flew as the two of them tore at each other. I was trapped watching the violence, everyone was yelling at them to stop, but no one was going to risk getting between two bitarogs. Nessa was bigger than Niratap and quickly gained the upper hand, pinning him to the ground. He bucked and kicked at her, his hind legs scratching her belly. Her jaws closed around his neck, and she slammed him down against the floor where his head cracked mercilessly. He went limp in her jaws.

"No." My voice was a whisper in the chaos.

Nessa's eyes locked with mine.

"No!" I launched toward them.

She shook him.

My father pulled me back against his chest thrusting his arm forward. A blast sounded through the room throwing Nessa off her brother. She snarled, charging at us only to crash into an invisible wall of hardened air. She roared, the sound echoing through the gym shaking dust free before she bashed against the wall.

"Shasha, go to him. I don't know how long I can hold her." My father said releasing me.

"Nira!" I slid in beside him.

Blood was splashed all over the floor around him, his fur matted around the neck where Nessa had found her purchase. I pulled his head into my lap stroking his muzzle.

"Niratap, I need you to wake up. *Mo grá.*"

His eyes cracked open and upon finding me and not his sister, his body relaxed. A sad sounding rumble rolled through me.

Shadows came to him as he rose and shifted in his most-human shape. Mitta grabbed his antler and yanked his head back inspecting the punctures and gashes that were already pulling back together.

"What in the actual fuck is going on?" She snarled at him, her face said she was angry, but her voice quavered with fear.

He met my gaze, and I saw the regret deep in his eyes.

"Watch out!" My father shouted as his wall faltered.

Niratap jumped up, shoving Mitta out of the path and stepping around me. He caught his sister in a headlock just above my head.

"Enough, Nessa. Enough."

She snarled and snapped her teeth in my face. I saw it then in her eyes. The hatred she had for me. I moved, tucking myself behind him. Nessa pulled free and shifted to match him, heat radiating off her body. Long red welts are the only proof of their altercation.

"How fucking dare, you!" She snarled, pointing at me.

"I haven't done anything to warrant you trying to kill your brother."

"You tricked him with that horrible scent of yours."

"Nessa, enough." He growled.

"Why did you abandon us Niratap? Why did you abandon me?"

"I didn't abandon you, Ness." He said, tucking me closer to him. "And Shasha hasn't bewitched me. Why are you acting like this?"

Her tail flicked in irritation. "You were supposed to

find a female from our species, Niratap."

"I haven't seen a female of our race since the crusades, Nessa. I couldn't jaunt off and find one back then either. I was a prisoner. A weapon of war. I don't know what you expected."

"Loyalty to your species."

"How can you talk of loyalty to our species when you hid in the wilds all this time?"

Her skin went rosy. "I was alone, and I was afraid, Niratap. I was hunted down like a wild animal, smoked out of my den and chased by dogs. I was thrown in a cage and transported on a ship. That horrible man bought me and he," her voice broke on a sob. "He and that ogre took turns on me. They broke me."

Niratap's tail twitched, I knew he was angry with her for whatever it was she'd said about me, but his heart ached for her and her suffering. I felt the tightness in my own chest.

"Then I smelled you and foolishly I hoped that you were there to save me. Instead, you were just as trapped as me and somehow in worse shape."

"Nessa, I can't fix what happened to you. I couldn't risk you. I couldn't risk the rest of my family."

"Those scientists tried to put your seed inside me and that's all you have to say to me. You couldn't risk it!" She shrieked.

My mother gasped. I peered at the doorway, the whole house had gathered, Allipo and Echo pushing past the group carting robes for each of them. Allipo didn't say anything as he handed Niratap the robe. Echo smiled softly at Nessa.

"Nessa."

"No, Niratap. You were scared, cowardly."

"Of course I was scared, Nessa." He shouted. "Only a fool wouldn't be scared. He was going to kill me, Nessa, just to prove he could. He almost succeeded."

"I know." She hugged herself. "And after all of that

you would be rid of me? You would throw me to the wilds again?"

Niratap pinched his brow. "No, Nessa. I lost you. I missed you. I mourned you. And then I fought to survive. I nearly starved to death several times in my youth without you. I thought you were dead. You actually being alive takes my breath away, but I will not let you abuse the family and love that I've found because you were alone."

"Niratap."

"No. You chose to hide. You didn't look for me back then. You can't tell me what to do now and you can't tell me who I can mate."

"Nira—"

"No, Nessa. We are done arguing over this. If you are keen on saving our species go find a male. Howen is too stoic for your wild nature and Shang will try to strip you of your wildness by force. Krishna may be the only one who will let you stay as you are, but he is religious, and you would be second to that. Casrian would have been your best match, but he has more than likely been killed."

"That's it?"

Niratap nodded, turning away carting me with him. "Yes. If there are more of us, they are hidden in the wilds, as you were."

"Brother, I'm sorry."

Nira sighed, guiding me to the doorway. "I don't want your apology, Nessa. I'm not the one who deserves it."

"But—" Nessa reached for him, but Echo grasped her wrist, shaking her head. Tears rolled over Nessa's cheeks. I wanted to know what she had said that had caused my mate to lose his temper.

Nira stopped at the threshold and gave a courtly bow to my parents. "My apologies for scaring you and delaying your return home with our spat. And V, thank you for intervening."

My father just nodded, wrapping an arm around my

mother. "We'll get out of your hair. Keep her safe."

"On my life, V." And with that we left the gym and the throng of worried faces.

In our room Nira kneeled before me, inspecting my skin and clothes before he pulled me flush against him. His body shuddered and I patted the back of his head.

"Please don't be afraid of me." He whispered against my neck.

"Never." I said against the shell of his ear. "I'm not afraid of you. I'm not afraid of your sister."

He pulled me tighter against him. "I'm sorry."

"Don't be. What did she say?"

"She doesn't approve of me taking a half-human creature as a mate."

"I gathered that, but what did she say?"

He shook his head sadly. "You do not deserve the hatred of her words."

"Be that as it may, mate, neither do you." He pulled away, my eyes locking with his. "Whatever she said I can handle."

He swallowed. "It started the day of the funeral. She called you a half-breed whore. Today it was a poorly bred whore, and it was too much. I—I lost my temper."

I gave him a crooked smile. "Obviously."

He huffed, a light smile coming to his face. I tilted his head back examining the red welts and puncture marks, already scabbed and fading. "They won't scar, if you're worried."

"I wasn't, more assessing you to see if I needed to snap back."

His brows furrowed. "I would rather you and Nessa not face off."

"Why? Do you think I can't take her?"

"No love. I know you can, but I would hate for you to get burned fighting with her."

"Like you did?"

"No. Where I am shadows, she is flame."

"Fire?"

"Yes, like our mother. Wildfire roars in her veins, if not for the synthetic venom she probably would have razed the building to the ground."

I shuddered and ran my hand down his throat. "I will not intentionally start a fight with your sister."

"Okay, I can accept that." He chuckled, tucking his head into the crook of my neck. His hands were shaking as they wrapped around my back. "Is it terrible of me to want you?"

I cradled his head to me. "No mate. It is never wrong for you to want me."

Deftly as always, he lifted me and sprawled us before the fireplace. His massive body hovered over mine as he kissed my neck and collarbone. His hand slid under the hem of my shirt as I pulled the sash of his robe free. He purred against my throat as my hands pushed the fabric off his shoulders. He lifted up, shucking the fabric from his body. I held him back, taking in the raised red scratches that crossed over his chest and stomach. They were bright against his white scars and honey-tone skin. He was breathtaking to gaze upon and he was mine. The scar across his face brightened his eyes, which stared at me with the same hunger I felt in my heart.

"You are beautiful."

He scoffed. "Not as beautiful as you, my love."

I smiled at him. "I think you are and that is all that matters."

He collected my hand and raised them over my head as he descended. He kissed the hollow of my throat causing my heart to skip a beat. "You are the most beautiful creature I have ever beheld."

"Nira." I arched off the ground pressing my body against his. I was met with a growl.

"I will take you at my leisure, love."

I wiggled against him. "Your leisure is too slow."

His claws skated across my skin as he kissed me. His lips softly swallowed my protests, his fangs gently prickled my lip, iron danced across my tongue. He growled as he pulled my essence into his mouth. I arched against him again, pressing his hard body against my core. He groaned and pulled back, licking my blood from his lips. His eyes glowed with lust.

"Nira. Please." I pleaded.

"What do you want?"

"I want to taste."

"What do you want to taste?"

I struggled against his hold. "You."

He smiled, taking his bottom lip between his teeth. Heat pooled in my core as he hovered over me. Our eyes locked as he bit down on his lip, letting his blood drip over my lips. The rich velvet iron hit my tongue, followed by rainy forests I had never seen and the smokey burn of old Irish whiskey. His essence warmed me, making my skin burn.

He kissed me again, shifting his hips in the cradle of my body. He groaned in my mouth as he pressed against my core.

"You are so wet for me." He hissed against my lips. "Just for me?"

"Only for you."

He pressed into me, a guttural sound coming from my lips as he stretched me. I would never be ready for his size in any shape, but he filled me so perfectly in each one that I never cared. Never cared if he was rough or gentle. Never cared when he came so viciously that it leaked from me for days. Never cared about the ache that came after. Loved the ache really. Today he was gently suckling on my neck as he kept his thrust easy and gentle. It frustrated me.

He wanted comfort and release, but still he was concerned about whether my body could take his onslaught. I twisted beneath him, trying to roll him over. Even with all the training I had been doing, he was still at least a hundred pounds heavier than me and much larger.

He groaned against my chest. "What mate? Are you trying to run from me?"

"No." I moaned as he bit down on my collarbone and sucked. "Roll over."

"Do you not like to be ravaged?" He teased, his breath dancing over the small hurts over my neck causing my body to sing.

"I want to ravage you." I panted. "You are being too gentle."

"I'm being too gentle?" He purred against my pulse.

I twisted again and he cupped my back supporting me as we rolled. I kissed down his chest before sitting up and straddling his waist. He slid deeper and both of us groaned at the sensation.

"Fuck." He growled his hands digging into my hips. "You feel so good."

I cocked my head to the side and smiled at him. His muscles strained as he tried to control himself, his head tipped back until his antlers kissed the floor. I ran my hand down his chest, enjoyed how his breath caught. How his cheeks colored with effort. "I like you like this. Under me."

His eyelids cracked looking at me with lust. "You vixen."

He gasped as I rocked my hips against his, the sound of him heating me, urging me to go faster. The feel of him deep inside me, hitting all the right spots. Filling and stretching, I got wrapped up in him, our hearts thundering in time. I don't know who made the move whether it was him or me who parted from the other and shifted us. Facedown in the plush carpet had me seeing stars and he pounded into me. His hands held my hips bracing me against his bruising force. Pain. Pleasure. Heat.

All coiled around me. Tighter and tighter until my body spasmed, his name a cry on my lips. He collapsed over me as he came. One hand planted itself by my face, the other wrapped around my waist; holding me to him as he filled me. Each surge of him brought another wave of dizzying ecstasy that leaked down my legs. He kissed my shoulder softly.

"You destroy me." He breathed.

"To reiterate past statements; the one seeing stars is the one that's destroyed." I kissed the side of his hand.

He kissed down my spine as he eased himself out of me. I felt the vacancy of him in my soul, followed by a gush of fluids.

"Fuck." I groaned.

"I definitely made a mess of you."

I peered over my shoulder at him. He stared at my body with longing and care that made heat return to me. "Are you going to just stare at me or are you going to clean me up?"

His eyes flicked to mine and were filled again with that lust. "Is that an invitation, love?"

"When has it ever been anything but?"

He smiled hungrily at me. "You are always so eager to please me."

"I get just as much from you." I said.

He shook his head before he scooped me up at the waist, resting my knees atop his shoulders, spreading me wide for him. I squealed, my fingers digging into the carpet, as his tongue swept over my core, lapping up our combined essence.

"Oh god."

He chuckled. The soft puffs of breath cold against my heated flesh. "I am no god, sweet flower, but you are an altar for worship."

"Am I?" Another pass of his tongue stole my breath. "Fuck."

"Yes." He purred against my core.

His devotions rolled another orgasm out of me. Tears of pleasure ran from my eyes, and when he eased me back down on the carpet, he kissed them away.

"Are you okay?" He near whispered, rolling my boneless body over.

"Yes, *mo grá.* I am more than okay. Worshiped and loved beyond words."

He smiled softly. "I am sorry for my outburst. Nessa just gets under my skin every time. She knows what buttons to push, even now after we've spent so much time apart."

"I hear that is what having siblings is like. You don't need to apologize, least of all to me."

He tucked an errant braid behind my ear. "I am sorry though. I scared your mother and had V not interfered, I'm not sure the fact we are siblings would have stopped her from actually hurting me."

I frowned but cupped his face. "You guys will find common ground again. Eventually."

He frowned looking up at the ceiling. "Survival has made us very different creatures."

"Doesn't mean you don't love or care for each other."

"No, it doesn't. However, we need to find a way to communicate with one another; preferably one that doesn't evolve into us tearing into one another. Imprisonment made me hard and quick to anger. Isolation made her feral and unyielding. Not a good mix to address one another."

"No, but it will get better, love. She's taken a shine to Echo, who is the last person I could see her connecting with."

He huffed a laugh. "Echo has a way with savage animals."

I swatted him. "Nessa is not a savage animal."

"Okay. You are right, but she is a bitch and unnecessarily cruel."

I sighed, sitting up. "I know you are both mad at

one another for things that don't matter." He growled. "And things that do. But she must have suffered out there all by herself. She probably had to scrounge and scavenge to survive. You were a prisoner, and they only gave you what you needed to survive. You both have lived terrible lives. I think you need to talk to her before we leave for Babylos."

The irritated wrinkle formed between his brows as he glowered at the ceiling, but he sagged with a long sigh. "You're right."

"I know I am. That is why you love me." I beamed at him.

He smiled roguishly. "That isn't the only reason I love you."

"You keep those paws to yourself." I said, scrambling to my feet and sidestepping out of his reach.

"My flower." He crooned coming to his feet with that savage predator's grace of his. "Why do you run from me?"

"Because, you animal," I laughed moving backward to the bathroom, "I have a training lesson with Mitta in a half hour and she hates it when I smell freshly bred."

He purred satisfactorily as he followed me. "I like that. The idea of you carrying my babes fills me with more emotions that I can identify."

"After, remember?" I said lifting my hand to meet his chest in the doorway.

"Yes. after."

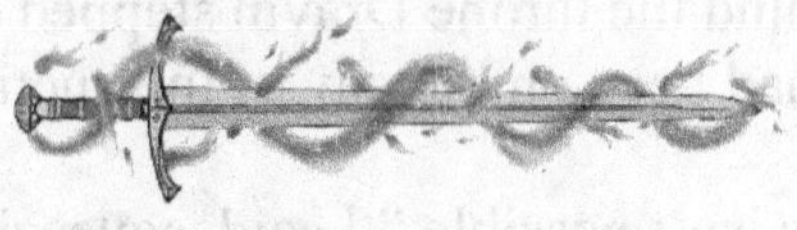

That night Niratap fell asleep before I could settle down. I shifted closer to him hoping the steady cadence of his breathing would ease me to sleep. Something wouldn't let my mind settle. I would have gone to the bathroom and splashed my face, but my mate had me locked against him. Even asleep it was as if he feared this wasn't real. That we had failed to rescue him from his terrible fate. I watched his peaceful face with my sleep-leaden eyes, glad he was sleeping with such calm. I don't know when sleep overtook me, but I woke up feeling cold. Our bed was empty, the fire had become soot under the mantle.

"Nira?" I called and there was an eerie silence in the house. I slid from the bed, the icy floor biting at my feet. Sliding my arms into my robe I moved to leave.

"Nira!" I called down the hall after opening our door. My voice echoed through the cavernous hall. I crept down the stairs, my barefooted steps the only sound. The house felt dead. I slipped on the last step into the foyer, catching myself on the banister. A viscous black ooze coated the bottom step and led behind the stairs into the ballroom.

"Nira!" Panic caused my voice to raise an octave. Where was everyone else? Were they hurt? Why was it so cold? Where was my mate? "Nira!"

There was a soft groan from the ballroom as I rounded the bottom of the stairs following the trail of ooze. The ballroom was poorly lit, but I saw him across the floor sitting in a throne-like chair. His head hung limply between his shoulders. "Niratap, what's going on?"

He groaned but didn't raise his head.

I took a step toward him. "Niratap—"

"I don't think he'll respond to you, girl." From the shadows behind the throne Dravin stepped out, as crisp and clean as he had been on the day of the auction so many months ago.

"This isn't possible." I said, squeezing my eyes shut.

"What's not?"

I glared at him. "I must be dreaming. You're dead, Dravin. Dead. I shot you."

The bullet wound appeared in his face and leaked over his jaw. "That you did."

He smiled a vulpine smile at me, grabbing my mate's antler and pulling his head back. My breath caught at the sight of him. Black handprints spanned over his body. His face pulled into a grimace and he had black tear trails leaking from his eyes.

"Niratap!" My heart hammered in my chest and a cold sweat peppered my skin.

"Such a shame." Dravin said, walking around my mate. "I thought he was tougher than that."

"Dravin, you let him go. Right now!" I shouted.

"Tsk tsk tsk." He said walking around behind the chair. A different man, dressed in a fine brown suit that almost matched his brown hair, came out the other side. His eyes were as black as the tear tracks down my mate's face. "Dravin is dead, he can't hurt him. I, however, plan on hurting him quite a bit."

"Who are you? What are you?"

"You don't know me." The figure said looking down at my mate, examining him. "But he is exquisitely familiar with me."

"Let him go."

He pulled Niratap's head back until his antlers clacked against the wood. "I've let him go for such a long time though and to be honest with you, I don't like to share my toys."

He brandished a knife and pressed the blade against my mate's throat. My voice came out a choked whisper. "No."

"It will be fun when I get to rip him from you and break him." He ran the knife against Nira's throat, and black blood oozed down his chest and out his mouth.

"No." I charged towards them and a shadow leapt at me. It restrained my arms and legs and chuckled in my ear.

"My master likes the feisty ones. He will like breaking you before he breaks your mate."

"No!"

"No!" My scream echoed around our bedroom. I felt large, warm hands grab for me and I leaned over the bed and heaved my guts onto the floor. Broad hands swept my braids behind my head and rubbed soothing circles across my back while I gagged.

"Are you alright, *mo grá?*" His voice covered me like a blanket with its thickness from sleep.

"Yes."

A gentle rap sounded on the door. "Enter."

Allipo cracked the door, Eloimaya behind him. "Is everything alright? We heard a scream."

"Yes." I said. Looking up at my mate, making sure he was whole. "Just a nightmare."

He frowned, his brows pulling together. "Quite the nightmare."

I looked down at the floor, covered with the spilled contents of my stomach. "Yeah."

He scooped me into his arms and carried me towards the bathroom. "Would you mind cleaning that up while I tend to her?"

"Of course, my Lord."

"I don't need tending." I growled. "I am perfectly capable of brushing my teeth on my own."

"Yes, you are, but I am still going to look after you." He carried me through the door and shut it softly behind him before he set me on the floor. His broad hands captured my face, thumbs wiping away tears I hadn't known I had shed. "Will you share with me?"

His quicksilver eyes searched mine before I pulled away to the sink. I splashed my face and swished the taste of bile from my tongue. He sat on the lid of the toilet and rested his head against the tile. He wasn't watching me, but I felt his worry in my heart. I dried my face, leaned against the counter and took a deep breath.

"I awoke in our bed alone. It was cold and so silent. I called for you and heard nothing. So, I went to look for you. Calling for you the whole way. I slipped in some slimy liquid at the bottom of the stairs. It trailed into the ballroom and there you were."

He shifted to look at me, but I couldn't face him with what had happened in the dream.

"You were sitting on a throne on the dais. And Dravin stepped from behind the chair. Taunted me. Touched you." A chill went down my back at the memory of my mate's face. "I realized then I was dreaming, because I killed Dravin. I watched the life leave his eyes. I told him to let you go, but then he changed. Shifted into another man, a man I didn't recognize. He told me Dravin wasn't going to hurt you, but that he would."

Silence fell as the end of the dream shook me. Niratap kneeled in front of me, our faces level, his eyes pleading with me. "Tell me."

"I watched him slit your throat." The words left me feeling hollow and broken inside. "A shadow restrained me and told me his master would enjoy breaking me."

Niratap growled at the wraiths of my dream. "No one will harm you, love. I will not allow it."

I cupped his face. "You can't save me from everything."

Sorrow sat unpleasantly in his eyes. "I know. It does not mean that I will not try."

I kissed his forehead before I wrapped my arms around him and sank into the steady warmth of his body. "I don't want to lose you. Not again."

He didn't respond. Didn't make promises he couldn't keep or promises that I knew he wouldn't keep. He just held me there in our bathroom on his knees. I was the only being he would kneel to and even that power was not enough to protect him from those who hunted him.

Chapter Twelve

Katrel

I knew this was a stupid idea. Even though it was mid-May, the breeze off the Atlantic was still frigid at the harbor. We had packed light; each of us with a single backpack, save the lord who also had a single suitcase. And even though he planned to approach my father without his shadows and mask, they were in place as he argued with the harbormaster, a greying dwarf with a no-nonsense attitude.

"We just need passage to Asuna." He growled.

"And I already told you sir there are no passenger ships to Asuna. Only cargo."

"Then we are cargo. We need to get to Asuna."

"And I need to get fucked by an incubus named Larry. Neither is happening any time soon."

I felt the rage rolling off him as he groaned. "Why? Is there a dollar amount attached to your cooperation?"

"No, no. No amount of money you could give me will sway me to lose my job."

Shasha stepped beside him and asked. "What would sway you?"

The harbormaster chuckled. "Besides an act of divine intervention or royal decree from the king of Babylos. Nothing. You aren't getting passage."

Royal decree? I stepped forward and pulled the amulet around my neck out of my shirt. "I am Crown Princess Katrel Gwendolyn Raloqen and I have summons from my father to appear at court. Will you grant us passage on a ship to Asuna?"

The dwarf's eyes widened as he stared at the amulet. The royal crest. The key for me getting back home.

He cleared his throat. "I can get you on the next cargo ship to Asuna. All six of you together?"

My body relaxed. "Yes."

"Very well. I will go make arrangements with the captain. You might be expected to earn your keep."

"That's fine. All of us are willing to work for passage."

He sighed pointing up to a weather-worn, brown building. "Wait in my office, Your Highness, I'll go find Captain Brast and we can arrange your passage."

"Thank you, harbor master." He waved us off and traveled down the docks to whatever ship housed Captain Brast. I loosed a breath I hadn't known I was holding.

"Thank you, Katrel." Shasha said beside me.

"Getting there was always going to be difficult." I looked back at the lord, at the tension in his shoulders. "We knew it would be difficult."

He sighed. "Yes, we did."

"Why aren't there passenger voyages to Asuna?"

"There are trade tariffs in place that prevent tourism basically. Very few are allowed in Babylos from the rest of the world. There are nearly zero non-elves. My father has done it that way to preserve our culture, while still trying to keep wealth flowing through the kingdom. It's been a knife's balance. There are steep fines on ships who illegally bring non-elves to the gates of the kingdom."

"What happened the last time you three traveled there?"

"We were stowaways." The lord said softly to his mate. "It was a rough nine days at sea and then we *may* have incapacitated the gate guards."

"Let's go wait in the harbormaster's office. I don't want to spend more time than I have to in this cold." I stated matter-of-factly, knowing full well that the Atlantic was always cold.

Captain Brast was not what I expected as a ship captain. He filled the harbor master's small yellow office; much like Lord Niratap did, easily as tall as Durgesh. Broad like an orc, but he had the angular sharp features of an elf. His skin was a muddy grey that made me think of a drow, a sub-race of elves known for their dark grey skin.

"So, you want passage to Asuna?" He said to me, his voice gravelly from salt air.

"Yes."

I held my head high as he looked me over. "Undek says you are the Crown Princess."

"I am."

His eyes finally left me and took in my companions. "These your guards?"

A cold laugh bubbled up from me. "I don't need guards. These are my friends and my sister."

He eyed Lord Niratap behind me, where he stood against the back wall. "Interesting company you keep. Is he tame?"

Lord Niratap snarled at the captain. "I take great offense to that comment. I may be a beast, but I'm not a savage."

The captain shrugged. "You can put just about anything in a suit and pretend it will behave itself."

Shasha shifted between them, a tiny barrier between the two huge males as her mate growled in irritation. She always astounded me with her bravery. "Lord Niratap isn't someone I would go against if I was wise."

Brast's gaze returned to me. "I know who he is. I know many who have been saved by him. I also know what he is and that is my concern. Having a predator aboard my ship, unrestrained, is not something I take lightly. Makes the crew anxious and an anxious crew makes mistakes."

Static laced the entire room as we collectively bristled. Shasha came around the desk and pressed her finger into the male's chest. She roared with that fire I so admired. "You will not put him in a cage! I will not allow you to! He is not—"

The lord pulled her against him and away from the other male. "Will it be a stipulation on us gaining passage?"

"Nira, you can't." Shasha protested, twisting in his arms.

He shushed her. "Would me in chains be a requirement?"

"That depends."

"On what?" Mitta hissed, coming to stand beside me.

"Some say you are a savior, a hero to those in bondage. Others say you're a monster who takes only what serves him and abandons all the rest. I just want to know who I will have on my ship."

"You will have me as I am. Just a man trying to keep his family safe."

The captain looked at each of us, sizing us up as allies or opponents. When his gaze landed on me again, he gave a soft nod of his head. "Very well." Our group breathed a sigh of relief. "However, you will be expected to earn your keep. Accounting for extra mouths without work is unacceptable. The Folkestone is a two hundred ninety-five-meter pananmax and she doesn't run herself."

"We would never have expected to not work." Bastion said, crossing his arms over his chest.

The captain nodded. "Follow me. We'll get you settled then I will make some arrangements. We set sail tomorrow at noon."

The Folkestone was a massive cargo vessel, loaded with shipping containers at the end of the docks.

"What are you hauling to Asuna?" I asked.

"A variety of things." The captain answered as we approached the gangplank. "Dry goods like rice, flour, and sugar. Casks of wine and spirits, small boats for fishing, cloth, furniture, mail. Some of it is for the beings that live in Asuna, and some is for Babylos itself."

"Do you venture into Babylos to sell goods?" Tummi asked.

"No. Mixed beings like myself aren't welcome through the gates of Babylos. You are both probably aware that your father doesn't approve of interspecies breeding."

I kept my gaze on the ship, but my heart seized. Shasha was in danger going into my homeland. That reality didn't sit well. Niratap wouldn't let us fall before our father and Shasha wouldn't let him come without her. They had debated, and argued, and fought those initial weeks after coming home from the hospital. I didn't want to put her at risk, not before my father. I paused at the foot of the gangplank and looked at my family. Bastion's hand fell to the small of Tummi's back and he smiled at me. Niratap and Shasha paused their hushed conversation about life at sea and looked at me. Mitta in the rear, her hands hovering close to her blades, ready for any threat that may appear. I had thought about the heat of the kiss and the ache of her words.

I was a mistake. Those words had been thrown at me my whole life. How dare I be born a daughter, a divine mistake on my family line. Leaving my home behind with no plan, with a sword from my teacher and no training, was a mistake. Praying to any higher power that would hear me

to have my father leave us alone was a mistake. I should
have known and the fact that it had shaken me to my core,
that I had thought that after three hundred years he'd leave
me alone. That was a mistake.

"If you don't want to risk it." I started. I had no
choice in this. I had to go, but they didn't. "If you don't
want to risk each other, this is the last time you can turn
around."

"Kat," Tummi said smiling sadly, "we are with you.
We're not going to abandon you to our father."

"I don't want—"

"Katrel." Niratap spoke. I looked back at my
longest friend; he smiled sweetly at me, and my heart
ached. Sacrificial, caring man. "We are going. You will not
have to face your father alone, and we will come home."

The captain cleared his throat. "As sentimental as
this is, I don't envy you. King Cardoc is as cruel as they
come."

"Have you had run-ins with my father?" I asked the
captain.

"Not personally no, but my mother told me about
him. She is a drow, a dark elf, and she always spoke out for
our people." He cleared his throat again. "Her people.
Cardoc has been good to elf-kind as a whole, but not those
that think differently. That love differently. My parents
didn't care, neither did those around them, but Cardoc
banished my parents. My father from Babylos and my
mother to Pamiršta because they were different. Because
my father was an orc."

I cast a glance at my sister and Bastion, at how he
held her close, at the bond between them that my father
would despise. I looked back at the captain. "What
happened to them?"

"My father used to be the harbor master." He
looked off into the grey sea. "He died at sea about a decade
ago. My mother had owned a boutique and made clothes,
but I haven't seen her since I was a boy. She used to write

letters, but when things got tight and the letters stopped. She didn't want to risk exposing me to Cardoc's wrath." I swallowed as the captain turned back up the gangplank. "I admire your group's bravery. Cardoc is a monster."

"You talk as if you know firsthand." Niratap said following the captain closely.

"Someone has to ferry the outcasts from Asuna."

Niratap shook his head but smiled down at his mate. "You may admire our bravery, but I admire yours."

He chuckled as we ascended onto the deck of the ship. Men and women ran about the deck, several paused as we passed, eyeing us as we followed Captain Brast. He led us into the bridge where there were several men standing about going over maps. They stood at attention as Brast entered.

"At ease." Brast said. "What are we looking at?"

"Captain." A young man with mouse brown hair spoke. "There is nothing alarming to report on the satellite. However, there are clouds starting to push from the south."

"Keep eyes on it, Thomas."

"Captain Brast." An orc male stepped beyond the others, he was almost as tall as the lord and built like a tank. His head was shaved with thick black tribals that started at his crown and disappeared down his neck. His tusks were bright against the sea-grey of his skin. "Who are your guests?"

"Vakmu, this is the Crown Princess and her friends. We are giving them passage to Asuna."

Bastion came to stand as the orc crossed his arms over his chest. "Looks like six shades of liability to me. Earthbloods can't be trusted, and the beast will complicate our entrance into Asuna's harbor, not in a cage."

"Our Lord will not be in a cage." Bastion growled.

"Why not Earthblood? You are being ferried as cargo."

Bastion's arms dropped, stepping forward. "He will not be bound. You do not have authority over us."

"Bastion." Niratap growled behind us. The words laced with the power he carried so well. "They are ferrying us to Asuna. Though you don't agree with the Ironblood, the Captain has a say in how we travel there and if his crew preferred it to grant us passage–"

"No." Shasha snapped, putting herself in front of her mate.

"No one is going to be caged." The captain said sternly. "Lord Bondbreaker is a guest on my ship and will be treated with respect. Vakmu Sharp is my chief mate, my second in command, he is difficult to get along with, but his support and loyalty are unyielding."

"Like a knife in the back." Bastion spat crossing his arms over his chest again.

"Bastion. Enough." Niratap growled.

"Bondbreaker may be a beast, but we might have to leash this Earthblood if he is yearning to fight."

"Is that a challenge?" Bastion moved to stand before the male an inch between them.

"Call off your dog." Vakmu growled as he loomed over Bastion.

Tummi wormed her way between them, pushing Bastion back as she muttered. "Age-old clan feuds aren't worth it, Bastion."

Vakmu laughed cruelly. "Little Earthblood needs an elf woman to fight his battles."

Mitta was past me in an instant, her curved dagger pressed against the orc's throat. "I would choose your battles wisely, orc. Going after Bastion is going after all of us. Now if you are done posturing, we can get on with it."

He held up his hands in submission. "Very well, rakshasi."

The captain sighed as Mitta sheathed her dagger and smiled at him. "Vakmu, will you condense the greenhorns into one cabin, the other will be for our guests."

"You want me to tell them they will be bunk-buddies?"

"Yes. They will be bunk-buddies. If they don't like it, they can get off my ship."

"Very well, Captain Brast." Vakmu left, two men following behind him.

"Bondbreaker, your boy isn't going to be a problem, is he?"

Niratap glanced at Bastion as he pushed past the rest of us to view the maps and charts that were tacked to the table. "No, he won't, but maybe for safety's sake we should keep them separated."

"Agreed." The captain said, turning to the table. "What skills do your people have?"

"All of us are trained in combat, but I doubt that will be of much need on a merchant ship traveling to the Elf Kingdom. Bastion has kitchen experience if your cook needs assistance. The rest of us are brute labor at your disposal and most of us are a quick learn."

"Even the women? The royals?"

"Definitely the women." Niratap said with a smile. "Especially the royals. Don't let their properness and femininity fool you. All these women are lethal in their own right."

Brast nodded. "I'll add you guys to day duty then, its mostly watching the sea and machinery. If the clouds stay south of us, it won't be an issue."

"But don't hold our breath."

"It's like you've been on a ship before." The captain smiled.

"Not for a very long time."

Chapter Thirteen

Mitta

"These will be your group's quarters for the voyage." The captain said as he showed us the cramped space with four capsule cots set in the walls. "I know it's nothing fancy, but it is always cramped on a ship. I can probably round up a couple extra pillows and blankets."

"Thank you. We'll make do with the space, captain." Niratap said with a smile.

"Good. I need to make the final arrangements for the cast off tomorrow. Settle in, rest, and be ready for tomorrow."

"Thank you, captain." Katrel said as the captain left down the hall. Disappearing through a port door.

"Four cots for six people is ridiculous." I griped, annoyed that the captain thought this was acceptable.

"It is what it is, Mitta, we will make do. I will take the floor." Shasha made to object, but he held his hand up. "No, *mo grá*, it is alright. I'm far too tall for these cots anyway. The rest of you can divvy the four cots."

"Bastion and I will share a cot." Tummilia said pointing to the top bunk.

"I'll take this top cot." Katrel said, tossing her backpack onto the bed.

"Then I guess that settles it." Shasha sat on one of the lower cots as Niratap rolled his suitcase to the wall between the beds.

"You're okay with this?" I couldn't fathom him choosing to sleep on the floor.

His eyes narrowed. "Mitta. Sleeping on the floor for three nights won't hurt me, firstly. Second, we're here on Katrel's propriety and not mine. If four cots and the floor is good for a princess, it's good enough for me."

"Can we please not address me as a princess." Katrel groaned from where she stood. "I only used the title to gain us passage to Babylos. I don't want to be a princess in the function my father wants."

"I meant no offense." He said with a dip of his head.

"I know." She sighed, stepping past me. "I'm going to explore the ship."

"Be careful." Niratap warned. She waved dismissively at him as she left.

I tossed my bag on the remaining cot and turned after her. "I'll keep an eye on her."

The lord thanked me as I trailed after Katrel. She walked like a warrior, her gait smooth and lethal as she prowled through the belly of the ship. She never glanced back at me as she peered into halls and the galley where men sat grumbling about having to buddy up.

"I don't care if she's a princess, I don't want to buddy with anyone." A human said as he tilted back in his chair.

"Nobody wants to buddy with you anyway, Jordan. Your feet smell like corn chips." An older man on the opposite corner of the table said, earning a round of riotous laughter.

"You know most people would be happy to have someone to cuddle with on the cold nights." She smiled ruefully at the men.

"Katrel, what are you doing?" I hissed at her.

"Having fun." She didn't even look at me as she answered and stepped into the galley.

"Kat." I followed behind not wanting her to cause more trouble than we could handle, as the human stood meeting her demure gaze with a glare.

"You the royal cunt that kicked me out of my bunk?"

"Oh, whatever is a cunt, sailor?" She said almost

meekly. Almost.

"I don't know who you think you are, Princess, but on this ship, we don't cry tears to get our way."

"You don't think I can pull my weight?" She pouted her lips.

I snagged her arm and pulled her to face me. "Katrel, if you're itching for a fight, fight me, but these men aren't worth it, and they don't deserve whatever you have planned for them. We are on this ship because of you, but don't put the lord in a bad position."

She glared at me but sighed. "Okay."

"Women. All bark, no bite." The human said sitting back down at the table, the men chuckled in agreement.

I flung a dagger with wicked speed, the blade digging into the table before him. The men were all silent as I stalked to the table and pulled the dagger from the wood. "Watch your tongue, just because I kept her from crawling into your skin does not mean I won't flay it from your body without a thought. Don't tempt me."

"You're her, aren't you?" The older sailor across the table asked quietly.

I smiled at him; the expression laced with venom. "And who would I be?"

"You're Mitta Rask. The Night Tiger."

It had been about a decade since I had heard that name uttered. The Night Tiger, the mercenary that was both brutal and quick when she was hired to end the lives on the black market. Most did not know that I had only gone after those who had abused their power, or that most of them had been people opposed to Lord Niratap and his goals to dismantle the beast we walked through. I just dipped my head in confirmation. "You best educate your fellow sailors about who sails with them to Asuna, or they may find the end of my knife."

The man nodded at my bluff. They weren't worth my fury. I just needed them to have a healthy dose of fear to keep the peace. I left the table, catching Katrel's arm as I passed and tugged her behind me to the deck. There were men about barking orders at each other as the last of the containers were loaded onto the ship. I pulled her to the starboard side of the ship that overlooked the grey sea.

I took a deep breath of the salty air before I turned on her. "What is your problem?"

"Excuse me?"

"You heard me? What is your problem? Being a princess is so hard on you that you must risk everyone by throwing a fit and starting a fight with a bunch of sailors that we are stuck with for three nights? Royalty got you down?"

"Don't patronize me."

"I'm not. You are acting like a spoiled child and none of us can afford shit to explode while we're at sea. We don't know how long we will be in Babylos, and we don't know what kind of insanity your father will unleash upon us. You need to keep your cool or you're going to get us all killed."

She looked out at the sea and frowned. "You didn't have to come."

She didn't understand that I did. It wouldn't have mattered if the lord had wanted me to stay behind to watch the manor. I would have come. I couldn't lose her. I looked out at the grey expanse. "No, I did. I won't let you face your father alone and it will be over my dead body that you stay."

She whimpered. "Mitta, I—"

"No." I turned away; my chest tight with all the things I wished I could tell her but couldn't. Not without breaking everything. I pushed off the railing pinning her with my gaze. "Just keep it together, alright? You can't go postal on everyone because you are in a bind. Cool your head before you come back."

"What are the different Orc clans?" Shasha asked Bastion as I walked into the cabin. The lord was gone, but everyone else was settling in. Bastion leaned against the wall while they chatted.

"Well, my family comes from the Earthblood clan, Ma always told me that our clan was the least blood thirsty of the warrior clans. Vakmu is an Ironblood. They are the most savage of the warrior clans, back when the world was always at war, Ironbloods would wear their enemy's heads on their belts. There are the Grassbloods that are predominantly mages. The Icebloods are cold thriving orcs that make weapons of ice that are sharper than any steel. The Necrobloods were warlocks that dabbled in necromancy, but they've disappeared from the earth. No one knows what happened to them."

"Where is the lord?" I asked, sitting down on the cot that was mine.

"He went to speak with the captain." Tummi said from where she lounged. "Where's Kat?"

"I left her on deck, she needed to cool her head."

"Did something happen?" Shasha asked.

"Just Katrel wanting to fight." I sighed laying back. "You know how she gets."

"Hot blooded." Bastion said.

"I hate when she's like that." Tummi said, playing with Bastion's unruly hair.

"She's unpredictable and all too predictable when she's like that." I said. Remembering all the times that she had gotten into an altercation or fallen into the sheets with a man because she was hot. "She's either throwing her fists at someone or fisting some random man's hair."

"She's always been self-destructive when she's

angry." Tummi said. "It got her smacked often enough by our father when we were kids, not that it was ever somewhere anyone would see."

My gut tightened; how could anyone harm their children like that. Katrel had an attitude on a good day and was a brat when she didn't get her way. Even so I didn't think it warranted beating her.

"And we have to make nice with that man?" Shasha said.

"We do." Niratap said from the doorway, carrying an armful of blankets. "We have to in order to ensure our survival. Cardoc could just as easily kill us as let us live."

"What did the captain say?" Bastion asked.

"He said that Asuna is a trade city, and all sorts of beings exist there both permanently and migratorily, so our presence there should go mostly unnoticed." He said dropping the blankets on the floor. "Until we approach the gate. Apparently, several beings made breaks through the portal and attacked the port city. Now royal guards are stationed at the gate."

"Royal guards are a problem. It will take away our plan of dropping in on my father. He will probably have us escorted to the capital." Katrel said from the doorway, she looked at the ground when I glanced in her direction.

"We adjust then." The lord continued. "We adjust the plan, our formation won't change, we will just have to be more alert."

"I still don't like you being in front." I said. "It puts you at the greatest risk, let me take the bolt instead." I could have imagined it, but I thought Katrel flinched at that.

"It may put me at the most risk, however we do not know what Cardoc knows about us. We don't know if he knows the girls are capable warriors. We don't know if he knows about my recent imprisonment. Putting me in front is about appearances, and Cardoc is all about appearances."

"He is." Tummi said. "I agree with Mitta though.

You already took an arrow for us once; you shouldn't have to again."

"I will though, as long as I am able." Niratap said, sinking onto the floor and stretching out his long legs. "I know you all have my back, and I am forever in your debt."

"You saved us too, you know." Katrel said, leaning opposite Bastion.

"Be that as it may, we are going to keep you free. A united front against a misogynistic ruler."

"We're going to be so heroic." Bastion said, glancing up at Tummi. "I won't let them hurt you babe."

She pinched his cheek. "Just stay out of our father's direct path please. He dislikes orcs as much as he dislikes humans."

"We are all in danger going to Babylos." The lord said contemplatively. "We should rest. Tomorrow, we cast off for Asuna and though the captain just wants us watching the sea, anything can happen on a ship in the Atlantic."

Everyone crawled into their bunks and the lord shifted some blankets on the floor. I watched him settle into the slim padding between the floor and himself. Shasha draped a hand out of her blankets to play with his hair. I rolled over to face the wall, and all the heartache and longing crept in, choking me in sorrow before sleep.

The next day was uneventful. Just the sea, lazy grey clouds, and an overly excited young woman. Shasha pulled Lord Niratap behind her from one side of the ship to the other. She wanted to watch as home faded into the distance and wanted to watch as we charged forward into the great expanse. The sea churned around us and ships passed us returning to port, and then it was just us, the sky, and the sea.

That night Bastion had helped the cook prepare dinner; it was a warm stew that the windblown bodies enjoyed. The sailor sang bawdy tunes and danced around the galley. Everyone had smiles on their faces when we retired to our bunks. Even with all the merriment my heart was heavy. I laid there staring at the wall willing my darkness to leave me in peace. Sometime in the night I heard whimpering and rolled to see the lord leaned into Shasha's cot whispering softly to her.

"Is everything okay?" I asked hushed.

"She was having a nightmare." He said with equal softness before easing back against the wall with a soft groan. His fingers gently stroked her hand. "She will be upset if she finds out she woke you."

"I wasn't really asleep."

He smiled softly. "I know. Trouble sleeping?"

I sighed. "My heart is heavy."

"I'm sorry, but I won't fall back." He said, focusing on the shifting form next to him. "If anyone gets hurt right away, I would prefer it to be me. I heal the fastest out of all of us."

"I understand that but—"

Shasha shifted from her blankets and blearily looked at both of us.

"What's the matter, *mo grá*?"

She mumbled something unintelligible before scooting out of her cot, wrapping her blanket around her, and plopping down on his lap, snuggling close to his chest.

He chuckled. "All right, my flower, I'll hold you."

She mumbled again before her breathing settled. Niratap rubbed her back in small soothing circles. We sat there in silence and watching him care for his mate, that old ache threatened to bring tears to my eyes. I sniffled to myself.

"Why don't you just ask her?" He queried in the darkness.

"I can't."

He sighed. "Why not?"

I swallowed and it felt like glass down my throat. Could I tell him about my foolishness as a youth? The promise I could never break. I trusted him with my life. Surely, I could trust him with Bran and Asira's memory. Trust him with my hesitation.

"I—"

"Will you two stop chattering down there; some of us are trying to sleep." Katrel groggily snarled from her cot.

"Apologies, Princess." The lord said with a mischievous grin. A pillow shot down at him which he caught.

"Don't call me that." She growled. "Now give me back my pillow and shut up."

He chuckled softly and tossed it back up at her gently. "I'm sorry."

"Go to sleep." She groaned and I heard her music start to play through her headphones.

After a moment the lord said. "I don't know why you refuse to go with your heart, but I know you love her. More than maybe is right, but maybe not. You'd never know unless you tried." He smiled softly at me, no judgment, or suspicion in his gaze. "Maybe whatever is holding you back is something that you can let go of."

Could I let go of Bran? Let go of his burly laughter and warm smile? Let go of his bravery and honesty that got me through so much? But losing him. Losing Asira. I didn't know if I could.

"I made a promise." I whispered, traitorous tears rolled over my cheeks. Gods I hated crying. I hated feeling this helpless and lost. "I don't think I can break it."

He didn't comment on my tears, just glanced down at the bundled woman before him. "I thought my life was over when I lost Deirdre. When I was a prisoner, I was lost. And yet here I am. Loved and cared for more than I deserve by my friends-made-family and this beautiful woman."

"But what if I can't have that?"

He smiled to himself. "You won't know until you try."

"I don't deserve her."

"Because of the station she doesn't want or because of your promise?"

"Both."

"Don't be afraid of it, Mitta."

"You make it sound so easy." I huffed wiping my eyes.

"Loving someone is never easy, my friend, but loving them from afar is much worse. Try to sleep, Mitta, we have one more day at sea and then navigating to Babylos. Be her friend if nothing else."

Chapter Fourteen

Shasha

My dagger weighed heavy against my thigh as we came down off the ship. Asuna was much larger than I had imagined for a floating city that acted as the portal to Babylos. Paved roads and tightly clustered houses under the oceanic sky peppered with gulls. The smells of salty sea air and fish were strong. The docks were full of life as cargo was unloaded and fishermen were pulling in with their morning catches. Mitta pulled my hood over my head as she stepped in front of me, guarding me as men and women moved past.

"Keep your face covered, my lady."

"Why?"

Mitta eyed an ogre that walked past with large, rolled wefts of fabric on his shoulders. "Because we don't know anyone here and we can't trust them."

I looked back up to the deck of the ship where my mate was masked, speaking with the captain. There was no hiding what he was, not with his height and antlers. He bowed his head to the captain and descended the gangplank. "Do you think we'll be safe?"

"I don't know." Mitta said as Katrel and Tummi took up the lead of the group. "I would rather run with an air of caution."

"Caution would be wise." Katrel said softly. "As soon as we get to the portal we will be at our father's mercy."

"Lead the way, my dears." My mate said, coming to stand behind me. "Let's get there first."

Blending into the crowd ebbing into the city center, we wove through the bustling bazaar where vendors of all walks and races sold their wares. Bright spices from all over the world, silks, and satins in all shades of color, meats and roasted vegetables that pulled me to them. Niratap placed a heavy hand on my shoulder after the second time I veered away from our group eager to see everything, smell everything.

"Careful, my Flower."

"I am."

He chuckled. "I don't want to lose you in the crowd because your curiosity knows no bounds."

"I am not an errant child that needs to be babysat."

"No." He said softly as he guided me to continue forward behind Bastion. "I never said you were, but I fear we may find enemies here."

I swallowed. That was something we didn't need. Running into enemies would highlight who we were and put us at risk. We needed to avoid that in order to enter the Babylos.

"Bondbreaker!" A familiar voice shouted brightly ahead of us.

Mitta swore as we recognized the finely dressed male. "It's Voxviraz."

"Bondbreaker!" The incubus waved at us animatedly. He was dressed in a cream-colored suit that had gold edges that pulled out the glint in his golden hair. His curved horns were a pale-cream pearlescent in the sunlight.

Niratap growled at the incubus as he shoved him into an empty alley and pinned him against the wall. "Voxviraz, could you not paint a target on my back again?"

The creature smiled wistfully up at my mate. Delicate strands of his spun gold hair fell in front of his face and over his blood red eyes that looked out at the world hungrily. "Apologies. No hard feelings about the auction?"

Mitta snarled. "You have to be fucking kidding me you spineless excuse–"

"Enough." Niratap snapped at her. "What did you want, Voxviraz?"

"Penance? Forgiveness for my cowardice? You were—"

"An easy target." Niratap stepped back letting the creature straighten his suit, and pat away the dust.

"Yes. Again apologies. I don't do well with angry mobs, I deflected."

"You're lucky I don't skin you alive right now." Mitta hissed.

"Mitta enough. What do you want? We have places to be."

"You are going to Babylos, are you not?"

"We might be."

He smiled knowingly. "There is an old ruin in the far north beyond the mountains. Before Babylos was split from the world of man, that ruin was home to my people. There is an artifact there that I would like to get my hands on. Unfortunately, the guard won't let me pass to collect it. Wouldn't even take a bribe."

"And you think that the guards will let us pass?"

"Why wouldn't they? You have the Crown Princess with you."

Everyone in the group bristled, no one outside the house knew who Katrel was. No one.

"How do you know you know who I am?" She hissed from behind me.

"My, my, fire tongue. It's almost as if your father hasn't kept eyes on you. Word spreads fast in the underground."

"Especially when you're shmoozing everyone with any kind of sway." Mitta growled.

"Information keeps schmoozers like me alive in the underworld, Night Tiger." Voxviraz growled back, flashing his very sharp teeth. Mitta's hand landed on her knife as she began to advance on the incubus.

I held my arm out to stop her. "I trust that you will

keep that information to yourself, Voxviraz.”

“Why, Lady Bondbreaker, if it keeps my head upon my shoulders, I would do anything.”

A non-answer. I asked. “What is this artifact?”

“The Amulet of Lilitu. It is said to enhance the power of suggestion that my race holds over others.”

“And why do you want this?” I pressed.

“It sounds like it would be the best way to start a mass orgy.” The creature shrugged non-committal. Another non-answer.

“What do we get in return if we bring you this amulet?”

The creature cocked his head and smiled. “A favor for your efforts.”

Niratap slid in front of me. “No.”

“I was speaking with the Lady.” Voxviraz glared up at my mate, though his smile didn’t fade.

“I don’t care.” He growled. “Favors like you are offering never come without strings.”

“Now Bondbreaker, you can’t expect me to slight the lady.”

“I do, actually.” He snarled, leaning into his face. His fingers shifted into claws that gouged the stone wall behind Voxviraz.

To his credit, he didn’t balk at my mate or his threat. “If you bring me the amulet, Lady Bondbreaker, I will owe you one favor, no strings attached.”

“And how am I to trust you?” I asked, slipping between the incubus and my mate, leaning into him and creating space there. “How am I guaranteed that there won’t be strings?”

Voxviraz eyed me, his smile never waning. “I see your lord has taught you not to trust the words from those with twisted tongues.” His forked tongue flicked between his lips.

I merely stared, waiting for an actual answer. Voxviraz sighed through his nose, his face falling. “Very well, my Lady. I offer up my blood seal of honor."

"What is that?" I asked as I felt Niratap tense behind me.

"I offer you a drop of my blood and I take a drop of yours. It is a binding contract between the two of us. I will swear a favor free of strings and you will swear to bring me the Amulet of Lilitu."

No one breathed. Fae were wily creatures. Demons were tricksy. Incubi were the homogenized version of both. If I accepted this offer, I would have an ace if we needed it. An incubus with connections in my back pocket, but was it worth the risk? Niratap's hands rested protectively on my shoulders.

"*Mo grá,* I do not trust him."

"I know." I stared into the creature's eyes; eyes so close to the color of blood. "I accept."

Niratap's grip tightened on me. "Shasha–"

"It's okay, my Love." I really hoped that I wouldn't regret this.

Voxviraz smiled wickedly, holding out his hand. "Your knife, my Lady?" I pulled the cragstone blade from my hip and offered it to him, his fingers were long and elegant. He took the blade and pricked my finger, then his own. "I, Voxviraz Penn, First Son of the Morning, swear of all that I am and all that I will be, that I will owe you, Shasha Nicole Dion, our Lady Bondbreaker, mate of shadows, one favor, no strings attached, upon the delivery of the Amulet of Lilitu."

My heart skittered in my chest. "I, Shasha Nicole Dion, the Lady Bondbreaker, swear to deliver the Amulet of Lilitu to you, Voxviraz Penn, for the payment of one favor no strings attached to be collected at my leisure."

The creature smiled knowingly at me, and he tapped his fingertip to mine. I felt the magic dance across my skin; it was a sensual caress of a lover. A delicate golden chain adorned my wrist as the magic coalesced, a matching one appearing on Voxviraz's.

"I see that your lord has taught you very well, my Lady." He purred examining the jewelry and handing me back my blade. "You worded your half of the bargain very well."

"What will you do now?" I asked, sheathing my blade.

"I will go and find a bed mate I fancy for the evening." He turned down the alley, opposite the bustling market, and threw a casual hand over his shoulder. "I will see you when you return, Lady Bondbreaker."

Niratap took my wrist in his hand and examined the chain. His eyes were hard, but I couldn't decipher his expression behind the mask. "I am alright."

"We shall see." He said softly, a growl laced on his tongue. "I do not trust him."

The gate to Babylos was guarded. Elven men clad in white-gold armor stood stoically with pikes in their hands at the intricate gate that divided the portal from the common folk that milled about. Beyond the gate was a large mirror that reflected everything back in stunning clarity. Katrel marched ahead of us towards the gate and the guards, who crossed their pikes in defense.

"None shall enter the Kingdom of Babylos by order of King Cardoc, Third of His Name." One of the guards said not looking at us.

"Move you brutes, I was summoned to court." Katrel hissed.

"None shall pass." The other guard said.

Katrel stepped back and squared her shoulders. "Step aside, soldiers."

Neither soldier moved.

"I told you to step aside, soldiers."

"On whose orders?" The first guard asked.

Katrel ripped off her hood. "By my orders. I am Katrel Gwendolyn Raloqen, Crown Princess of Babylos, and my father has summoned me and mine to court."

The guards exchanged a look. The second guard stepped to the center of the gate while the first guard ducked past and into the silvery mirror, its surface rippled.

"Where did he go?" Niratap asked.

"He went to find the captain. He will be the one to decide if your group may pass or if you will be arrested for lying to the Crown Guard."

"I'm not lying to you. I am the Crown Princess."

"Kat." Tummi took her hand. "It's okay, we'll wait."

Fifteen minutes passed, before the surface of the mirror wobbled. Fifteen minutes of Katrel pacing back and forth before the gate like a caged wild animal. Fifteen minutes of watching her stalk back and forth before the guards, with a menacing fire growing in her eyes. The elf man that came through the portal was tall, dressed in the same fine armor as the other guards, except his armor was inlaid with whorls of darker gold and a grand helm set atop his head, protecting his face from view.

"Finally." Katrel snarled at the man. "How dare you make me wait."

"As hostile as ever, Princess?" His voice was rich and smooth like chocolate on the tongue, even as it echoed in the helm.

Tummi took a step back into Bastion, tugging her hood farther over her face. Katrel hissed at him. "Who are you?"

The knight's captain bowed at the waist to Katrel. "Apologies Princess, but have you forgotten me?"

When he stood, he pulled the helm off his head. Radiant golden hair was tied back from his face that was composed of sharp cheekbones and jaw. His eyes were the same shade as the oceanic blue sky. Katrel took a step away from the man who offered her his hand.

"You're a captain?"

"Yes, Princess."

Niratap stepped past me, looming over Katrel and the man. "Katrel, who is this?"

The male smiled smugly up at my mate and hot ire filled my belly. "I would ask you the same question sir, but to answer you. I am Revan Cistern, the Crown Chosen, Heir Apparent, and the Crown Princess's betrothed."

I saw the flick of my mate's tail beneath his cloak. "I am Lord Niratap Bondbreaker, and these are members of my household. We are escorting the Crown Princess."

"Thank you for delivering her to me." Revan said. "I will see that she is brought before the king."

"No, you misunderstand me, we will continue to escort the Lady." Niratap said standing at his full height, letting his shadows slip free from the bottom of his cloak. A towering force before the knight, his smile not fading from the panes of his face at the threat.

He just nodded his head. "If that is the princess's wish."

"It is." Katrel said. "May we?"

Revan bowed to Katrel. "Yes, Princess."

Katrel led us through the portal mirror. Niratap brought up the rear. not trusting the guards to not turn on us. Stepping through the mirror surface was like walking through a wall of water. It clung to my skin and hair until I cleared the other side. Niratap's hand closed over my shoulder as he blinked in the bright light. I watched in awe as my mate pulled back his hood and untied the mask. The shadows wisped off his skin, revealing his honey-tone to the sun. He always took my breath away with his beauty.

"Welcome to Babylos." Revan said as he stepped around us. "This is the city Cardstona."

The city around us was built of pale stone and shining blue glass. The portal was located on a hilltop that looked over the land and the blue tiled roofs of the city.

The air was scented with salt and the sea was to my right. To my left beyond the towering buildings were vast fields and farmland. Before me, in the distance I spotted another city before a mighty forest that seemed to go on forever and beyond that were tall mountains. We followed Revan, who talked incessantly about the city to us, how it was both a trade city and military outpost, to the wall where horses waited saddled for us. All of them were fine, elegant limbed creatures, whose fur was fine shades of silver and white. Niratap towered over all of them as he walked through them. The horses were not scared, only curious of the monster before them, more trusting then the warriors that watched our group.

"Shasha." He called from where he stood before the darkest of the horses, a deep blue who demanded my mate's attention. "He should be your mount. He is the kindest of them all, his disposition is a match for Guinness."

"Who will you ride?"

"No one I'm afraid, though these are beautiful horses. None of them could carry me. I will run beside you."

Revan trotted over on a silver mare. "Firenze is a good horse. He will treat you well, Lady. Apologies that we don't have a mount for a creature of your stature."

The way that he said 'creature' made the smile drop from my face. Niratap said. "An oversight, we did not send word before our arrival."

"Pity. I'm sure that King Cardoc would have been here to welcome you if he had known. He will still be excited to accept you in Illishara." He said, turning away and heading to the front of the group.

Somehow, I doubted that as Niratap helped me onto the back of the horse and tied down our belongings to the saddle. "I don't like him."

"I don't think anyone does." He said, tightening the last strap on the saddle and sweeping his cloak over my lap, his black dress shirt and slacks contrasting harshly against the pale stone. "Keep hold of my belongings?"

"Of course."

"My heart?" He asked, his eyes soft.

"Always."

He kissed me sweetly, stepping back as the shadows swept around him. His clothes landed softly in my lap under the cloak, the tendrils of shadows played with my braids and caressed my face. The sable-grey beast that now stood in his place shook out his fur, the dark scales of his forelimbs shimmered in that oceanic sunlight and cast dark iridescent light in shades of blue and green.

The guards backed their horses from him, like the beast before them would go for them. I reached across the little space between us and pet the soft fur between his ears, a rumbling purr answered me. When I righted myself in the saddle, I met Revan's piercing gaze before he turned and led us through the massive oak gate. Had he read me as a weakness to my mate? Only time would tell how things would go.

We rode hard. Over rolling meadows and vast fields of wheat. Crossing a mighty river over a white stone bridge. Closer and closer to the giant monolith that was the capital city. Illishara sparkled against the dark woods beyond it, a gleaming monument to this kingdom.

With hoods pulled over our heads we entered the picturesque city. Niratap stalked between me and Bastion as we made our way to the castle up the main road. The walls of the buildings ranged from white to pale grey. Shops lined the road with big windows and stained-glass doors that captured the light and made it dance on their wares. Katrel sat ramrod straight behind Revan. Followed by myself, Nira, and Bastion, with Mitta and Tummi in the rear. The guards watched my mate restlessly, a fox in a hen house.

I peered at my mate, his moonlight eyes meeting mine. I could feel his caress in that look, feel his strong hands and hear his promises of safety. They didn't trust him, but the rest of us; they weren't afraid of. A foolish thing.

When we passed through the pearly gates before the palace, shadows swallowed me, loving hands on my face and a chaste kiss as the parcel of my mate's clothes disappeared from my lap and he took his most human form. Fiddling with his cuffs until they sat just so on his wrists. Lethal grace layered over him even with his charming face. When his cuffs were settled, he offered me his hand. It was care that I didn't need, but that I loved and knew was necessary to prove who I belonged to.

"Thank you, my love." I said, taking his hand and letting him pull me into his arms.

"Remember you are a weapon, like any of us." He hissed in a whisper. "Do not let them look down on you because you are a woman. Because you are human."

"Never." I whispered back. "I know I have fangs now."

He smiled as he sat me down; Katrel came to his side. "Are you ready for this?"

A dip of his chin. "No going back."

We gathered into formation with Katrel on my right, Tummi on my left, Bastion and Mitta behind. My mate bravely headed our party, prepared to take a bolt if need be. I grasped his tail lightly, feeling both his softness and his strength.

"*Mo grá.*" He whispered peering over his shoulder.

"Nothing. *Is liomsa tú agus is leatsa mise.*"[30]

"*Go dtí mo anáil dheireanach.*"[31] He murmured to

---

[30] You are mine and I am yours.
[31] Until my last breath.

me. "You ready?"

"Yes." I dropped his tail and squared my shoulders.

Revan led us up the bone white steps into the castle. Through warm sun-toned oak doors, the floor was a white marble inlaid with shimmering gold. A crimson carpet lay upon the center of the hall that matched the banners that hung. A great, golden many-eyed serpent with a flaming crown.

"What is that?"

"A biotatá, it's a flaming serpent that lived in the founding of the Flame Empire, in the beginning; they are rumored to be extinct now. Crimson and gold are the colors of the royal family. At least for as long as our family has held the throne." Tummi murmured to me a distant smile on her face.

I nodded. Somehow despite the depictions of fire and strength, I only saw the color of blood. Only saw pain. I shuddered at the thought of what waited beyond another set of oak doors where music played lightly over the flood of conversation. Revan smiled as he thrust the doors open.

Beyond them was a grand hall, with two-story ceilings that had intricate antler chandeliers that burned with golden fae light. Men and women chattered in clusters wearing fine clothes from all periods. Men in courtly clothes to fine suits like my mate liked to wear. Women in modest poofy Victorians to sleek gowns that glimmered in the light. Along the walls knights observed the guests that danced and chattered. Beyond them all was a dais upon which two thrones sat, behind them was a larger banner with the royal seal.

The crowd parted as Revan led us up to the dais and they murmured on a knife's edge, their eyes tracking the male at the head of our party. I peered around him at the man we approached, King Cardoc Raloqen, the Elf King, Katrel and Tummilia's father. He was lounging back in his throne carved from a rich, honeyed wood, dressed in a deep maroon surcoat and night-dark black pants and boots. His dark mahogany hair was shorn at the line of his sharp chin. Dark eyes that, when the light caught them just right, flashed orange, gold, and copper, like when he lifted his head to examine our group. Beside him a fair woman with long, silver-blond hair and eyes like stars sat in a long pale blue dress. Standing just behind the king on the other side was a man with long straw blond hair that was tied back from his fair face, his eyes were a grassy green.

"Revan." The king's voice was deep and cold as he spoke.

Revan bowed at the waist. "My King."

"What have you brought to court with you?"

Katrel stepped away from me, lowering her hood to face her father. The crowd murmured in both shock and confusion.

Revan cleared his throat. "I present the Crown Princess Katrel Gwendolyn Raloqen."

Chapter Fifteen

Niratap

He sat there idly, the presence of his children nothing more than an inconvenience to his evening. I did not like the way he looked at Katrel as if she meant nothing. I ground my teeth as I bowed my head in a show of respect.

"King Cardoc, I—"

"Silence, beast."

My tail swished in annoyance. I kept my head bowed and tried again. "King Cardoc. King of the Elves. I beseech your grace with a request to release your daughter."

"I said silence, beast." I met his ember filled gaze, the crowd of courtiers around us began to murmur. "Katrel, what is the meaning of this?"

"Father, I answered your summons."

"We have come to ask that you grant Katrel her freedom." Tummilia said from my other side, lowering her hood.

He leaned forward glowering at the girls. "Freedom?"

Katrel took a step towards the man, her voice strong. "Yes father, I—"

He held up his hand, dismissing her. "My people please continue the festivities in the courtyard while we discuss our family matters."

The courtiers bowed to the king before taking their leave out of the great hall. It wasn't until it was just us and the royal knights before the king and the hall's doors closed that he addressed us.

"You really are a disappointment, Katrel. I

explicitly told you to leave the trash where it was and instead you bring this riffraff into my home and embarrass me in front of my court."

"How can you treat them like that? They're your children!" My mate hissed behind me. I reached behind and pressed her back.

The king eyed me from his throne, and the look said enough about what he thought of me. The beast that stood before him asking for freedom. "My children failed me when they were born with holes between their legs."

"Cardoc."

"That is King Cardoc to you, beast."

I couldn't keep the bite out of my words as I stepped forward. "King Cardoc, I am Lord Niratap Bondbreaker, and I humbly ask that you hear our plea and release the Crown Princess from her duties so she may live her life as she chooses."

He smirked at me. "A lord from the world of man has no sway in my kingdom. Especially one who is a monster, no matter how eloquently you speak and dress, that is all you will be in my court."

I swallowed as the clink of armor echoed throughout the room. The guards were preparing for orders to kill me. I closed the distance to the foot of the dais and kneeled before him. I heard my mate gasp behind me. "Be that as it may. I ask for your penance to allow her to go free."

I didn't raise my head as he stood and came to stand before me. "You're a brave creature." He murmured his fingers dancing over a prong of my antler. His calloused fingers closed around my chin roughly and angled my head to look upon him. "What are you?"

"I'm a bitarog, Your Majesty."

"I have slayed many of your kind for the sole joy of killing, and yet you prostrate yourself before me." He angled my head one way then the other. "You're much smaller than other bitarogs."

I felt the familiar tang of binding magic trill over my body and coat the back of my tongue. The king could cast magic without uttering a word, half a thought and I knew he could have killed me if he wanted. The magic sparked over me and fizzled out; I had never thought I would be thankful for the weight of Dravin's manacles.

"For a creature known as the Bondbreaker, you seem to already be someone's property."

I made to growl, but the scent of all the seasons flooded my nose along with metallic blood. The sounds of swords being unsheathed trailed down my spine. Shasha, my mate, had come between me and the king, her cragstone blade pressed to his throat, the smallest trickle of blood sliding down his pale neck.

"Unhand him." She demanded.

My heart thundered as her rage poured into me, hot molten ore under my skin. She had sensed the magic, had not been able to stay idle and had not wanted to risk me. My heart cracked at the thought.

The king looked down at her, judged her as she appeared. A human girl brandishing a knife for a monster, the binding magic crackled again, and again fizzled out as my own protected my mate. Cardoc's eyes narrowed, as I wrapped my arms around Shasha's waist.

"Interesting. You should keep a tighter leash on your belongings, beast." He said releasing me and stepping back.

"She is not a possession." I growled, backing away and tugging Shasha with me. She expertly twisted the dagger in her hand ready to attack. "She is my equal."

"Hmm. Stand down." Cardoc said to the guards as he straightened and pulled a handkerchief from his pocket to dab at the small cut on his neck. He frowned at the blood that stained the fabric, and then eyed the group. "Why should I grant your request, beast?"

"You are King of the Elves; you do not need your daughter to be a brood mare for you to name an heir." I said. Plan A was going swimmingly.

He looked down at us, and I could see the wicked gears in his head turning. "I will ponder your request, but until then you will stay in my kingdom under my watch. In the event I choose to grant said request."

"Thank you." I said with a bow of my head taking another step back from the dais.

"Oh, don't thank me yet, Bondbreaker. You may just give up this radical mission before I make a decision. Cyran."

"Yes, my King." The soft natured man beside the throne said.

"Make arrangements for the princess and her guests. I'm sure her rooms can be emptied if they are occupied."

"Yes, my King."

"Behave yourselves in my home." He said, turning back to sit on his throne. "I'm not above killing, monsters especially."

"Of course, King Cardoc."

We followed the soft-spoken man through the halls until he paused. He took a deep breath before he turned on us. His green eyes swirling with wildness I hadn't expected the male to have. His face twisted into a rage.

"I told you not to come back." He growled at Katrel. I stepped in front of her instinctively.

"Mind how you speak to her." I growled.

He eyed me unafraid, but that vigor fell as he pinched the bridge of his nose. "Why did you come back?"

"Niratap, it's fine." Katrel said, gripping my arm as she passed. "I had to."

"No, you didn't!" He shouted as she came before him. He looked heartbroken, hopeless. "I tried so hard to keep you away. I told you to stay away. I told you that you should never come back."

"He threatened her, Teacher." Tummilia said as she came around my other side. "We couldn't ignore his request."

The man's demeanor fell even more at the girls before him. He wrapped his arms around them. His eyes met mine as he held the girls and there was both sadness and pride in those emerald eyes. The way he clutched them to him showed they were more precious to him than to their own father. "You are either very brave or very foolish."

"Both is a better assessment." Shasha said wrapping her arm around my hips.

"I take offense to that, love."

"Why?" Mitta pressed. "It is one of the truest statements there is. Who is this?"

Katrel stepped back from the male. "This is Cyran Crane, the Crown Scholar and our teacher."

He gave a gentle bow of his head and offered his hand for me to shake. His hand was calloused as my own and not at all what I expected of a scholar. "I apologize for my outburst. I was working on trying to push Cardoc one way. He is stagnant when it comes to tradition."

"We have other reasons for coming, as a scholar I know you can help us." Tummi said, looking back at us.

I cleared my throat. "We need some information on an entity that is hunting me."

"An entity?"

"We think it's a being called the malice." Mitta said. "We have wards on the property that keep it in the outskirts in the physical sense, but it has been plaguing the lord's dreams."

"We need to know what it is so we can stop it before it can catch its prey. I don't want to know what it wants with my mate." Shasha added with a frown.

"You keep that information to yourself, Lady. Cardoc does not need more ammunition to go after you and him." He smiled. "That knife to the king's throat was a statement enough. A brave, but foolish claim."

Shasha pulled me closer, and I asked. "Have you ever heard of such a creature?"

"Personally no, but my father might have. Each scholar in the castle usually has a special interest. Mine is ancient history and traditions, but my father." He paused, his face going serious. "My father's specialty is of a darker flavor."

"Cyran, do you know any traditions that I might be able to use to gain my freedom?" Katrel asked.

The scholar closed his eyes, his fingers dancing along his robes as if he was scanning the spines of old books. He paused as if he had found the tome he wanted. "I think I know just the tradition to use." He frowned. "However, you would still be at his mercy. I'll show you the tome I have in mind. The head of housekeeping is already tidying rooms for your group. I told her four, but I don't know how you're partnering up."

Tummilia pranced to Bastion's side and grabbed his arm. "Bastion will stay with me."

The young male blushed. "Tummi."

"I will stay with Katrel." Mitta said. "I don't trust the king to not try to harm her."

"That is probably the smartest thing anyone from this group has said."

I frowned, but we continued after the scholar.

"Has anything changed while we were gone?" Tummi asked as we rounded a corner.

Cyran's tone was flat as he said. "No. Nothing of importance has changed. Maybe some staff has changed."

The library was a massive dedication to knowledge.

The room was bright and airy even with the heavy scent of old tomes and dust, and walkways crossed the vast expanse of the open space above our heads. The floor we were on had a walk spanning across a plunge deep into the ground, brightly lit with fae lights. The walls as far as I could see were lined with books of varying ages. There were several stacks along the floor and desks that had piles of books and scrolls on them. The amount of knowledge here was beyond any that had ever been heard of. The only sounds were the whisper of robes and the scratching of quills. Cyran murmured to another scholar as we took in the massive space.

"Welcome to the Great Library of Illishara." Cyran said with a sweep of his arm at the space.

"How many books are there?" Shasha asked as she came to the railing.

"I do not know. The library has been in existence since before the era of elves, when only the gods walked the earth. At least that is what the stories say."

I smiled at her wonder. "All the knowledge in the universe is here in the Kingdom of the Elves."

"I wouldn't say all the knowledge, but a vast majority of it, yes." Cyran said proudly as he turned to where the stairs led to the floors below. "Follow me."

Down and down, we went into the depths of the library. He turned us down a long hall lined with books and doors, opening one. It was an office lined with shelves of books with an old mahogany desk in its center, a stack of books and scrolls upon its ancient surface. Katrel looked lovingly at the desk as if it held so many memories. A window that let in bright late afternoon light held a vignette of gondolas shifting up and down the canals of Venice, two well-loved green couches sat before it.

"I remember," Cyran said, running his fingers over the books along the wall. "When you girls were little and played hide-and-seek."

"Getting to the Crown Scholars' desk was always

endgame." Katrel said, her smile wistful as she ran her fingers over the old wood.

"The only thing that changed was who got here first." Tummi said sitting on one of the couches.

"I always enjoyed the sounds of you girls laughing through the library. Some of these scholars are a tad stuffy. Ah, here it is." Cyran pulled a thick black book off the shelf and set it upon his desk moving several scrolls to the floor. The embossing on the book read *The Warriors Way: A Record of Knight's Traditions Under the Roaring Flame.* The scholar flipped through the book, hunting for his idea. "Here, this is what I think you can use to gain your freedom. *The Trials of the Flame: The Sovereign's Test.* It's an old test that used to be used to knight males from lower-born houses. That being said, I think it is something that Cardoc would go for since it links back to his great-grandfather, the last son of the Flame Emperor."

"What are the trials?" I asked, curious to what kind of feats Katrel would have to do in order to earn her freedom.

"That is what I meant by she would be at his mercy. The king gets to pick the trials, traditionally there is a test of bravery, a test of strength, and a test of wit. Cardoc would have control over the trials, and they could be anything from full combat to killing an enemy of the crown, or worse."

Katrel frowned at the tome. "Do you think he would take it? If I asked him to test me for my freedom?"

Cyran's brows furrowed. "I believe he would, if anything solely for the enjoyment of seeing if you failed."

I frowned at that as there was a knock at the door. I read over the description of the test.

"Enter." Cyran said straightening as the door opened to reveal another elf male. He was similar in appearance to Cyran but aged with deep frown lines around his mouth and crow's feet around his eyes that shone the same deep green and his straw-colored hair was silvering at the temples.

"Crown Scholar." The man said with a dip of his chin.

"Father." Cyran said with an equal dip of his chin. "This is my father Cairn Crane, Senior Scholar of the Occult Arts. He may have an answer to your question, Lord."

"A query for me and my expertise?" His voice was smokey and smooth, but something about him slithered under my skin.

"Do you know of an entity known as the malice?" Mitta asked from where she scanned over the trials next to Katrel.

"The malice, it does sound familiar." He mused, his fingers doing a similar motion to what Cyran's had earlier. "I have a tome in my office that contains information on such a creature. If you would like to follow me to my office in the depths."

Mitta straightened from her spot. "My Lord?"

I nodded my head; Shasha grabbed my hand and squeezed. "Will you share with me what you find?"

My brows furrowed. "Are you not going to accompany me?"

"No, I have things I want to ask Cyran. Some things I want to learn."

I nodded, tucking an errant braid behind her ear. "Very well, my flower. Lead the way, Senior Scholar."

"Cairn is just fine sir."

"Very well, Cairn. Mitta."

"Yes, my Lord."

I followed behind the scholar with Mitta behind me, deeper into the darker reaches of the library. The light became thinner as we descended. The scent of paper older than time and of old iron turned my stomach. The shadows around us seemed to watch as we passed.

"Why is it so dark down here?" Mitta asked behind me, just as on edge at the phantom eyes dancing over our skin.

"The tomes with darker content seem to prefer the shadows, keeps them from wandering."

A shudder trailed down my spine as I asked. "What made you interested in the darker parts of the world?"

"Death always piques the interest of near-deathless things." He shrugged, turning down a hall. "The darker things just appealed to my nature. Why your interest in the malice, young lord?"

"We believe that this entity is stalking my home and influencing dreams of those in my care. I want to know if there is a way to stop it."

"Hmm. How peculiar." He turned into a dim office where faelight candles flickered. His office was dark, his vignette window of the night sky, the stars sparkling. "If I recall correctly the malice is an occult horror."

"Occult horror?" Mitta asked as the scholar looked over the books on his desk.

"Yes." He answered pulling a book from the bottom of the stack on his desk. "Horror and abominations are not things that are born of this world, they are made. Created by beings that are no longer of the nature they were born. Necromancers can also create such creatures, but the cost is much higher if you are still connected to this plane of existence. Have you enemies that are not fully of this world?"

"I may, but none that I am aware of." I said as he opened the tome.

"Interesting." He flipped through the book until he found the section he was looking for. "Here it is. The malice is an abomination horror directly linked to a lich, the only beings that have the power to truly control them. It is an eater of fears and feasts on the pain of its victims, in service to its creator."

"What is a lich?" Mitta asked, coming to peer into the book.

"A lich is a being that has separated their soul from

their corporeal form in an effort to become truly immortal. Not many have been successful in such a process.”

"What does one do to become a lich?” I asked, my unease deepening.

"With the use of rare substances in a magic ritual, that render the casters soul bound to one or more items in the world, a phylactery, where upon they can be resurrected should their physical form be destroyed. I have heard that occasionally if the ritual is partially completed one could still become a lich, but it takes their new form years to come into fruition. The soul must marinate in its home object for a time.”

"Is there a way to get rid of the malice?” Mitta asked, scanning the pages.

"I would assume that the only way to be rid of the malice is to get rid of the lich controlling it.”

I sighed. "Meaning I have an enemy I don't know, who is immortal, and coming after my home.”

Chapter Sixteen

Shasha

Watching my mate leave with the elder scholar curled heavily in my heart. It wasn't that I didn't want to know what the malice was or why it would be after him, I had questions that I wanted to ask that I hadn't been ready to share.

"You had queries for me, young lady?" Cyran asked. The Crown Scholar smiled softly at me; his energy seemed to put me at ease. So much like his father in appearance, but nothing like him in the soul.

"Do you have information on bitarogs?"

The others glanced at me from where they had positioned through the room, and I felt my hands start to shake a little.

"There are several books on monsters." He paused his brows furrowing. "Are there things that your mate refuses to tell you?"

"No." I said quickly. "There is limited information on his kind in the human world, most of it has been destroyed or manipulated by the church. There are things that I want to know that he doesn't know, because he was robbed of the opportunity to learn. I want to understand him, biologically, so I can better protect him."

The scholar smiled at me softly. "I see, come with me, child, and we'll find you some books to read."

"Do you want me to come with you?" Bastion asked from where he leaned against the couch next to Tummi.

I looked at Cyran. He was at ease in our presence, and I felt like he meant me no harm. "No Bas. I'll be okay."

"Okay. If, you're sure." He said.

"Bas," Tummi said placing a hand on his thigh. "Our teacher has been nothing but good to us before. I don't see him harming our lady."

"Never." Cyran said with a bow of his head. "I want the same things for your group. For you all to go home and be happy, away from influence of Cardoc."

I smiled at him. "Lead the way."

Cyran led me up back to the main level and across the long bridge to the other side. He paused before an alcove and reached for books and scrolls, stacking them in his arms. "You and he are an interesting pair."

"What do you mean?" I asked, taking the scrolls off the top of the books in his arms.

"Interspecies couples are frowned upon in our kingdom, traditions based in purity."

"Why does that make us interesting?" I asked as I followed him back across the bridge.

"Because I never thought a human and a monster could coexist in such a way. As partners or lovers without being victimized by the other."

"We aren't perfect." I said as we came down the stairs. "We've put each other in very dangerous and precarious positions. Both of us anger quickly and both of us tend to be cruel when we're like that. Even so, he has been kind when I'm not deserving and honest even when he didn't want to be."

"You care for him deeply, then?"

"We are two sides of the same coin. He is my air and water. He is my home. I don't care what traditions we break or beings we offend. He and I are just right, and I will die defending it."

He smiled as he let me pass him into his office. "You are a very brave young woman. I know many men that are not that brave."

I shrugged. "He would do the same for me."

He hummed to himself. "I can't see a monstrosity like a bitarog doing that for another."

"Teacher, he's not nearly as monstrous as he may sound." Katrel said from where she sat on the couch looking over the accounts of the trial.

"You all seem to care for him quite a bit." Cyran said, setting the books on the side table.

"He saved our lives." Tummi said. "Everyone who works with Lord Niratap was once imprisoned and in one way or another we owe him our lives and loyalty."

"He is a good man." I said as Cyran handed me the first book. "*Monstrous: A Guide to Monstrosities.*"

"It should have most of what you are looking for, my lady."

I scrolled through the table of contents and frowned. "Bitarognius is the closest thing I can find in here."

"That would be correct, that book is a scientific reference on monsters, though it is several centuries old. Most of the other books are books that have accounts on interactions with bitarogs." Cyran said, unrolling a scroll at his desk.

"And the scrolls?" I asked.

"Anatomy, though I don't think the depictions you will find—" he paused thinking. "Comforting."

"Read it to us, Shasha." Bastion said, sitting next to Tummilia.

I flipped to the section the book indicated and cleared my throat. "'The Bitarognius commonly known as a bitarog is a class one sentient sub-fae beast monstrosity.' Class one?"

"Meaning apex predator." Cyran said from where he scanned the scroll.

"'As such, they are known to be hostile if approached and should be avoided at all costs. They are an amalgamation beast that is part canid, part feline, part ruminant, but most deadly and importantly, part draconic. The beasts themselves have natural rapid healing, linked to their biological attunement to magic. However, they are susceptible to toxins and poisons. It is recommended to carry aconite arrows if wandering the wilds to slow the creature down if you come into contact. If hunting bitarogs, basilisk venom has the strongest effect against them.'" I looked up at the group. "What's aconite?"

"Wolfsbane." Katrel said softly.

"Keep reading love." Tummilia said.

"'Both male and female bitarogs are massive monsters to meet in the wild. Males tend to be anywhere from six hundred to nine hundred pounds in their beast forms and females six hundred to one thousand pounds, depending on their regional subspecies.' How much does Nira weigh in his beast form?"

"I weigh about five-hundred thirty pounds." He answered from the doorway. "Why, *mo grá?*"

"You're small."

Bastion broke into a cackle as my mate gaped at me. "Excuse me?"

I felt heat warm my face and I barked at Bastion. "Not like that! He is well endowed in that department, you pervert. For a bitarog he is small. I asked Cyran if there was information on your race here, so maybe we could fill in the blanks that we don't have."

Cyran chuckled behind his desk and asked. "Did my father answer your questions?"

"Yes." Nira said, sinking into the cushion between me and Katrel. "However, I have more questions than when I started as well."

"What is the malice?" I asked.

"An abomination horror created by a lich." Mitta answered. "Problem is we don't have a known lich enemy."

"What is a lich?" Bastion asked.

"Liches are undead sorcerers, who have separated their soul from their bodies for a chance at immortality." Cyran said, his brows knitted together, before he sighed. "You must have many enemies, Lord, if you don't know if one is a lich."

Niratap shrugged. "Having enemies has just been

part of the job."

"Which has been?" Cyran asked, meeting my mate's gaze without flinching.

"I have become a philanthropist, of sorts, if only to further my goal of ending slavery and use of non-human creatures as currency. Tangentially that comes with many risks as most of my dealings take place on the black market. Enemies are a risk and always have been."

"If you put the princesses in danger—"

My mate closed his eyes. "Both of the girls are more than capable of defending themselves."

"How? They have had no training in swordsmanship and weaponry."

"Not in the Elven Kingdom, but it has been almost three centuries since they lived here. They know how to fight, how to kill if they must. Katrel is one of the most skilled warriors in the organization we've built, and she beats me more often than I beat her." Both girls smiled at their teacher, who deflated into his seat, but didn't press the issue. Nira looked down at me. "Continue."

"'In addition to their size, bitarogs have six-to-nine inch fangs, five inch talons, and horns or antlers, depending on the subspecies. Bitarogs appear to be just as varied as humans. Subspecies include Northern, East Mountain, East Tropic, North Eng, Desert, West Tropic, and Western Mountain. Bitarogs from each subspecies can have varied horns or antlers based on their heredity.' What subspecies would you fall under love?"

"My best guess would be north eng and east tropic."

"You're mixed?" Cyran asked, rolling out another scroll and weighing it down.

"Yes, my father was a refugee from South Asia after the first bitarog hunt." Cyran just nodded, returning to the scroll. Mitta was looking over his shoulder at the contents.

I continued. "'The largest of the subspecies appears to be western mountain aligning with the region's large ruminants of the west continent, but the northern subspecies is a close comparison as well. The smallest subspecies is the desert variety, compacting size for survival in their harsh environments.

"In recent observations it seems that bitarogs form tight family units, with a single mated pair and their children. Males are more aggressive and territorial than females and will defend their family groups viciously, females seem to only be aggressive when cornered or defending their young.'"

"That's interesting." Mitta said pointing at the scroll Cyran was reading. Nira cast her a glance. "Oh sorry. I didn't mean to interrupt, but did you know you have a two chambered stomach? It says here on this scroll that it helps the digestive process of bones and heavily fibrous vegetation. Please carry on."

He smiled at her and wrapped an arm around my shoulders. "'Bitarogs are fiercely protective of their partners most of all and will attack unprovoked if they perceive a threat. Mating rituals of bitarogs have not been observed at the writing of this volume, but it is assumed that partners court each other for several weeks before bonding to one another.

"Shape shifting has been observed in various degrees, but limited states. It appears that the creatures have at least two forms, beast and an almost human shape, save their size and adornments, but some bitarogs have been observed to have a mediary form between that is used for intimidation.

"A bitarog's life expectancy is unknown, most are hunted and killed before they reach laming years. They do not thrive in captivity and in order to be bent to the will of a master they must be broken. Stubbornness with obedience is common. Pain is a preferred method of breaking the spirit. However, after a time they can snap and are no longer affected by whips and binding spells.'"

Niratap tensed beside me and an ache entered my

heart. A couple sentences had made him relive his brutal life. I placed my hand on his thigh to reassure him. The moonlight pools of his eyes met mine and they were haunted by those memories, both old and new, and that made my heart crack for him.

"You are not there anymore."

He leaned down and pressed his brow to mine. "I know, my flower, but the weight never leaves."

I frowned and there was a knock at the door. A fair-skinned elf in a soft brown dress, her brown hair up in a croquet stood with her head bowed. Her voice reminded me of a fall time breeze. "The princess' suits have been cleaned and have fresh bedding along with another room in the same hall as you requested, Crown Scholar Cyran."

"Thank you So—"

"Solaris!" Tummi shouted, leaping from the couch and near tackling the poor woman. "You look so beautiful. Oh, how I've missed you."

"I have missed you too, Princess."

"Please just call me Tummi. We were thick as thieves growing up. You simply must tell me everything I've missed. What young men have your fancy?"

The woman cracked a soft smile, but it was Cyran that spoke. "Solaris is working with Keerane in the hope she might one day take her place."

Tummi elbowed her playfully. "Going for head housekeeper I see."

She giggled. "Oh, stop it, Tummi. You're going to get me in trouble."

"No, I won't."

"Solaris." Cyran interrupted rolling up the scroll he and Mitta had been looking at.

"Yes. Crown Scholar Cyran."

"Will you take the princesses and their guests to their rooms please? I have some research I would like to do before the evening meal and the king requires me."

"Of course."

"What did we interrupt when we arrived?" Katrel asked.

"Just a meeting with landowners, city leaders, and the arch council."

Katrel frowned but made for the door. "Still stuffy old bastards?"

"Things rarely change, my dear." Cyran said softly, rolling up the scrolls.

"Follow me." Solaris said, walking down the hall arm in arm with Tummi.

"Lord." Cyran said as I set the book upon his desk. "You keep those girls safe."

"I swear to you as I did to them. On my life, we will be leaving this land together." My mate said as his hand fell to the center of my back.

"Such promises when you have the most to lose here." Cyran's green eyes locked with my mates.

"They are worth the risk." He said softly, before his eyes flicked down to me. I felt his fear and worry about what was to come. It thudded deeply in my heart. "Come, my flower, well get left behind."

"Thank you, Cyran, for your help."

He handed me a book. "Some more reading about the beast you claim at your side."

"He is a man." I couldn't keep the sharpness from my voice, my heart fluttered.

"We shall see." Was all he said before turning back to the scroll before him and we ducked out the door to follow our friends. Tummilia chatted happily with Solaris as she led us through the halls of the castle.

She stopped before dark doors, a faint smoldering scent filled the hall. "Crown Princess, your room."

Katrel frowned but opened a door that was singed on the inside, in flashes and whorls as if a great fire had burned the door and room. With a sigh she entered her room, Mitta following behind.

"Tummi, your room, and the next room is for the

lord. Are there enough rooms for you?"

Tummi smiled at her and kissed both her cheeks. "Yes, Solaris. Thank you so much."

"Just call if you need anything, my friend."

"We will." She assured her as Mitta waved us into the room.

Once the scarred doors were shut and we had gathered around the dining table by the great balcony windows that overlooked the glimmering city below, Katrel sighed.

"I'm not going to make it." Her voice broke into a harsh laugh. "This is stupid. So stupid."

"Kat." Tummi said gingerly, walking to her with her arms open.

"No. Don't. Please." She pleaded, holding her hands up, her eyes teary. "This was too risky from the start, and I foolishly dragged all of you here to die."

"Like hell." Bastion growled sitting in one of the ornate chairs by the table. "And even so I'll fight like hell to get us out."

There was a mumble of agreement and Niratap said. "Regardless of what happens we will get you home."

Katrel rubbed her face, sighing again. "So, the trials?"

"What did the book say?" Tummi asked.

"Just that there were three trials: tests of strength, bravery, and wit. The rest of what was written in there were some of the notable feats. Slaying a harpy queen. Swimming to the bottom of Edge Lake for a siren egg. Finding a flaw in a great work. All the events were things picked by the flame emperor and a couple were by Cardoc the First."

"So," Mitta said looking out over the city, "he could pick anything. Make you perform any three feats to win your freedom."

"Or he could trick me into doing what he wants."

"So, our options are what?" I asked. "You give in?

206

We try to flee? Or do we stand and fight?"

"You make it sound so easy, my Lady." Katrel glowered at me and began to pace. "What if the worst happens?"

"What is the worst, Katrel?" Niratap asked from where he leaned against the wall. "Us dead and you tied to a marriage bed?"

"Exactly." She said exasperated, still pacing and worrying her thumb. "Our father isn't going to fight fair; he is going to manipulate the entire situation. He is going to make it so that I lose the little freedom I have and my family." She froze and looked at us, her eyes teary. "I can't lose you. I can't."

"Kat, we aren't going anywhere without you. Whether it is home or the grave, we are going too." My mate said softly.

Another round of agreement from the group.

"Kat. You are one of the bravest people I know." Her sister said. "You can beat him, I know it, you have that spark."

"Tummi, I—"

There was a knock at the door.

Mitta pulled a blade from her hip as she cautiously approached the door. "Who is there?"

A soft voice kissed with starlight answered. "Can a mother not see her children?"

Mitta opened the door and the slender ethereal beauty that was the Queen of the Elves floated into the room. Tummi beamed at her mother, the gentler of the two sisters. Katrel turned her back glancing over the city be-low.

"*Äiti*."[32] Tummi said softly, going to her mother.

"*Rakas tyttäreni, niin täynnä tähtien valoa.*"[33] She said, cupping Tummi's face in her hands and kissing the bridge of her nose. "Look at you, you've grown into such a

[32] Mother
[33] My sweet daughter, so full of starlight.

beautiful woman."

"You are even more brilliant than I remember, *Äiti*."

The queen looked past her younger daughter to the smoldering one. "Katrel."

"*Mère*."[34] She responded morosely in French, a language I recognized but could not speak.

"*Laisse-moi te regarder, Feu de forêt.*"[35]

"*Pourquoi? Pour que tu puisses me dire à quel point je t'ai encore déçu?*"[36]

"*Feu de forêt non. Je souhaite seulement revoir mon enfant, qui me manque depuis trois siècles.*"[37]

Katrel chuffed, turning around. "Have you mother? The last time you saw me you told me you wished I'd stayed away. That I should have left in the night and never returned. That the most foolish thing I could have done was step back through that portal home. Would you still rather I be gone? Am I still not wanted?"

The room had gone so silent that I was sure everyone heard as my heart cracked. Mitta's stoic watchful expression slid into a glower. Katrel didn't know how Mitta longed for her, I was certain Mitta didn't even know. The queen frowned at the smoldering woman she bore and let the single tear roll down her face.

"*Je te voulais,* Katrel. *J'ai toujours voulu vous deux.*" [38]

"Then why did you let him sell my sister like a common whore!" Katrel shouted, near screamed at her.

"I did not know." The queen placed a hand over her heart, her sleeve falling back revealing a deep purple bruise around her wrist, the shape identical to a hand.

"Lies!" Katrel screamed.

[34] Mother
[35] Let me look upon you, Wildfire.
[36] Why? So, you call tell me how I've disappointed you again?
[37] Wildfire no. I only wish to see my child, who I have missed for three centuries.
[38] I wanted you, Katrel. I have always wanted you, both of you.

"Mon enfant, je ne le savais pas."[39]

"Arrête de me mentir!"[40]

More tears fell from Ciserie's eyes. *"Je te le promets, ma traînée de poudre. Je ne savais pas."*[41]

"Kat, stop." Tummi murmured but it was swallowed by Katrel's shouting.

"How could you not know? He paraded us around to that man and sold her! Sold both of us. All vies for power he doesn't need because he is a king."

"Katrel, I swear on the stars."

"Don't lie to my face." Katrel's eyes were watery, but she refused to let the tears fall. Her voice fell into a hiss. "You let him do all those horrible things to us. You let him beat us as children. You let him parade us at events like cattle. You let him. You. Let. Him."

Niratap shifted past me and put himself between the mother and daughter. "That is enough, Katrel."

She glared up at him, but I saw the fire die. "It's not fair."

He gazed softly down at her. "Life is not fair, Katrel. Everyone in this room is a testament of that. Even your mother."

"But she—"

"Enough."

Katrel stormed past him and out the door. Mitta with a bob of her head in my mate's direction, followed her. To keep her safe or the people of the castle safe, I wasn't sure. My mate sighed through his nose as he turned and offered the queen a deep bow.

"I apologize for her outburst. Katrel has a lot on her mind."

The queen wiped the tears from her face. "You defended me, why?"

A swish of his tail as he stood and pointedly looked

---

[39] My child, I did not know.

[40] Stop lying to me!

[41] I promise you, my wildfire. I did not know.

at her wrist. "Because Katrel is not the only bird that's being pushed into a cage."

The queen hid her wrist beneath her sleeve, before she circled my mate. I bristled at the critical scan she gave him. "What are you to my daughters, beast?"

"I am their friend." He said simply with a dip of his chin.

"He rescued us, *Äiti*." Tummi said from behind her.

The queen ignored her daughter, her eyes locking with Niratap's as she asked. "You would risk everything for them? For their freedom?"

"Yes."

She cast a glance at me. "You would risk her?"

Niratap swallowed. "She has given me no choice."

"There is always a choice." She barked looking back at him.

"Did you have a choice, Your Majesty?"

Her eyes widened. "Why does that matter?"

"Because you were defending choice and that bruise upon your wrist tells me you haven't had a choice in a very long time and be it forward of me, but I wish to save those that need saving."

She smiled softly, turning to the door. "I am beyond saving, Bondbreaker. Please save my daughters from the fate that Cardoc has planned for them. Help them find their freedom. If they have that, then I can endure."

"*Äiti*."

The queen kissed Tummi on the cheek. "*Rakkauteni sinua kohtaan on tähtien joukossa.*[42] Tomorrow after the courtiers leave, we will dine together. No matter what it looks like it is a test for all of you. Be on your guard. Especially you Bondbreaker, Cardoc will be going after you, trying to stop you from freeing my daughters. I pray to the stars that you have a plan to get them out."

With that the queen left and we discussed the trials again, even with Katrel and Mitta missing. In agreement

---

[42] My love for you is among the stars.

that the trials were Katrel's best chance of beating her father, we retired to our own rooms. My mate paced the expanse of the room, his long legs eating up the space as he thought.

"It will be okay, *mo grá.*"

He paused before the massive bed and looked at me. "How can you be so sure, my flower?"

"Because I believe in us. Regardless of what Cardoc throws at Katrel for the trials she will come out victorious, of that I have no doubt. If it gets to be too harrowing for her, I know you will do everything in your power to help her."

"And you are okay with that? You are okay with me risking it all?"

"No, but I know you, mate. I know that regardless of my feelings about this you will stop at nothing to get those girls free. Even if it costs you your life. Even if it costs us."

"Shasha."

I shook my head, willing the tears away. "I will be here to fight with you, for them, for us."

He came to the bed and cupped my face in his hands. "You are too good for me."

I chuckled. "Too bad you're stuck with me."

He smiled then kissed me softly. "I wouldn't have it any other way."

Chapter Seventeen

Tummilia

Home. I was home and yet I felt like an outsider. Katrel was scared and angry with everyone. She had screamed at Niratap when she had finally returned to the rooms, I could hear her through the walls. Bastion held me close as she raged next door. Fire raging against shadow. I wondered if she was truly mad at him or if he was just taking her anger to spare others. To spare Mitta.

I wondered when that started. When had the stoic warrior who had taught us to fight, to wield weapons, and be strong; had grown to look so softly at my sister? How long had she had the longing and love in her heart? How had I only just now noticed the way Mitta looked at my sister with such heartache?

After the slam of two doors and a quiet apology, the hall quieted. Everyone settled into the peaceable evening, but the thoughts of maybes and hows plagued me.

"Have you ever noticed it?" I whispered to the male behind me.

"What?" Bastion grumbled into my shoulder halfway to sleep.

"Mitta and my sister?"

He buried his face in my unbound hair. "What do you mean?"

"The way Mitta looks at her, as if she was the moon in the sky."

He huffed, shifting away and rolling me beneath him so we were face to face. He asked. "Are you meddling?"

"No."

He kissed my brow. "Really?"

I glowered, kissing his sensuous mouth. "No. I was just wondering if you had noticed."

He smiled at me shifting more to straddle my hips. "I mean not like heated stares, but I have noticed Mitta is harder on your sister than anyone else. Gives her extra instruction."

"Maybe she just wants to make sure she's on her game?"

He shrugged. "Maybe. Maybe she's been pining after your sister for as long as I pined for you. Maybe longer." He ran kisses from my jaw down the side of my neck.

I pressed my hand to his chest. "Bas, we shouldn't."

"Why?" His cheeks were flushed as he pulled back to look at me.

I swallowed. "If my father—"

He pressed a finger to my lips. "I'm going to stop you right there. That man has no sway over who you bed."

"That man is the ruler of this kingdom and my father."

"He's also the man who sold you into slavery and the man that beats your mother." He sighed, rolling off me onto the bed. "You saw that bruise on her wrist."

I had. "Nothing changes."

I felt him look at me as I stared at the ceiling. "You know that's not okay, right?"

Tears welled in my eyes. Gods did I, and when I spoke my voice cracked. "I know."

"He beat you girls growing up, didn't he?" Bastion asked so softly.

I nodded, the tears rolling over my cheeks. Bastion wiped the stray tear from my cheek as it shone in the pale firelight. I rolled into him burying my face against his chest, his strong arms wrapping around me, pulling me close.

"Tummi." He said my name so sweetly and I could hear all the promises he was making as he said it. "I will not let him harm you."

"But what about you?"

"What about me, love?" He peered down at me with that crooked grin to warm my heart. "I'll manage."

I reached between us and grabbed his face. "Now that I have you, I don't want to lose you."

"I'm not going anywhere, love." He pressed a kiss to my palm. "Not even the dark realms can take me from you."

I ran my thumb over his tusk, marveling at his beautiful, loving face. "What did I ever do to deserve you?"

"Everything and nothing, love."

I placed a hand over his heart. Looking at the array of small fading scars, some I knew, some I didn't. "Somehow I feel like I'll never be enough for you."

He tipped my head back and his eyes shone in the thin light, storm clouds that eased me into safety. Thunder laced with all those unspoken promises. "I feel the same, but let's not be in those dark places right now."

I smiled sadly at him. "But we are very much in one of those dark places, Bas."

"Babylos doesn't have to be dark, love."

"As long as my father is king it will be for me."

"You don't have to stay in this broken court." He said gazing at me with such intensity. "You haven't been part of this court for a long time."

That twanged through my heart as loud as thunder. I kissed him, rolling on top of him, nestling his thick body between my legs. "You, Bastion Day, warm me, heart and soul, and I am so lucky to call you mine."

I ran my hands over his stomach, and he arched against my touch. His soft hair tickled my palms, his skin warm over the muscles beneath. Velvet over stone. My nails scrapped his nipples, his breath hitching. I drug my nails down his chest eliciting a gasp from him. A soft desperate sound. This dance he had started for us. This reversal of roles made me feel empowered. Made me want and not feel disgusting for that want; for enjoying the heat spreading from my core.

"Tummi, please." He begged as I caved, rolling my hips.

"I love that, when you beg for me." I purred as his hands gripped my hips. A strangled cry came out of his mouth as I ran a finger along the hem of his pants. I leaned forward, my hair falling over my shoulder, the curtain dusting down his side. "So precious, the sounds you make for me."

A gasp as I grazed my nails up his sides, his head falling back into the pillows. "Tummilia."

"Ah ah ah." I chided, kissing the underside of his jaw and licking along his throat. "What do you call me?"

He groaned under me, rolling his hips against me as I nipped his collarbone. "Please, Mistress."

Euphoria flooded me at the desperation in his voice. I ran my hands down to the hem of his pants. "Good pet."

I crawled down his body kissing a trail over his fevered skin, as I slid him free of his pants. I nipped at the sensitive flesh of his body. He groaned deep in his throat as he fisted the sheets holding himself to the bed, when I knew he wished to buck. His toffee sweetness was already beaded at the tip. A weak part of myself wanted to steal it from where it gleamed but licked up his length instead, listening to his breathing become irregular and feeling his fluttering pulse beneath my palm.

I looked up at his beautifully built body, my eyes devouring his hard muscles and long burly limbs. The trail of dark hair that dusted up his center to the sparse patch on his chest. His beautiful eyes heavy lidded as they watched me.

"Please." He nearly whimpered as my tongue traveled up his shaft. I stopped before his weeping head and eyed him carefully.

"Please what, pet?"

His head fell back with a groan as I ran my tongue

over him again. "Please taste me, Mistress."

"My pet, I am tasting you."

Another gasp as I made another pass, the bead growing heavy and rolling down over his broad head, the toffee taste heating my core. "Please suck me, Mistress."

I flicked the ridge of him with my tongue. He groaned arching up underneath me. "I don't think you want it enough."

A guttural cry met my ears, almost a choked sob.

"Now pet. You must keep it down. Don't want everyone knowing how you beg for me."

A pained grunt followed by a whimper greeted my ears as another bead of the sticky sweetness appeared. Cruelly I spread the liquid over his head, coating both him and my finger.

"Watch me, my sweet, sweet pet." I purred. He obliged, lifting his deeply flushed face to watch as I swept the fluid onto my finger and sensually slipped it into my mouth.

"Fuck, Tummi." His head flopped back against the pillows. "You keep teasing me like that and I'll cum before I can feel—"

He arched, the sentence breaking off into a deep throated groan as I sucked on the tip, pulling more of that delicious sweetness onto my tongue.

"Fuuuuck." He ground out. His large hands threaded into my hair as my tongue did long slow passes across the head. I stroked him with one hand and the other braced on his thigh, the muscles straining as he fought his instincts.

A pained cry left his lips as he tried to push my head away. "Tummi I'm going to—"

I raked my nails along his thigh as his hot seed fired into my mouth. I tried to swallow every drop even as it leaked around my mouth down his length and my chin. He was delicious, sweet, and creamy. The soft gasps and pants of breath as I cleaned the rest of him had me molten.

"Tummi." He begged; eyes heavy with lust. "Please."

I kissed up his still hard length. Then the soft grove of his hip and the trailed over his stomach. "Please what, my pet?"

His hands tightened in my hair. "May I, have you?"

The simple ask always warmed my heart. He let me take from him until I had him needy, until he was destroyed, but he always asked. I smiled at him.

"Take from me, Bastion."

"Do you mean that?" His eyes widened as he asked me, his hands dropping from my hair. My words having a sobering effect on both of us, but—

"Yes."

"Tummilia, are you sure?" He sat up and I eased back, kneeling eye level with him.

"Yes Bastion. Take from me your own pound of flesh. For you have also suffered at the hands of others."

His thunderstorm eyes were locked with mine until he swallowed. Closing his eyes to attempt to hide his emotions, I saw the shame in the way his shoulders fell. The guilt in the way he clenched his fists. Then he looked at me.

Chapter Eighteen

Bastion

She was beautiful. As radiant as a star on the horizon, outshining the sun and moon with her brilliance. She had never let the things that happened to her shadow that brilliance either, but my heart twisted at what she offered. Her long, summer field hair framed her slight body in a halo of gold and those star bright sea blue eyes watched me. So clearly seeing all the shadows in me.

"Bastion."

"I don't want to hurt you." I was scared I would, by taking her on the way my orc instincts demanded.

She smiled; the soft tipping of her sensuous mouth warmed that dark part of my soul. "Do you need me to tempt you, *mon cher*?"[43]

All thoughts eddied from my head. "What?"

Her bright little laugh warmed me from those shadows that had crawled into my heart. As she slipped from the bed, and I followed sitting at the edge. She teased the slim straps of her nightgown off her shoulders. The soft fluttering of the garment falling to the floor captured my eyes. I stared at it on the floor as it was joined by a pale pair of lace panties and I prayed to all the gods to give me strength, so I didn't scare the beautiful woman who bared herself to me. Slowly my eyes ate up her long, beautiful legs to the softness of her groin up her toned stomach topped with her full soft breasts, her nipples rosy in the pale firelight. Her waist-long, summer-wheat hair cascaded behind her in soft golden waves and those blue eyes that were the waves of the stormy winter sea.

My mouth went dry. She was beautiful. A goddess

---

[43] My dear.

of all that was bright and lovely. A star embodied in a being.

"You are so beautiful."

"Bastion." She flushed a deep rose.

"You are." I smiled softly. "Come here."

She sashayed towards me, coming to rest between my knees, her hands falling to my thighs, where her fingers traced wicked circles. Breathtaking even in that and it was devastating that she was mine. My hands came to rest at the small of her waist and pulled her closer into me pressing my brow to hers.

"My devastating beauty." I murmured.

"*Kylla rakkaani.*"[44]

I smiled. "You speak too many languages."

"I do not. There are still dozens that I don't know or speak well." She protested but smiled.

"Tummilia." I let my lust and need muddy my voice. Her skin pinked further at the sound, a delicate puff of air in her response to her name. "I need you as an orc needs."

"Then take it." Her voice was velvety with the need in her, but I needed her to understand. There was thousands of years of taking in my blood. Even after the enslavement of my race, war drums still called for blood in my ears, things I had never experienced demanded a taking. My orc instincts wanted to claim her, take from her.

I took an unsteady breath and in a harsh whisper I said. "I want to conquer you and that kind of taking is not kind or gentle. My blood calls for the violence of it and it scares me."

"Then take it from me."

"Tummi–"

She pressed her finger to my lips, silencing me. "Do you want me?"

"Maddeningly."

"Then take from me, I offer myself freely and

---

[44] Yes, my love.

without fear."

I closed my eyes and breathed in her sunshine scent, spring and magic and life. I felt my instincts barrel against the cage I had locked them in. They demanded I claim her in all the ways I could. That I conquer and pillage. "Fuck."

She locked her hands around my neck. "Bastion."

"I need you."

She shifted whispering in my ear. "Then take me. Please."

I moved faster than either of us perceived flipping her face down onto the mattress and kicking her feet apart for me. She yelped playfully as I pinned her arm behind her back and kissed between her shoulder blades. My other hand traveled down her soft side and over her beautiful ass. My finger sliding into that slick wetness between her thighs.

My voice was guttural as I whispered into her shoulder. "You are so wet for me love."

"Bastion." She whimpered as I pressed my fingers into her, her heated gaze piercing me.

"Shh." I murmured as I brought my moistened fingers to my mouth and tasted her.

"Oh gods." Her eyes fluttered closed in anticipation.

I shifted, sliding my thickness between her legs. Those war drum instincts bellowed inside me, poised for conquest. I growled. "Tummi. Look at me."

Her eyes open a fraction as she fought against the pleasure at my preparations.

"What is the safe word?"

She smiled at me. "Axolotl."

I smiled. "That's my good girl."

I let my instincts free and thrust into her with an unkind force. She yelped into the bedding trying to stop the cry from being heard. Let them hear me take what is mine. I slammed into her body with unrelenting need. Her body accepting the assault of me at the brutal pace the drums set in me. I felt her grip me as she shattered beneath me. Her heated groans and moans muffled by the fluffy sheets of her bed.

I leaned over her and whispered. "Don't fucking move."

She nodded. I pulled free and she groaned at the vacancy.

"Don't move."

I kneeled behind her devouring the sight of her dripping core. All for me. My breath cooled her, and I delighted in watching her quiver. I kissed the supple back of her thigh inching toward her moist slit. Her back arched as I plunged my tongue into her, lapping at the tender flesh. She panted my name breathlessly as her body shook. I pulled that sweet bundle of nerves into my mouth, drawing a ravaged cry from her throat. I cupped her thighs as her legs buckled when she came again. I pulled away, standing and flipping her over to face me. Her body flushed as I eased myself between her legs. Her pleasure addled stare begging me to continue.

"I'm going to claim you as mine, Tummilia Raloqen. Savagely like my people have always claimed those we keep."

"Yes." Was her breathless reply. "Please."

"You will be mine." I ground out locking her legs around my hips, pressing the broad head of myself at her entrance.

"Yes." She arched against me, her glorious breasts bobbing with the movement. I bent forward, taking one of those pretty pert nipples into my mouth. Her hands threaded into my hair as she tried to buck into me. "Bastion."

I released her flesh with a pop, our faces only inches apart as I said. "You will be mine. Tummilia. Mine and only mine."

She smiled at me. "Claim me."

"*Ah moraha gok rah ashurhi uhah kurashk eh, Bastion Day, shkah arthkah kakk sar eh mnara mo sur et*

221

morkoh sur ehurkoh." I pressed slowly into her, as she tried to grind onto me. "*Eh goh no urdka sho asta et rok hushokur mah ehshkah mnukaarth, urkoh sur nukarha utkar kar kaha.*"[45]

She writhed against me. "Bastion."

I kissed her as I seated myself fully into her. "*Kha kar ka kharok sur mo sur, et karha kharok shekha kahrashkah mnarha.*"[46]

She moaned, her skin glittering in the firelight. Her nails scraped my scalp. "*Kha kar ka kharok ah khasha duh kut mo sur et narharuh, urg karha kharok ehka ek durha.*"[47]

Her head fell back, a sound of ecstasy leaving her lips. "*Kha ka kharok ah khasho duh, ro sur duh no duh karhaurkoh kharok urg sururkoh kharok rah eh kharok.*"[48]

"*Kha ka kah, et kha kharok ashkurhi sur urdka urghi agrha us grog eh ashkarhi sur.*"[49]

"Bastion." A repeated desperate prayer, my name on her lips.

"*Tummilia Raloqen asta eh tash hri, sur gah ehurkoh et eh gah sururkoh. Ragah et gahrouh datka eh sar moraha rah moraharsar. Eh kharok sho nukarha utkar sururkoh kahkarha. Eh knarok shog nukarha utkar sururkoh rokahro. Eh knarok shog duh sururkoh duhrokkaroha osh durgha et no uhah sur tashkah urhag durgha man takro.*"[50]

---

[45] By the breath that is held before the battle, I Bastion Day, of the Earthblood clan lay my soul upon you and make you mine… I who bow beneath the bright stars and mighty mountains of my homeland, claim you against all other males.

[46] No other male will lay upon you, or they shall forfeit their lives.

[47] No male will be permitted to look upon you with disrespect, for they shall meet my blade.

[48] No male will be permitted to force you to bend to their will, for your will is my will.

[49] No male, blood or no, shall hold you lower than the station at which I hold you.

[50] Tummilia Raloqen, star of my holy sky, you are mine and I am yours. Wholly and fully until my last breath is breathed. I will stand

She came violently around me. A wonton scream, I captured it with a kiss. Mine. She was mine. That word ricocheted through me and the rightness of it pulled me along with her. I dumped both my soul and my seed deeply into the beauty that allowed me to claim her. I fell deeply into her, and I could drown in this sensation of belonging that being there, with her, in her, connected to her that overtook me. I lifted her and sat upon the bed, not ready to leave the warm cocoon of her love. When we parted our kiss, our sweat slick brows pressed to one another. There was a light knock at the door.

"Who is it?" Tummi asked, her voice bright like starlight in her eyes.

"Just checking to see if you guys were alright." Mitta's voice said through the door.

"More than alright." I called to her. So much more.

"Alright." Mitta responded and I could hear the laughter in her voice. "Just keep it down."

"Sorry." Tummi said as she smiled down at me.

We were quiet as footfalls disappeared from the hall. I kissed her lightly. "You are divinity, *eh asta hri*."[51]

"What is that language?" she said softly.

"Orcin. It is the language of orcs."

"What did you say to me?"

"It was a soul vow."

She blinked at me. "A soul vow?"

My heart clenched in fear. "You are my heart-match, Tummi. You are mine and I am yours. In my tongue I have claimed you as my instincts and heritage demand."

She smiled dreamily. "Yours."

"Yes."

She stroked my cheek, only love dancing in her eyes. "Mine."

against all your enemies. I will stand against all your hostility. I will stand as your defender in dark times and kneel before you in worship and in times of victory.

[51] my star in the heavens.

I smiled, the sudden weight leaving my chest. "Yes."

"What is the vow, I do not understand Orcin."

I smiled. "By the breath that is held before the battle, I Bastion Day, of the Earthblood clan lay my soul upon you and make you mine. I, who bow beneath the bright stars and mighty mountains of my homeland, claim you against all other males. No other male will lay upon you, or they shall forfeit their lives. No male will be permitted to look upon you with disrespect, for they shall meet my blade. No male will be permitted to force you to bend to their will, for your will is my will. No male, blood or no, shall hold you lower than the station at which I hold you. Tummilia Raloqen, star of my holy sky, you are mine and I am yours. Wholly and fully until my last breath is breathed. I will stand against all your enemies. I will stand against all your hostility. I will stand as your defender in dark times and kneel before you in worship in times of victory. My star in the heavens."

Tears rolled over her cheeks. "Truely?"

"I vow this to you, *eh asta hri*." I said, wiping the tears from her face.

"Bastion, you honor me." She says softly. "I feel this overwhelming sense of rightness when I'm with you. I feel loved and cherished and worthy. How did it take us this long to find one another?"

I gave her my goofiest grin. "We were afraid of taking the leap, *eh asta hri*."

"I love you." She said, sliding off my lap. I groaned as she slipped free of me. She smiled impishly at me. "Do you want a bath?"

"I would love one."

The bathing room was more modern than I had expected when I had peered into the space earlier. A modern toilet, a luxurious counter and sink, a rainfall shower that was lined with river stone and moss and a deep sunken pool of a bath. It was already full and magically heated.

Tummi peered at me over her shoulder as she stepped down into the pool, until the water lapped at her waist. "Of all the things I've missed, this is one of them."

"A magic pool?" I asked, following her into the water, a smile on my face.

"Well, yes." She smiled at me as she sat down at the back edge of the pool. The water rested just over the swell of her breasts. "What girl wouldn't enjoy a magically heated pool in their room?"

I chuckled sitting down next to her. "Would you ever stay here?"

She pulled her knees to her chest. "No. I love my people and my mother, but I have so much more of a life outside of this forsaken palace. Not that my father would keep me around, he would probably sell me off again if I stayed."

Hot anger crawled under my skin. "I won't let him hurt you."

She huffed. "I'm more worried about him hurting you than me. I'm a disappointment. In my father's eyes you are a lesser being."

I shrugged, draping my arm around her shoulders. "He can look down at me all he wants. I'm an orc, Tummi, my race is known for battle and bloodshed. Our language is fairly primitive and outside of modern groups, the clans are primitive."

"Just because your race has historically been one way doesn't mean that you are that way." She said, casting her cream-colored legs over my lap.

"Everyone only ever sees a grunt." I said softly.

She cupped my face pulling me to look at her. "They are missing the man."

I smiled at her. "They are missing a star."

When we sat down at the king's private dining table, unease and anger curled in my stomach, made me wish for the idle days we had spent in the library pouring over books. Cardoc Raloqen sat at the head of the table clad in a red surcoat and black trousers, his face a mask of coldness. The queen at his left, clad in a pale grey high-necked gown, had smiled softly as we had entered. Katrel sat next to her mother, then Tummi and me at the end. Cyran, the scholar, sat at the king's right and fiddled with his linen napkin as if he had not expected to be ordered to witness this meal. Lord Niratap sat next to the scholar, Shash at his side and Mitta across from me.

Upon each place setting were crackers with a fancy spread and half of a yellow tomato. A slim man dressed tidily with an apron tied around his waist addressed the table. "Tonight, our eminence has requested a multiple course meal to welcome his children home. For our hors d'oeuvre we have a simple wheat cracker with a sage and garlic cream cheese and halved golden crown tomatoes that were grown in our greenhouse this winter. And we've paired it with a spicy Bloody Mary spritzer. Enjoy."

He bowed and left, the table was stiff as the king ate his food and eyed us all as we dug in. Three crackers to whet the appetite.

"How many courses are meals like this anyways?" I asked Tummi as the lord moved the cocktail away from his mate, she glared at him but it had no venom.

"Five or six depending on what father feels like." She smiled at me warmly as the next course was brought out.

"The next course." The servant announced. "Is a chilled butternut gazpacho made from squash harvested this morning."

Shasha said to her mate. "Cold soup?"

He chuckled. "It's gazpacho."

"It's soup."

"Yes."

"But it's cold." He chuckled and shoved a spoonful into her mouth before she could continue.

"Why the formal dinner?" Katrel asked her father.

"Can I not host my guests at my table?" His tone made my skin crawl.

Katrel frowned and chuffed. "My family, chosen and otherwise, at the same table."

"Well then." The king said, leaning back. "It's not every day that I have such a—varied lot around my table."

The lord's eyes narrowed, but he said. "Thank you for your hospitality, King Cardoc."

The king smirked before lifting his spoon full of soup to his mouth. "Gazpacho is lovely this time of year. Katrel, I'm glad you decided to join us before the betrothal."

Katrel glowered at the soup. "I'm not marrying Revan."

The king didn't even react. "We shall see."

Katrel dropped the spoon in the soup, splattering it across the table. She sat taller in her chair, chin set. "I will not marry him."

The king met her gaze, for a king descended from flame his icy gaze made even my heart flutter. "That is not becoming behavior for a princess."

"I am not staying here." Katrel said, holding her father's stare, even though her voice wobbled. "I will not stay here, and I will not marry that knight."

"Katrel." The queen said quietly, her voice slightly hoarse. She cleared her throat subconsciously and I could have sworn the scholar flinched. "The fates are yet to be determined."

Katrel opened her mouth, but Tummi said. "Mother,

are you feeling unwell?"

The queen smiled brightly at her younger daughter as she sipped some water. "No, I've had a rather uneventful day and haven't spoken much."

The lord cocked his head slightly. "Had we known your day was so lonesome we would have ventured from the library to keep you company."

The queen locked eyes with Niratap. "I will keep that in mind while you're here, young lord."

The lord's smile was genuine, but when he returned to his meal a shared silent look passed between him and his mate. The meal continued with that taunt silence, a guitar string ready to snap. The waitstaff placed the next course before us.

"Our salad course tonight is a simple mixed green bed topped with an aged cheddar made by artisans on Creators Island and Innuram flowers, dressed with a balsamic vinaigrette that is made in house." The servant announced. The queen and the scholar stiffened at the mention of the blooms.

"What is innuram?" I asked Tummi, who had moved the flowers off her salad.

"It's a flower that only grows in Babylos. It has a spicy taste, and I don't particularly enjoy it, but it is one of our father's favorite spices when he hosts others at his table."

"Innuram is said to be born of the flame and helps weed out enemies, though it is also said to be an aphrodisiac. It has a robust spicy, but earthy flavor similar to saffron." The king said from his seat ignoring the words his daughter had spoken to me, but frowned as Niratap also removed the flowers. "Flowers not to your liking, Bondbreaker?"

"Apologies, I don't care for flowers, for eating that is. I find my pallet doesn't appreciate their subtle notes."

"Pity."

Niratap took a bite of the salad, but I could see the

ire burning in his eyes at something in the king's tone. I wished I was as good at reading the subtleties of voices, it felt like the lord had gleaned a vast array of information from one word or phrase. Shasha leaned forward in her seat to address the scholar.

"Cyran, I appreciate the other tomes that you found for me today, they were very informative."

"I'm glad they were to your liking, Milady. I may have another book on myths that you could read in my office."

"I would like that."

"Tummilia, I have a book I would like to share with you as well." The scholar said before he sipped his wine.

"Oh, what is—"

"Katrel." The king said, speaking over the younger daughter. His voice swallowing hers. My hand covered Tummi's as she quavered. The king's eyes marked the action and glared at our joined hands.

"Father." Katrel's tone was flat.

"What did you even do with the time and freedom I allowed you to keep?"

She met the king's gaze and to stand between the two of them would be to spontaneously combust. "I trained. My body and mind."

"Both girls have been integral in the organization that I run." Niratap supplied, sensing that guitar string straining further.

"And pray tell what is it that your organization does?"

The lord sat his fork down and sipped the wine. "The organizations main aim is to shut down the black-market trade in creatures, and we rescue and relocate those that have been victimized by the market itself."

"Such a noble cause." The king said contemplative as the servants left the room. "Though I don't see how a key-bone player, princess or no, and the trash I cast aside could aid in such an organization."

I stood throwing back my chair and shouted. "She is not trash!"

"Ah, the brute speaks." The king smiled a cunning glean in his eyes. I felt everyone's eyes on me.

"A brute I may be, but she is a living being and your daughter."

"Bastion." The lord said, authority laced in the word.

"You will not address her as trash."

"Bastion." A growl this time.

"You will not speak about her as if she is not here."

"Bastion." A snarl. I cast a glance at the lord, wisps of ever-present shadows crawled over his hands and neck, and a primal part of me wanted to balk at the face of the predator there. Each word was a pointed blade aimed at me. "Right your chair and sit down."

I obeyed his order but hissed, pointing at the king. "You're okay with him speaking to her like that? About her like that?"

The servants clustered by the door and watched through the little window, their eyes darting between us and the king. A muscle feathered in the lord's jaw. His voice laced with leashed reprimand. "No. However, we are guests in his home. You were raised better, Bastion."

"But—"

"No." He snarled before he bowed his head to the king. "I apologize for the boy's outburst."

"Don't apologize for me like a child. I—"

I saw the lord's shadows undulate behind him, but it was the creamy pale hand on my arm that gave me pause. I looked at the woman who had my heart, tears in her eyes. "Enough, Bastion."

"Tummi—"

"I see." The king mused softly.

My eyes snapped to his beguiled face, unable to contain the rage. "What?"

"I find it amusing that the waif of the royal family

found herself a brute trench rat to warm her bed." I tried to rise, but both Tummi and the lord's shadows held me in place. The queen reprimanded her husband, her voice barely over a whisper. He paid her no mind as he continued. "Orcs are only good for grunts. You haven't fought on enough battle fields, boy, to speak against me, and I would hold that tongue of yours before I cut it out. What clan do you hail from? You are so fair skinned you're clearly not of the Ironbloods because you would have been slaughtered before you whelped your first cry. Grassblood seems a bit too soft for that rage that you hold. An Earthblood is most likely, but I am surprised that they let you live into adulthood."

"My heritage is none of your concern."

The king smiled as he waved at the servants. I looked down the length of the table at where Mitta sat, her face was tight-lipped as she watched the servants bring in the next course.

"Our main course," the servant started nervously, "is roast venison hunted from the southern wilds, served with a mushroom risotto and grilled brussels. All dressed with thyme and innuram butter sauce."

Mitta said from the end of the table. "You have a penchant for that flower, King Cardoc."

"It is my favorite." The king said softly with a smile on his face that didn't reach his eyes.

"It has a fine flavor." Mitta answered.

"I'm glad that you like it." The king said, sipping his wine before his eyes fell to me. "Now then, boy, what is your heritage?"

I swallowed my bite of venison. "I'm an Earthblood."

"Hmm." He mused chewing. He swallowed. "And your parents are both Earthbloods as well?"

I fisted my hand in my lap. "They are."

"Gentle natured orcs then. Father a cook of some sort and mother a scullery."

"My parents are both cooks, but they are also warriors. They fought in both the world wars after they had been liberated from coal slavery." I hated the rutting way he looked at me.

"The Days are formidable." The lord supplied, before he coughed. All of us looked at him in concern, except the king whose smile didn't fade as he ate another bite of food.

"Are you alright?" Shasha asked, looking up at him.

He took a sip of his wine. "Yes. Just a tickle in my throat."

"I do hope that the food is to your liking. My chef worked tirelessly for us today."

"The food is delectable, Your Majesty." The lord again bowed his head to the king, before taking another drink of his wine.

An unearthly silence choked the table as we ate, most everyone was focused on either their food or shifted to the king or the lord when he coughed, apologizing each time that the tickle in his throat wouldn't let up. Something in the room had shifted and I grew increasingly uncomfortable as the dishes from the main meal were cleared. Something was very wrong.

Chapter Nineteen

Katrel

The lord coughed across from me again and silver rimmed his eyes a bit at the force, Shasha watched him with near terror in her eyes. He again assured everyone that it was just a tickle in the back of his throat. My mother and teacher were watching him as well as if they expected something terrible to crawl out of his skin. Something was off.

"Father." I said sitting straight in my chair, hoping that stealing my spine would still my nerves.

Slowly my father peeled his gaze away from Niratap. "Yes, Princess."

The conniving way he said that. I swallowed. "I have a proposal for you."

My friend coughed again, as the servants brought out dessert. It was a chocolate tart with candied violets and a lavender colored sauce drizzled over it.

"I—"

The servant cleared his throat. I glared at him sharply as he spoke. "For dessert we have prepared a dark chocolate tea tart with candied violets and innuram lavender sauce, served with coffee."

"Thank you, Grayson."

"At your leisure, Your Eminence."

"Father."

"Yes, child. You had something you wanted to propose to me?"

I swallowed again. "I want to win my freedom."

He blinked. "And how would you win your freedom?"

"I would like to preform The Trials of the Flame."

If my offering intrigued him, he did not show it as he took a bite of his dessert, his eyes shifting from me and cast around the table holding on where the lord took a bite of his dessert. Most everyone else also took a few bites of the decadent dessert my father had requested. All except Mitta who watched the lord with bated breath. I peered at what she was seeing on him, hidden in the peaks of scars around his throat were red splotches slowly crawling up his skin.

The lord set his napkin on the table and cleared his throat. "Apologies, King Cardoc but I have to excuse myself."

"Nira?"

He looked at his mate as he shifted to stand, his pupils blown and said. "Something is wrong."

"What's wrong?" There was panic in her voice as Mitta stood. The redness was rapidly spreading across his neck and face.

"What did you do?" My eyes locked on my father who had that rage inducing smirk upon his face.

"Whatever do you mean?"

Niratap pushed up from the table and tried to take a step, his knees buckling below him sending him crashing face first into the floor. We bounded out of our chairs. The servants snickered from behind the curtains and doors.

Shasha was beside him in a breath as a pained choking sound escaped his lips and his claws raked across the stones. I returned my attention to the man I knew was responsible. "What. Did. You. Do?"

"I shared a meal with my guest, Katrel." He frowned at me. "It's not my fault the beast has a weak constitution."

Niratap pushed himself to his knees, his body shaking violently. My mother shifted in her seat, like she was about to go to aid, but the stern hateful look my father gave her had her meekly returning to her seat. "What did you poison him with?"

"I did not poison anyone." He feigned a shocked expression. "How foolish of me, innuram with its lovely notes, doesn't agree with beasts. It seems to be slow acting as it enters their systems. You can put any brute in a suit and pretend he's not a monster."

"How dare you." Venom laced Shasha's voice as she stood pointing her dagger at my father. "How fucking dare you."

"You will find, child, that he is nothing more than a monster."

"No, the only monster I see is you."

"Enough, Shasha." Cardoc smiled at her as Bastion pulled her arm down and willed her away from the foolish death that would come from attacking the king outright.

"You have my word, Cardoc, that if this causes any permanent damage to him, I will personally carve your heart out myself." Shasha hissed.

With a gentle push, Mitta urged Shasha to lead us from the dining room to our quarters, putting us between her and my father. Mitta supported one shoulder and Bastion the other as they half dragged the moaning lord from the room. Tummi paused at the door waiting for me, not about to leave me alone with him.

"Father, think about my idea, please."

"Let's discuss it." He smiled at me before taking another bite of the dessert.

"Not tonight. I am going to tend to my friend, we can discuss it tomorrow."

"Tomorrow is a gathering of the nobles; my day will utterly be filled, my dear."

"At your earliest convenience then, father." As much as it pained me, I bowed to him. "Goodnight."

"I would be careful where you put your loyalties, Katrel. He is just as liable to bite you as protect you."

I paused at the door. "That may be so, Father, but he is still the only monster in this castle I'm not afraid of having at my back. Goodnight."

Tummi and I walked down the halls, following the grunts of our companions, the half feral groans from the lord. Guards and servants gave us a wide berth as we wormed our way to our rooms. It was outside the lord and lady's suite that Tummi wrapped me in her arms.

"You were very brave."

I frowned. "I don't feel brave."

"You were." She said, pressing a kiss on my cheek. "Let's go help our friend."

We entered the washroom where Mitta and Shasha fussed over the lord. Mitta digging through her first aid items, Shasha unbuttoning the lord's undershirt, the skin beneath an angry red filled with hives. Bastion paced by the bathing pool.

"Why?" He snarled.

"He was trying to goad us all night." Mitta snarled back. "Your outburst defending Tummi became the focus, not the food. Cardoc had this planned already."

"But why is it only affecting him? You ate the flowers and you're not in agony." His question was punctuated by the lord's groan, his face pinched and breathing shallow.

"I'm a shifter, jackass. Not a beast." She snarled at him.

"Where can we help?" I asked as Shasha slid the open shirt from under the lord.

"Just steer clear, he's liable to puke all over us anyway." Mitta said blandly as she moved to his side, a brown bottle in her hand. "My friend this is going to burn like a mother fucker, but it's the fastest way to get the poison out of your belly. Shasha come to this side, so he doesn't trample you."

"Peroxide?" She asked as Mitta unscrewed the bottle.

"It agitates the stomach lining and causes the body to evacuate its contents." She answered, tipping the lord's head back. "It will only be a few tablespoons, but it will happen quickly."

"I'm going to hate this aren't I?" He growled at her.

"Oh, most definitely. Open up." He frowned but obliged as Mitta poured the astringent in his mouth. "Swallow."

It was only a few moments until he swung to the toilet, back bowing, as he retched into the bowl. Shasha wet a rag in the sink and came beside him, pulling his hair back and dabbing his brow with the rag. A sheen of sweat coated his body as he heaved and heaved, flushing the toilet threefold. He hovered there as an occasional dry heave racked his body. His arms quivered as they clenched the porcelain, panting.

He spat before flushing a fourth time and gingerly sitting back. He huffed through his nose. "I don't know if I can stand."

As close a plea for help as it could be, I made to move but there was a quiet rap at the door and Cyran, followed closely by my mother ,peaked in. Cyran cleared his throat.

"We wanted to make sure you were alright."

"I've spent the last hour heaving my guts. Do you think I'm alright?"

My mother swished around Cyran and approached the sweaty lord and gave him a long look. I watched both him and Shasha recoil slightly under her gaze. As she looked upon his new and old scars, the hard life he had lived. Her hand reached out and everyone held their breath as she rested it against his cheek.

"Such a hard existence you have had." Our mother's hand glowed against the lord's face. Shasha's hand was in easy reach of her dagger as mother said. "I can't rid you of the scars, but I can ease the pain in your body and aid your organs to process the rest of the toxins out of you."

He sagged into her hand as her magic flowed into

him easing the strain in him, her other hand cupped the other cheek. Shasha asked. "Why do this if your husband just tried to kill him?"

She frowned as Cyran said. "She did not know until it was too late." His brows furrowed at my unasked question. "Neither of us did."

"And you expect us to believe you?" I hissed.

"Why would we come to check on him? Why would your mother bother healing him if we meant you all harm?"

"That is the question." I said crossing my arms, but the lord relaxed further into my mother's touch, enough so that Shasha went to lean against the wall. Her eyes never left where the Queen of the Elves held her mate's face.

Cyran sighed sitting on a bench beside Tummi. "Cardoc is cruel and conniving."

"We know that." Bastion said.

"But he has done many things to protect his people."

"He has also isolated and held them back." Mitta said.

Cyran frowned. "I didn't say that I served the king as a choice."

"Then leave." I said.

He looked at my mother who eased her hands away from the lord. "I can't."

"Your loyalties may be the only reason you breathe." Niratap said, wobbling slightly as he looked at our mother. "Thank you."

"It was the least I could do."

Niratap caught her hand and pushed back her sleeve. The dark bruise had faded to a greenish yellow but was still distinctly the mark of a hand. He asked. "How likely is it that there is a dark mark on your throat?"

Shasha came to stand beside him, her face pulled into a frown. "He hits you."

"Ciserie." Cyran said standing, his legs eating up

the distance between them.

"Oh, don't fret Cyran, you don't need to mother hen me." She waved both men off and glowered at Cyran. "It's not a secret that the king takes his endless rage out on his meek wife."

"Mother." Tummi's face was devastated.

"It started after Katrel was born and only got worse as time went on." She looked sadly at us, her daughters. "All of it was to protect you girls."

"Why stay?" Shasha asked the queen.

She smiled mirthfully at her. "Because even if he hates me, he will not allow me the freedom of that choice. Cyran assures me that Cardoc will take up your request, but I fear he will pit you against things that out match you."

"I have my family at my side." I said, holding my chin high.

"I'll try to keep him distracted." My mother said. "Keep him occupied so he leaves this family alone."

"Mother, we don't want you to sacrifice your life." Tummi objected.

She ignored my sister and pinned me with her gaze. "Tomorrow dress in a knight's regalia and ask to perform the trials before the nobility and viziers. He will be forced to accept it."

Cyran frowned. "I will find you some regalia and deliver them."

I fought back tears. "Thank you."

"Be strong and brave, my child." My mother said softly before dipping her chin at us. "Lord Niratap, I suggest that you rest. A soak in the bathing pool will help your joints."

"Thank you, Queen Ciserie."

"In close conversation, just Ciserie is fine." She smiled at us. "Goodnight."

"Goodnight." We said as my mother slipped from the room quietly.

Cyran watched her go. "You are all very lucky.

Innuram isn't fatally toxic to beasts, but it does cause discomfort and can force them to take on their natural shape. I think the king was hoping that you would lose control and go for anyone at the table."

"He underestimates my control."

"I think we all did." Cyran said as he turned to leave. "You are going to have to be on your guard now, he will not make that mistake twice."

"Noted." The lord said as he used the counter to push to his feet, his mate coming to his side.

"Call if you have need of us." Mitta said, looking him over once before heading for the door. "Take the queen's advice."

He sighed. "Yes, Mitta."

Everyone followed after Mitta, but I paused at the door.

"Yes, Katrel?" He asked softly.

I turned. Shasha supported him as they moved closer to the pool. "I don't want you there tomorrow. I've already put you at risk."

He straightened to his full height. "I will be at your back. I refuse to be a weakness for you."

I smiled sadly. "The moment I claimed you as family, you became a weakness. Whatever is to come will come at a cost, I don't want that cost to be any of you."

"We will be there beside you." Shasha said softly. "You are stronger than he knows, and you will be okay."

"I hope that you are correct, Milady."

Chapter Twenty

Katrel shut the door with a quiet click. Niratap rested his hand on my shoulder, giving it a gentle squeeze. I looked up at his face. His eyes, still watching after them through the door, were serious and sad. I stroked the small of his back, willing him to look at me.

"How are you feeling?"

His eyes softened. "A bit shaky I'm afraid, but I shall be alright."

My hand traced idle circles at the base of his spine. "Do you want to soak?"

"I was told by two members of authority to, so I better. The queen may not chastise me, but Mitta will tan my hide if I don't do as she instructs." He chuckled softly.

My lips twitched upward. "Very well, my Lord. Would you like my assistance?"

He shifted, standing to face me. His gaze took me in and when his voice filled with lust and smoke rolled over me, my core heated. "There are many things that require your assistance, mate."

"And how may I assist you, my Lord?" I asked, my fingers finding the button of his pants. "What kind of assistance does my mate require."

"Exactly what only you can give me."

I freed him from his pants, sliding the fabric down his long legs. "And what is it that only I can give you."

His hand cupped the back of my head. "You, if you'd be so inclined. I have spent the last hour ungraciously emptying my stomach."

I smiled at the predator who smiled back at me. "Be that as it may. I would happily take you, mate. Anytime.

Anywhere."

I slid the straps of the gown I had worn to dinner over my shoulders. The warm yellow gossamer falling from around my body. His nostrils flared as he hungrily took me in. I backed into the pool the water warm against my legs. He grasped the handrails leading into the pool, following me into the depths. The water stopped just above my breasts at its deepest.

We circled each other in the pool. Hungry. Pale scars stark on his honeyed skin. His muscles flexed under that beautiful skin. He grimaced, pain sluicing through his face. It was a bucket of ice over me.

"Sit."

"I am fine."

I frowned. "Sit."

He sighed. "Very well."

With a soft groan he lowered himself to the seat at the edge of the pool, then stretched his long legs out before him. I stepped closer to him seeing how stiff his movements were, so close again. "Are you in pain?"

He avoided my gaze. "I am just old, my love."

I frowned. "You are not that old, Niratap and you are still recovering."

He looked at me then as I reached for the bottles and vials that lined the back of the pool and a rag. He asked as I sniffed from one of the bottles, it smelled of lavender. "Do you think I am incapable of protecting us?"

I wet the rag and poured on the sweet-smelling soap. "No, I don't think that, but you tend to throw yourself on the sword even when you don't need to." I ran the rag down the side of his neck. He leaned into the touch. "Moreover, I think you're pushing yourself when you aren't fully healed."

He glowered but I could feel the stiffness of his joints easing. Much like I could feel the tightness in his throat when the poison started to get to him, and the unsteadiness that almost had knocked me down in the room. He said. "I am well enough."

I met his eyes. "I worry about you."

A soul-deep sorrow made my chest hurt; the emotion barely flickered in his eyes. "I don't mean to cause you worry."

I ran the cloth over his chest, my eyes remembering all the pain that his life had already been. "I know."

He captured my hand in his, and it was dwarfed in his grasp. "Shasha."

I met his gaze, those silver eyes glowing in the thin light. "I do not want you to have to suffer anymore."

He gave me a soft smile. "I am trying so very hard to be worthy of your light."

"You don't have to try." I slipped over him, straddling his legs. "I am the one who isn't worthy of your gallant heart."

"Gallant?" He smirked, wrapping his arms around me.

"Yes. My knight." My safe place. My home. My heart fluttered.

"There are plenty of men and beasts that would disagree with you." He said, stroking idle circles on my back as I traced the basilisk scar.

"They are bad men and beasts then because you are nothing but generous and kind."

He smiled softly, leaning in to kiss my cheek. He murmured. "Never think less of me."

I turned, pressing a kiss to his lips, meeting him with the same intensity that burned in his eyes. "Never. You are mine and you are good."

He swallowed and pressed his brow to mine. "Mate. Mine."

I felt him harden beneath me, but I asked. "With the mate bond can we sense each other?"

He blinked. "I—I am not sure. I know between the Lycans it is common between alphas and their mates; some can even communicate with one another through the bond."

"Do you think that ours could do that?"

"Our bond is still young. There is a honeymoon phase, the sinking, I think it's called where the bond grows and strengthens. It's why we struggle with simple kisses quickly evolving into bedding one another or when we are under duress we want that comfort of the other's body."

"How long does this sinking last?" Heat was coiling in my gut for him.

He rolled his hips against me in answer to the need readying in me. I groaned before he answered my question. "I do not know. It can vary with the Lycans. It could be a few months; it could be years."

"Years of needing you maddeningly."

"I hope it's more than years. For as long as I breathe, I will need you." He reached between us and eased himself in me in emphasis. He rocked under me. "I will always need to feel you. I will always need your scent in my nose and your taste on my tongue. I will always need to be wrapped in you. I will always need you. Mate. Mine."

"Mine." I groaned against his lips. "Forever mine. Only mine."

"You are all I have been looking for. The master of my heart."

I pressed my hand to his chest. "No."

He stilled his ministrations an edge of concern in his eyes. "What?"

I cupped his face in my hands. "I am not your master, of your heart or otherwise. You have been held underneath others for too long. You are mine and I am yours. We are equals."

"You are too good for me." He said, his eyes were full of wonder.

"I could say the same."

I rocked my hips, and he buried his face in my neck. "*Is tú mo theach.*"[52]

I groaned as his fangs grazed my pulse, followed by

[52] You are my home.

his tongue. "I love you."

"And I you, *mo grá*. May I taste you?"

"Please."

His fangs sank into my neck. It was a sharp pain that made me gasp and then waves upon waves of pleasure as he pulled my essence into him. My fingers sank into the sable strands of his hair, nails scraping against his scalp. My body spasmed in his hold, clenching tightly around him. He groaned deep in his throat as his body found release and he filled me with his seed. He pulled back, lapping at the open wounds, his magic pulling my skin closed and unblemished. I captured his mouth, my tongue exploring the iron and flowers and forests that was us.

We parted, breathless and stunned. I studied his beautiful face. Eyes full of devotion, an acolyte to the temple of our love and he was mine. "You are magnificent."

He chuckled. "Says the goddess."

"What do you think Cardoc's motive was to poison you?" I asked, sliding from his lap and scooping up the rag to wash myself.

"I don't know. He can't bend me to his will, and I am an obstacle in controlling his children. From what I know about royal courts it could be a test for me, for the group, for Katrel."

"Test for what?"

"My tolerance to the innuram. The group's ability to watch out for each other. Where Katrel stands."

"Well, we failed to watch out for you."

"The king intentionally goaded Bastion. Out of all of us the king figured he would be the easiest to rile up. Though for all my restraint if he had said terrible things about you, mate, I am unsure if I could have stayed in my chair."

I frowned at him. "I'm glad he didn't. The last thing we need is you in that kind of situation."

He huffed. "I would defend you against him.

Cardoc may be king, but he holds no power over us."

"Except a swift death." I threw the rag at his face.

He caught it with ease and shrugged. "Mayhaps, but I would fight it every step of the way, if only so you could live."

"Self-sacrificing, fool." I muttered.

"A fool I may be, but I am only a fool for you." He responded, setting the rag on the edge. "That being said, I understand. It is why you brought your blade to Cardoc's throat in the throne room."

I swallowed. We hadn't talked about it, my insane defense of my mate before the king and court. The act itself was reason enough to be executed and yet he hadn't. "Yes. I felt his magic curling around you, I watched as he examined you like a prized cow, and I couldn't stay idle."

He nodded, looking up at the ceiling. "I was alright. I am used to that kind of treatment."

Something hot shot through me and I shouted. "You shouldn't have to be!"

He didn't flinch and continued to stare at the ceiling. "And you shouldn't have to come to my defense."

"I will always come to your defense." I snarled. "You are mine, Niratap, mine. It is my heart that beats in your chest. It is my home you walk around in. You are all the stars, the sun, and the moon in my sky," my voice broke, "and I will not lose you again."

He looked at me then and such sorrow filled his eyes. "Shasha."

"No. I cannot feel that again. I cannot feel that void where you once were again. I almost lost you not once, not twice, but three times. I can't Niratap. I can't. I can't go through that again. I won't."

His expression was unreadable. "I don't want you to have to do that again, but the path we walk is not without its risks. Especially here."

"I know."

He shifted closer to me. "I can't promise you that I

won't fall on that sword."

"I know."

He kneeled there before me. "I can't promise you that I won't fail."

"I know."

His hands cupped my cheeks, his thumbs brushing away my tears. "I can't promise you that dying is something I can't do."

I took a shuddering breath and tried to blink away the tears. "I know."

"What I can promise you, *mo grá*, is that I will fight to stay by your side. I will fight to remain on this side of the soil, if only so I can bask in the light of your smile." He pressed a kiss to my brow. "I can promise you, that my love for you is what has kept me going for many months now and the thought of losing that is the most terrifying beast I have ever faced. That I can promise."

"Such promises."

"From my heart to my heart."

I pressed a kiss to his lips. "We are a mess."

He chuckled. "Yes, we are."

Only when we were pruned and fully exhausted did we travel from the pool to the bed. I fitfully tried to find sleep and even with him wrapped protectively around me, a veritable shield against our enemies, I could not find it. Even though I knew his magic would alert him if anyone we didn't trust came into the hall. Something sinister still floated in that inky abyss beyond the decadent walls of the castle and in those folds of sleep. The malice still lingered there in those places where Niratap couldn't escape by himself, and neither could I.

When the watery grey light of dawn began to dance around the room, I slipped from the bed, my mate peacefully sleeping there, lost somewhere safe I hoped. After seeing to my needs, my mate still hadn't roused and as I crossed the main space of the ostentatious suite we were staying in. I saw that the door to our rooms was ajar.

Something oily and dark danced along my senses.

"Who's there?"

"Shasha." It sounded like Tummi calling me from the hall.

"Tummilia, what did you need?" I asked, going to the door.

She stood down the hall and waved to me. "I want to show you something."

I slipped my boots on and followed her as she dipped right down the hall crossroads. "Tummi, wait up."

I jogged down the hall and turned and she waved at me from the next crossroads and turned left. "Hurry, Milady."

"Tummi, wait!"

I broke into a run following her straw-colored braid as she dashed out a set of glass doors into the mist laden garden. I spun wildly looking for my friend.

"Tummi!"

"I'm in the orchard." Her voice floated from the thick grove of trees. "Hurry!"

I ran past trees deeper and deeper into that grove. Some trees slumbered, some were in full bloom, and others had branches weighted down, heavy with fruit. I would ponder the strangeness of that later. I followed the soft rustle of leaves as Tummi led me deeper into the orchard-turned-forest. The rich loam of the elf kingdom evolving into the rough, rocky dirt so much like home.

"Tummi! Where are you?"

"Shasha!"

"Tummi!"

"Shasha!"

"Shasha! Shasha! Shasha!" The forest echoed around me and laughed. I saw her standing at the opposite end of a small clearing.

"Tummi!"

"Tummi! Tummi! Tummi!" The forest chittered and laughed.

"Shasha this way!" She disappeared beyond the edge.

"Shasha. Shasha. Shasha. This way. This way. This way." And more tittering laughter.

I stopped in the center of the clearing. So, like the one at home where the dryads slept. I spun around searching for Tummi among the tangled branches and brambles.

"Tummi?"

"Over here." Her voice called in front of me.

"Over here." It echoed to my left.

"No here." My right.

"Here I am." Behind.

"Stop messing with me!"

"Stop. Stop. Stop. Me. Me. Me."

"Stop it!"

"Stop it. Stop it. Stop it."

"Enough!" I screamed and the forest went cemetery silent.

"Are the spirits of the forest picking on you, our lady who walks with shadows?" The sweet lilting voice of Willow asked.

"Willow?" I turned to where the sweet faced dryad stood. "What's going on?"

"You are dreaming mate to the breaker of bonds." Birch said at my other side.

"This is a dream?"

"It is. It is. Our lady of the seasons." Maple chirped.

"So, I'm asleep."

"That would be correct, companion to the scariest thing in the forest." Hawthorn said.

"Is there something wrong with the blankets of dreamland?" Rowan asked.

"No."

"Or are you just scared, one who tastes of all the flowers of the seasons?" Oak asked from directly behind me. I turned to look at the dryads as they closed in on me.

"Yes. Yes. Are you scared lady of the seasons?" Willow asked.

"Are you scared? Are you scared?" The others chimed as they closed in on me.

"You guys don't have to crowd me."

They reached for me and Hawthorn asked. "Do you really taste of all the seasons, oh Lady of the Shadow?"

I backed away. "Stop it."

"May we taste you, oh Lady Bondbreaker?" Rowan asked as her leaves began to rot and fall away, black ooze sliding from her eyes and mouth. The others quickly followed suit, leaves falling all around me as I backed away.

"Why did you bring that vile darkness to our forest? Why did you let it seep between rock and root and fester, one of the shadows?" Oak asked as they converged.

"Why? Why? Why?" The girls asked in the sing-song way that normally made me smile, but here it sent gooseflesh across my body.

"Will your blood be the cure of this blight?" Oak asked her fist clamping shut inches from my face, and I teetered backward over an edge that had not existed moments ago.

I plunged into the icy moss-grey water, the cold forcing the air from my lungs. The water seemed to pull against me as I fought to the surface. Above, the mist had settled heavily around the sudden body of water, the branches of naked trees reaching up like boney hands. The eerie feeling of being swallowed made my heart race, and the deep gulps of air I took in didn't alleviate the dread. My heart doubled in pace as a scaled hand wrapped around my leg and drug me under the water. After the bubbles cleared from my vision, there was a pale fat mare with long teal seagrass mane and tail before me. It cocked its head at me and smiled in the most unholy of ways.

"Well. Well. Well. Welcome to death, Lady

Bondbreaker." The creature purred through the water.

My eyes widened at the voice.

"Oh, how I will enjoy the taste of your flesh on my tongue."

Creseda.

"Then I will take your mate."

Hot rage roiled through as I reached for my dagger. It was not there.

"Pity you don't have your blade. It might have been the only thing that saved you from joining the bones at the bottom of my lake."

I needed to think fast. I needed a weapon. I needed air. Swimming to the surface would make her toy with me and I would drown before I could escape my dream. So, I dove. Swimming as hard as I could while Creseda laughed and laughed and laughed, until the soft murky bottom came into view, bones of all types sticking up from the muck. "Swimming down will not save you. Only prolong your suffering."

My hand closed around a thick femur bone, probably belonging to a horse or other large quadruped. I waited until her dark shadow descended over me. I wrenched the bone from the bottom, leveling the other end at her. The bone had been broken so the beasts could suck the marrow out, and the jagged end sunk deeply into her equine belly. I would not be some monster's dinner. Inky black blood flowed from her belly making the water opaque, I kicked up towards the surface, my lungs starting to burn.

"How dare you. How could you?" Sounded her watery gasp behind me. "Killing me won't protect you or your mate."

I peered down at her as she sunk limply to the bottom, beyond the cloud of blood. The cloud pulsed and throbbed, pulling together into a solid shape of a man. His brown hair danced around his face, his brown eyes unassuming beneath me, but his ghastly broad smile sent chills down my spine. He began to walk towards me through the water. A dream, this was only a dream.

"Why do you flee from me?"

The water became thick around me.

"I thought you were brave enough to face death."

I fought, my limbs going leaden as my progress to the light all but stagnated.

"At the very least I thought it would be harder to kill you."

Bubbles slipped between my lips and floated rapidly to the surface.

He was behind me then, his hand closing around my throat. "I wonder what the beast would do, if you never took another breath."

I closed my eyes, more and more of that precious air escaped from my nose and mouth.

"I wonder what his broken cries would sound like. How losing you so early would break him."

I struggled, my eyes opening to see a familiar scarred hand plunged into the depths, reaching for me.

"I wonder what you taste like outside of the dream world. My pets wonder too."

Shadows twisted around me from the deep. No. No. No. I twisted in his grip, kicking him away from me. I frantically fought the water, reaching for that hand and that salvation.

"Soon you will be mine. You and your mate."

I broke the surface.

My eyes opened and I gasped for that life giving air, coughing as my body choked it down into my lungs. Shaking hands rested on my shoulders as the visage of my mate came into focus, panic honing his features knife sharp, in that grey predawn light.

"Shasha." The pain in his voice cracked my heart.

"Mate." I croaked.

"Mine." He pressed his head to mine. "I thought I had lost you."

A sob cleaved from me at the lost hopeless feeling that seeped between us. My oxygen starved lungs ached as if I had indeed been drowning. Warm tears tapped across my cheeks, a shaking breath danced across my lips and the quivering in his body was more noticeable.

"Nira."

"You weren't breathing. I couldn't find your pulse or hear your heart. You wouldn't wake."

I reached between us cupping his face, my fingers wiping away the treks of tears. Even though I held him in my hands and my lungs hurt and my heart pumped wildly in my chest now, he had thought I was gone.

"My love."

He shook his head those night bright eyes gleaming. "I thought you were gone. I thought—" He swallowed, unable to say the horrible things he thought. Light footsteps sounded beside the bed, and he growled. Near feral with that lingering panic.

"It's okay. It's me." Mitta said softly, her hands raised. "May I check her out really quick, my Lord?"

He pulled back, eyeing me and there was a tightness to his skin that told me his control was slipping. I stroked that face until his eyes met mine. "Mate, let our friend look me over."

"The hall is clear. Bastion is watching the end." Tummi said from the doorway. Niratap's jaw was tight, and violence lingered in his eyes.

"Niratap. I am alright. I am here."

He stiffly shifted off me and lay on the bed next to me on his belly. His face turned to me with predatory intent, and I knew deep in my soul that if anyone made a wrong move, he would lash out to protect me. Even against our family. Mitta eyed him and the taunt muscles of his back, poised to strike if need be. I eased into a sitting position, my chest heavy.

"What happened?" Mitta asked, pressing her fingers to my neck searching for my pulse. Niratap growled. "Territorial males."

I place a hand on his shoulder, the rock of muscle feathered under my palm. "I must have fallen asleep, and I had a nightmare."

Mitta frowned. "A horribly vivid one if you stopped breathing."

I ran through what had happened, told them about the dryads, Creseda, and the man in the lake. "I think it was the malice."

Another growl from the male at my side.

"It was trying to drown me." I said as Mitta examined my eyes, turning my head back and forth.

"That would explain the 'not breathing'." She said, dropping her arms. "You're okay though, maybe a bit tired from that harrowing dream."

"She is not okay, Mitta." He rasped beside me, rising. "She stopped breathing, and I could not hear her heart beating."

"I know." Mitta held her hands before her non-threateningly. "She is alright now. There is nothing physically wrong with her. She is breathing normally, and her heartbeat is strong."

"Mitta—"

I placed my hand on his chest. "Mitta, I think we need some time to settle ourselves without an audience."

She stepped back and bowed. "As you wish, Milady. I will go watch the hall."

"Thank you, Mitta." The door closed behind her with a click, and I looked at my mate. His skin to tight for his body. His eyes, though they seethed with rage at unknown enemies, were wrapped in sorrow. "I am all right."

"Is that what it felt like when I died?"

My heart skittered. "What?"

Silver limned his eyes. "You felt like you were gone. It was like my chest had hollowed out and I was empty."

I curled into his chest, the memory of that pain sluicing through me. I nodded.

He wrapped his arms around me, holding me tightly. "I'm sorry."

Chapter Twenty-One

Mitta

When the grey light finally warmed, I returned to
our room. Katrel was standing before the wardrobe mirror,
her warm brown hair unbound and cascading down her
back as she straightened the sleeves and collar of the deep
crimson jacket. The knights' regalia had not been designed
with women in mind. She had tucked the fine white shirt
underneath the jacket into her pants. She had opted for her
high waisted skinny jeans that hugged her curves instead of
the men's pressed pants that lay discarded on the bed, the
knight's boots shined before them on the floor. She was
absolutely lovely.

"You look regal." I said, coming behind her.

"It feels off wearing this. What if he tells me no?"
She looked at me pleadingly in the mirror, her copper eyes
lost.

"He can't, that's why they told you to wear the
regalia. Prove yourself to him, Katrel. The rest of us know
you are capable."

She glanced back at herself in the mirror adjusting
the collar again. "You make it sound so easy."

"I believe in you." I said, collecting one of the
dining chairs. "Sit and I'll braid your hair."

She didn't argue as she eased into the chair. I
brushed back her wavy tresses before starting at the crown
of her head. She was a gift and no one in this rutting
kingdom seemed to know that. It was frustrating to find
that lost look in her eyes and not be able to comfort her. I
huffed to myself.

"This must be difficult for you."

"What?" I asked.

She fiddled with her jacket smoothing out the breast where the biotatá was embroidered. Such a ferocious symbol for such overall peaceful people. "Being stuck in this room with me."

I finished off the braid and went to grab the boots. "Why would you think that?"

"We—we haven't talked about it."

"About what?"

"The kiss."

That blasted kiss. I could still taste her on my tongue. The thought filled me with both heat and frost. She wasn't mine. She couldn't be mine. Bran. Asira. "What about the kiss?"

She turned in her chair to watch me, her cheeks taking on a rosy glow. "That it happened. Why it happened. What I walked in on."

Fuck me. I had needed a release, and her name had been on my lips. She tracked me as I walked in front of her and kneeled. "And what did you walk in on, Katrel?"

"I—you—" She swallowed as I kneeled before her. I needed to touch her. "I can put the boots on by myself."

"Let me." I hooked the back of her knee and ran my hand down to her ankle to lift her foot. The hard-won muscles feathered under my touch, and I wondered if those muscles would feather under my tongue. I tried to take a breath to steady my nerves, but her scent permeated it. Marigolds and smoke. I slid the boot up her calf and moved to the other.

"So, the kiss?"

"What about it?" Bran. Asira.

"Why did you kiss me, Mitta?"

I sighed. Finishing with boot and sat back. Bran. "It was a lapse in judgment on my part and I'm sorry."

She swallowed. "Oh."

The sound made my heart ache. Asira. "Kat."

"No, forget I asked." She moved to stand. I pressed my hand to her knee.

"Wait."

"Why?" She glared at my hands. "You said that I was a mistake, that kissing me was a lapse in judgment."

"That is not what I said."

"That is exactly what you said."

She tried to stand again, but I rose, pinning her to the chair. Face to face with her I growled. "That's not what I meant. It was never what I meant. I said that the kiss was a mistake. That the kiss was a lapse of judgment. You are not a mistake, Katrel. Never once have I thought you were a mistake. You are my friend. You are beautiful. You are a gift."

Her eyes were wide as she took in my words. "Mitta."

"It is not for lack of wanting, or that I find it distasteful. But—"

"What is it?"

I shook my head. Damn my foolish heart and damn this beautiful woman. "I made a promise that I cannot break."

Her brows scrunched. "What kind of promise?"

I sighed, pulling away. "It's a part of me I'm not ready to share."

She frowned and I just wanted to make her smile. Just wanted her to be happy. She leaned forward brushing her lips against mine. Not really a kiss, but it froze me in place. She whispered. "When you're ready I'll listen."

My heart thundered in my chest. "Katrel."

"Fuck it."

She pressed her mouth to mine and the smoke and marigolds filled my nose and mouth. My hands traveled into her hair at the back of her head. The silken threads tickled my fingers. Her hands moved to my shoulders, then slid down my sides. I wanted this so badly. I wanted her so much it hurt but—

I broke the kiss. I pulled back trying to steady myself. Steal my nerves. She looked at me forlornly. "It's not that I don't want you, because trust me I want you."

"Mitta."

I forced myself to step away, to move out of her scent. "It's not that I don't crave you or love you. I just can't have you. You are not mine and you can never be mine."

Saying it out loud broke me. She sniffled, wiping her eyes. "Okay. I won't push you today." Her voice wavered as she took a shaking breath. "I need you with me today to face him. I need my friend and my teacher at my side so I can win my freedom. We can figure us out after."

"Kat—"

"No." She wiped her eyes again. "Later, we can talk later. Now does my face look puffy?"

"No, your face isn't puffy."

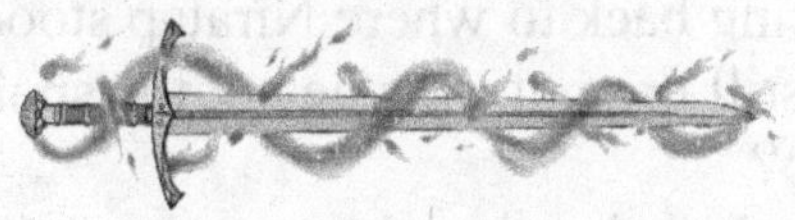

When eleven tolled, we congregated in the hall. The lord and lady hung close to one another, Tummi and Bastion stood behind them. The morning's events still lingered in Nira's eyes, leaving them haunted in a way that I had only seen a few times in the last few centuries.

"You're staying behind." Katrel told him. "I don't care if you want to protect me, I need to face him on my own to make this request."

"As you wish, however, we are going with you into that lion's den, I won't leave you undefended."

"Fine." Katrel hissed. "Stay at the back of the room."

She turned and led the charge to the throne room, her braid lashing side to side like a whip. She paused before the door, the rest of us behind her, a united front. I placed my hand on her shoulder.

"I'm scared." She admitted.

"You are stronger than he knows. You can do this."

"We are right behind you, Katrel." Shasha said.

She took a breath, pressing her hands to the wood. "Okay."

With a heave she shoved the doors wide. The nobles and viziers fell silent as we entered. The others fell back along the wall as Katrel and I marched before the dais. The king shifted to look down at us as she stopped before him. His eyes narrowing as he took in her attire, the nobles and viziers murmuring about it.

A cruel smile graced his lips. "Princess, it is rude to interrupt my meetings with the nobility."

Katrel bowed her head. "Apologies father, but I have a request."

"So, you are speaking for yourself today." He asked, glancing back to where Niratap stood. "I can see that the beast is still present, was he not the spokesman for your ragtag group?"

I fisted my hands at his tone but let Katrel defend us. "He is a lord, father, and he has weathered far worse than the stunt you pulled last night. I have a request."

A muscle clenched in his jaw as his cruel smile fell. "What is your request Katrel; I have business that you are intruding on."

Katrel took a knee before her father and kept her head low. "King Cardoc Raloqen, Third of His Name, King of Babylos, I beseech thee and request to perform the Trial of The Flame to prove myself to you and win the freedom to choose my fate."

The murmuring increased as the crowd took in her words. The king's face showed nothing as he crooked a finger at Cyran, who stood back behind the throne to step forward. The scholar had stopped by our room late last night with the regalia and told Katrel how and when to ask her father this question. Now he was advising the king on the merits of letting her perform the trials; how, if they were deadly enough, he might not have to worry about the rest of us. How it would put Katrel in her place if she failed and had to bend to his will. They whispered between each other and eventually the king nodded.

"Rise, daughter. I will grant your request, and as I ponder it, I know what your first trial will be."

Katrel stood. "You do?"

"Yes, there is a legendary blade that was once used by the flame emperor himself. Aetherius, it was called. It was lost many eons ago in a cave on *Magav Hiiglane* in the Herod Mountains. Your first trial is to travel there, retrieve the sword, and bring it to me."

Katrel bowed at the waist. "Thank you, father."

He chuckled. "Don't thank me yet, daughter. Both the mountains and the wilds are full of beasts that are almost as likely to eat you as the nobility." Courtiers laughed. "I would err on the side of caution when you venture into the north."

Chapter Twenty-Two

Katrel

I stared up at the man upon the throne. "North through the wilds and into the Herod Mountains."

"I would assume that you will want to spend the rest of the day preparing for your journey. Cyran will be available to you when we break for lunch in the hour. I assume you will have questions about the terrain and the beasts that roam the wilds." He smiled cruelly at me. "I wish you the best of luck, daughter. Now, leave me to my business."

"Yes, father." I bowed again before turning on my heels. I hadn't noticed when we entered, but now I could see that the royal guard were armed with ellervine, an enchanted rope that was used to subdue creatures by neutralizing their magic. Dread filled my belly as we neared our friends.

"Oh, Bondbreaker." The king called over the space, his tone laced with courtly mockery. "I do hope you are feeling better."

The lord stiffened by his mate. "I am well, Your Majesty."

"It was a shame that your constitution wasn't strong enough to make it through all of dinner; the evening cocktail was to die for."

Niratap smiled and it was edged with challenge. "Pity, I'm sure we would have had a fine go at it then. Maybe next time."

"Certainly." The king crooned. "I had lovely arrangements prepared for you."

"Of that I had, no doubt." Niratap bowed his head. "Thank you again for your hospitality, King Cardoc."

My heart thundered in my chest as I bid the lord through the door ahead of me. I could feel all within the hall watching me as I paid more respect to a beast than to them. I could feel their sneers and judgement as I walked out the door. Felt it even after the servants closed the doors and we walked down the hall toward the library. My heart continued to pound like a rabbit's as we entered Cyran's office and I sat before the enchanted glass, which overlooked a wide cerulean sea.

"I hate him." I whispered, letting my head fall into my hands.

"He accepted your request." Niratap said plainly, leaning against the wall of books. "And retrieving a weapon doesn't seem that hard."

"You don't understand. The wilds are full of beasts and wild things that are dangerous."

"Katrel." The lord said while the rest of them settled on the couches. "I will try to not take offense at the implications that you do not think that we can handle a few beasts when I myself am a beast."

I glared at him. "No. There are scarier things in the wilds than you."

He smirked at me. "Really?"

I rolled my eyes. "Yes, there are cockatrice and wyrms and, and—"

"And?" His smirk fell but that wildness still gleamed in his eyes.

"It's dangerous and after last night—"

He groaned and turned to the window. "I am fine."

I huffed through my nose. "Now, but we all know my father was trying to put you in a precarious situation, that would have ended with you being dead or in the dungeon."

He continued to stare at the illusionary window, his tongue traveling over his fangs, a threat of violence creeping into his eyes.

I hissed. "Don't even say what you're thinking

about saying. Because I can guarantee that every single woman in this room will beat the ever-loving shit out of you."

His brow rose, but he didn't respond, staring at the illusion of that calm, beautiful ocean. But I knew he saw his mate turn her head to eye him over her shoulder. He cleared his throat when he turned his head from the window. "Then, Princess, how do we proceed?"

I fisted my hands. "Right now, we wait for Cyran to be done. After we plan and prepare and so help me, Niratap, if you call me 'Princess' one more time I will hurt you."

He flashed me that wild smile. It was a smile that would give enemies pause if they met it on the battlefield or even through fancy dinners. It was that smile that made me remember painfully that he wasn't the man who stood before me, but the beast he proclaimed he was. Just as wily as any fae creature or courtier I had ever met, my Lord and friend. "I would like to see you try, Prin—"

His mate threw a pillow at the male and hissed. "Stop antagonizing her. How long does it take to get to the mountains?"

"I know it's a day's hard ride to Ehiza, the hunting town just outside the wilds. From there I don't know. Horses don't go into the forest."

"Why?"

"Horses refuse to enter the wilds." My sister said ominously. "Some say that there is a curse in the wilds that repels domesticated creatures. Others say the horses know what lies within the woods and prefer life."

"Wyrms and cockatrice are all but extinct in the rest of the world, why are they still here?" Mitta asked.

"Story goes," Cyran said, entering the door. He flopped down at his desk and dumped an armful of scrolls across its surface, "that when the flame emperor used the star's power to separate Babylos from the rest of the world that the wild things came with it. There are also draconic creatures, cryptids, and harpies in the wilds."

"Oh joy." Bastion said. "Everyone loves harpies."

"The harpies you shouldn't run into," the scholar chuckled, "as long as you don't get turned around in the forests. The harpies reside on the cliffs to the northwest. On your trek you will mainly have to worry about notdeer and aracks."

"Excuse me, what?" Shasha asked, her eyes both wide and eager.

"Notdeer," the lord explained, placing a hand on her shoulder. "Are creatures that resemble deer but are not deer."

"Well obviously." She rolled her eyes at him.

"They are predators that coexist with the deer population in the wilds. They prefer humanoids but in recent years they tend to attack anything that goes for their herd." Cyran said as he weighed down a large map over his desk. "Aracks are spiders the size of bears, or bigger, that will eat anything."

"Gross." Mitta said, striding to the map. "So, we're going to this mountain, and it should take us four days to get there approximately."

"If you don't run into any trouble, yes, it should only take you four days to get to *Magav Hiiglane*. I'll have stable hands prepare your horses for tomorrow."

Shasha moved to the table, scanning the map before she pointed. "This is where we need to go."

The rest of us crowded the scholar's desk. Shasha pointed to the far north peninsula where the shifting sands of Sucuba Desert was situated between the Herod Mountains and the Eastern Sea. Over the crumbling tower marker for the Incubus Ruins. I said. "It's at least two days from the mountains."

Cyran nodded. "If you are going to the ruins, your best and quickest way back here would be along the coast. It's a five-day journey to the delta by Ehiza."

"What kind of things lurk in the desert?" Niratap

asked.

"Mostly horned serpents and maybe some wyverns. It has been quite some time since anyone went that far north."

"Why is that?" He asked.

"The risks outweigh the benefits. The last time anyone was up in the mountains was a hundred years ago, when the king tried to establish a mining town."

"What happened?" I asked.

"The wilds happened. There was one survivor."

The lord frowned before he returned to the window. "The mountains, what are the risks?"

Cyran gazed up before returning to the map. "There are serpents, fiends, wraiths, and trolls. Rumors of basilisks, hydras, and dragons."

"Running into any of those rumors could be the end of us." Mitta grumbled. "I don't have any antivenom left from our last encounter with a basilisk. Hydras are extinct in the world of man. Dragons have separated themselves from man the best that they can."

"The wildlife is the least of your worries in the Herods. The weather can change rapidly and the paths through them are confusing. Caves and drop-offs that can cost you your lives."

"Tell me about the sword." I asked. "What about Aetherius?"

"Aetherius, the sword of the Flame Emperor." Cyran grabbed a scroll and rolled it out on the western side of the map. "It is said that it was gifted to him by the mother and creator to lead the elves out of destruction. The blade was forged from the fire of the earth and the light of the stars and gifted to the greatest line of elves to live. After the Emperor and his consort separated Babylos from the world of man, the flame emperor and the consort fell, and the sword was lost."

"What could have felled such a king?" Tummilia asked.

"The legends don't say. His tale just ends, and history picks up after Cardoc the First's coronation." Cyran shrugged.

The lord huffed. "For such a history-focused race, the lack of information is disheartening."

"I agree." Cyran said. "I have spent most of my life hunting for answers from before the separation and the missing years between the fall of the flame and rise of Cardoc the First."

Niratap stared at the window as it switched to a green meadow. "Very strange indeed."

"So," I pressed Cyran. "What are our odds?"

"You want me to calculate the odds of you succeeding?"

"I want to know what our odds of survival are."

Everyone looked at me and it was like a collective breath was held. Cyran sat back in his chair with a contemplative look. "If you are lucky and manage to avoid the wilds of the forest, survival is two to one odds. If you run into a creature and have to engage the numbers slide rapidly the other way."

"And succeeding?"

"Katrel, I have the utmost faith that you will succeed and return here. I am confident that you will defeat your father."

I swallowed. "Thank you, teacher."

"You have your friends with you and already I know that they are just as serious about getting you home as you are."

Shasha smiled at me. "We will be with you every step of the way."

"Thank you."

The sun hadn't even crested the hills when we ventured out of the gates of the castle grounds. Our breath fogged as we traveled through the near-empty streets. My people. Even if I didn't want to sit on my mother's throne and bear the future, I was still loyal to these people. People who smoked in their doorways or peered through their windows as they watched us pass. What would happen to them if I did succeed? Would my father just appoint Revan as king? Would Revan be a good king to the people as my father had been? These people were the only ones he did right by.

Mitta came to my side as we hit the poorest streets. "What are you fretting about?"

"What is to come."

"If you succeed or fail?"

"Yes."

"About you or the people?"

I swallowed, she always seemed to know. "My people. I may not want to be their queen, but I still worry for them."

"You are good. That is why even though you don't want to stay, you worry about them."

The gate out of the city creaked open before us. "I worry that I will fail them either way."

"You won't." Mitta smiled at me, bright as the sun that finally kissed the horizon. "I know you won't."

I smiled at her before twisting in my saddle to look at my family. Behind me, Niratap loped next to his mate and behind them my sister and Bastion brought up the rear. They had been so brave to follow me here, to risk everything for my shot at freedom. I took a deep breath. "We ride for Ehiza. It will be a long hard day. I hope to make it there before sunset, so there will be no breaks except lunch."

Bastion nodded. "Lead the way."

I cracked the reins and willed my horse into a gallop over the plains past grazing cows and sheep, past farms showing their beautiful green as seeds sprouted from their depths, past orchards in full bloom, past the hum of bees and calls of birds. Even as the kingdom grew, ever-changing and adapting as the world of man, the soft sighing plains still sang in the cool spring breeze.

The sun's climb was the only marker that we were traveling and by the time it hung high in the sky my body was slick with sweat as it heated the earth. We slowed our horses and broke for lunch by a small stream. The horses munched happily in the swaying grass, but the nob of cheese, hunk of bread, and apple was underwhelming.

"Why does the Elf Kingdom not have vehicles?" Shasha asked, staring out across the grass where the horses ate.

"Elves are strong believers in balance." Niratap answered. "Yes, guns and cars make surviving easier, but they are not kind to the earth, water, and air. Babylos is relatively cut off from the vast resources that the world of man has squandered on such things."

She nodded. "If man wasn't so greedy, our world could look like this."

"If man wasn't greedy, love, many things would not be as they are."

"Humans grew hungry because the elves had everything." I said. "I remember Cyran telling us that was why the creator, and the earth sent calamity to the world. The elves took advantage, and man was starved for the things the elves had: wealth, power, food."

"And the humans rebelled." Tummi added from where she sat filling the canteens. "They took up arms with sympathizing elves and other beings and rebelled. The earth was stained by the blood of all those beings and the earth and creator wept. They caused great floods and shook the earth; disasters that had not yet existed fell upon the living beings until the bloodshed stopped."

"Ending bloodshed with more bloodshed." Shasha shook her head.

"The creator and the earth didn't want their children to suffer, but in order to end the fighting they knew it was necessary." I continued. "After years of war and a single year of calamity the Flame Emperor, the last elf king, and a king chosen by man were met by the creator and the earth. Both were given weapons not for killing, but for righting the world and bringing about balance. The King of Elves was given a mighty blade and the King of Man a mighty spear. And so, men and elves separated and united under their kings, peace flourished."

"But unlike elves who live long lives and remember things as they were and used to be, men do not. Within a century of that great horror the men of the world separated, and the cycle of greed and hatred repeated." Tummi frowned as she handed Shasha her canteen. "The Flame Emperor with his captured Queen of Starlight went to the peak of *Magav Hiiglane* and begged the earth and creator to give them the power to move the elves away from the world of man."

"What happened?" She asked after a long swallow of cool water.

"The earth and the creator said they could, but that relinquishing of the world had a price." I continued. "It cost the Flame Emperor and the Star Consort all their magic. Every ounce in their bodies and souls. Stars are full of magic, which was why the star consort had been captured when she fell. Her magic had made the flame emperor unstoppable; her power gave him the ability to unite the elves under one banner."

"When the magic is drained completely like that, you die." Niratap said plainly and his mate looked at him wide eyed.

"And that is how the sword was lost. They both died on that mountain and the sword was lost, but no one really knows." I said looking up at the clouds drifting over the sun. My body ached. "We need to get moving soon."

Everyone nodded and began packing up. The lord

laid many swift kisses to his mate before collecting the horses from the tall grasses. I marveled at them, their devotion and love. Something all beings wished for. What I wished for. I glanced at Mitta who stared at the horizon, eyes hunting for danger.

Dusting the dirt from my ass, I pondered what she had said. That she wanted me, the breaking of her voice matched the breaking in me. She wanted me, but she couldn't have me. What or who would keep her from me? In all our many years together, Mitta had never gone to her bed with another and never did she venture into others beds. Even now she insisted on sleeping in the chaise in my room, instead of encroaching on my space in the massive bed.

I rolled my shoulders before mounting the storm-grey stallion I had picked. Mitta's chestnut mare bounced up to her, ready to run again, at ease with the tiger before her. Mitta slid the beast an apple slice and petted her soft nose. She was all the embodiment of that other shape. Grace and ferocity and cunning. My heart ached for her.

"What's wrong?" she asked, coming to my side.

"Nothing that can't wait." I said checking the others as they fell into formation. It could wait. I could wait. "Let's ride."

The afternoon sun beat harshly against my face as we rode through the plains. The tall spring grass sighed through our winds. Sweat trailed down our bodies both humanoid and beast, the lord's panting becoming more and more labored as the sun dipped into the final descent to the earth. This trek had been hard on him. It would continue to be hard on him.

As the sun kissed the horizon, Ehiza came into view. The township was full of hunters and harder-hewn elves who lived off the wild land and traded in meat and hides. It wasn't often that they had royal visitors, and our small band had not been announced; the thought had passed my mind as we had left this morning, but by then it had been too late.

Just as my eyes noticed the glint from the guard wall, it was too late. The arrow sung as it swept toward us. No, not toward us. Toward Niratap. I turned my head as the arrow flashed past me.

"Watch out!"

He swung wide as the arrow speared toward him. The arrow sunk into his hip and sent him to the ground, in a cloud of dust, roots, and stones. I yanked on the reins as Shasha screamed, her own horse not even at a full stop before she leapt from his back and ran to her mate.

Looking back to the town I saw six horses heading our way. I pushed my stallion back toward the town, Bastion coming up at my side and we rode to the retinue that was coming our way, bows and swords drawn. I would worry about my friend after.

I pulled the royal crest from my shirt holding the amulet up. "Stop in the name of the crown!"

The bows and swords lowered as we met them. The male at the head of the party on a black horse snarled. "Who are you?"

"Crown Princess Katrel Gwendolyn Raloqen. Why did you fire on my party."

The male frowned. "There is a beast in your company, Princess."

"Yes. That beast is a lord from the world of man and my friend."

"Apologies, Princess, we did not know you or your—" he paused as noticed Bastion at my side, "varied party were coming this way."

"Apologies for not alerting you of our arrival. Who

are you?"

The male wisely bowed his head. "Lathai Gormon, lead hunter and steward of Ehiza."

"We will meet you at the gates," I said turning back to our group. "I need to see to my friend."

"An interesting choice of friends you have, Princess."

I didn't deign an answer as I rode back to where our horses stood around the group as Shasha and Mitta hovered over the lord. "How is he?"

"I'll have to cut it out of him." Mitta snarled from where she poked at the bloody grey fur. "The shaft broke in the tumble."

"Damnit. Can you walk?"

The lord's silver eyes met mine and he shifted his clawed talons under him. He rose, towering over all of us in his beast form. He tested a step, his right hind side drooped in a limp, but he was able to move. Shasha left his side, only to hand the reins of her sweet horse to Bastion, before returning to her mate. She placed a gentle hand on his side and walked beside him. Slowly we crept towards Ehiza, the gate braziers a beacon in the growing dark.

"We're almost there." Shasha said softly to Niratap who huffed in response. I turned my head and peered at them over my shoulder.

"When we get you taken care of," she said, stroking the side of his face, "I'll find whoever shot you and give them a taste of my blade."

He gave her an incredulous look.

"What? You can wantonly defend me, but I can't do the same."

He chuffed in agreement.

"That's not fair." She barked at him as he shook his head.

I smiled to myself. He would be okay as soon as the arrowhead was out. As we passed through the gates Lathai bid us to follow him. The people from town had gathered;

men had their bows and swords at their fingertips, women
held back their children as they gaped at us, hands palming
daggers. Not at us, but at my friend as we made our way
into the stables.

"The last stall is clean." Lathai said. Niratap
growled at the male as he passed. We all understood what
he meant.

"Bastion," I said dismounting, "you and Tummi
tend to the horses."

In the stall Mitta pulled a knife from her hip and
pointed the tip at the lord's face. "You fucking bite me and
I will shorten your favorite part."

The look he gave her in answer was all jokes as he
snapped his jaws playfully at her face. His mate pulled him
by the ear. "Knock it off."

He laid back in the hay chuckling to himself. Mitta
struck swiftly and without mercy, slicing into the fleshy bit
and the juncture of his hip. The roar echoed around the
stables; yet the horses barely nickered at the sound. I
caught the confused look Lathai cast through the stables.
Questions, so many questions, burning in his eyes. Mitta
slipped her finger into the gash and yanked the arrowhead
free. The male's eyes widened further as the edges of the
wound pulled together. It was still too slow a progression, I
held my breath until the pink flesh closed.

"What is that?" Lathai asked me, just as shadows
exploded through the stables. The others in the stable
screamed.

As the shadows receded, Niratap stood, a smirk
sitting gently on his lips. His mate tugged the edge of his
shirt up checking his hip, a pink line sitting just over the
ridge.

"I am fine, *mo grá.*" He said.

"I had to check myself, you ass."

He chuckled, leaning down to press a kiss to her
brow. "I love you too."

"My Lord." I said, his eyes finding my own.

"Who is this?" He purred at me; danger woven in his voice.

"Lord Bondbreaker, this is Lathia Gormon, the Head huntsmen and steward of Ehiza."

"Do I have you to thank for the arrow I took?" he asked smoothly, his hand gripping his mate's shoulder, holding her back.

"No, I did not loose the arrow."

"Pray that my mate doesn't find out who did; she plans to flay them alive."

Lathia glanced at Shasha, more wary of the beast at her side. "Mate?"

"Yes, now if you would point to the man who shot him, I would like to make good on that threat." Shasha plastered a pleasant smile on her face.

Lathia cast me a glance. "She can't be serious."

"She is." The lord said. "The last man that wounded me, she killed."

I laughed at the look of shock on Lathia's face. "Come now, steward, I wouldn't have traveled without a lethal force at my back."

"But she is a woman and a human."

"Looks can be deceiving." Mitta said, wiping her hands of blood.

"I don't know what you and your group are here for princess," Lathia said.

"Katrel. Lathia and I am on a trial to retrieve a sword for my father. We only need shelter for the night, a safe harbor for our horses, and a rough heading to the *Magav Hiiglane*."

He eyed the group. "Princess."

"Katrel."

"Katrel, I don't think you will find a place that will welcome your ragtag group in for the night."

"And why is that?" Shasha hissed, still being held at bay by the lord.

"Because, no elf household would take in a beast,

an orc and two humans. Regardless of whether or not they were with the Crown Princess."

Mitta laughed. "You think I'm human, love."

"Mitta." The lord's voice was edged in warning.

"What!" she snarled her features teetering toward feline.

"Mitta." I said, coming to stand before her, whiskers pressing against her skin. "You don't have to prove how beastly you are."

She settled, if only just enough that she didn't rip anyone's throat out. "Fine."

"Lathia, find us lodgings for the night and tomorrow were going into the wilds and heading for *Magav Hiiglane*."

"I hear what you are asking—"

"I wasn't asking." I said to him, "It's an order."

The man glowered but bowed his head. "As you wish. Give me an hour and I'll see what I can do."

"Thank you." Niratap said with a bow of his head.

Chapter Twenty-Three

Shasha

As Lathai left us in the stables, my mate's grip on my shoulder loosened. He said. "He seems pleasant."

"He's annoying." I countered. My fingers still itched with the need to draw blood.

"I am alright. No need for the bloodlust, love."

"Don't tell me when I can and can't fight for you." I snarled, jabbing my finger into his chest.

He smiled sweetly at me. "Shasha. I would never."

I shoved him, though he didn't shift. "How dare you."

"At least they're fighting here." Bastion murmured to Tummi.

"As long as fighting doesn't turn into fucking we'll be fine." Mitta added.

I groaned. "We will not and do not."

"You sure about that love?" Nira asked, smiling wickedly.

I sighed in a long-suffering way. "You're impossible."

He cupped my cheek. "You love me."

"I do, but I'm not above beating you for your nonsense."

"I wouldn't expect anything less." He murmured as he leaned down.

"I'm mad at you."

"I know." He pressed a kiss to my brow.

"Gods, you're insufferable."

"You didn't say that the other day." He pressed a kiss to my cheek.

I swatted at his face. "The worst."

He chuckled, as he straightened. "Be that as it may, we need Lathai at least for tonight and when we come back."

I sighed. "Fine, but I'm not playing nice. I don't like the way he looks at you like—"

"Like a monster." He said softly.

"Yes." I said stepping around him and sitting on a bale of hay.

"We can all agree that we don't like him." Katrel said from where she stood leaned against the stall doorway. "The lord is right though. However much we dislike him we need him for this leg of the trial."

"Do you think he would guide us to the mountains?" Mitta asked, the skin of her face still too tight.

Katrel shook her head. "The hunters don't stay overnight in the woods."

"Why?" Bastion asked from where he set his saddle.

"Because predators hunt at night." Niratap answered, leaning against the wall next to me. "And given what we know about the wilds, there are a plethora of things that would eat elf hunters."

"So, what is the plan?" Tummi asked, setting down another saddle.

Katrel sighed. "Right now, I'm hoping he can get us lodgings for the night that aren't this stable and a hot meal."

"Hot food would be nice." I said.

"So, we're waiting." Mitta glared at the front of the stable. "Waiting and praying that the fact that you are the Crown Princess is enough to sway them not to flay the lord."

"They won't flay him." Katrel growled.

"Really?" I snapped. "Because they did shoot him with an arrow."

Katrel leveled a gaze at me, but Niratap said. "Fear

is a powerful motivator, for all sorts of reactions. I feel that the fact they let us into the stables at the very least, is a testament to Katrel's sway."

"Sleeping in a stable isn't terrible," Bastion said as he wiped his face with his shirt. "If you can get past the smell."

"Speak for yourself." Mitta and Nira said at the same time.

I laughed.

Mitta chuffed. "If I wanted to smell animals while I slept, I would have found a satyr to warm my bed."

Tummi smiled, mischievously. "Allipo tried, once."

"And only once." Mitta growled.

"I'm fairly certain you shaved a decade off the male's life." Niratap said sinking onto the hay bale with me. "He started getting grey after that."

"Psh." Mitta said. "He was drunk, he didn't even remember it until you lot told him."

I leaned into my mate while the others joked around with one another. "Are you okay?"

He wrapped his arm around me and tugged me closer into his petrichor and whiskey scent. "I am alright. Sore, but my healing is getting faster, even with the hiccup from that atrocious dinner."

"I'm going to kill him if he hurts you again."

"Now, now my vicious little flower, we can't have that."

"And why not?"

"Because even though Cardoc is not our friend, he is not truly an enemy and when Katrel beats his silly trial the kingdom will still need a leader."

"Precarious."

"Indeed." He stroked my side idly.

My gut twisted a little as the others kept rehashing Allipo's missteps. "What's wrong?"

He paused his ministrations a moment then picked his stroking up as he spoke softly. "I'm not entirely sure. I have a strange feeling."

"Hmm."

"How did you know I was pondering it?"

I shrugged. "I just had a feeling; it's been quite frequent as of late."

"I wonder?"

"What?"

He pressed a kiss to my head as Lathai came back into the stables. "I have a few questions for your father when we return home."

"Oh?"

He stands facing the steward who has stopped next to Katrel. The steward frowned and said. "I have a few questions."

Katrel turned to face him. "What questions?"

"Not for you—Katrel. For him."

My mate tilted his head to the side and a placid grin danced across his face. It is an expression of both curiosity and menace that I know he is aware of. "And what are your questions?"

Lathai swallowed. "Firstly, what are you?"

I frowned, but my mate straightened to his full height. "Not that it matters to our request, but I am a bitarog."

Lathai nodded at that response, his eyes flicking to Mitta and then me. His gaze lingered on me a little too long and made my skin crawl. "Them?"

My mate's eyes narrowed, but he answered the question. "Mitta is a rakshasi and the head of my security and our medic. Shasha is half human, half elemental, and my beloved mate."

My eyes reached my mate's face, but Lathai nodded and asked. "Do you mean any harm to my people?"

I looked back at the man pinning him with a glare. "How—"

Niratap places a hand on my shoulder. "That depends."

"On?"

"Do you mean any harm to my family?"

The air was charged with his question. Lathai watched us as he took everything in, his eyes repeatedly falling on me, as if me being his mate was a testament to his kindness and motives. The scrutiny of his gaze made me uncomfortable. Niratap shifted so he was standing slightly in front of me, his protectiveness warming a part of my heart that roared to his defense.

At last, Lathai blinked, nodding his head. "Very well. Follow me, I'll show you where the baths are and show you where you will be staying."

"And where would that be?" Mitta snarled, her voice full of distrust.

Lathai sighed and looked to the ceiling, as if praying to the gods that he could survive us. "At the lodge. My home."

Lathai showed us the communal baths and explained that we were welcome to use the facilities but stressed that modesty is still expected in the baths, which I found strange if they are public. Tummilia told me that they were common in Babylos as a whole, even with modern commodities bringing about private baths. Then explained that they were heated through magical means and the water was healing and sacred.

After the baths, we approached a large, stone building, which I could only assume was the lodge. Men and women were standing outside the building laughing and chatting as we walked up. The sudden silence as they noticed us made my skin itch. Lathai ushered us inside quickly reassuring his people that we weren't a threat. The inside of the lodge was large and rustic, with exposed beams and a plethora of exposed wood. Tables and a bar are set against one side of the grand room, a couple sits at a table eating steaming bowls of stew with crusty bread. The woman behind the bar blanched at the sight of us but nodded her head at Lathai before she dipped through the doorway behind the bar. There were hunting trophies mounted along all the walls, varying antlers, and taxidermized birds and fish, but it was the large reptilian skull mounted above the fireplace that caught my eyes.

"The last dragon to fly in the skies of Babylos." Lathai said to me, marking my gaze. I felt my mate tense behind me.

"Why is it the last?"

"No dragons have been seen in Babylos for almost three millennia." He nodded to the skull. "My great-grandfather killed that beast after it decimated the village."

"Dragons don't attack unless provoked." Niratap said in a hiss behind me, his knuckles cracking as he fisted his hands.

Lathai looked over at me, at my mate, his eyes narrowing. "I wasn't alive then; I can't speak to what happened prior to the hunting and slaying of the dragon."

I reached back and clasped my hand around his fist, rubbing my thumb comfortingly until the tension eased from him. "Even so."

"If I ever come into contact with another dragon, I will keep that in mind."

"Lathai." The woman who was behind the bar came up to him with a glass of water in her hands. "These are our guests?"

"Yes, Farryn." He said accepting the water from her and taking a hearty swallow before he gestures to Katrel. "This is Crown Princess Katrel."

The woman started, her voice almost squeaking. "Lathai, why did you make the Crown Princess wait in the stables?"

"They needed a secure place to tend to the—" He caught himself, his eyes flicking over me again, to my mate. "Lord."

"Why was—" The words died as she followed Lathai's gaze, her color fading.

"Who is this, Lathai?" My mate's voice was sharp and direct.

"This is my wife, Farryn. She runs the lodge and is a healer."

Niratap stepped around me and I hated it when Farryn flinches at his approach. I see the hesitance in his motion and instead of taking her hand he dipped into a half bow. "Lord Niratap Bondbreaker, my dear."

She shifted behind Lathai, as Nira rose and Katrel pressed him back, taking control of the interaction and introductions. "Lord Niratap is my friend, and he means you no harm. This is his mate Shasha, my sister Princess Tummilia, Bastion Day, and Mitta Rask the lord's head of security and medic."

Farryn's fearful eyes darted about the group, she stepped past her husband and gave a respectful bow to Katrel. "You have an eclectic array of friends."

"What is that supposed to mean?" I hissed, pushing past Niratap and in front of the woman. She stood a few inches taller than me and smelled like grass. "What is wrong with her friends? What is wrong with me? With my mate?"

Nira pulled me back to him, his hand firmly on my shoulder. I wanted to snarl at these people who looked at him like he is nothing, that treat him as if he is nothing more than a beast. He rubbed his thumb against my pulse, and that rage in me settled to a simmer.

"I apologize for my mate." He said softly. "She is protective of me and recently has become very acquainted with her fangs. She doesn't hesitate to bare them."

"Thank you for the meal, Farryn." The man sitting at the tables said, the woman waved as they made their exit.

"Anytime, Hagen."

"Now that introductions are done, can we sit and discuss what we need to—" Nira's voice drifted off at the patter of little feet. Upon the stairs stood a small child with bright eyes and the same tawny hair as Ferryn. She froze as she beheld him, the monster in a man's skin. Niratap stepped around them to speak to the girl. "Come here child."

Lathai tensed, reaching for his sword. Katrel pinned the blade in his scabbard. She hissed. "That is unwise."

He snapped. "Leave my daughter alone, beast."

"He's not a beast." I snapped at Lathai as I followed after my mate, though I was curious as to what he saw in the terrified little girl. She cowered beside the banister, her eyes a captivating silver.

Niratap kneeled and held out his hands to her. "Come here, sweetheart. What is your name?"

"Solana." Farryn barked at the girl. "Go back to your room."

The girl receded a step, and I felt the defeat my mate did in his heart at her fear. I stepped past him, charging up the steps and sitting beside her. I smiled brightly at her. "Solana, that is a pretty name."

The girl looked at me doe-eyed, then returned her gaze to my mate before sitting beside me on the stairs.

"You know you don't have to be scared of him."

She inhaled deeply and exhaled a long breath.

"I know he looks scary," I continued at the subdued child, "but he's only ever scary to adults."

She turned to look at me, disbelief apparent in her eyes.

"I promise. He's really sweet."

Her delicate little fingers touched her face.

"He only bites bad guys."

She cracked a soft grin and looked down at him again.

"He really loves kids and has a weakness for them."

My mate smiled up at me and the girl, his eyes not leaving her small face.

"I'm sure if you asked him, he'd carry you on his shoulders, let you steer him by his antlers."

He chuckled at the absurd expression she gave me and nodded up at her. "She speaks the truth. Come here."

She swallowed but stood and cautiously descended the stairs to stand before my mate.

He cocked his head at her. "May I pick you up?"

The girl nodded.

Nira swept her up in his arms. "Solana is a pretty name. Do you know what it means?"

She shook her head.

"It means sunlight. Your skin is so fair, have you played in your namesake at all."

She shook her head.

He frowned momentarily. "How old are you?"

The girl holds up her fingers.

"Seven!" He said excitedly. "You're so tall for seven."

She beamed at him.

Nira turned his attention to her parents. "Does she not speak?"

Farryn shook her head. "She was attacked by a wild fae at four and it stole her voice."

Niratap frowned at the girl. "It didn't steal her voice. It sealed it away. I can unseal it, if you grab me some water."

Farryn nodded softly, looking a bit dazed, taking the glass from her husband before hurrying behind the bar. When she brought the water back to my mate, he took a sip and offered the glass to the girl. She took a swallow and handed the glass back.

"This may sting a bit, sweetheart. Are you ready?"

The little brave face she put on as she nodded, made my chest squeeze. Nira's eyes glowed ethereally, and the shadows danced, twisting around his legs and up. They dipped into the water, making it black. The little girl squirmed as the shadows climbed up her body wrapping around her small legs.

"The shadows are a part of me, child. They won't hurt you." He said softly as he handed her the cup. "Hold this."

She looked into his eyes as he used his sharp fangs to cut his thumb open and with a practiced hand drew on the girl's throat. His magic crackled in the air and pulsed around us. His eyes filled with a softness that not even I received.

"Drink." He told her, nudging the black water to her lips.

She made a face but began to drink. She winced as she swallowed.

"I know, little one. I know." He soothed until the last drop was gone. Once she swallowed it a smattering of sparkling lights exploded from where they stood like a singular firework in the night. When the light faded the shadows slipped back into my mate's skin.

"Solana." He said sweetly.

She opened her eyes.

"You can speak now, but take it slow, your voice might be a little scratchy."

"What—" her voice rasped a bit, but she swallowed and tried again. It was light like a bell. "What is your name?"

He smiled. "My name is Niratap, but you may call me Nira, my little friend."

"N—Nira." She smiled at him. "Would you really let me ride on your shoulders?"

He chuckled. "Yes, I would."

"How?" Farryn asked dumbfounded, treks of tears falling down her cheeks.

"I could smell it in her. The magic. And believe it or not, it's fairly common for wild children to get silenced by the fae. Right, Bastion?"

"In my defense," Bas grumbled from Tummi's side. "Taegan was the one that started picking on the hob, not me."

"Didn't your parents teach you not to speak ill of the dead." Mitta countered with a vast grin over her face.

"It's the truth." He said with an almost whine. Nira laughed as Tummi patted his shoulder consolingly.

"Solana." Farryn wept.

"Hi, momma. The nixies played a trick on me."

Lathai tilted his head. "Nixies?"

"Yes, papa. The nixies in the barrow by the river."

"And what did these nixies do?" My mate asked, his voice light and loving but I saw the flash of violence in his eyes.

She looked shyly at him. "I can't tell. The nixies said they would drown me if I told."

"I won't let those wicked nixies hurt you, love." He said to her, shadows creeping over his hand. "What did the nixies do?"

"The nixies have a water horse friend that said their troll friend said they found a treasure in the ruins up north. The nixies talked about going on a trip to steal the treasure. Nobbs said that they should take a bunch of the kids from the village to trade for the treasure because trolls like to eat children."

Nira frowned. "And who is Nobbs?"

"Nobbs is the big nixie that takes care of the rest of them. Nobbs is mean."

"Is Nobbs the one who locked your voice away?"

She nods. "He pulled my hair too."

"What a mean little nixie." My mate said moving the girl from one arm to another. My hands tingled slightly, and I narrowed my eyes at him. He met my gaze but shook his head softly. I wondered if he realized yet that I could sense that buzzing in his arms. The aches that took up residence in his shoulders.

"Nobbs isn't little. Nobbs is taller than papa and has

great big hands and tufted ears.”

“Okay, okay. Did they get the treasure?”

“I don’t know, I haven't been back to see them.” Her face fell a bit at that.

“It’s okay. What color is Nobbs?”

“Nobbs is black with shaggy hair, and sometimes he plays with me as a dog, the other nixies are too small to change their shape like that.”

My mate nods. “I see, little one.”

“He bit me once because I wouldn’t follow him into the wilds. I told him my papa would be mad if I went into the wilds.”

“Give me your hand. *Tugaim duit mo scáth a chosaint. Go gcoimeádfaidh sé slán thú fiú nuair nach bhfuilim anseo a thuilleadh.*”[53] His shadows whirled around her small wrist forming small black and quicksilver beads.

“It’s so pretty.”

“Wear it always and it will keep you safe from harm.”

“I will wear it forever.”

He chuckled. “And no more playing with the fae. Nixies or otherwise.”

She frowns. “But—” He gave her a fatherly look. “Okay.”

“Now it is awfully late, and you should be in bed.”

“Do I have to?”

“Yes, I think you do, but how about this? I’ll let you ride on my shoulders, and you can lead me to your room.”

“Okay!”

He helped her scurry around to his back and she took hold of the tines of his antlers. “Okay, Solana, lead the way.”

She guided him up the stairs tugging gently on his antlers to turn him up past the landing.

---

[53] I grant you the protection of my shadow. May it keep you safe even when I am no longer here.

"Be careful with him, Solana." I called after them.

"I will." She called back waving at me.

I smiled as he ducked down the hall, the little girl giggling the whole way. It was only when I heard the click of a door opening that I stood and walked down the stairs to where the others stood clustered together.

"Why would he do something like that?" Farryn asked, still staring after them as if she could see him tucking her seven-year-old into bed.

"Why wouldn't he?" I asked her.

"He was shot by the guard. He had to be treated in the stables that he had to limp into. Why would he free her voice and ask nothing?"

"There is an ask." Katrel said.

Lathai and Farryn looked at her. Lathai asked. "What would you ask of us, your Grace?"

"We need help." She said, uncrossing her arms.

"Anything." Lathai said softly.

"We need a heading. The fastest way to *Magav Hiiglane* and a safe place to stable our horses."

"We can take care of your horses while you are gone but are you sure you need to go to *Magav Hiiglane*. The way is dangerous and that is only accounting for the terrain."

"This we know." Mitta said with a nod.

"Why do you want to venture that deep into the wilds and into the most dangerous terrain in Babylos?"

Katrel took a deep breath. "I am attempting the trial of the flame to win my freedom, my first trial is to retrieve the legendary blade of the flame emperor, Aetherius."

Lathai's eyes widened, but Farryn asked, wiping her face. "Why are you trying to win your freedom? You are not a prisoner; you are a Crown Princess."

"And being Crown Princess to the Raloqen line means I am nothing more than a brood mare for future kings. My autonomy is not a concern to my father or the man he picked for me. I would rather put my life at risk to help those I can in the world of man with my found family than be bound to a marriage bed."

Lathai scoffed. "King Cardoc cannot force your hand, that is cruel and unreasonable."

"But he has." Tummilia confided. "My sister either follows my fathers deranged orders, completes this trial, or submits."

"Could you not just deny his request?" Farryn asked.

"It's not a request." Katrel lamented. "It's an order and defying it would cost all the things and beings I love."

"So, we came as a family to try to guarantee her freedom one way or another." I said.

Lathai nodded and continued forward. "Much of the wilds are not mapped and the creatures that roam them are even more deadly than your friend."

"I have faced plenty of terrible things in my life." My mate said as he descended the stairs, rolling his shoulders.

"Is she—" Farryn asked.

"She's asleep. I know we are on a time crunch, Katrel, but I would like to serve some justice for the little one."

Katrel cocked her hips. "I should have known. Nothing really changes in three hundred years, does it?"

Niratap frowned and Mitta said. "The phooka is the one you want to see isn't it. This Nobbs."

"Phooka? But Solana said they were nixies?" Farryn questioned.

Niratap wrapped his arm around me, pulling me to his side. "Yes. That is the kind of creature she described Nobbs as. Phooka are not dangerous to adults and though it is their nature to be cruel to children, it shouldn't be. Creatures who are oftentimes helpless should help those weaker than them not brutalize them."

"That is a very model view of how things should be, for one such as yourself." Lathai said, his voice carrying a sort of awe.

"I was once one of those helpless ones and I do not wish that for anyone." Nira said and my heart ached. "There is too much cruelty in this world, regardless of the realm."

Lathai nodded. "You all must be hungry after your travels."

"Famished." Tummi said with a broad smile.

"Come. Let's sit at the long table and discuss. Farryn, will you?"

"Of course." Farryn said, turning to the kitchens.

"I'll help you." Bastion said, following behind her. "If you'll allow me."

She started a little at his offer, but Nira said. "Bastion works in the kitchen back home quite often. His parents run it."

She nodded, and they continued through the door behind the bar. I pressed a hand on Nira's arm as he pulled out my chair.

He looked down at me and cocked his head, question in his eyes. *Yes, mo grá?*

I frowned at him, my brows creasing. *Are you alright?*

A subtle shrug and a nod. *Yes, sore but I am alright.*

I sighed. Taking the seat he offered me and letting him scoot it into the table. He sat beside me clutching my hand in his. It still caught me off guard when he opted for more casual clothing, especially when it left his honeyed arms bare, his pale scars visible to the world. His thumb stroked the back of my hand reassuringly. Looking up at his face marred and beautiful, and mine, my heart jumped.

He leaned in, his lips dancing against my ear. "Be careful mate, you keep looking at me with those eyes and I might do something regrettable. You'd enjoy it, but—"

"Could you not?" Mitta hissed on his other side. "We're getting ready to eat, don't ruin all my meals with your stench."

He chuckled softly, kissing my temple. "Apologies, Mitta."

She huffed as Bastion and Farryn carried in trays with steaming bowls of stew and crusty bread. My mouth watered as they set them about the table. Lathai thanked his wife as she took the tray from Bastion and went back to the kitchen. The stew was gamey, but in a delicious earthy way, mellowed by robust tubers and herbs.

"So, your task is to go to *Magav Hiiglane,* in search of the legendary blade, Aetherius, of the Flame Emperor. Is your father mad?" Lathai asked.

"He thinks it an impossible task, where I will either perish or come back home to bend for Revan. The tallest peak is where the sword was last known to be, so that is where I will go."

"And you are prepared for notdeer and cockatrice and tarasque?"

"Tarasque?" I asked.

"They are a relic monstrosity." Niratap said, dipping his bread in the broth. "An old-world monster like myself. They are cunning and large, but not with the capacity of human intelligence like my own race or the animal intelligence that the basilisk has. They are baser creatures, and their only drive is survival. Hunt, kill, eat, and procreate."

I nodded. "Beasts and monsters aren't really high on my list of worries when it comes to this."

"I agree." Katrel said, staring into her stew as if she could divine the path. "What are the chances that this is a wild goose chase?"

Lathai shrugged. "The loss of the flame happened over ten thousand years ago; it could be."

"Ten thousand years is a long time for a sword to be lost." Bastion said around his stew. "Who knows if we will even find it intact; it could be rusted to oblivion."

Lathai shook his head. "Aetherius is a sword created by the gods, it will not rust and fade away to time.

The spear of man is in a museum now under another name than what it was given. Unaffected by time as I've been told."

"So even with the passing of an age, the sword will be whole?"

Lathai nodded. "If what the legends say are correct and it was indeed lost on *Magav Hiiglane* that is where you must travel. I would tell you to follow the river, however, that will add an extra day at least to your trek."

"I would prefer not to travel close to the water with wild kelpies in the waters." My mate said.

"I also don't want to add any extra days to this venture." Katrel said to him. "Leaving my father alone to plot the next trials too long makes me nervous."

Niratap nodded in agreement and Mitta asked. "So, traveling through the forest is the quickest route?"

"Unfortunately. However, there is a stream that also flows from the mountains that you could follow north. It's a half day journey into the wilds."

"Would you be willing to guide us there?"

"No, but I can have one of my hunters guide you there. Vidarr is one of the best. They can lead you there easily and make it home before dark."

"And the stream can lead us to the mountains?"

"I believe so. If the stream veers too harshly you just have to keep a northerly heading. Easier said than done with the canopy, I suppose."

"Then we have our heading." Nira said, leaning back in his chair. "A day to deal with the phooka and nixies, rest, and prepare supplies to trek into the wilds."

There was a hum of agreement, and everyone busied themselves with finishing their meals. Katrel excused herself for the baths after Farryn had showed us to our rooms. The sweet woman apologized profusely for the bed not being long enough for my mate. He assured her he would be fine, even if he ended up sleeping on the floor. Dirt and sweat clung to my skin and I felt gross, looking at the clean sheets of the bed.

"I think I want to bathe."

"Then go to the baths my love." My mate said from where he had sat beside the bed on the floor, stretching his long legs.

"You do not want to accompany me?"

He smiled, looking at me through his lashes and my stomach flipped. "Though our romp in the bath at the castle was world ending; I do not think that the people of Ehiza would appreciate me taking you in their public space."

"We don't have to fuck each other in the baths. What if I just wanted your company?"

He leaned back with a groan. "*Mo grá*, I love you deeply and madly."

"But?"

"But I don't want to be that exposed here."

The flip of my stomach solidified into discomfort. He was exposed here, with just his fair face and demeanor to protect him from attacks, but his body, covered in the scars of his hard life, was a sobering reminder. The stark bands of skin on his wrist and neck were already on display. I frowned at him. "I'm sorry, I wasn't thinking about—"

"It is alright, love. You do not see me as monstrous, something that both floors and comforts me, but those outside our family will see my scars and assume one of two things. Either that I am weak or that I am dangerous even unprovoked. It is not for lack of wanting, but I would rather not put us at risk here."

"Nira, I—"

He held up his hand. "It is alright, Shasha. I can handle how others view me; I have for a long time and now I need to pick my battles. Being exposed around people who could view me either way and act either way is not something that I want to deal with. Especially if it puts you at risk."

I wanted to argue that he didn't need to worry about

me, but I knew he worried about me with his every breath, as I worried about him with mine. "Very well."

He waved me to him and when I was standing between his legs, he looked up at me, devotion in his eyes. His strong hands held me in his space, resting on the back of my thighs. Just the two of us. The only beings in this moment. "You are my everything. Mate. Mine. Go take your bath. I will be here waiting for you."

"I love you." I said, cupping his face in my hands, a shadow of stubble on his chin.

"And I you."

I leaned down, kissing him deeply, letting him fill my soul with his warmth and love. I was always going to cherish this in him.

Chapter Twenty-Four

Katrel

The heat of the bath finally seeped into my bones, the grime, sweat, and dust from the day leaving my skin. How was I going to do this? The talk of traveling into the most hostile territory of my homeland, of maybe not finding the mythic blade of my forefather, it had started a chill in my bones that threaded into my blood. My hands still felt icy to the touch. I sighed, sinking deeper into the magically heated water. I had no idea how long I had been soaking. When I stood to shift to a different part of the pool a familiar gasp echoed off the stones. I peered over my shoulder at Shasha, who stood at the edge of the pool.

"I'm sorry–"

"Don't apologize. Just get in, Shasha." I barked though I hadn't intended to sound so harsh with her.

The gentle splashing of her descending into the pool was the only sound as I shifted closer to where the water flowed into the pool, needing the extra heat for the chill that had renewed in me.

"I know it is ghastly to look at." I said softly. She sat opposite me sinking deeply into the water.

"Niratap says the same about his scars. I think the same thing about my stretch marks. It's your skin, Katrel. It tells the story of your life."

I cocked my head at her. "When did you become so wise? I have three hundred years on you, and I am terrible with what you just said to me."

"Maybe all you ancient, wise beings are wearing off on me." She said with a chuckle.

"It has to be Rogmesh, because the rest of us are not that smart. Especially Niratap. He may be cunning and brave, but the male is dumber than all creation."

She laughed. "He is, but I love him."

I smiled at her. "I'm surprised he didn't come with you."

"He—" She chewed her lip in thought. "He didn't want to be that exposed in mixed company."

I nodded. "I understand that. Elves tend to be a prideful, judgey bunch."

"Are you not worried?"

"In all honesty I really don't care what they think of me. If they see me as I am or as they always have; isn't up to me." I said rubbing my hands together under the water. "Lathai astounded me by just listening to my criticism about my father and agreeing that his ideas for me are wrong."

"It helps that I am not your father's biggest fan, Katrel." I turned as Lathai lowered himself into the water. He was well muscled as I expected from a hunter, across his pale chest are four jagged scars. He wades toward us, but stopped at a respectful distance, Shasha still sank a bit deeper into the pool. Lathai nodded his head at me. "What caused that?"

I glanced at my shoulder where the twisting burn scar edged over, I turned slightly to show him my back. "The cost for saving my sister from the cruelty our father sold her into."

Lathai paled. "Who did—how did that happen?"

"The who is long since dead and not of concern. The how." I swallowed. "I was dipped in acid."

"How did you survive?"

"My agony, along with the suffering of my sister prompted Niratap to free himself from his bonds and slaughter those who held us captive. I know everyone outside of his family views him for what he is." I flicked my eyes at Shasha, her own eyes wide as I bore myself to Lathai and her. "He is a good man."

Lathai nodded. "Bad men don't take care of

children or break spells on them.”

Shasha smiled. “I’m glad that you see that.”

“Niratap has always had a weakness when it comes to children. That is why taking Taegan and Nevin was so important to him. When we broke up rings, if there were children, Niratap was the one who personally saw to caring for them and organizing with social services.” I smiled at Shasha. “He’s a big softy.”

“He is and a cheese.” Sweet laughter bubbled from her. “I couldn’t have found a better man.”

I smiled at her. “I envy you two at times.”

“Why?”

I shook my head, casting Lathai a glance before I said. “I am amazed at how open you are with each other. How free. I wish I could do that for myself.”

“Hopefully soon you can.” Shasha said softly. “We just have to survive this.”

“What are your other trials?” Lathai asked from where he rubbed the dirt of the day away.

“I don’t know.” I said. “He gave me this one to keep me busy while he pondered the others.”

Lathai glanced at me with a scowl marring his face. “It is a dangerous thing that he asked of you. He knows that.”

“The mountains are that treacherous?” Shasha asked.

Lathai nodded. “No one ventures out that way for good reason. The wilds are dangerous.”

“You said that earlier.” Shasha said, splashing water carefully over her neck. “Is it because of that scar?”

“Caught the sharp end of a barghast about twenty years ago. Farryn wouldn’t let me venture far from home after, especially now with Solana in our lives.”

“She seems sweet.” Shasha said happily.

“She is, though she’s not much of an outgoing child.”

“Befriending wild fae and being tricked by them

will do that to someone." I said matter-of-factly. "I
understand that it is dangerous, which is precisely why my
father sent me. He expects the threat of danger to frighten
me, even though I have spent the last three hundred years
fighting in wars and going undercover to save people from
terrible things. He underestimates me. Speaking of the man,
why do you dislike my father?"

"Why do you want to know? Plan to sell me out as a
dissenter to get in his good graces?"

I scoffed. "I could bring your head back to him on a
pike and it would not change his view of me."

Lathai's eyes widened with a healthy dose of fear.
Shasha chided me. "Katrel."

I shook my head. "I wouldn't. However, my father
already had a low opinion of me when I was born, no
matter what fear I claim for myself, no matter the talents I
have or the skills I've perfected. I will be nothing but a
broodmare to his line. I'm only going through these trials
for a chance at freedom, not a guarantee."

"Is the weight of the crown that heavy for you?"
Lathai asked softly.

The crown hadn't scared me when I was a child.
When I thought that one day I would be heir and would be
able to lead my people forward. That reality was crushed
quickly in my pubescence when boys and men were trying
to worm their way to my father through me. Men my
father's age. I sighed. "The weight of the crown was not a
heavy burden, the weight of only being a womb was. The
weight of knowing that the only value that I had to my
kingdom was my body. That weight I have hated with my
whole being the entirety of my life. So, I became
impossible to approach, by the men and boys that were
vying for a chance to be the next king. How shameful it
was to be born female, in the kingdom that I loved. Crown
Princess Katrel the man hater."

Shasha frowned, glaring down at the water. Her
voice shook with rage, which I was intimately familiar

with. "You are more than what you could possibly provide for them."

"I know." I said, trying to fight off tears that burned my eyes. "Both I and my sister were paraded around for men to covet. Men my own age and men our father's age. All for whatever fruit they may seed in our wombs. I carried that as a young girl, and I felt betrayed."

"That is an unfair weight for a child to carry, that was why you never came back." Lathai said.

"It is. I knew he would want to claim me eventually; I just didn't think he would summon me home so soon." Traitorous tears rolled down my cheeks. "I thought I would have more time."

We were silent for several minutes, me sniffling softly and the burbling of the main fountain that fed most of the pools the only sounds. Lathai cleared his throat before he spoke. "I disagree with your father on a fundamental level. I don't agree with his stance on trade, sealing us off from most modern conveniences for the sake of tradition. It doesn't sit well with me. He limits the amount of technology that can come into the realm and rarely does that make it beyond Cardstona or the capitol. I don't think women should be subservient to their husbands, many of my most skilled hunters are women and we would be lost without their keen eyes. Women notice more than men do. Under Cardoc's rule I fear for my daughter's future especially. I know Cardoc is trying to shelter our people from war and drugs, but at what cost?"

Shasha nodded. I swallowed. "Revan will be just as terrible as my father on the throne and though a more noble king would be better for the kingdom, I don't see my father swaying from his choice if I win."

Lathai nodded, already accepting that fate. "I know. The least I can hope for is that my daughter loves someone here that will appreciate and love the skills she has, or she gets to escape to the world of man where I know she won't have it easy, but at least she would have a friend."

He smiled at Shasha when he said that. It was true, wherever Solana ended up Niratap would shelter her. I smiled as well. He was a good friend to me and my sister. I was harsh with him too often, something I would rectify when we were home. If we made it home.

With a sigh I stood and, even after our conversation, was pleasantly surprised when Lathai averted his eyes, respectfully. I tucked myself into the plush robe, tying it tight for the brisk walk back to the lodge. I made to leave, when Lathai spoke.

"For what it is worth, Katrel, I think you would have made a fine ruler."

I froze at the door. Me? A ruler? My heart skipped a beat, before I answered. "Thank you Lathai. For your kind words and help."

"Thank me when you win."

"Niratap, slow down!" Shasha hollered after her mate. "They don't know you're coming to wreak havoc; you can wait for the rest of us."

He growled but stopped his angry prowl. He had woken rather terse, but he and Solana had chatted a bit this morning and something that had been talked about had him extra on edge.

"Apologies, mate. I want to fix this quickly."

She caught his tail and gave it a playful yank. "What's your rush?"

His jaw was clenched with the simmering in him. "This Nobbs, though that is not his true name, was trying to take her, to spirit her away with her name into the bowels of the barrow."

"Is that what she told you this morning?" Shasha asked.

He nodded. "A grave mistake on his part."

I frowned catching up to them. "You plan on taking his name?"

"Yes. By force if I have to."

"How very fae of you, friend." Mitta said at my side.

He chuffed at her. "It is part of my classification, so I do have some of those tendencies. Down this hill is a fae that will pay for hurting that poor girl. For stealing years of her life just for some fun."

Tummilia asked from behind me. "And we're supposed to supervise the nixies?"

"I doubt the nixies will interfere; they know when they are outmatched." Mitta said in answer.

"May we continue?" Niratap asked, with a sweep of his hand.

Shasha laced her fingers through his and kept him at a pace that we could follow. I didn't blame him for his rage, something in that little girl made her increasingly easy to love. The thought of her being yanked into a fae court made my skin crawl, and I knew that I wouldn't interfere with whatever he was going to do to the phooka. The barrow came into view soon after we began to descend the hill. The large mound of earth once used to house the dead, now the home to the fae that had claimed it. Nixies splashed in the river that wended close to the barrow, their laughter a melodic ringing of bells. Atop the barrow sat a few others just watching the merriment. Niratap approached them, Shasha letting his fingers slip through hers as they neared.

"I'm looking for the nixie that goes by the name of Nobbs."

"And who would be asking?" The nixie in the center spoke, his eyes not leaving the river's edge.

"I would." The lord snapped.

At his tone the male in the center turned to look at him. "And you would be?"

"Are you Nobbs?"

"I am."

Shadows whipped out from Niratap's body lashing around the male's limbs, a startled yelp coming from his lips as those shadows raked him down the side of the barrow. The nixies that were beside him fled to the water's edge to watch with the others.

"You will release her, phooka." Niratap snarled as his shadows brought the creature before him.

The creature smiled. "And who might you be?"

"I will be your jailer by the end of this exchange. Release Solana from her binding, now."

"Threatening fae is a dangerous thing to do, shifter."

Niratap slipped his hands into his pockets. "As is testing my patience when it comes to the girl. Release her."

"Make me."

"With pleasure." Niratap sneered, stepping in closer to the fae. "Do you know what I am?"

"Some kind of shifter trying to win a pointless battle."

Niratap's chuckle was dark, wicked even. His fingers shifted into his long talons. "I am a bitarog and I'm about to be your nightmare."

Shasha winced as her mate raked his claws down the front of the phooka, his shrill scream piercing the sky. Blood wept down his torso and he thrashed violently in the grasp of the shadows, hissing. "Release me, you half-feral beast."

"No."

More thrashing and hissing. "I will eat that child the next time I lure her out of that infernal village."

Niratap struck, the deafening crack of bone sundered across the water and made my stomach flip. White bones protruded from the creature's arm, and he bellowed in agony. Niratap leaned in close, whispering into the creature's ear. Nobbs paled, and I knew he had asked for his name. A true name gave another being power over you, complete control.

"I will not." The creature shouted as Niratap eased away from him.

"Tell me your true name, phooka."

"Never."

Niratap cocked his head to the side and watched, amused as the shadows started to twist his good arm. The creature screamed and screamed as his flesh twisted and when his joint popped, I braced for the crunch, as his arm snapped with the tension.

"Name?"

"Nobbs." He sobbed, pathetically.

"No. Your true name." The lord said as the shadows began to twist his left leg.

Shasha placed a gentle hand on her mate's back. I wouldn't have been surprised if it was shaking. She had seen him feral in defense of her, but she had never seen his ruthlessness. One of the many reasons he was feared as much as he was respected. He didn't look at her, didn't acknowledge her. I knew that he couldn't. That he would give the phooka a chance to take advantage of the one he held most dear. The screaming was interspersed with whimpering sobs before the creature's knee gave a sickening pop. Through the whimpering he mumbled something.

"What was that?" Niratap asked.

"Nobskein." The phooka spat. "Neethers."

"Nobskein Neethers." Niratap purred the name, and I felt the magic of it sing through the air. "You will release the girl from whatever trappings you have her wrapped in, firstly. And second, what was the treasure that you were stealing from the trolls? Answer me true."

"I release Solana Gormon from her contract with me and mine, from this moment forward." The shadows dropped him on the ground in a heap of mangled bones. He sobbed in agony.

"The treasure?"

Weeping the creature said. "In the barrow."

"What is it?"

"It is an amulet that the trolls found in the incubi ruins in the desert. It's very beautiful and full of magic. It's yours if you want it."

"Oh, I planned on taking it regardless." Niratap looked back at us and beckoned us to the mound of earth with its small stone doorway. Mitta closed the distance and ducked inside. "Do you know what it is?"

"Just an amulet, I know nothing else. Are you going to kill me?"

Niratap cocked his head again as he looked down at the creature. "It crossed my mind, but I'm not that kind of monster. I'll let you keep your life, but you will stay away from the town and its children."

"I will."

"Nobskein Neethers I command you to swear it upon your life."

"I swear."

"Swear the fealty oath!" Niratap snarled.

The creature swallowed. "I, Nobskein Neethers, swear under the holy sun and divine moon that I will not hunt the children of the elves and will let them live in peace under the penalty of returning to the earth if I fail in my oath."

Mitta exited the barrow, the dazzling amulet glittering in her hand. It felt like Voxviraz did, both menacing and seductive. Shasha moved past the lord and the broken phooka to take the amulet. She examined it carefully before looking back at her mate, whose tail twitched in agitation.

"How do we know if it's the one we're looking for?" She asked.

He didn't look at her; just continued to glare at the creature at his feet. He asked. "Do you know what temple the trolls sacked?"

"Lilith or something like that, they weren't very clear."

"Lilitu?" Niratap pressed.

"Yes, that is what the kelpie said." Nobskein whimpered. "Lilitu, the goddess that the fiends worship."

Niratap at last looked at his mate, stepping around the broken creature. He slipped it from her hands and into his pocket as he whispered imperceptibly in her ear. She nodded and pressed a gentle kiss to his cheek. He met her eyes and the intensity of that stare. The devotion that I saw there. I wish I had something like that. I hadn't found it outside of my kingdom and I doubt I would find it here either. If I failed. Revan would use me to further the royal line. Claim me as my father had claimed my mother. I shivered at the thoughts.

"Are you going to leave me like this?" Wailed Nobskein.

Niratap huffed. "I suppose not. Mitta would you set his limbs and knee."

"Of course, my Lord."

"Tummi. Could you heal him?"

"Yes." My sister elbowed gently past me.

"Heal him enough that he won't die from his injuries."

"Yes, my Lord."

"Leave the knee mangled so he can remember his oath."

"Of course."

Niratap cupped his mate's face as Tummi and Mitta got to work. The cracking and grating and screaming wormed under my skin needling at my resolve to stand there. I swallowed and took a breath. I could withstand this.

Niratap said without breaking Shasha's gaze. "Let that pain be a reminder not to test me further. The oath will be the least of your worries if you fuck with me. Understand?"

Nobskein nodded, his face wan and a sickly green.

"Do you understand me, Nobskein?"

"I understand you, Lord."

Shasha's eyes narrowed at her mate as he turned to leave. Whatever silent conversation they had been having, had not gone in her favor. She stormed after him across the clearing not ready to be done.

"We're leaving." He said as he walked past me. A haunted look in his eyes. I did not envy him for the harsh conversation they were going to have. Tomorrow we would be leaving for the mountains, with a hope and prayer we would come back home. I hoped we would.

Chapter Twenty-Five

Shasha

How dare he. Yes, the brutality with which he had handled the phooka was shocking. I had never seen him so cruel. Not that I faulted him for it. I knew when we had left the lodge he was out for blood, but I hadn't expected that.

His words he'd whispered to me as he had taken the amulet from me still ran wild and untamed in my mind.

"I am sorry, mo grá. I am sorry you had to see that. He cannot have my mercy not after what he tried to do to that little girl, what he succeeded in doing to her. I'm sorry I wasn't forthcoming in my intentions for the day. This is one of my faces and I am sorry that makes me a monster."

"You are not a monster." I said with a kiss.

He had just stared at me, his gaze equal parts awed and haunted. Even as I willed it into my eyes, *you are not a monster, you are not a monster, you are not a monster.* He had only cupped my face gently and I felt him trembling while he gave his threats and orders. Then he walked away.

He was ahead of the rest of us. Keeping his distance while he came to terms with what he had done. I frowned at his back, wanting to get into that space and reassure him. Panic had made him twitchy and that had made my heart race uncomfortably in my chest, almost battering against my ribs. I didn't like it. Both the sensation and that he still feared I would turn away from him at the simple show of brutality. He was always so careful with me, not that I minded his doting, but the man had a way of forcing himself to be the villain. He was mistaken, but the twisting in my gut told me he wasn't ready to forgive himself. That was another thing we needed to share; I wanted to know if he felt what I felt. I thought I was feeling him, his emotions and the shifting aches in his body. We wouldn't have that conversation soon with his mood. I sighed.

"Don't fret, Milady. It's not you that has him in knots." Katrel said softly to me.

"I know." And I did but it didn't make my heart slow. "I wish he would talk to me instead of twisting himself in knots."

"Men aren't good at the talking thing."

"Hey!" Bastion barked behind us. "I take offense to that!"

Katrel chuckled, but there was a cold edge to it. "Bastion it's okay, the adults are talking."

"Kat!" Tummi chided. "Just because you're older than him doesn't mean you can talk to him like that. He is an adult."

I smiled softly at Bastion, he had been distant since Taegan's funeral, a weight that had bogged my mate down. He should have told him sooner, but I understood why he didn't. Bastion had taken the news about as well as Niratap had. Grief that had him crawling into my skin, the only comfort I could offer.

Bastion returned my smile even as he continued to glare at Katrel, Tummi a comforting presence at his side. I was glad they had found each other. I hoped Mitta and Katrel could find some common ground. There was tension there that I was sure everyone was aware of. Back at the lodge Solana charged towards Niratap as soon as he was through the door.

"Nira! Did you find treasure?"

He crouched down as she approached, running into his outstretched arms. She was oblivious to the blood that we both saw on the hand he had used to wound Nobskein. He tucked that hand into his pants pocket to hide it from the child.

"We found something, though I don't think you will find it that interesting." With his other hand he pulled a small sky-blue stone from his opposite pocket.

"Oooooo." She cooed, taking the stone. "Did Nobbs and the nixies give you trouble?"

He smiled softly. "You won't have to worry about Nobbs or those nixies anymore."

"Really?"

"Yes, but I want you to stay away from the fae regardless. They are very dangerous."

She frowned. "I liked the way the nixies braided my hair."

He chuckled softly, pressing a loving kiss to her brow. "My Shasha also braids very well. She does her own hair."

The girl beamed up at me over his shoulder. "Really?"

I smiled. "Yeah, I can braid your hair, sweetheart."

"Can you put flowers in my hair?"

I saw what he was doing. "I can."

"Nira, will you tell me a story? While Shasha braids my hair?"

"While I do love that idea, I will have to pass on it for today."

"Why?" She pouted.

"I am very tired."

My heart skittered in my chest. He was being honest with the child; I felt that heavy weight in my body. Had that show of brutality taxed him so? "Solana, let him rest. I can tell you a story while I braid your hair."

She pouted at me. "Okay."

Nira pressed a kiss to her brow before he stood. He turned and looked at me with those silver eyes that stretched into oblivion. He pulled me to him, his clean hand cupping the back of my head. There was still fear in those eyes, but understanding laced through them as well. "Later, *mo grá*."

"Later." It was a promise.

When I finished telling Solana not one, but three stories her mother ferried her off to help in the kitchen before the dinner rush. The little girl excitedly retold the story of goldilocks to her mother. Farryn smiled at me as they left.

I went down the hall and stood before our room door, listening for any indication of the man beyond the door being awake. I felt him. The sensation of him in my skin was jarring but comforting all the same. His breath was easy in my lungs, restful.

I walked farther into the lodge's many roomed hall. Tummi and Bastion laughed in their room. Katrel and Mitta's door across the hall was ajar. I knocked.

"Yes?" Katrel called.

"Hey." I said, pushing into the room. "I—I don't want to bother him when he's sleeping, and I don't have anywhere to go."

Katrel smiled sadly at me. "He does that. Almost every time."

"He's done that before?" I don't know why I asked. I knew he had to unleash that part of himself.

She nodded, leaning back in the bed to stare at the ceiling. "How do you think he garnished the fear that allowed him to walk freely through the black market?"

"I meant the hiding. I know it was more than what he is that garnered the fear on the market floor."

She frowned. "Yes. He has always been standoffish when he has had to be brutal. I think he needs it to remind himself that he isn't the bad guy. Sometimes it takes longer than others."

I sat on the edge of the bed. "Do you know anything about mate bonds?"

She barked a laugh behind me. "No. Between the two of us, you are the expert."

I sighed. "That's my problem. The dream walking was one thing, but there's more now and I don't know what's going on."

"More?"

"I can feel him. It's more than his presence. I feel his emotions. I feel his pain. Niratap and I haven't had a chance to talk about it." I rubbed my face and held my head in my hands. "I don't know if he is feeling it too or if I'm just going crazy."

"You're not crazy." Katrel said softly. "I'd give him a couple more hours and then go slip in there. I know you want to talk to him and knowing my friend, he really does want your comfort."

I laid back on the bed. "Sometimes I question whether he wants me with him or not."

"He wants you there." Katrel said softly. "He's just afraid he won't be able to protect you."

"Even after I saved him?"

"Especially after you saved him."

I sighed. "Men."

Katrel laughed. "Don't hold it against him. You were a wild card none of us were expecting. He loves you and just wants you safe, happy, and healthy."

"I know." Tears pricked my eyes, and I hated that my voice wobbled. "Those things can't happen for a long time though."

Katrel didn't speak for several moments. "You're probably right and the path to that point is a long one with plenty of pain ahead. I wouldn't still be with Niratap if I didn't think he could succeed."

"Even now?" I asked. "He's still not recovered from the basilisk or from being tortured."

"Yes. He's noble to a fault regardless of how his actions may seem at the time. He is good. An ass at times, and stubborn, and I wish he would ask for help more than he does, but he is good. That is all I need to know in order to follow him. I like having the freedom of choosing that he gives me. He never expects me to follow blindly and after what he did for me and Tummi, I will always be in his debt.”

“And what about your birthright? What about being queen?”

“I’m not wholly opposed to ruling Babylos, but I would want to pick my partner and rule by my terms. Not be a womb for the next Cardoc.”

I nodded. “You should get that right.”

“Choice has always been important to Niratap. In our situations we were robbed of it and now he protects it and he doesn’t let us get bullied into not having it.”

“You shouldn’t be forced into doing anything. I knew he was out for vengeance this morning and I wasn’t prepared, but it was necessary for that little girl and the rest of the children of the town. I don’t inherently agree with the amount of force. However, once it started there was no going back, and I wasn’t going to undermine him. Even if I didn’t have a choice at that moment.”

“That was one of the things that we fought about after he brought you home. Your lack of choice. He hadn’t given you that, and we were not kind to him about it. We didn’t agree with him owning you. Those arguments are probably floating through his mind right now because he didn’t give you a choice and you were scared in those moments.”

“I was, but not of him. Never of him.”

“Scared of the violence he used. You know he’d never use that against you.”

“I know but it was still startling. Still shocking.”

Mitta stepped into the room; her face etched with worried lines. She paused when she saw me. “I hope I’m not intruding.”

“You’re not.” Katrel said flatly. “It is your room too.”

"We were just talking about this morning." I added.

She sighed, sinking into a chair. "He's still hiding away I take it."

I nodded. "I think he is actually asleep though."

"Well, that's good. That he's resting, not that he's hiding."

I shrugged. "He's so concerned with me being afraid of him and he doesn't realize that I just want to be with him. I don't care if he's ruthless or cruel when it is required of him because I know he is a good man."

Mitta smiled. "He is."

"How did talking with Lathai go?" Katrel asked, sitting up to face her.

"Well enough. I met with Vidarr. They seem to be wise, though they are younger than I expected."

"Are they sure of the path?" Katrel asked.

"Yes. I was shown roughly on a map, I'm still not comfortable but we're out of time."

"Two nights in uncharted land will do that." I said.

"It's so much more than that." Mitta sighed again. "As long as we're together."

"We can conquer anything together."

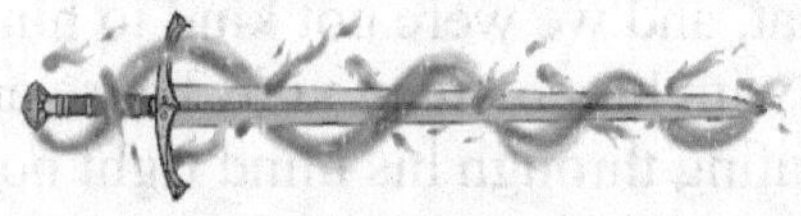

It was dark before I made it back to our room. Niratap was curled in the mound of blankets we had fashioned into a bed. The actual bed was made and tidy. I hadn't slept in it last night, preferring to be curled against him. I set the bread and cheese that I had brought up on the table before I crept toward him.

"Nira?" I whispered, stepping over his tangle of legs careful not to crush his tail. He didn't stir even as I crouched and curled up next to him. My back to him with space between us. I sighed. "I'm sorry. For whatever it was today that caused you to hide. I'm sorry."

His arm banded across my stomach and pulled me against his firm body. His voice was rough and edged with sleep. "Why are you apologizing? What do you have to be sorry for?"

I stroked my thumb over the back of his hand. "Nothing."

He sighed into the back of my head. "I'm sorry for making you worry. I'm sorry you had to see that."

"I am not afraid of you." His sharp intake of breath told me everything. "And I'm not afraid of what you did. I am yours and you are mine. Nothing you do will change that."

He pulled me tighter against him. "*Is leatsa mise agus is liomsa tú.*"

Though his lilting Irish was still hard for me to understand. I knew he had repeated my words. "Yes. I am yours and you are mine."

He nestled closer, pressing a kiss to the nape of my neck. "I'm sorry."

"Stop." His tongue was hot on my neck, sending my pulse skittering. "Stop apologizing to me."

"Why?" His hands roamed sliding under my shirt and slipping beneath the waistband of my pants.

"Nira."

"Yes, mate?"

"You're impossible. You know that right?"

"I need—"

I rolled my body against him, a deep throated groan an answer to my question. "What do you need, love?"

"You, always you."

I twisted in his grip, our faces a breath away from one another. "I need you to listen to me."

"I do listen to you." He moved to press a kiss to my lips.

I blocked him with a hand. "Niratap, what is wrong? Why are you so afraid that I am going to leave you?"

His eyes sparked with the sharp pain that shot through my heart. "Because everyone I have ever loved has been hurt or forcibly taken from me and I do not want to lose you. I—I never want to feel that broken again."

I cupped his scarred face in my hands. "I cannot promise you that the world will not try to rend us from one another. I cannot promise you that Cardoc, or the market, or whoever this lich is trying to get to you, will not try to break us apart. I cannot not promise you that we will survive. I can only promise you that I love you with every fiber of my heart, my soul, my essence and I will fight to keep you with me. So do not mistake my fear of the world as fear of you. Do not mistake my anger at the terrible things that happen around us as anger at what you have to do to end it. Do not mistake my tears for those who are suffering as tears that I am suffering. As long as I have you, Niratap, as long as you are mine and I am yours, I am nothing but happy and honored to be at your side and nothing, absolutely nothing, that you or others do, will be able to take that away. I will not let them take me away."

He stared at me with those warm pools of moonlight that were equally full of love and sorrow. His hand cupped my face and no matter where the worlds took us; no matter what life had in store for us, I would follow this man anywhere. We were as sure as the sun and moon rising day and night. A constant, sure thing. He pressed his brow to mine.

"*Ta mo chroi istigh ionat.*"[54]

"What does that mean?"

"You are my heart."

I closed my eyes breathing him in. I would never tire of that wild smell of rain. "You are mine."

"I know you don't want to hear my apologies, Shasha, but I don't know how else to be."

"I'm not asking that you change, Niratap. I just

[54] You are my heart.

want you to know that I will be with you always."

He rolled on top of me, sinking his body between my legs. His lips met mine in demand. He was begging me to stay with that kiss. Begging me to never leave him alone. I sent a prayer to any god that would hear me to let us be. Let us stay together no matter what. We had both almost died to save one another. We both were willing to sacrifice everything to keep one another. We had already fought for it and that should have been enough. Gods, I hoped it was enough.

Chapter Twenty-Six

Shasha

That next morning, we set off. Vidarr was a slight elf who stood no taller than myself, gender-ambiguous with bright green eyes, a sweet smile with a scar, and a lilting voice that was soft like the sunrise as we traipsed into the forest. The golden light filtered eerily through the spring leaves that swayed in the breeze. We ventured deeper and deeper into that dewy green, the trails narrow and overgrown, full of the stamps of wildlife that traveled them.

"What do you think we'll come across?" Mitta asked Vidarr, breaking the early morning quiet.

"I hope nothing." Vidarr said without looking back. Their voice was warm but graveled with the early hour. "There are plenty of creatures that roam the forest. The cockatrice and notdeer are my biggest concerns, though they are typically nocturnal creatures. It will be more of a concern when you guys break for camp."

"Should we travel through the night and camp during the day?" Niratap asked.

"No. I would not travel through the night at all. The creatures here will stalk you and traveling, you will be easy to separate. Camp at night and if one of you can put up a barrier do it. Cockatrices aren't fond of fire, and the not deer shouldn't attack if you are grouped together."

"Emphasis on the shouldn't." Bastion quipped.

"Shouldn't." Vidarr smirked over their shoulder. "As you know, Lathai and I have warned you that this is a risky endeavor that you are on."

"Do you think we should give up?" Katrel half growled.

Vidarr turned, walking backward to speak. "Never. I want nothing more than for you to succeed in this. Prove to Cardoc that we are more than wombs to be bred."

"You think that winning my freedom will grant the kingdom that?" Katrel pressed.

"No, but I hope that it will." They said, facing forward again. "It would change the lives of many if it does."

"Cardoc seems unmoved by what the girls have accomplished back on the other side of the portal. What do you think beating him at his own game will prove?" Niratap asked.

"Everything." They said wistfully, turning at a break in the trail.

"I don't understand." Tummi said.

"If the Crown Princess," Katrel sighed at the title, "can prove that she is strong and capable, that will tell the kingdom that females as a whole are strong and capable. It could most ideally set into motion a revolution."

"Giving them a voice in what they do with their bodies and their lives." I added.

They nodded. "There are many women in Ehiza that hunt; most are better than the men."

"Lathia said you were one of his best hunters." Nira said, ducking below a low branch.

"I am. Lathai has the skill of seeing potential in everyone and he pushes everyone in the community to strive for greatness. All roles are open to everyone." They wormed their way through some brush and bramble.

"If this liberation happens, what would that entail?" Bastion asked.

"At worst women will have more protections and more variety in how they live their lives. At best things will equalize as a whole and those that have been banished will be allowed to come back home."

"From Pamiršta?" Tummi asked.

"Yes, and the world of man."

"How many souls have been lost?" Mitta pressed.

"Too many."

"Do you think it would–" Niratap started to ask.

Vidarr raised a hand to their lips, shushing our conversation. Niratap stalked to their side sniffing the air. He growled, his shadows trailing across the ground and into the brush. He turned to the left, his eyes scouring through the trees for whatever they had found. I drew my knife as the forest fell deathly silent, not even the bugs sang. The sisters quietly flanked Nira, and I felt Bastion and Mitta come to my back.

"We're being hunted." Mitta said to me after scenting the air.

A white serpent leaped from the greenery, and Vidarr fired an arrow through its head, spearing it to a tree. It thrashed there violently before it stilled with a dying hiss.

I relaxed. "A snake."

Vidarr peered at the animal and spat on the ground. "A feathered asp, they are rarely alone."

"There are more of them?" Bastion asked, glaring at the snake.

"Most definitely and a cockatrice."

"Great." Katrel growled. "Just what we need an hour and a half into this journey."

"It is rather close to the town. I will have to let Lathai know." Vidarr said softly. "Be vigilant and guard your eyes."

I swallowed and Bastion asked. "Our eyes?"

"Cockatrice have eyes that can paralyze you." Tummi said next to him.

"We move forward quietly." Vidarr said, knocking another arrow as they moved forward.

We moved on as the sun rose higher and higher in the sky. No other snakes appeared and neither did their master cockatrice as we came to a clearing, the sun high above us as a small stream trickled by.

"This is where I leave you." Vidarr said. "If you follow the stream, it should lead you to the mountains."

"You will be fine going back on your own?" Niratap asked.

"I will. The cockatrice does not frighten me. Neither do the snakes; they are just obstacles on the path home. You are the ones who will need to be careful. Keep a strong barrier at night and keep close to each other."

Niratap bowed his head. "We will. May I?"

He reached out his hand, palm up, offering it to them as shadows danced along his fingers. Vidarr stared at his hand, before tentatively placing their hand into his. *"Tugaim cosaint mo scáthanna duit, chun tú a threorú slán abhaile."*[55] The shadows wrapped around their wrist and formed into a soft band, and Nira released them.

"Thank you, young lord." They bowed deeply. "May the road rise to meet you."

He smiled at them. "May the sun shine warm upon your face."

They returned the smile. "Until we meet again."

And they left.

We didn't break long in the clearing, moving along the small stream into the never-ending dense woods. The afternoon sun was hot even through the trees. The light played through the spans of spring leaves and danced on the water.

"Do you think we are being hunted?" I asked no one in particular.

"Can we not talk so cryptically, Shash?" Bastion growled behind me. I could see his eyes roll at the back of

---

[55] I grant you the protection of my shadows, to guide you safely home.

my head.

"Probably." My mate answered me. "However, they may only be watching to see where we go and what we are. Most should leave us be."

"You hope." Mitta said beyond him.

Niratap shrugged. "I am the scariest thing in the forest. At least currently I smell nothing other than deer and birds."

"That's cause enough for concern." Katrel snapped. "Between notdeer and harpies, I would rather not."

"Ha. There are no harpies or notdeer in the vicinity."

"Your little shadows telling that to you, my friend?" Mitta said over her shoulder.

"The shadows are watching out for us." He said softly.

"I'm not concerned about the creatures in the shadows; the lord will keep us safe." Tummi said.

"Neither am I, but he is fun to tease." Mitta laughed.

"I guess I'm not safe anywhere." He chuckled, softly.

We all laughed. I stepped on a stone and my ankle rolled. The pain was sharp and I swore. Niratap caught me before I hit the ground.

He scooped me up into his arms. "You need to watch yourself, love."

"I'm fine. I just tripped on a stone." I groaned as he took my pack.

"Humor me, mate." He nuzzled my cheek and continued with the sun.

He carried me as the sun dipped lower and lower in the sky until we came upon a small clearing. His arms ached as he set me gingerly on my feet, the throb mirrored in my own shoulders.

"Are you alright?" I asked as he stretched the soreness loose.

"I am fine, mate."

"This place will have to do for tonight." Mitta said. "It's flat enough to sleep."

Niratap nodded, setting our packs down. "Agreed. I'll gather some firewood."

"Nira, let me help you." I said testing my ankle.

"No Shasha, rest that ankle." He smiled softly. "I will be fine."

"Stay close." I urged.

"I will." He pressed a kiss to my cheek. "Set up our bedrolls."

I watched him as I rolled out the mats. His long body dipping in and out of the brambles; his arms filling with small branches. I rolled my shoulders, trying to alleviate the buzzing there and the tingling in my hands. We needed to talk about this. This connection, that I loved and hated, had me so worried about him with the near constant phantom pains that shot through my body. Maybe I was going crazy.

"Are you going to be able to build a barrier?" Mitta asked as he came back into the clearing.

"Yes."

"The magic isn't going to tax you?"

He frowned at her. "I will be fine, Mitta."

"I just want to be sure; your pride could get us killed."

He scoffed as he started to build the fire. "Do you think I would put all of us at risk like that? I know what my limits are."

"Could have fooled me." Katrel said.

He sighed, irritated and remorseful. "I am sorry for what I have put you all through. I do not need a reminder of it, but it is my nature. I promise you that I can keep us safe with my magic."

"How does the barrier magic work?" I asked.

"It's much like that wall that I used at the auction to protect us from bullets."

"The one that caused your body to attack itself?" I asked frowning.

"My reserves are replenished, my body is healed, and it won't need to be as thick to keep creatures out."

"Nira, I don't want you putting yourself in a situation where we don't have the medicine or tools to keep you on this side of the soil." I growled.

"Trust me, mate. I will not risk myself in such a way that leaves you unprotected."

"It is not a lack of protection I am worried about!" I shouted at him, the whole camp taking a breath at my outburst.

He sighed at the skeleton of sticks that was to be a fire. "I am okay, love. Sore, yes, but I am well enough to do this. I promise you."

I frowned. "I just want you safe."

My chest ached as he lifted his face to me. His face pinched in anger but also defeat. "I know." He stood then stretching his long body. He surveyed the clearing before closing his eyes. He took a big breath and held his hands out palms down. Shadows pulled from the edges of the clearing, climbing up his legs to gather in his palms.

"*Guím ar na scáthanna is faide a chaith an ghrian ag dul i dtír sinn a chosaint ó dhochar.*"[56] The shadows fell from his hands and spread like spilled ink across the ground. "*Iarraim ort sinn a bhac ó radharc agus ó fhuaim. Go dtí go bpógann an ghrian an talamh arís.*"[57]

Shadows rose forming a globe over us. Blocking out the light for a moment before the wall shimmered and let the fading light dance over the camp once more. He rolled his shoulders and shook out his hands before opening his eyes.

"Are you well?" Mitta asked.

---

[56] I beseech the shadows cast longest by the setting sun to shelter us from harm.

[57] I ask that you block us from sight and sound. Until the sun kisses the earth again.

"I am." He gave her a curt nod, before he faced me. His face was carved cruelty, but his eyes were soft, vulnerable.

I looked away from him and continued setting out the bedrolls. He sighed and kneeled to go through our packs. Regret twisted in my stomach, and I felt terrible to have doubted him. Where was the line where it was doubt and not concern. I huffed to myself and laid back on the bed roll, staring up at the setting sun as Mitta got the fire going and Bastion strummed his guitar.

"I don't know why you brought that." Katrel growled.

"Entertainment. Even though I love you all, we don't have new stories to tell."

"There are plenty of stories Shasha doesn't know." Tummi said.

"Plenty of embarrassing Bastion stories to tell." Katrel added.

"Hey now, that's not fair."

Niratap nudged me with the bag of rations from my pack. "Eat."

"What about you?" I asked sitting up.

"You eat first."

I pulled a piece of dried meat from the bag. "Eat."

He frowned but took the meat, tearing off a section with his fingers. Watching me as I pulled an apple from the bag and halving it with my knife. I handed him one. "I'm sorry."

"What for?"

"For doubting you."

He chewed the meat thoroughly before swallowing. "You didn't doubt me. You just worry for me, and I do realize that I don't make that easy."

"Unbearably."

He smirked and offered me a section of dried meat. We ate in amenable silence. Bastion strumming away on his guitar; singing as the sun disappeared from the sky and the stars blew it up. My eyes traced over the familiar sky as I curled into my mate's side, his breathing steady and relaxed. If only we could stay in this relative peace because even with the journey still long and arduous ahead of us, I wanted to just lay with him under the sky. I pressed my cheek to his chest to listen to the strong beat of his heart.

"What is on your mind, *mo grá?*"

"I just want this with you, always."

He chuckled lightly, pulling me close. "Adventure?"

"No."

"Then what, my heart?"

I smiled to myself. "Peace."

"That is a hard ask with all we have against us."

"I know." My voice went watery as tears edged my vision. "Do you think we will find it?"

He shifted me so he could look at me, his calloused thumb brushing away the errant tear. "Shasha, I don't know. What I do know is that I will fight with all that I am to get us there."

I pressed my cheek into his hand. "We. We will fight for it."

"I don't expect you to fight my battles."

"I know, but I won't let you fight alone."

He pressed a kiss to my brow. "I know. Now rest mate. We have a long day ahead of us."

I fell asleep to the sound of his heart beating beneath my ear.

He hadn't lied to me as we trekked the wilds the next day, the terrain grueling and uneven. After lunch Nira shifted into that wildest shape of his and demanded that I rode on his back. He ardently refused to let me walk, so astride his back I went and we continued on. Katrel and Tummi teased his male need to provide for me, and I chuckled when he growled in playful annoyance at them. This shape was easier on his body somehow. Even with my added weight, his movements were smoother and more at ease. I stroked the sable grey strands beneath my fingers, loving the softness of them.

I needed to talk to him. I needed to know. Feeling him in all aspects was becoming taxing on my mind. If I understood, maybe it would ease my stress and maybe I wouldn't be so afraid. He peered at me over his shoulder quizzically, his silver eyes sinking deep into my soul. He saw me. He saw that I was twisted up in knots over something. We would talk soon. I could see it in that look. I reached forward and scratched behind his ear. He purred at the touch, the vibration sluicing through me. I frowned at him, and he just chuffed happily to himself.

When the sun started to dip low, we found a clearing, smaller than yesterday's, to bed down for the night. After gathering firewood and rolling out the beds, Niratap shifted, pulling the shadows again from the depths of the forest around.

"You good?" Bastion asked him as he rolled his shoulders.

"Yes." Nira answered, his lips pulling into a frown.

Bastion held his hands up in innocence. "I was just checking. Don't bite me."

The corners of Nira's lips pulled a little closer to a smile before Mitta said. "I don't like this spot you picked."

The phantom smile disappeared. "Why, Mitta?"

"There's too much foot traffic through here. All kinds of animals from deer to whatever made that." She pointed to a large, round feline paw print.

"A chimera and it's a few days old, most of it is deer and probably notdeer." He shrugged. "The barrier should keep those creatures away."

"Should is not a guarantee, Niratap!" She growled

and poked him in the chest.

"I'm confident that we can handle those creatures should they somehow get through my barrier. If it eases your concern, Mitta, I will take first watch."

"It doesn't, but fine." She growled but smiled when she flopped down on her bedroll.

He chuckled, grabbing his pack and pulling the rations sack free. "So persnickety, Mitta."

She huffed but said nothing as everyone settled in for the evening, eating our meager ration meals and Bastion serenading us until the sun settled over the horizon. The crackle of the fire was the only sound for company then as I tossed and turned. Unable to sleep I stared into the blackness of the world beyond the barrier. The fire's crackle was the only sound when Nira lay behind me, finally off his watch. He pulled me close, kissing my neck.

"You should be asleep, *mo grá*."

"It's hard to sleep without you." I murmured.

He nuzzled my neck. "I'm here now."

I leaned into his warmth. "I find now that I don't want to sleep with you near anyway."

He chuckled. "Mate now is not the time to mess with my baser instincts."

"If I'm on watch I better not see or smell anything, you heathens." Mitta growled from her post by the tree.

"Mitta, there is no need to worry. The barrier will keep the unsavory creatures away from us. Rest."

"I am resting, but I will watch." She said smiling at me. "Keep your clothes on."

"I wasn't going to give him my flesh." I looked up at him. His face was tight with exhaustion. "I did want to talk with you, if you would be open to it."

He kissed me sweetly. "Of course, my love."

"You do need to rest through." I cupped his cheek.

"Let us talk, then we both can sleep."

I nodded, laying back against the bed roll. "Things between us are changing."

He tensed. "Shasha, if you are afraid that I would turn my claws against you, I would never. I would sooner cut my own heart from my chest."

"No, mate." I said softly. My hands covering his. "I am not afraid of you. I will never be afraid of you. You are my everything and nothing you do will change that."

He audibly swallowed, his voice dropping low. "You honor me, every day you choose me."

"And I will choose you every day. Never think otherwise." I swallowed my fears, trying to overcome what I wanted to say. "Our bond. I think it is changing, and I want to know if you feel it too, if you felt me like I feel you."

"How do you mean?" He asked, and I palmed my knife.

"I've been feeling your emotions, even when they aren't painted on your face. I've felt your pain. When your joints ache I feel it in mine."

"Shasha—"

"When Cardoc tried to poison you, I felt the burn in your belly. Do you feel it?" I gripped the blade in my hand tightly. He hissed, twisting me underneath him, my knife bouncing across the ground.

He glanced at his palm, his skin unmarred and looked down at me, at my hand. "Why would you do that?"

"You felt that?"

"I did, but why would you harm yourself to prove a point?" He glared at me as his magic zinged through the air and warmth flooded my body. I felt the flicker of panic in his heart.

"It is just a cut. A flesh wound."

He frowned pressing his brow to mine. "The wound that almost took my life last fall was just a flesh wound. Do not do that again."

"Nira. I did not mean to cause you distress. I just wanted to know."

"Then ask me, but do not hurt yourself again."

"You're one to talk. You've been tied in knots since we arrived in Babylos. Over everything. It's been so much more than the way your cuffs sit on your skin."

He sighed, resting his head against my shoulder, and a sharp crack ached in my heart. "I'm sorry."

I pressed my face to his neck, biting down on his flesh. The spot on my own neck that mirrored his tingled lightly. He groaned as I pulled away and kissed the spot.

"No fucking." Mitta scolded.

"No." I said softly. "Not tonight."

"I—"

"Want me?" I lifted my hips against him, his hardness present there. "Not tonight."

He sputtered. "Woman, you torment me."

I laughed. "And Mitta will skin you alive if you try to bury your favorite appendage."

"It's not my favorite, it's yours."

"Shh." Mitta stood, drawing her sword.

"What is it?" Nira asked lifting his head.

"I don't know, but there are many of them."

Nira shifted as a doe peered at the barrier. "A heard of deer."

Nira stood watching. "Not just deer."

A large stag nudged the doe forward, but something about it was just wrong. It peered at us scenting the air. "What is it?"

"A notdeer."

The stag leered at us, a second set of eyes opening upon its brow. The tips of its antlers pressed against the barrier, unfurling against the one-way wall into—

"Are those hands?" Bastion groaned. "Am I having a nightmare?"

"No Bas, this is very real." Mitta said as I got up.

"Shasha—"

"What? It's on the other side of the barrier. It can smell us, but it can't hear or see me." I said, approaching the strange monster. "When will I ever get a chance to

330

observe one of these again?"

He frowned at me but didn't come to my side. I looked at the wild creature again. By all passing glances it would pass for a deer, though it was taller than an elk and unnervingly thin like it was starved. It huffed against the barrier scenting me on the other side. The green slit eyes flared as its black forked tongue slid from its mouth slapping wetly against the wall.

"That's gross." Katrel said from where she had slept.

"And fascinating." I replied.

"Only the girl obsessed with monsters would find that fascinating." She quipped.

"I want to know if the drawings in the text that Cyran showed me were accurate. I'm increasingly curious as I get introduced to more and more wild creatures. They fascinate me."

The creature chuffed, its breath fogging the barrier. Seams split down the center of its jaw to its chest and along the sides. It opened like it was a blooming flower, a gaping maw filled with serrated teeth and sharp fangs descended from its jaw that oozed a viscous liquid. It may have been wrong, but I found the terrifying creature beautiful. Even as its jaw flexed against the barrier as if it tasted us.

"Help me." A child's voice came from the maw.

"That's just wrong." Tummi pointed out.

"Hello? Help me." The notdeer continued.

"I will admit that is a very effective way to capture prey." Niratap observed, placing a hand on my shoulder.

"Help me. Its dark and I'm scared."

"Definitely a nightmare." Bastion said, lying back down and covering his face.

"Help me. It's coming after me. Help me."

"I don't think any of us are getting more sleep tonight with that there." Mitta said, sheathing her sword. "Can you scare it off?"

"Help me. Help me. Please. Somebody." A

woman's voice called into the void.

"Gladly." Shadows danced around me and into the barrier wall. The shadows snaked around the not deer's legs and the creature screamed a very human sounding scream. It thrashed against their hold.

"Beautiful." I gasped as the side of the creature lit up. "Bioluminescence."

"Let me go! Help me! Help me!" It thrashed free, and fled, into the void of the night, the actual deer following it.

"Satisfied." Niratap asked.

"For now." Mitta said staring after the creature. "Now all of you go to bed; dawn is still a few hours away."

Chapter Twenty-Seven

Bastion

The dawn came too soon and after a night plagued with visions of hand antlers—hantlers—handlers—I yawned to fight off the shudder. We had made impressive time through the wilds following Vidarr's instructions, and as the foliage thinned and then opened to rocky dirt, the terrain starting to pitch uphill, I felt silly for doubting the young elf. Gone was the softer loam for hard clay and shale, the shade nonexistent as we trudged up the carved game trails into the foothills.

"I was hoping there would be more cover as we headed into the mountains." The lord said pausing at the crest of a hill.

"Let's hope we can find a cave tonight that is unoccupied." Mitta said as she passed him.

"Unoccupied would be preferred." I groaned. "I don't want to have to cuddle with something that will eat me."

"That's funny since you've been cuddling with my sister every night." Katrel barked behind me.

My face heated and Tummi turned to face her sister, her cheeks rosy. "Katrel that's not—"

"Don't try to say that's not what's happening. We all heard you the other night in the castle. Stone walls may be thick, but they're not that thick." Katrel said and I could hear the smile in her voice. Teasing, she was teasing us.

I cleared my throat, with warm cheeks I smiled at Tummi. "Your sister wasn't the only one enjoying that feast."

"Oh, I'm well aware." Katrel said, passing me. "It's good that you both enjoy your meals."

Tummi looked at me absolutely horrified. "I—"

I pressed a kiss to her lips. "I love you. *Asta hri.*"

"You."

"Me?" I asked, kissing her cheek.

"You're—"

"Come on lovebirds." Shasha called from the hilltop.

Tummi sighed and pressed a kiss to my lips. "Brute."

"I love you too." I wrapped my arm around her shoulders. "Together."

"Together." She beamed as we continued up the hill past the lord and lady, where they stood watching the forest behind us.

"Are we being followed?"

"No, something just feels—"

"Off." Shasha finished as she turned to squint ahead of us.

"That's unsettling."

"You mean you weren't unsettled by the notdeer?" He asked with a smirk on his face.

"Can we not talk about the fucking deer!" I groaned, stalking down the rocky hill.

We hiked through the foothills to the base of the rocky mountains, the megalith of *Magav Hiiglane* in the distance; its peak cutting through the clouds that drifted lazily over us. The path was winding, and I felt the air begin to thin as we climbed in elevation. Katrel and Mitta headed the party now, the lord and lady bringing up the rear. We did not pause, eating cheese and dried meat as we walked. I glugged water from my canteen and offered it to my heart.

"I have my own canteen, dear."

"I know but humor me."

She smiled sheepishly at me as she took the canteen and took a couple small swallows before handing it back. "Thank you."

"*Eh asta hri sur naharuh eh.*"[58] I murmured exaltedly.

"You're native tongue fascinates me." She said with a dreamy smile on her face. "Why don't you speak it more often?"

I pondered her question for a moment. "My parents never wanted it to be a barrier between us, so growing up it was something we did just as a family unit. Orkin is the language of war times and has always been associated with violence. Outside of orc-kind no one hears or sees the reverence that goes into the language. Ma never wanted our mother tongue to be weaponized against me. When I've been undercover it helped me interact with other orcs. Being fair sets other orcs on edge."

"I hear it." She looked up at the sky. "Languages have a way of doing that. Elder has long since been forgotten, there are some scholars that can read it, like teacher, but the sounds of the tongue have been forgotten to time."

"There are many languages that are dead and dying." Niratap said behind us. "Irish is like that. I find that time does that to languages when the people who speak them are treated poorly. Careful, love." He caught his mate by the wrist as she skidded on some loose shale.

"Thank you." She murmured to him.

"Orkin isn't used vastly and each clan has a dialect. I don't know enough of the diversity of my people to try and protect that knowledge. The language and some songs are all that are left of the mysticism of the Earthbloods."

"Would you sing us a song?" Shasha asked.

"Oh yes, sing us a song." Tummi said with a

---

[58] "My star in the heavens you honor me."

bounce.

"Yes, minstrel, please croon for us." Katrel teased.

I rolled my eyes, but picked the song I knew the best, a simple tune called Battle Song. *"Ashkurhi mo duh kurashk morahamnara. Khasha theg ashkurhi sur kahtestheg rok. Kanamnaraosh kut kog udkah et asta et kana. Mnuha mnara kogsur ahkha ashkurhi mo kurashk morahamnara. Khasha theg ashkurhi sur kahtestheg rok. Ah ehkasho ashkurhi udkah kurashkarth et osh ara shakha kamnarasho urgha kah. Mnaraeh sur kha kut ut karhaah. Khasha theg ashkurhi sur kahtestheg rok. Ashkurhi mo duh kurashk morahamnara."*[59]

"That was beautiful, Bas." Shasha said.

"Thanks." I smiled despite myself. "It's about going into battle and keeping your cool. I only know the first couple verses though. It's part of a bigger ballad, Dad knows more of the verses."

"A song for battle." Mitta said softly. "I know a couple of those in my mother tongue and—"

"And?" Katrel pressed

She shook her head. "It's nothing. Just small things from my youth that cropped up."

There was something almost bitter in her voice. It was something I had started to notice, along with the way Mitta's eyes trailed Katrel with longing. I wondered if that was how I had looked before Tummi and I had finally fallen into one another. Was she holding herself away because she did not think that she was worthy? I stared after the woman curiously blooming in my heart. I had needed a push to talk to my heart so maybe—

"Are you two going to fuck anytime soon or are you

---

[59] Hold on to the battle song. Let the drums keep your heartbeat steady. Moon watches from above and stars with her. Home feels far away but hold on to the battle song. Let the drums keep your heartbeat steady. As the dawn breaks over the battlefield and the night's fire cast the sun in red. Know you may never see it again. Let the drums keep your heartbeat steady. Hold on to the battle song.

just going to simmer in the sexual tension forever?" I blurted.

"What?" Katrel turned hissing at me.

"I mean it's pretty obvious that you two have a thing for each other. I was just wondering when, you know."

Katrel's skin pinked as she glowered. "That is none of your business, brat."

"Well, I was just saying—"

"I don't fucking care." She snarled, I didn't understand the hostility she tossed at me. "Shut the fuck up, Bastion."

"I was just asking a question, Kat, you don't have to go feral on me."

"Excuse you?" She stormed toward me.

"What?"

Her hand stung across my face, and despite the rage on her face she had tears in her eyes. I stared at her as her sister and the lord started in on her. Something cracked in my chest. Had they rejected each other? Had they ventured into each other and saw a mistake? Had I ripped open a closed wound? I just stared at Katrel until Mitta's voice cut through the din of voices and was a physical blow to my heart.

"Is it really that obvious?"

Everyone went quiet at the injury in her voice.

"I didn't mean—"

Mitta's eyes narrowed. "That's not what I asked you."

I swallowed "Yes."

Mitta unbound her hair and turned away finger combing the brown strands. She started to braid it as she continued moving down the path. "We need to keep going."

"Mitta I—" Tummi grabbed my arm as the rakshasi warrior disappeared down the hill, shaking her head. "I didn't mean—"

"I know, love." Tummi said.

"I just thought—"

"I know, love."

As darkness descended that night, we curled under a small overhang. The lord's barrier thicker to hold back the biting chill that came with the roaring winds that picked up when the sun disappeared past the mountains. I stared out at the stars that night on watch, listening to the wind and soft sounds of sleep; wondering what I could do to fix my fuck up from today. A ghostly figure sat next to me.

You doing good, B?

I sighed. Taegan's ghost wouldn't leave me to my own thoughts.

You really fucked up today then huh?

I nodded, and peered over to where everyone slept. I whispered. "I outed Mitta and Katrel to everyone."

Everyone already knew that. Mitta has always paid extra attention to Katrel. Our whole lives.

"But why not act on it? Why just pine after each other?"

Like you with Tummi?

I glared at him. "Okay fine. What are you doing here?"

I can feel your melancholy through four realms.

I rolled my eyes. "Yeah, right."

Just apologize. Mitta has her reasons.

"And you're not gonna tell me, are you?"

"Tell you what?" Mitta asked.

I started. "Nothing. Nothing. I'm sorry, Mitta."

She sat beside me, those brown eyes piercing. She sighed and looked to the stars. "I can't have her."

I frowned. "Why?"

"I can tell you, but you must keep it a secret. I haven't told anyone else. Can you do that?"

"I can." I said.

Her eyes pinned me again. "Can you?"

Tell her.

I swallowed. "What about a trade? A secret for a secret?"

Her eyes narrowed. "What is your secret?"

I swallowed. Fuck this was scary. "I can, uh, talk to ghosts."

A faint smile tugged at the corners of her mouth. "Like who?"

"Like Taegan who is fucking obnoxious and only shows up to pick on me." I growled at my specter of a friend. "My grandfather a time or two, not that either time was very pleasant, and sometimes victims from my undercover work. Beings that suffered under the guy that enslaved the lord last. His children. Sometimes there's people who I don't understand floating around."

Tell momma tigress that I miss her lullaby.

"Taegan said to tell his momma tigress he misses your lullaby."

Her eyes widened. "I only ever sang one lullaby to Taegan."

Bíum Bíum Bambaló.

"*Bíum Bíum Bambaló.*"

A tear trekked down her face. "Holy gods, you can talk to ghosts."

"Yes."

"Can you call on them?"

"No, and I can't send them away either." I tossed a glance at Taegan, even though Mitta couldn't see him.

"Do you see ghosts around me?"

I swallowed. "Yeah."

She closed her eyes. "Who?"

"A girl. She changes in age and follows you around. She's shushed me more than once."

Mitta smiled and nodded. "Anyone else."

"When you're angry there's a man there, big burly guy. He talks occasionally, mostly just your name. The rest I don't understand."

She wiped her face and smiled sadly at me. "A long time ago, way before you were born, around the same time Katrel and Tummi were born, I had a mate and a child. I lost them before I was enslaved and brought to the new world."

My heart broke. "What happened?"

"We lived in a small village in a sheltered valley. My mate was the chief's son and a brave man; eight years my senior, but, Bran, he was my everything at eighteen. Soon after we were paired, our daughter was born. We gave her a mighty name; with the hopes she would step into it."

"What was her name?"

"Asira. It means mighty warrior. Two winters passed us and on the eve of the longest night, the first winter after Bran's father passed, we were attacked. They took us by surprise. Homes were set ablaze. I—" she wiped her teary face. "I was on watch on the opposite side of the valley; by the time I made it back to the village everyone was dead or gone. I found Bran in our house; he had Asira clutched to him. She was dead. He was almost dead. I pulled him into my arms and made him a promise that my heart would always be his. He died in my arms."

"Mitta, that's terrible. I'm so sorry."

She shook her head. "It was a long time ago."

"And they're why you won't pursue a relationship with Kat?"

"One of the reasons. The most important one, but she is also too good for me. Too noble. Too brave."

"But she loves you. The rest doesn't matter."

"What is love if not endless and vast?"

"Exactly. You can still love those you've lost while opening your heart to Kat."

"Love or lust. I promised Bran on his dying breath,

and I can't break that oath."

"So, you're just going to be alone for the rest of time?"

"Mayhaps. Go get some sleep kid."

"But—"

She shook her head. "It's alright Bastion, I could use some time with the stars."

I frowned but stood. "Aright, but Mitta you should think about whether this oath is for love or if it is just punishing both you and Katrel."

She huffed. "When did you become so wise?"

"When I needed to stay alive and after an annoying ghost told me it was time to grow up." Taegan smiled at me as I turned to venture back to the group. "I don't think your mate and your daughter would hold it against you if you let yourself fall in love with her."

Chapter Twenty-Eight

Katrel

The roaring wind made sleep hard to come by, even as Bastion curled behind my sister and tugged her close to his chest. His cheeks pink from the cold and his eyes heavy.

"I thought you were on watch?" I asked

"I was." He said pressing a kiss to her cheek when she wiggled closer to him. "Mitta kicked me off. She wanted some time with the stars."

"That sounds incredibly lonely."

"She wanted to be." His grey eyes met mine. "Do you love her?"

I frowned. "My sister? Obviously."

"I know. Not who I was asking about."

"Why do you want to know?"

"Because I want to know if I really need to apologize to you or if you're just being a bitch."

"Bastion!" Tummi growled, swatting his arm.

"Shut up and sleep, Kat. If I have to walk another twenty miles exhausted, I will be so pissed." Shasha snapped from behind the large mound of fur that was her mate. He huffed his agreement.

"Sorry." I locked eyes with Bastion. "You're a dick."

He shrugged. "Your sister likes it."

Tummi pressed a hand to his mouth, mumbling. "Gross. Go to sleep."

He chuckled and kissed her hand. "Alright, love."

She curled into him, patting his cheek. "Quit picking fights. Kat, go to sleep."

I settled back into my bedroll, the sounds of

peaceful breathing and the howl of the wind the only
sounds for quite some time. I took several deep breaths to
steady myself before I whispered to the wind.

"I do."

"We're not stopping for lunch."

"But Katrel." Bastion whined. "We've been going
since before dawn."

"I don't care, Bastion. We're a day out from the
mountain and who knows how far we'll have to trek or how
deep we'll have to search."

"Yes, but we've been hiking uphill since dawn and
we're going to have to scale cliffs here soon if my eyes
don't deceive me."

He wasn't wrong, there was a bend coming up and
after it the scale was treacherous.

"We should rest, Katrel." Niratap said from the
back. "So, everyone can make that climb."

I gritted my teeth before turning and walking
backwards. "Fine, we'll rest before—"

My foot hit air. The world tilted. Mitta lunged. The
night darkness exploded. The velvet caress of shadows
looped around my limbs and my shirt pulled tight around
my body. Mitta and Niratap had caught me and pulled me
back onto the ledge. Both were panting as I sank down on
the ground.

"A break then?" He growled.

"Yeah." My voice was small as I looked into the
void I had stepped into, and the one-hundred foot fall I had
been spared from. "A break."

The group let out a collective sigh and broke for
lunch, chatting amongst themselves. Mitta sat beside me
and offered a slice of apple.

"You, okay?"

I took the slice, my hand shaking slightly. "Yeah. Thank you."

"You really think I would let you fall to your death?"

"Well, no."

"You need to be careful." She chastised.

"Excuse me?"

"I know you don't want to waste time."

"The longer we're gone the more time he has to plot, and I don't trust him—"

"None of us trust him." Shasha said behind us. "But we are with you, and we will keep you safe."

"It's what family does." Tummi added before drinking from her waterskin.

I chewed thoughtfully on the apple slice. They were risking everything for me and my sister. Had already been threatened repeatedly and attacked by my father. A wicked king who only wanted subservience. If I failed my father's test, I would fail all of them. Risk all of them.

"Hey." Mitta said, pulling me from my thoughts.

"What?"

"I know it's scary, but we're here. We won't let anyone take you away."

I swallowed. "You sound so sure of that."

"She is." Niratap said from above me as he glanced at the cliff face. "We won't allow him the luxury of taking advantage. You will be successful in these trials; whatever they may be, and then we will go home. Together."

That word had been his promise. Together.

After everyone had eaten, we attacked the mountainside, scaling across the gap with only Niratap's shadows to keep us safe, his magic anchoring us to the brittle shale wall. Even with his protection it was slow progress.

"Careful Shasha." Niratap said behind his mate. "Test it before you move on."

"You know." She grunted, pulling herself up next to me. "The free climbing lesson would have been more beneficial, prior to scaling a cliff with at least a hundred-foot drop."

"If you can chat, it's not that hard." Mitta growled ahead of me, easing up the lip that was starting to form.

"So shut up so we don't fuck up." Bastion snarled, as his foot slipped on the shale.

"Careful babe." Tummi snapped as she sidled up to him.

"I'm fine."

Mitta cleared the edge and offered me her hand. "Come on, Kat."

I gripped her wrist, and she hefted me up. "Thanks Mitta."

"Yeah. Shasha, love, take my hand." Mitta and I pulled while Niratap pushed. She moved past us out of the way, breathing hard.

Niratap shimmied onto the ledge using his claws; he reached out for Bastion and lifted the boy over the edge and did the same with Tummi. We rested, covered in sweat and dirt, passing the water skins between each other. I stared at the legendary mountain hoping that the sword of all our legends was there.

That night we settled into a cave. Hiking deeper into the mountains and pushing hard into the heart of the peaks. *Magav Hiiglane,* a foreboding overseer to our progress. Even as the sun set, painting the beastly mountains ablaze, I felt as if the mountain was watching me. And maybe it was watching me as I approached its mighty face, looking for a legend.

This test was a fool's journey. He hadn't given a

timetable, though we expected it to take at least a week for the journey; the king expected me to fail. The lord stood from the fire and kissed his mate's head, then shifted into that beast shape of his to watch the wind kick the dust around outside. He lay there tucked inside the mouth of the cave.

"Love, I think we'll be okay for a little while."

He peered over his shoulder, his silver eyes narrowed.

"Hey now. You don't get to be huffy with me."

He snorted.

"I have blisters on my hands and my ankles, and I will come and kick your ass."

His tail swished with a chaotic glint in his eye. She charged up to him.

"Mate. You need rest too."

He huffed at her.

Shasha buried into the lord's fury side and sighed into his warmth. "You're impossible. You know that right."

He expelled a wolfish laugh and nuzzled her before returning to his vigil. His ears shifted with every skittering of stones outside the cave as if every pebble could be a beast coming to eat us.

"I can take a watch if you want, my Lord." Bastion said, sitting up from where Tummi was curled next to him.

Those unnervingly intelligent eyes fell on Bastion before the lord shook his wolfen head in refusal.

"Well, let me know." Bastion said and eased back down onto the bedroll, wrapping an arm around Tummi.

"He's a stubborn man." She said quietly against him. Niratap huffed again but didn't stir from where he lay watching the darkness.

"Aye." He grumbled, kissing her brow. It warmed my heart that he cared for her so. "He need only ask, and any of us would take a watch."

"Bastion, just shut up and go to sleep, one of us will take a watch in a few hours." I growled from the side of the small fire.

"And one of us will." Mitta scowled in Niratap's direction. "Shasha is right, you need rest too, my friend."

Niratap huffed again. Foolish stubborn male. Everyone quieted down, Bastion and Tummi soon fell asleep followed by Shasha who was nestled into the lord's side. The safest place she could be. I poked at the fire listening to their soft breaths.

"Mitta, I—"

"You should rest." She said softly.

"We should talk." I looked up at her where she sat propped against the wall, a knife in her hand as she prepared to sharpen it. "About what Bastion said."

She ran the stone across the blade. "No. We don't."

"Mitta."

"No, Kat. Not here. Not in current company, fur covered guards have ears."

Niratap huffed at that, and his tail swished across the ground.

"That's fine. You be offended, you nosy brute." She growled at him.

Another tail swish and a soft chuckle was his answer.

She smiled, running the stone over the blade. "We'll talk soon. Just not tonight. I have things I need to figure out first."

I swallowed. I hated this tension looming between us, a chasm where my heart was screaming from one side and hers the other. There was something there, she had told me as much, but she had also called the kiss a mistake. The actions and words were twisting me apart.

"Get some sleep, Kat. We have at least ten miles before we get to the mountain. Rest."

"Okay."

One would think the mountains would be cooler, but I was very mistaken. It wasn't even noon yet, but still the sun baked the earth and us with it; even within the densely packed pines at the base, the mighty mountain was sweltering.

"Gods have mercy." Bastion groaned.

"Oh, quit complaining, Bas." Shasha grumbled back.

"Shash, it's so fucking hot though."

"And complaining about it won't make it rain or anything, so shut it."

"But Shasha. I'm dying." He whined.

"Then die quietly, Niratap is covered in fur and is perfectly fine." She barked.

"Why is he spending so much of the hike in his beast form?" Tummi asked.

"It's easier on his joints, carrying the packs is easier, and his senses are sharper." Shasha explained.

"He's quieter too." Mitta sniped next to me.

Niratap growled and everyone laughed. Shasha scratched him behind the ear.

"Stay offended, my friend. It suits you." She smirked.

He chuffed and was met with more laughter. It was a soft sense of ease that overcame me as we exited a thick copse of trees and over the sunbaked shale. We could do this. We would find Aetherius. I would beat my father. I would be able to go home. I would be able to have a life after this. Cresting the hill, a cave came into view.

"Do you think this would be a good place to stop and rest?" I asked moving closer to the cave mouth. "Maybe start searching for the sword."

"Looks good to me." Mitta said standing beside me as a blast of shadows wrapped around us.

"Wait." Niratap said as the cool cavern air brushed past us. He sniffed air.

"What is it?" Mitta asked.

"Do you smell that?" He asked, a crease forming between his brows.

Mitta huffed the air. "Sulfur, metal, and ash."

I frowned. "What is it?"

"A draconic creature." Niratap said, pushing past us.

"And what does that mean?" Shasha asked.

He swallowed. "It could be anything. A drake. A wyvern."

"Or a dragon." Mitta hissed. "It could be a dragon."

Chapter Twenty-Nine

Allipo

The furious banging at the door was not what I wanted to wake to, as the dawn broke and I had to untangle my limbs. Mostly I was surprised it didn't rouse Eloi, who was nestled deep in my pillows, her sunlight hair splayed around her like a halo.

The banging continued, distinctly authoritative in cadence and demanding attention. I sighed, sliding off the bed and into a robe. The knocking thickened in sound, apparently the sheriff was growing bored having to wait for someone to answer the door at daybreak and had switched to his baton to beat against the doors.

"I'm coming, I'm coming." I muttered, opening the door, greeted by the red puffy face of Rodger Clemmens. "To what do I owe this lovely pleasurable wake up sheriff?"

"Where is that beast?"

I frowned, crossing my arms over my chest. "The lord is away. What can I help you with?"

"Bullshit. You've had beings coming and going for months. Where is he? Bondbreaker?" He shouted over my head and was met with silence.

"As I said the lord is away. What do you need, Rodger? You don't normally venture all the way to manor to plague us."

"What is killing the cattle? I have responded to ten mysterious cattle deaths since November."

Well shit the malice was becoming more active. "I assure you Rodger, that if Lord Niratap knew what was going after the cattle and deer he would deal with it. However, seeing as the lord is not here to address the issue,

I regret to inform you that I know nothing of your plights."

He straightened. "I didn't say anything about deer."

Double shit, damn my loose tongue. "Regardless, I have no solution or explanation for you."

"What did you bring home before the raid? After?"

"I assure you that Lord Niratap hasn't made any otherworldly purchases in the months immediately preceding or since the raid. He has been recovering from injuries he had received from said raid and now he is away attending to another issue."

Rodger jammed his finger into the center of my chest. "You can't protect him forever. I will see him behind bars for this."

I swatted his hand away and leaned into his face. "I doubt that sheriff. I doubt that very much. In all your years as sheriff you have never once proven that Lord Niratap has broken the laws in your peaceful little town. He has been nothing but respectful to you and the people of the town. Furthermore, he has gone above and beyond to keep the nefarious people out of your peaceful little town because, beyond your understanding he is a good man. Regardless, he's not human, and you do nothing but treat him as less than dirt."

His face puffed, his breath smelling of cheap diner coffee. "He is a threat."

I cocked my head. "Is he sheriff? I find that our Lady is more ferocious than him. She did take down a crime boss by herself with one bullet. To get him away from the lord of course, but I do believe she would stop at nothing to keep him safe and free. You won't prevent her from that."

"That little half-breed doesn't scare me."

I pushed him down a step. "You will respect the lady of this house. You have overstayed your welcome, Rodger. I'll give the lord your regards. If I remember." I made to shut the door, and the sheriff planted his boot in the space.

"Allipo, I don't know what it is, but something bad is coming."

"I wouldn't have coined you a psychic, Sheriff." I said, examining my nails in boredom.

He frowned. "I'm not, but something is not right."

"I will keep that in mind."

He pulled his boot free. "When will he be back?"

"I'm unsure; a month, maybe more." I shrugged.

He nodded. "Okay. I'll be in touch."

"Don't." I huffed and shut the door.

"What did the sheriff—"

I screamed and like a scared senior I clutched my chest. "Rogmesh, how do you fucking do that!"

The orc smirked. "Oh, quit clutching your pearls like a fifties housewife and tell me what the sheriff wanted."

"The malice is killing more deer and cattle. We've been preoccupied between the raid and the threat of Babylos; it had become a back burner issue."

She leaned against the wall, crossing her arms over her chest. "The sheriff is just concerned."

"Yes, but Rodger will be breathing down our necks now. I hope they find information while they're gone."

"They will."

"I don't doubt that. I just hope that it is substantial." I rubbed my temples. "I need to go over the security footage, check the lord's email, reach out to some of the guys undercover, call the ironworker Staspar told me about."

"All of that before coffee and pants?"

"No, I will have both before I sit in front of a computer." I smiled at her. "I know I'm dashing in my robe Rog, but I don't think your husband would approve."

"You're not my type, Allipo." She smirked stepping away from wall. "I'll start a fresh pot. Bagel and eggs?"

"Yes, you're the best, Rog."

"Go put pants on, Allipo."

I laughed as I ventured back down the hall to where the dawn, trapped in the body of a woman, lay sprawled in my bed. She sleepily watched as I moved before the armoire, a smile on her face.

"Good morning." She yawned.

"Morning. You can go back to sleep, lovey."

"Why are you awake?"

"Rodger was beating at the door." I said pulling clothes from the hangers.

"The sheriff? What did he want at dawn?"

"To be an obnoxious bother like usual."

"Allipo."

I sighed, stepping into my pants. "He was pressing about the malice, the killings of cattle and deer. He's concerned for the people of Grahamsville. Which I can understand, but—"

Her arms wrapped around my waist and kissed my shoulder. "It shouldn't be at the cost of our peace, just because we aren't human."

I glanced at her. "Exactly that. Now that I'm up I might as well start my day; I have much to do. The manor and the organization don't run themselves."

I took my breakfast in the study; going over statements, funneling money into the necessary respective locations, and reading the countless emails that flowed in every week. There had been no news of an in-person market popping up; the forums and chat rooms were either silent or still talking about the auction disaster last fall and the raid. Between the two, a lot of big names had been taken down. Baby steps, I guess.

I jumped as a call came through.

"Yes, Kallin?"

"I thought you were expecting me?"

"I was." I groaned. "How are things, now that you're back?"

"Things are slow, the boss got busted and the other generals are lining their pockets. This group is bound to collapse at this rate."

"Busted how? Have you found his source?"

"They don't take too kindly to cop-killing in the west. I don't see him getting out of it. I haven't found his source, but with the quality of merchandise we've been pushing, I'd say they're artifacts now. I don't think we're moving scales from a living dragon."

I sighed. "Damnit. Lord Niratap will be disappointed. Do you think you can rock the boat enough to destabilize it completely?"

"Maybe if I play my cards right. Mathias and Jonas are not friendly with one another so as unmanaged generals they are volatile, bound to make mistakes."

"If you can do it safely, bring it down."

"Directions from the lord?"

"From me. The lord is currently occupied with another issue and is away. Any murmurs of a market popping up at that end of the country?"

"No, after all the late and off-season stuff that's happened on your side it's been quiet. Most of our sales have been for drug running."

I leaned back in the seat. "Not ideal. If you hear anything let me know."

"Can do, Al."

"Stay safe."

"You too. When the lord's away, his tenants are bound to play."

"That's cryptic and not what I need today."

"Lighten up a bit you old goat. I'm just playing."

"I'm not much older than you."

He laughed, ending the call. I scoured more emails for anything of note; finding a few vacating notes and evacs. Everything was looking up to snuff, when Echo flitted on iridescent wings into the office, her face panicked and panting.

"Allipo, we have a problem."

"Fucking Kallin!"

Beneath my hooves the ground was still damp and muddy from the rain. Shouting and cries of anger graced my ears as I stormed out to the barn. Eloimaya and Dheg were arguing with the kelpie.

"Leave!" Dheg roared.

"Make me!" Creseda barked with a vicious laugh, gnashing her teeth at Guinness.

"Creseda, you hurt that horse, and the lord will personally see you dead." I snapped.

She smiled at me, showing off her broken glass teeth. "And where is our fearless lord and his whore?"

"Bitch!" Dheg dropped Guinness's reins and charged, tackling the kelpie into the muck. She thrashed under him as he grappled with her. "You will not speak ill of our lady like that. You—"

"Dheg!" I shouted. "Release her and settle the lord's horse."

He let go but glared at me. "But she—"

"I know, Dheg. The lord's horse. Please." My voice shook as I loomed over the kelpie. "Creseda, you were explicitly told not to return, by order of Lady Bondbreaker. The fact that you have ignored that direct order, is a direct violation of terms of your station as leader of your people."

"You do not have the authority to strip me of my power." She hissed.

"Of that you are correct." I crossed my arms as she came to stand. "However, the lord will hear of this transgression."

"Where is he?" She shrieked.

"Away. What is it that you need?"

"I need nothing from you, steward." She hissed, shoving me back, hard enough that I stumbled into the mud.

"Then leave." I growled standing up, flicking muck off my arms. "The lord will see you when he returns."

"And when will that be?"

"To be determined. Now leave."

She huffed, brushing the dirt off her arms. "I won't stand for being dismissed by a steward."

I glowered at her. "I could knock you back into the dirt, if you'd prefer."

She scoffed and started her march back towards the forest where two werebeasts waited for her. "I won't forget this."

"Then you won't forget that you will answer for your insubordination."

She slipped into the woods without another glance.

"I had it handled." Dheg growled, as he stroked the stallion's nose.

"Obviously." I pinched the bridge of my nose. I grimaced. My hand smelled of manure.

"I can hose you off in the barn." Dheg offered as he led Guinness into the pasture.

"Fine, I would hate to track this through the manor."

Echo laughed. "We wouldn't want that. The lord would wonder why the whole house smelled of horses."

I laughed. "That he would."

The cashmere sheet felt second to heaven, when I

had at last finished the day. It was heaven compared to a basement floor or a cell. Though finalizing movements for the organization was low in things I found pleasurable, with everything that was happening since the raid this winter, playing chess was important. Three informants said that their marks were going dark waiting for the dust to settle, and several others were parting from their marks as their organizations fumbled and collapsed with arrests. Everything was accelerated and it was good for our goals, but I worried about what desperation would come from this.

The door clicked softly as my heaven came to bed. She sat on the edge beside me undoing the long braid she had her hair in for the day. I fingered the hem of her shirt, absentmindedly.

"You can shower if you want."

"I'm okay. You're the one who was thrown in the muck." Eloimaya said.

"And got hosed down in the stables." I groaned.

She smiled. "How was business today?"

"Arduous. Several of our undercovers are cleaning house. Many of the bosses have been wrangled in the last few months, and the groups are dissolving without leadership. We'll have to go down to collect the packages tomorrow; there are some items that need to go in the vault."

She nodded. "And the artisan?"

"He's going to come in the fall when his latest project is up. He's sure he can save the failing structure, but he won't know until he sees it."

"That's good." She turned to face me and asked. "Do you think she's dangerous?"

"Creseda? I think she can be given the room to brood. She's upset that Niratap didn't even consider her as a partner, let alone that he mated a human."

"She's only half human."

"Semantics." I waved idly at the ceiling. "I think

she will wait to raise literal hell until Niratap is back, just to garner his attention. Hopefully. Just another thing to watch for, plan for."

She finger-combed her sunlight hair. "Are you tired?"

"Exhausted, my heart."

She smiled sweetly. "Too tired for me?"

A drunken smile spread across my face. "Never that tired."

She slid from the bed, slipping from her jeans, the sapphire lace undergarments were a tease to my loins. She straddled me and began untucking my shirt. "You're always dressed so well."

I chuckled at the dash of irritation in her voice. "Is that a bad thing?"

She paused in undoing the buttons, tilting her head looking down at me. "It makes you very fuckable, but it also makes it very hard to fuck you."

I unlatched my belt, letting my knuckles graze her thighs and core. She was already molten. "Oh, does it now?"

She shuddered over me, her fingers faltering over the button. "Tease."

I smiled lazily at her. "You know what I will give you. So let me tease you a bit."

She finished the buttons of my shirt and quickly popped the button of my slacks, sliding them down my legs and off my hooves. She straddled my waist and ground her hips against mine, a strangled groan left both of our mouths.

"Silly satyr, you are not the only being that is a tease." She slipped from her shirt exposing the matching sapphire blue garment, which she quickly undid to free her supple breasts to me. She hovered over me, her pretty carnation pink nipples dangling. I reached for her, but she caught my wrists. "Now, who said you could touch me."

"Is that your prudish elven raising speaking?"

She smirked. "No. If it was my traditional raising, I would not be in this bed nearly bare before you."

I flipped her and kissed down her chest. "Well let's get you completely bare and let me taste you."

Her skin pinked as my lips danced over her. A breathy moan cresting those soft lips when I sucked one of those deliciously pink nipples in my mouth, rolling it between my teeth. My hand wandered to that tantalizing apex of her hips, teasing her through that sheer lace that she had donned no doubt to torment me. She was wet and needy for me and as my fingers wriggled her from that lace I kissed my way to that glorious valley between her thighs.

Her delicate fingers wrapped around a horn, halting my progress. "Allipo."

"Now my sweet, glorious dawn." I groaned, meeting her heated gaze through my lashes. "Please let me have these few moments of heaven after the day that I've had."

She laughed breathily. "You're a brute."

"There's that traditional raising again." I brushed my lips over her delicate hip bone. "It's like your prudish ancestors are blocking me from beyond."

Her grip loosened. "I should have taken you up on that shower."

I beamed at her. "Oh honey. Shower or no, I am going to eat that glorious cunt of yours and after you come on my tongue several times, I will burry my body in yours until you forget your name."

Chapter Thirty

In the depths of Illishara's jewel of knowledge where the shadows moved on their own and the tomes spoke to one another; the dark-looking glass rippled as a figure came to appear there. The figure was a six-foot-tall man, whose face was ghoulish and body a half-wasted corpse. His eyes were dark in color, as if they had once been brown, but light didn't brighten them, and were sunken above the holes that had once been a nose. His mouth, what remained of it, was twisted into a scowl.

"Cairn." The figure said, as its ethereal bony body took form.

The scholar didn't look up from his work. His face painted with a placid smile. "I was wondering when you would show yourself again."

"You've been expecting me?" The figure's voice was raspy, the sound of papers getting shuffled.

"I have been. It's been three years since we last spoke." Finally, the scholar looked up at his ghoulish guest. "You look like shit."

"Ha. You told me this would grant me immortality. I've been festering in a jar for two hundred and sixty years and this body is weak and no match for the power you promised I would have."

"You were slain before you could finish it."

"I didn't realize that creature was so willful."

"Unknowns, but the other one I gave you on a silver platter, with that blood alone you would have had true immortality."

"She was—"

"Too pretty not to play with? Must you always have to play with your food?"

"Hardly." The figure glowered, as well as the half

rotten flesh upon it could. "Now my ingredients grow bold from years of freedom."

"I sent you an agent to undermine them."

"A woman at that." The figure spat with a hiss. "Useless things."

"Keep your vitriol to yourself. The child will do her job and do it well."

"And what of the ingredients."

"They are preoccupied right now. Should they survive Cardoc, they will be within your grasp again. You cooked for almost three centuries, I don't see how waiting a few more months will change that."

"Your brat needs to do what she was told."

"She is working on it. Patience."

"My phylactery is sitting on a shelf in that vault. I need it in order to regenerate fully, and I'm getting sick of waiting. I'm sick of being a shambling corpse."

"All in good time. I will reach out to her tonight; however, your beast may be quicker in motivating her."

The corpse figure smiled. "A nightmare of a reminder may be good for the child."

The scholar smiled. "Quite."

Chapter Thirty-One

Mitta

Cautiously we ventured inside the cave into the heart of the mountain. The scent of sulfur made me queasy as it thickened the deeper we went.

"Watch your step." Niratap called softly behind him.

"Do you think—"

"Bastion, be quiet." I hissed, cutting him off so our footsteps over the gravel were the only sound. He glared at me, but I needed to be able to hear.

Down and down and down. My heart skittered in my chest as we plunged into pitch blackness; I choked on the panic that seeped into my body. I tried to settle myself, pulling deliberate drags of air into my constricted lungs. The flash of a cold stone cell. An iron box. The smell of blood. The laughter of men. Crying. Screams.

A warm hand closed over mine and a zing of rightness eased the panic. Katrel didn't have to say anything, her familiar callouses pushing back the darkness and lessening the ache in my chest. It was unfair that just her touch chased away the demons of the past. It was unfair that I wanted it and couldn't have it.

I tugged my hand free as a faint light pierced the black. The cave opened up. Large mounds of gold and gems reflected the warm light cast by sconces and pyres scattered between the mountains and along the cavern walls.

"What is this place?" Shasha asked, stepping past her mate.

He gripped her shoulder. "A dragon's trove."

"Perfect place to hide a magic sword." Bastion said

taking in the space.

"And a dangerous one." I said. "I can see why the sword was never retrieved."

"We proceed with caution." Niratap said. "Kat, you're with Bastion and Tummi, take north side. Mitta, Shasha, and I will take the south."

"Tread lightly, we don't know if we're alone." I said following behind the lord and his mate.

We wove between the piles of gold, laced with ancient weapons, gemstones, and armor.

"A kingdom's trove." Niratap mused, picking up a diamond the size of his palm.

"Kingdoms. Plural." Shasha said, eyeing the diamond before moving forward. "Who even decided that stones and minerals have worth?"

"The elves or the dwarves." I said toeing a Spartans helmet. "Both races are known for their craftsmanship with precious metals."

"But they're just rocks and bits of metal."

"A question that has been asked for millennia and never answered." Niratap said, opening a chest full of deep blue sapphires.

"So, I know we're looking for a sword, but what are we looking for?" Shasha asked, eyeing a scimitar.

"A sword," he said with a smirk, "A broad sword more than likely. Ancient, probably shining with divinity."

"There!" Shasha shouted, pointing at a blade that was sunk into an old chest full of glittering fire red rubies, atop one of the taller mounds around the mountains of gold.

Shasha scrambled up the collected treasure, her mate watched her carefully as coins and gems rolled back down. "Be careful Shasha. Especially when you come down."

She sat on the top and panted. "Okay."

Light danced off the blade as if it was a prism and gleamed with many hues across her dark skin. She hefted the sword from the chest, scattering the rubies.

"Katrel, does this look right?" Shasha shouted across the cavern.

"It does a little. Come down and let me see." Katrel called back, weaving her way through the mounds of treasure to where we stood.

"Be careful." Niratap shouted, as she slipped the blade through her belt. It was then the mountain of gold shifted, coins skittered as something opened a large red eye, right behind Shasha.

"Shasha!" Niratap shouted charging to her as she turned to stare at the brilliant red eye. She said something, but the words were swallowed by the song of thousands of gold coins cascading off the deep bronze body of a dragon.

"Shasha! Run!" Niratap shouted, reaching the bottom. He didn't make it past there as a bronze tail swung, throwing him back into another pile of gold.

"Niratap!"

The dragon rose, shaking gold from its body. Shasha fell back on the pile staring at the massive head the size of a minivan. Niratap dislodged himself from the gold and charged. A feral snarl ripped from him as the dragon pinned him beneath its massive paw. He thrashed against the creature's hold, shadows whipping about the ground. The dragon's gaze fixed on where Shasha came to stand, brandishing her knife.

"Release him." She growled.

The creature's massive eye shifted back to where it held Niratap pinned. Its lips moved as it spoke in a voice that had not been used in a long time. "Why?"

Shasha's eyes widened. "Because he means you no harm."

His deep laugh shook the dust from the cave walls. "I fear not the fangs of such a small beast."

"Then release me, dragon!" He shouted.

"Silence!" The dragon roared, pressing down until a pained cry came from the lord. I swallowed, this was bad. "I am speaking with the girl."

"Please stop. You're hurting him." Shasha's voice was firm but wavered slightly.

"Why do you care?" The dragon asked as he surveyed her.

"He is mine." She said.

"Yours?" The dragon again looked at Niratap. A pulse of raw power thrummed through the space, the force of it knocked me off my feet when it struck Niratap. His body ricocheted off the floor, his eyes rolling back before he stilled. Shasha collapsed, her knife falling from her hand and sliding to the cavern floor.

"No." Tears streamed down her face as she stared at his limp body.

"I see. You have bound your soul to his. How peculiar." The dragon sniffed her. "Especially for an elemental."

Shasha glared at the creature. "I'm only half elemental."

"Even more peculiar."

"Why?" She snapped.

"That you are only half with the power that I smell in you. Why you would settle for a lesser creature is new and very strange."

"He is not less than me. We are equals."

The dragon again looked at Niratap, closing his talons around him and picking him up, his body limp in his hand. The dragon turned him in his palm, examining with sharp eyes. He pressed the point of a talon against the lord's chest. Old, raw magic thrummed violently through the cavern. Niratap's back bowed in the dragon's palm. He screamed. Shasha screamed, shifting to her knees.

Niratap thrashed and twitched in the dragon's hold as that magic invaded him forcing his body into its wild shape. When the shift was done the dragon presented him to Shasha, laying him upon the gold.

"Even now you are equals?"

She didn't answer, simply pulling that large wolfish

head into her lap, stroking him softly. Their conversation from the other night rolled through my mind. They could feel each other, their emotions, their pain. I swallowed, braving a step. The dragon's eyes landed on me as I took another.

"Rakshasi warrior." His voice boomed over me as I picked up the cragstone knife. He could smell what we were, and it was both terrifying and mesmerizing.

"Why did you wake?" I asked, standing.

"There were thieves in my home."

"We are not thieves." Katrel said coming to my side. She was too close, I angled my body in front of hers, one eye on her and one on the dragon.

The dragon sniffed. "I was wondering if you would ever come."

Katrel frowned. "You were expecting me?"

"For many, many millennia, yes." The dragon said, shifting his mighty paws over one another. "A champion" he called you then."

"What are you talking about?" She growled.

"The story must have been lost." The dragon said, cocking his head.

"What story?"

The dragon lowered his head to look at us. "The flame emperor told me, all those years ago, that one day a champion descended from both his children would come in search of the sword. They would have the power to alter the course of history for the land. You, young elf, have both fire and starlight in your veins."

"What do you mean?" Katrel asked.

"Who are your parents?"

"King Cardoc Raloqen the Third and Ciserie Stormblood." Katrel said, eyeing the dragon as he nodded.

"She descended from the one I watched after her parents gave all away."

"Our mother?" Tummi asked.

His nostrils flared, eyes dilating as he took in the

other princess. "You, I did not suspect. A daughter of just starlight."

Something clicked in my mind at that, but Katrel pushed on. "Tell us this prophecy you speak of."

The dragon's eyes narrowed at her, but he spoke softly. "I have lived many eons and have watched the world grow and shrink as time has gone. I've watched the rise and fall of the elves, the dwarves, the rise of men, and the separation of the elves from the rest of the world. I have been a constant like the sun."

"Before the separation, Emperor Conláed of the Flame and his Starlight Queen Lucette came to me, Teovelass, the eldest dragon of Babylos, to beseech my wisdom. I was the one who told him of the rending, the costs and risks. Conláed was a good and just king who just wanted peace for his peoples. Man quickly forgets the promises they make, and Conláed was worried his people would suffer, that his children and grandchildren would suffer."

"You said children. The flame emperor only had one son after the war." Katrel said.

The dragon eyed her before he said. "Lucette had worried about the boy, Einar. He was not like his father, the battlefield and bloodshed had stained his soul at a young age, with the loss of his mother during that terrible war. She was slain when men first began to fight back. She was an easy target. The boy and his father were the only royals who survived that first war. Lucette worried that the boy would try to erase her and her daughter, Hesperia. She voiced her concerns to Conláed who didn't want to believe that his son was capable, but I could see he was also worried. I advised the Starlight Queen that she have her daughter, and her young family, go into hiding. Let Einar run the kingdom and pick up the pieces after. It was her best chance at survival."

"What happened?" Bastion asked. All of us rapt with his story of the past.

"The rending happened. Conláed gave all that he was to separate Babylos from the world of man. All his fire. All his love. All his life. Lucette took the throne in her husband's stead promising a future without pain or fear. Einar had other plans. After the chaos of being cut had settled, Lucette built the portal between realms with Hesperia. Then she returned to me, the Queen of Starlight, and beseeched me to watch over Aetherius, the king's blade, for it should not fall into the hands of wicked kings."

"Soon after that exchange Lucette was slain by Einar, in the bed she had shared with his father. He sent those loyal to him to hunt down his half-sister and her family. They slaughtered her like an animal."

"Her family?" I asked.

The dragon smiled as close as a creature of his shape could. "They escaped in the night. And through the centuries the daughters of the star married into nobility, for all of them held Lucette's beauty. Males regardless of their race seek out beauty."

"So, you're telling me," Katrel hissed, "that our mother is a descendent from the Star Queen? Who we've been told from a young age was a prisoner to the emperor. You're telling us that all the history we know is a lie? That they were equals and loved each other."

"They were never equals. Stars do not fall in love with mortal creatures, they do not leave their blankets of night to mingle with them, they do not give up their divinity, and they haven't since Lucette was murdered. They have been silent watching over their sister's children."

"If they were watching out for us, then why was Tummilia sold away?" Katrel snarled.

"Do you think your life would be what it is now if they hadn't?" He asked her as the lord groaned.

"*Mo grá.*" Shasha said as the monster in her lap shifted.

The lord shifted, lifting his head to take in his

mate. His most important focus and when he was done surveying her, he looked to where we stood before the dragon. Checking to make sure all was well. His ears folded back as he locked eyes with the dragon and growled.

"Are you done acting like a child," the dragon hissed, "or will I have to render you unconscious again?"

Shasha grabbed one ear and yanked him to her. "Enough."

He snorted indignantly at her.

She rolled her eyes in response.

He snorted again.

She kissed his nose. "Snort at me again and I'll tan your hide."

He chuffed, in a warm playful way, before he turned his eyes to the dragon.

"You wish for me to release your form?"

The lord dipped his head.

"I believe that you will be more hostile to me with your words than you are with your fangs."

"You are not incorrect." Shasha said with a sigh. Niratap glowered at her. "However, I would like it if he had the free will to choose his shape."

The dragon eyed them for a moment. "Very well."

Shadows slithered through the scattered gold coins as the shape of the man returned, wrapping his body for some modesty. The lord glowered as he pulled his mate close to him, both cradling her and placing his body between her and the dragon.

"Why did you attack?" The dragon queried.

Niratap eyed him. "Because I feared for my mate's safety."

"Had I done something to warrant such a reaction? Had I threatened her at all?"

I could feel the venom in his glare. "I did not know and not knowing is a risk I will not take with her."

They watched each other for several moments

before the dragon blinked. "Understandable. I do not wish you harm, as you are not thieves but the cadre to the champion of the star and flame. You are welcome in my home."

"Teovelass?" Tummi said, pressing forward.

"Yes, Starlight?"

"Tell us more about the Star Queen."

"She was beautiful and graceful. Wise beyond the years of her mortal form. Most of all she was kind, a perfect partner to her king."

"What of her magic?"

"Stars do not possess magic. They are magic. Pure and raw. It has the power to heal, to make, and destroy. You have that power in you, child of the night. Do not be scared of it."

Katrel's brows furrowed. "What of the flame?"

The dragon watched her with an intensity that made me uneasy. "Flame is a destructive force, child. Flame has erased much of history when wielded by tyrants and conquerors. It is a mighty weapon and wielded by the just, it can bring about a new era. Do you have Conláed's just and righteous heart or are you your father's daughter?"

"What does that even mean?" She asked. Her voice carried a raw edge that cut me.

"You will have to decide, champion child."

"I don't feel like a champion."

"Maybe you are yet to be a champion."

"Teovelass. How do you know? How can you tell what we are?" Shasha asked.

"He can smell it in us." I said.

"You are wise, rakshasi. It is more than smell. It is a deep thrum of your nature, your essence dancing against mine. You are wise in mind, but your heart is fickle and torn. Stuck between two promises."

I sucked in a sharp breath, he knew. He knew; on those eddies of magic that were our souls, he knew. I asked in a hushed voice. "Do you know the way?"

The dragon shook his head. "Only you can forge your path."

Chapter Thirty-Two

Niratap

"What does it feel like?" My mate asked beside me, her eyes full of that wild curiosity. "Our essence?"

"Each of you is different. Your essence is the song of everything, the seasons, their elements, everything. A rarity even in your kind. Your," Teovelass chewed on the words he wanted to describe me with, "mate is the song of an old, shrouded forest. The young orc is of both the earth and heavens, kissed by divinity. The rakshasi is of ice and steel as most of her people are. The princess is of the night sky and the champion the flame of a falling star."

"Is your sense of essence how you locked my mates form?"

"In part."

"How?" She beamed at the dragon.

He chuffed a laugh. "So curious you are, child of all. I followed his essence to his true form."

"How did you know he was mine?" The words made my heart flutter.

"His pain is your pain." Teovelass said matter-of-factly. "Your essence and his are intertwined, beating with your hearts, anchoring your souls."

"Does our bond extend my life? Does it keep him anchored in this world? Does it protect him from those who wish to cause him harm?"

"Bonds like yours are mysterious and never in my time has a bitarog mated an elemental of your caliber. You are not yet at your crossing."

"Crossing?"

"When elementals come of age, mature into their powers. You will have many gifts to master with how your essence sings."

"How—"

"*Mo grá.*" I grasped her chin. "You don't need to ask him about everything."

"But—"

"No, love."

"You are also a young creature." I met his gaze. "Should you survive the animosity you are doomed to face, your power could rattle the place you call home."

"Doomed?"

Teovelass nodded. "Draconic creatures have always been both feared and prized for their power. You and I are no different there. I would wager that you have lived very few days where you have not been some being's prize."

"And you?" I pressed, already understanding my fate. Hating how Shasha had been dragged into a life of misery and fear for loving me. She placed a hand on my cheek, pulling me from those thoughts.

Teovelass cleared his throat and closed his eyes as if he had to peer into that distant past, his tail flicked in irritation. "I have only been hunted once and Einar did not fare well in that endeavor, but before that, no. I was born in the time where my kind were revered. Keepers of the peace. Counsel to the first kings. Guardians of time."

"And now?" Mitta asked.

"Now I am the last of my kind."

Shasha frowned. "That must be a lonely existence."

He blinked at her. "I do not need your pity."

She puffed at him. "It's not pity."

He cocked his head. "Then what is it?"

She looked at me and I said, "It's understanding."

He watched us with those calculating eyes. "Very well. You, the cadre of the Champion of the Flame, are welcome to stay here for the evening. You may leave in the morning."

"And Aetherius?" Katrel asked and I eyed the blade beside my mate. Fire rubies were inlaid in the golden hilt which had been wrapped in a leather braid. The blade was etched in swirls and whorls and down the fuller there were strange markings; words from a language long forgotten.

"Aetherius is the sword of the flame emperor and only the champion can wield it to its full potential. Are you a champion, Katrel Gwendolyn Raloqen?"

Her voice gave away her doubt, but she held her chin high as she said. "I don't know."

Teovelass nodded. "A test then it seems."

My body ached by the time the group curled up to rest. Shasha curled against my chest. Her hands had tried to work the pain from my body, but quickly tired and soon she was asleep. I pulled her close to me, she mumbled something unintelligible, a protest or a thanks, I didn't know. I tucked an errant braid behind her ear, with a finger. Her beautiful earthen skin was soft beneath the digit.

"You care for her very much." The dragon, Teovelass murmured.

I looked up and met the crimson eyes. "I do."

"Then why bring her to such a dangerous place."

I smiled at my sleeping mate. "I made a promise to the champion. We made a compromise. She is more than capable to handle Babylos."

"Do you not fear that Cardoc will take her from you?"

My heart seized in my chest, the jolt of panic roused her enough to wrap an arm around my waist and mumble something. I stroked my hand down her spine. "I fear it, but I will not allow it to happen. She won't allow it to happen."

"But what can one power-locked elemental and a beast do against the King of the Elves?"

"You underestimate the strength of a woman

defending what's hers."

He chuckled softly as he laid his head over his paws. "Perhaps."

It was only the soft rasp of Shasha's breath and the crackle from the braziers for some time. My thoughts dancing from the malice, who even here crept into our dreams and stalked us from the shadows. These trials that very well may doom us all or free the girls from their royal shackles. Would Cardoc honor them? Was he that kind of man? To the family waiting for us to come home and those scattered around the world. What were they facing and managing without us? Had there been markets with our absence? Was my sister still hissing at everyone else? To that mysterious enemy lich and what he wanted from me. What he wanted with my family. What was he waiting for?

"Nira."

I stopped stroking Shasha's back, the rumbling voice pulling me from my thoughts and back to Teovelass who watched me with hooded eyes.

"Why do you refuse to rest?"

"Much weighs on my heart and mind."

"Tell Teovelass of your worries, so you may rest. You are useless to your family weakened by exhaustion."

He was right, but— "Speaking fears out loud makes them realities and I am not ready to face some of those fears."

"Then ask me for counsel. Ease a worry so you may rest."

It was sound reasoning. "How does one know an enemy if that enemy is unknown to them?"

"The question would be who your enemy is. For one to be an enemy one must know the other enough to form hostility towards them."

"But I have not interacted with a lich. Not once in my life."

"Then which one of your enemies had vanished over time?"

"Plenty have, but I don't know which of them had connections or resources to even begin the process to become a lich. Let alone one who would come after me so violently. What would they want with me?"

"Your draconic nature."

"What?"

"Bitarogs are hybrid beasts born of multiple creatures, but their draconic nature made them prime ingredients through the centuries, still dangerous but easier to capture and kill than true dragonkin. That draconic magic and blood makes you long lived. That longevity in you is what they are after."

I pondered that. Who wouldn't want a longer life, more time to do what needed done. More time to love. I kissed the top of Shasha's head. How many times had I wished for death, wishing for the pain and suffering to end. Now I hoped that I would have enough time for the beautiful woman beside me.

"If I knew who it was, I would be better equipped to protect my family."

"You know them. It is the only way to have an enemy. What do your enemies crave that you possess or keep them from?"

"Power. Control. Myself. Revenge."

"Any of those enemies who would be desperate enough for all of that to sacrifice what they are for a chance?"

"A few."

"Then you have your pool of enemies to look into when you return to the world of man. Now rest. None will enter my home without my knowledge."

"Thank you, Teovelass."

"Don't thank me, Breaker of Bonds, you will still need to seek this enemy out."

"Yes." I pressed my nose to Shasha's hair, her scent of everything soothing me. "But I have a way now and I can keep her safe."

He hummed and said. "At the cost of yourself I fear."

"Mayhaps."

I awoke cold and my heart careened through my chest at that. The once magically lit cave was dark. The mountains of gold, Teovelass, my family were gone. Shasha was gone. I felt her next to me, but I was so cold. My breath fogged before my eyes. A dream then, this had to be a dream.

I snarled, the hairs along my arms prickling. "Malice, where are you hiding?"

Claws scraped down the rock walls and echoed around me. "The breaker of bonds is not afraid of being alone?"

"I am not alone." Shasha's heart beat next to mine, even if she was missing from this hell. "What do you want from me?"

"I desire your fear." A phantom hand slid across my back.

I whirled around to nothing. "What does your master want?"

"Master wants your suffering." A yank on my tail had me spinning again. "Master wants your submission."

"You can tell your master that I submit to no one."

A dark papery laugh echoed across the dream. My body burned with a sudden rush of electricity as shadowy hands clasped my shoulders and the hiss of the malice slithered through my ear. "Master will claim you as he has always claimed, and you will serve your purpose."

I tried to rear back, but my body wouldn't listen. "Release me."

The malice sunk its claws deep in my shoulders, a

pained cry crossing my lips. "I do not hold you, master does. Master tells me to find your fears and I do. Master is very excited to take your sweet little female away from you."

My heart bottomed out. "Leave her alone."

"She is your greatest weakness. Master will take her from you." Shasha's screams echoed through the chamber, my name on her tongue. "Master will use her to break you."

"No." I tried to wrench my body free, but I was paralyzed.

A silken shadow of a tongue slid up my neck. "Yes. Master will break her."

"No."

"Niratap!"

The malice chuckled as I screamed.

Sweet kisses pulled me from the nightmare, my name a gentle prayer on her lips. She had straddled me, pinning my hands to my sides. I took a breath through my nose, the tang of blood not present.

"Nira?" Everything I had ever dreamed of was in that sweet voice.

"May I hold you?" My voice was thick in my ears.

She loosed a shaky laugh before shifting to free my hands, which I snaked around her waist without opening my eyes, burying my face in the crook of her neck. She rubbed along my ribs.

After some time she asked. "Was it a bad one?"

"No. Was my reaction?"

"Only when you bucked me off the bedroll." She kissed my temple.

"Apologies, *mo chroí*."[60]

Another gentle kiss. "We have an audience."

"I just need this."

"Does that abomination haunt you often?" Teovelass's rough voice asked beyond my lids.

Laying back I huffed, watching as the firelight pulled the golds from Shasha's eyes and she smiled sweetly; Teovelass looming behind her with his knowing gaze.

"It's becoming more frequent that my nightmares belong to the malice." I answer cupping my mates face. Mate. Mine. Safe.

"Do you have many nightmares?" The dragon asked.

"My life has been plagued with adversity; my sleep is mostly plagued with the memories of such."

Teovelass nodded. "You are susceptible to the power of the creatures of shadowed places. Darkness is both your strength and weakness."

I frowned. "I have come to terms with what has happened to me."

Teovelass just blinked before he said. "Past traumas make you skittish of the future, whether you have accepted them or not."

"I do not fear my darkness."

"Ah, but you do fear what your darkness can do to others?"

<hr>

60 My heart.

Chapter Thirty-Three

The grumbling voice of our dragon host pulled me from sleep, restful for the first time since coming to this godforsaken place. I rolled to see he was speaking to the lord and lady.

Niratap glowered at his mate. "It doesn't matter, I am in control of my darkness."

"When you are awake." Shasha countered.

His tail flicked in aggravation. "I am not the only person to have nightmares."

She frowned. "True and you are also not the only person who gets violent when they have them."

Teovelass puffed a breath between them. "You will not fight in my presence. Mates should not fight at all."

"Is that your opinion or your wisdom?" Niratap growled.

Teovelass huffed, tendrils of black smoke curling from his nostrils. "Blood mates can feel each other through the bond and though your bond, like yourselves, is young you can feel what your partner feels. It is unnecessary and selfish to fight with that knowledge."

Shasha's shoulders fell, but Niratap's tail flicked again. Shasha wrapped her arms around his shoulders and kissed his cheeks until the rigidness left his body and he tugged softly on one of her braids. I smiled at them; they had been through so much already and yet they were here facing the worst my kind had to offer. For me and Tummi.

The dragon's gaze landed on me. "Are you ready to be a champion child?"

I sat up and met his gaze. "I don't know how to be a champion. A warrior, yes. A disappointment as a Crown

Princess, definitely. How am I supposed to be a champion for my people?"

"Only you can decide how you champion for your people. You might surprise yourself, young one; you may champion for your people by championing for yourself."

"Winning my freedom will not do anything for my people."

He stretched his mighty wings over us. "Are you so sure of that?"

"A single person cannot change the world."

"Ah, but you believe a single beast can change how humans look upon others."

I tensed under his gaze, the words finding their mark. "It's different."

The wings settled, but his gaze did not. "No, it is not."

"How can you say that it isn't?" I challenged, approaching where the lord and his mate were seated.

"You believe in the young lord's vision, do you not?" Teovelass pressed.

"I do."

"Do you believe that he can achieve it?"

"I do."

"Then you believe that one being can create great change, fire's child."

"I believe he can make a difference. What does winning my freedom prove to a corrupt king who will very likely not grant me the freedom I'm fighting for?"

"Very true, but are you still going to fight?"

"Yes."

His tail swept from around him, setting the sword in my hands. "You may take Aetherius when you leave."

"You had not decided if I was worthy until now?"

"I had not." He pointed to a cavern opening opposite the entrance. "That cavern will take you back to Ehiza when your group is ready to depart."

"What about you?" Shasha asked as he folded his

paws.

"I will remain as I have for the last several millennia."

Shasha frowned. "It sounds like a lonely existence for one as magnificent as yourself."

He chuffed at her in a serpentine laugh. "The existence of the final ones always is."

We left soon after the group had all risen and eaten breakfast. Teovelass sinking into his trove. This cavern was lit in a pale-blue-green light cast by bioluminescent algae. It thrummed around us to its own heartbeat.

"This is so pretty." Shasha said, the light dancing over her skin.

"It's moonbloom algae." Mitta said beside me. "It's very rare, usually only found in cold climate dead volcanoes."

"Is *Higlane* an old volcano?" Shasha asked.

"That is a question for the dragon that's older than time." I sniped.

Mitta frowned beside me. "It's possible with the underground network of caves."

I frowned in return, but the lord asked. "What is the plan Katrel?"

I took deep even breaths. They were following me. I had seen the bruises that Teovelass had left the lord with. Even as he had dressed after the stories, his body splotched with deep purple and blue. I clenched my hands, willing myself to calm, to ease their shaking. I was leading them through this foolishness, leading them to risk their lives.

"If this does lead to Ehiza, I think it wise to impose on Lathai's hospitality for a night and send word of our return to the king via falcon."

"Will you tell him of your success, Kat?" Tummi asked.

"No, I won't tell him about Aetherius or Teovelass. The dragon's safety should be a president because the king will want to claim him as a trophy and in case, we need to seek his guidance"

"Do you think you will need his guidance before the summer solstice?"

Gods, summer solstice was only twenty-two days away. Just over three weeks. Three weeks to earn my freedom and get us home. I didn't know if I could do it. I didn't know if I could champion for my people and my family. I took a shallow breath. "I don't know."

Silence fell over the group, a chokehold on my thoughts that came back to all the risks I was dealing to those I loved. Be a champion for my people, what did a dragon know of me to suggest that I was capable of such a thing? How was an unloved princess supposed to champion for a people? Cave dwellers like rats and newts ran along the thrumming walls and floor, a lanky creature hissed and scampered down an adjoining cavern, his footsteps splashing along the small stream flowing from it.

"A knocker." The lord said from the back his dark-seeing eyes watching the creature.

"Do we follow it?" Mitta asked softly, looking down the cavern as well. "Or do we stay the course?"

The lord blinked in the blue gloom. "Knockers aren't known to be hostile, but they are rumored to cause cave-ins. We should stay the course."

My thoughts continued to spiral as we walked on, the hours ticking by to the sounds of our feet. I was a coward. I couldn't do this, but everyone was depending on me to show my father, to show the king, that women can be great.

Sooner than should have been possible the afternoon light broke through the dimming glow of the moonbloom as the cavern opened to grassy hills, the stream veering downhill to the river borrows.

"Well then." Bastion huffed. "Six hours of walking is much preferred to the six days."

Ehiza welcomed us warmly, and after quickly dispatching a letter to the king, we retired to the lodge again. Solana was practically glued to Lord Niratap's leg, he indulged her by telling her fantastical stories only half based on truth. She smiled brightly at him with each tale. I had always loved watching him interact with the children he encountered. Gone was that darkness he carried, even when he was veiled in shadows there was a softness to him with them. He was partway through a story featuring the wild folk of the forest that had Solana giggling wildly that Farryn asked the lord. "Are you planning on having children?"

His eyes sharpened at the question, a flick of his tail the only sign of annoyance, but he smiled. "If that is what fate has in store for me."

"What of you, young lady?" She pressed Shasha.

The lady set her glass down. "My mate and I have spoken about it. We hope for it, but after. After we achieve the very dangerous goals we have. After that. After life is not so dangerous, then we will find such peace."

Farryn frowned, but Lathai said. "I will send up prayers to the stars for you. That when peace finds you, that it is easy for you both."

The lord nodded, a shadow in his eyes as he hefted the giggling girl on his shoulders. "I will take this young one to bed. The sun is asleep and so should be its light."

"Nira, I'm not tired." She whined gripping his antlers as he left the table.

"Hush, my little ray of joy, it is bedtime for you."

"Fine." She groaned, leaning over his head. "But you will tell me another story."

He chuckled up the stairs. "Of course, Solana."

When their voices had faded Farryn eyed Shasha. "You would bear that beast children?"

Mitta and Bastion snarled, but the lady held up her hand. She eyed Farryn with the weight of her title. "You still don't trust us, trust him."

"I do not trust things that hide their fangs."

"Fangs or no, that beast as you call him saved your daughter, gave her his protection, and is now tucking that little girl into bed."

"That is immaterial to his nature."

She scoffed with the strength of a queen. "Is it now?"

Farryn did not balk from that gaze. Shasha, with the little courtly training she had, blinked, smirked and took a bite of food. After she swallowed, she spoke, her voice full of mirth. "To answer your rude and prejudiced question, yes, I would bear that *man's* children, for he has proven to me more times than I can count that just because he is a monster that doesn't make him monstrous and he is more of a man then many of the males I have had the displeasure of meeting in my young life. I would take him over any humanoid, any day."

My heart swelled, bravery like hers was worth following, just as her mate's loyalty was worth following. Farryn said disbelievingly. "Any male?"

"Any male." She stood. "Now if you'll excuse me. I will join my mate."

The lady left the table, her footsteps light. I watched her out of the corner of my eye as she ascended the stairs and disappeared from sight. I looked back at Farryn whose face was puffed in anger. I said. "Did you think that it was wise to ask Lady Bondbreaker such a question?"

Her cheeks pinkened at my focus. "I do not recognize her as titled."

I blinked. Farryn had been standoffish and shy, but the hostility was a development. "You should, for both she and her mate were titled by myself and my sister. He is one of my longest friends."

She swallowed and bowed her head. "I meant no

offense, your Highness."

"Whether you meant it or not, you have succeeded in just that. Just because I speak plainly with you does not mean that you have free reign to act this way. I expect better from my people, especially those who have shown kindness and hospitality to my family prior."

"I apologize."

"I do not want it. I don't know what he did, or they did to warrant this kind of reaction because from where I stand, Lord Niratap has been nothing but kind and fair with your town even after your watch shot him upon our arrival. He has freed your daughter from a fae entrapment and been nothing but gracious with you. Lathai, you have also been very quiet in this exchange. What happened?"

"Lord Revan paid us a visit while you were in the wilds."

Tummi froze at the mention of the putrid male. I asked, "Did he threaten you?"

"Lord Revan delivered a summons to the royal palace for the summer solstice. The summons was for a royal wedding." Bile coated my tongue as Lathia looked to his wife, whose rage was as palpable as her fear. "He said that we should feel inclined to separate you from your group for him."

I frowned. "Revan is a brute, but you have nothing to fear from him. There will not be a royal wedding."

Farryn hung her head. "I am sorry, Katrel. I fear for my family."

I clasped her hand across the table. "Me too, Farryn. I am terrified every day that I am here, and I cannot wait to go home with my family. But I promise you that I will not allow my father, nor Revan, to hurt yours."

Chapter Thirty-Four

Shasha

I met him in the hall as he pulled Solana's door shut with a soft click.

"Asleep already?"

He chuckled softly, tucking a braid behind my ear. "Yes. I got her tucked in and part way through the story *The Little White Cat* she was out."

"The Little White Cat?"

"It's a tale of a young prince and princess that escape giants with the help of—" he smiled down at me, cupping my face.

"A little white cat."

He booped my nose. "Exactly."

I looped my arm around his waist, guiding him to our room. "Are you alright?"

He let me lead, his eyes looking anywhere but my face. "I am."

"Farryn get under your skin?"

He shrugged. "No. Her question ruffled my fur a bit, but I could smell her fear. I have the feeling they were paid a visit by that knight."

"Revan."

"Yes. I couldn't detect his scent, but I fear they were threatened."

"I don't like that knight, not that we have had pleasant interaction with authority anyways."

He chuckled. "I don't think Farryn acted out of malice."

"I agree." I turned before our door. "I was unsettled by it though."

He leaned over me, his callused fingers tipping my

head back to look at him. His eyes filled with wild delight. "How may I settle you, love?"

An equally wild smile danced over my lips. "I'm sure you know how to settle me."

One hand slid down the side of my neck as he purred at me. "I'm sure I know a few things."

"Do you, my Lord?"

He pressed his face against mine, he had a fine stubble that tickled my cheek. "Open that door and let me show you how much I know." My breath shook as his tongue danced over my pulse, and his hand shook as the other found my hip. "Come mate. Let me settle you."

I turned the doorknob, the door swinging into space as he held me. "My Lord."

"My Lady." His voice was velvety in my ear.

"The door is open."

"I know." A soft kiss against my throat. A graze of his teeth.

"Are you testing your resolve or mine?"

He chuckled. "Maybe both."

"I would insist that his lordship make a decision." I felt him smile against my throat; his tail pressed into my back.

"Why is that?"

"Because I need you and if you don't take me now, I will help myself."

"To me?"

"No."

He growled possessively, edging me into the room. "Can't have my mate wanting."

"Oh, I'm fully capable of getting off without you."

He nipped at my neck kicking the door closed. "My sweet flower. I can't wait to have you."

"Show me."

"With pleasure."

He lifted me into the bed, his hips sinking between my thighs. His hand roved hungrily across my skin and under my shirt, bunching the thin material and sports bra up over my breasts. The other tangled in my braids to tilt my head back giving him better access to my throat. My hands tingled and a tightness flared through my core. He groaned against my pulse, delighting in the sensation. I bucked against him reaching for my pants button. His hand collected my wrists and pulled above my head.

"So eager."

I arched in his hold. "Please."

"The mating bond," he crooned across the damp flesh of my neck. "Makes this an interesting exchange."

"You feel me and what you do to me?"

"Yes, and I feel my hands on your body."

I tugged my hands free, reaching between us to undo the snaps on his shirt. Faintly the tickle of fingers danced over my ribs and when I had freed him, I pressed my hand over his heart. Heat bloomed over my own.

"Fascinating." I gasped as he pulled back to look at me, his eyes full of heat.

"Is liomsa tú agus is leatsa mise."

You are mine and I am yours. The words brought goosebumps to my skin, they were vows to one another. It was as true as the thrum of our heartbeats, promises that no matter what came our way, we would have one another. I knew it with the certainty of the sun.

"Claim me, mate."

He growled falling on me, his fangs finding purchase along my throat. I raked my nails down his back as my body went rigid and boneless at the same time under him. His hand deftly undid my jeans, as he pulled my flowers and seasons into him, and slid me free of the garments concealing my lower half.

"Nira, please."

He released me. The zing of his magic, an electricity against my skin, as he sealed the bite mark with a wet sweep of his tongue. He eyed me with wonder and hunger before he descended down my front.

Hot wet kisses, sharp nips from fangs, skin pink from hungry claws, had me yowling, my whole body sparking with ecstasy. One broad hand cut off my shriek. I gazed down at him poised just below my navel. The raw predator edge to his silver eyes made my body ache.

"Though I love hearing you cry at my touch, *mo grá*, there is a child sleeping not many doors down. I ask for your silence while I taste you."

I whined behind his hand. Gods.

"I'll reward you." A sweet kiss against my skin. "For your silence."

Fuck. This male. I nodded.

"Good girl." He smirked and lowered his head, kissing a trail down my thigh.

The first press of his tongue had me arching off the bed, biting my lip to keep from screaming. He slid an arm under my hips and pulled me closer, angling me for his best access. He sucked my clit between his teeth, and I bit down so hard I could taste blood. He purred against my core in satisfaction, his tongue plunging into me, curling to stroke that perfect spot. I saw stars. My legs clamped around his head holding him to me as he sent me crashing over the edge. This fucking male.

After I rode out another rush of euphoric cunnilingus, he kissed his way up my body. His magic healing small hurts along the way. He took my mouth. His tongue swept, tasting my blood like he had tasted my body. I tasted myself on him, floral and wild. He licked his lips. Hungry eyes taking me in as I panted on the bed.

"You did so well, my sweet."

"Niratap. You better get out of those pants."

He chuckled. Pressing a kiss to my lips before he stood. "So eager for me?"

I propped myself up to watch him as he slid free of his clothes, the massive length of him bobbing. "You look pretty eager if you ask me, mate."

He smirked. "And how would you like me?"

"Would you like to sit on the floor or the bed?"

"What I would like is to be buried inside you." Restraint echoed in his voice.

"The bed then." I patted the mattress before I stood shucking off my bunched top and bra. "Sit in the center for me."

He obliged, gracefully crawling into the bed and slipping a pillow behind his low back. There was nothing graceful or attractive as I crawled on the bed and stood over him, gripping his antler for support. He watched me with that predatory look that made my body quiver. A hand caught my knee lightly; support should I need it.

"What are you planning, my flower?"

I cupped his face. "You'll see."

Slowly I slid my body down enjoying the way his eyes locked with mine, his hands trailing up my legs, cupping my ass. I reached between us and positioned him.

He growled when I didn't sink over him. "Are you going to torture me?"

"I might." I stroked him.

His head fell back with a grunt. "Woman."

I pulled him forward, pressing my brow to his meeting that hungry gaze. "What am I?"

He blinked. "Mate."

I slipped him between my folds. "What am I?"

"Mine." He growled, claws pricking along my cheeks.

I kissed him. "That's right and what are you?"

"Yours."

"That's right." I slipped the crown of him inside and he hissed.

"*Is liomsa tú agus is leatsa mise.*" I breathed, seating him deep within me. Held his brow to mine as he watched me take all of him, as he stretched and filled me.

"Fuck." He ground out in a strangle moan. "Shasha."

"You. Are. Mine. Mate." I ground my body against

him with each word. "Always."

"I love you. More than words." He panted. "*Mo chroí. Solas na réalta go léir i mo spéir. Mo bhaile. Mo gach rud.*"[61]

I rocked against him, using his antlers to pull myself. The heat that pooled through me caused me to pant at him in return. "I don't know what you said, but all of it. I want all of it. All of you. Like this. Always."

His hands traveled up my back, claws pricking the whole way. The sensation caused us both to groan. "You are everything I have ever wanted, mate. Everything and more. I can't see life without you in it. I don't want it without you."

He bucked into me, and I shushed our cries with a kiss. His tongue and mine fought for dominance, as he thrusted, winding us tighter and tighter.

I yanked his head back, breaking our kiss. He growled as I kissed and suckled his neck. My voice was full of euphoria as I begged. "Please."

He grunted. "Anything for you, *mo chroí.*"

With an efficient swipe of a claw, he flayed his neck for me. I lapped up the wild rain and whiskey of him. Savoring every pull as he pushed. He was a high that I would never tire of, never wanted it to end.

His hands pressed me against him, my body rolling off that euphoric cliff and pulling him right behind me. His body throbbed, filling me with him. I felt that hot seed trickle down my thighs. The knot of our bond tightening as the wound closed and I peppered his throat with kisses. My hands fell from his antlers, letting his head fall forward against my shoulder. Our shared breath came in hot pants as we returned to our bodies.

He pressed a kiss to my temple. "Are you alright, love?"

"Wrecked, but yes. Are you?" I shifted back

[61] My heart. The light of all the stars in my sky. My home. My everything.

meeting his gaze before he hissed, his still hard member twitched inside me.

"Destroyed." He kissed my brow.

My fingers traced over the pink scratch that would be gone tomorrow and hickies that were already fading. He watched me, shivering as my fingers passed over the darkest bruise, the tickle mirrored on my own skin.

"Sorry."

"Don't apologize. I could drown in your touch." I laid my head on his shoulder and he stroked my back, a comfortable silence fell as we soaked each other in. I don't know how long we sat like that wrapped in each other. Nira's voice was thick as he asked. "Would you like them to stay."

"What?"

He chuckled. "The hickies. Would you like them to stay?"

"No. It makes me sad that my marks don't stay long on you." I placed my hand over his heart. "My mark is in here and that is all that matters."

He kissed my shoulder and rolled us, his hips pistoned softly and I groaned. He braced his arms on either side of my head and on a deep throated laugh. "You are a treasure, my heart."

"I love you."

He pressed his brow to mine. "So much."

Lazily he made love to me, our souls coiling around each other. It was a devotion. Something vast and wild and reverent. If I was religious, I would have claimed that the warm light between us was holy. He curled behind me when we were satiated, holding me close as if I would disappear. I pet the arm he had banded across my stomach.

"Are you alright?" I asked into the darkness.

"I am well." He said into my hair. "Are you?"

"I am." Even though the bliss of our joining was fading and the weight of what we were facing settled in.

"What is on your mind, *mo grá*?"

"Everything and nothing."

He pressed his head against mine. "Are you worried?"

"Yes. Do you think that we'll be okay?"

He stroked his thumb along my rib. "I hope that we will, but time will tell."

I turned to look at him. "How can you be so relaxed about it?"

He kissed me. "I find that there is little reason to let my worries consume me. Especially here."

I nodded. It did seem pointless to worry when we were already hip deep. Katrel could master this, she could win her freedom, but— "What will it cost?"

"I wish I had an answer." He swept a braid behind my ear and kissed me. "Sleep, love."

Dawn came too soon. An end to stolen moments for us and parting from our allies. Mitta had glowered at both of us when we had made it downstairs. She didn't comment, but I knew she smelled what lingered on our skin. Lathai, his family, and the village saw us off. Solana clung to my mate with all her might not wanting her friend to leave.

"You are sure that you will go?" Lathai asked Katrel again.

"I'm not afraid of my father." It was bravado, but the lines bracketing Lathai's mouth softened.

He asked my mate. "You are sure about returning?"

Nira bowed his head. "The princesses are my family, and I intend to keep them safe."

"Niratap." Solana whined from where she was wrapped around his leg. "Do you have to go?"

He kneeled down, gently prying the girl from his

leg. He smiled at her and tucked her soft tawny strands behind her ear. "I do, sweetheart."

She frowned. "Because you have to protect the princesses, right?"

"Yes." He stroked her little arms with his thumbs. "They don't have a nice father like you, they need me to have their back."

She sniffled. "Will I see you again?"

He smiled sadly at her. "I would love nothing more."

She turned to her father. "Daddy, can I see Nira again?"

Lathai looked at Niratap before he turned his eyes down to his daughter. "On the summer solstice we'll be in the capital city. If he is still here, you'll see him."

Katrel said rather coldly. "You'll be coming then."

"It is a royal summons." He said matter-of-factly. The threat to his home was too great to ignore. "We will be there regardless of the outcome."

Nira cleared his throat before pressing a kiss to her brow. "We'll see each other again, my little ray of sunshine. Be brave."

"I will." She beamed as he nudged her toward her parents.

He stood, a light ache wobbled my knees and bowed deeply to Lathai and Farryn. "Thank you for your hospitality and kindness. It was refreshing. You honor us."

Lathai guided his wife into a bow. "You honor us, Lord Bondbreaker. Thank you for everything you have done."

Many of the other villagers followed his lead and bowed. Not to the princesses, but the beast lord who had saved a child. Nira's tail twitched. "Thank you."

He turned then and came to my side helping up on the mighty horse who had Guinness's temperament. He stroked my thigh gathering his shadows.

"Whatever comes, mate?"

"Whatever comes."

He pressed a soft kiss to my brow before stepping back. The shadows swallowed him in a whirlwind of billowing black tendrils. His clothes slid into the saddle bag with phantom hands. Solana squeaked from where she stood by her parents, surprised at the darkness that had swallowed her friend. I smiled at her, unafraid, and as quickly as they had erupted the shadows dissipated, some curling through his grey fur and around his antlers. He shook out his coat, sinking into the wild shape. Black talons dug into the dry soil, the dawn bouncing off the dark scales as he stretched his long canid body.

"Solana!" Farryn shouted, from where Lathai held her back. The young girl had ventured into the half circle of horses to look at the large beast there.

Niratap cocked his head to the side and ventured a step towards the girl. She yielded a step back. He chuffed laying down and lowering his head to the ground, tail flicking playfully. She giggled and edged a few steps closer.

I leaned down from the saddle. "He likes to be scratched behind the ear."

Niratap huffed at me but flopped onto his side.

"Solana don't get any closer to that beast." Farryn sniped.

"With all due respect, stop worrying. His shape is different, not his mind." I hissed as Solana came up to him. "Go on sweetie."

"It won't bite me?"

Niratap huffed indignantly.

"No. You couldn't let go of him a few moments ago."

"That is not Niratap."

I smiled. "How do you know?"

Solana eyed Nira, who, beyond his size, was the picture of non-threatening. Reaching out, her small fingers sank into the grey fur along his side.

"It's so soft." Nira lifted his head, her eyes catching his. Those eyes that never changed, both kind and haunted. Solana smiled. "You're soft, Nira."

He huffed at her before bumping his nose to her forehead. She wrapped her arms around his muzzle and whispered to him. When she released his face he licked her, sending her giggling before she walked to her parents. He stood and bowed his head to them once more, then nodded to Katrel, who turned her horse back towards the glowing city of Illishara.

Chapter Thirty-Five

Katrel

We rode through the morning, breaking at the creek as we had on our way to Ehiza. Niratap didn't bother to shift, drinking deeply from the creek itself. His dark iridescent scales sparkled from where he waded into the water where he snapped at fish that drifted by Shasha, who giggled as she ate an apple.

"My Lord."

He looked up at me, at the formality that we had mostly left at home.

"Revan threatened Lathai and his family."

He nodded, like he had figured something like that had happened.

"Farryn acted that way at last night's meal because they were told to separate us."

He huffed.

"I wanted you to know."

Silver eyes locked with mine. He had made to give them as much protection as he could before we had departed. I knew that, had heard his quiet conversation in the predawn before most had woken. He had told Lathai to be prepared for anything, especially come solstice. Had warned him of what lay hidden in the bowels of *Magav Hiiglane* and of the secret cave that led into the heart of those mountains. Niratap nodded and returned to the fish in the creek.

"Do you think that they will be alright?"

He sighed, but didn't look up.

I looked up at the vast expanse of the sky. "I told them, I promised them they would be."

"Did you think that was wise?" Mitta asked as she

stood to collect the horses.

"I don't know. I want to keep them safe."

"I thought you didn't want to be their princess." Bastion said from where he filled the canteen.

"I don't, but I do not wish the people of Babylos ill."

"The crown is not the heavy weight." Tummi said. "It is the nightmare of ending up like our mother."

Her words were a heavy weight. "The crown is not heavy at all. I want to choose who I am with, and I want the freedom to own my own body."

Bastion frowned, looking between the both of us. "Everyone deserves that."

Illishara was brightly illuminated as we were ushered in by the gate guards, the sun sending the white stone ablaze. People watched from their homes and businesses as they had when we had first arrived. Wrapped and hidden, Aetherius a heavy weight down my back. Mothers tucked their children behind them, hiding them from who they perceived as the most dangerous being in their midst. The soft fall of that predator's paws behind me had me lifting my chin as we rode into the palace grounds.

Stable hands stood waiting to take the horses. At the stairs into the palace, Cyran stood, his face grim. Shadows erupted, the stable hands freezing their approach as I turned in the saddle as Niratap stepped from the enfolding darkness, reaching for his mate. His eyes wholly focused on her as he lifted her from the saddle and set her upon the ground, sliding her down his body the whole way. I longed for that kind of unfaltering devotion. Mitta handed the reins of the roan to the petrified stable hand.

"He's not nearly as terrifying as he looks."

I smiled as I dismounted. Niratap growled. "Neither are you."

Mitta shrugged. "They haven't given me a reason to be."

She was right. I had spent the last couple centuries being in awe of the warrior, who had taught me everything I knew. The myth of the night tiger lingered in chilled alleyways of the human lands, the blade of the Bondbreaker. In those earlier, more cutthroat years of the new world, having her with us had been a blessing. She was fearless and ruthless. The Blade of the Bondbreaker indeed. I approached Cyran who bowed.

"Crown Princess."

"He's waiting for me, isn't he?" I asked.

The scholar nodded, looking past me at my family. "He is in a foul spirit."

"Joys."

"Did you find the blade?" He asked in a hushed whisper.

"I wouldn't have come back if I hadn't."

Cyran nodded, folding his arms behind his back and turning into the doorway. "Good. Keep your head high."

Mitta put a hand on my shoulder, electricity skittered down my spine as she said. "We are with you."

The throne room was darker than I was accustomed to, the antler chandeliers dark. Only the braziers on the dais and a few scattered torches blazed through the room. He lounged on the throne, clad in black and idly sipping a dark wine as we entered. I stopped before the dais, bowing at the waist. A man's bow. I raised my head to meet his glower.

"Father."

"Princess, I see you have claimed your ancestor's sword." He glanced behind me. "And kept your friends."

"I have." I drew the blade, the metal reflecting the light. "Both are secured."

He hummed, drinking what remained in the glass. "Tomorrow at noon be in the area, your next trial will begin there."

I bowed again, holding the sword steady. "Very well, father."

"I'm surprised you managed it so easily." He said standing and approached us. "The next one will not be."

"I would expect nothing less." I said sheathing the blade. I held my breath as he assessed me, coal dark eyes analyzing . I held that gaze, though my soul was begging me to break it, begging to run as he smiled knowingly at me.

"Hopefully you can hang on to both as you proceed."

A threat. "I plan to."

He nodded, stepping past my true family. "Goodnight Princess, I will see you in the arena."

He left. My heart collided wildly with my ribs and Bastion clapped me on the back. "That went well."

I took a breath. "It did, which is unsettling. He did not seem all that interested in the blade that he has coveted his whole life."

"Scholar." Niratap asked. "What do you know?"

Cyran dipped his chin respectfully. "I only know that he visited the menagerie after he received word of your return."

"And Revan?" Tummi asked with a frown.

"Revan was sent to deliver invitations to the nobility and township leaders," Cyran frowned. "For the royal wedding."

"There will not be a wedding." I said.

Cyran nodded. " I hope not, for all our sakes."

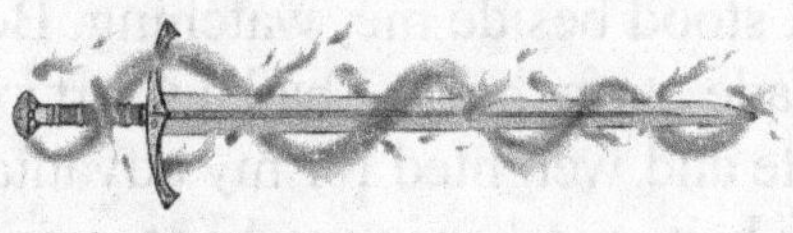

Noon that next day came far too soon. I had slept fitfully wondering what horror my father would unleash for me. What creature he would make me face as entertainment. Crowds from Illishara lined the arena, chatting and cheering waiting for the show to begin. Incense stained the air; both Mitta and Niratap bemoaned the thick scent of cedar and patchouli that blocked their senses before we had even entered the arches. Two guards stopped us before we crossed into the mouth of the area, both fair, one with blonde hair that stuck out from the bottom of his helm; the other had a wicked scar across his cheek.

They bowed and the blonde spoke. "Crown Princess Katrel, I was asked to escort you to the battle gate."

I swallowed. "Very well."

"Your entourage was asked to be seated above the gate. I will see them there." The other guard said.

Tummi gave me a reassuring hug. "You are strong and brave and resilient."

"Thank you, sister."

Niratap eyed the guards but said. "Raise hell, my friend."

The fire in me whispered that it would, and Aetherius hummed at my back in answer. "I will."

"Be smart." Mitta said. "Remember what I've taught you. Be brave."

I met and her gaze, giving her a single nod before turning back to the guard. "Lead the way, knight."

Down a hidden corridor and a spiral stair, I came to stand in the shadow of the arch before the dirt expanse of the arena. I could see most of the stands where the crowds of people were sat; my family above me even though I could not see them. I swallowed and checked my weapons as the knight stood beside me, watching. Besides the legendary blade at my back, I had a short sword at my waist, reliable and weighted for my advantage, two knives tucked in my belt, another in my boot, a dagger strapped to my arm, and three throwing pins that held the braided bun in place. I ignored the weight of the cragstone blade sheathed along my breastbone—Shasha had nearly begged me to take it for my safety—a blade that could kill most anything.

"You wear those weapons like you know how to use them." The knight said beside me.

"Because I do."

He scoffed. "Aren't you a little old to be playing pretend, Princess."

I frowned. "You'll see. I bet that my skills rival Revan's." I bobbed my chin to the king's box, where he stood watching the crowd. He must have returned this morning from his deliveries.

He laughed. "I bet not."

"What is your wager?" I asked.

"A week's salary. Yours?"

I smirked, pushing bravado into my voice. "My dowry."

For the first time since he'd greeted me, the knight was uncomfortable and swallowed. "You jest."

"I might."

"I cannot accept your wager."

"Fine." I smiled, looking out the gate across the expanse of dirt. "Just your salary then?"

"Your Highness, it would be a miracle if you survived this." His voice wavered.

"I have faced many beasts in my years away. What the king has planned I assure you I will handle. Unless you are afraid that you will be broke for a week." I smiled, peering down my nose at him.

He swallowed again. "It is improper."

"You seemed so sure. Oh well, your loss."

He looked out at the arena filling quickly with patrons. "This is suicide."

"Maybe."

"Are you sure you want to do this, Princess?"

I looked at the male, his fine boned elven face and watery grey eyes. "I would rather die in that arena than marry that knight."

He swallowed and bowed. "You are reckless."

I shrugged. "It has never stopped me before; it won't stop me now."

The king entered his box, and the crowd cheered wildly as he waved at them. I wondered if they would cheer if they knew he used his daughters as breeding stock. If they knew he had sold one into slavery. If they knew he beat his wife. He shushed the crowd so he could address them.

"Welcome, welcome, people of Babylos!"

Another cheer roared from the stands. He silenced them with a hand.

"Thank you for indulging me on this fine spring day. As most of you know, my daughters have returned to us after a long time away. My eldest has challenged me to give her trials to prove she is capable of independence."

I scoffed at his words.

"Today you will bear witness to her second task. A Trail of Strength as decreed by our forefathers. A fight to the death."

A gasp of shock rolled through the crowd.

"I know. I know. A dangerous task indeed, but I have been assured by my daughter that she is capable and that she has learned many skills of survival in the human lands. Now, I present my daughter, Crown Princess Katrel Gwendolyn Raloqen."

I stood tall and glanced at the knight, while the crowd cheered. "It's a shame that I won't be able to take your paycheck."

"Princess."

"Tell Revan to choke." I said before I stepped out into the blazing light of the arena, to the crowd's cheers.

I glared up at my father, who smiled at me deceptively. "Welcome Princess. Your second trial, child, will be a duel against one of the most ferocious creatures to have ever walked the earth."

The gates opened across the dirt expanse of the arena and the incense pyres were snuffed. I braced myself for whatever force my father had in store, whatever beast lay beyond those doors. The sunlight illuminated a man, chained and kneeling, his arms suspended above him. His long blonde hair was dirty, stringy, and hung limply around the cracked paddle shaped antlers atop his head. His skin was ghostly pale making the dark bruises that covered him stand out in stark contrast. I knew that man. I knew him. Knew his laugh. Knew the scars upon his skin. Knew his touch. There was a snarl from the stands as the smoke cleared completely, that all but confirmed it. The man raised his head and the verdant green eyes that shone out of that wan face stole my breath. Casrian.

I looked to where Niratap and the others stood in the stands. His face pulled in a painful mix of anger and sorrow as he gazed at the chained broken man that he had called friend. It was when his eyes met mine that I saw the regret, the pain that sliced deep through his heart. He was choosing which one of us would live. He looked back at the being that had once meant so much to him, and sadly looked back at me. A slow exhale of breath. A few muttered words to his mate. And when he pinned me with those cold moonlight eyes; he simply nodded. I knew how to defend myself against his species. I knew their weaknesses, his weaknesses, and that was how I would survive. I would survive. I had to survive. Casrian would not leave this area.

"Imagine my surprise when you brought another one to me, though he is obviously poorly bred and weaker than this specimen."

Niratap snarled from the stands. "Cardoc!"

My father just smiled that cruel smile. "Let the battle begin. To the death."

The chains that held Casrian in place slid free, his hands falling to the ground. He looked so broken, sorrow in his own eyes. A whip cracked in the darkness, and he snarled, coming to stand. Even from across the arena his megalithic twelve-foot presence rattled me. Casrian was massive, his imprisonment having no effect on his muscled body. He snarled at the elves behind him. Snarled as a whip cracked again forcing him into the light. Snarled again as powder was thrown into his face. He roared, scratching at his eyes and face. The gate was closed before him. He shook that mighty head and the five-foot span of his antlers. He looked at me then, red irritation staining his eyes and mouth. What had they given him? A feral growl emanated from my friend.

"Katrel!" Niratap shouted behind me. "It's Innuram. They've dosed him with Innuram."

Fuck.

Chapter Thirty-Six

Mitta

My heart stopped. No. She was going to get killed. Casrian was a brute of a male, easily pushing two thousand pounds in his beast form. I took a step forward, ready to jump in the arena for her. Niratap clapped a hand on my shoulder, halting me.

"She has to do this on her own."

"The fuck she does." I snarled. I couldn't stand by. I couldn't lose her. Blood-soaked memories twisted my insides.

"Mitta." He said, squeezing.

"Fuck off, I didn't know you to be a coward." I turned to face him, his hand not lightening.

He glowered at me. "Use your head, Mitta. We interfere and we're all dead."

He bobbed his head. I had sudden clarity in what he meant, a dozen royal guards in our section stood watching us. Watching me want to vault into that arena. I glanced across the stands to where Cardoc sat, smiling at us. He knew we wouldn't stand for this, knew that, and prevented us from helping.

"Cardoc planned this; we cannot intervene."

"Fucking bastard." Bastion growled, his hands in fists at his side.

Casrian roared and my heart fluttered, panic oozing through every pore. "We're going to watch her die."

"Katrel will be fine." Tummi said as I looked out over the arena, dread pooling in my gut. "She is fast on her feet, and she can beat Niratap."

"No offense to the lord, but Casrian is easily three times as big."

"None taken. You're not wrong, Mitta. Casrian is a beast of a bitarog."

"Does she stand a chance?" Shasha asked.

"I don't know."

Casrian's body thrashed as the innuram started taking hold, his body shifting disjointedly. Shasha gasped, her hand grabbing Niratap's wrist as Casrian fell, a leg shifting before an arm, his ribcage bulking up painfully. He snarled, shaking his head, his antlers digging into the earth and kicking up dust.

"Casrian!" Katrel shouted, drawing her sword. "Casrian!"

She needed to attack now! End this before it could truly begin, but this was her friend, our friend. The skeletal, half shifted beast lifted its head, jaws snapping viciously. I shuddered, even Niratap's half shifted form disturbed me. Living beings should not look like half desiccated corpses and those corpses should not move. Casrian stalked towards her, with predatory intent, the tall spinal bones of his back a brutal sail.

"Casrian, it's me!" The beast only bellowed at her, the sound soaking into my bones. "It's me! Katrel!"

Casrian chuffed, head low as he prowled closer. I whispered. "He doesn't recognize her."

"No, he does not." Nira agreed, giving my shoulder a squeeze. It was all the reassurance he could give me.

"It's the drugs, Mitta." Bastion said. "It's the drugs."

"Casrian, please. I don't want to hurt you." Katrel shouted, facing him as he stalked forward, pacing back and forth across the dirt.

The male snorted through his half-formed face. Casrian was canid as the lord was with large jowls full of sharp jagged teeth, saliva hanging from between them. But Casrian was more bear-like with his bulky barrel chest and cresting spine, necessary for the muscle attachments that held that massive antlered head. He snarled and charged.

"Katrel!" I screamed. "Run!"

She didn't. She held her ground as the beast barreled towards her, brandishing her sword before her with both hands.

"Kat! Please!"

She did not move. She faced him as he raced toward her. His maw of teeth on display.

Niratap's hand held firm on my shoulder. As he grew nearer, I didn't feel like I was breathing.

The arena fell into a fearful silence. Only the grunts and pounding of Casrian's feet upon the earth reverberated in my ears, battling the sound of my pounding heart.

I screamed.

Dust kicked up around where Katrel stood as he met her on the field. Please, creator, don't take her from me.

Chapter Thirty-Seven

Katrel

I swallowed. I heard Mitta screaming and I wanted to turn. I wanted to hear what she was screaming at me as Casrian, my friend, charged. I heard his old laughter in my ears even as he bellowed. Each second of his approach felt like a year, dust flying behind him. I remembered him coming to my bed; we hadn't been physically compatible, but he had wrought pleasure from my body, and I his. He had told me of the frosty north land of his birth as we laid in the afterglow. He had been boisterous and bold. He had been brave and reckless. He had never worn a mask and always tried to pry me from mine.

"You aren't really this angry all the time, are you?"
"Come on, Kitty Kat, hiss and spit or get over it."
"Show me who you are."

I held the sword before me, braced my feet and waited. He was close enough now that I could see his pupils were completely blown. He wasn't that male who loved so fiercely, had wanted to love me beyond the comfort of my bed. I'm sorry, Cas. I'm so sorry.

Dust whirled around me, clouding my vision. I blinked the debris from my eyes. The tip of my blade sat inches from the center of his head, thick golden-brown fur and skin were stretched tight over that mostly canid head, the ends of his muzzle were mostly exposed bone. Thick saliva dripped to the ground; his puffs of breath were soured with rot.

"Casrian."

"Little elf." He rasped in a voice both young and old; human and not.

"Casrian. It's me, Katrel. Your friend."

He rumbled deep in his chest. It vibrated through my blade and up my arms. "I have no friends here."

Tears threatened my eyes. "No, you do. I am here. Niratap is here, and Mitta. Tummi and Bastion are here."

He growled, his tail thwacking against the ground in rage. "I have been forgotten."

The dust finally settled; I spared a glance up to my family. Mitta's face was ashen and Niratap's pained. Everyone else looked afraid. I should be afraid.

"No, you haven't, my friend." Slowly I lowered the blade and reached out my hand. "We're here. We found you."

"Princess, though I am fascinated by this pitiful exchange, this is a fight to the death." Cardoc's voice barked from the stand.

I swallowed. "Casrian. Let me help you."

His eyes flicked to Cardoc warily. "You are here to kill me."

"I don't want to hurt you, Cas."

"You're here to kill." He growled, shaking his head. "Kill. Kill. Kill."

"Casrian." My voice cracked as I reached for him. "Cas, please don't listen to him. I don't want to hurt you."

"Hurt. All elves do is hurt."

"Cas, please. I don't want to hurt you, friend. Please. Cas. It's me, Kitty Kat."

"No." He growled. "Kitty Kat didn't want to come. Kitty Kat didn't want me."

Tears rolled down my face. We had fought the last time I'd seen him. He had wanted me to go with him, west to where he was looking to raise hell. I had told him no. He had pressed and I told him to leave, that I didn't want to build a life with him. That had been three years ago. Fuck, had he left and been snatched up and locked away here?

"Cas, please." I was begging him to yield.

"Kitty Kat told me to leave." He shook his head, turning away pawing at those sad green eyes. "I left and elves caught me. Elves brought me here. Elves hurt. Elves hurt."

"Katrel, I tire of this." Cardoc chided from his box. "Just put the poor creature out of his misery."

"Stop talking."

"Kill the monster so we may feast, though I was hoping for a show."

"Stop."

"Come now, slay the—"

I pulled a pin from my hair and hurled it. The ping of it hitting the throne echoed through the arena. He didn't move a centimeter. "Stop fucking talking."

"Did you think that wise, child?" He glowered at me.

"The only monster I see in this arena," I snarled pointing my blade at him, "is you."

Fire flared in the braziers. "Insolent child. You will pay for your actions."

"You don't scare me." Fire flared around me dancing on the ground.

He laughed. "It is not me you have to be scared of child. I am not the opponent you face in the arena."

"You tortured him. Broke his spirit. Casrian is a good male."

"He is a beast and the sooner you see that, the sooner you'll learn. Archers."

"No!" I screamed over the whine of bowstrings.

"Ready."

"Stop this."

"Fire!"

"No!"

Archers fired upon Casrian. Arrows stuck into him from all angles. His cries were half human, half wild bellows, as he clawed at the arrows stuck in him.

"Elves hurt. Elves hurt. Elves hurt." he snarled, turning toward me, blood dripping from his maw. "Elves hurt."

“Cas.”

“Elves hurt.”

“Cas. I’m your friend.” I yielded a step.

“Elves hurt.”

“Cas, please.”

“Hurt elves.” My friend wasn’t there anymore.

I pulled the sword before me. “Cas, I don’t want to do this.”

“Hurt elves.”

“Casrian.”

Screams rose as he charged. I had to wait. I took a breath. Each foot closer my window approached, but I would get gored if I missed. Move too soon and he would divert and catch me before I could recalculate. Too late and I'd be flung or caught in those gnashing teeth. People were screaming, Mitta was screaming. I rolled out of his path, his massive body colliding with the white stones of the arena.

“Run!” Niratap shouted.

I heeded this time, bolting across the arena while the stunned bitarog righted himself. I had to outsmart him, that was my only chance. My heart pounded loud in my ears. He was bigger, stronger, and faster than me. I had to be smarter I–

“Katrel! Look out!” Shasha shouted.

I whirled around. Just in time to see the massive paw coming towards me.

Chapter Thirty-Eight

My stomach roiled as Katrel was flung across the arena. The scent of her blood hit me moments later. I pulled against the arms that held me back, clawing at them. I was screaming, a roaring filling my head. The king laughed. He fucking laughed. I would kill him for this. I'll kill you. I'll kill you.

Cool soft hands cupped my face, silencing the rage. "Breathe, Mitta. She's okay."

"Tummilia."

"Look Mitta, she's okay."

I peered past her into the arena where Kat pushed herself to stand. Blood dripped down her arm from a deep laceration as she pulled the two knives from her belt, the sword on the other side of the male before her. People cheered as that calm calculation faded over her face. A killing kind of calm that I had trained into her. She had to be a weapon.

"What is his gift?" Shasha asked her mate.

"Casrian's gift is manipulation of light."

"He can manipulate light?"

"It's much like how I can manipulate shadows. His methods are dangerous, and I can only hope he is too far into the wild that he doesn't use them."

"What does that mean?"

"I fear we are about to see." Bastion grumbled, pointing out at them.

I looked at Casrian, a bright sphere glowing between his antlers. Shit. Shit.

"What is he doing?"

I swallowed. "He's concentrating the rays of light

so he can fire them.”

“Hold up.” She said disbelievingly. “You’re telling me that he can fire lasers?”

“More or less.” Bastion said.

“She doesn’t stand a chance, does she?” The sphere continued to grow upon his head.

“If she is clever enough.” Niratap answered.

With the first blast of light, Katrel spun out of the way and charged. The second, she dodged with a leap. The third she rolled beneath, coming close enough to slash her dagger across the too tight skin of his face. He rose up on his hind legs, a towering eighteen-foot beast. She slashed along the back of his legs earning a feral roar. His tail thrashed, knocking her to the side causing her to drop one of her blades. He landed with a boom as she came to stand pulling the knife from her boot. She hissed at him going in again. She sidestepped his swipe ducking under him and slashing at his belly.

“Katrel move!” Niratap boomed. The last place you should ever be is under a bitarog with all their razor-sharp talons and claws.

She dove to the side and rolled away from the slam of his paw.

The copper tang of blood hung heavily in the air as they faced each other again. The sphere of concentrated light throbbed between his antlers. It was a blessing that it took time to weaponize rays of light, that he had to concentrate for the gift to be more than a party trick. Katrel flipped a dagger, not taking her eyes off him, before she launched the blade at him and ran. She reached between her breasts and drew the cragstone dagger. She needed a killing blow, needed to get close enough to wound him with the dagger.

He gave chase. She flung the other dagger at him blindly. It embedded itself into his shoulder. Casrian bellowed, collapsing into the ground and rolled end over end. Katrel dashed out of his path drawing the mythic blade from her back.

Over the din of cheers, a voice keened. "Channel your fire into the blade."

I looked for the voice that called out again. "Channel your fire."

Katrel spun looking for the voice. "I don't know how."

Casrian stumbled to his feet, the injured limb unable to support his weight and sent him back to the ground. I saw him then, running across the lip of the arena opposite us, Cyran. He leapt and spun past the two guards that tried to slow his approach.

"Katrel, channel your fire into the blade."

"I don't know how, Cyran."

Cyran moved to dodge the grasp of a guard. "The blade is an extension of your body. The fire is an extension of your will. Combine them."

Katrel shifted her grip, watching Casrian with one eye. Seconds felt like hours. "I can't."

Cyran was caught by a guard and screamed as he was being hauled away. "Get angry, Katrel!"

Casrian stood unsteady on his wounded legs, eyes locking on her. The crowd cheered as he roared at her and began to run. She turned to face him, still trying to connect with the sword.

"She's panicking."

Chapter Thirty-Nine

"Channel your fire into the blade. Channel your fire."

I spun looking for the voice finding Cyran fleeing from guards. I shouted. "I don't know how."

Casrian began to stand again, and I watched him while tracking our teacher as he out maneuvered the royal guard. "Katrel, channel your fire into the blade."

"I don't know how, Cyran."

"The blade is an extension of your body. The fire is an extension of your will. Combine them."

I shifted the blade in my hand, trying to summon the fire in me, trying to find an ember. "I can't."

Cyran was caught by a guard and screamed as he was being hauled away, fighting each step. "Get angry, Katrel!"

Casrian's roar was almost swallowed by the roar of the crowd. Shit. I was out of time. Shit. Shit. Shit. Get angry. I was angry, but I was scared. I was scared. I was scared and as Casrian charged me, I froze. This was it. I was going to die.

"Katrel!"

What would happen then? Would my family be able to flee? Would my father kill them?

"Katrel!"

Would any of them make it? Would Tummi be forced to take my place? Would Niratap be forced into bondage because of me?

"Katrel! Move!"

I ducked on instinct alone, a scream escaping my lips. I lunged upward, heaving with my whole body. Metal sunk into flesh as the ground met my back. The air was knocked from my lungs, and I squeaked under the mass that was Casrian. The pommel of the sword had hit me in the side and at least a couple ribs had cracked with the impact. I tried to shift, but I was lodged beneath him. His blood soaking me or was it mine?

"Please. Kill me." The weak male voice whispered. I fought for a breath. "Cas."

"Kitty Kat." That carnal voice, full of warmth and affection. "I don't want you to die."

"Casrian, you brute." I choked on the sob working its way up my throat. "I didn't want to hurt you."

"I know, Kitty Kat." He coughed, the force digging me into the dirt. "I smell that cragstone on you. End my suffering, love."

"Cas."

"Right into my heart, love."

I pried the knife from between our bodies, I screamed at the pain that flooded my senses. Broken ribs and broken fingers. "Cas."

"It'll be quick."

I angled the blade, his heart thumping erratically in my ear. "I'm sorry, Cas."

"I know, Kitty Kat."

"Cas." I sobbed.

"I love you, Katrel."

"I love you too, Cas."

"You didn't, and that's okay."

"Cas."

"Please, Kat. End this."

I tried to nod, but the space did not allow much. "Goodbye, my friend."

"Goodbye, my Kitty Kat."

I thrust the knife with as much force as I could into that pounding drum above me. It skittered and thrummed down that killing blade. The cruel stone banishing the magic that knit flesh and bone together. There was a shutter. A sigh. And—

"Thank you."

Chapter Forty

Mitta

"No!" I leapt for the edge of the arena as Casrian tackled Katrel, both going down in a cloud of dust. Strong arms wrapped around my waist and held me in place. "Let me go! Let me go! Kat! Kat!"

"Mitta, steady yourself." Niratap growled in my ear.

Tears threatened my eyes. "Niratap, release me. I can't lose her, too. I can't."

"Let the dust settle, Mitta." He growled. "I'm worried too, but we have to wait."

The dust settled in the arena, dusting the hulking body of Casrian, blood pooled around his as well. The male was breathing softly. The tip of that ancient sword jutting from his side, a punctured lung was not a fatal wound. In the stunned silence that was the arena we could hear his grumbling, but his words were lost to the distance. Were they talking? The whole arena held its breath. Held its breath as Casrian shuddered and sighed. A death rattle that was felt through the realms. The lord's grip loosened on my body, his arms shaking. Dead. Another of his waning race was dead, but was Kat? I slipped from his arms and that mass of cooling flesh shifted.

"Kat." All thoughts eddied from my mind as her hand clawed at the earth and the arena erupted with cheers.

"Kat!" I leapt from the stands into the dirt arena and dashed across the expanse, colliding with the lifeless corpse of my old friend.

"Kat." Pushing against the behemoth I heard her voice beneath. "Someone help me!"

Shadows curled around me as the massive hands of

a half-shifted Niratap tucked under the warm body. "On three, Mitta. One. Two. Three."

Together we hefted Casrian's body to the side. Katrel laid there blinking in the daylight, tear tracks cutting through the blood on her face. She looked at me with such sorrow in her eyes.

"I didn't want to hurt him."

"I know, Kat." I said to her, reaching out my hand.

Her gaze traveled past my shoulder to where Niratap stood. "I didn't want to kill him."

"I know." His voice was sad, but human. "You didn't have a choice, Katrel."

Niratap pulled the blades from Casrian's corpse, the wet sound rent new tears from her eyes.

"I didn't want this." She sobbed, finally taking my hand and curling into my chest.

I looked to Niratap, who was glaring at the king's box and snarled. "Are you entertained?"

With that, Cardoc left the king's box to plot the next method of torture for his daughter. I ran a hand down Katrel's back soothing the sobs that were unearthly quiet.

"Can you walk?" I whispered into her hair. My throat was raw from screaming.

A nod and a barely audible, "I think so."

"Okay," I pulled back to look at her. There was a small laceration above her eye and a bruise on her cheek. "Let's go get you checked out."

"Right." I pulled her with me to stand. She took a step with her head held high, another and she crumpled. "Fuck."

Niratap grabbed her elbow. "You won. Everyone is watching, so you *will* walk out of this arena."

A cursory glance proved his words. No one had left with the dismissal of the king. They watched on in quiet conversation with each other.

"Keep that chin high. Show them you're not afraid. Show them you'll keep winning. I've got you."

Together we helped her hobble across the arena. A call rose from the people. It started softly at one end, a female voice rising above the silence. The sound grew with each step, a chant that sank deep into my bones. Her name became a roar as we entered the archway, a song that her people cheered.

Niratap scooped her into his arms as we crossed the threshold of shadow, murmuring softly. "I got you. You did great. I got you."

Our friends met us outside the arena and together we rushed through the castle to our quarters. Cyran was already pacing before the doors, dressed casually for the first time I'd ever seen. He had a blackened eye and split lip.

"Is she alright?"

"She'll be okay." Niratap said, letting me open the door. "She just needs to be looked over."

"I'll summon a healer." I didn't bother arguing with the battered man, my focus wholly centered on that brave woman as the lord set her gingerly into a chair. Her shirt was ruined, coated in that too dark blood the bitarogs had.

"Thank you, my friend." She murmured.

"Of course." He dipped his chin turning to his mate who held out a pile of clothes.

"You're getting rather good at that." Bastion said. "Slipping from your clothes with half a thought."

"It seems like a practical skill to have while I have limited resources." Niratap answered

"Okay Mr. Limited Resources," I snapped kneeling in front of Katrel. "Go get dressed. Someone grab me a basin with warm water and towels."

"Yes, Mitta." Tummi and Bastion scuttled off. Shasha and the lord moved to the side, and he dressed quickly and dispersed his shadows.

Gingerly I placed my hands on her knees. "Tell me what hurts, Kat."

She stared at me for what felt like hours before she

rasped. "Everything hurts."

Chuckling, I broke our stare. "Okay, well what hurts the worst?"

"My left hand and my ribs."

"Let me see that hand."

She lifted the gnarled thing, her thumb, ring, and pinky finger bent at odd angles. I took the hand gingerly feeling out the bones. She hissed through her teeth but didn't pull away.

"I'm going to have to reset these fingers before someone can heal them."

She took a deep breath, looking toward the ceiling. "Do it."

I fixed her pinky first, the least broken of the three. Tears ran down her face and she took another breath. The ring finger I had more difficulty getting the bones set; the bones had twisted. She whimpered, gulping down air as I reached for the thumb. It was two clean breaks in the small bones of her hand but setting them took her over the edge. She screamed, the cry loosening sorrow in my heart.

"I'm sorry."

Her breathing was shallow, and her voice was high and tight with pain. "No, you're fine."

"Here's your water and rags, Mitta." Bastion said, setting them down beside me.

"Thank you." I stood. "That shirt has gotta go."

She grimaced, but nodded as I withdrew my dagger. Slicing up the garment, I swallowed the desire that bubbled up through me as I exposed her blood-stained skin and the soft swell of her breasts, behind the wrap she had looped. My eyes ate up every inch of skin and my mouth went dry. *Mine.*

I swallowed again, trying to banish the errant wild thought. My hands shook as I peeled her out of her shirt. The thoughts eddied away as I exposed her left side, black bruises along her ribs, her skin torn and oozing.

"Are you dizzy?"

"No."

"Is it hard to breathe?"

"It hurts, but no."

Taking the rag, I dipped it in the water and began wiping away the blood from her shoulders and arms. She had a laceration in her arm and bruises, so many bruises, but she was relatively unhurt.

Footsteps stormed down the hall and our friends flanked my back as the door burst open.

"You males, out." The woman hissed.

"Keerane, they will stay."

"It's improper in your state of undress, your Highness." She bobbed her head.

Niratap scoffed, keeping his body between us. "We're staying. State your business."

"Keerane is a healer. Let her by. I trust her." Katrel growled.

I looked at the older elf woman, she had sharp emerald eyes and that ethereal beauty of her race, with her mousy brown hair done up in a high frizzy bun. She glowered at the males who moved aside and cleared her throat. She smelled of linen soap and wildflowers, though the flowery smell might have just been her basket of blooms she carried with her.

"Status?"

I cleared my own throat as I cleaned a wound. "She has three open lacerations. One tear on her left side, one slice on her right bicep and a small one above her right eye. She has a couple cracked ribs on her left and her left hand has several broken bones that I've already set. She more than likely has a sprained knee or ankle, but I haven't made it that far in my evaluation. Everything else is bruising and minor abrasions."

"And were you just going to bare the princess before these males?"

I bristled, but Katrel hissed. "Keerane, both males have committed partners. Both males have seen women

424

before. My body is of no surprise to them."

She scoffed coming around behind Katrel to set her basket on the table. "Well, I—" She trailed off , staring at the scars that were Kat's back.

Kat frowned, her eyes meeting mine, then she looked at her bruised hands. "I was dipped in acid a long time ago."

Keerane placed her hand over her mouth. "How long? When?"

"Long enough. Soon after I left."

The woman nodded and examined Katrel's back in silence. Gingerly she placed a hand on the bruised skin above her broken ribs, golden light spilled from between her fingers. Her magic smelled of warm grass, the bruise tightening under her touch. Katrel winced as she moved away. She sealed wounds and lessened bruises, working her way around to face the princess. I sat in the free chair closest to Kat. Mesmerized by the healers ability.

"It could have been much worse, had that beast gotten ahold of you." She murmured.

Katrel frowned at the woman. "He was my friend."

"Your friend? That monster?"

"Casrian was a good male." She said solemnly, I remembered she had bedded him not too many years ago. "He was a good person."

"I don't see—"

Interrupting, her voice sharper than the lady's cragstone knife, Katrel said. "Keerane, you should tread very carefully with what you think of saying next. I care little about what you think of me and my decisions. However, you will not speak poorly about the people I care about, regardless of their race."

She blinked and bowed her head. "Apologies, Your Highness. May I?"

Katrel lifted her hand to the woman. Keerane's brows rose. "You set the bones beautifully."

I spared a glance to lord Niratap, who frowned. I

said softly. "Thank you. I've had a lot of practice."

She gingerly set her hand down and kneeled touching down her legs. "It will be tender for a few days."

"Alright."

"I would rest for a couple of days."

"Alright."

She squeezed her ankle, Katrel winced. "I mean it."

"Fine." She barked. "I'll rest."

Keerane nodded as she stood. "Take a hot bath, wash the grime off yourself. Rest. I'll have some tea brought up to help with the residual pain."

"Thank you, Keerane."

"We admire your bravery, your Majesty."

"There was nothing brave about what I did."

Keerane bowed her head. "I will check on you tomorrow."

"Thank you, Keerane."

She dipped her head again before she left, the door clicking shut behind her.

"Are you good on your own or would you like assistance?"

She stood testing her healed joint. "I can manage. Will you bring me some fresh clothes, Tummi?"

"Of course, sister."

With a weak smile, she carefully stepped away, only slightly limping, and into the bathing room. I wanted to care for her, even when it was not my place. Even when the vows I'd swore kept me rooted, I wanted to be there to care for her.

426

Chapter Forty-One

Bastion

Casrian had fought the poison every moment of that fight. I had seen it. As the toxins ripped through his body his mind fought. His death had been a mercy. What had he suffered here in this horrible place? What would we suffer if Kat couldn't win her freedom? My skin itched uncomfortably with those fears.

Mitta snarled, pulling me from my thoughts. "Okay, Mr. Limited Resources, go get dressed. Someone grab me a basin with warm water and towels."

The male spirit that followed Mitta stood by the door, watching her and shaking his head. He pointed at her and sighed.

Hún hefur svo mikið pláss í hjarta sínu til að elska mig og prinsessuna. [62]

I wanted to understand what he said. Tummi placed a hand on my shoulder and said. "Yes, Mitta."

I followed her into the bathing room and sighed as she closed the door. Too many things were happening too fast. "Are we–"

"Don't." she said digging through a cupboard and pulling out rags.

"*Asta hri.*" [63]

"Bastion. We can't start thinking like that. Kat has made it through two grueling trials. We can't doubt that we will make it out of here. We can't worry about what would happen if–"

"But what happens if–" I hissed, flexing my hands.

"No." She shook her head as she collected the bin.

[62] She has so much room in her heart to love me and the princess.
[63] Star in the heavens.

"No, Bastion. I can't. I just can't. If I lose hope now, what then?"

"Tummi, I–"

"Unless you're going to apologize, Bastion, don't." She muttered, filling the basin.

"What next then?"

"What do you mean?"

"What are we doing next?"

"Well, we're going to take these supplies to Mitta. Then after I know Katrel is taken care of I want to find Cyran and ask him what he knows about the star."

"You think he will have information on them?"

"If not, he knows where I can look. Take the bin."

"And what are you looking for exactly? Teovelass said that the flame emperor's kid wiped them from history."

"That may be, but only the scholars live in the library. I doubt Einar got rid of everything. Come on." She said pushing through the door.

"Here's your water and rags, Mitta."

"Thank you. That shirt has gotta go."

A cadence of footsteps outside the door pulled the lord from his mate to stand between where Mitta was working and the door. I came beside him, crossing my arms as a woman, her mouse brown hair done up in a thick frizzy bun, pushed into the room, Cyran standing in the hall behind her.

"You males, out."

"Keerane, they will stay." Katrel hissed.

"It's improper in your state of undress, your Highness." She dipped her chin, but I saw the judgment in her shrewd green eyes.

The lord scoffed but did not move. "We're staying. State your business."

"Keerane is a healer. Let her by. I trust her." Katrel growled and we moved out of the way. The lord watched the healer closely.

"Status?"

Mitta prattled off a list of injuries. Broken ribs, cuts, bruises, sprains. She had been so lucky. I had seen bitarogs rip through enemies. The lord himself had shredded through beings to protect others. Kat bested him in hand-to-hand, but they had trained together for so long—

"And were you just going to bare the princess before these males?" The woman hissed at Mitta.

Mitta's hands froze where she was cleaning the slice along Kat's ribs. Kat looked up at the woman, eyes narrowing and full of authority. "Keerane, both males have committed partners and both males have seen women before. My body is of no surprise to them."

She scoffed, moving behind Kat to the table, her basket full of flowers. "Well I—" She trailed off horror in her eyes as the locked onto Katrel's back.

"I was dipped in acid a long time ago." I looked at Tummi whose head lowered to look at the floor.

"How long? When?"

"Long enough. Soon after I left."

I rubbed Tummi's back to comfort her. I was a child compared to the two of them and my lifespan, if I lived into old age, would be just a blip. They had suffered so much at the hands of men. Greedy men. Men who craved control and power over anything else. Men who prowled the shadows. Men like me.

My hand stilled on her back. She looked up at me, her face tightening in concern. "Bas."

I shook my head.

"It could have been much worse," Keerane murmured softly, as she worked, the flowers wilting in the basket, "had that beast gotten ahold of you."

"He was my friend."

"Your friend? That monster?" The woman sounded genuinely shocked. I rolled my eyes.

"Casrian was a good male." Kat said sadly. "He was a good person."

"I don't see—"

Kat snarled sharply. "Keerane you should tread very carefully with what you think of saying next. I care little about what you think of me and my decisions. However, you will not speak poorly about the people I care about, regardless of their race."

"Apologies, Your Highness. May I?"

Keerane took Kat's hand and continued her work. Tummi poked me between the ribs. "What's going on?"

"Nothing, Love."

She glowered at me. "You are a bad liar, Bastion."

"It's not something that matters right now." I answered quietly.

"You are thinking something bad about yourself again, aren't you?"

I sighed. "I might."

She folded her arms across her chest. "I don't understand why you are like this. I mean—"

"Fine." Kat barked. "I'll rest."

Keerane nodded, standing and collecting her things. "Take a hot bath, wash the grime off yourself. Rest. I'll have some tea brought up to help with the residual pain."

"Thank you, Keerane."

"We admire your bravery, Your Majesty."

"There was nothing brave about what I did."

"I will check on you tomorrow."

"Thank you, Keerane." Katrel said, before the woman ducked out into the hall.

"Are you good on your own or would you like assistance?" Mitta asked her softly.

Kat stood, testing a step. "I can manage. Will you bring me some fresh clothes, Tummi?"

"Of course, sister." Tummi moved to the wardrobe as soon as the door closed.

The lord opened the door letting the scholar in. "That was very brave of you, scholar."

He met the lord's gaze with the fearlessness of a warrior. "She needed help."

"Don't let Kat hear you say that." Shasha said from the bed. "She hates that."

"She should have used her fire."

"To be honest," Tummi said, pulling out of the wardrobe with an armful of clothes. "I didn't know she had fire magic."

"She roasted this room before she went to rescue you." Cyran growled. Mitta furrowed her brows and the male, Bran, wrapped a phantom arm around her. "I had hoped she would have fostered that skill into a weapon."

"Magic is a terrifying skill to manage." Niratap said, leaning against the door. "It does not matter what kind of magic it is either."

"It is still something she should have bloomed. Not having control of a destruction class magic is dangerous and she has sequestered it."

"I do not blame her for being afraid of flame." Niratap said softly. "The shadows I wield were not so easily mastered."

"She is the daughter of the Raloqen line, it is to be expected she would carry the emperor's flame in her blood."

"I do not have flame magic." Tummi said before the bathing room door, knocking. "I am also a daughter of the Raloqen line, wouldn't that also be true of me."

"There has never been more than one child to the throne. Your birth was unprecedented."

"Well even then, there is barely a lick of magic in me." She said before she pushed into the bathing room.

"You would think the blood running through both their veins would influence their gifts." I said, watching Cyran glower at me. "Why wouldn't Tummi have just as much magic as her sister?"

"Teovelass said that he only smelled starlight in Tummi though." Shasha added. "Maybe there is more to it that we don't know."

"Who is this Teovelass?" Cyran asked warily.

"The dragon that lives under *Magav Hiiglane*." Tummi said, coming back into the room and shutting the bathing room door behind her. "He told us a different history, the true history of our people. I was hoping that you would help me explore the archives for information, teacher."

"What are you looking for?"

"Anything you can find about the Emperor's Star."

Cyran blinked. "Very well."

Chapter Forty-Two

Katrel

The bath eased the ache in my bruised body, the heat seeping into my joints like a salve. Casrian was gone. I had mourned losing him once already but knowing his fate; knowing I was the cause of his vacancy in the world rent at the pieces of my heart that had always belonged to him. I sank underneath the water, hiding the tears that tried to run down my cheeks. His laughter just a memory now.

"You are so beautiful, Kat." He whispered in my ear, sweet whiskey on his breath.

"Stop." I pushed against his chest, trying and failing to get him to drop me.

"You know, I've always wondered what your skin feels like."

I stopped fighting him. "What?"

His emerald eyes were hooded with lust and alcohol. "What do you feel like?"

Heat clouded the dread that had taken residence in my heart, false confidence took root. "Want to find out?"

"I bet you—Wait, what?"

"I said 'want to find out?' Come on Cas don't tease a girl with a good time."

He set me down and let me lead him away from the dancing and revelry. He kissed my neck and held me like a treasure. When his hands had exposed my scarred body, he kissed each hurt as if he would remove them from my body. My soul.

"You are so beautiful, Kitty Kat."

No. I surfaced, sputtering a bit.

"I know you're not okay, but I'm here if you need me." Tummi said from the counter.

I wiped the water from my face. "I know."

"I brought you the comfiest thing I could find. Follow Keerane's instructions."

"I plan too."

"Okay." She turned to the door. "Was it terrible for you? When father sold me?"

Another open wound. "He sold the only person who had ever meant anything to me. It destroyed me."

She nodded. "I know I don't say it often, but thank you."

"I would do it all over again you know?"

"I do." She slipped out the door, leaving me to my thoughts.

I sank into the water. Mitta had screamed my name, had come to my aid when I was sure my father would let me suffocate under Cas's body. Was that kiss really a mistake? Did she really not want me? She had said that it wasn't for a lack of wanting, but did she want me? What kind of promise from the past would hold so much weight as to keep her from loving me? Who would keep her from loving me?

What would it matter if she could love me? There was no guarantee that the king would allow me to have my freedom. No promise that we would get to walk out of here. Niratap had said months ago that Cardoc would tie me to the marriage bed if he couldn't get me to go willingly. I stared at the ceiling, the hauntingly familiar celestial motif was meant to be relaxing, but it just made me feel small and insignificant. Who was I to question the hand that I was dealt? Who was I to question whether or not I deserved what my heart desired?

There was a knock at the door.

"Yes?"

"Are you alright, Katrel?" Mitta.

"I am." I faced the door were she crept in.

"The lord and lady retired for the evening and Tummi and Bastion went to the library with Cyran. Did you need anything?”

I gazed back up to the ceiling. “No.”

“How is your hand?”

I flexed my fingers. “It hurts, but it feels fine.”

“How’s your breathing?”

“It aches when I breathe deep, but it’s not too bad.”

“I’ll leave you to your soak then.” With dip of her chin she turned.

“Why are you running?”

She peered at me over her shoulder. “I’m not running.”

“You always seem to be running when it comes to me.” Her screams echoed in my ears.

Glowering she asked. “What do you mean?”

“When I’m in danger or hurt you’re running to me but when I want clarity or comfort you run away. Why is that?”

“Katrel, this is not the proper time for that.”

“When will there be a proper time, Mitta?” I snarled. “When I am dead?”

“Why would you say such a thing?” Pain and fury rolled into those bronze eyes.

“I ache, Mitta.” My heart was too full and much too empty. “I ache deep in my soul, and I thought you would be there, and you are running. Always fucking running.”

“I cannot–”

“That is what you always say. You cannot love me. You cannot be mine. You cannot want me.”

“Kat–”

“No!” I stood splashing water across the stone floor. “You do not get to stand there and tell me how you only care about me when it is convenient for you. You don’t get to tell me that it is not for a lack of wanting me, but that you cannot have me. Take me, Mitta. Take my scarred and battered body and soul. Take. Take and do what you please.”

She swallowed. “I cannot take what is not mine.”

"But it is yours if you would only take it! You kissed me, Mitta! You kissed me and it sparked this longing in me. Longing I have never felt for any male. Longing I have never felt for freedom. Take it! Take me!"

"I cannot, Katrel."

"Yes, you can. You can if you would just try, Mitta."

"You don't understand."

"What is there to understand? You either care for me or you don't. You either want me or you don't. You either love me or you don't."

"It's complicated."

"I don't care how complicated it gets; I still love you." My hand clamped over my mouth.

Tears rolled down her cheeks. I could count the times I had seen her cry in three centuries on one hand. "I cannot give you what you need."

"I need you."

"I can't."

I had never felt like this. It was as if all that I was and all that I had ever wanted and needed eddied away, leaving me hollow. My heart thundering between my ears, but also oozing from my pores and into the near scalding water that had turned frigid. I turned frigid.

"Leave." My voice was flat even to my own ears, devoid of what I wanted to feel.

"Katrel. I–"

"I said leave."

"Let me explain."

"No, I don't want to hear how I can't be your person. You are my person, Mitta! You will always be my person, even if I can't be yours, so leave. I do not care where you go, just leave."

She retreated through the door, my heart gripped painfully with each step she took away from me.

Chapter Forty-Three

Niratap

The angry shouts from Katrel's room pulled my attention away from Shasha's hands trailing over my chest.

"What is it?" She whispered kissing along my collar.

"Fighting." I said, shuddering as her tongue trailed up my throat.

"Who?" Her breath tickled behind my ear.

"Katrel and Mitta."

"Let them fight, maybe they'll figure their shit out."

A door slammed and I shifted her from my lap. "I doubt it, tiger incoming."

"Damn it." She flopped down dramatically as the door opened. Salt curled into my nose as Mitta's bleary face slid into our room.

"I'm sorry." Mitta sniffled and bowed. "I don't mean to intrude. I just—"

"You don't need to apologize, Mitta." I unfolded myself and went to her side.

Tears rolled down her face, which she viciously wiped away. "I just need a moment."

"Take as many as you need."

Her breath sawed out of her. "Why is this so hard?"

"Loving people is hard." I slid my hands into my slacks, glad Shasha hadn't made it to slipping me out of them.

"It shouldn't hurt this much. I have never had love hurt me this much. Why does it hurt so much?"

"Why are you not just honest with each other?" Shasha asked, slipping her hand into my pocket, weaving her fingers between my own.

Tears seeped from her eyes. "I have been honest. I have told her that I am enamored with her. I just can't have her."

"Why is that?" Shasha pressed.

Mitta shook her head. "The wounds of my youth are mine and mine alone to bear. She does not need my sorrows distracting her while she is trying to win her freedom."

"If you opened up to her, she might surprise you." I spoke gently and Shasha squeezed my hand.

"It serves no purpose right now." She hissed. "It would only serve as a distraction for her."

"But it would serve you." Shasha pulled her hand free. "It would serve to ease this ache in you both."

"I refuse to be a burden on her."

Cupping her face, Shasha said. "You are beautiful and brave, and you deserve to be happy."

Mitta frowned, pulling Shasha's hands from her face. "I will never be happy, but thank you for that wish for hope. My happiness died long ago."

"Mitta—"

She shook her head wiping her eye again. "May I use your bathroom for a moment?"

Shasha's heart cracked and a cavernous feeling weighed in my chest. "You may, but Mitta—"

"Thank you for caring for my weary soul. I will attend to my needs and be out of your hair." She turned away.

"Mitta?"

"Yes, my Lord?"

It killed me to see her so broken. "We are here if you have need of us."

"Thank you, my Lord." She slipped into the bathing chamber with a soft click of the door.

Shasha shook with agony for our friend, as I guided her back to the bed. I had been so absorbed in my goals that I had never noticed the attraction between the two girls.

438

Thinking back, it was blatantly obvious that the girls cared deeply for one another, but what drove Mitta from claiming everything that I was sure Katrel had offered? It was not my place to ask, nor was it my business.

"Why can't they just love each other?" Shasha asked.

"Love does not come easily to those of us who have never had it in quantity or quality. I had a difficult time convincing myself that it was love that I felt for you."

"As opposed to what?"

I smirked. "Hunger or lust."

"You would have eaten me?" She smiled through her mock horror.

"I might have. Early on I could not tell what needs my instincts wanted to fulfill."

"Carnal ones it seems."

I huffed a laugh. "Well yes, I did meet those needs with you first."

"And I hope that you continue to find those needs met with me."

"Oh, I definitely plan on meeting them." I growled, pressing my lips against her throat, desire flooding both our bodies. "But after we are alone."

"She would be so angry." She whispered breathlessly.

"She would."

The door to the bathing room opened. The white feline stalked out, bronze eyes watching us momentarily before she dipped her head and moved towards the door to the hall. There was a hollowness in that gaze that I had never seen outside of the mirror. I cleared my throat to ease the tightness that took residence.

"You can stay here if it is easier, Mitta."

The tiger paused her retreat and shook her mighty head.

"You are just going to lie there in the hall, aren't you?" Shasha pressed. "Guard her door and wait to be allowed back in?"

Mitta huffed, opening the door and exiting into the hall. The latch snicking back into place was a boom in her wake.

"Her heart is broken." Shasha rubbed her hand down my back.

"It is her own doing that causes it."

"Do you think they will make up?"

I swallowed the hollow feeling still weighing down my heart. My mate's heart, her eyes, held so much remorse for our friend. "We can only hope."

She shifted back into the bed, slipping under the covers to try to hide from the chill that iced our blood. "I am tired."

"Rest then." I said slipping under the blankets with her wrapping my arm around her shoulder. "I will be here."

"I know." she rested her head against my chest. "I love you."

"I love you."

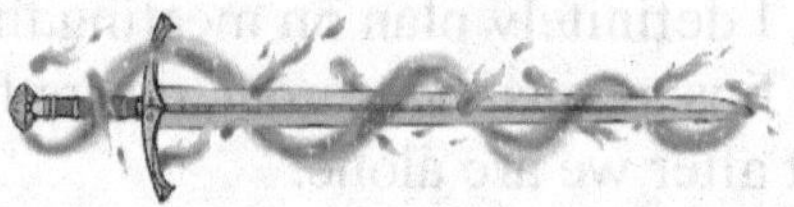

Idly I played with Shasha's braids, her breath a soft puff against my chest while my thoughts were too busy to let me sleep soundly. What in your past is so terrible, Mitta, that it would keep you from allowing yourself to love that fire-spirited woman like you wanted? A small worry when we were sleeping in the lion's den, waiting for him to become hungry enough to no longer need us for entertainment. Injustice polluted the court and most turned a blind eye to it to avoid the wrath of the king. It filled me with rage that simmered in my blood. Shasha shifted fitfully as she sensed that anger through the bond. The bond that grew with intensity each passing day. Would it make us stronger or would it be a great weakness in the other?

When she had sliced her hand in the forest, the sting of steel kissed my own; pain dulled in potency, but uncomfortably sat in my skin.

A firm knock on the door pulled me from my thoughts "Enter."

Bastion eased into the room and dipped his head. "My Lord."

I sighed. "Everyone has been so formal today."

"I'm sorry." His face tightened. "Why is Mitta in her oversized tiger form just lying in the hall barring entry into Katrel's room?"

"They fought and wounded each other's hearts in the process. Did your search for information prove fruitful?"

"Yes and no. Cyran pulled many ancient texts, some with vague references to Lucette's kindness or The Flame Emperor's bravery in battle. There were several tomes that Cyran said were missing or in his father's study in the depths."

A chill settled in my bones. "Did you go to the depths?"

"No, Cyran didn't want either of us in that dark part of the library. He said he would request them from his father and inquire on the missing volumes, in the morning."

"Very well." Still limited answers, limited solutions.

"I–" Bastion shifted uncomfortably.

"Yes?"

"I have been meaning to apologize for things that have escalated because of my presence." The boy was always so apologetic for things that weren't his doing.

"I am well, Bastion. The moments of discourse that have accosted me are not your doing and you do not need to harbor any guilt for the actions of a cruel man."

"But had I not let the king rile me up, maybe we would have noticed your discomfort sooner and avoided the aftermath."

"Though I thoroughly hate the taste of bile and peroxide, I am alright. The king's scheme failed, and I am alright, Bastion."

He frowned at me. "Fine. I will leave you to rest then."

I nodded my head. "Go take care of Tummi, Bastion."

Chapter Forty-Four

Shasha

Three days of scouring ancient books in the library surrounded by dust and aging paper. Three days of waiting for Cyran's father to surface with the texts that he had. The tomes he had brought to Cyran's office were talking more about starlight as an ingredient in spells, but not one mention of the lost line of female descendants of the Star. Three days of hunting and returning to our rooms with more questions than answers. Three days of Mitta standing guard before the princess's door. Three days of silence from Katrel and a deepening sorrow in Mitta's eyes.

It was on the trudge to the library the fourth day, after Cyran met us, his face grave. "We have a problem."

"That is not reassuring." My mate growled, his unease twisting in my stomach.

"Cardoc has decided that in two days' time there will be a ball. All the local nobility will be in attendance. He has opened the invitation to your group as well."

"A ball does not spell danger to me." I said softly.

"It is probably one of the most dangerous events there are." Niratap's voice dropped menacingly, and the rolling monsoon of anger and fear made my bones quake. "Are we to be guests or entertainment?"

"Guests was what I was told. However, knowing the king as I do, I would not hold it past him to twist it the other way."

"We will prepare for a ball, then." Tummi said, glancing at her sister, who had finally joined us. "I'm sure we have gowns that will fit, or that can be altered quickly. We may even be able to find something for you, Shasha."

I smiled. "I have a dress."

My mate cocked his head. "You packed a dress?"

"A woman always brings her Sunday best." I winked at him. "At least that's what my mother says."

He smirked. "What dress did you bring, *mo grá*?"

"You'll see."

"As fun as the prospect of a ball seems, it being in two days would put us three days till the solstice." Bastion crossed his arms across his chest. "And still no word on what Katrel's final trial will be."

"What is he planning?" Katrel asked the scholar. It was the first time she'd spoken since her fight with Mitta.

"I do not know." Cyran eyed our group. "I would advise caution. Nobles are already arriving today for—"

"A royal wedding." Disdain coated Katrel's voice. "Where even is he?"

"Who?" Cyran asked cautiously.

Katrel frowned, cocking her hip to the side. "My betrothed."

"At this time of day, he's in the training yard with the knights—" Katrel turned on her heels and stalked back down the hall. "Where are you going?"

Without turning, she patted the ancient sword at her side and said. "To teach the male a lesson he won't forget."

"Katrel, I don't think that wise." Mitta said, following after her. Katrel ignored her.

Niratap leaned his head by my ear. "Will you make sure they stay out of trouble?"

I faced him, our noses brushing as his pooled moonlight eyes met mine; lust and fear fighting for dominance in him. "So trusting of you, my Lord."

"Well, I trust you much more than the scorned lovers." He said softly, Cyran made a noise in his throat. "*Mo grá*?"

"I'd love to watch her show that asshole a thing or two."

He smiled. "You will tell me all about it?"

"Of course, *mo chori*."

He kissed me softly. "Good. Don't get left behind."

"Find something in your search." I kissed him back before taking off after the girls. "I'll keep them from killing each other."

I caught up to the girls as they rounded another corner, Mitta pleading with Katrel to reconsider.

"Kat. Will you please just stop for a second and think? He could seriously hurt you and if the worst happens—"

"Mitta, I don't think that train of thought is good for what you're trying to convey." I puffed and she glared at me.

Katrel paused before a set of glass doors that overlooked the training courtyard. Two dozen elven men were paired off, sparing one another, the blonde douche bag stalking between the groups correcting forms and offering advice.

"I do not think this is wise." Mitta hissed.

"I don't care if anyone thinks it is wise or not." Katrel snapped. The first words she's spoken to Mitta in three days, though they were broad enough to wound. She swallowed. "I am going to show him that, in the case the worst does happen and I have to give up my freedom to save my family, I will be a nightmare of a wife to him and he will not tame me into my mother. I will not willingly bow to a man who is weaker than me. I know everyone thinks this is a terrible idea that I shouldn't paint a larger target on my back, but I refuse to lay down quietly in that marriage bed."

I placed a hand on her shoulder. "We are with you."

Her copper eyes flashed in the early morning light, showing the fire in her. "I don't want you to get caught in a dangerous situation."

I smiled at her. "Nira wanted me to come to make sure you two stayed out of trouble."

Her eyebrows twitched upwards. "Really?"

"Yes. Besides, with how our mate bond is evolving,

I'm sure a very angry bitarog will arrive to rectify it if anything truly goes wrong."

"Let's hope that doesn't happen." Mitta murmured. "It would put him at risk, which is why we shouldn't be here."

"If you do not want to be here, you can leave." Katrel hissed. "Since you enjoy running."

Mitta's eyes narrowed, pain lacing them. "Let's get this over with then."

"Let's." Katrel pushed open the doors.

The first couple groups of guards noticed us, pausing the sparring to bow as Katrel descended into the courtyard. Revan's back was to us where he corrected a young knight's posture. The knights bowed in a wave as she led us through them, her head held high. The young elves who were taking instructions noticed Katrel and bowed deeply.

Revan twisted, smirking before he bowed at the waist. "Good morning, Princess."

"Revan."

He stood, the smirk still painted on his face. His eyes filled with a masculine delight as they ate up the three of us, taking in my hips, Mitta's curves, and Katrel's chest. Disgust curled in my stomach.

"I am a captain, and now with our pending wedding, heir to the throne."

"Right." Katrel looked down her nose at the male.

"What brings you here to squire training, Princess?"

"I wanted to see if you were actually worthy of the title my father is handing you."

"Oh." He frowned.

"What, Revan?" Katrel stepped into his space. "Are you afraid of me?"

Arrogance flared in his face, a lupine smile crossing his face as he gazed down at her. "Why would I ever be afraid of a woman?"

"You should be afraid of us." I said, pushing past

him to the weapons rack.

"Women are the weaker sex. I don't see how a rakshasi or a princess would be a cause for concern, let alone a half breed."

Katrel stomped on his foot pulling his gaze back to her. "You will mind how you speak to my lady."

"Is that a request, Princess?"

"It's an order, Revan."

"I don't take orders from women."

"Gross." I spun the sword in my hand.

"Especially abominations."

Katrel kneed the male in the groin, before Mitta could even retort. He folded over himself, with a groan. She pressed a knife to his throat pulling his head back by his golden hair. She hissed. "Mind how you speak to my lady."

A couple of the squires snickered and the rage in his face was lethal. "Fine."

"Fine, what?"

"Fine, Your Grace."

She dropped the male and sheathed the dagger in her belt. "Would you like to spar, my Lady?"

I smiled. "Of course, Your Majesty."

Aetherius sang as she unsheathed it. "Find one that fits?"

I shrugged. "I am much more comfortable with my dagger, but yes; though I find it slightly unfair that you have a legendary magic sword, and I have a practice blade for children."

"Take it up with the lord." She flipped the sword in her hand. The squires watched as we began our dance, circling each other like sharks. I wondered how many of them had watched her fight with Casrian. How many would learn from what we showed them, just sparring. I wondered if Revan would take the bait.

Katrel struck and I met her blow for blow, trying not to give up any ground within the ring. Mitta stalked around the ring watching us carefully, fully becoming our teacher. Sweat rolled down both our faces as we met strike for strike. I attacked her weaker side, but she caught me each time, deflecting and making me concede a step. She spun kicking my feet out from under me, the sword flying from my hand. I hit the dirt and reached for my dagger. As my fingers curled around the hilt, Katrel buried Aetherius in the dirt by my head, the sharp edge of the blade nicking my neck.

She panted over me with that fire raging in her eyes. "You're dead."

"Every time."

She pulled Aetherius from the earth, careful not to nick me again, before she offered me her hand. "Lord Niratap is going to have a come apart at that."

"It's just a scratch." I said even as I felt the welled drop of blood roll down my neck. Squires clapped around us.

"Have Mitta check it out." She said softly, her eyes flitting over my shoulder.

I turned as Revan approached, clapping for show. "Well done, Princess."

I held my ground between them. "You should lessen that tone of yours."

"Oh?" He smirked at me as I drew my dagger. "Why should I?"

"Because she outranks you."

"A technicality."

"A technicality?" I hissed, but Katrel placed her free hand on my shoulder as she eased ahead of me.

"You want to prove otherwise, Revan?"

"I could never raise my sword to you, Princess." he bowed at the waist. "We are grateful for your display, but the squires have much to learn and—"

Katrel used the tip of Aetherius to tilt the male's head up to look at her. "Are you afraid to lose?"

She was baiting him, and it was working, his eyes

narrowing with malice. I turned walking to the edge of the ring where Mitta was flexing her hands. "He's not worth your breath, Katrel."

"Maybe you're right my lady: only a coward would deny a challenge." The squires began murmuring.

"Are you sure this is what you want, Princess?"

Katrel shrugged. "I don't like men telling me what to do."

"Very well." Revan stood drawing his sword: it was an elegant weapon, inlaid with a gold flaming serpent down the center. He crossed his blade with Aetherius as he stepped into the ring, his movements refined as he stepped into her space. "Your father will hear of this."

"Good, I hope he learns to fear me, too."

Katrel shifted a step away and slashed his blade tip into the dirt. She kicked out against his ribs and sent him stumbling with a grunt.

"Stop dancing with me Revan, you were never very quick on your feet."

"Princess, my patience is running thin."

"Good, maybe you will actually act like a challenge for a few moments."

He roared lunging for her with wide swings of his sword. He was angry and it made him sloppy. Katrel didn't have to try to parry or block his attacks, her movements agile as she slipped away from him over and over again. A broad sweep of his blade missed her but sheared the end of her braid setting her chestnut strands free. They broke apart. Revan panted in ragged heaves, his sword hanging limply in his hands. Katrel was sweating, but her breathing was steady and even as she swept her hair over her shoulder.

"Do you yield?" He huffed.

"Over a haircut? You're kidding."

He shifted his stance. "You will not defeat me, Princess."

Katrel matched him. "You sound so confident of

that, Revan, even as you try to catch your breath."

"Bitch." He charged, the sword dragging in the dirt.

Aetherius sang as it collided with his blade. Katrel, shifting her blade and twisting his sword from his hand, smiled at his failed maneuver. His sword skidded across the ground to where the squires stood in awe. "That's no way to speak to the Crown Princess, Captain."

He lunged for her with a roar; she easily side-stepped the desperate attempt to tackle her.

"I wonder what the king will say when he finds out his heir was bested by a woman."

"When you are my wife, you will learn your place." He growled into the dirt.

She fisted his hair, wrenching his head back and pressing the edge of Aetherius against his throat. "I will never be your wife."

"We'll see about that, Princess."

"I am not a prized cow that can be bought and sold." She removed Aetherius from his throat, before she thrust his head into the dirt. "And you are not captain material."

Katrel stood and smiled at the two of us. She had drawn a line in the sand. Claimed herself as a free being. It was as we walked back through the castle halls that a foreboding sense of dread sank into my heart. She had succeeded in her mission to humiliate the male, but what would happen when he retaliated? The dread wound tighter and tighter as we approached the library. Niratap greeted us at the door, wrapping his arms around me, lifting me, and holding me close. He set me down quickly and tilted my head to the side with a finger to my chin so he could examine the thin slice on my neck. He frowned.

"What happened?" he growled.

Katrel bowed her head. "I apologize, my Lord. I was careless when we were sparring."

His eyes narrowed and I felt his need to protect me. "I am alright. It's just a scratch."

"I would say that is more than a scratch, *mo grá*."

"A cut then. I only bled a little and it doesn't hurt."

He leaned over, pressing a kiss to my neck and the tingle of his magic smoothed my scabbed skin. "You are certain?"

"Yes, my love, I am certain."

His eyes scrutinized my face, for my honesty. Whatever he found was satisfactory. "Very well."

"Have you found anything?" Mitta asked, pulling his attention away from me.

He shook his head. "Nothing of note, Tummilia was relaying again what Teovelass had shared."

"We are out of time to go back and ask more of the dragon, as well."

"Yes." He said, frowning. "We are out of time."

451

Chapter Forty-Five

Tummilia

Fruitless had been our search for anything on the Star Queen and her legacy. The lord had left the table to reunite with his mate, as I shared what Teovelass had told us again with Cyran. For any kernel that would spark recognition. He was just as perplexed as us.

"I can't think of another tome or section of the library that might have any information about the star line. If what the dragon said is true, not that I doubt what his ancientness said, Einar successfully destroyed half of the royal lines from history, the more powerful line at that."

"So, what are you saying?" Bastion asked. "That the descendants of the star have more claim to the throne than the descendent of the flame?"

"In the grand scheme of things? Yes. Stars are a focal point of worship between many races, a queen descended from a star would be a force to be reckoned with. They could, if they chose to, take over." Cyran extrapolated.

"Meaning mother could if she wanted?"

Cyran swallowed. "If she had the power, yes."

"You could Tummi, if you wanted." Bastion said.

"What could Tummi do if she wanted?" Katrel asked. I scanned her quickly. Dusty black boots, black fencing pants intact, as was her top. Not a scratch; one worry eased away.

"Cyran is just as perplexed as the rest of us, but if your mother or sister or even you wanted, you could take over the kingdom, the world even." Bastion answered as the others came to the table.

"A drop of starlight is a powerful thing." Cyran said

cryptically.

"As an ingredient." Niratap said, his voice tight with annoyance. "As a being they would be near unstoppable."

"Therein lies the problem, neither princess is connected to their power." Cyran growled, meeting the lord's annoyance with his own. They had been battling like that for the entire hour that the rest of the group had been gone.

Katrel scoffed. "It's not like we have had the chance to master any kind of magic."

"If you could connect to your power without your emotions getting in the way, you could channel that energy into Aetherius and overthrow your father." Cyran barked, with a glower as Katrel pulled out a chair beside me.

"You're talking of treason, teacher." I whispered. Bastion nodded his agreement.

"I am speaking the truth. If your sister could tap into the emperor's flame she could overthrow her father with her power alone, a drop of starlight in that would be the undoing of the empire as we know it."

"That is a lot of pressure to put on one person." Niratap said with a frown, as he pushed Shasha's chair in.

"It is, but heavy is the head that wears the crown." Cyran said, returning to the book before him. "As much as it pains me to say, that crown is the main cause of your father's cruelty."

"As the Crown Scholar isn't it your job to make sure he is just?" Shasha said, reaching for a scroll.

Cyran sighed as he flipped the page. "Yes. Technically, the Crown Scholar's job is to advise the king in his affairs. However, my father had, long before my time, poured poison in his ears. He doesn't listen to my advice on how to run the kingdom."

"Then why appoint you as Crown Scholar if he doesn't want your advice." Bastion grumbled, grabbing another book from the stack on the table.

"To keep an eye on him." Our mother's soft voice said from between the stacks.

"Your Majesty." Cyran stood quickly and bowed at the waist.

"*Äiti*."[64] I smiled at her as she floated into the space. Her gown was a near pearlescent white that made her fair features glow and the dark bruise marring her pale cheek prominent. Anger and sorrow warred in my heart at the sight.

She looked around the area, before she smiled at our teacher. "Lift your head, my friend, we are clear."

"What kind of relationship do you two have?" Niratap asked. The question found a wound in *Äiti*, her face pinching into royal scrutiny.

"Why do you ask, young lord?"

Niratap sat pulling the text that he had been scouring towards him, shaking his head softly. "I have some assumptions and educated guesses, but I do not wish to cause harm."

Mother swallowed as Cryan stood and glowered at Niratap. "We are friends. Though it displeased our parents and the royal house. We have been friends since we were children."

The lord held Cyran's gaze and dipped his chin. "My apologies. I meant no offense."

"Apology accepted." *Äiti* said, softly. "Are you all prepared for the ball?"

Mitta scoffed. "Considering we heard of it this morning, no."

"Queen Ciserie, have you come to give us advice on survival for the night? Or perhaps give us guidance on what your daughter's next trial will be?" Shasha asked impertinently.

"I only wanted to see what had pulled you all into the library." She said, folding her hands before her.

"Research, obviously." Katrel growled, lifting a

<hr>

[64] Mother.

book from the stack.

"Katrel." I snapped, slamming my hands on the table. "Can you not be cruel to our mother. Knowing what we know, I can't understand why you continue to be so mean."

"Girls—" *Äiti* whimpered.

"The fact that you continue to support someone who let all those terrible things happen to us—"

"She didn't know."

"It doesn't matter."

"Girls, please–" Mitta hissed.

"It doesn't matter? Where was our mother when you walked off with Revan when we were presented to the court, you at fourteen? Where was she when father beat me for wanting to learn to wield a sword?" She hissed, her voice rising and echoing across the stacks. Embers blazing in her eyes.

"It's terrible what we endured, but it's not her fault, Kat."

"Where the fuck was our mother when you were sold into slavery?" She stood, pointing angrily at our mother and flame—actual flame—danced in her hair. "Where was the outrage? Where was the love? Where was she?"

"Katrel!" Cyran shouted quickly, trying to cover the books.

"Tell me, Tummilia! I'll tell you where she was, because it wasn't in the throne room. It wasn't in the hall. She was in his bed, while you were sold!"

"I don't care about that." I shouted at her standing. "She is our mother!"

"She abandoned us!"

"Katrel, that's enough." Niratap growled, shadows twisting along his arms.

"She didn't protect us from him." She snarled, flames crawling down her own.

"Katrel, you need to calm down." Bastion pleaded.

"She let him treat us like trash and throw us away."
Her eyes widened as if she hadn't realized she had ignited.

"Katrel." *Äiti* whispered, tears trekking down her
face.

"Don't you dare." Katrel hissed as the fire in her
flared dangerously.

"I never wanted you to be hurt." She stepped closer
to the table.

"Don't lie to me."

"I love you both very much."

"No. You don't."

"Katrel." I tried to soften my voice to calm her.

"No Tummi, you don't get to defend her. She wasn't
there when we needed her most."

"Wildfire." Our mother said softly, reaching for her.

"You weren't fucking there!" She shouted, tears in
her eyes.

"Kat." Mitta said also reaching for her.

"No!"

Darkness and heat flared simultaneously and
violently around us, deafening the light and sound. The
shadows suffocated the flames, the taste of ash coated my
tongue as I screamed. When the shadows receded, I saw
that Niratap had moved his mate behind him, protective of
her most of all, sweat beaded his brow, his breath coming
in shallow pants, and his hand shook. Too much. He'd
given too much, and everyone froze.

"Nira." Shasha's voice was so small behind him.
His eyes locked on Katrel, who coughed softly. "You need
to sit down."

Shasha righted his chair and eased him into it. Mitta
shifted from where she had stood over to the lord. "What's
wrong?"

"I'm fine." He rasped.

"You're not."

He scoffed, lowering his head to the table. "Just
give me a moment, Mitta."

Mitta looked at Shasha, who shook her head. "I can't tell. I—I just feel unsteady."

Mitta pressed her finger to his neck, measuring his heartbeat. She sighed after a minute. "Rest for a few minutes. I think you brought yourself to the threshold and are in a syncope attack. I think he'll be okay."

She patted him on the back before shifting to look over my sister who had placed her hands on the table, the wood around her fingers singed. "Are you alright? Did you–did you burn yourself?"

"I'm fine." She hissed, pulling away, glaring at her handprints on the table, before she turned to leave. "I'm fine."

Cyran seethed. "Katrel, are you–"

"Don't." I said sharply as she left. "Don't."

"She could have burned down the entire library." He shouted.

"But she didn't." Niratap growled, shifting as his mate ran her hand down his spine trying to soothe the trembling.

"Only because you stopped her."

"I contained the flame." He glared over his arm, his eyes unfocused. "I did not stop her. I don't know if any of us could have stopped her."

"What do you mean?" *Äiti* asked from where she stood, shaking behind Cyran who was fretting over the books and scrolls that had all remained untouched.

Niratap sighed leaning back in the chair with his eyes closed. "I mean, she was angry and spiraling and nothing anyone was going to say to attempt to calm her down would have worked."

"I knew she was angry with me," *Äiti* murmured, "but I didn't realize that she blamed me for it all."

"*Äiti.*"

She shook her head, turning away. "No, Tummilia, I have failed you both so much."

"*Äiti.*"

She left. Her dress a whisper across the stones.

"That was a nightmare." Bastion grumbled flopping down in our bed.

"The seamstress who fondled you to get you fitted?"

"No, the library."

I frowned. "I wish it hadn't come to that."

"I know that she's got trauma, but don't we all at this point?"

I glared at him before I slipped into my nightdress. "It's complicated. Katrel was groomed for a purpose, and she has abhorred it every day. It skewed all her relationships, even ours."

"Why yours?"

I sat on the edge of the mattress and stroked the back of his hand. "I am the second child. A princess by blood only. Katrel is the first born. The Crown Princess and heir-bringer to the throne, since I was born a girl, all the pressure for the future of the kingdom fell on her shoulders, her womb, at five. I was free of that burden. Free to pick my own husband, from the young lords, of course. Free to go have a family. Free to explore arts and literature and be a cultured debonair woman. Katrel had to be molded into the mother of the future heir to the throne and a subservient wife."

He sighed softly. "And she's so afraid of failing that she is pushing everyone away."

I nodded. "She's always been like that."

"What happened?"

"To Katrel? I think she just became hard to protect herself, not feeling when she feels too much."

"I understand that. I meant what she said, when you

were presented to the court. When that pompous asshole pulled you from the ball."

I swallowed as I remembered the night when I finally learned why my sister was so angry. "Revan was charming. Kind to me, even after Katrel turned him down for a dance. He danced with me and made me laugh. He snuck me wine from the buffet and offered to walk me to my room for the evening, when I tripped over my own feet. I don't remember what we talked about at the beginning of that walk. I don't remember walking down the hall that led to the treasury." My breath shuddered as it came back in harsh clarity. "I do remember him pushing me into an alcove. I remember him pinning me against the wall and his hands wandering while he told me I would like it. At the time I didn't know what the 'it' was, I knew what sex was, but I hadn't expected his hands to rove over me like that, to pull my skirts up against my protests, to kiss me to silence those protests."

Bastion shifted in the bed, pulling me back against his chest. His heart hammered violently against my back as he growled. "If you ask it of me, I will kill him."

"Bastion."

"I will kill him for you. I will flay his skin from his bones after I break every one of them. He will not know of anything other than my vengeance." His hands shook against my abdomen. "He will bleed for hurting you."

"You can't kill him. Revan is a trained captain of the guard and chosen heir to the throne. Killing him would be your execution order."

He kissed my neck. "I am not afraid of death. Not when it comes to you."

"I am afraid of death." I murmured. "Especially when it comes to you."

Chapter Forty-Six

Bastion

Tummi twirled in the pale blue gown that the seamstress, Rena, had altered to make room for her more womanly body. Gossamer floated on the air as she danced about. I smiled before the seamstress tugged my collar.

"Do you like it?" She asked softly, her eyes dipping low. She had been like that when she was taking my measurements for the dressy outfit that Tummilia had requested.

I stretched my arms over my head. "It feels great. *Asta hri,* what do you think?"

Tummi stopped her spinning and smiled at me. That smile could light up the sky. "You look lovely, Bastion. You do fine work, Rena. He's rather handsome, don't you think?"

"If it is to your liking, Your Highness, I will take my leave." She curtsied and quickly left.

Tummi frowned and pressed a gentle kiss to my lips. "Pay her no mind, love."

"What does that mean?" Her tumultuous sea-storm eyes met mine.

She swallowed, a pale angry blush dusting her cheeks. "They don't like you. With me."

"Ah." I shook my head. "You act like that's something I'm not used to."

"It shouldn't be like that, Bas!"

"I'm an orc, Tummi, a brute at best. People's opinions of me really don't matter, love."

"I don't want people thinking less of you."

"Ahk." I cupped her face in my hands. "I don't care. I don't care what anyone but you thinks of me, love."

"Bastion."

I pressed a kiss to her brow. "Only you, *Asta hri*. I am okay with what I am. Don't cry for me, alright?"

She nodded "Let's go see everyone else and get this night over."

She turned to leave, but I caught her wrist and pulled her to me. "I am with you, love. I won't let him do anything to you."

She smiled at me. "I won't let them hurt you either, love. Come on, they're waiting for us."

In the hall, Mitta stood before Katrel's door, the slim black gown hugged her body with a plunging cut out that showed the intricate tiger tattoo down her back and her hair coiffed elegantly. Her eyes narrowed as we stepped closer, the kohl around them making them sharper. The male appeared at her side with a bright smile. "What's with the face, Bastion? You look like you have never seen me in a dress."

I swallowed. "To be honest, Mitta, I've never seen you in a dress like that."

She scoffed, a smirk coming to her face. "Honestly, Tummi I don't know what you see in him. Boy's daft."

Tummi giggled. "I guess it's a good thing that he's handsome."

She shook her head. "Will you go check on your sister, dear."

"She still not talking to you?" I asked.

Mitta's face tightened painfully. The male behind her placed his ghostly hand on her shoulder. "No."

Af hverju velurðu að þjást af hjarta mínu?[65]

"Go ahead, babe." I said softly to Tummi. She smiled as she slipped into her sister's room. I cleared my throat. "What language is it that you grew up speaking, Mitta?"

"Icelandic. Why would you ask such a—" Her eyes widened, she whispered. "Bran? He's here?"

[65] Why do you choose to suffer my heart?

I nodded. "I can repeat back what he says if you would like to talk to him."

Tears welled in her earth-toned eyes. "Please."

"What do you want to say?"

"Bran, ég sakna þín og hjartað mitt verkur stöðugt til þín."[66]

Mitta, ég er alltaf hjá þér litli tígrisdýr.[67]

Mitta smirked as I repeated to the best of my ability.

"Ég þekki hjarta mitt. Ég ber þig og Asira alltaf með mér."[68]

Bran smiled sadly at her. *Af hverju velurðu að þjást af hjarta mínu?*[69]

Mitta started at the question. *"Ég — þú lést af því að ég var of hægur. Ég læt þig deyja."*[70]

Nei. Þú gerðir það ekki. Ég var feginn að þú varst öruggur. Gaman að taka á þér höggið.[71]

"Fokk Bran. Ekki láta mig gráta rassinn þinn."[72]

He smiled softly at the memory. *Mér þykir leitt að þú skulir hafa þurft að vera einn svona lengi.*[73]

"Já. það hefur liðið langur tími án þín. Ég sakna þín svo sárt að ég var næstum búinn að gefast upp. Bara til að sjá þig aftur."[74]

Aldrei. Aldrei segja það aftur. það hefur verið friður minn að vita að þú lifir þegar ég var fallinn. Aldrei halda að þú sért óverðskuldaður lífið sem þér var gefið. Þú ert konan mín og ekkert sem gerist mun breyta ástinni

---

[66] Bran, I miss you and my heart aches for you constantly.

[67] Mitta, I am always with you, little tiger.

[68] I know my heart. I carry you and Asira with me always.

[69] Why do you choose to suffer my heart?

[70] I—you died because I was too slow. I let you die.

[71] No. you didn't. I was glad that you were safe. Happy to take your blow.

[72] Fuck Bran. Don't make me cry you ass.

[73] I am sorry that you had to be alone for so long.

[74] Yes. It has been a long time without you. I miss you so painfully that I had almost given up. Just to see you again.

minni. [75]

"Bran—"

Þú hefur elskað mig nógu lengi, Mitta. [76]

"Bran." I felt the cracking of her heart in my heart.

Nei, þú hefur elskað mig nógu lengi. Ég spyr, nei. Ég bið þig að brjóta eið þinn og elska þessa prinsessu af öllu hjarta. [77]

"*Ég get það ekki.*" [78]

Þú getur. Fyrir hana geturðu. [79]

Mitta fanned her face fighting the tears in her eyes. "*Hvernig gastu sagt mér að yfirgefa þig?*" [80]

Þú ert ekki að yfirgefa okkur, Mitta. Ég mun alltaf vera maðurinn þinn, maki þinn. Asira mun alltaf vera dóttir þín. Við munum alltaf vera hér með þér, bíða eftir þér. Þangað til, litla tígrisdýrið mitt, þarf ég að láta þig elska aftur. Ég þarf á þér að halda, eins og þú varst. Mér er sárt yfir sorg þinni. Vinsamlegast hjarta mitt. Elska aftur. Fyrir mig. [81] He pressed a phantom kiss to her brow. *Elska aftur og ég mun vera hér til að heilsa þér þegar það er kominn tími til.* [82]

She looked almost startled, but nodded. "*Allt í lagi ástin mín. Ég mun reyna.*" [83]

---

[75] Never. Never say that again. It has been my peace knowing that you live when I had fallen. Never think you are undeserving of the life you were given. You are my wife and nothing that happens will change my love.

[76] You have loved me long enough, Mitta.

[77] No. You have loved me long enough. I ask, no. I beg of you to break your oath and love that princess with all your heart.

[78] I can't

[79] You can. For her you can.

[80] How could you tell me to abandon you?

[81] You aren't abandoning us, Mitta. I will always be your husband, your mate. Asira will always be your daughter. We will always be here with you, waiting for you. Until then, my little tiger, I need you to let yourself love again. I need you to be happy, like you used to be. I ache at your sadness. Please my heart. Love again. For me.

[82] Love again and I will be here to greet you when it's time.

[83] Alright my love. I will try.

Takk hjartað mitt. Ég mun vera hér með þér en elska hana eins heitt og þú getur.[84]

"*Ég elska þig, Bran.*"[85]

Þar til síðasta stjarnan deyr, Mitta.[86] With one last smile at her he faded away.

"He's gone."

She dabbed at her eyes, trying not to smear the khol. "Thank you, Bastion."

"Don't mention it. He's been begging to talk to you for a while. I just—"

"Can't have everyone asking for the dead." She smiled at me. "Does my make-up look like shit?"

Her kohl had bloomed a little, but it only gave her a smokey eye. "No, you are beautiful, my friend."

"Will you go check on the lord and lady. They are perpetually late."

I snickered. "Yes, they are, the lord has to fiddle with his clothes too much."

She laughed. "Isn't that the truth."

I knocked on the door.

"Enter." Shasha said warmly.

"I heard all of that, kid."

I laughed as I stepped into their room. "We know. It was intentional."

He huffed from where he stood before the mirror, straightening his cuffs. His mate giggled. "He does primp quite a bit."

"You are the one who distracted me. Parading out of the bathroom in that fucking dress."

I glanced at Shasha as she stood and smoothed the gold sweetheart dress that hugged her hips, before it fell in a puddle at her feet, a long slit exposing a dark thigh wrapped in a gold cuff. Her braids were loose, framing her

[84] Thank you, my heart. I will be here with you but love her as fiercely as you can.
[85] I love you, Bran.
[86] Until the last star dies, Mitta.

face and gold beads and makeup made her eyes shine in a honeyed tone. I sketched a bow.

"You look devastating, my lady."

She smiled at me. "You look rather handsome as well, my friend."

"Tummi had it made for me." I smiled at her as I stood straighter. "You ready for this?"

She sighed as the lord came behind her, pulling her chin back to look at him. "Ready as we'll ever be. Right, *mo grá*?"

"Right." Hunger and heat radiated in the lord's eyes.

"If you guys need a couple minutes, I can step out."

"Don't give him ideas, Bastion."

"Mitta would carve the skin from my body if I walked out there smelling freshly fucked."

"You're damn right!" She shouted through the door.

We laughed before the lord guided his mate out into the hall. Katrel glared at the group over her shoulder, her crimson gown dipped low in a swoop down her back, exposing the extensive scarring that she normally hid.

"That is a brave choice." I said softly.

She frowned at me before she began to march down the hall, her heels clicking on the stone. "They need to see. What was done to me, they need to see it. None of them know and I want those bastard males to see what they did."

I swallowed. "She is in a mood already."

Tummi looped her arm through mine as we followed after her and Mitta. "Do you blame her?"

"No, but I didn't expect that."

Tummi shrugged. "Let's just get through tonight. One step at a time."

"What are we to expect?" Niratap asked behind us.

"Well, when we enter the ball, we greet the king, everyone does. A bow and then I assume we will claim a wall while the procession goes, unless father has designated a spot for us on the dais."

I frowned. "Sounds fabulous."

"I doubt that will happen. I hope it doesn't happen. After the procession there will be music, dancing, and libations. Sometimes there are announcements or declarations and sometimes there is entertainment. It's the same as any ball really."

"That is my concern." Niratap growled.

"Though the nobility is cruel, there is an air of sophistication at a royal ball and never once has there been creature abuse as entertainment." She frowned when we turned down the wing's adjoining hall. "I would have told you to stay behind if I was concerned with that happening, my Lord."

"Do you think there's a chance he'll try something?" Shasha asked.

"There is always a possibility." Tummi mused. "It is my hope that he refrains from the theatrics while the rest of the gentry are here."

We turned down another hall, this one filled with banners. "Hopefully there will be decent music." I said.

"Classic elven music. Ballads and such."

I groaned. "Damnit."

She giggled. "Maybe you could sing for us then."

"That would probably paint a target on my back." I said as we came up behind Katrel and Mitta who stood in silence at the entrance to the last hall between us and the throne room.

"I think you should do it." Katrel said softly. "The gentry could use something interesting for a change."

"Don't take any unnecessary risks." The lord cautioned me. "We don't need to be separated from one another."

"Especially because all eyes will be on us." Mitta said over her shoulder as we approached the doors.

"All of them." Katrel said, taking a deep breath. She nodded to the guards. "I'm ready."

The doors opened. "Announcing Crown Princess

Katrel Gwendolyn Raloqen and Princess Tummilia Raloqen and their traveling party."

I huffed. "A footnote in history I guess."

"I don't know what you expected." Tummi said at my side.

"A tad more than a traveling party. 'Bard from the realm of man' would have been nice."

Tummi laughed and the room's attention shifted from Katrel to us, tension easing from her shoulders.

Nobles filled the throne room, dressed in their finery. Most sneered as we passed them to approach the throne. Cardoc sat with that serpentine grin on his face, a grin that would have made the biotatá on the royal crest proud. Katrel dipped into an elegant bow that exposed her back to the king. I watched as he sneered at her in disgust before I dropped into a bow myself. Of all the males in the world that I had met, he was the vilest. Treating his children as if they were game pieces on a chess board. The expression was gone when we rose.

"Welcome, Princess." He said with a dip of his chin.

"Father. I hope the day has treated you well."

He lounged back in the throne, his crimson robes shifting with the movement. "It had. Until a squire told me that you and your band of females had crashed their practice the other morning."

"We may have done so."

He scoffed. "May have?"

"I had already proven myself as a fighter in the arena. I did not see any harm in my teacher, Lady Bondbreaker, and myself using the training grounds."

"And sparring with Sir Revan?" There were shocked murmurs amongst the crowd.

"I wanted to see if he has earned the title that you wish to bestow upon him."

He smirked. "And what did you find?"

Katrel cocked her head to the side. "I found that

though Lord Revan is sufficient in the sword, he is cocky, and it blinds him to the whole picture. One could say that it is a poor quality in a king. To be so full of oneself that they cannot see the whole picture."

The king frowned. "I will consider that, daughter. Enjoy the festivities. They are in your honor after all."

Katrel dipped her head. "Of course, father."

She turned to lead us off when the king said. "And Katrel."

"Yes, father."

"Dance with your betrothed tonight."

"Father I—"

"That is not a request."

"Very well, father."

He waved us off and as a group we followed Katrel to a corner of the room away from the throne dais. She pressed herself against the wall and released a large breath of air. She twisted her hands in the gossamer layer of her gown.

"A dance with him won't be terrible, Katrel." I said, crossing my arms across my chest glaring at some ogling nobles that passed by. "This whole thing is just a farce to try to get you to fold to his whims and—why does the music have to sound like a dirge?"

Tummi snorted a laugh, earning more pointed looks of disgust. "A dirge?"

"Yes. This is funeral-march territory."

The others laughed, except Niratap who watched the crowd carefully. Even Katrel cracked a small smile. It was probably the first non-hostile expression I had seen on her face this entire trip.

"So, go change it."

"Katrel, that is dangerous." Niratap growled, his face curdled with disdain.

Katrel shrugged. "I'll dance with the asshole, and it will pacify him for a while. Show these stuffy fucks some fun."

"Before or after your dance?"

Katrel dropped her hands, pushing away from the wall. "I don't care, I'm going to go find him and get this over with so I can bathe in bleach later."

"Be careful." Mitta called after her as she slipped into the crowd.

Niratap fiddled with his cuff. "I don't like this."

Tummi smiled gently at him, understanding written on her face. "You are not trapped. None of us will let you be hurt here."

His face pinched as Shasha placed a hand on his back. His eyes found me, pinned me under that lethal edge. "Are you going to go through with it?"

"With getting on that stage and singing? Yeah, I think I will."

He scanned over the crowd again. "Alright. Be careful."

I dropped my arms. "Are you going to be okay, my Lord?"

His eyes cut to me and even though I couldn't decipher the torrent of emotions that swirled there, I did see the haunted edge of one who was accustomed to a cage. He cleared his throat and gave a weak smile to his mate. "I will be alright. Go."

Tummi grasped my arm, tugging me behind her to the stage. "Leave him be."

"I wish that haunted look didn't exist."

"You have to remember, Bastion, he was tortured and abused at events like this. He was used as entertainment for wealthy assholes like the crowd around us. He's here to keep us safe and to support Kat, but I can guarantee that he is reliving his abuse."

I swallowed, trying to ease the choking sensation that lodged in my throat. Sometimes I forgot that the man I looked up to, had suffered long before my time. "How are we getting me on the stage?"

"Solaris plays cello in the royal ensemble, when

they finished this movement I'll ask her."

"You think they'll let me?" I was strangely nervous.

"They won't tell their princess no."

We slipped up beside Solaris as the last lift of the song started. Tummi waved and Solaris smiled, expertly keeping with the music. I was impressed with the ease with which she interacted with the princess. As the song finished, Tummi caught her attention.

"Your Grace?"

"Solaris, I have a request."

"What is it, your Grace?"

"My man here sings rather beautifully, would you humor me, by letting him sing a couple songs."

"The king would never allow it."

"I'll take the heat from the king."

She gazed up at the dais where the king chatted with a noble and Scholar Cairn. "Your Grace, I don't think that is a wise idea."

"Please Solaris."

"Solaris, what's going on?" Another musician hissed before he noticed us. "Oh, your Grace, I didn't see you there."

"It's not a problem. My partner here sings, and I was trying to convince Solaris to let him join you for a couple songs."

Both musicians looked towards the king, who laughed at something the noble said. "You can sing, right kid?"

"Yeah."

"You know music?"

I scoffed. "Well, I sing and play instruments, so yeah."

"Something old or modern?"

"Something modern. Spice up the funeral march that is this ball."

The male musician looked again at the king, before looking back at me with a smirk. "Fine. Don't get us killed, please."

"Deal."

He extended his hand and hoisted me up onto the stage. Murmuring picked up amongst the crowd and the king's eyes landed on me, his laughter dying. I took a deep breath, to them I was the enemy, and this would be a dance. The lord and lady stood against the wall between us and the king. Katrel was against the opposite wall watching the crowd, still searching for the knight. Mitta was nearby watching after her. Tummi came to stand in front of the stage, smiling up at me, encouraging and warm.

It was then, looking at my starlight, that I realized that no matter what happened tonight we could die in just a couple days. It hadn't truly set in when we had been traveling treacherous waters and through monster infested forests, facing a dragon, dancing between nobles who saw me as a lesser being, but standing here on a stage in this foreign land before the love of my life. It hit. I swallowed.

I turned to the ensemble and moved to the piano-like instrument. "Okay, the song I want to do is slow and jazzy." I played the first starting notes and rhythm. "It follows with the vocals."

"So, follow your lead?"

"Yeah. I'll count you guys in."

I turned back to the crowd, all the judging eyes of elven lords and ladies honed in on where I stood. I rolled my shoulders and looked back at my star. A guiding light in this sea of darkness, my joy, and my future, all in her wild blue eyes. I took a steading deep breath and counted into the first beats of the feeling that *asta hri* was for me and "Tennessee Whiskey" left my lips, for her and only her. There was no microphone, but when I looked at her it was just the two of us in a sea of bodies and sound.

I finished the song, there was clapping and appraisal from the band and the crowd. A strange kind of euphoria settled in as I looked over them, some clapping and smiling with surprise. I smiled at Tummi, and she nodded at me;

her eyes begging me to sing more. I turned to the band and tapped out the tempo of the next one. "Love Me Harder". It was edgier and it was an ask to that bright light below me. "Simple Man" came to me next, and it felt right: brandishing my soul to the enemies that moved in closer. Tummi's face was a beacon swaying to the music and my heart felt so full that the next came easily. "Home." It felt like a promise as she danced alone before the stage, singing along. Couples paired up and swayed together or spun around the room. Laughter and love radiated from the dance floor; Shasha was even able to pull Niratap away from the wall to dance. One more. One more song then I would go dance with that woman who was my life, the woman that left me "Speechless".

When the song finished, I bowed to the crowd and the king. There was applause, but the king just smirked and continued to speak with Cairn. I thanked the ensemble for letting me sing. The male at the keys said I could mix it up with them anytime. It was a blur of motion as I slid off the stage and lords and ladies came to talk to me. Asking about where I learned to sing like that and why I was stopping, but I only had eyes for Tummi. I pulled her into my arms, and she crushed her lips to mine, before the stage and all that were present. There was a collective gasp across the room then a smattering of cheering and laughter.

I set her down and she beamed at me. "I love you."

"And I you, *asta hri*"

"Will you dance with me?"

"I thought you'd never ask."

Chapter Forty-Seven

Katrel

My sister glowed in Bastion's arms as he spun her across the floor. He had wooed most of the nobility into dancing to his songs. It helped that Tummi was well liked by most of the nobility, with her soft agreeable nature. Even as children, many thought that she was the better of the two of us. Her bright acceptance and love of Bastion was protection in its own right. Mitta approached me with a glass of sparkling wine in her hand. She was so beautiful. The slim fitting black dress accentuated her hips. Just the sight of her soft kohled eyes and red painted lips heated my core.

She stood beside me and sipped her wine. "You look nice tonight."

I swallowed. I was still mad at her. My heart still hurt at what she had said.

"You're still angry with me."

I looked out at the floor, wanting very much to disappear.

"I–I said some things the last time we spoke that I know hurt you. I know that and I want to right that with you. I want to tell you why it has been that way."

I shifted a step.

"I know that you are hurt. Please let me explain."

"Why." The word felt like sandpaper on my tongue. Revan finally appeared beside my father; his eyes pinned on me. He nodded to my father before beginning to approach.

"I want to tell you everything, but not here."

I scoffed. "Whatever." What did the reason matter when the outcome was the same?

"Do you not believe me?"

Revan prowled through the crowd towards us. I was hurt and angry, but I would not let him threaten her. "It's hard to when one feels so fucking unwanted."

"But, Kat—"

"And the only thing that hurts is the knowledge that you will never look at me the way I look at you."

I stepped away, not wanting to see what my sharp words did to her beautiful face. Revan smiled at me. His eyes devoured the expanse of my dress, lingering at my chest. "Hello, Princess."

"Enjoying the view, Revan?"

"Very."

Gross. "You here to claim your dance?"

"And more if you'll allow me." He extended his hand.

"We'll see."

I took his hand and let him lead me onto the floor. Nobles moved away, many whispering amongst themselves. The scarred Crown Princess. Tainted. Unruly. Wild. Revan's hand came to rest over the pale scars that covered my back. I looked up at him as the first notes of the waltz number started.

"They are unsightly, but they don't bother me."

"But they're unsightly? My scars?"

"Well, a princess should be perfect in both looks and demeanor."

"And I'm not."

"Far from it, Princess, you are a challenge. One that I will gladly take on."

"Really? You think you can win against me? I didn't realize that you were a glutton for punishment."

He spun me out and when I was pressed against him again, he said. "Maybe I am, but I will be happy to tame that wildness in you."

"I don't think your ego could handle losing that battle."

"Who says I'll lose?"

He dipped me.

"I will not be your obedient wife."

He eased us into the next movement. "I would never expect the biggest viper of the court to submit willingly."

"You're all talk Revan. If only you didn't have such small assets, you'd be more interesting."

"I can promise you, Princess, that there is nothing small about me."

I locked eyes with Mitta over his shoulder, her lips pulled in a thin line. "You'll just have to prove that."

"Is that an invitation, Princess?"

"Think of it as a challenge."

"Is it enough of a challenge that you'll invite me to your bed?"

"Maybe after this dance."

He spun me again and my eyes found Mitta. Was it worth it to stay angry? Was taking Revan to my bed too cruel? Would it wound Mitta as her rejection had wounded me? Did I care? About her, yes. About myself? Pressed against this male, I didn't know if I did anymore. The song ended and we bowed to one another. He offered me his arm.

"Shall we, Princess?"

I took a breath. Mitta turned away from where she was watching and disappeared into the shadows. If she did not care, why should I?

I took his arm. "Let's see if you're all talk."

Together we left the throne room, and I felt the king's eyes on me the entire way back to my room. Having him in my space felt strange, like my heart was sinking into my stomach. He peered down at my face with a triumphant smile.

"Are you scared, Princess? I can be gentle."

"I'm not afraid of you Revan."

"Good." His hand twisted into my hair pulling my head back as he herded me to the bed. "It's no fun for me if you don't fight back."

My nails dug into his arms through his shirt as he pressed a punishing kiss to my lips. I tried to turn my head, but his hold in my hair tightened as he sought entry into my mouth. He parted from my mouth and kissed down my neck.

"I thought you would be gentle." I hissed as he pulled back to look at me.

"I said I could be." He smiled at me, unsheathing a dagger with his free hand and pressed the tip to my sternum. "Not that I would be."

Fear crawled under my skin, but I kept my face stoney as I said. "You will not tame me."

"We'll see about that, Princess." He sliced through the crimson fabric of my dress, exposing my body to him. His eyes eating up my flesh from my breasts, tripping over the lance scar under my ribs, down the small strip of fabric of my thong that covered my sex from his eyes. "At least the front of you is still mostly unmarred."

I frowned at him. "I liked that dress."

He shrugged. "You're a princess, just have another one made."

"Don't look so smug."

He tossed me by the hair onto the bed, strands of it escaping as I glared at him over my shoulder. He smirked at me as he undid his belt and released his penis fisting it and pumping. The dagger was still in his other hand. "I will enjoy this."

"You can't treat me like that."

"In our bed, I can treat you however I want."

"This is my bed." I growled, turning to face him. "And last I checked Revan; I could revoke this challenge at any time."

He shrugged. "I will make you mine, Princess."

I laughed in his face. "You really are an idiot, aren't you? It doesn't matter how big you think your prick is Revan. I am not marrying you."

"It's almost like this trial has given you the illusion of choice." He grabbed my leg and dragged me to the edge of the bed, the tip of the dagger swooping under the string that held the fabric in place. "You were promised to me long before you decided to run off to the world of man and debase yourself with lesser beings."

"I never debased myself. I was not a whore. I had consensual sexual encounters with men."

"There cannot be that many noble born elves in the world of man." He sliced through the strings on both sides, dropping the dagger on the floor.

"I made it a point to avoid elves." I groused, trying to squirm away.

"I bet that lord and orc had a go at you." He said, kneeling between my legs, pulling me close.

"Don't speak ill of my friends. Niratap saved my life, I'm indebted to his compassion, and I helped raise Bastion. I changed his diapers for Christ's sake."

"Being indebted is a decent enough reason to sleep with someone."

"You disgust me." I barked trying to arch out of his grip. His arm wrapped around my waist, pulling me tight against his hard member.

"That's right, Princess, try to run, it makes me want you all the more." He notched himself against me. "You'll enjoy it in the end."

He thrust into me roughly and pain lanced up my spine. I thrashed against him as he fell upon me. His mouth was hot on my skin and his hands were vice grips on my hips.

"You are so tight, Princess."

Tears pricked my eyes, but I refused to cry in front of this male. His pace was punishing, each thrust was a fist against my body, my soul. His grunts and groans were a vulgar melody in my ears. I wrapped my legs around his back, slowing his pace and easing the sharpness of his body slamming into mine.

"That's right, Princess. I knew you'd like it."

I played along, arching my back and moaning. I could pretend.

"You feel so good, Princess."

He couldn't last that long. I could get through this night. Get through this moment. Lick my bruises after.

"I can't wait to put a king in you."

I cringed. Never. I would not be a broodmare for the kingdom. No matter how much I loved my people. I would not.

"I think we would make a handsome prince. Don't you think, Princess?"

I swallowed my protest. "I don't think so."

He glared into my eyes and there was no kindness in this male. I had suspected as much, but now that he was buried inside of me, he had no reason to hide it. "I like that you still deny me. I will claim you, Katrel. You will not deny me for long."

He pulled away, flipping me over, lifting my hips with a scoop of his arm. He pushed into me with a sigh.

"No." I pushed up from the mattress.

He pushed me down. "No? You're mine, Princess."

"Revan, stop."

He fisted my hair, pulling my head back as he thrust into me. "That's not a very nice way to ask."

"Please, Revan, stop."

"I figured you've fucked around like a whore. I might as well treat you as one."

"Stop."

"Not until I've had my fill."

"Revan, please I don't want this."

He pushed my head down into the sheets, silencing my begging. "I'm going to put a child in your womb."

I was not going to cry. Absolutely was not going to cry. I was going to survive this. I was going to survive and face my final trial. Then I was going to go home, to deal with real villainous people. Not petty nobles who didn't understand suffering. He finished, thrusting several more times until he went soft. He flopped back on the bed with a groan. I slipped from the bed and padded to the bathing room. I sunk into the ready hot water wanting only to cleanse him from my skin. I began scrubbing and scrubbing, until my skin was raw.

I didn't know how long I was in there, cleaning him off my body, suddenly very thankful for contraceptives from the realm of man. I stared at myself in the mirror at the damage that male had inflicted on me. The shallow cut down my sternum and the starts of bruises all down my body, from his hands and bites. I slid into my robe covering the marks that dotted my skin. It was what I deserved, wasn't it? After dragging my family into this shit show, putting them in danger, pushing my emotions on Mitta. I swallowed and exited the bathing room, expecting Revan to have become bored with my absence and left.

"I was wondering when you would come back for more." I froze. The male lounged in my bed, stroking himself.

I frowned, drifting to my wardrobe. "I expected you to be gone."

"Why would I leave my wife?"

I scoffed. "I'm not marrying you and you have overstayed your welcome."

"Overstayed my welcome? I thought proving my assets was the challenge, now that you know of my endowments, come show me how much you enjoy me and ride my cock."

I opened the wardrobe shaking my head, reaching into my bag for a dagger. "I have seen much more impressive dicks in my life. Yours is nothing to boast about. Now get out of my room."

He shifted on the bed, his feet hitting the ground. As he marched towards me, he snarled. "I'll fuck that attitude out of you."

"You fucking touch me, Revan." I snarled, whirling

around and brandishing the dagger. "I will cut that sad little worm off your body."

He stopped halfway between the bed and where I stood. "You wouldn't dare."

"Fucking try me." I stepped towards him. "Get out of my room."

"Your father will hear about this."

"Fuck you and fuck him." I advanced another step. "I am not scared of either of you. Get the fuck out of my room!"

"I'm not leaving."

"Get. The. Fuck. Out."

"I think not." There was a knock at the door. Revan shouted. "Go away."

There was another knock. He swore storming to the door and wrenching it open.

Chapter Forty-Eight

Mitta

She left the throne room with Revan, by choice. My stomach soured as I crept around the edge of the room watching the crowd of nobles spin around the dance floor and gossip. I came across Niratap in the shadows, flexing his hands and rubbing at his shoulder.

"You shouldn't do that here."

He dropped his hands, and his silver eyes slid to me before returning to the dance floor. "I'm fine."

I followed his gaze across the floor finding Shasha dancing with Bastion, her eyes darting to where we stood. I scanned the crowd quickly, finding Tummi chatting with Cyran by the refreshment table.

"Is it getting more frequent?"

"No." He sighed. "It's just me. I'm having a hard time with all of this."

"Is that why the lady keeps looking over here to check on you?"

He chuckled. "She's worried. I'm not doing well with the ball. It hasn't gone unnoticed either."

I glanced to the throne, where the king lounged watching us. "You can't go anywhere without making enemies, can you?"

He smirked at me. "Technically he was already an enemy prior to this."

"It would be nice to not have to watch our backs at every turn."

"Maybe someday, Mitta. Maybe someday." He scanned the room quickly. "Where is Katrel?"

"She left with the knight."

His eyebrow rose. "And you're not following after

them?"

I wrapped my arms around myself. "She doesn't want me there. She made that very clear."

"Are you sure? Maybe she just needed you to explain why you two have been going back and forth."

I glanced at him. "Are you trying to pry into my past, my Lord?"

"Never." He raised his hands in surrender. "I do not need to know your past, Mitta, but if you want to love Katrel you will have to tell her."

"I was planning on it, but she—"

"Is hurt and scared."

"Well, I—"

"Mitta, for being the one who told me to pull my head out of my ass with Shasha, you're terrible at listening to your own advice."

I opened my mouth to protest, but under his scrutinizing gaze I shut it. "So, what do I do?"

"I don't like that she is alone with him."

"You want me to interrupt them?"

He sighed. "If you love her like I think you do, Mitta, I expect you to do much more than that."

I looked up at him. "Will you be alright?"

He nodded to where Bastion and Shasha danced. "He has wooed most of the nobles with his singing, I don't believe Cardoc will make a move on us tonight. Go and get your *princess*."

"I'll tell her she needs to carve out her pound of flesh for that."

He smiled. "Go, Mitta."

I nodded, slipping around the edge of the room, feeling eyes boring into my back. I glanced back over my shoulder before leaving down the hall, the king smirked at me, dark eyes watchful and plotting. I did not like the look that he gave me and wondered if leaving the ball had put a target on my back. A chill ran down my spine, as I moved through the castle.

I lifted my hand to knock on the door when I heard them speaking beyond the door.

"I'm not marrying you and you have overstayed your welcome." She sounded perturbed.

"Overstayed my welcome? I thought proving my assets was the challenge, now that you know of my endowments, come show me how much you enjoy me and ride my cock." My nails dug in my hands to the point of pain.

Katrel said flippantly. "I have seen much more impressive dicks in my life. Yours is nothing to boast about. Now get out of my room."

"I'll fuck that attitude out of you." He growled, his steps stalking toward her voice.

"You fucking touch me, Revan, I will cut that sad little worm off your body." She snarled, her tone taking on that sharpness she weaponized.

"You wouldn't dare."

"Fucking try me. Get out of my room."

"Your father will hear about this."

"Fuck you and fuck him. I am not scared of either of you. Get the fuck out of my room!"

"I'm not leaving."

"Get. The. Fuck. Out."

"I think not."

I knocked.

"Go away." The knight growled.

I knocked again, and the door flew open before me. The nude knight stood at attention before me.

"What do you want, rakshasi?"

"This is the room I am staying in, so I'm going to bed."

"Find another place to sleep for the night. I am spending the night with my betrothed."

"The fuck you are." Katrel snarled. I peered at her over Revan's shoulder; she was brandishing a dagger at the male. She was in a robe with the collar open at the top, exposing a line of bruises down her neck and chest. The sight made my blood boil.

"Princess, don't make a scene."

Katrel's brow rose at the audacity, but I said. "I think you should leave."

"What are you going to do about it?"

"At the moment nothing. Unless the princess asks it of me. However, she did tell you to leave, you should respect her wishes."

"You can't tell me how to treat my wife."

"No, I can't, but the princess is not your wife. You two are currently in an arranged engagement, but she owes you nothing. So, grab your clothes and leave."

He squared his shoulders in the doorway. "I'm not going to be pushed around by a woman, especially a woman who thinks she's a warrior."

I took a deep breath. "The fact that I could flay your skin from your muscle, alive, with my bare hands should give you plenty of reason to be pushed around by me. The only reason I haven't is because she has not asked it of me. So do the smart thing and leave before my fragile patience runs thin and I maul you for the fun of it."

"You wouldn't dare."

"I like the taste of blood in my tongue, knight. I wouldn't test me."

He swallowed, backing to the bed. He kept one eye on me while he dressed, mumbling about how it wasn't right and that the king would hear of these transgressions. I stepped into the room, watching him with the same predatory focus. I stopped when I had placed myself between him and Katrel.

"You will pay for this." He hissed.

"I have seen children that scare me more than you ever will. Leave and close the door behind you."

He slammed the door, knocking a fine dust from the frame. I waited until the echoes of his steps disappeared, before turning to face Katrel. Her copper eyes were filled with uncried tears. Cautiously I took the dagger, which she still held aloft. It fell to the floor in a clatter. My hand swept the edge of her robe to the side and examined the bites and bruises across her neck, chest, and shoulder. A shallow cut marred the space that dipped between her breasts. Her cut dress was discarded at the foot of the bed.

"Are you alright?"

Her bottom lip wobbled, she shook her head.

"Are you in pain?"

Another shake of her head, but I saw an errant tear roll over her cheek.

"Let's go sit down, okay? I have some salve in my bag for bruising, they'll be gone tomorrow." I guided her to the edge of the bed, before collecting the medicine from my bag.

I returned, opening the tin of salve when I froze. "Do you want me to do it, or would you like me to leave?"

"Please." She grabbed my wrist with both her hands, her voice cracking into a sob. "Please, don't leave me."

"Okay. Okay, love, I won't." I dipped my fingers into the salve, gingerly rubbing it into her skin. "I'm not going anywhere."

I worked my way over the bruises, being mindful to keep her covered as I came to kneel between her legs. I frowned at the finger shaped bruises that tranced her hip bones and thighs. The sadist had brutalized her. She had chosen to let him come to her room, but even the invitation could have been revoked. She hadn't expected him to abuse her as he had, it was evident in the bruises and her silent tears. Katrel wasn't one to freeze when in danger. Though I couldn't blame her for being angry with me. I had resisted and pushed her away. Right into his fucking hands. I sighed.

"I'm sorry." She whispered.

"You have nothing to be sorry for, Katrel." I said, capping the salve and setting it to the side. "I am the one who should apologize."

"No, Mitta. I was cruel, throwing myself at you when you were very obviously not interested in more."

"I never said that I wasn't interested in more, Katrel."

"No, you said you couldn't. You couldn't have me. You couldn't love me. You couldn't want me. I kissed you and I didn't respect you telling me no and I pushed and pushed. And when you didn't respond to my pushing, I blew up on you and made my issues your fault."

"It is alright. I've had the gift of some clarity in my heart. I have a lot to tell you if you feel like hearing me out and maybe after that we can try."

"But I kissed you when you didn't want it."

"Katrel."

"What?"

"I kissed you first."

"But—"

"I never said that I didn't want you, that I didn't wish I could have your hands and lips all over me. I made a promise to someone a long time ago, an oath, that I was terrified I would break and damn us both. That I would lose their memory if I let myself be happy. I kissed you back because I wanted to, against everything that I was trying to hoard in my soul. I wanted to."

"Tell me."

So, I did. I told her of my mighty Bran, who I learned to love and cherish; of my fierce little Asira who didn't get a chance to live up to her great name. I told her of a village bathed in blood and fire; of dying words and final breaths. I told her of my wandering through ice and smoke. Of being captured and traded and beaten. I told her of my pains and sorrows and regrets. I told her about how she warmed my days and filled me with a longing I didn't know I had the capacity for. A longing that I was afraid of, afraid to learn what it would do to the ghosts of my past. Tears traveled both our faces by the time I was done with my story. I looked at my hands. Afraid once more, that all that I was would disappear if she rejected me.

Her calloused fingers tilted my chin, so I would look in her eyes. "Do you love me?"

"I want to. If you will allow me."

She tugged me closer to her face, her voice low and husky. "I can't promise I won't make you question."

"I can manage my own fears."

"I've never been monogamous. I may wander."

"Let me be your home to return to."

"I can't promise that I won't hurt you."

I swallowed. "I can't promise that I won't either."

"I want you."

"I want you. I have wanted you since I met you. In you I found a piece of my heart that I didn't know was missing."

"Is it just because I'm pretty?"

I scoffed, smiling as I said. "There is a profound difference between kissing someone because you find them attractive and kissing someone because words can no longer express how you feel for them."

"I'm bad for you."

"Katrel. When I look at you, I ache. I look at you and I just love you, and it terrifies me."

"Why?"

"It terrifies me at what I wouldn't do for you."

"And what would you do for me?" She leaned closer and there was almost no space for air.

"Anything."

"Then fucking kiss me already."

I sighed. "I never thought you'd ask."

I closed that last breath between us, her lips were so soft. I cupped her face, drowning in her wildfire scent. She kissed me back, her tongue demanding entrance to my mouth. She tasted of summer wine and spice. Her hands shifted into my hair tugging at the base of my head. She panted as we parted, both of us breathless.

"May I touch you?"

"Please."

Her fingers shook as she slid the strap of my dress from my shoulder. Those copper eyes locked on the rise and fall of my chest. When the other strap was free she tugged the apex of the collar down, exposing my breasts. She tucked an errant stand of hair behind my ear, her fingers trailed down my neck and between my breasts. My skin pebbled a trail under her touch.

"You are so beautiful."

My face heated, and I looked away. She cupped my face, pulling me back to face her. "Don't hide from me. Not anymore."

"Katrel, I—"

"Shh." She stood before me untying the sash at her waist. The garment fell open baring her body to me, a rosy blush bloomed across her chest and slowly ascended up her neck. Those imperious eyes held me, question and longing floating in them.

"You are beautiful." I choked.

She placed her palm against my cheek, thumb stroking idle circles. "Mitta, I've wanted this for so long and now I don't know what to do. Isn't that silly."

I press my lips against her hip's soft curve, a breathy gasp escaping her lips. Her salty smokey scent was sharp with my proximity. "You are not silly."

Another kiss across the bruise on her hips. "I am. Perfectly opening up right before I might be imprisoned or die."

I kissed my way over her navel, dread mixing with arousal in my gut. "We are with you."

She swallowed. "I know and it terrifies me."

I kissed her other hip, tempted to dip between her thighs; to erase the torrent of dark thoughts in her head. I looked up at her, her face perfectly framed by her breasts. "I promise you Katrel, I will ensure you are safe."

"Mitta, I don't want you to risk everything for me."

"Katrel. You are everything to me."

Her expression twisted to pain. "I—"

I gave in. Pressing a kiss to the top of her pubic bone before slipping my tongue between her lips, her coarse hair tickling my nose. She's sweeter than I expected, wet and ready for anything. A shocked groan came from her mouth as she doubled over me, hands twisting into my hair. I flicked my tongue over that sensitive bud hidden there. My name was a cry from her lips. My hands wrapped around her muscular thighs for support. She trembled under my touch, her nails raking over my back.

"Mitta, I—oh holy stars." Her knees gave out. I clutched her to me, relishing her sweet smokey taste but angry that the male's scent and briny taste lingered on her body. She was mine.

I let her sink to the bed, the possessive thought burrowing deep into my heart.

"Mitta."

I couldn't claim her like that. I couldn't. She didn't want the weight that came with it.

Once more she tilted my face to meet her gaze. "What's with that face?"

I narrowed my eyes. "What face?"

"The terrified face. It's not the face that the woman who just licked me to completion should have. What's wrong?"

"I want to claim you."

"What do you mean?"

"I want you to be mine." I swallowed. "My heart aches for you to be mine. I can't stand the smell of anyone else on you."

She smiled wistfully. "You want me to marry you? Mate you?"

I started a bit. Marry her? "You wouldn't want that. You have been against marriage since before we came here."

"I am against marriage to males who think me an

object and pawn for their success."

"Kat, I don't want to hold you back."

"Then hold me up. Be there for me like you always have and love me while you do it."

"Kat—"

"I think that I would like that with you. I want to be yours."

"Really?" My heart skipped in my chest.

"Mitta. I have craved affection from you for nearly two centuries. Anything at this point is a gift."

I rose, easing her back on the bed, hovering above her "Katrel Gwendolyn Raloqen, Crown Princess to Babylos, will you take this small wildling as yours? To cherish and honor until the deepest darkness claims you."

"I do. Mitta Rask, Last member and Chiefess of the Frosted Mountain Clan," My heart swelled. "Will you take this wildfire as yours? To cherish and honor until the deepest darkness claims you?"

"I do."

"Then kiss me, Mitta."

I did and when we parted that sealing of our souls, I slid my hand down between us. "I plan on much more than just kissing you."

"Oh really?" She asked, sighing as my fingers dived into her wetness.

"Yes, wife." There was a rightness to it that I couldn't explain. I went to kiss her again, but she stopped me.

"I want you to promise me something."

"Anything."

"No matter what happens in the next few days, to me." I went to protest but she silenced me with a finger. "I want you to promise that you will get our friends out, that you will get my sister out. That you will get yourself out. No heroic moves. No knightly grand gestures to save me. Just get the family out."

"Kat, you're asking me to leave you behind if the

worst happens."

She nodded, smiling sadly. "It is my deepest regret that I dragged you all here with me. Please, Mitta."

The pleading in her voice killed me. "You have my oath, Katrel. On my honor I will make sure our family gets out."

Tears rimmed her eyes as she stroked my hair. "Thank you."

"Katrel. I'm not going to leave you behind either."

"I'm not included in that oath of yours. As it stands, I'm the only thing keeping all of you, especially Niratap, alive. I will not be the cause of their deaths. You will get them out with or without me."

There would be no argument. No trying to get her to not sacrifice herself for our family. So, I kissed her. "You have my oath, wife."

"Show me what two centuries of love feels like tonight. Tomorrow we'll face what comes."

A possessive growl rumbled in my throat. "With pleasure."

I stood sliding out of my dress the rest of the way, straddling her waist and covering her with hot open-mouthed kisses, dragging my fangs over her sensitive flesh. A wildfire made flesh. That was what she was, the antithesis of the ice and snow I was born in. Her hands twisted in my hair pulling me up her body to her mouth, even as my hands descended. She kissed me with fervor, and it was dizzying.

"I have wanted this." She groaned as I slid my fingers into her. "Wanted you for so long."

I kissed her collar. "Me too."

She was lithe, lean beneath me, but not weak. Her breath rattled out of her, my name on her tongue. "I want to worship you. Please let me."

I smiled against her skin. "Make me."

She thrashed under me and groaned at the friction it added. "Mitta."

"Show me how strong you are, my sweet flame."

She arched off the bed, twisting and leveraging me over and underneath her. She panted over me, her amber waves falling over her shoulder draping us in her scent.

I smiled, rising up and kissed her cheek. "You win, my flame, do as you please."

She kissed down the column of my throat and to my breast. She sucked my nipple into her mouth, rolling it between her teeth. I arched off the bed as her fingers worked my other breast. She licked over where she inflicted her little hurts with her teeth. She continued down my body, licking, and sucking, and biting my unmarred skin. Dusting kisses over the scars and old hurts that she had no claim to but worshiped all the same.

"Kat." I groaned as she bit down on my hip.

She kissed the small hurt hungrily looking up at me through her lashes. "May I continue, or do you want me to tease you?"

I let my head fall against the mattress. "I can think of no better torture than you continuing."

She eased my thighs apart, kissing along the sensitive flesh there. I fisted the sheets as her tongue lapped up my slit, taking my wetness into her mouth. She sucked my clit into her mouth and the air left my lungs in a rush, as she worked the bundle of nerves. Her name was a plea on my tongue as stars sparked behind my lids. She slid her fingers into me, one at a time, stroking that explosive spot with need. I writhed beneath her, finding release and arcing off the bed, body spasming like I had been electrocuted.

She guided me back down, slowing her strokes before she eased her fingers out of me. She licked my fluids from her fingers, sucking on each digit, releasing with an extravagant pop that caused my blood to heat anew.

"You taste like something I have been missing my whole life."

I reached for her. "Come here and kiss me. I want to be lost in us."

She crawled up my body, smoldering eyes locked with mine, face framed by her gorgeous hair. She kissed me and I tasted myself on her tongue, the salt and frost of my youth. I drowned in her, in us and I tumbled into everything that could be, everything that I had always wanted was there written in her kiss.

I don't know when that soul rending kiss ended, if it ever really did. We curled into one another and with her tucked against my chest breathing softly in a gentle sleep, I felt both at ease and utterly shaken.

"I love you." I whispered into her hair pressing a kiss to her head.

"I love you too." She murmured against my throat. "Don't forget your promise."

"I won't."

It was a promise that I didn't know if I could keep.

Chapter Forty-Nine

Shadows lurked in the corners of the scholar's office; his work illuminated by candlelight upon the desk as he waited. The shadows of the looking glass writhed as the corpse-like figure appeared.

"Well?" His voice was clearer this time, less gritty.

"She is yet to check in with me. I expect it anytime now."

The creature growled, pacing in the cavernous darkness. "You said she was reliable."

"If she wants to keep her mother alive she will."

The creature smirked. "You are still cruel and conniving in your old age."

The scholar frowned, glaring at the glass. "I am older, but I am not at death's door. I still have many years in me to trade in chaos."

"I cannot wait to see what you will unravel. How are the whelp's trials going?"

"Better than expected."

"Pity. I'm sure the king is up in arms about it."

"He's been plotting heavily the last few days. I'm sure his majesty will rig this last trial so there will be no winning. However, he hasn't voiced those thoughts with me." The other side of the glass flickered with firelight. "Here she is. Report."

The woman glared at the scholar through the glass. "How is my mother?"

"She is well, eating and drinking, her nursemaid even got her out of the house for a little while today."

The girl swallowed, glancing at the door behind her. "I don't have much time."

"Then your report child."

She nodded. "I haven't located the relic yet."

"Pity." The scholar frowned. "Guess that sickly mother of yours will have to go without care."

"Please don't."

"I gave you a job to do; our benefactor is not pleased with your lack of results."

"Lack of results? I have been undercover for years trying to get here. I have been abused and raped and have gotten where you want me to be. But I lack results?"

"Don't test me, child. I will throw your mother out on the streets to waste away at the mercy of her sickness if you speak to me like that."

The girl hung her head. "I'm sorry."

"Find the relic. We need it to move forward with our benefactor's plans."

"Yes. I understand. I will continue my search." With that the mirror went dark the connection severed.

The creature chuckled. "You hold her leash so tightly friend, no wonder you have her obedience."

The scholar frowned at his friend. "Yes. Quite."

"What other chaos have you been manufacturing, friend?"

"If you stick around for a moment I will show you." The scholar willed the glass to shift, moonlight fracturing in the water. The pale corpse-like eyes and toothy smile framed in kelp-like teal waves. "Creseda."

"Master Cairn." The kelpie bowed her head respectfully.

"A kelpie, Cairn?" The corpse said bemused.

"She is in a position of power within the machinations of the beast's circle."

"Happy to serve you both." She crooned through the water, bowing where she floated in the water.

"How are things progressing?"

"I tried to take a shot at manor's keepers. The older satyr is most loyal to the lord, but even he has a weakness. I am sure to find it with more prodding."

"What are your plans to cause distress?" The

495

scholar pressed the carrion-fed creature.

"I have amassed a group of shifters that are sympathetic to my rejection at the hands of the half-breed bitch. We will strike the human town at the base of the mountain, breed more distrust with the citizens there. It will limit the aid that they will be able to muster to go against you, your darkness."

The corpse creature chuckled. "What a clever creature."

"You honor me with your praise."

"Continue with your plans. Prove your worth to me and you will receive much more than praise."

"Yes, your darkness."

The kelpies image went dark, and the scholar again faced his monstrous benefactor. "All is going according to plan."

"I had little doubt in your ability to create chaos for me, Cairn."

The scholar leaned back in his chair and appraised the wraith of a man beyond the realm. "You are going to bring the creature to his knees, aren't you?"

"I am going to make him bend and then I will break him."

"Remember you need him alive to finalize your transformation."

The creature waved him off. "I don't need to kill him to break him."

The scholar chuckled. "We shall see if they make it out of Babylos first."

"Until our next discussion then."

"Of course."

A dip of its chin was the only acknowledgement before it turned and retreated into the cavern. The glass went dark. The scholar looked over his research at the scribing of ancient necromancers and their successes and failed attempts at creating what they were trying to achieve. A lich was easy enough to make, the life force of a powerful long-lived being. Many had been successful with basilisks or lesser draconic creatures. And a drop of wild magickal power; most had gone with hellfire or dragon's breath, but the liches were fragile and their forms unstable. A drop of pure undiluted power, a drop of a star, and the life of one of the longest-lived creatures, besides a dragon itself, would aid in the birthing of one of the greatest creations the world had ever seen. If the scholar's guesses were true, his friend would become a god. A lich god with the power over life and death itself.

And what chaos they would create.

Chapter Fifty

Allipo

Eloimaya was quiet today, she had been for several days. It was odd to say the least. I cleared my throat as we pulled out onto Main Street.

"Yes, Allipo?"

"Are you alright, love?"

She swallowed. "I'm fine."

I frowned. "You've been quiet. I just want to make sure that if I did something or said anything that upset–"

She placed a hand on my knee and squeezed it. "No, love. My family has been in my thoughts a lot lately with everyone away in Babylos. It makes me think of what I was forced to leave behind."

I covered her hand with my own. "I'm sorry, my love."

She smiled sadly at me. "No need to apologize. It is no one's fault but my father's for being cruel and wicked. I was an object for his gain, not his daughter."

I pulled up in front of the post office and parked. "You were a victim of the system. All of us have been at one point or another. You will be okay now, love. You are safe and no one can hurt you anymore."

Her smile was tight. "I hope you are right."

I smiled softly at her. "That is all we have. Hope and each other. Come on, Pedro said there were a lot of packages and some things that I need to sign for."

"And Rogmesh said we needed to get coffee." she added.

"Right, we have much to do today."

The post office of Grahamsville was mostly empty at the early hour. Pedro waved through the window as we entered. I gave Eloi the key to the PO Box and went to the counter.

"Hello Pedro."

"Hello Allipo. Is the lord still away?"

I nodded. "Yes, though I am hoping they will return soon."

"Very good. There are a few of us in town that prefer it when he's around. Fewer weird things seem to happen."

"Tell that to, Rodger."

Pedro chuckled as he stacked boxes on the cart he used to help us load. "He still giving you guys trouble?"

"Always. You'd think that despite the fact that we have been here since before he was born, and the town hasn't been razed to the ground that we were out to get him."

Pedro grimaced. "Little harsh, Allipo?"

I sighed. "The bastard has been banging on the manor door every few days since the lord left. Demanding to know when he returns and what he plans to do about whatever monstrosity is roaming about killing the deer and cattle."

"Do you know what is killing the cattle?" Pedro asked his face going ashen as he handed me the clipboard to sign for the packages. "My papa lost a heifer and calf a couple weeks ago."

"The lord has some ideas. It is part of the reason he is away at the moment."

"I hope he finds what he needs."

"We all do. Do you know what anything is?" I gestured at the packages.

"All I know is that the top two are fragile and filled with liquid."

I sighed. "Alright."

"One of the liquid ones is from Kallin." Pedro said, going over the manifest. "There's a note on the manifest that says, 'for the vault.' What does that mean?"

"That whatever it is, is dangerous enough to warrant being under lock and key."

Pedro eyed me. "And he thought it smart to mail it?"

"It made it here unharmed didn't it." I smiled at the boy.

He gave me an incredulous look. "Fair. In the back of the hearse?"

"Yes. Eloi anything of interest in the paper mail?"

"There are a couple letters to the lord and the rest is just junk. Oh, there is a letter from a metal working company."

"Finally." I reached for the letter earnestly. "Fucking finally. You know how long I've been waiting for this company to get back to me about restoring the railings on the north side of the manor? Phenomenal."

"What does it say, my love?" Eloimaya said, tucking the letters in her bag.

Pushing out the door to the street I tore the envelope open, quickly scanning over the text. "They say they will be available this following spring and are very interested in working on our historic home."

"Good news?"

"Yes, but the north side balconies are badly deteriorated. They are dangerous."

"It's just a little longer to wait, and then in the fall next year you can design those rooms to your hearts content."

"Very true. It will be grand news to tell Lord Niratap when—"

"Satyr!"

"Oh, for fucks sake, Rodger, what now?"

"Where is your lord?"

"He is away. Like I told you days ago, repeatedly."

"Where the fuck is he?" The sheriff snarled at me.

"He is not here."

"You tell me now or I will arrest the whole house."

A humorless laugh left my lips. "You're joking."

"I know you aren't fond of him, Sheriff Clemmens, but that seems excessive." Pedro said, easing the cart back onto the sidewalk.

"Pedro, your father lost his best milk cow and her calf from whatever they brought into the woods."

"Oh, definitely. Those bodies were definitely eaten by a basilisk or a hippogriff." I rolled my eyes. "You need better material, Sheriff. Lord Niratap is away, and I can assure you what is going on here is one of his priorities. I'd expect and hope that he and the others will return soon after the solstice with a plan."

"Assure me? I don't trust your conniving tongue, satyr."

"He has a name, Sheriff." Eloi hissed beside me. "He speaks true, the lord is away looking for answers. I understand that it is scary, but you cannot accuse us of something solely on the grounds that we are not humanoid enough."

"What is it that your lord does that he has all these resources? Nothing good I assume."

I had had enough. "If you must know, Lord Niratap has old money. Hard fought for and hard won, just like his freedom. He is a good male, a just male, who takes what he earns through stock trade to help those who like him have been trapped in terrible situations. If you took the time to remove your bias you would see that, not the predator you think him to be. At every turn you are hostile to the members of our house, to our friends, and even Lady Bondbreaker's parents; you ought to be ashamed of yourself."

"Why should I be ashamed about my bias towards monsters?"

I frowned. "It makes you a bad cop."

"Excuse you."

"We are good people." I shouted, my blood boiling.

"You aren't people."

I tucked Eloi behind me. "What?"

"Rodger, you can't be serious!" Pedro pleaded. "That is horribly prejudice."

"When have they done anything for us? For humans?"

"They are a part of the community, Rodger." Pedro protested.

"And I would be rid of them if I could." He huffed.

"Well, I will aid you in your day then, sheriff." I hissed, easing Eloi into the car. "We have other business to attend. Thank you for loading our packages, Pedro."

"Anytime, Allipo." Pedro answered as Rodger snarled about how he was the appointed law official and that he would be listened to. His questions would be answered. "Oh, papa asked me to see if Echo could come down and preg-check his goats. She's more accurate than the vet ever is and cheaper."

"I will ask her when we return home." I smiled at the young man. "Tell your father she is quite fond of that cactus drink he makes."

"Ah, Agua de Kefir. I will let him know." He smiled.

"Where are you going?" Rodger hissed as I opened the driver's door.

"Grocery shopping if you must know. Go disturb the peace elsewhere, Rodger."

"Allipo Comotis!"

He smacked the back of the hearse as I pulled away from the curb. My knuckles were white on the steering wheel, the leather squeaking under my grip. I had to drive away, before I did something that I would regret. Eloi placed a gentle hand on my knee, her thumb stroking gently.

"He really is a brute. At least he knows your name."

I sighed, shaking my head as I turned into the town grocery store. "He's biased, but he is a good sheriff. The people in the county elect him and he is well liked. Honesty

502

besides his pessimistic view and antagonization of the lord, I like him. He's just set in a mindset."

"It's an outdated mindset."

I parked and looked at her breathtaking face. "It is, but one that persists."

Inside the store Solette waved from behind the register. "Good morning, Allipo."

She was a sweet, dark-skinned girl who always wore her hair straight. She was about the same age as Lady Shasha. "Hello, sweetheart."

"Carter has that coffee Rogmesh ordered in the back; I'll grab it as soon as I as finished with Mr. Rainier."

The old man sneered, but I nodded. "Thank you, we'll do the rest of our shopping and be up."

"What else was on the list?" Eloi asked walking beside me.

I pulled the slip of paper that Rogmesh had thrust into my hand before we had left. "A few kinds of dried beans, spices, coffee, sugar, and flour."

Eloi sighed. "I'll grab another cart."

I chuckled. "You saw the amounts then."

"Yes." She waved a hand at me. "Go grab the flour and sugar and I'll meet you with the beans."

I chuckled. "You're going to make me grab that all on my own."

"You're a strong man, Allipo, I think you can handle it."

Some of the tension eased as I ventured to the baking aisle. She was a balm to my more neurotic tendencies, and an anchor to my anger. Had Eloi not been with me, I would have just gotten myself arrested. I rolled my eyes at the prospect of actually hitting the sheriff. Hefting the bags of flour into the chart, I thought of all the nightmares that crept in the shadows around us. I wondered if the malice and its master were trying to distance the town from us. It was our closest form of aid, though beyond distressed animals, mail, and necessities the bonds between us were weak at best.

The ground shifted beneath my hooves and dust flitted down from the ceiling titles. I turned my head to the front of the store where people stood looking to the north, pointing at something in the distance. Another rumble and I stepped forward as people began to run outside the windows. Eloimaya poked her head around the corner of the aisle, concern pinching her brows together. I saw them then, werebeasts charging after people, chasing them into buildings. A fireball blasted past, colliding with a car in the parking lot. Solette and Carter stepped closer to the window to stare at the chaos unfolding outside.

"Get away from the glass."

The warning came too late as another rumble shook the ground beneath me and a blast of magic made the glass shatter into the store.

I opened my eyes to screams of chaos and the scent of blood. A light had fallen in the blast knocking me to the ground, my arms and back were covered in small cuts. I pushed the fixture away, rising to my knees. The front of the grocery store was littered with glass, fallen lights, and broken displays. Fire blazed in the car that had been ignited in the parking lot.

"Eloi!"

A couple of soft coughs were the only answer.

"Eloi! Solette! Carter!" I shouted moving to the front of the store.

"Allipo." Eloi whimpered from the end display the blast had sent her into.

"Are you alright?" I asked, pulling her up.

"A couple scrapes. I hit my head pretty good on the way down."

"Allipo, help." Solette cried beyond the registers.

"Solette, honey, are you hurt?"

"I think I'm okay. I'm stuck under the ball cage."

I saw the wire cage crammed in the space between two of the check lines. "Is Carter with you?"

"I can see him. He's in the cubicle of the register. Carter, are you okay?"

Cater didn't answer. "I'm coming to get you guys out. Hang on."

"Carter. Carter, can you hear me? Carter, are you okay?" Solette pleaded with her coworker as I began to shift debris out of the way so I could right the ball cage. Glass crunched under my hooves. "Oh god. Is he dead? Please don't tell me he's dead."

"He's probably just unconscious." I said.

"Keep talking to him, Solette." Eloi said beside me. "We're going to get you both out."

"His mom just got out of the hospital. He can't be dead." She wept. "Carter, please wake up. Carter."

Eloi crawled over the counter trying to get access to him. She reached into the space as she spoke to him. "Carter. Carter. I need you to wake up."

Gunshots reverberated outside between the snarls and screams. I snarled, moving the last of the debris. "Fuck."

Carter groaned. Solette cried harder. "Carter. Oh god, thank you. It's okay Carter. They're getting us out, it's okay."

"How's he looking, Eloi?" I asked as I peered at how Solette was pinned.

"He looks okay. His arm might be broken. Carter honey I need you to talk to me."

He coughed softly. "Everything hurts. What happened?"

"There's been an attack. We're going to get you guys out and get you to safety okay."

"I can't feel my hand."

"His arm is pinned under the cage." Eloi said gravely.

"Shit. Hey Carter."

"Yeah?"

"I'm going to get you out of there okay, but it's going to hurt like a motherfucker."

His voice went weepy. "Okay."

"I need you to try to stay conscious, okay?"

"I'll try."

"Solette if you can push at all, we can get this out faster and get you guys looked at."

"Okay." She sniffled. "Tell me when."

I curled my fingers into the wire. "On three. One. Two. Three."

Carter screamed as the wire cage was pulled loose.

"One more push, Solette. One. Two. Three." Another hard pull and the cage came free. I tossed the warped metal to the side. "Mind the glass, Solette."

Eloi slipped onto the floor next to the kids. "His arm is definitely broken, Allipo."

"Okay." I helped Solette to her feet and gave her a quick look over. "You just got a couple scrapes and more than likely a goose egg on the back of your head."

"Is Carter going to be, okay?"

"I'm going to take a look. Mind the glass." She nodded and eased her way over the debris. I kneeled next to Carter. Blood streaked down the side of his wan face, the ball cage must have hit him on the way down. His left arm hung limply at his side, twisted at a gnarly angle, his skin a bright purple. "Hey, Carter."

He kept his eyes locked with mine. "Hey. Is it bad?"

"Your arm is broken, probably in a couple places. I'm going to have to move it so I can set the bones. Okay? It's going to hurt."

"Yeah."

"Okay. Can you sit forward for me? I'm going to have Eloi untie your apron so we can use it for a sling."

"Yeah." He shifted forward with a wince.

"Thank you, bud." I felt his arm gently. "Good news, the breaks feel clean."

"Joy." He grimaced

"Okay. I'm going to set this for you. On three."

"Okay." He puffed a few breaths.

"One. Two. Three."

He screamed. I placed his arm gently across his chest and tied the makeshift sling to hold it in place.

"Was there anyone else in the store?"

"Tommy was here, but he was on his lunch break. There wasn't a mid-shift scheduled today."

"Good. Let's get you two out of here. Eloi call the house; we need backup down here."

I pulled Carter to his feet. Working our way out into the parking lot, Eloi relaying information to Rogmesh over the phone, she would rally everyone, get down here as soon as they could and meet us at the hospital. We eased the kids into the hearse, carefully buckling Carter in.

"Where are we going?" Solette asked.

"I'm going to drive you guys to the hospital so you can get looked at."

"Can I call my mom?"

I dug my phone out of my pocket, the screen cracked but it was working. "Here sweetie."

"Thank you."

"Well. Well. Well." A snarling voice crooned behind me.

I rounded on the voice pulling my side piece. A werewolf stood there; one I did not recognize. "Who are you? Why are you doing this?"

"Our leader sends her regards."

"Where is Creseda?"

"She is going to lead us shifters to greatness." Saliva dribbled out of his maw as he spoke. "How dare that mutt of a lord think her an unworthy partner. Picking a human is foolish."

"You cannot speak to the lord's desires. The fact that you would follow Creseda in this foolishness shows your weakness of character." I slid the safety free.

"Where is the lord?"

"He is away."

The werewolf huffed. "You hide him from us. Your mistake."

"No, your mistake." I fired. Two shots, one to the heart and one to the head.

"You shot him."

"Get in the car, Eloi." I kept my gun trained on him.

"You shot him."

"Eloimaya. Please get in the fucking car. I only have regular bullets in this gun."

"What?"

"I shot a werewolf with regular bullets. He will regenerate and be sore. So, please get in the car so we can get the kids somewhere safe."

She blinked before running around the car to the passenger seat. I backed to the driver's door, watching the rise and fall of the male's chest as the bullet worked its way out and tinked on the asphalt. He would be fine, shortly. Slipping into the car, I locked the safety. Shifters snarled and hissed through the streets around us, looking for people who weren't in the shelter of broken buildings to chase. I pulled out of the parking lot listening to Solette console her mother in the back.

"No, Mom, I'm okay. Mr. Comotis is taking Carter and I to the hospital. Stay home until things calm down. I'll call you again. I promise. I'm okay. Carter is going to be okay. I know. I will. I love you. Bye, Mom." she sighed, holding the phone through the privacy window, for Eloimaya to grab. "Thank you."

"Anytime, sweetheart." I said, taking a residential street to avoid the flooded main road. "I'm glad we were there to get you out."

"You shot that werewolf. I thought you guys saved as many beings as you could. Why? Why are they doing this?" Carter asked.

"By the sound of it the shifter community is upset with the lord's choice in a partner." I tossed a glance in my mirrors. "I don't know why they attacked the town, though."

"That kelpie that no one likes is the leader of the shifters isn't she." Solette asked.

"Creseda. Yes, she is, the lord and lady threatened to take her title a not too long ago, because she was acting out and attacked the lady's mother. Eloi?"

"Yeah." Both our phones in her white knuckled grip.

"Were okay, love. Call X and see if he can bring in aid."

She nodded, looking down at my phone and calling.

"No, it's Eloi. Allipo is driving. We have a situation. The shifter community has mutinied; they've attacked Grahamsville." She shook her head. "No. It's been mainly infrastructure damage, I haven't seen any corpses. Okay. We'll be at the hospital. No, we're okay. A couple kids were injured at the grocery store. Yes. Okay. Okay."

"Well?"

"He's going to mobilize a team. He asked if we could hold out for a bit. I said yes, but I'm not really sure. They'll helicopter in at the hospital as long as we can secure it."

I glared out the window. "We can try. I only have one clip. Are you armed?"

"No, we were going to the post office and grocery store. I didn't think I would need to be armed."

The hospital came into view. "Let this be a lesson then, if we leave the manor we're armed."

She nodded. "Understood."

As we turned toward the emergency wing. I saw

two kelpies, one pale and one dark, being held at bay by Pedro's father, Guillermo, one was bleeding from the side of her face. A woman was ferrying small children into the doors.

"Eloimaya, I want you to get the kids out when I park and help that woman get the littles inside."

She nodded as I sidled up beside Guillermo and parked. Eloi hastened to her task as I switched off the motor, easing Carter ahead with Solette's help and herding the small kids inside. I stepped out training my gun on the kelpies.

"Allipo."

"Guillermo."

"Tell me the sheriff is wrong and you're not in league with this."

I rolled my eyes. "Fucking, Rodger."

Chapter Fifty-One

Allipo

Guillermo chuckled. "The man really hates Lord Bondbreaker, doesn't he?"

"Unfortunately. It's not the battle I want to fight." The pale kelpie advanced a step, I fired a round into the concrete in front of her, earning a hiss. "Where is your leader?"

"Lady Creseda is occupied." The pale-skinned kelpie hissed, licking her lips. "What is it to you satyr, want to join the coup?"

"After all Lord Niratap had done for you, this is how you plan to repay him?"

"He promised Lady Creseda greatness." The dark one snapped.

"He promised her safety and life outside a cage."

"Lady Creseda has earned the greatness that Lord Niratap denies her." The pale one snarled.

"Deserves greatness. She was promised." The dark one agreed.

"So, you will follow her to your deaths? Imprisonment?" The pale kelpie hissed, but the other looked scared at my words. "Is that what you want? To be locked away from the water?"

"Scatha, maybe we should listen to the satyr."

"Laita, you coward. Lady Creseda will achieve greatness. His Darkness will reward her and us for our bravery." She sunk down reading to charge. "And no flea-bitten satyr will get in our way."

She lunged at me.

I fired. The single shot drove home between the kelpie's eyes, she landed before me with a wet plop. "Ω μεγάλη, Τηθύς συγχώρεσέ με."[87]

A wail came out of Laita, and I took aim. "You killed my sister!"

"She made her choice. If you value your life and freedom, you will go home."

Another wail. "Scatha!"

"Laita." I said gently. "I don't want to hurt you, but I have a duty to the people of this town. There are children in there who are scared. I must protect them. Make the right choice. Go home."

She swallowed. "My sister."

"I will not let anyone take her body. Go home and I will make sure she is returned to you." With a sad glance at her sister's cooling body, she changed into a dark-colored mare, eyes glowing a seafoam green before she fled.

I sighed through my nose, as Guillermo came to investigate the body. "This day is a nightmare."

"*Si.*"[88]

"Do you know how people are faring?"

"Most are just scared. I've seen some minor injuries."

"Where's the sheriff?"

"He was on the other side of the hospital securing the entrance. Once it's secure he was coming to help."

"Great. Will you poke your head in there and have them bring out a gurney so we can take her to cold storage?"

"You're going to do as you said?"

I nodded. "I may be a wily satyr, but I am a man of my word. I didn't want to kill her."

"But a threat is a threat."

"Guillermo."

"Right. I'll be right back."

I rolled the kelpie onto her back and swept brackish hair out of her face, blood oozed from the hole in her

[87] Oh great, Tethys forgive me.
[88] Yes.

forehead. "I didn't want to kill you. I didn't want to hurt anyone, but I couldn't let you hurt the people of this town."

I placed two worn coins onto her chest. The doors opened behind me as I swiped her eyelids shut. "May your journey across the river be gentle."

"Allipo." Eloimaya's voice was gentle.

I scooped Scatha from the ground and gently set her on the gurney, pulling the sheet over her. "Put her in cold storage. Someone from the house will come to claim her after things settle down."

The nurses mumbled their agreements before moving back toward the doors right as Rodger came barreling through. He eyed the sheet covered body and then glared at me.

"What did you do?"

"Something I had to do." I sighed.

"Who was under that sheet?"

"A poor soul who made a poor decision in following a zealot. Now, if you please, Sheriff, there are other things to attend to besides you blaming my family for your misfortunes."

"You can't just kill people without consequence." Rodger aimed his gun at me. "Drop your weapon."

"Rodger, let's go inside and discuss this. I don't want to play chicken with you. I'm not interested."

"Drop the weapon."

"We are on the same fucking side ,Rodger." I snapped, holstering my gun at my back.

"Sheriff. *Por favor*."[89] Guillermo said coming back out the doors. "He is a hero. Defending children and good people from kelpies. He did what he must."

Rodger's protests almost drowned out a pulsing rustling sound. "Be quiet."

"What did you just say to me?" Rodger shouted.

"For fucks sake, Roger, please shut up. Something is coming and I need to hear."

[89] Please.

Graciously he stopped, listening with human ears. "I don't hear anything."

"Shh." The sound of scales over stone sent a chill down my spine. So, few serpentine creatures still roamed the world of man, all of them great and terrible. "Everyone inside now."

"Why?" Rodger asked

"Get inside now."

"What is it?"

"Something dangerous. Now go." I pushed Eloi ahead of me as I herded them inside. Glass and steel would not keep them safe from whatever horror appeared. "Lock the door."

"What?" Eloi grabbed my arm as I hit the button to stop the door. "No, you can't be serious."

I pressed a kiss to her lips. "Do you trust me?"

Tears pricked her eyes. "Yes."

"Then lock the doors. I have to keep everyone safe."

"Allipo don't do anything foolish."

I gave her a soft smile. "Never, my love."

This was painfully foolish without knowing what creature approached. What had Creseda bargained with to bring such terror to a small town? The scrape of scales over the asphalt pulled my eyes to a beautiful woman. Her face was of my homeland, soft and supple though dappled with grey scales. Her eyes were red and I felt stones fall into my stomach. Her hair, twisted and thrashed atop her head, was a marker of her gruesome race, a gorgon.

I closed my eyes as the creature approached. "You are a long way from home, sister."

"You are either very brave or very foolish, satyr."

She said her voice a ravaged hiss.

"Perhaps I am both." I smiled as she coiled around me. "Why are you here instead of your home?"

"What care does a satyr have of the fate of a gorgon?"

"I wish not to fight with you, sister."

"Is that why you hide your gaze?"

"I may be foolish but I'm not stupid. Though I know you to be beautiful, I enjoy my flesh as it is."

A hissing laugh answered me. "Hard to frolic with stone legs. Should I leave you to stand here and continue my task to reap terror upon mortals?"

"What could a kelpie offer a gorgon to do such bidding?"

"Oh, no kelpie bargained with me, though she is favored by the one who bargained with my sisters. My loyalties were bought by one full of dark powers, he promises much to the lair of gorgons. Power, wealth, people to rule, all that my sisters and I wish." Her scales were a soft sighing in my ears as she coiled her serpentine tail.

"What was this dark power's price for such rewards?"

"He searches for much that the gorgons do not have, a drop of starlight, a beast with dragons' longevity, a vessel of his essence, a land long lost to him, vengeance and ruin for those in his way. Much of this is foreign to my sisters and myself, but he gave us the freedom to search and cause terror in our wake. Though I've grown bored in wondering for things so foreign to me. People run from me, and I do not take joy in the suffering of innocents. What do you make of that satyr? A gorgon grown bored with the screams of men?"

"I would venture to say you long for the quiet caves of home, sister."

"Do you miss your meadows and white stone pillars, satyr?"

"White pillars fell long before my time, but I do miss the meadows and simpler times."

"Why stay if you miss it so?" The baying of weres kicked up anew.

I swallowed. "Though my soul wishes for those simpler times where there were only meadows, wine, and frolicking; I have found a family from all the misfortunes of concrete and steel and here I have a purpose to complete. Peoples that I care for deeply and wish to protect."

"These humans who cow at the sight of something far greater than they?"

"Aye, most are good people and there is much to be done in securing our freedom, sister. Those who are not good wish to strip us of all that makes us great, to make themselves great. Your stoney gaze being one such tool."

"These not good peoples, they hide in the darkness do they not?"

"Most often, yes." I felt her face floating before mine.

"Do you believe this being of darkness plans to use my sisters and I for the reach of his goals?"

"What other beings would lure you out of the safety of the caverns to search across the earth for items unknown to you? Why risk the few members of your kind to search for such things when promises are easily broken by those who are not good?"

She hissed, her breath smelling of shellfish. "You say my sisters and I have been had?"

"I say that you have been tricked out of safety. Frightening good people makes their protectors turn to their blades and worse. Return home gorgon. Return to the safety of your caverned island."

"And my sisters who roam the world?"

"Go search for them or return home and hope for the best."

"The best being that they grow bored of tormenting innocents or come across a well-spoken satyr who will point them home?" The tongues of her snakes tickled my skin.

I smiled, even as the baying hounds neared. "That would be most intriguing to find another well-spoken satyr across the seas. I hope that all your sisters come home to you."

The gorgon pressed a kiss to my cheek. "I shall return then to the safety of my home, with the hope that my sisters will come to their senses and keep their heads."

"I will keep you in my prayers, sister."

She chuckled softly, her body uncoiling from around me as she slithered away. "I will pray for you as well, satyr, for the werebeasts will leave me be, but I wonder if you will be able to talk yourself out of their frenzy; if Dionysius will grace you."

"Dionysius doesn't abandon his satyrs."

"I hope you are right."

When the sounds of scales shifting disappeared under the pants and calls of approaching werebeasts closed in, I opened my eyes. Werewolves, berserkers, kelpies, and so many more that we had pulled from tanks and cages paced anxiously around. A berserker approached, his bear's body standing as tall as the lord.

"Where is the lord?" he snarled.

I folded my hands behind my back, my fingers closing around the butt of my gun. "The lord is away on business in Babylos. I do not expect him back for a few more weeks as it were."

"My quarrel is not with you, satyr. Do not lie to cover his tracks."

"I do not lie. The lord and lady are away. Go home and leave the people of this town be. Your quarrel, as you call it, is not with them."

The berserker's shoulders fell. "I taste no lies from you, Allipo."

"That is because I do not lie. Go home."

A werewolf behind him snarled. "Lady Creseda

demands retribution for titles not bestowed upon her.”

“The fact that you have followed the kelpie woman blindly speaks to your intelligence.”

“Lady Creseda champions for the shifters.” Another barked.

“Lady Creseda promises us greatness.” Another added.

“Then where is she?” I snapped. The kelpie had worn through all my kindness. “Where is this fearless leader of yours who guides her people to attack a small town with a single sheriff? Where is the coward that would spur you on to attack the meek and defenseless, let alone the very people who have orchestrated you the freedom to do so?”

I was greeted with snarls and barks of rage.

“You turn your back on the very beings that rescued you and for what? So, some kelpie with delusions of grandeur can lead you back into a cage?”

“Silence, satyr.”

“You know not of who you speak.”

“Lady Creseda promises to give us rewards for our loyalty.”

I scoffed. “Then you are fools who will deserve what comes for you.”

“Is that a threat, Allipo?” The berserker growled.

“No.” I said pulling my gun and aiming. “It is a promise.”

The berserker eyed the weapon with a blink. “You plan to kill us?”

“No.” I didn’t want to, but I would protect the people of this town.

“Then why brandish a killing weapon?”

I shifted and fired before a wolf that had been edging his way forward. “Because I have a duty to uphold, and I plan to honor the lord in doing it.”

“Even in his absence?”

“Especially in his absence.”

The berserker stepped back into the fray of beasts. "We are ordered to terror."

"And I will stand against that."

"You are outnumbered."

"You underestimate the power that a satyr has."

Wolfish laughs rolled over me. Power and will to call upon the gifts of a god. Lord Niratap never approved of the gift, the divine curse that many of my kind had forgotten in the confines of servitude. Satyrs were agreeable foolish laborers, cruel entertainment, fodder for greater beasts; beaten down, many had forgotten of their patron from the old world. I closed my eyes to the laughter and mocking and reached to that deep part of me connected to the god of satyrs.

"Καλώ τον Σάτυρο θεό. Διονύσιε, ω δότρια του κρασιού και της παραφροσύνης, ευλόγησέ με με τη δύναμη της τρέλας σου για να νικήσω τους εχθρούς μου. Στο όνομά σου παρακαλώ."[90]

There was always a moment before the power rose when I feared that I may be abandoned. A moment where all my wiles and wit left me bare in the chaos that existed around me. A moment where the laughter of shifters sunk deep beneath my skin, nestling close to my bones. A moment that was short lived before I felt that brush of insanity across my spine, like hands twisting under my skin. The blinding power of madness, both weapon and curse, caused laughter to wildly bubble out of me.

Then the screaming began, and it took all that I was to hold onto myself as the power thrummed from me. The screaming continued as the sounds of a helicopter flew overhead. The screaming tore at the hands I held myself with as the insanity lit my blood on fire. Agony raged through my body and mind as the screaming lessened until it was just one voice screaming. My voice. My screams.

[90] I call upon the satyr god. Dionysius, oh giver of wine and insanity, bless me with the power of your madness so I may defeat my enemies. In your name I beg.

Just as quickly as the power had sunk into my
bones. It was gone. The blinding light of madness released
me. The world tilted dangerously to one side. Blackness
was all that greeted me at the end of my fall.

The beep of machines was a knife behind my eyes,
a new stabbing with each tone. I groaned rolling away from
the incessant beeping.

"Allipo?"

I cracked an eye, light another stab in my brain. The
sweet cadence of Eloi's voice calling out for aid was a balm
against the pounding in my skull.

"Allipo?"

"What happened?" I covered my aching eyes with a
hand.

"You don't remember?"

"I remember the town being attacked, are the kids,
okay? Carter and Solette?"

"The kids are good. Carter doesn't need surgery,
you set the bones perfectly. Solette is with him while they
fit him for a cast."

"The weres?"

"Xaevean brought a host, arrests were made, and
everyone is alright."

"Any fatalities?"

"None." Xaevean said coming in the door, the
heavy footfalls of the Days behind him. "All in the
attacking party were arrested with no fight, thanks to
whatever you did, and everyone in town has been
accounted for."

"Just one fatality then." I said.

"Who?" Rogmesh asked softly.

I sat up, blinking against the bright lights. "A kelpie

named Scatha. Her body is down in cold storage. When this gets settled down, I promised to return her to her sister."

Xaevean nodded. "I have buses coming to take those we arrested into holding."

"How many?" Durgash grumbled.

"Thirty shifters."

"I would think it would take more to throw even a small town like this into the chaos the day has brought." Rogmesh said.

"Aye." Her husband agreed.

"The rest must have fled back to the community, and they should stay there for a time, I'd assume while they regroup." Xaevean said from his post against the wall. "I can put a tac-team in to watch the settlements. However, I don't want to step on Niratap's toes. Have you heard anything?"

I shook my head, the motion making my vision swirl. "No, but Babylos is its own pocket dimension, they have little internet and even less cell service. As soon as they are on their way home, I shall receive word."

"I worry for my daughter."

"She is in good hands. Lord Niratap won't let anything happen to her."

"I know but I still worry." Xaevean ran a hand over his head which was back to his normal puff of hair. "Her mother worries."

I nodded. "I understand."

Rodger stormed in; a nurse was close behind him. She slipped past and began checking my vitals and removing leads. Rodger cleared his throat "Are you alright?"

"Is that genuine concern I hear?" I glowered at the sheriff.

He frowned. "It was genuine, believe it or not."

I scoffed. "Right."

"Look I know I've been less than friendly to your house, but—"

"Rodger, I have a splitting headache and don't want to have an altercation because you think you're in the right."

He folded his arms across his chest. "Well fine. Thank you for your assistance with whatever that was. I—"

"What do you want?" I snapped. "I don't have the patience for you and your fake thanks or apologies. I assume Xaevean has already reached out for aid to rebuild the town, and the manor is on board if there is a need for hands, labor, or financial aid because unlike you the rest of this town hasn't treated us like trash."

The nurse winced at my tone, but Rodger carried on. "It is no fault of mine that that lord of yours is so untrustworthy."

"Why is it that you single him out? Is he not humanoid enough for you? As it stands, sheriff, I would trust Lord Niratap much more than you any day."

"Oh really. The man that you serve versus a servant of the law."

"Law unto himself."

"Listen here you—"

"No, you listen and listen well, sheriff. The lord is a good man, and I will not stand idly by while you repeatedly try to drag his name through the mud."

"He is a monster."

"In species alone. That is all that matters to you, isn't it?"

"He's a predator, worming his way into the hearts of people so he can eat them."

"Your view of his kind is skewed by a history of hatred."

"History that was well warranted."

"To a narrative of oppression."

Xaevean placed his hand on Rodger's shoulder. "That's enough. From both of you. Niratap is a good man, Sheriff."

"But he kidnapped that young lady and turned her

into a sex toy."

Xaevean's face softened with a soft laugh. "That young lady is my daughter, and she is as wild and untamable as the wind. She loves him, and the bond between them is built on love. I've known Niratap for some time and though his methods often butt up against my work he produces results. He saves countless lives, risking his own life more often than his people's. I wouldn't have my daughter with anyone else at this point."

Rodger blinked at Xaevean. "You can't be serious."

Xaevean nodded. "I am. My daughter loves him. He loves her, to a fault. That is all I could ask of her partner. Come on, Sheriff, let's go talk about repairs and I'll get you in touch with the National Guard commander that will be overseeing the aid."

Xaevean gave me a smile as he walked the sheriff out. I sighed, rolling my neck.

"He means well." The nurse, Ingrid, said softly.

"I apologize for my outburst, dear."

"No, you don't have to. Everyone knows that the sheriff is hard on you all. He means well."

"I wish he would look beyond his bias to see what we are trying to do."

"It's hard for anyone to look beyond a bias if they are bound in pain." Her tone was sharp, even to her own ears as she apologized profusely. "Sheriff Clemmens' mother was killed by a creature, and it follows him like a shadow."

And there it was. The last piece of the puzzle that I needed. An understanding that put us on opposing sides. He didn't know us. Couldn't allow himself the space to without feeling like he was disrespecting his mother. Much how I had resented humans when they had killed my father. I knew that anger and it had taken me almost an entire century to move past that anger. Anger that kept me alive while I was in the fighting ring. After things return to normal, maybe we could bridge the gap.

Chapter Fifty-Two

Bastion

Sweat stung my eyes, as I faced Shasha again. She had her braids done up behind her head, her eyes focused, her breath coming is shallow pants.

"You've gotten fast."

She smiled at me. "I don't believe we've ever actually sparred, Bas."

"I think you're right."

"You should see her quickdraw, Bastion." Niratap said from where he sat, flipping through a tome.

"I bet she is almost as fast as you."

He smiled. "Somedays faster."

Mitta and Tummi walked past us. Mitta barked. "Take a break, you two."

"How's your sister doing?" I asked Tummi, wiping the sweat off my brow.

She glanced to where Katrel stood with Cyran, who was dressed casually in beige pants and a white shirt, in the farthest part of the courtyard. Deep in concentration. "Not as well as she would like."

"What are they trying to do?" Shasha asked, sitting beside the lord.

"They are trying to get her to connect with the flame magic in her blood." Mitta said, watching Katrel. "Cyran thinks he can help her guide it through so she can utilize it."

"Fledgling power is a dangerous thing to master." Niratap said softly.

"It is." She agreed. "But it could be an edge that we will need for whatever the king has planned."

"Or it could backfire; we still don't know what

Cardoc is planning, and tomorrow is the summer solstice."

Mitta glowered at him. "Yes, but it could be a boon. If she can—"

"If she can." Niratap pointed.

"Do you doubt her ability?" Tummi asked with a frown.

"It is not that I doubt her ability." He said softly watching Katrel's shoulder fall as she failed yet again to summon the flame. "I doubt that she will be able to overcome her fear."

Mitta sighed. "You are right, though I hate that you voiced it."

I stretched my arms over my head, while they continued to discuss the ramifications of whether or not this was a good use of time. That was when I saw him. The apparition stood watching over Katrel, dressed in red that matched the royal crest, his hair the same honey chestnut that Katrel had. I walked over to them, eyeing the man.

"How are you doing?" I asked.

"So, fucking fantastic." Katrel snapped.

सा भीता भवति।[91] The apparition said beside me.

I shook my head at him, causing his brow to rise. "No luck becoming a candle?"

Katrel looked to the sky in disbelief. "Must you?"

"I meant no offense, but what's keeping you from accessing it?"

"I don't know."

Droeneuh jeut neudeungo lon? Peuë droëneuh neubantu ulôn bak neupeurunoe putroë nyan?[92]

I shook my head again at the different language, another I didn't understand, and he frowned. "Is it because you're afraid?"

She glowered at me as Cyran said. "If it is fear in your way, you will not be able to channel the magic in your blood."

[91] she is afraid.

[92] you can hear me? Will you aid me in teaching the princess?

Eh sha nukarmo sur knarock khasha eh?[93]

My eyes widened at the spirits use of Orcin. "Okay. So why are you so scared."

"I am not, scared."

"Katrel." Cyran sighed. "You will not be like your father."

Kama sha udsha kama sheer et ta udka kog ahdsho eh sha atka kama.[94]

"Maybe if you opened up to the flame and centered yourself."

"Like you're an expert on magic."

I frowned. "Just try it and don't be a bitch."

She flipped me off and faced Cyran again. The apparition moved behind her, easing his body into hers. Katrel jolted but relaxed again. Her face pinched with focus as the apparition lead her movements and helped her summon the flame in her blood. The orange ball of flame formed in her hands when she opened her eyes. It flared in her hands as her eyes widened with disbelief.

"How is this possible?" She was shocked.

"I told you just to ease into it." I said as the others came to observe.

"Okay." Cyran said. "Draw Aetherius and channel your fire into the blade."

The ball of fire banked, lingering flame flickered at her fingers as she drew the blade. She clasped it between her hands and focused on the blade. The flame eased from her fingers and up the fuller, causing the ancient inscriptions to glow before flames danced around the blade.

Cyran smiled. "Well done."

Katrel smiled, her face giddy. "I can't believe I did that."

"It's a good step forward. Now reel it back and do it again."

---

[93] I can help if you will let me.
[94] If she can center her mind and open up to the flame I can show her.

She followed those instructions. Her breath was a bit shaky as she drew the flames back into her body. They repeated the push and pull of flames for over an hour, all of us watching with awe. Gradually the apparition eased out of Katrel, until he stood beside her whispering in her ear in French. Encouraging her as she went through rounds without him. Could she hear him? Did she know someone else was helping her? Who was this male?

"Alright. I think that will be good." Cyran said, wiping sweat from his brow.

"Do you kno—"

Cyran shook his head at her question. "No. Your mother is worried, both of us know that he is plotting something."

"Tomorrow is the solstice." Niratap said softly.

"He is trying to trap you." Mitta agreed.

Katrel swallowed, looking over us. Eyes pausing on Tummi before holding on Mitta, who frowned at something unspoken between them. "Thank you. For everything that all you have done for me."

"Don't you dare." Tummi hissed. "We don't do goodbyes."

Katrel smiled softly at her sister. "It's not goodbye. I just wanted to tell you all. Just in case I don't get the chance."

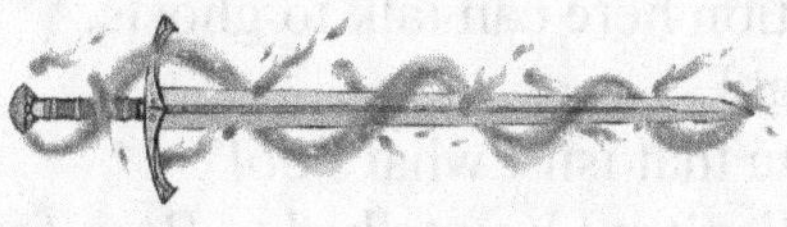

"Are you worried?"

Tummi paused her pacing to look at me. "Why wouldn't I be? Our father hasn't summoned Katrel for a task, no one knows what he's plotting."

"We'll take it one day at a time."

"But—" there was a knock.

I rose from the chair to answer it. "Yes?"

"Bastion, let me in." Mitta hissed beyond the door. She practically shoved her way into the room.

"Jesus, Mitta!"

"What did you do?" She growled at me.

"What did I do? What are you talking about?"

"In the training ring this morning, Katrel was struggling to even produce a spark, you walk over, and she suddenly gets it."

"I don't have a lick of magic in me Mitta, I didn't do anything."

"Who helped her?"

"I don't know. He spoke old languages that I wasn't familiar with."

"What are you talking about Bastion?" Tummi asked.

"You haven't told her?" Mitta asked.

"Told me what? What hasn't he told me?"

"Mitta you are the only person who knows that. I shared that with you in confidence and to give you peace."

"What if I didn't need peace? What if I was happy in not knowing?"

"You were stuck and he just wanted you to be happy. It paid off, didn't it?"

"Oh, you meddlesome boy."

"Full stop." Tummi said, pushing between us. "What the fuck are you taking about?"

"Bastion here can talk to ghosts."

"What?"

"Mitta that isn't what I do!"

"But isn't it? You talked to Bran for me, bridged between life and death. Told me about Taegan. Who helped Katrel with the flame?"

"I don't know who he was, he just offered to help. Katrel just needed to relax. She was so twisted up with fear that she couldn't do it on her own."

"You can speak to the dead?" Tummy asked.

"Who was it?" Mitta demanded over her.

"A man dressed like a noble. It could have been an ancestor, a court member, I don't know."

"Enough!" Tummi shouted. "What did he look like?"

"He was tall, soft features, the same hair and eyes as your sister. He was dressed in the royal crest's colors."

Tummi went to the shelves along the wall and pulled a large book from the shelf, flipping the pages as she came back to us. She pointed at a page before turning it for me to see. "Him."

On the page there was a portrait of the spirit I had seen. Beneath the picture was his name in a detailed scrawl. Conláed Raloqen the Flame Emperor. The flame emperor. "Yes."

"The great flame helped my sister."

"The great flame?"

"It's a folk name. Emperor Conláed helped my sister with her flame. Wow. Just wow."

"You're not acting like I expected." I said as she turned to sit at the table.

"How was I supposed to act?"

"I don't know. I think most people would freak out to find that their partner can talk to the dead."

She smiled at me. "I'm not surprised; a little angry if I'm honest. Why didn't you tell me sooner."

I rubbed the back of my head self-consciously. "It's not the best leader when I introduce myself. 'Hi, I'm Bastion. I like easy mac, music, and I get tormented by the dead."

She laughed.

"Why are you not surprised?"

"I was there when you were born. I watched Saabraa breathe life back into you. It just makes sense that you would be on the precipice between life and death."

"You're not scared?"

"Why would I be scared of the man I love?"

"Why did we wait so long?"

The door clicked with Mitta's silent exit, leaving us to swoon over one another. No matter what happened I was going to keep this woman safe.

Chapter Fifty-Three

Niratap

I was adrift. My nightmares, though lessened here, still lingered. The darkness was suffocating. Shasha's scent anchored me even as my mind floated in the black. A familiar dread seeped into my skin.

Master approaches. The hiss of the malice licked my ears.

"Why do you torment me?"

A laugh echoed. *My master wants one weakened. Easy to take over. Easy to break.*

A foul taste crawled over my tongue. "It will take much more to break me than your master thinks."

Master has charged me to make it so. Pretty mate shall be an easy way to break you. She is fragile.

"You leave her alone." I snarled.

The grating laugh echoed around me. *Master approaches. Most excited to hear her cries.*

My heart thudded in my ears as I roared into the void.

Normally when I woke for the summer Solstice the fluttering of wings and clip of hooves greeted my ears. Not the soft breaths of my mate still sleeping softly before me in a bed not our own and the screams from my dream still echoing in my head. The dark of the night not quite ready to yield to the dawn.

I pressed a kiss to her crown, inhaling the

wildflower scent of her that made my blood sing. What was I going to do? This unknown enemy was coming for me, and they were planning on using Shasha to win. Loving her had put her in harm's way again. That terrified me more than a lich coming after me. Shasha in danger crawled under my skin like a swarm of worms.

She stirred in my arms and her voice was heavy with sleep. "Why are you fretting?"

I kissed her crown again. "I am not fretting."

"I can feel it, you know. The distress you have. Share."

This growing connection between us also terrified me. "I had a nightmare."

She sat up and glared down at me with impertinence. "Are you well?"

I reached up to stroke her shoulder. "I am. Unnerved but I am."

In the faint light I saw her brows pinch. "The malice?"

"Yes." Fear crawled along my spine though I tried to ignore it; she saw.

"Nira." She cupped my face.

I sighed. "I'm afraid. Not for myself but for you. They plan on using you to get to me and I don't want that to come to fruition. I don't want you to be at the mercy of anyone, let alone a lich."

She eased me onto my back, straddling my hips, a vixen's smile on her lips. "I am not defenseless, my love."

"I know." And I did. She had come to save me, time and again. From Draven, from Cardoc, from myself. But— "I am scared that you will be in danger, that whatever that danger is I will not be able to protect you. That we will lose each other."

She laid her body over mine resting her head over the thrum of my heart. Her fingers tracing over the basilisk scar. "I share your fears, but as long as I have you with me and I am with you, everything will be okay."

No matter the storm or battlefield she settled the rage in my heart. I pressed yet another kiss to her crown. "You amaze me."

She tilted her face up to look at me. "Why do you think that?"

"Plenty of reasons."

She smiled. "Tell me."

I laughed softly. "Oh, I couldn't say. I'm a mated male you know."

Playfulness danced over her face. "Oh really. I had no idea."

I nodded. "Yes. I couldn't be disloyal to her."

"Well, tell me about this mate of yours?"

"Is this where we joke about bathroom photos?"

She laughed, that springtime joy pouring out of her like champagne. "Bathroom photos?"

"You know, where the men talk about their families over the divider and show each other wallet photos of their kids."

"Do you have wallet photos of your mate?"

"I might."

"Tell me."

"Okay, yes. I do." I had slipped the small photo of us dancing into my wallet soon after her mother had given it to me.

"You do not."

"I do."

"I want to see it." She made to move off me, but I held her hips in place.

"I thought you wanted to know about my mate."

She returned to her rested position. "I do. Tell me about this mate of yours. Is she beautiful?"

"Very."

"How beautiful?"

"She is the most beautiful woman I have ever met."

"What makes her that beautiful?"

I swallowed, looking into her earthen eyes. "She has

these gorgeous brown eyes that light my soul on fire."

She fluttered her eyelashes at me.

"She has lips that are soft as rose petals and each kiss from her feels like it could last forever."

She kissed along my collarbone.

"She is wickedly smart."

A huff of a laugh.

"Insanely curious to a fault."

"Is that a bad thing?"

I smirked. "No, she has this openness that sucks me in. I never had the chance to be that curious about everything. I learned very young that the world was a very dangerous place and that being afraid would keep me alive. It has kept me alive."

"But?"

I took a shaky breath. "But my loving and generous mate, she makes me feel alive; like I am living for the first time. Every day I get with her is precious and I would live through every terrible thing that has happened to me again to spend just one more day with her."

Her smile took on a sad weight. "You know she would never ask that of you?"

"I know, but I would suffer terribly for just one day more."

She shifted to look down at me. "And I will do everything in my power to make sure you don't have to."

She kissed me, both sweet and sad. "Let's go back to sleep. The sun has not yet awakened, and we should rest."

She curled into my side. "We're going to make it through this love. As long as we're together."

Someone was knocking incessantly at the door soon

after the sun had risen. I felt Shasha shift from the bed. Heard her feet pad across the floor to the door.

"Hello?"

I shifted in the bed to watch as she opened the door.

"What?"

Sweet smelling smoke quickly filled the room. I moved for the door, but the world spun and the flood disappeared under my feet. I heard Shasha scream as I hit the floor.

"Are we taking both of them?" A male voice asked.

"No just the girl. Those were our orders."

"No." I croaked on the smoke that was making my vision spin. A man stood over me, face mostly covered by a cloth.

"Please let her go."

"The king sends his regards." He kicked me in the temple, and everything went dark.

Chapter Fifty-Four

The dawn had pulled me from Mitta's arms and comfort of my bed to the training field. I pulled from the warm well in my blood, a pocket of flame that had lain dormant to my fear. The flame was shaky and unrefined, but I could still call it forward. Could still pull it from my skin to dance.

I had avoided the heat in my veins. Afraid the power would make me like my father, afraid that the flame would char my soul and make me a monster. I knew now through trial and error that it was a part of my soul, the brilliant part that wanted to dance in the wind. The hot part that wanted to protect my family as much as I did. The warm but misunderstood part of my soul that just wanted to be loved.

The flame danced over my hands and sparked brightly. Yesterday it had been a bright orange, today it was a deep crimson and focused into a tight ball. I wanted to master this. I wanted to own this part of myself. Cyran had said that it was key to not being ashamed of it, trusting it to protect me and those I cared for.

I drew Aetherius and willed the flame to curl around the blade, like a fat cat in the sun. The flame twisted easy at my direction and crackled as I went through stances by myself. I would master this. I would right the wrongs of my ancestors. I wound end the tyranny of my father's reign. I would escape what tradition dictated was my fate. I would–

"Kat!"

Tummi ran into the training ground, panting heavily. I pulled the fire back into myself. "What is it?"

She doubled over choking down air. "Something terrible has happened."

"What?" I scanned behind her for danger. "What happened?"

"I'll tell you on the way." She beckoned me to follow.

Running through the castle, past nobles and staff, Tummi said. "I left early this morning to meet with Cyran in the library, he was called away soon after we met up, so I took the tomes he had found for me and went to wake Bastion."

We turned down the wing to our rooms and a sinking dread sunk into my gut.

"But Bastion wasn't in our room. So, I knocked on your door to see if you or Mitta knew where he was. You were gone. So was Mitta, but your room looked like a fight had broken out. So, I went to Niratap to see if he had heard anything."

I glanced into our rooms. Tummi's room was empty. I froze. Mine was disheveled, chairs toppled, the tea set and other porcelain lay broken across the floor. Blades scattered among the shards of glass. I swallowed, someone had taken her. Had they taken Bastion as well?

"Kat!" Tummi called from Niratap's room.

I pushed myself past the fear gripping my heart, making it hard to breathe, and entered my friend's room. That fear ratcheted up as Tummi rolled Niratap's head out of a pool of congealed blood, his face pale and pinched with worry. Shasha was nowhere to be seen.

"Please tell me he's breathing." I whispered.

"He is, just unconscious with a head wound." She dabbed at the cut with a rag and I saw a deep purple bruise marring the side of his face. "Thank the stars."

"What happened? Where is everyone?"

"Kat, I don't know. Do you think father had something to do with this?"

I felt the blood drain from my face. He wouldn't.

He couldn't. No, he would and could and he had definitely played a role in the cracking of my heart.

"Kat?"

"It's my trail. He took them. He took our family to use against me."

"No."

I turned, bolting from the room.

"Katrel! Fuck." Tummi's footsteps followed behind me as I charged to the only place he would be.

I burst into the throne room doors, slamming them against the marble walls. Lords and ladies decorating the ball floor looked at me in varying expressions of shock or disgust. Guards rimmed the walls decorated in their royal armor and armed with ellervine and cragstone. The crowd parted as I pushed forward, Tummi at my heels, as I approached our father on his dark throne; our mother the picture of subservience beside him. The doors were shut behind us, locking us into whatever it was we were to face.

"I was wondering when you would join us, Princess."

"Where are they? Where is my family?" There were gasps among the crowd, but I didn't care anymore. "Where is Lady Bondbreaker? Where is Bastion? Where is Mitta?"

I hated that my voice broke at her name.

"Well, you see, daughter, I have planned this final trial just for you." He smirked, waving his glass of wine to the guards. "Bring them in."

Guards led in four identical beings and forced them to their knees before the throne. I could not tell if they were male or female. I could not tell their race. There was no distinguishing between the beings—and why were there four of them? If this was my family, they had been enchanted to confuse me and who was the fourth?

"What is this?" I asked.

"This, Princess, is your final trial. Since you want to cut yourself from the royal line, I found it only appropriate that you cut out part of that freedom as payment."

"No."

"Before you are four beings, all who matter to you in one aspect or another."

"No."

He smirked. "Now let me finish, you impertinent child. One of them must die, but I give you the choice on which one you kill. I'll even give you the boon of sparing one from your choice."

"You cannot expect me to slay someone I care about."

"Then you will bend to my will. You will bend and wed Revan and bare the throne an heir as is your duty."

"I will not do this. You cannot make me."

"I can and I will, child. Guards."

The song of steel unsheathing caused my knees to wobble underneath me. He wouldn't.

The guards each grabbed the hooded figure before them and their head back exposing their throats for their blades. The blades rose to deliver on his threat, there was murmuring around the room.

"Stop. Please stop." I cried.

"Are you giving up?"

"Katrel you can't give up." Tummi said softly.

"I can't do this Tummi. Bastion is up there. Mitta is up there. Shasha is up there. Niratap can't lose her. You and Bastion have finally found each other. Mitta—"

"I know." Tears fell over her cheeks, her face becoming blotchy. "None of them are going to blame you for the blow."

Her own heart was breaking at her words. I could hear it in the way her voice cracked. "Tummi."

"You can do it, take the boon. Save one for sure and then choose."

"Tummi, I can't."

"Katrel." The king said, sounding bored. "The guard's arms are growing tired."

I closed my eyes. "I want to spare Lady

Bondbreaker."

"Unfortunately, I don't know which one is her." He smiled at me. "You must pick, Princess. One to guarantee life and one to meet death."

I took a step forward. I couldn't do this. I could lose everything if I picked wrong. If Shasha fell to my blade, Niratap would never forgive me. If Bastion was the unfortunate one Tummi would be heartbroken. If I killed Mitta, I would follow her into the ether. We had denied each other for far too long and now that she was mine, I would not lose one moment of the life we'd promised each other. I did not know who the last loved one was. Was it a trick? Was it just some poor soul picked to make this harder for me? A glimmer of hope in a hopeless situation.

Four cloaked figures, two choices to freedom. Would I make the right choice, or would I lose it all in a heartbeat? I walked closer, but they were identical. Hands bound behind their backs, hoods over their faces, masked under magic. I prayed to the stars, begged them to guide me true. Shasha could not fall under my blade; Niratap had suffered enough.

Who could it be? Was it a puzzle that I had to figure out? Would he put her first or second or was she last to throw me off? I reached out my hand. He would have put her third in line. Would have placed her in the least obvious spot. He didn't hate elementals or humans. Bastion would be placed first, first to speak out against him blatantly. He would have put Mitta second with the hope I would think it the dummy and the dummy was last. Yes, that had to be it. I reached out my hand and pulled the hood away.

I was wrong.

Chapter Fifty-Five

Tummilia

My heart cracked as Katrel pulled the hood away, dispelling the enchantment on the lucky one. My lucky one. Bastion's eyes were wild and once he saw me; his shoulders fell in relief, like he had been more worried that I was in danger. I had never been in danger here, hated by my father but loved by the court.

My knees went boneless, and I sank to the floor. Kat, with tears in her eyes, cut him loose and he was kneeling before me teary eyed, pulling the gag from his mouth to murmur his relief that I was safe. That I hadn't been hurt, even as his eye was dark with a shiner, dried blood streaked below his nose, and his lip swollen. I had told her to sacrifice my heart, to save Shasha, knowing that if Bastion had gone, I would have gone with him. Did Katrel know that? Did she know and that was why she had picked him? Could she not lose me that badly? He pressed a tusk heavy kiss to my brow, his tears dripping onto my cheeks.

Katrel wasn't facing us, her head bouncing back and forth between the hooded figures. She had to kill one of them now. Mitta or Shasha or someone else. She had to choose. She had to—the doors banged open again with a feral snarl.

"Cardoc!" Niratap stood at the entryway.

"Bondbreaker, how lovely of you to join us. I was wondering if that kick to the head had done you in."

"Where is she?"

A dangerous grin curled over our father's face. "Who?"

"Don't play with him." Bastion barked.

"Where is she? Where is Shasha? Where is my mate?"

"Oh, how delicious." Father purred.

"Where the fuck is my mate, Cardoc." Niratap stepped into the throne room, his face bruised and contorted with rage. "I will not let you hurt her."

"Oh, I would never hurt an innocent girl. Katrel has the honor of choosing to spare your precious mate. Though I won't feel bad if she dies, that slice from her blade stung."

"Release her." He shouted with the thrum of power that sent the shadows skittering around the room. Nobles yelped in fear, one lady fainted.

Father frowned and snapped his fingers. "No."

A guard stepped out from behind a pillar throwing the ellervine lasso with deadly aim. The rope slid gracefully over Niratap's antlers and cinched tight around his throat as the guard pulled back, yanking Niratap off his feet. There was a painful crack as his head bounced off the marble floor. He snarled as guards descended on him, but it lacked ferocity.

"Now, Princess, finish your trial. Who will suffer the cost of your freedom?"

Aetherius hung limply in her hand, her eyes scanning, scanning, scanning. She didn't know who she was going to pick. She was panicking.

"Kat."

"I can't do this." Her voice so soft under the Niratap's growls.

"Do you yield to your duty, Princess Katrel?"

Her hand tightened around the hilt of her sword. "Never."

"Then choose."

One more pass over the three remaining figures. A moment of pause as her eyes landed on the first figure, who was knelt before our mother, her hand pressed to her mouth in shock. Shock at something she had discovered. Katrel shifted closer to the figure, a dark smile returned to our father's face.

"I'm sorry. Please forgive me. I hold you no ill. Forgive me."

She plunged the blade through the figure's chest. The figure did not flinch as the blade was pulled from their chest. Blood spurted under the hood staining it red. Katrel grabbed the hood and exposed our teacher. Our mother wailed, standing and she near fell down the dais steps. Father rolled his eyes at the display.

"Release the others." Katrel demanded, watching out mother pulling at Cyran's binds.

Father waved a dismissive hand, and the guards pulled the hoods free. Mitta had bruises on her cheeks and a slice across her brow, she rolled away from the guard before he could restrain her again. Katrel cut her bound hands, her face was twisted in rage at the state of the warrior she loved. Shasha's eyes had locked on where her mate, restrained on the ground, was snarling.

Rage sparked in her eyes as she swung her head back into the guard's groin. The guard toppled over, and Shasha disarmed him, cutting her bonds before pointing the sword at the king.

"Release him." She hissed.

Father just eyed her from his lounged position. "This is the second time you have threatened the king of this land with a weapon. It is a crime punishable by death."

Niratap thrashed with a wild snarl. His face was pulled back over his fanged mouth, his skin looking tight as the ellervine kept him from shifting. "You will not."

"It is tradition and law." Guards closed in around Shasha, blossoming from the crowd.

Shasha scoffed. "You would seek the wrath of my mate?"

"Your mate is currently at my mercy." He waved a hand towards where Niratap was restrained. A guard moved from the shadows with a long spear in his hands. The spearhead was the same dark colored glass as Shasha's favored dagger.

Shasha's face went ashen. "No."

"Enough." Cyran coughed, mother had released him from the gag. "False king."

"Cyran, please." Mother pleaded.

"What was that scholar?"

Cyran shifted and coughed weakly but looked up at the king with disdain. "You are a false king."

Father shifted from his lounged position to eye the dying scholar. "Says the adultier."

There were whispers around the nobles. Cyran laughed weakly. "Says the wife beater."

Gasps and chatter spattered through the nobles that stood away from where Niratap fought the guards, the binds cutting into his skin, causing him to bleed. Shasha spun keeping the guards at bay.

"You accuse the king of beating his queen."

"Many already suspect that you beat the woman who birthed you children."

"You're still trying to hide the truth." Father shook his head, glaring down at me. "Does she know she is a bastard?"

The blow rocked through me suddenly. I looked at Cyran anew. His pale blonde hair a lighter shade of mine, his nose so similar to my own. Most of my features were much like my mother's, dark storm blue eyes, night sky eyes, a fair skin, but her hair was the color of starlight. The golden hue of my hair could only come from one person. It was then that I remembered something that Teovelass had said. Katrel held both flame and starlight in her blood, but I—I had only had starlight.

"It can't be true." I breathed.

"Oh, but it is." The king said. "I am not your father, Tummilia. You are the product of adultery, the daughter of a whore and a scholar."

"Do not speak of her like that." Cyran hissed, before he coughed.

"Weakness. A weakness I tried to rid myself of, but as weaknesses tend to do, it uprooted my house, even after I tried to tame the wandering womb of my wife."

"The only weakness in this court is you, Cardoc." Mother hissed at him.

Rage filled his face. "You dare disrespect me?"

"I have never respected you." The words were calloused, and the nobles chattered like trapped birds.

"I shall remind you of your weaknesses, Ciserie." Flame curled from Cardoc fingers, before he launched them at her.

The screaming started. My voice raging over the crowd with *no*.

Chapter Fifty-Six

Katrel

I reacted, stepping before the ball of fire and lifting the bloodied Aetherius to block the blow. The blade absorbed the fire, flaring beneath the heat. People were starting to shout, a mix of curses and cheers. Divided.

"You are not worthy of that blade."

"I earned this blade, unlike you father who sent me on the errand expecting me to cow at the challenge."

"Women are weak and so should stay."

"I am not weak, though long I have believed it to be true."

He laughed at me. "You were supposed to be a boy."

I braced myself between my father and my mother. Knowing that Mitta was at her side trying to stop Cyran's bleeding, trying to save the scholar. I heard his wheezing breaths. He would die without a healer. "Your flame was no match to a star."

"What are you talking about?" He laughed. "Stars bend to fire."

"No." Cyran wheezed. "Stars are more powerful than flames ever could be. For flames die and stars do not."

"What do you know of such things, scholar?"

"I know that before the age of man, when the world was one, a star fell from the sky and fell in love with a king."

Cardoc sat in his throne amused at the words of the dying man. "All of us have heard this story, but if this is how you want to spend your final moments, I won't deny you."

Cyran scowled, but with a cough began his tale.

"Our great burning flame, Conláed Raloqen fought bravely against the siege of man with his only son at his side. Gone was the child's mother killed in that first uprising and though they battled fiercely many fell to man. It was this bravery and dedication to his people that caused the star to fall. Conláed fell for the glimmering star, named Lucette. The sky and the great creator descended and gifted the leaders of each faction mighty weapons. Conláed's blade imbued with his fire enabled him to lead elves to a time of peace. With Lucette at his side, as his wife, he led his people through an era of peace, and she bore him a daughter drenched in her light."

"Changing a small detail to prove something philosophical, is a waste." Cardoc hissed.

"I am only telling the story true, as it hasn't been told for millennia." Cyran coughed again. "But unlike the elves who have long lives and longer memory, man is neither and soon war returned to the elves. A century passed at war and the mighty flame grew weary of the bloodshed."

"And he used the star to separate Babylos from the world of man. His son taking up his mantle to lead the people." Cardoc finished the history that had been told since birth. Not the truth.

"You are wrong." I said.

"Am I?" Cardoc frowned.

"Continue Cyran. Tell them the truth"

"With the guidance of an ageless being, Conláed gave up all that he was, for his people. Trusting his wife to keep the kingdom together in the separation. The emperor's son felt slighted and so he hunted for the star and her daughter. He slayed them in cold blood to claim the throne as his, ending the line of star." He coughed and wheezed. He was dying and this story had captured the ears of the nobles, against the deference of the king. "But as luck would have it, his murdered sister had a family who escaped into the night. A young noble who left everything behind to protect his celestial daughter."

"What is the point of this story?"

Cyran tried to rise from under the caring hands that were trying to staunch the bleeding. His skin pale and wan as he coughed. There was so much blood. Too much blood.

"The point." I faced my father, glaring at him. "The point is that you do not have claim to the throne that your forefathers spilled innocent blood for."

"Is that a challenge?"

I reached for the flame of my ancestor. The flame of a just king who wanted to right the wrongs that his children had done to his people. I felt him there with me, he had been a presence at my shoulder this whole time, the nagging feelings to keep going. Keep fighting. The flame answered that call to keep fighting, igniting Aetherius with bright hot flames.

"Maybe it is." I brandished the flaming blade. "Maybe it is time for you to step down, father? In your waning years as it is."

The whispering murmurs of nobles ceased, and it was in that silence where only breath and crackling flame sounded that my father blinked. Then he laughed.

"And who would lead the kingdom? You? Your bastard sister?"

I swallowed. "No. Neither of us. Though we love our people, neither of us want to be leashed to the throne. Our lives have purpose already."

"Then who would take up your mantel? Who will stand on the throne? Who will bear the weight of the crown?"

"I–I don't know." I was unsettled by the thought that maybe I was wrong.

"You don't know. Who will back a royal who doesn't know?"

"I would find someone worthy of the title."

"And who would you pick?" He stepped down the

stairs of the dais. "A commoner with a noble heart? A bendable creature of breeding?"

Snickering began among the nobles, rising as an uncomfortable pressure around me. "The tyranny must stop."

"You think me a tyrant daughter?" He stopped just out of the reach of my blade.

"I know you to be one. Only a tyrant demands his daughter bend to the will of another man. Only a tyrant traps his daughter in tests he believes she will not conquer." I said.

"Tests that you have performed beyond expectation."

I took a breath to steady myself, letting my voice rise with each truth. "Only a tyrant gives that daughter no options. Only a tyrant beats his wife into submission. Only a tyrant sells off a member of his house into slavery."

"That trash was never my daughter." He shouted, drawing a blade that clashed with mine. "She was never a member of this house!"

"But she is my sister!"

Flame twisted up my father's sword as we came to blows. His fire was brutal and cruel, and it raged against mine.

"You never loved like a father should love."

"Love doesn't rule a kingdom."

"What about your parents?"

"My father was a king just as I am, and my mother was subservient."

"What about your wife?"

"Ciserie was nothing but pretty breeding stock for her father's station. She failed in her purpose, not once but twice."

"What about me?"

"You were supposed to be a boy. You were not worthy of my attention."

I roared and we met viscously, flame and steel a

song in my blood. I would not cow. I would not bow. I would not give up. I would not allow him the chance to rule over my family or my people. Today his reign would end.

Chapter Fifty-Seven

Tummilia

Cyran was my father. Cyran Aeralei Crane, Crown Scholar, was my father. My father. I saw the man from my childhood in a different light. Kindness given freely to crocodile tears. Love given freely with sneaked sweets during lessons. Protection without the demand for payment. Cyran was my father.

My father was dying. Blood was starting to pool around him, Mitta had sacrificed the pitiful threadbare shirt to try to stanch the flowing crimson. He was dying. He was dying, his head gently cradled in my mother's lap. His blood stained the pale royal grown, her pale fingers which stroked his face. She was apologizing for, what I didn't know. Her lips just kept whispering to him. *I'm sorry. I'm so sorry.*

Katrel was yelling at the king, screaming at him. Her blade full of flame as she stood before him, challenged him. He had stood before her and laughed, meeting her challenge as a king, not her father. All her life Katrel had just wanted to be loved, to feel like she meant something to someone. She hadn't seen all these years that she was. She hadn't seen the bonds grown through hardship. She respected and cared for Niratap, but she had never allowed her heart to see that he cared about her. She hadn't seen Mitta pining for her for almost three centuries while she denied herself. She hadn't seen the family at her back. She hadn't until they had wanted to expose their necks to the executioner.

I turned my head to the others. Niratap thrashed in the hold of the ellervine that wound around his throat and limbs, digging in deep, the friction causing him to bleed.

He had ceased his battle briefly to allow Cyran space to share the truth. A truth that rocked the court. I had heard it in the gasps and murmurs of the nobles. Niratap snarled, his eyes focused, not on the clashing of flame encase blades, but on his mate.

Shasha was trapped, surrounded by eight knights with swords drawn. The knight she had disarmed was closing in behind her, his arms open. Two swordsmen attacked and the unarmed man grabbed her. A wild snarl echoed across the hall, echoed in my heart as the knight pulled Shasha's arms behind her. She kicked and arched against the men. She was yelling, screaming at them to let her go, let him go. It rose to a keening as Niratap gained some leverage and flung a knight into a pillar. He was pulling towards her, towards the center of his universe. The cordage around his throat cinched so tight that it caused his voice to croak over her name. The spearman plunged the cragstone edge into his back, his pained cry choked as he thrashed. He was defenseless against them and at their mercy.

Bastion had stood, snarling and yelling, but refusing to leave my side. He loved so fiercely, so bravely with his sweet but battered heart. He was the proof that parents could love each other and bestow that love onto their offspring. Bastion, my Bastion. There had been fears that Cyran had pointed out in one of our sessions in the library. That memory flashed across my mind. I hadn't thought much about what he had said.

"So, an orc?"

"Is that a problem?"

Cyran didn't speak for some time. "No."

"Then why mention it?"

He sighed. "It is just a short time of happiness is all, if you make it out of here."

"He's only forty-four he's not old for an orc."

"True, but your lifespan is so much greater than his. He will be lucky to reach your length of life already."

Would he be lucky with the work that we did? Would he see that many suns? Or would life's work, this journey, be the end of his pure loving heart.

Nobles were screaming. Nobles were laughing. They had wormed their way around the periphery, the guards between them and Niratap. The sounds he was making were closer to the beast in him that was held at bay by the ellervine, a harsh wheeze hung at the end of each snarl. They gawked at Katrel and Cardoc, whose blades and flames had pushed them even farther back. They had little interest in what was going on, beyond their entertainment. They did not care that the king was fighting his daughter for the right to the throne. They did not care that a mated pair were being kept apart at the behest of their king. They did not care that the queen was covered in her lover's blood. They did not care that that lover was dying, that the Crown Scholar was dying.

"Stop." My voice was just a whisper in the roar around me.

Shasha kicked a knight in the head knocking his helm free, to clatter on the marble floor. She cried out in both pain and rage as the men gripped her ankles. They were trying to restrain her. She fought them every step of the way, a hellcat of a woman repeatedly out-maneuvering nine men. The spear stabbed Niratap in the back again, a choked howl crashed against the stone. Katrel dodged a savage blow from Cardoc blade that chipped the marble step of the dais. Cyran coughed, his breath becoming more and more shallow with each passing second. Mitta was trying desperately to stop the bleeding, to save him. It was a miracle he had lasted this long, that he had been able to tell everyone the truth, whether or not it made a difference. Katel had fatally wounded him, but she had given him time, in missing his heart she had given him that. He feebly reached up and stroked mother's face. It was a goodbye.

"Stop."

A knight approached Bastion, sword drawn and

ready to draw blood. Bastion was unarmed, his only drive was protecting me. I was drowning in all that was around me. My heart was pounding in my ears, my stomach tied in knots. What was I going to do? No one was listening to me. No one heard my pleas to stop this. Stop the chaos around. Stop the harm. I just needed it to stop, and I was angry. Angry that I was being ignored. Angry that my family was hurting and bleeding and dying. That anger roiled in me hot and bright, much like the searing flames that sparked between my sister and her father, as he gained the upper hand. He pushed her back and up the steps of the dais. Katrel lost her footing while avoiding a slash from Cardoc. Aetherius bouncing away from her across the dais. Cardoc loomed over her.

"You have lost." He panted, pointing the blade at her chest.

"Enough!" I shouted and the anger rolled out of me, a wave that washed over the room knocking over guards and nobles. The wave of power glittered with flecks of turquoise light. It was pure magic. It was pure starlight.

Chapter Fifty-Eight

Mitta

Power crashed over us, like a wave breaking against the cliffs, knocking me back over the dais step. Ciserie braced her body over Cyran. He was fading fast. Where did this wave come from? I pushed against the throbbing and the stinging in my wrists. I looked at them, the red marks from the ropes fading under the flecks of light. The light was healing the small hurt. I looked to where Cyran lay. Ciserie had also seen the flecks of healing light, she was reaching for them as they drifted by, catching as many of them as she could and pressing them into the wound. The deadly wound, that was starting to close.

There was shouting at the other side of the room, and when I turned my head, the ropes that had held Niratap back were gone, dissolved by those bright flecks of light. Blood still trickled down his back as he faced the dozen guards that were brandishing their swords at him. His tail flicked with irritation, shadows starting to recover from the hold of the magic ropes. Shasha twisted out of the grasp of the guard that held her hands behind her. They were distracted by the gems of light that were floating around, clustering on hurts both big and small.

My name was called from across the dais. Her face was the first thing I saw, those beautiful cheekbones and bright copper eyes. There was a cut across her brow, a moment in the scuffle where she had miscalculated and been injured. Those bright turquoise lights clustered there.

"Mitta." There was fear and a sad acceptance.

I saw everything then. I saw her father standing over her, hatred twisting his face into cruel, harsh lines.

"No."

"Remember what you promised me." She smiled sadly at me. Even as the tip of Cardoc's blade pushed closer to her chest.

"No!"

"You made an oath." She said tearily. "You promised me."

Oaths, promises deeper than anyone could make. The oath would bar me from keeping her and she had accepted it. She wanted me to keep that oath, to keep our family safe. An oath had held me away from her until just a few days ago. I saw Aetherius then, a few meager feet from my hand. Would she forgive me if I broke my oath? I didn't know. Would she be angry? She would. She wanted me to flee, to take our scrappy family from this kingdom to the safety of home. Without her, and I didn't want to live life without her. I took up Aetherius.

"Your family as you call them will not leave this kingdom alive. I will send them home in pieces." Cardoc laughed at Katrel's haunted expression.

"No. I beat your tests. I earned my freedom." She shouted as I stood, the waves of energy and light lapping against my legs, twisting around the blade and weaving with the flames still ignited.

He lifted the sword, preparing to strike her down. "And you lost it when you challenged me."

I was in motion, running across the platform. Slashing the blade out in sweeping arch of flame and light, it collided with Cardoc's blade sending him backwards down the steps. "Leave her alone!"

"Mitta, don't." Kat pleaded behind me. "You have to get them out of here."

Niratap had incapacitated most of the guards around him and was facing off with the spearman that stood between him and Shasha. She was kicking trying to get loose from the two guards that held her ankles. Bastion was defending Tummi from a guard with his bare hands light and blood covering them. Tummi was glowing her eyes glowing the same bright turquoise as the flecks of light. Cardoc came to his feet glowering as he picked up his sword.

"Who are you to challenge me, rakshasi bitch."

"I'm sorry, Kat. I can't leave you behind."

"Mitta."

I took up my stance, facing the king. "I am Mitta Rask, last member of the Frosted Mountain Clan and Chiefess. I am the Night Tiger, silent assassin of the black market. I am Lady Tiger defender of the faire. I am the Oathbreaker and I will be leaving here with my family." I glanced over my shoulder at Katrel. "All of my family."

"You will not leave this room alive. The princess will fulfill her duty to this kingdom, whether she wishes to or not. She has no claim to my throne and no one to take up the mantle she doesn't want."

"No, Katrel will be leaving this kingdom with her family. I will not allow you to tie her to a marriage bed to be a broodmare."

"That is her only worth." He lunged, clashing his sword against mine. "She has no value to me other than that."

I pushed him back and swung with the flames and light. "She is worth so much more. She is brave. She is kind. She is honest."

He blocked each slash blow for blow. "Petty attributes of weakness."

"She is anything but weak." I raised my blade to block, seeing an opportunity. I twisted, tucking his blade under my arm and pulling the sword from his hand. I slashed upwards across his chest, sending him to the ground. I stood over him and brought Aetherius to his throat. The room fell into a shocked silence. Cardoc was king no longer

"Finish me, then leave Babylos without a leader to guide them."

"You are not worthy of this blade." I said, but did

not lower the blade. "I will not take your life for your folly."

"Because you are a coward?"

I pushed the blade against his neck, the ever-sharp edge drawing blood. "No, because you will not be a martyr for the cruel."

"I am king."

"No more." A familiar elegant voice said.

"Mother." Katrel said softly.

I looked up, watching Cardoc in my periphery. Ciserie had slipped out from beneath Cyran, her light-colored gown stained with his blood and approached Tummi light still ebbing from her body. The queen kneeled before her daughter tucking loose strands behind her ear before she cupped her face and kissed her brow.

"That is enough, *tähtien valo*.[95] That's enough."

The great sea of power faded, leaving only the flickering floating lights which still searched for small hurts to mend.

"Bastion." Ciserie said softly looking up at the boy whose bloodied hands held the sword he had pried from the knight who lay unconscious at his feet. "Come care for your heartbond."

Bastion moved behind Tummi and wrapped his arms around her as Ciserie moved away. Tummi's eyes ceased their eerie glowing and she sagged into his chest with a sign. Ciserie then turned to where I stood with Cardoc under the blade. Her face cold with distaste and stars glittering in her bright eyes when she looked down at him.

"Cardoc, your cruelty is done. You will renounce the throne and leave."

He laughed at her. Even trapped beneath my blade. "You have not the power to banish me."

"Is that what you think?" She said softly. "Who will stand beside a dying flame?"

[95] Starlight.

There was a shift in the energy of the throne room. Knights who remained conscious had lowered their hands and blades. Shasha had slipped free, her body pressed to Niratap's and the cragstone spear broken. Nobles had come out from their cowering, Lathia and Farryn among them. All of them were watching Ciserie standing over the man who used to lord everything over her.

A feeble voice broke the silence. "Long live the Star Queen. Long live Queen Ciserie Daughter of the Star. Long live the Star Queen." It had been Cyran, who with Katrel's help was sitting up, glaring out across the room at the fallen king.

Chapter Fifty-Nine

Niratap

"Long live the Star Queen." Lathia's voice said, the sound echoing around the room. "Long live, Ciserie."

I wrapped an arm around my mate, who had once again saved me, defending me from another slice from the spearman and the call was echoed by knights who raised their swords to the air and nobles who bowed in reverence and servants who had come out of their hidden doors. The call echoed around the room, off the marble floors and high arched ceilings.

We approached, my eyes narrowed at Cardoc and his cruelty that was now at its end. The sharpness left as I met the queen's eyes, I saw it again in that imperious gaze, the strength of a woman long suffered but exceptionally capable. I bowed, as gracefully as the wounds slowly being stitched together by flecks of starlight would allow.

"Long live Queen Ciserie." I murmured softly. "High Queen of Babylos."

Color had drained from Cardoc's face at the words, softly spoken, but heard by the entire court. It was such a small phrase, but the weight of it was the shift of power in an ancient kingdom. Katrel moved, cradling Cyran to her side and approached where we stood.

She dipped her head before her mother, not wanting to drop the scholar at her side. "Queen Ciserie, High Queen of Babylos, I ask of you to renounce my claim to the throne to live my life freely. I ask to be a princess no more."

Ciserie considered her daughter with an air of aloofness. "I grant your request to renounce your claim to the throne."

Katrel's shoulder sagged with relief. "Thank you,

your maj–”

"However, you will still be a princess to the kingdom of Babylos."

"But I–"

Ciserie held up a hand. "You will remain a princess, Wildfire, as you will remain my daughter. Princess Katrel Gwendolyn Raloqen, the Flame Princess. Your sister will also remain a princess, Princess Tummilia Aeralie Stormblood, the Star Princess."

At the utterance of her true name Tummilia opened her deep blue eyes that now, like her mothers, had flecks of stars floating in them. She looked first to Bastion, the boy who fought for her and loved her without wavering, then to us. Cyran smiled softly at her as tears crested in her eyes at the sight of him standing. He was her father, not the broken man at my feet. I felt the heat that started to roil in that hateful man. There was a flash of flame that I quenched with my shadows. His scream echoed in the bubble of blackness. Nobles moved back and the knights prepared to act, but Ciserie with a soft smile and wave of her hand, cast their worries aside.

Her soft voice carried over Cardoc's pained screams "Mitta. Give Katrel the blade."

Mitta obeyed, offering Katrel the blade and taking Cyran's weight from her. Strain pulled at my control over the shadows, but I fought my weakening reserves. Battling the ellervine ropes and cragstone had drained most of my magic.

"Nira. That is enough." Shasha whispered

"Not yet." I said softly, not looking at her.

"Mother, what do you want me to do?" Katrel asked, casting a worried glance at me.

"You will take the rest of Conláed's flame. Strip your father of it."

Katrel swallowed. "How?"

"Aetherius will guide you." Cyran said softly, Cardoc's screams fading into soft whimpers. "You did it earlier when you defended your mother and I."

"When you are ready, the young lord will release his shadows." Ciserie said, eyeing me. "I would make haste though; he seems to be running out of magic."

Katrel took a deep breath and centered herself, the flames of the sword connecting to hers again. "Okay."

My knees wobbled unsteadily when the shadows fell. The smell of burnt flesh, hair, and cloth uncoiled in the smoke. His hair was singed, the back of his hands burned from where they had covered his face. Flame had eaten through patches of his fine clothes and the skin was red and angry; some spots even blistered. Katrel set the tip of the blade in the center of his chest, the flames shifting to an eerie blue.

"Cardoc Raloqen, third of your name, you are hereby stripped of your title of King of Babylos. No longer will your bloodline cause harm to the people of this kingdom and with the permission of the High Queen I remove the sacred flame from your blood."

"Please." Cardoc begged, moving his injured hands. "Please daughter, don't take my flame. Don't take away the power of our bloodline."

Katrel's face was hard and cold as she looked down at him. "You never listened when I begged you for mercy. You never listened when my mother begged for mercy. I will not grant you mercy now. The flame emperor's bloodline will no longer be corrupted."

The blue flame spread over Cardoc, tracing over the veins and arteries of his body. The flame burned brightly, but did not burn the whimpering fallen man. Just as quickly as the flame had ignited his body it receded up the sword and into Katrel. The force of the flame rocked her back a step and she shut her eyes as it settled into her skin. I watched the bright blue trail under the skin of her face before it faded below. She blinked a couple of times before looking up at us, embers danced in her copper eyes. Ciserie smiled, before looking down at Cardoc.

"Cardoc, count yourself lucky that despite your cruelty to me and my children, I allowed you to keep your life and your freedom. May it be long lived, so you can find penance for your centuries of misdeeds. Guards, see to it that his burns are tended and when he is healed see him out of the castle grounds. I do not care where he goes from there."

He made a pitiful sound as two guards scooped him up and half dragged him from the throne room. Ciserie sighed but moved with a soft ethereal grace to stand before the throne. She clasped her hands before her blood-stained gown and looked out at the nobles, the lords and ladies of the land.

"I know that you may not want me to lead you and our people." She spoke clearly, her voice carrying over all that was present. "I will swear to you that no matter your decision I will support you as I can in whatever capacity. If you don't want this shift in leadership, I am sorry to tell you that there is no avoiding it now. Cardoc did many good things for the people as a whole, but he has also locked his people away from the world and the expansion that has been created in the realm of man. We as a people are long lived but sheltered as we are we have stagnated."

There were soft murmurs of agreement.

"As your queen, if you will allow me, I will pledge for more trade opportunities for all our communities. I want to open up education for those who do not live in Illishara. I want to meet the needs of our people as a whole and I want to reunite families that Cardoc and his father had torn apart for their selfish reasons. I want to bring them home."

Nobles pushed forward to the dais with a cacophony of questions, that grated against my ears and my nonexistent patience. I snarled. "Enough!"

Silence followed and Shasha said brightly, casting me a sideways glance. "Queen Ciserie will answer your questions in due time. However, many of us are covered in blood and bruised. I believe that we should take a break for the remainder of the day and celebrate the end of solstice as only a new kingdom can."

"Who are you to order us girl?" Some lord snarked from the middle of the park.

Shasha bowed and cocked her hip to the side. "I am Lady Bondbreaker."

"Your title is not recognized here."

"On the contrary." Ciserie said over him. "The title was bestowed by both the princesses, and I will recognize the Lord and Lady Bondbreaker as members of this court, and I agree with Lady Bondbreaker's suggestion. There has been too much hatred and bloodshed. I bid you all to rest, tonight we will watch the sun set on the old Babylos. Tomorrow we will hold court, and I will answer your questions."

Bastion had taken Tummilia to her bed, the girl weak and slipping in and out of consciousness. When she was rested, they would join us. The rest of us entered Shasha's and my lodgings and Mitta twisted me, lifting the loose stained dress shirt to examine the thick itching scabs on my back. She chided. "Honestly."

"Please save your berating on my foolishness and singleness of mind. My mate was in danger, and she was my only concern." I said my voice sounded hoarse from slowly recovering from the crushing.

Shasha frowned at me but said nothing as she sat at the table next to Katrel.

"Painfully lucky, they missed your vital organs, and it seems that Tummilia's starlight healed most of the injury." Mitta continued checking over where the ropes had dug into my skin, all mostly healed or scabbed over. "I fear the day that luck of yours runs out, Niratap. Who knows what—"

"Mitta." Katrel snapped, her eyes softening at Mitta's expression. "Please let the fool sit and rest. You have much time to berate him about his recklessness."

"I just—"

"I know." Katrel smiled. "The Oathbreaker then?"

Color bloomed across Mitta's face. "You asked me to do something that I couldn't fathom doing. I couldn't let you die. I couldn't leave you behind."

I moved to sit on the chaise, slow going with the aches that ran rampant up my back. I had been foolish, but Cardoc had drugged us and stolen Shasha and placed her in the line of fire. It was something that was punished, but I would never forgive the man for the cruelty he had beset upon my family. Worry not my own twisted in my stomach; looking up I saw Shasha chewing on her lip and watching me with intensity.

"I will be fine, mate." I gently rubbed my throat.

"You are in pain, and I don't like it."

Everyone looked at me then, I held up my hands in a plea. "I will be alright. I ache, but my body is recovering."

"Slowly." I heard the worry in her voice now.

"Yes. My magic was greatly depleted by the ellervine. The wounds to my back were made with cragstone and will heal more slowly. I am fine."

"Niratap, you self-sacrificing asshole." Her voice was teary as she got up from the chair and fled to the bathing room. Mitta stopped me from following.

"Not yet my friend. She has had a hard day and needs a moment alone. She is not angry at you; she is worried and you belittled that worry."

I sighed, easing back into the chaise. "It was not my intention. I just don't want her to fear that I am in danger. I hurt, yes, but not in a way that will be the death of me. The itching of my skin and head are more likely too."

"You head laceration hasn't healed?" Mitta's brows

knitted together as she stepped closer.

"No, my scalp just itches uncomfortably."

"Don't stress Mitta, he's probably about to shed his antlers." Katrel said, leaning forward and bracing her elbows on her knees. "Hopefully after we get home. I would hate to travel with him lopsided."

I glowered, but Bastion said from the door. "She's right. You are mighty cross when your head tries to lean one way or the other. We taking bets on which side goes first? I say fifty bucks it's the right one."

"Deal, I raise you sixty if it's the left." Katrel said with a grin.

I pinched between my eyes. "Fucking hell."

"Jokes aside." Bastion said sitting in the chair Shasha had left. "What are we doing next?"

"I think it wise to stay at least a couple weeks to see how Ciserie fairs." Mitta said. "Cardoc isn't a threat, but that doesn't mean some other noble won't try to undermine her."

"I agree. That and we can tend our wounds and rest for the trip home. Hopefully Captain Brast will be in Asuna."

"You think he will give us safe passage home?" Katrel asked.

"I believe he will."

"We should find his mother." Bastion said. "She is a drow, where do those who are banished go?"

"Into the wilds." Katrel shrugged. "Though I've heard rumors of a township on the other side of Edgelake."

"It is something that we can talk to Ciserie and Cyran about it tomorrow, for now I think we all should get some rest. Regardless of how welcoming they may be, I will probably decline Ciserie's invitation to festivities."

Bastion nodded. "Tummilia is exhausted."

"And how are you faring kid?"

He smirked. "Hand hurts a bit, but there's barely a scratch after Tummi unleashed her starlight on everyone."

"What will come of that I wonder?" Mitta said, checking Bastion's hands for herself. "Tummi full of starlight and Katrel with the emperor's flame."

"I would say the sisters are a force to be reckoned with." I furrowed my brows. "It may also put you both in danger with this unknown enemy we are facing."

"What do you mean?" Mitta asked concern tightening her face as well.

"Starlight is one of the mythic ingredients in the creation of a lich."

"But our mystery enemy is already a lich." Bastion said. "Why would a lich go after Tummi?"

"Cyran and I had theorized that the lich after me is incomplete, having not completed the power ritual. The information we found was limited. Necromancy is outlawed magic in the rest of the world. I doubt we will find more information at home." I sighed, a twinge of pain seizing up my back; my tail gave me away.

"You should rest." Mitta said, glancing at the bathing room door. "Maybe soak and check on your mate. She is worried about you."

Mitta took Katrel by the hand and led her out of the room. Bastion paused in the doorway and looked back at me.

"Do you want a hand?" he asked.

I shook my head. "I will be alright, kid. Go look after Tummi."

"Okay." He waved as he turned out the door. "Be careful with yourself, old man."

I huffed as the door clicked shut. Standing again would be an issue, the muscles in my back still spasmed painfully while the wounds slowly healed. I pushed onto my feet, even though my body protested and leaned my head against the door listening to her soft breaths through the wood.

"I know you are angry with me, *mo grá*. Open the door so we can talk."

Silence met me.

"Shasha, please. Open the door."

"You already know how I feel. Why should we discuss it?"

I sighed. "Shasha, please."

The door cracked; she looked up at me with a steely expression. "Why?"

"I know what you feel, but not why?"

Her eyes softened a little, the edge of her lip twitching up. "Are you really that dense?"

"I have to prove to you repeatedly that I am? Especially when it comes to you."

She let out an exasperated sigh. "Males. Come in and sit before you fall down."

I obeyed, groaning as I sat, the muscles of my back screaming at it. "I'm sorry."

"You don't even know why you're apologizing." She said standing before me with her hip cocked to the side.

"For being a fool. I don't want you worrying about me. I will be alright."

"I know you will." She said sharply. "That doesn't mean I am not going to worry about you when you are in pain. Wait here."

She dipped out the doorway into the main room. I counted myself quite a fool for thinking she wouldn't worry with the pain acting as a beacon that I was in-fact not okay. Of course she would worry about my wellbeing. I understood now that me belittling my pain had belittled her feelings of concern. Again, we had come dangerously close to losing each other. I never wanted any of my darkness to hover over her. I did not want death to be her watchful companion. I never wished for any of that for her. She returned, clean light clothes over one arm and a silver tin in her hand. She set them upon the counter and pulled a basin from below the sink, dipping it into the bath before setting the steaming bowl beside me and dropping a washcloth into the basin with a splash.

"What is in the tin?"

"A salve that Nikki gave me while you were in the hospital. She said she hoped I wouldn't have to use it, but she ran a guess that it would be needed at one point or another." She said softly pushing her way between my knees to undo the buttons of my shirt. "I debated a long while on bringing it, but now I'm glad I did."

"She is a good ally to have."

"She's nice. Did you know she's a biologist, studying rare creatures for the bureau?"

"You two talked?"

"We did. I did threaten her at least a couple times when you were getting treated after the raid. After things had settled and you were conscious again, my father got us in touch with one another. She was glad that you were recovering and said I was lucky because you are so charming."

I smiled. "Charm can get you out of sticky situations."

She huffed, stepping away and pulling the shirt off. "I will have to remember that when you're trying to charm your way out with me."

"It works most of the time."

She huffed, coming around the front. "I'll remember that."

I smiled at her. "My charm isn't going to get me out of anything now is it."

She smiled, grabbing the rag from the basin. "Nope."

Behind me she gently pressed her fingers to my back. I tensed under the touch. The heat from the cloth helped soothe the ache. We sat in silence for some time while she lovingly cleaned the wounds and rubbed the salve over the healing scabs. She came around to face me once more, a stubborn set to her face. She tilted my head up and wiped the dried blood from my face. Her eyes intense as she looked me over.

"You scared me." She said.

"I did not mean–"

"I know." She dropped the rag into the basin with a plop. She did not release my face "When they were taking me away, I saw him kick you. I felt your consciousness slip through my fingers. I screamed your name and felt only darkness and the beat of your heart. I knew you were alive, but you felt so far away."

She closed her eyes, and I saw the traitorous tear that rolled down her cheek. "They took me kicking and screaming through the haze in my mind. They gagged me and took me out of my clothes and bound my hands and I was scared of what was going to happen. I was so scared." She looked up at me then. "I was so scared that you were going to die in that room."

I cupped her cheek with my hand, smearing that tear with my thumb. "I was scared. So scared that I did not care who I had to tear through and what horrible things I would have to do, as long as you were safe and in my arms, again. I just kept reaching for you. Fighting for you."

"When the rope slid over your neck and your head hit the marble, I just wanted to charge across the room and save you, but I was trapped there watching you struggle, and you were just so angry."

"I was angry. I could smell you in that room. I could feel your fear and anger as clear as my own and seeing what Cardoc was making her do." I shook my head. "My only thought was getting to you."

She turned her face to my palm, kissing it. "We are going to be the death of ourselves, aren't we?"

I kissed her brow. "I fear that you are correct, my love."

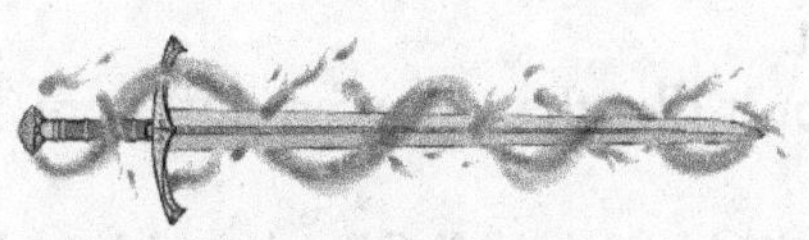

Two weeks passed in a blur of court meetings and motions. We tried to keep the peace between opinionated nobles who wanted to know about trade and landholdings and common folk who wanted to see their families again. Many had fled to the mainland, but most had fled to Pamiršta, the hidden place that Captain Brast had spoken of. A township that had grown over the centuries for those that the long line of Cardoc's had banished, Edgewater was the only village that interacted with them. We traveled there with Ciserie to offer an olive branch.

Edgewater was similar to Ehiza, built beside Edgelake surrounded by farmland and plains. The people were kind to us, but wary of me. It no longer bothered me when others watched me with fear in their eyes. I had honed it into a weapon that had been the forefront of my identity in the market; the shadows and mask making me mysterious. The gawking and whispers of fear echoing around me rolled off easily, but Shasha bristled with each remark she heard about me, and I felt the static along my spine. I watched her frown at each one as we passed them.

Edgelake was shrouded with heavy mists, the water fell perpetually over the edge of the world. Bastion scoffed at that, but Ciserie explained that when Babylos was cut from the world of man a great void was left off the east side of the country. It was treacherous living as close as Edgewater was, the captain of the trade ferry added. Pamiršta had grown in the farthest corner from the capital as they could, the town skirting the Edge. A single lantern on an isolated dock greeted us through the mist, our only light to disembark from the boat.

"I will return tomorrow, Your Majesty."

"Understood. Journey safely home."

With a nod the man pushed out and disappeared into the mist.

"I don't like that we were left here." Mitta grumbled.

"It will be alright." Ciserie said pushing forward down the path. "He promised us safe passage and he is good. He agreed to an increase of boats back and forth across the lake to harbor those who wanted."

"What do you expect to find out here, mother?" Katrel asked.

"I expect that we will not be welcomed warmly, though I am sure word of Cardoc's fall has reached this village. I hope that we will be able to welcome those who want to return to their families. I want to give them what they need if they do not wish to leave."

I agreed with Ciserie's motivations, but I also understood Mitta's concern for safety in the early weeks of the queen's reign. "We are just staying one night, Mitta. I am certain we can pull it together for one night."

Mitta sighed but took the lead with Katrel guiding us down the well-worn path to the village.

Pamiršta was not what I had expected to see. Buildings stood constructed of stone and wood; where I had expected a tent city was an actual town. The paths through the town were paved with cobblestone and a fountain bubbled at the center of the square. Children laughed and ran by some with elf ears, some with orc ears. The people were diverse shades happily going about their day with little care that the royal family had paid them a visit.

A drow woman paused, noticing us. Her skin was a muddy grey and her eyes were dark. She smiled and came forward. "Welcome to Pamiršta. You are safe now."

Ciserie smiled. "I remember you, Nosche Brast."

Nosche paled, recognizing Ciserie; she bowed at the waist. "Queen Ciserie. I apologize, I didn't recognize that it was you, it has been so long."

"It is quite alright." People noticed us now and their faces were a mix of fear and hope. "I would like to address the people of this place."

"You are in the right place, Your Majesty."

Ciserie nodded, clearing her throat over the eerie silence that fell over the crowd. "People of Pamiršta, I have traveled here to tell you that Cardoc reigns no longer, and you are freed from your banishments. I want to offer you the option of returning home to your families and I want to offer aid to those who wish to stay."

They peppered Ciserie with questions from what had transpired that Cardoc would renounce the throne to what they were required to do to return home. Ciserie told them of Katrel's trials, of the Oathbreaker who defended her, of the Starlight Queen and the Flame Emperor. Shasha slipped her hand into mine, tugging it to grab my attention.

"That woman is the captain's mother."

I nodded. "She is."

"She should come with us to see her son."

"I agree, but it is her choice."

Shasha slipped from my side to where the woman stood, listening to Ciserie and her daughters. She spoke into her down pointed ear in a whisper. The woman's eyes went wide as she listened to Shasha, tears pricking at the edges of her eyes. She nodded at Shasha's words. It would be a heartbreaking reunion indeed. Long live the Star Queen resonated over the crowd.

We ate a hearty dinner and Nosche Brast, who was both heartbroken and happy for the chance to return to what remained of her family, led us to the small hostel where the newcomers where housed. The rooms were small as were the beds, but as least it was dry. I leaned against the wall, easing to the floor. Shasha frowned. Her unhappiness burned in the center of my chest.

"It is one night, *mo grá*."

"And six more on the ship."

"It can't be helped; they don't build things to my

size. I am accustomed to it."

"I don't like that you have to choose the floor to sleep."

I smiled and beckoned her closer. Her knees pressed to my chest, her hand settling on an antler tine as she looked at me. I ran my hands up the back of her legs. There was anger simmering in her and sorrow and it filled me with a warm ache in my chest. I pressed a kiss to her stomach. "I know you are angry at the world for not being accommodating to me. There was a time when I was angry at the world. Very angry at my circumstances, not having a bed wasn't one of the things that I was concerned about."

Her lips tightened and pain bloomed in my chest.

"I was angry that I was trapped. Angry that I was cold. Angry that I was alone. Angry that I was hungry. A safe place to sleep was the least of my worries. So, sleeping here on the floor propped against the wall, though not the most comfortable place to sleep, it is acceptable for a few nights."

Tears rolled over her cheeks. She moved to wipe them away, but I caught her wrists, and my cheeks caught her tears. The tightening in my chest made it hard to breathe but gazing into those teary eyes I saw that every transgression against me, every broken bone, every scar had led me to this woman.

"I know it is not ideal, but we make do with what we have. We are survivors. It is what we do."

Chapter Sixty

Katrel

We were leaving Babylos two bodies heavier. Well one body and one bag of ashes. Cardoc had left Casrian's body to rot in the arena; most likely a way to control me, had he won. My friend's ashes were nestled lovingly in my bag, so we could take him home. Home. It had been decided that Captain Brast's mother, Nosche, would travel with us to Asuna. The hope was that the captain would be there waiting for us. I was heading home. Home with all my family intact. My true home with Mitta.

Mitta.

I watched her where she stood and chatted with Nosche who sat astride a palomino. Watching her I had to wonder if her words of love and marriage held. Not because she had broken an oath, an oath I am glad she did, but because I didn't know if the words had been said in love or lust or pity. I just didn't know. I just—

"She seems very nice." Mother said, coming beside me.

"She seems kind. Niratap will make sure she gets reunited with her son."

"I was talking about Mitta."

A jolt rammed down my spine. "I don't know what you mean."

"Don't you, Wildfire?"

I didn't face her, just watched as Mitta mounted a roan stallion. "I do not deserve her."

"Who says?"

"She is everything that I have ever wanted in a partner." The truth pulled tears to my eyes. "She is too good for me."

"I will blame your father for this."

I looked at her then. The starlight blue brightened her pale skin and the luminosity of her eyes, flecks of light floating there. A diadem sat softly over her brow, a placid smile on her face. "What do you mean?"

"It is the power of weak men and to push those who are stronger around them down, to make them think less of themselves. You are not what your father has made you believe, my child. You are worthy of the flame in your blood. You make your ancestor, you make Conláed proud."

I blinked at her. "I—How—I don't understand."

"I cowed to your father to keep you both safe. To keep you safe, the first princess of the Raloqen line and Tummilia the first princess born of love."

"How long have you and Cyran—?"

She smiled, a tear rolling down her cheek. "He was going to marry me, before my father sold me to yours. I can now. I can marry him and not have to fear for his safety. I can be happy, and I want you to be happy, Katrel. That woman loves you, so let her and be happy. You won. You earned that happiness."

I hugged her. My arms wrapping around the willowy figure of my mother, my head pressing into her shoulder, and I hugged her. "I'm sorry."

She wrapped me in her arms, her hand rubbing soothing circles over my spine. "I love you, Wildfire. You are forgiven. There is nothing for you to be sorry about, but you are forgiven. Be free."

A strong hand gripped my shoulder, pulling me away from my mother. I saw that it was Cyran. I turned and hugged him as well. The man had been a better father to me than my own had. I had grown up not knowing it, but now I realized. He gave me a gentle squeeze.

"Don't be a stranger, okay?"

"It's hard to get here."

"I know. Hopefully it will get easier."

"Thank you."

"Whatever for, Princess?"

"For everything. For your patience, your kindness, and your love. Without it I–" I swallowed hard. "I may not have made it this far."

He looked at me with so much love and warmth. "You were strong enough from the beginning. You just needed a push and a sword."

"Told you she was a big softie." Bastion said, walking up with his guitar strapped to his back. I wiped my face and smiled at him.

Cyran clapped him on the shoulder. "You take care of these girls, alright?"

"Yeah, but to be honest I think these girls will end up taking more care of me."

Tummi ducked under Cyran's arm and hugged him tightly. "We'll take care of each other."

"Girls. Bastion. Let's go." Niratap called from the horses

"Coming." Tummi called back, turning to hug our mother. "I love you both. We will write."

"You better."

Tummi and Bastion waved as they descended the stairs. I looked back at my mother and my chosen father. It was a strange thought. In only a couple of months I had changed the course of the lives of this kingdom, putting them safely in the hands of the couple before me. Mother would nurture the people of Babylos like she had always tried to nurture us, and Cyran would teach them the truth. I had freed our people and opened the world to them, but even though I was free to live my life, I felt like I hadn't done enough.

"Am I really free to go?"

Mother's brows tightened with concern. "Why wouldn't you be?"

"I just feel like I haven't done enough."

"Katrel." Cyran said softly. "You have done more than enough, for yourself, for your sister, for your family, for your mother and me, for your people. You will always be welcome here. Always be able to come back and be a princess if you choose."

"Or you can stay with your family." Mother said. "Live a happy life, Katrel. That is all that a mother wants for her children."

"But what about Cardoc and Revan?"

Mother frowned at their names. "Both have lost their station and been punished. Cardoc has no power and Revan, though skilled, is nothing without his father's backing, which he has lost."

"But–"

"Go and live your life, Katrel." Cyran said, smiling broadly. "We can take care of things here."

I couldn't help but smile at them. "I love you. Both of you."

Mother covered her mouth as tears flowed from her eyes, Cyran wrapped his arm around her, tugging her close and smiling at me. "We love you too, Wildfire. Always."

In Asuna, news had spread of Cardoc's fall. The streets were congested with elves bartering with the merchants for goods and information of their loved ones. Several elves recognized us and several asked if we knew where their loved ones were. So many had been cast aside by my father; it broke my heart.

"The Folkstone is in port." Niratap said behind us, indicating where the boat was.

Nosche pushed past us to look at the freight ship, teary eyed. "My son captains his father's ship."

"He takes pride in that as well." Niratap added. "He is a good male, your son."

"His father was a good male." Nosche said softly.

"Let's go meet him then." Tummi grabbed Nosche's hand pulling her along.

Mitta laughed as Bastion followed behind them. He called back. "Don't worry, I got them."

The docks were bustling as freight was moved off the ships and merchants bartered; Captain Brast was surrounded by such merchants. I wondered if they were telling him about the power shift, given his dazed look. Tummi called out to him, waving frantically. He looked at her his face still pulled in that mask of confusion. Then he saw his mother.

I thought goodbyes had been hard but seeing him run up to the slight woman and pull her into a tight bear hug, lifting her into the air, it warmed my heart painfully, even more so when we traipsed down the dock and saw tears trekking both their faces.

"This is amazing!" He said brightly and dazedly. "How?"

I smiled at him. "You said you missed her, and we found her."

"And I wanted nothing more than to come see my little boy all grown up." Nosche said gently as he sat her down.

"Mom, dad he—"

"I know." She patted his chest softly. "Orcs have long lives, but your father wasn't a young buck when we met, and it's been over a hundred and fifty years since I last saw him. I had hoped, but I knew it was unlikely, Hayden."

Brast wiped his tears away. "He missed you so much. I was so young, but you look just as I remembered you."

Nosche smiled sadly. "You look just like your father, a little younger and not big around the middle as he was. He would have been so proud of you; for all the good you have done."

He beamed at his mother, before looking up at us.

"Are you ready to go home, Bondbreaker?"

"Very." Niratap said behind us; people gave him a wide berth.

"I'll get the greenhorns shifted around for your group." The captain looked down at his mother still clutched in his arms and then back to us. "I'm glad that you made it out alive."

We wandered onto the ship while we waited for our accommodations. I stood at the bow taking in the salty sea breeze and cry of gulls. We were going home, and everything seemed right. I wondered if things would be different now that Mitta and I had opened up to one another or if they would go back to the way it was before; loving and avoiding it.

"There you are." I turned to find her walking towards me, her hair back in its normal braid. She smiled warmly. "I was looking for you."

"For me?" I asked, turning to face her completely.

She blinked, her smile sliding a bit as she stopped a few feet away. "Yeah, unless you want to be alone."

I looked over my shoulder at the ocean. "No. I was just marveling at the feeling of freedom."

She caged me against the rail with her body. Every part of her lined up with every part of me. "Are you happy with all this freedom?"

My heart skittered violently. "I'm scared of it, actually."

Her eyes swam with questions. Her lips were so welcomingly close, but so very far away. "What scares you, Kat?"

I swallowed. "No more secrets?"

"I have none."

I took a breath. "What are we?"

She angled her head at the question. "What do you want us to be?"

"I love you."

"I love you, too."

"I want you."

"I want you, too." She smiled again.

"But I'm scared that when we get back home that you won't anymore."

She chuckled mirthlessly, before pressing her lips to mine. The kiss was soft but demanding. It was like a promise she was pouring into me and her hands caught my hips, pulling me against her. I cupped her face, taking it for all the unspoken things that danced between us. When we parted I rested my brow against hers, breathing her in.

"Never doubt my heart, Katrel." She said, echoing the promises of her kiss. "I love you. You have all of me if it is what you want. I will take whatever you have to offer me, whatever you want to gift me. I will be whatever role you are comfortable with. If that is friend or lover or wife–"

I pulled back to look at her. "Wife?" I echoed the promise and vows we had made.

"If it is what you want. I will make it official in whatever way you wish. In my heart I am yours."

"Kiss me again, wife."

"Gladly."

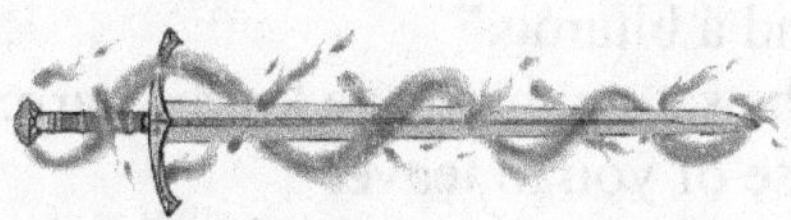

It didn't take long after we got onto the ship for the men to be moved and everyone claimed their bunks. Mitta set her bag on the lower bunk but climbed into the bunk above smiling down at me.

I leaned against the wall as Niratap settled on the floor. "What are we going to do when we get home?"

He looked at me seriously. "Firstly, we will check in with Allipo to see if we missed anything. After that I believe everyone else can return to their normal routine."

"Everyone else?" Tummi asked from her bunk, where she was curled into Bastion's chest.

Niratap nodded. "I will more than likely be drowning in requests for my presence and K was in the process of pulling the last few strings holding the ring he and Taegan were in. I'm hoping that it will collapse without the need for me to intervene. However, given the threats I was given I will more than likely be required."

"And my parents will want to see us as well." Shasha said settling into her bunk.

Niratap scratched his scalp at the base of his antler. "Yes, that too. I have some things I wish to discuss with Xaevean as well."

"How much do you think happened in what two and half months?" Bastion grumbled from the bunk.

Shasha looked at me then went back to her mate. "A lot can happen in a couple of months."

He smiled softly at her, lowering his hand. "Yes indeed, *mo grá*."

"All of you made it back alive I see." Vakmu said from the doorway

"You sound surprised, Vakmu." Mitta growled from beside me.

"I didn't expect it. Especially from a couple of princesses and a bitarog."

Shasha sat up; her gaze knife sharp. "I think it would be wise of you to leave."

"And why is that sweetheart?" Vakmu crooned.

Niratap's tail flicked in irritation, but it was Tummi that spoke to the orc. "You cannot speak to the lady like that."

He laughed a deep belly laugh. "I'm not threated by a bastard."

There were shouts of protest, but it was Bastion that flew off their bunk and charged the male.

"What you going to do, you pathetic Earth—"

Bastion's fist connected squarely in Vakmu's nose. A high-pitched crack rang as the bone collapsed.

Chapter Sixty-One

Bastion

I hadn't thought. I had just reacted, leaping off the bunk. It wasn't until hands wrapped around my arms and hauled me back that I realized what I had done. Vakmu lay sprawled awkwardly in the hall, gurgling. His nose was broken and bleeding. One of his tusks was missing. No, it wasn't missing, it was in my hand. I struggled against the arms that held me back.

"Enough, Bastion." Niratap snarled in my ear.

"I'll kill you." I screamed.

There was more shouting. Men clambering down the hall of the ship.

"Bastion, you need to calm down." Mitta snarled.

"I'm gonna fucking kill you!"

Soft hands set lightly on my face. Sparkling blue light dancing around me. Time slowed as Tummi's face came into view. "Stop."

"I—"

"I know." She smiled, her face tight.

Sailors lifted Vakmu off the floor. Someone was shouting for the captain. The lord guided me to Shasha's bunk with a gentleness that made my body feel intensely fragile. I stared at the tusk in my hand numbly as the shouting eased, the captain finally coming down the hall.

"What is going on?" Brast's voice boomed over us.

"The orc kid went crazy and started beating on Vak." One sailor said.

"He ripped out Vak's tusk, Captain." Another said.

"Bondbreaker. I thought you said that you would keep the kid in check."

"I did. That is why Vakmu is still breathing."

The captain huffed and spoke to Vakmu. "What happened?"

Vakmu groaned, but didn't speak.

"Take him to the infirmary."

"Yes captain."

"And the rest of you get back to work, the ship won't unload itself."

It was after the sailors' voices faded from the hall that the captain spoke again, his voice hushed and tight. "What happened?"

"Vakmu said the wrong thing about the wrong female." Niratap said plainly, easing back to the floor, in front of me. "Though I hadn't expected Bastion to leap from the bunk to correct the behavior. Right, Bas?"

I stared at that tusk in my palm. I didn't remember coming off the bunk. I didn't remember attacking Vakmu. I didn't even remember what he had said. My hands were bloody, and my knuckles ached. My chest was tight, and my heart thudded against my ribs. My hands were shaking, and I felt lost.

"Bastion." Tummi said with a frightened sounding softness.

I swallowed. "I–I don't know."

"What does that even mean? You don't know?" Brast snarled.

"Brast." The lord growled, but when he spoke to me his voice softened. "Bastion where are you?"

What kind of question was that? "On a ship. We're on a ship heading…"

"Where are we heading?"

Everything felt so far and so close all at once. I just glowered at my hands. Where were we going? Why were we on a ship? What happened? What fucking happened? Why was I so angry? Why did that make me scared? My chest felt so tight, my vision black around the edges.

"Bastion. I need you to breathe."

I sucked in a deep breath, the oxygen making my

head spin wildly. When had I stopped? I closed my eyes and waited for the world to stop throbbing.

"Bastion."

"Yes?"

"Keep your eyes closed."

"Okay." Someone's hands took hold of mine, taking the tusk from me and wiping them with a damp rag. What had I done? What had I done? What had—

"Bastion. I want you to keep those eyes closed, but tell me where we are?"

"We are on the Folkstone. We're—we're going home."

"That's right. We were sitting in the bunk talking about what we were going to do when we got home."

"Yes. You are planning on diving back into work."

He chuckled. "Thats right. Then what happened."

I fisted my hands, tightly. My voice turning menacing. "Vakmu."

"What did Vakmu say?"

"Vakmu insulted Tummilia. He insulted my heart match. He called *asta hri* a bastard."

"How did that make you feel, Bastion?"

I shook my head. "It is not important how I feel. He–"

"Bastion. What happened?"

Everything flooded back in red. "I was angry. I reacted. I wiped that fucking smile of his face. No one talks about my woman like that and gets away with it."

"I don't think he will be smiling again anytime soon."

"I don't feel bad about what I did either." I added with a whine. Part of me hated how childish that sounded.

I opened my eyes. Niratap was crouched before me watching me. "Welcome back, kid." He looked up at the captain who just looked at me and nodded before he left. "Everything is alright."

"But I–I beat the shit out of him."

"To be honest with you, kid, if you hadn't, I would have." He smiled warmly at me. "Get some rest, kid."

He stood with a groan and Shasha was at his side. "Where are you going?"

"I'm going to talk with the captain, love."

"I'm coming with you."

"Very well. The rest of you relax; the next week will be filled with long days at sea." Together the lord and lady left the room to find the captain.

Tummi eased me back onto the bunk, curling herself protectively around me. "I don't blame you. It was foul what he said, but I can protect myself, Bastion."

I shook my head, closing my eyes to the swirling heat in my blood. "I know you can *asta hri*, but I will not tolerate any *skag* disrespecting you."

"*Skag*?"

"Trash. No one is allowed to tell you that you are worthless. Not if I am there."

"Bastion."

"Tummilia. I will kill men for less when it comes to you."

The sky was clear, and gulls cried above us, a couple crew members were fishing off to my right. One more day and New York would be in view, saltwater, a memory I could put behind me. Vakmu had been released to duty yesterday and I had made myself scarce as possible. Captain Brast had put us on duties on opposite sides of the ship to keep the peace, but Niratap had assured me that Vakmu would leave me alone. The grey skinned arms that joined me proved that was wrong.

"What do you want?" I hissed.

"I deserved it."

I glanced at his face that was scabbed and bruised, stitches stood out against his brow. "Did you?"

"I attacked another male's heartmate. I deserved what you did, I deserved worse."

"I shouldn't have, but I'm not sorry I did."

"I would do the same. You are surprisingly honorable for an Earthblood." He held out a cord to me. His tusk tied at the end. "You bested me as a male, take it and get your marks."

I accepted the cord. "Clan marks. I'd have to find an elder for that and there aren't many of them left within the Earthbloods."

Vakmu just continued to stare out at the ocean. "Ironbloods are the same. Warbands aren't like they used to be. The clans aren't like they used to be."

"Aye."

I don't know how long we stood there in the agreeable silence, before Vakmu turned to leave.

"Vakmu." I called after him watching the proud step of his stride.

He grunted.

"You aren't a horrible male."

He laughed, waving. "Neither are you, Bastion Day. *Het su tash sur.*"[96]

I smiled, turning back to the ocean, watching as the sun glittered brightly over the water. "You too, *skag.*"

[96] Warm days bless you.

Chapter Sixty-Two

Shasha

I hadn't realized how homesick I had been until joy sparked through me to see the small, isolated town at the base of the mountains, people waved as they walked by on the sidewalk. The tinted windows were the only proof to who sat within. Niratap watched them with a scrupulous glance, a sense of suspicion crawling under his skin.

"It's different." He said softly.

The front of the grocery store had a fresh coat of paint and new windows, the roads had been repaved, and the church had scaffolding against it, but nothing seemed out of place. "What do you mean?"

"Something happened here while we were gone."

"How can you tell?" Tummi asked.

His eyes scanned again. "Firstly, Rodger hasn't stopped us yet."

"It makes it sound like you miss the bigot." Bastion said popping up between our seats. "Though it is weird."

Niratap shrugged. "Allipo will debrief me when we get back to the manor."

"How did he sound when you called?" Mitta asked.

"Winded." Niratap's eyes narrowed. "It doesn't tell me much."

"That old goat is rather distracted with Eloi at his side."

Nira smirked. "I figured that was why he was winded."

The rest of us laughed except Mitta who groaned in annoyance. "Males."

"Joking aside, something happened, and it wasn't good. Until we know what it was no one goes to town."

"You think they've turned against us?"

"No, Katrel, but I don't trust the traumatic look that everyone seems to carry."

Allipo was on the phone arguing with someone when we rolled up the gravel. His face twisted in a cantankerous grimace at whatever was being said. Eloi opened my door, while he snapped at whoever was on the line.

"I don't care what you have to do about it. I told you the lord just barely returned home, he hasn't even walked in the door, and you are demanding to speak with him."

"Hello, my friend. I missed you." Eloi said wrapping her arms around me.

"Hello Eloi. All is well?" I nodded to Allipo.

"Then fix it!"

She smiled sadly at him. "It's been a rough couple of months while you've been away my lady."

"What happened?" Niratap asked as he got out.

She gazed at Allipo who was frowning at the sky, listening to the poor soul on the other end. "Dissention."

"That's not very clear, dear."

She shook her head. "Allipo handled most of it."

"Who?" There was no room for avoidance in my mate's voice.

Eloimaya frowned again. "Creseda."

"Where is she?"

"We don't know, my Lord. She is in the wind."

"Allipo."

The satyr turned as he ended the call and bowed deeply. "Sorry, my Lord. The gang war on the west coast is getting bloody, all the operatives are jumping, some without checking in with their handlers. I have been fielding calls all week."

"That is a separate situation that I will address later. What happened while we were away?" He snarled and it was a voice that even caused me to pause.

Allipo swallowed as he stood. "Creseda and several others in the shifter community staged a coup. They attacked the town."

"Was anyone hurt?" I asked.

"There were some minor injuries, a couple broken bones."

"Any fatalities?"

Allipo looked down. "Just one. A kelpie."

"And Creseda is in the wind?" I asked. Tightness coiled its way along my spine, as Nira's tail flicked angrily, an ache closing over my heart.

Allipo nodded. "Yes, my lady. The citizens holed up in the hospital, quickly reacting and moving somewhere safe. Eloimaya and I were in town and assisted where we could while we waited for backup."

"Allipo protected everyone from the shifters and a gorgon."

"A gorgon?" A jolt of fear cut through the anger and sorrow that danced under my skin.

"Yes, my Lord. She was not part of the siege on the town with the shifters, she was sent out by some dark master. She did not give me a name. Gorgons are old world and mostly talk poetically or in cryptic phrases. I convinced her to return home."

"And she went willingly?" I asked.

"She had grown bored looking for things she did not understand."

"What was she sent to find?" Niratap asked his brows pulled tight over his eyes.

"A drop of starlight, a beast with dragon longevity, a vessel of his essence, land, and vengeance."

"Fuck." Nira twisted away, pulling the tie out of his

hair, and untwisting the strands. "Fuck."

"What's wrong my Lord? What does it mean?"

"The lich that is after me has conned gorgons to hunt for his ingredients." Niratap raked his fingers over his scalp, I felt the pressure of his nails over my own. "Fuck. To hunt for me. For Tummilia. Fuck. Fuck." His emotions were flaring so rapidly, I couldn't keep up with the roiling. Shock. Fear. Concern. Worry. Dread. Rage.

I moved to cut off the frantic pacing and the thrumming that started in my heart. "Nira, we can face this. We'll face it together."

His pupils narrowed on my face. "Shasha, we are talking about a powerful enemy. More connected than Draven. More powerful than Cardoc."

"I understand that, but Nira—"

"I am not putting you in their path."

My own anger flared against him, two flames battling for dominance. "I will be with you against this enemy and every enemy. *Is limosa tu agus is leatsa mise.*"

He bared his fangs. "*Is liomsa tu* and I will not have you in harm's way again. Never again."

"Niratap, I chose you and all that comes with it. The danger, the risks, all of it, because I love you."

"Love is not enough." He snarled.

The words weren't meant as a blow, but they slashed through my heart. Pain shot through me cold and sharp. The rage and fear that had pushed words from him melted from his face. Horror took its place, his brain catching up to his words. I felt my stomach bottomed out with shame. I turned away.

"Shasha."

"You've said enough." I snapped tears burning behind my eyes.

"Shasha." He grasped my arm.

"No Niratap." I snapped wrenching my arms from his grasp, tears escaping. "No."

His hands fell to his sides, he flexed those long,

elegant fingers at a loss. "Shasha. I didn't mean–"

"No, you did, you meant it and I know that it comes from a place of fear, but Niratap." I growled. "Niratap, I am not defenseless. I am not weak. I am not less because I'm only half elemental and mortal. I will be with you no matter the threat. No matter what you say."

"Shasha I never—"

"I don't want to hear it." I turned away from him storming off to the stables. "Just leave me alone."

He didn't follow me. No one did. In the stables I pulled Guinness out of his stall and brushed him. Nira's emotions twisting with my own tightly; anger and regret and hurt danced between us. I pushed against the force of his feelings as I saddled Guinness. I just needed a moment alone, a moment of peace. I didn't have to ask Guinness where to take me, but the familiar path to the meadow flew past as we traveled through the woods. Eventually Niratap faded from my senses. Our bond had a range then and I could finally breathe out from under the weight of his regret. Though it wasn't intentional, my absence from him would be a punishment and even though I loved him fiercely I couldn't get past what he had said.

Love is not enough.

He had shouted the words at me. Meant them in that moment of anger and fear. And maybe my love wasn't enough to keep us safe, but that didn't mean he could doubt my convictions of being there for him. For fighting for him. For trying to help him fight his battles.

"I don't get it, Guiness."

The horse knickered beneath me.

"I love Niratap. He is a part of me and I'm a part of him, but sometimes I think we are two souls floating away from one another. I wonder sometimes if we rushed into each other."

Guinness huffed.

"I know he just wants to keep me safe, but I want the same things. If he would just let me be there for him."

Guinness paused ears flicking about to the sounds around us.

"What is it?"

Guinness snorted and continued down the trail. I strained to listen to whatever it was he had heard, but I only heard the cadence of insect cries in the summer heat. It wasn't until the meadow came into view that I relaxed again. The grasses and tall flowers swayed in the breeze and with the drone of bees and hoverflies. It was peaceful. It was peace, a slice of it through the chaos that was becoming my life. I slid off the saddle and walked with Guinness to the side of the pool.

"I'm not really angry with him, Guinness." He pressed his nose into my shoulder. "I just felt like he was pushing me away. I don't want him taking all the hits for me. I want to be there for him, by his side. Not just a warm body that he may or may not return to."

Guinness huffed into my hair.

"I know he just wants to keep me safe, but I don't want to lose him again. Not when I'm trying to be strong enough to protect him."

Guinness tugged one of my braids and I slung the reins over him.

"Thank you for bringing me here. You can stay or you can go back. Nira will come fetch me if you leave."

Guinness folded his ears back.

"Okay, my friend, go graze. I'm going to go for a swim."

He huffed at me again, before he turned away to sniff the flowers and munch on the untouched summer grass.

I thought of Nira as I slipped out of my clothes, folding them in a neat pile with my dagger atop it. I had already forgiven him. I knew that. He probably knew that too. Diving into the clear blue water with the brightly colored water fae dancing around me I wondered when he would seek me out. I knew eventually he would grow tired of the space. We hadn't had much space from one another since the beginning, excluding his imprisonment. We had so much to navigate still. Things normal couples talked about like marriage and kids. Things we hadn't shared like my fears of aging without him, about leaving this plane and leaving him behind. We didn't know what my lifespan would look like either, once this coming-of-age thing happened.

I surfaced sucking in a big breath of air, before laying back to float. What would that be like, I wondered. Would I be able to windfall like my father and create barriers of hard air. Or would nothing happen at all and the human in me win, it was both exciting and terrifying to think about.

I floated there in the cool water watching the sun travel the afternoon sky. I was comfortable there even though I felt my skin pruning in the water. It wasn't until the clouds turned a dusky pink that I climbed out of the water, collecting my clothes and heading into the cave. Maybe I would stay here tonight enjoying the peace and comfort that came from the sounds of insects and bats. Guinness followed, his hooves clicking softly on the stones, his soft nose bumping my shoulder in the dark."

"You aren't going to leave me, are you?"

I heard him shake and snort.

I laughed. "Okay, sweetheart."

I pulled the lantern and the worn blanket from the saddle bag and laid then out on the cool ground. Laying down to dry. Guinness occasionally sniffed me and snuffled a braid. His presence was equally as comforting as my mate's. I dozed, the glow of the sun fading into night.

I felt him. The twist of worry danced over my skin and the pang of regret echoed through my heart. Soon the near silent click of his talons on the stone was slow, cautious as if he thought I would send him away. Rolling to my side I watched as his glowing eyes approached and he stopped at the edge of the blanket laying down. I turned the lantern on.

"You've come to apologize and beg for forgiveness."

He huffed, but didn't lift his fluffy head. His hot breath rolled over my skin causing it to goose.

"What if I'm not ready to forgive you?" I already had.

His ears folded back.

"What if I want to stay mad?" I wasn't.

He closed his eyes. I rolled to my back.

"What if I wanted to punish you?" I slid my hand down my body, watching as his eyes heated. Guinness snorted, his hooves clicking as he left.

Niratap shifted forward.

"No." He froze those heated eyes watching. "I'm going to punish you, remember."

He huffed as I sat up shifting my body so he could see me clearly. Exposing myself to him. He licked his lips.

"You really hurt me with what you said."

Ears folding back, his eyes locked onto mine, the desire still burning through me, but that twist of regret acted in my heart. I spread myself wide for him, but his eyes never left my face.

"I know you're scared and worried, but I am your mate. You don't get to push me away."

A high-pitched whine came from him, as he adjusted.

"I'm going to be by your side the whole way. I'm not going to let anyone take you from me."

He growled, talons sinking into the earth. My brain took me back to the throne room, when his voice had echoed around me, asking for me. No, demanding my return. I felt so much for him, at that moment. I had been scared, worried about his safety. Had Cardoc ordered it he would have been dead, an easy target unconscious and vulnerable. It scared me to know he wasn't invincible, even when he acted like he was.

"You understand that I won't stand behind you to be protected anymore. I'm going to face your enemies by your side. They are my enemies too."

He looked away. Concern was ice through my veins.

"I will not. I know you worry about me, but I will not stand idly by and let you get taken by this lich. You hear me?"

He sighed.

I sighed too. Laying back on the blanket as tears threatened my vision. "I hate seeing you hurt."

He stood turning away from me. Had he shifted?

I covered my eyes. "Where are you going?"

Pain laced through me; his voice was raw. "I–I am sorry. I can't put you at risk."

A sob broke free. "So, you're just going to leave?"

"I don't know what to do, Shasha."

"Do you love me?"

"You know the answer."

"Say it. I need to hear you say it."

"Shasha, I love you. You are the air in my lungs and the blood in my veins. You are the one person I cannot lose. "

"Then why are you walking away?"

"Because I don't know what you want from me." He snarled. "You spread yourself to torment me, but your words say you're angry. You came to our place but didn't ask to talk it through. I–I don't want to fight with you."

"Come back." I stared at the shadowed cavern ceiling. "Please."

I wasn't sure if he would. In the silence I was afraid. I closed my eyes to the sound of him, his steps, his breath, the soft grunt he made as he sat beside me.

"I don't know how to fix what I said." He said solemnly. I looked at the long line of his spine and the muscles that quivered under the patchwork of scars.

"You don't need to fix anything."

He looked over his shoulder at me. His face was drawn and dark circles hung under his eyes. "Are we okay?"

There was dread and worry tying knots in my heart. "Why wouldn't we be?"

He hung his head in his hands. "I—I am terrified, Shasha. This enemy is dangerous."

"I'm not afraid of danger. I don't care if they are more connected than Dravin or more powerful than Cardoc. I don't care that they are hunting for ways to become more powerful. I will be with you and together is how we will be from now on."

"Shasha, a lich is hunting for me. A lich powerful enough to summon a horror to haunt me. Cunning enough to persuade gorgons to hunt for him. They have already found weak links in the organization and are destabilizing it as we speak."

"The lich doesn't have me, and they don't have you."

"I don't know if I'll be enough to keep you safe."

"I can protect myself."

He sighed. It was a long-suffering sound. "Your skills have grown, but not even I am prepared for this enemy."

I rose, wrapping my arms around his shoulders. "Together. We'll face it together."

"They want to pull us apart." He lifted his head.

"That's impossible. You are part of me and I'm part of you."

He smiled, but it didn't touch his eyes.

I pressed a kiss to his temple. "I am with you, no matter the enemy, no matter the danger."

"I am afraid."

"And I'm not? Nira, I only thought of you when those guards hauled me away. I was terrified that they would go back and hurt you. And I am scared of this unknown enemy, but I know you are not going to back down. You have our family to protect. The organization to hold together. There are so many beings that depend on you. The weight is unimaginable but let me help. Let me carry the burden with you. Don't make it easier for our enemies to pull us apart by pushing me away."

He twisted, pinning me beneath him. The speed stealing my breath as did the tenderness at which he protected my head. He pressed his brow to mine, my eyes dancing over his features from the pale scars to his thick lashes. I reached up, tracing the curve of his cheek with my finger. It was damp.

"I love you, Niratap." My voice came out a whisper. "No matter what happens."

"Shasha—"

"Will you just kiss me already? There are so many what ifs, but there is only this one truth that matters. I love you. So, kiss me."

He did. His tongue swept over mine while his hands trailed over my shoulders. My legs wrapped around his waist, and he groaned into my mouth. Kissing down my throat, his tongue passing like a brand over my skin. He pulled me against him, cradling my spine with one hand this other pulled my head back, giving him more access.

"I want–" He growled.

"Take." I panted.

The flash of pain was lightning that sparked a wave of wild pleasure. My nails dug into his shoulder.

"Please."

He growled against my throat, the vibrations echoing through my whole body. He let go pulling back to look at me. A crimson line trickled down over his chin, his tongue darted out, lapping it away.

His voice was feral. "What do you need, mate?"

"I want a taste. I want you."

He reached past my head, then offered me my dagger. I gazed into the liquid silver pools taking the blade. He dropped his head, kissing the tender spot on my neck.

"Take."

"I—"

He drug his tongue over my throat. "Take."

My hand shook. "I–"

He clasped my hand and gently pulled the blade against his neck, slicing the skin. "You won't hurt me."

He took the dagger, setting it aside. Blood trickled down his neck.

"It's not closing."

"It won't for a while." He said softly. "Take."

He licked my neck again before his teeth sunk into the flesh again. I bucked against him, and his claws drifted down my back. I wrapped my arms around him with a cry. I lapped the trickle of blood, and the world spun with rain and whiskey on my tongue. Magic zinged across my skin.

"Mine." He growled.

"Yes." I groaned against his throat.

He rocked back lifting me enough to slide himself into me, catching my moan with a kiss. I tasted myself on his tongue, the tang of copper, and the bouquet of blooms. I got lost in us. In the ache building between my legs. In the sting of the love wounds on both our bodies. In his whispered promises of love and safety. Tears came to my eyes as we crested, I clung to him, the bond between our souls singing. He was mine and I was his and everything made sense when it came to that.

He curled around me, kissing every spot of skin he could find. "I am sorry that my words hurt you, mate. Mine."

I trailed my fingers through the silken strands of his hair. "There is nothing to apologize for. I know that it came from a place of fear."

"I still shouldn't have said it." He met my gaze. "I shouldn't have projected that fear at you."

I kissed him, easing him onto his back. The angle slid him deeper and brought both of us to gasp. I looked down at him, the epicenter of my life and felt only love for the man beneath me. I rocked against him, loving the view of his head kicking back and the way his face twisted with pleasure. I ran my hands over his chest, fingers tracing his scars, wishing I could take all that pain from him. I wanted his suffering to end with me. I knew that it was impossible for it to end. Impossible that my will and body would end the suffering he had survived for centuries and continued to push through.

I only hoped that my love was enough. That I was enough to end his suffering.

Chapter Sixty-Three

Niratap

Dawn came too quickly. Dawn always seemed to come too quickly when I just wanted to drown in her. The cut in my skin had finally clotted, even as she had fallen asleep, she had fretted over the oozing wound. It had been worth it. She was always worth it, but the dawn pinking up the grey sky told me there was work to be done.

I ran my hand over her back. "*Mo grá,* it is time to go back."

She mumbled a protest curling into my chest.

"I know. I would love to stay in peace with you, but there is much that we need to do."

She glared at me through her lashes. "It is unfair that we can only get a few hours of it."

"I know. After."

"After seems so far." She stretched rolling over.

It did and as she dressed, I pondered when we would find moments like this again.

"Did Guinness leave?"

"He did."

"He was satisfied with my safety then."

"He knows nothing will happen to you when you are with me."

"The scratches down my back say otherwise." She wasn't wrong, bruises and scratch marks peppered her skin.

Folding the blanket I said. "Well, nothing that you don't welcome."

She kissed my cheek. "Okay fair. Are we walking back or are you going to carry me?"

"I'll carry you. It will be quicker, and we can share a meal before I fully dive into working."

"Alright."

I took that wildest shape, shaking out my fur. The infernal itching sent an uncomfortable shiver down my back, kicking and scratching at it didn't relieve it. I needed the antlers gone, because this was only adding to the stress.

Shasha's laugh danced around me. "You, okay?"

I huffed, laying on the ground so she could climb on. She scratched behind my ear, my head tilting into the touch. She laughed again.

"Your antlers are really bothering you, aren't they?"

I dipped my head.

"I'm sorry that it's so itchy."

I looked over my shoulder at her, her sweet smile warming my heart. I loped towards home, her hands threaded tightly through my fur. She was sunshine in my life, even when she was the source of much of my worry. I didn't want to have her in harm's way, but I also realized that she was far past letting me be her shield. She had made that evident the moment she had come between me and Cardoc. I didn't want her to be mine either.

I was done. Mentally I was done. Done with requests, with panicked emails, with even more panicked calls, with reallocating resources, and with Allipo hovering over my shoulder, blocking my access to the liquor cabinet. It was after one such unsettling phone call with two agents on the west coast who were monitoring the drug trade. One of them particularly worried over turf wars and power vacuums that were popping up since Dravin's near public death and raids on his properties.

I pinched the bridge of my nose. "Can we be done for the day, Allipo?"

Allipo flipped through the meticulous notes he had

been taking in my absence. "There is still much to do, my Lord."

I sighed. "What else?"

Allipo glanced at me over his glasses. "Are you well?"

I considered the satyr. "I am just tired."

"Letting your mate bleed you is probably part of that."

I scoffed. "Hardly."

He smiled. "We have inventory for the vault, and you need to return Voxviraz's call."

"The incubus can wait, as can the invent—" Leaning back in the chair I tipped violently to one side. "Shit."

"Niratap!"

"I'm fine. I'm fine." I rolled towards the weightier side of my head. My elbow ached from where it had cracked against the floor and my knee ached from the desk. I lifted myself up pulling my off-balance head from the ground. "I just dropped an antler."

I propped myself against the wall, as the sounds of footsteps echoed through the library. Shasha, Mitta, Echo and Nessa came through the doorway. I frowned, bracing the antler still attached.

"Are you alright?" Mitta asked sharply.

"I am alright." I said as Shasha dropped by my side.

Nessa burst into laughter, folding over herself.

I sighed. "Truly mate, I am alright."

"Are you sure, brother? Are you not feeling lopsided?" Nessa twisted her head to the side and cackled.

"Very funny, Nessa." I growled. "So funny I forgot to laugh."

Shasha glared at her. "Nessa, laughing is kind of rude."

"Oh, if my brother can't handle being teased at his age then he is more immature than I thought."

I tugged lightly on my right antler, with the hope that it would come off as well. "I can handle your teasing, Nessa, but the witch's cackle is a bit excessive."

She glowered at me, her laughter dying. "At least I'm not going to walk in circles for the next week."

I tugged on the antler again, not wanting her to be right. "Touché."

She smirked, before turning away. Echo smiled at us before walking after her. Another tug and finally the antler came free. I closed my eyes as my vision swam.

"You, okay?"

"I will be." I rubbed the stinging muscle in my neck. "It just takes a moment to find my balance again."

"Was it the right or the left?" Katrel asked from the door, a smirk was in her voice.

"The left." Mitta answered.

"Fuck yes. Bastion! Where are you brat? You owe me sixty bucks!" She shouted satisfied that I was uninjured.

"Do you need help to stand?" Shasha asked softly.

"No, I will be fine. Thank you though." With a grunt I stood, stretching the muscles of my neck.

"You need to be careful, Niratap." Mitta said, crossing her arms.

"I know Mitta."

"I mean it. The next fifteen weeks. Vitamins every day."

"I know." I growled.

"Why?" Shasha asked.

Mitta looked at her, her face pulled into annoyance. "While his antlers grow, his body pulls minerals from his bones, especially his ribs. His bones will quickly become more brittle and the last thing I want to do is set ribs, while your growing antlers. His healing will be stunted as well. No taking bullets. No avoidable risks."

I sighed. "I will be careful Mitta."

She groaned, turning to leave. "Somehow, I doubt that. Before you leave to visit Shasha's parents I need to stock your blood. Before your body goes into overdrive, please."

"Yes Mitta. I will be there later."

"You will." She said walking out the study doors. "I'll hunt you down otherwise and drag you there."

"I'll bring him down." Shasha said, placing a hand on my low back.

Allipo righted the chair. "Do you want these to go to the craftsman?"

"Yes. I want his best work for my mate's blade."

"I will take these and get them shipped." Allipo bowed, antlers in hand. "I'll let you rest. That phone call and inventory can wait."

"Thank you." I said as he hurried from the room leaving me with my mate. "I am truly okay, Shasha. Better now since the itching will subside for a few days."

She worried her lip, stepping over to the window. "When are we going to visit my parents?"

"Soon I imagine. Have you called them?"

She shook her head. "Mom will just ask me a million questions and I don't know what I want to tell her."

"V is glad that we are safe, and everyone made it home okay."

"But everyone didn't make it back, Niratap." She said softly looking out at the cemetery grove.

I swallowed. My eyes fell on the much too small urn on a shelf for the mountainous male it contained. Another set of phone calls that I had to make. I turned to the cabinet. "You are right."

She didn't move from the window as I pulled the scotch and two glasses from the cabinet. A tightness taking hold of my chest. "It could have been you."

"But it wasn't." I said solemnly, pouring the scotch.

"But it could have been." She wiped her face.

I walked to her side, offering a glass of scotch. She took it, swallowing the amber liquid in two gulps. She held her hand by her face, fighting off the cough. I took a sip myself, letting the burn coat my throat and settle the unease in my stomach. "But it wasn't. Casrian was boastful and arrogant. I'm not faulting him as a person, but he was reckless."

She scoffed and set the glass on the windowsill. "And you're not?"

"I try not to be. Though more often than not I am not successful and if it comes to you, I don't care how reckless or dangerous something is. You are my priority."

Her eyes met mine. "And you are mine, Niratap."

I pressed a kiss to her forehead, pulling her scent into my lungs. It was more grounding than the scotch ever was. "I know, *mo chroi.*"

Her arms wrapped around me, pulling me close. I let her cry, rubbing soothing circles down her back. I understood what she meant, what she feared. That I wasn't immortal or invulnerable. I could be killed and the weight of her mother's words from Beltane settled into my bones. *In this where you burn the world for her do you include yourself in that?*

"This weekend we will go see your parents for a few days."

She wiped her face as she pulled away. "Are you sure?"

"Yes. V and I talked a little on the phone this morning, but I want to ask him more questions where he can't deflect, and I think we need some time away from all of this." I gestured vaguely at our surroundings with the glass.

"But you have so much work to catch up on."

I tilted her face up. "I do. The work will still be there next week, pack a bag and we'll leave tomorrow."

She gazed into my eyes and my heart fluttered.

"I know that I have made several poor decisions in the time we have been together, *mo grá*, but I want to be better for you. Let me."

She blinked and nodded, stepping away from me. "I

will let the others know we will be gone this weekend."

I leaned in, pressing a kiss on her cheek. "I love you."

She smiled. "I love you too."

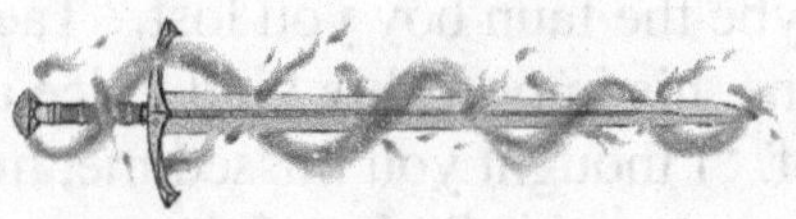

Everything was hazy. My head felt heavy as I tried to blink the fog from my eyes. A jolt of panic sparked through me. I couldn't move. Cold iron manacles encircled my wrists and ankles, the scent of blood filled the air around me. Darkness was all my eyes could see. I tried to get my lungs to pull in air, but I couldn't breathe. Everything was sore and my strength was gone. The bonds were so tight I couldn't even thrash. Where was Shasha? Where was my mate?

"I got one." The shivery voice of the malice cooed.

"Leave us alone."

"I told you last time that wasn't something I could do." White glowing orbs appeared above me. "Master wants you to suffer."

"I don't care what your master wants. They are an abomination."

The malice laughed coldly as candles ignited around us, illuminating the underground cell. "Who will be your tormentor tonight, breaker of bonds?"

"Release me."

"The first love?" Its unnatural shape wavered, and it was Deirdre's serene face that looked down at me. It was her delicate fingers that trailed down my bare chest, as the creature crawled on top of me. Her voice cracked the part of my heart that would always love her. "Don't you miss me, Nira."

"Stop this." I closed my eyes.

"Or maybe the holy man that broke you." A fist

connected with my jaw, my head whipping to the side. I saw Father James' leering face and felt the rings that adorned his meaty hand as it connected again. "Pain is the only thing that beasts understand."

I spat the blood off the table. "Enough of this."

"Maybe the faun boy you lost." Taegan's soft grey eyes met mine, his impeccably kind voice driving a knife into my grief. "I thought you missed me, my Lord."

"Please stop this." I hated that my voice wavered.

"But we've just started. It was such a shame when his sweet little life was cut so short." Taegan's eyes fell from his sockets, wetly bouncing off my stomach and hitting the ground with a wet plop, his ears followed. Black blood leaked from the empty spaces. "I had good eyes and ears, when I was alive though."

"Stop." I arched off the table. "Stop."

"Maybe your old master would be an acceptable torturer." Atton loomed over me gripping my face. "This didn't scar you nearly enough, you insufferable beast."

The familiar thorns dug into my skin. "Stop this."

"But we've only just begun." He hissed. "I will enjoy wringing the willfulness from you."

"Stop. Please stop."

"I love listening to you beg. I wonder if that pretty mate of yours will beg for me."

"No! Leave her alone! Please. Please."

"Does she beg for you when you fuck her? I bet she does. I bet she screams so beautifully."

I felt his hands on my throat. Spots started to obstruct my vision. I closed my eyes as his flesh started to decay.

"Will she beg for me when I fuck her? When I break her?"

"Stop."

Shasha was screaming, her voice begging for it to stop. I heard the crack of bones and her whimper. "Which hole do you prefer, beast? Or should I just make another?"

Hands still held my throat, closing it off from all air. Hands trailed over my arms and chest, almost a lover's touch. Some of them dug at my skin, slicing and cutting. I felt them on me. I felt them inside me, twisting and reaching for some secret thing only they knew about. Voices laughed at me. Screams echoed around me. Shasha's pleas for mercy. Allipo's cries of betrayal. Tummilia's grief filled wails. Mitta's roars of anger.

I sat up in the bed, gasping and choking trying to pull air into my lungs. Shasha slept quietly beside me, her breath even and undisturbed unlike my mind. I hung my head in my hands, trying to erase the sounds of her screams in my ears and the feeling of phantom hands exploring my body. Whoever the malice's master was, they coming for us and I feared that we wouldn't make it through this.

"Are you ready?"

I chuckled. "I can handle your parents, *mo grá*."

She smiled at me knocking on the door. "They're a lot."

"So are you." I pressed a kiss to her brow as she scowled at me.

"Ass." She worried her lip. "Your antlers."

"I'm currently sans antler and it will only throw off your mother, who I suspect won't notice after she sees you."

I chuckled again as the door opened and Ventris stood there, his blue eyes sparkling with delight. He shouted into the house. "Jazz!"

"X who's at the door?"

"Woman come see." He sighed at her, before he looked over his daughter. "Are you well?"

Shasha smiled. "I am."

"And you?" He asked me, eyes flicking up to the top of my head.

"I am also well."

He nodded, understanding. "Your mother will be very happy to see you. Jazz!"

"I'm coming! Who's—" Jazzera, threw me for a loop every time I saw her with how she looked like her daughter. They had the same face and coloring; Shasha's eyes were just darker than her mother's. It was like peeking into the future.

"Hi, momma."

"Babygirl." Jazzera near tackled her daughter in a viscous hug. "I was so worried about you. Were you hurt? Were you well fed? Were you safe? How long have you been back? Why haven't you called?"

Shasha half laughed and half groaned at her mother's onslaught. "Not terribly and I'm already better. Yes, we were well fed. As much as we could be. A couple weeks now. We've been busy helping the town and trying to rout out members of a coup."

"Your father told me that things had been bad at the manor while you were away. Is everyone okay?"

"Yes." I answered for my mate.

Her mother turned to look at me, her eyes widening seeing me for the first time. "What happened to your antlers?"

"Normal shed should happen about every half century or so." I offered her a reassuring smile.

"It's different. What does it feel like?"

"Mom!" Shasha shrieked mortified. I chuckled.

"Itchy and I often get crushing headaches as they grow back." Shasha looked up at me with a crease between her eyes.

"You didn't tell me you got headaches."

"It is a small thing. In ten weeks, I will be done growing them and spend a day uncomfortably itchy, to shed the velvet and everything will be good as new."

"Ten weeks with headaches sounds absolutely miserable." Jazzera said.

"It is, but it is part of life for my species at least for my genes. Nessa got off easy with the same horns as our father. She doesn't have to shed and go through this process."

"Why is that?" she asked.

"Our parents were two different sub-species of bitarogs. I took after my mother with deerlike antlers and Nessa has the horns of our father, more antelope. I find it rather unfair to be honest with you." I nodded towards the interior. "May we come in?"

"Oh, yes of course." she said scooting away from the door.

Shasha and V stepped inside together, so he could wrap her in a warm hug. I followed behind, dipping under the door frame and standing at my full height, which felt strange in the Dion family home.

"Not having them seems to have its perks." Jazzera said as she shut the door.

"Indeed." I moved across the space and set our bags at the base of the stairs.

"You brought bags? You're staying?"

"For a few days." Shasha looked down, twisting a curl with her finger. "We figured it would make up for not calling right away."

Her mother's sharp cry of excitement hurt my ears, but I was happy for her. Happy for my mate whose worry faded away. Her mother hugged her again, before they ventured into the kitchen to talk about our journey and what to make for dinner. Ventris shook his head as I watched them disappear.

"Was it bad?"

I shook my head. "No. Though Cardoc made the whole thing difficult and painful. He is no longer king, and the girls get to keep their freedom and their partners."

"Partners?"

"Mitta and Katrel have sorted out their differences and are together. Just as Tummi and Bastion did before we left."

"Finally." He chuckled. "I thought they would never get past it."

I smiled. "Thank you for coming to my family's aid while we were gone."

"Don't mention it. Allipo did amazing defending innocent lives. That being said, I think he and the sheriff almost came to blows multiple times."

"He conveniently left that part out."

"Figures." V peered into the kitchen, smiling at his family. "I have to thank you."

I cocked my head to the side. "What for?"

"For saving my daughter so I could get to know her. For loving her like you do."

I smiled. "I should thank you, for not listening to your father."

His smile turned sad. "Yeah. Fuck him anyways, he wouldn't know a blessing if it broke his jaw."

"Let's join them then." I tipped my head towards were the women talking about making a roast for dinner. "Enjoy our blessings."

Chapter Sixty-Four

Shasha

My parents were overjoyed that we had come to visit. My father spoke of the attack and about how those that had been arrested were currently sitting in cells at the head bureau office in DC. Niratap wanted to question them about Creseda's whereabouts, since the community was both divided and half missing. My father said that wasn't a good idea, explaining that there had been a powershift and new management was heavily investigating into black market operations, especially quote unquote vigilantes. I scoffed, but Niratap agreed to lie mostly low. They discussed the pros and cons of said new management and considered what was to come of it, if it would interfere with our operations or travel to and from Asuna. V didn't have answers.

I was still coming to terms with it. The fact that V, Xaevean, was my father. He looked like the impressions I had had, especially now that his hair was growing out and he started to loc it, but I didn't really know him. I trusted him because Nira trusted him despite not knowing the complexities of their relationship. I was open to loving him because mom had forgiven him for his decision to leave us. I truly hadn't formed my own opinion of the man yet. It wasn't until we were curled together in each other's arms on the floor of my room, Niratap's heart a steady drum under my ear that I asked him.

"How did you and my father meet?"

His voice was heavy with encroaching sleep. "Would you be upset if I told you he was trying to arrest me?"

"I wouldn't be surprised."

He chuckled softly. His breath dancing over my hair. "It was about a hundred years ago. It was soon after I had freed Allipo from the Blackhand; I was scoping other fighting rings in the city, looking for those like Allipo who were trapped and being used. They were more common then, entertainment for factory workers and other fools who wanted to make a quick buck. It made it easy to avoid the darkness that was poverty. It was the wrong place wrong time scenario; they were busting the owner of the ring for money laundering of all things. Mafia activity is what got us in close quarters."

"How did you avoid getting arrested?"

"Well, your father was just a cop then, playing human. He would bounce between towns and districts every few years, answering the beck and call of his father. I simply asked him how an elemental made it onto the police force. He shot me in response."

I twisted in his arms. "He what?"

Niratap chuckled. "He shot me. It wasn't until after I was crammed into a cell and the girls came to fetch me that we actually talked, discovering we were on different sides of the same team. Our relationship as allies helped when he joined the FMBI about forty years ago, and they had attempted to arrest me again."

"Why didn't you tell me this sooner?"

He shrugged. "It wasn't of the greatest importance. I want you to form your own opinions of the people we work with. I will advise you on some yes, but overall, I want you to be independent. After we found out that Ventris was your father I kept things to myself. You deserve to make your own relationship with him, regardless of how we interact. You deserve to have that with your father."

I pressed my head against his chest. "I don't know him."

"Then get to know him. Talk to him. It doesn't have to be about the work that we do. Ask him about his family, though he probably won't have very good things to say about his father."

"They're no contact. I know."

"Ask him about them. He has brothers and a sister, and he loves his mother dearly."

My fingers trailed over his chest, tracing his scars. "When do I find time to ask?"

"You make time for it, love. Now sleep."

I opened my eyes the following morning tucked in tightly in the blankets. Niratap had already headed downstairs, and the smell of coffee and bacon wafted through the house. There was a soft knock on the door.

"Oh, you're awake." Mom said softly. "Why are you sleeping on the floor?"

"Nira doesn't fit on the bed and regardless of if I start the night in a bed, I usually end up in his arms at some point."

She gave a soft smile. "Breakfast and coffee are ready."

"I'll be down in a minute."

"You guys doing, okay?" She asked as I wriggled out of the cocoon that Niratap had put me in.

"We're fine." I grunted, finally getting free. "Why do you ask?"

"Things seem tense that's all."

"We've had some disagreements, but I think we're good. He can probably hear us just so you know."

"I asked him this morning. He gave me a similar answer."

"We both agree. It seems like we're good." I shrugged, slipping on jeans and a comfy t-shirt.

She came in, shutting the door and whispering.

"Shasha Nicole Dion. What happened while you were away?"

"Nothing. We're good."

"He seems down. Is it the antlers or something else?"

"He lost some people last year and he's still recovering from what Dravin did to him physically. He is naturally stoic."

Mother frowned. "If you say so."

I sighed. "There's a lot going on and I don't want you to worry. Let's go eat breakfast."

Downstairs I pressed a kiss to Niratap's cheek before I went to make myself coffee. He mumbled a good morning as he read through emails on his phone. Tension floated through the bond, more bad news, more panic, more unease. My father set a stack of hotcakes on the table and sat next to my mother who was eyeing Niratap's face. He set his phone face down as sat down with my coffee.

"Nothing good?" I asked.

He sighed. "More panic and unrest. I will have to travel to California and Idaho soon to try and settle things and Voxviraz sent the dates for his showcase along with a cryptic mention of you."

"Why is Voxviraz asking about my daughter?" Ventris, my father, asked.

"I may have made a deal with him for a favor." I said into my coffee.

"What kind of favor?"

"An open favor with no strings."

"Favors always have strings." Ventris scooped eggs onto his plate.

"She worded her bargain well. Voxviraz will have to be very careful trying to worm more out of her trade."

Silence took over the table as we served ourselves and ate. It was an almost normal breakfast. Almost.

Ventris leaned back looking between the two of us. "You let her make a deal with a demon?"

My mother choked on her coffee.

"I don't *let* your daughter do anything." Nira said, standing to take his plate to the sink. "She made the decision herself, against my advice."

"What?" My mother sputtered looking at me.

"I thought the deal would be advantageous, especially since we were successful on our end."

"Demon deals are dangerous." Ventris snapped.

I collected the other empty plates and platters and joined Niratap at the sink. "I know. I took that into account when I made it."

"What are you going to ask for?" Mom asked.

"I haven't decided yet, but I have some ideas."

"Just leave the dishes in the sink. You two are always doing the dishes while you are here."

"It is the least I can do." Niratap said softly.

Mom batted us from the sink. "Later, Niratap. Later, you are a guest."

He listened, sitting back down at the table. "If you say so."

We sat there in the kitchen talking for some time, drinking coffee. Mom and I listening to Niratap and Ventris talking about agent movements and power vacuums. Mom occasionally asked questions to clarify terms so she understood what they were talking about. Her face twisted when drugs were explained, or they spoke of illegal trades from women and guns to drugs and body parts. They were both serious and methodical as they spoke about multiple facets of each of their organizations, some of it I could follow, most of it went over my head.

Niratap shifted in his seat, looking to the front of the house. "Jazzera, were you expecting anyone?"

"Not now. Decan said he would come over for Sunday dinner."

"V." Niratap pulled his firearm, the sleek dark steel not something I had seen him pack.

"Gotcha."

"What is it?" My mother paled when she saw the guns both men had pulled as they got up from the table.

"Shasha, stay with your mother." Niratap said firmly as he got low beneath the living room window and my father pressed against the door.

"Who is it?"

Niratap peeked over the sill of the window. He frowned, the tension slipping from his body. He stood and cleared his weapon, tucking back into the waist of his pants and shaking his head.

"Well?"

"It's all you, V."

"That doesn't tell me who is out there."

Niratap ducked into the kitchen and sighed. "It's your parents."

"Fuck me."

"Xaevean." My mother hissed

"Sorry, Jazzybaby. Why is he here?"

"That is for you to ask." Niratap said leaning against the island. "They are your family after all."

I looked between my mate and the door where my father stood. Niratap's eyes narrowed, but he bobbed his head. I understood that he didn't think highly of my paternal grandfather. From what I had been told, I wasn't sure I wanted to know him, but there was still a part of me that wanted answers. It was that part of me that pulled me into the living room as a polite knock sounded on the door.

I moved forward as he opened the door, beyond the screen was a man who could have been a leaner version of my father. His hair was tidy and short, and he was dressed in a tailored navy blue suit; dark sunglasses hid his eyes. Beside him was quite the opposite of what I imagined the wife of a senator would look like. She had long dreads that were coiled atop her head half-hidden under a teal cowl that both contrasted and complimented her jam-colored dress, which fell in many layers fringed with gold. Her wrists were adored with golden bangles and her thin fingers were decorated with multi-colored rings. Her near white-grey eyes froze me in place.

"What do you want? Why are you here?" Ventris snapped.

"Really Xaevean, is that any way to speak to your parents." The man took off his sunglasses and he had the same lightning blue eyes that my father had.

He scoffed. "There was a reason I went no contact with you. Hello, Momma, it's very nice to see you."

The woman looked at my father and gave him a soft smile. Her voice was velvety but seemed laced with danger. "It is nice to see you to, sweetbreeze."

"With the pleasantries out of the way, let us in."

Ventris crossed his arms. "No"

The man sighed. "Xaevean, why is it always so tedious with you? None of the rest of your siblings give me this much trouble."

"I'm terribly sorry that you haven't burned bridges with Malich, Teion, or Kindra."

"Xaevean, as the oldest you should be–"

"I am not the oldest." He shouted. "Zakari was the oldest."

"Even you speak of him in past tense."

"He died with honor even though he was doing what you told him to. "

"Zakari was a good son. He listened."

"And this is why I haven't spoken to you in twenty years."

"It's neither here nor there. For once I am glad that you didn't listen to me. I want to meet my granddaughter."

Ventris shut the door in his face.

"Xaevean that is not how you treat family." Mother snarled as she walked into the living room. "I don't care how terrible he was to you."

"Jazz. He is not walking into this house."

"Yes, he is." She snapped reaching the door handle.

He put his hand on hers. "He wanted to take me

away from you.”

“He already succeeded in that, Xaevean. I lost you because of him.”

“He wanted us to kill our daughter.”

“I am right here.” I said.

“Shasha—”

“I want to meet him.”

Niratap said from the kitchen. “V, just open the door. You can kick him out after.”

Mom pulled the door open. “Come in. We’d love to have you.”

I sat with my father on one side of the table, my grandfather and grandmother on the other. Niratap had made a fresh pot of coffee and set it on the table. He had made my grandmother a cup of herbal tea, then came to stand behind me.

“I’m surprised you remembered, Bondbreaker.”

“I may be busy Aria, but I would be ashamed if I forgot you preferred tea.”

My grandfather scoffed, taking a sip of his black coffee. “I see that you are still pretentious.”

“Not nearly as pretentious as you, Severine.” Niratap returned.

He glowered over the rim of the cup at my mate. “Why are you even here?”

“He is Shasha’s—” My mother looked between us.

“Mate.” I said to my grandparents. “Niratap is my mate.”

My grandmother nodded like it made sense, my grandfather glowered looking at my father. “You let her debase herself with a lesser being?”

It was so silent you could have heard a gnat scream.

I looked at him, this stranger who was supposed to be a pillar of a community that I was a part of who thought the being that was the center of my happiness was less. I frowned.

"They picked each other before I even knew they were together." Ventris said, eyeing my mother who was twisting a towel in her hands.

"Niratap is a good man." I said. "I trust him with my life."

"Was that before or after you gave him your body?"

"Father." Ventris snapped.

"Severine." Niratap growled. I felt his hands on the back of my chair.

Severine's eyes sparkled brightly. Niratap's hands shook as if he was fighting against something as he released the back of my chair and stepped back. Glancing at Nira over my shoulder I saw his jaw locked and his face curled into a wrathful sneer. The veins in his neck protruded with effort.

"Stop." Ventris hissed. "You will not use that in my house."

Severine just set the cup of coffee down and crossed an ankle over a knee before he addressed Ventris. "Look, son, I am not here to wax poetic with you or rehash our sordid history. I am just here to meet my granddaughter, the only thing worth noting to me in your existence, and to extend an offer to train and house her once she crests her maturity."

"Why would she want to live in your little town?" Niratap growled through his teeth.

"Because she is the next pure elemental and she will need to be taught extensively by her people."

"Wait, what?" Both Ventris and I said at the same time.

"How can, you be sure?" Ventris asked.

"Your mother has seen it."

Ventris fell back in his seat. "But she is only half-elemental and though our family is a strong line, I am just an air elemental."

"Terribly disappointing as it is, maybe the genetics just skipped you."

"How is that even possible?"

"Do not question the threads of fate, Xaevean." My grandmother said softly and though her voice was steady the room warbled with power.

"What does that mean?" I asked them.

She smiled at me. "You will be more powerful than you can comprehend, child."

"A regular elemental has control of one of the many facets of power that rule the world." He cast a glance at my father. "Other *gifted* elementals can control upwards of four elements. In rare cases some of those gifted elementals can have extraordinary gifts such as compulsion or foresight. A pure elemental has the skill to master all the elements and more than likely several of these extraordinary gifts."

"How do you know?"

"Aria has the gift of foresight. She has seen your gifts, but she still fails to tell me anything."

"Those visions are not for you, husband." Her mysterious eyes met mine. "We have much to discuss, Shasha, dear. When you are ready?"

"I have so many questions."

"In good time." She smiled warmly at me.

"Unless you wish to come with us now?" Severine said with a smile. "However, I will tell you that Halivaara has a strict policy on outsiders."

"So, I couldn't go?"

"As my granddaughter you have special privileges." He looked above my head at Niratap. "However, your *mate* wouldn't—"

"Then I won't go." I said firmly.

"What?" Severine sounded genuinely shocked, sitting forward as the sparkle in his eyes faded. "You would suffer through your crossing alone? You would try to learn the skills without aid?"

"I would. I don't know you and to be honest I don't like the way you treat my father or my mate." I looked at Nira and he gave me a sweet smile. "If my mate can't go I won't."

"You can't be serious. No one has ever gone through the crossing alone." He frowned.

"She is not alone, Severine. She has me." Niratap said placing a hand on my shoulder giving me a gentle squeeze.

"You won't be able to help her through it." He said matter-of-factly, glaring over my head. "You have no idea what element could manifest first."

"And you do?" My mother asked from the kitchen.

"No, but if she is with us, she would have a support system, a team of elementals that could circumvent a disaster and care for her."

"And we aren't capable of doing that?" Ventris asked.

"I would be surprised if you were capable of much, Xaevean."

"Enough." I snapped, earning a sour look from Severine. "I don't care that you're my grandfather, you don't get to come into my parents' house and cause them problems. You don't get to treat my mate like garbage solely because we are a different race. And no one gets to argue over me like I'm some kind of commodity. I am a living, breathing person, no one's possession."

"And yet you have let that monster bind you to him."

"Don't talk about him like that." I slammed my hands on the table. "I have stabbed men for less. I chose him. Me. It was my decision to form the mating bond. It was my decision to be in a relationship with him."

"And what of the magic around your neck?"

"The magic—" I touched my throat. It hadn't been that long ago that that magic had saved my life. The only time he used it was at the auction.

"I can see it, you know. The chain he has around your neck."

"It's for my protection."

"Is that what he told you?"

"Severine, that's enough." Nira snapped.

His eyes sparkled again. "You will stay out of it." Niratap growled behind me.

"Poor sweet girl. Roped in and tricked by a monster. Is that how he pulled you into his bed?"

"I wasn't tricked."

"Really then? If it wasn't a trick, he'll release you, right?"

I knew he wouldn't. The magical tether between us had kept me safe, protected me from real monsters. I didn't wish to be rid of that protection. "That is neither here nor there."

"That isn't an answer." I swallowed. Niratap squeezed my shoulder. "Let him go. Let him speak for himself. Please."

"Why, so he can pour honey in my ears?" Severine scoffed. "I think not."

"Let him go." Mom barked at him.

The spark in his eyes grew as he turned at her. "I will not be told what to do by a woman, let alone the one my idiot son gave up a dynasty for."

I slapped him. I had had enough. He was treating everyone but me like trash and though I hated it, both Niratap and my father had the skin to take it. My mother didn't deserve it. "Get out."

His face moved from shock to an anger that promised cruelty. His eyes sparkled at me. "Sit down. You don't raise your hand to me."

I didn't sit down, didn't feel whatever it was his power did. "Well, you forced my hand. Get out of my parents' home. I never want to see you again."

The spark died in his eyes, and he frowned. "Very

well. Aria, we have overstayed our welcome."

She sipped her tea and then said. "I knew you would posture us out of a good conversation with our only grandchild."

He swung a menacing glare her way. "Then why not stop me?"

She leveled a more menacing glare at him. "I don't like to interfere with your stupidity, Severine. It is the only thing that keeps you humble, and therefore tolerable."

He frowned at her but stood up and offered her his hand. She smiled at me as she stood. "Very well. We will leave, but when you find that you can't do this with your means. Call me and we'll get you taken care of."

He offered me a card and I let it hang in the air between us. "I won't call you."

He set the card on the table. "We'll see about that."

"Threatening her is in poor taste Severine, as is gaslighting her." Niratap said, coming to my side. "I'll show you out."

"We can see ourselves out of this hovel."

"I will talk to you soon, Shasha dear." My grandmother said as Severine led her from the kitchen.

I stared at the card on the table as the door closed. I just stared at the obnoxious embossed letters of his name and number. I couldn't trust him. He would try to use me. My own grandfather. I sat numbly in the chair, still staring at the card. My father stared at the card as well, his chin propped in his hand. Finally, he sighed and leaned back in his chair to stare at the ceiling.

"I'm sorry."

"Don't apologize for your father, V. You can't take the blame for him being a snake." Niratap said, clearing the cups from the table. He smiled, pulling something from the teacup and setting it on the table before me. "This is for you."

"What is it?" My mother asked. She pried herself from her daze. She had deflated against the counter after my grandparents had left.

The item was a simple silver ring with a black stone setting. The stone had a mirrored surface.

"A scrying ring." My father said. "Your grandmother did say she would speak to you soon. Cryptic as that is."

Niratap eased my mother into a chair, his gentleness made my heart soft. "She always had that flair."

"How is she going to talk to me with a ring?"

"Your grandmother is more than just gifted with foresight. Your grandmother is Psychyk. It is more complicated than her being able to see the threads of fate, she had the power to manipulate fate if she was so inclined."

"I am certain that was what your father was hoping to use when he had sought her out to marry."

"Probably and she probably already knew those where his intentions."

"Why would he just want her for her abilities?" I pressed.

My father sighed again, today aging him rapidly. "Don't get me wrong, I love my people, our people, but they had this nasty propensity to marry for breeding and strength. Your grandfather is descended from a line of royalty. As close to royalty as elementals get. Your grandmother from a long line of mystics just as old and strong as the royals. Both of them have access to multiple elements and extraordinary gifts."

"That still doesn't explain why he thought he could use her."

"Your grandfather has the power of compulsion." Niratap said from the sink. "Meaning that he can enact his will on others. Severine has always been a politician and is known as the snake for a reason. I'm sure that was his plan for Aria."

"Compulsion is what he was doing to you?"

He looked over his shoulder at me. "It was. On me

and your mother."

My stomach twisted in rage. "He tried to use it on me."

"He did." The flair of anger was woven through the words.

"It didn't work."

"Then you are lucky." My father said. "Not many are immune to compulsion and probably the best thing you got from me."

"Aria is also immune to his gift, much to his disappointment."

Mom looked at the card on the table, her eyes still a bit too wide, and her hands trembled as she reached for it. "It was so strange. I was trying to come to the table, but a glass wall was in front of me. My body and my brain were separated, and I was beating on the glass trying to get out. Then the wall was gone, and I couldn't do anything." She turned to where Niratap was washing dishes. "Was it like that for you?"

A jolt of panic danced over my heart as he paused in setting the rinsed dish on the counter. It wasn't like that for him. It wasn't glass walls that held my mate back, but chains. He cleared his throat and sad blandly. "No. it is not like that for me."

"Then what—"

"Mom." She turned back and I saw the innocent curiosity in her expression. I shook my head, rising from the table and joining him at the sink. I bumped into his side. My eyes narrowed as he flinched from me. He tried to hide it, lifting a sudsy hand to scratch his head, but I saw it. "I can rise and dry."

He gave me a strained smile, before handing me a dish. "Alright."

I would never forgive my grandfather. No one could treat my mate like he had. No one could get away with causing the tension that edged along his spine. No one had the right to make him so uncomfortable in his skin. No one

had the right to make my mate flinch from touch as if he
expected to be struck. No one.

Epilogue

Nessa

The car finally crunched up the gravel, announcing my brother's return home. It was unfortunate that they had shown up while he was away. Unfortunate for me, because I had been promptly herded to my room and locked in, with the faun standing guard. Two days of hearing their voices echo through the halls. Two days of smelling them throughout the house. One smelt of sand and steel, another of rich spices, the third smelled of rain and stone. He was the one I wanted to meet, his scent reminding me of home. They were here for me, though they spoke of me as if I belonged to my brother. The satyr placed them in a different hall than me, but I wanted to see them. I wanted to see these males.

I opened the door, and the faun looked at me from where he leaned against the wall, talking to Echo, the only being in this house that didn't annoy me. She smiled at me.

"Going somewhere, Nessa?" The faun asked.

"This is ridiculous." I huffed. "My brother will be angry with this treatment."

The faun gave me a smirk. "I think he will be satisfied that we kept you from three males looking for a womb to lay their seed."

He was right, but I hissed. "You can't keep me here."

"The lord will decide when you meet them. If you meet them."

Ash danced over my tongue. "You can't tell me what I can and can't do."

"Nessa." Echo said softly. "The lord just returned, let him address the other lords to see what they are actually here for."

I scowled. "I want to hear what my brother says."

"No, I was told–"

"Dheg, baby, let her listen from the stairs." Echo pressed.

The faun frowned at her but sighed. "Fine." He pointed at me. "Not beyond the stairs. The lord has sway, but he is outsized and out matched against the other three."

"Understood."

I followed them down the hall. Despite my cross nature I did not want harm to come to my brother. I would flay anyone who tried to harm him. In the months that my brother had been gone, I had learned more about what he had been doing in his absence from my life. I learned of his suffering and the war he was fighting. A war I had become a victim of; I wondered why my brother fought so hard for beings that would have looked down at him. Echo and Dorilody had told me that Niratap didn't see race when he went into battle. He did not care if it was humans or elves or bitarogs on the other end of his claws. He only cared if they were using their power to enslave and abuse others. It was something he couldn't forgive. He was one man trying to save the world from itself; it was both brave and foolish.

I sat at the landing. The satyr glowered up at me as he opened the door for my brother and his mate. She was worrying her lip at whatever they were speaking about as they entered, and my brothers tail flicked in irritation, the expression of contemplation shifting quickly to suspicion then to anger. His eyes found me and his frown deepened.

"Where are they?" He asked the satyr.

"In the dining room."

"How long have they been here?" His legs eating up the floor to the doorway.

"Two days."

He turned on the satyr. "Why didn't you call me?"

"You were with the lady's family and though they have been persistent and annoying they are our allies, and I didn't think it would be an issue for them to wait to speak with you."

Niratap's eyes flashed to me and then returned to the satyr.

"Dheg has been guarding her rooms. I put the males in a separate hall."

My brother sighed heavily. "Nessa."

"Yes."

His face was pinched in irritation. "I am sure you understand why these males are here."

"I am aware."

He huffed a dry laugh. "I won't allow them to use you."

It was my turn to laugh. "I am not a weakling that needs to be coddled."

He frowned. "Come listen but stay out of sight."

I moved down the steps following behind him, pausing just outside the doorway as he entered.

"Gentlemen."

"Niratap." The English voice answered.

"Howen. Shang. Krishna. Why are you here?"

"I think you know why we are here." The English voice said.

"We want the female you have claimed." One of the eastern ones snapped. His voice was sharp like a blade.

"Now, now Shang. He has mated with her. I can smell the seasons on him. She must be quite the beauty for Niratap to claim her for himself. He is not the kind of male who would hold a female from the scrutiny of his friends." This other male had a lightness to his voice, that reminded me of our father.

Niratap growled. "No, I would not hold a female from you, we had an agreement on the discovery of a female."

"Then why have we learned of this female you mated, without honoring our agreement at that, through gossip channels." Shang snarled and I wondered if they were here for me or to judge my brother. "We are entitled to take her from you, mated or not.

"That is not something that will happen." Niratap snarled back. Shasha sidled up close to me listening as well. "My mate will not be subject to your cruelty, Shang."

"You dishonor this group, by hiding her away from us. We had an agreement." Shag shouted beating against the dining room table.

Shasha whispered to me. "Do you think they are looking for you or me?"

"I think that the males are ignorant and assume that I am his mate."

She smiled. "Probably, and the questions have turned to attacks. Nira won't back off his defense."

"Exactly. He will have to figure it out on his own."

"I have not hidden my mating from you. If the gossip channels have failed to tell you what has happened to me in this last year, that is not on me or my mate."

"And what pray tell happened, Bondbreaker?" The English voice said over the scrape of a chair.

"If you must know Trailblazer, I–"

"I do not care what may or may not have been done." Shang interrupted. "How long have you been mated?"

"Since the end of November, Smuggler."

"Is she already full with your babe?" The other male teased.

"No."

"Is she scared of males?"

"Surprisingly no."

Niratap's voice took on a boastful tone that made his mate smile. "I'm going to peek."

"Then why do you hide your mate from us?" The Englishman asked.

"Because she does not deserve to be attacked by three males she doesn't know. I want to know why you thought gathering in my home was a wise idea. You yourself said that us gathering would be an exceedingly dangerous, Howen, or did you forget your own fearless leadership?"

"Watch where you step Niratap." Howen said sharply.

"In my own home, Howen?"

Shasha slipped into the dining room, and the males were instantly silent.

"Leave us human. Your presence is unwanted." Shang said dismissively.

Niratap snarled. "Do not speak to her like that."

"I will speak to her however I please."

"Not in my house you won't."

"Enough." Howen barked. "Girl this is not a place for you, go resume your duties."

I could hear the expression on her face as she addressed those males. "No male tells me what to do in my own home, firstly, and second you will not disrespect my mate in that home as well."

"Shasha—"

She carried on, ignoring the warning in my brother's voice. "Furthermore, if you are here for me, you will find that I have fangs and will fight back."

The last male, Krishna, laughed; it was a light and refreshing sound. "My, my it looks like we have misunderstood that glorious rumor train. You must be the fire-hearted mate we keep hearing about."

"I am."

"You are not a bitarog." Shang said.

"No. I am half-elemental."

"Do you have no respect for your species, Bondbreaker?"

"I have plenty of respect for my species, Shang. I have chosen a mate; it matters little to me what her species is."

"Typical of the mixed breed."

There was a sharp inhalation of breath and a bang. I

looked into the room. Niratap stood between me and the table. A wheaty blonde male stood opposite him at the head of the table. He was taller than Niratap dressed in a fine dark brown suit and his antlers that of a fallow deer that I hunted at home, his eyes an icy blue. Another male still sat at the table; his warm sienna features pulled into a mocking smile. He was dressed in a pale blue garb I'd never seen before. He resembled our father with his dark hair and long coiled horns. The last male I couldn't see. I pushed further into the room, Niratap stopped me before I moved past him. Shasha had the last male pinned to the toppled chair under her dagger. The male's face was disinterested as he met Shasha's gaze. He had a sandy complexion with dark hair and clothes. His antlers swooped from the crest of his head the prongs short.

"You will not disrespect my mate. Not in his own house and not in front of me." She seethed.

"Dangerous little viper." He said.

"I'm not above killing for my mate."

"Niratap, I apologize for my less than savory words."

"Shasha, let Shang up, please."

She moved to stand at my other side, while the male righted himself and the chair. His face was all sharp angles with dark eyes. His gaze was critical as he looked me over. I didn't like how he smirked when he finished his appraisal. The male opposite him had round soulful brown eyes, his smile was warm with the whisper of mischief. A red dot was painted in the center of his forehead. The male at the head of the table blinked when my eyes found his, the bright color sucking me in. He was quite handsome with a strong set jaw and soft lips. He cleared his throat looking at my brother.

"Apologies Niratap. Yes, we had agreed that congregating was not the greatest idea. We assumed that the other bitarog that was rescued with you was who you had mated."

Niratap was careful to hide his grimace. "I can understand were the information channels got confused. This is Nessa, my older sister. Nessa meet the last known males of our species. Shang, Krishna, and Howen."

Each male bowed their head with their names. Krishna was the first to speak. "You are lovely, lovely. Simply lovely, Nessa."

Niratap sputtered, guiding his mate to the table.

Shang returned to his seat. "I don't think flattery will bring her to your bed, Krishna."

"Flattery is always worth a try as is generosity. The Buddha says—"

"I'm not going to deal with your mysticism today. Save it for your devotees." Shang snarled. He was an assertive male, but he was cold and calculating.

"I hardly doubt your cruel nature would interest her, Shang."

"Enough." Howen growled from the head of the table. "We will not speak of her as if she is not here. Nessa, please sit. There is much we need to discuss."

Acknowledgments

A huge thank you to all my readers, for helping me live out my dream, and for sharing my books with others.

To the authors, artists, creators, and musicians that fuel my creativity. I devour content like its water so the list of you is beyond comprehension but thank you.

My husband, Allen, for just being my person. For giving me your blessings so I could focus on my art. For loving me when I haven't loved myself. I can't thank you enough for being the greatest gift in my life.

My mother for being the wing woman I never knew I would need and for being one of my biggest supporters. Thank you for birthing me, obviously, and being a rock for me, even though you haven't read these books yet.

Amanda. You are such a light in my life. I love you. I hate that you live so far away. I am so grateful for you, endlessly grateful, for all your love and friendship.

My friends because there are too many of you to name, who are always asking when the next one is coming, here you go. Thank you for being there in whatever facility you have been. Know that I hold you all in my heart and no matter if we talked yesterday or six years ago, I love you guys and I think of you all the time.

Side note, I am not a linguist. Please forgive my transgressions of translation.

Author Bio

S. R. George is a witch and storyteller who grew up loving to read. From a young age she has wanted to tell the grand adventures her mind takes her. Love stories are a favorite of hers, especially if they have fantasy aspects to them. Now she wants to share her chaos with the world. She currently lives in Idaho with her husband and two cats.